HC

WAR IN HEAVEN

Also by Gavin G. Smith from Gollancz:

Veteran

WAR IN HEAVEN

Gavin G. Smith

GOLLANCZ

LONDON

First published in Great Britain in 2011 by Gollancz
An imprint of the Orion Publishing Group
Orion House, 5 Upper St Martin's Lane,
London WC2H 9EA
An Hachette UK Company

A CIP catalogue record for this book
is available from the British Library

ISBN 978 0 575 09470 3 (Cased)
ISBN 978 0 575 09471 0 (Trade Paperback)

1 3 5 7 9 10 8 6 4 2

Typeset by Deltatype Ltd, Birkenhead, Merseyside

Printed in Great Britain by Clays Ltd, St Ives plc

The Orion Publishing Group's policy is to use papers
that are natural, renewable and recyclable products and
made from wood grown in sustainable forests. The logging
and manufacturing processes are expected to conform to
the environmental regulations of the country of origin.

www.gavingsmith.com
www.orionbooks.co.uk

To Lena & Jack Smith
Two members of an extraordinary generation

Prologue
Dog 4 Eighteen Months Ago

There's nothing good about being buried in a pile of bodies for seventy-two hours. Try to ignore the stench. Try to ignore what soggy, rotting flesh feels like against you. Try to ignore the feel of larvae hatching and crawling around, particularly when the maggots make their way under your inertial armour. Try to ignore the creeping cold. Try to ignore the cramp from staying in the same position for that long. Try to ignore the post-mortem movements of the dead guys you're bunked up with. Three days of speeding and sleep deprivation, try to ignore the obscene urge to giggle.

'Still, it could be worse – it could be raining.' Try to ignore Mudge breaking comms silence to highlight the added misery of the driving rain. Rain that was causing us to sink into a soup of mud, flesh and body parts. He only did it because we were close to being compromised. Still fucking irritating. Unprofessional. A grin spread across my face at the thought of being unprofessional and I just managed to stifle the urge to burst out laughing.

Try not to ignore what you're doing and where you are. That was made easier by Them. They were helping us remember by taking the bodies from the piles They had made and impaling them on spikes of metal cut from the warehouse walls of the overrun supply depot. They were arranging the impaled, mutilated dead in a spiral pattern.

An attractive arrangement, both industrious and difficult to ignore.

However, the more bodies They spiked, the closer They got to finding us, buried under the corpses. This was an issue. Though if I was honest I was more concerned with the tenacious maggot that seemed dead set on crawling up my arse, but then sleep deprivation was making me giddy and the maggot tickled.

It had been a big push as part of a planet-wide offensive. The depot had been twenty-five miles behind our lines. The trenches had buckled and They had surged through and kept going. We were struggling to retreat fast enough.

The depot had been a major one. Over two thousand people had worked here. It had cargo mechs, road and rail links and facilities for heavy cargo shuttles. It had also contained all the food and ammunition for that part of what had been the front. They had walked through it.

1

Then some bright spark in Command, who I can only assume has no knowledge of special forces and what they are for, tasked us to recce the depot. Before we got there I could have told him that it was overrun with Them. Hell, Command could probably have got a shot of it from orbit if they had tried hard enough.

A hairy gunship ride. A night insertion, in the short night of a planet in a binary system, and then a hard tab to set up an Observation Post. The OP set-up had not gone well, the area was too heavily compromised. Hence the buried in bodies and hiding rather than any form of useful recce. It was just a matter of who was going to be compromised first. I was pretty sure it was going to be me. I felt that lucky.

It wasn't. It was Gregor.

Shaz, our quiet Sikh signalman from Leicester, brought the tac net up. Immediately windows showing the view from each of the other seven members of the Wild Boys appeared in the Internal Visual Display of my cybernetic eyes. Gregor's guncam was kind of interesting. It seemed to be pointing down at the mud and corpses as if it was being held off the ground and shaken.

There was an explanation from Mudge's feed. The odd-looking journalist's camera eyes showed Gregor being held up by his neck. The Berserk holding him was using a pincer-like appendage on its weapon gauntlet to try to crack open the hard armour breastplate that Gregor was wearing. Attempting to get at the meat. It was like watching someone trying to open a tin can, an angry, struggling tin can.

I don't know why it surprised me. I had been expecting it. I was still startled when the Berserk pulled away the corpses covering me. Did I hesitate? It felt like it, but time moves differently when your reflexes are boosted as high as mine. Still, it felt like I looked at the Berserk's off-kilter appearance for a long time. They were mostly humanoid, I guess, a kind of chitinous armour over a smooth black material that looked like some kind of solid liquid. They had heads but no visible features.

It didn't even have the common courtesy to look startled at finding a heavily armed SAS trooper under the pile of corpses, but then we were already compromised, and if one knows they all know.

I was aware of Mudge firing his converted AK-47 at the Berserk holding Gregor off the ground. The smartlink putting the cross hairs, in theory, where the bullets were going to hit.

'Watch your fire,' Gregor sub-vocalised across the tac net. He sounded calmer than I would have with a Berserk trying to peel me and an overexcited junkie journalist firing in my general vicinity. Still, I had my own problems.

I raised the Heckler & Koch Squad Automatic Weapon and pointed it at the Berserk and then made a mistake. I fired the underslung grenade launcher at the alien. The chambered grenade was a thirty-millimetre High Explosive

Armour Piercing grenade. At point-blank range, the velocity and the armour-piercing tip of the grenade meant that it punched straight through the Berserk, leaving a hole I could see grey sky through.

I felt that if the Berserk had any sense of humour it could at least have done a double take at the sizeable hole in its chest, but it just kept reaching for me. I pulled the trigger on the weapon again, but the grenade launcher's unreliable semi-automatic feed system jammed. The Berserk's long talon-like fingers wrapped around my face, its clawed nails trying to break through my implanted subcutaneous armour. I worked the pump on the grenade launcher, ejecting the jammed round and chambering another.

I started screaming. The Berserk's nails had penetrated the armour and blood was pissing down my face. It hurt. That was reassuring. It's nice to still have nerve endings, I guess.

I pulled the trigger again. A flechette grenade. A better choice. In a hail of hundreds of razor-sharp, needle-like penetrators, the Berserk ceased to exist. That was all right – there were a lot more.

I moved into a kneeling firing position. Almost absent-mindedly I started firing. It was a target-rich environment. Or, as we preferred to say, we were surrounded, by fucking thousands of Them.

Squeeze the trigger until that Berserk falls over. Move the weapon, fire some more. Repeat until overrun and you're sitting on your very own rusty metal spike.

While my hands and smartlink were occupied I tried to get an understanding of the situation. Frankly, it was shit. The rest of the patrol were rising from their piles of bodies covered in viscera and looking like monsters out of some pre-Final Human Conflict horror viz.

Gregor was gamely and repeatedly stabbing the Berserk who had him in the head with his triangular-bladed sword bayonet. Black liquid was spurting out and covering Gregor's arm with each violent thrust. The Berserk dropped him. Gregor landed on his feet and kicked the Berserk, knocking it back slightly. This gave him just enough room to bring his railgun to bear on its gyroscopic harness. He triggered a short burst at point-blank range into the Berserk. Destroying it. Turning it into a puddle of black liquid junk of whatever passed for DNA with Them.

'We're fucked!' Mudge shouted helpfully. 'Again!' He was laughing. I found myself envious of his drugs. Fire, change target, fire again. I was taking multiple hits from black light beams and shards, but the integrity of my armour seemed to be holding.

'Nobody dies until we're out of ammo!' I shouted. Brilliant leadership, I thought.

I could hear Shaz's voice over the tac net. He'd recorded a request for fire support and evac and put it on repeat, as he was busy. He was slowly backing towards me, firing short burst after short burst from his laser carbine. Each hit, and he couldn't miss here, turned Berserk flesh into black superheated steam. His voice was like a mantra but it wasn't very calming. It was an old song we'd sung time and time again. Our request was so futile that Command weren't even granting it the dignity of a reply. They were just ignoring it.

Mudge's tactical assessment seemed right on the money. Not bad for someone who was ostensibly non-military. Fucked we were. Most of Their forces were still trying to batter the fuck out of our forces, who couldn't retreat fast enough and were periodically being overrun.

We had a lot of Berserks doing what Berserks do. They ran at us firing shard and black light weapons with a view to closing with us and tearing us apart. This made Them easy to kill but eventually we'd run out of ammo or they'd overwhelm us. On top of that I could see a couple of Their Walkers, large biomechanical mechs, moving towards us. Even a few of Their ground-effects armoured vehicles wanted in on our imminent deaths. If we were really lucky, then the GE vehicles would be carrying yet more Berserks. All of Them looked like indeterminate shadows in the rain.

We were laying down blistering fire all around us but were slowly being herded into a last-stand situation. I put the cross hairs from my smartlink over one of Their Walkers and used that as lock for both the Light Anti Armour missiles in their tubes on either side of my backpack. The two Laa-Laas launched themselves into the air. I switched to the next target and fired another burst from my SAW.

Something bumped into my back. I didn't need to look to know it was Bibs – Bibby Sterlin, the patrol's other railgunner. She was a powerfully built thrill-seeker from a nice middle-class corporate family. Like Mudge she didn't have to be here.

Bibs let off stuttering burst after stuttering burst from the support weapon. Belt titanium-cored penetrator rounds were propelled at hypersonic speeds by the electromagnetic coil in the heavy weapon's barrel. When they hit a Berserk it was like watching an angry child tear up paper, only very, very fast.

'This fucking sucks!' she shouted, somewhat redundantly, I thought.

'You sound surprised!' I shouted back. My sound filters were struggling to deal with the rapid hypersonic bangs from the railgun. 'Reloading! Aaah fuck!' My IVD went blank as the black light beam hit me under my helmet, turned my skin to steam and partially melted the subcutaneous armour on my face. A shard round caught me in the leg just below my armoured kneepad. The inertial armour didn't harden quick enough to stop it and the round pierced my subcutaneous armour as well. I saw actual blood. Again.

Bibs moved around to my side and covered me as I ejected the spent cassette from my SAW and rammed home another two hundred vacuum-packed, caseless, nine-millimetre long, armour-piercing hydrostatic rounds. I was firing again.

Shaz was next to me now. Superheated air exploded as he fired burst after burst from his laser carbine.

'Reloading!' he shouted as he ejected the battery. I shifted my field of fire to compensate. He rammed another battery home behind the bullpup-configuration carbine's handgrip and immediately started firing again.

David 'Brownie' Brownsword, the world's quietest Scouser and our medic, was firing his weapon. He was covering Ashley Broadin, a tough, bald, bullet-headed Brummie and our combat engineer, as she ran to the closest approximation of cover she could find. She then returned the favour. It looked like they were wading through corpses. More Berserks were sprinting towards us.

On the run I watched Brownie raise his SAW and make a lock with the smartlink. Both his Laa-Laas launched, and I was aware of their spiralling contrails as they flew into one of Their GE armoured vehicles and exploded, crippling it. But more Berserks were spilling out of the back.

Mudge skidded in behind me. He and Gregor had been conducting fire-and-manoeuvre fun and games similar to Ash and Brownie's.

'Do you know what would be fucking useful?' he asked. I'm guessing it was rhetorical. He was on one knee firing burst after burst to either side of Gregor, who was wading through corpses as fast as he could to get to us.

'Watch your field of fire, Mudge,' Gregor sub-vocalised again over the tac net.

'If I had Laa-Laas as well. Wouldn't another two missiles be useful in situation like this?!'

'Time and place, Mudge!' I shouted as I fired my last grenade, hoping it was a HEAP. It was fragmentation. I got a couple of Berserks but didn't dent the Walker that was about to establish firepower superiority all over us.

Mudge was right but it wasn't my decision. Command were pissed off at us enough for having a civvy around. They weren't going to encourage him by equipping him with heavy weapons.

Dorcas was the final one to reach us. The loud-mouthed marksman, on exchange from the Australian SAS, skidded in next to me, displacing Bibs. He endeared himself further by showering us with a wash of mud and rotten viscera.

'I was hoping to stay hidden,' he said grinning. I knew he didn't mean it. I was pretty sure that adrenalin, combat drugs and bravado were all that was covering up his pant-shitting fear of imminent death. Just like the rest of us.

Dorcas's sniper railgun was still disassembled in its sheath across his back. There was no need for finesse here. He had his Steyr carbine and was doing what the rest of us were doing: finding the nearest target in his field of fire, hitting it with burst after burst until it fell over, then moving to the next target.

Anything got too close then he fired the underslung grenade launcher to give us a bit more breathing space.

We were bunching up. It meant we were a target for the first area-effect weapon They brought to bear on us, but we didn't have much of a choice. They were herding us and didn't care about casualties.

The amount of hot flying metal we were putting into the air was awesome. At the end of the day, however, special forces or not, we were infantry, and there was only so much hardware we could bring to bear.

Gregor was concentrating his fire on the Walker, keeping it off balance, the impacts from his railgun causing ripples all up its strange, almost liquid, biomechanical flesh. He finished it off with both his vertically launched Laa-Laas. Immediately another one strode into view.

We were gone. It was all over now bar getting rid of our ammunition before we died.

Still, it could be worse. It had stopped raining after three days.

1
Crawling Town (Again)

Why was I thinking about Dog 4 again? Just another gunfight, though it had been a hairy one. Another fucking last stand. My arm ached. The prosthetic one.

'It's the purity!' Mudge was practically howling at me. 'I mean, not the purity of the powder. This shit is probably cut with rat poison. But the colour, the whiteness of it, so, so virginal.' He was very excited about the large pile of coke he had on a piece of plastic on his lap.

'It's white because it's bleached,' I growled. I was desperately trying to find my way through the sandstorm. For such a large disorganised convoy you'd think that Crawling Town would move slower. Instead I had to rely completely on information from the four-wheel-drive muscle car's sensors.

The three-dimensional topographic map on my Internal Visual Display told me where all the surrounding vehicles were. Hopefully. They all looked unreasonably close to me. All I could see was a solid-looking wall of airborne dust and dirt. In theory Rannu was out in that shit on a bike. Every so often a huge wheel from one vehicle or another would appear close to our car and cause eddies in the dirt.

Mudge snorted a line of the white powder. Cold turkey had been a bad, bad time for him

'You really missed that, didn't you?' I asked.

'You've no idea, mate. You want to do a line?'

'No, Mudge. I don't really feel like switching off my nasal filters in the middle of a huge poisonous dust cloud.'

'Suit yourself.' He shrugged and did another line up the other nostril.

We'd already seen a number of accidents. Well, less accidents more automotive Darwinism. Mainly smaller vehicles, like ours, misjudging their place in the scheme of things and getting ground up by larger, much heavier vehicles with bigger wheels/tracks. I wasn't surprised

7

that accidents were the number-one cause of premature death in Crawling Town.

Still, in the body-count stakes car accidents had fearsome competition from the toxic and sometimes irradiated environment of the Dead Roads. I'd found this out the hard way the last time I had visited. The Dead Roads was the blasted and polluted wasteland that ran down the eastern seaboard of the United States. The result of the Final Human Conflict some two hundred and fifty plus years ago and unregulated industrial pollution in the wake of the country's financial collapse.

Coming in a surprising third for cause of death in Crawling Town was the internecine feuding between the various nomad gangs, while we were here to see if we could increase the number of deaths caused by violence. I had an old and cold reason to do this. A score to settle.

I had been happily enjoying my retirement from getting shot at in the colonies fighting in the never-ending war against Them. No, that's a lie. I was miserable, but I really didn't know any better and so was everyone else. Also it was the sort of misery that was easy to cope with. Then my old CO, Major Rolleston, a thoroughgoing bastard of the highest order, had decided to complicate my life by sending me after a Them infiltrator. We had assumed it was a Ninja – squaddie parlance for one of Their stealth killing machines. One had killed most of the Wild Boys, my old SAS squad.

It wasn't a Ninja. That would have been less complicated, though more fatal. It was an Ambassador. It was being sheltered by a group of prostitutes who worked in the Rigs, the shanty town made up of derelict oil rigs in the Tay River off the shore of Dundee. That was how I met Morag and really, really complicated my life by disobeying Rolleston. Fleeing with Morag to Hull (I only get to see the nicest places, a holdover tradition from my army days) with the downloaded essence of Ambassador, we agreed, sort of, to help Pagan, a computer hacker, create an electronic god out of humanity's communications network.

Rolleston was of course delighted with my disobedience, betrayal and apparent treason against humanity and dispatched all sorts of interesting people to find and kill us. This included, but was not limited to, Rannu Nagarkoti, a Ghurkha ex-SAS man, who was currently riding through the sandstorm somewhere, and the Grey Lady, Ms Josephine Bran, the scariest operator in the scary world of black ops.

Hull got burned. Pagan, Morag and I fled to New York. I came a close second in my arse-kicking at the hands of Rannu. He then joined us. I'm sure there are easier ways. I met my old friend Howard Mudgie – Mudge to his mates. We also got the support of Balor, the insane pirate king of the ruins of New York, though this had taken some persuasion and, for reasons still unclear, me getting the aforementioned beating at the hands of Rannu. Balor was a heavily augmented cyborg who had had his body sculpted to look like a sea demon from some old mythology. Mudge put us on to two pilots I really wanted to speak to, Gibby and Buck. They'd both worked the same shady world of special ops that I had. They had been Rolleston and the Grey Lady's taxi drivers, the taxi being a heavily armed and armoured vectored-thrust gunship. Gibby and Buck had been the last to see my best friend Gregor on Dog 4 after he'd been infected by one of Their Ninjas during its death throws. The two pilots were hiding out in Crawling Town. That's why we'd come here the first time, and some bad shit had happened to me for no good reason I could think of.

Gibby and Buck had told us that they had taken Gregor to the Atlantis Spoke, one of the city-sized orbital elevators that ring the planet on the equator. We found Gregor in a lab deep below the surface of the ocean being experimented on by Rolleston's employers, the Cabal. The dying Ninja had somehow joined with Gregor, transforming him into a hybrid form of humanity and Them. The Cabal were a shadowy group of upper-echelon corporate execs, military types and intelligence operatives. So we had some of the most powerful people in the world after us, and we were in the company of a human/Them hybrid and wanted for betraying the entire human race.

What we found out was that They had not started the war, as we had always been led to believe. It was us – or rather it was the Cabal. Not only had they started the war, but they had taught Them – who as far as I could make out were some kind of harmless vacuum-living space coral – to fight. They had done this through what Pagan called negative stimulus and what I call blowing the shit out of them.

So we'd been conned for sixty years into fighting a war that was manipulated so as not to end. I'm still a little hazy as to why. I'm guessing it had something to do with power, control, greed and all that good stuff. Mudge, however, claims it was to do with sexual inadequacy on the part of the members of the Cabal. Mudge puts a lot of the problems of people he doesn't like down to that, though Morag did point out that the majority of the Cabal were male. The Cabal were also working on their own version of God called Demiurge. Only instead of guiding the net to sentience and electronic omniscience (a word I'm sure no self-respecting squaddie should be using as much as I have been) they just wanted to control it.

So as our situation got worse and worse we came up with more and more desperate plans. We decided to program God to always tell the truth but to be under nobody's control. I know why we did this but often I feel it would be useful if we'd retained control of the electronic deity. We took over a media node in Atlantis at gunpoint and released God into the net. Now suddenly all information was available to everyone. Mudge then used the node to broadcast the evidence of the Cabal's crimes against humanity and Them.

After a worldwide televised argument with Rolleston and Vincent Cronin, the Cabal's corporate mouthpiece, the good Major and the Grey Lady made a concerted effort to kill us. In Buck's case they succeeded. In what felt like a one-sided exchange of violence it also appeared that the Major was somehow augmented with Themtech. He was pretty much walking through railgun fire.

A lot of pissed-off people's secrets had been revealed. There were also a lot of people baying for the Cabal's blood. As most of the Cabal were fat old men being kept alive by machinery they weren't too hard for the vigilante crowds to deal with.

Ambassador had told us that They wanted peace. We wanted peace. Hurray, the war's over. Except Rolleston and Cronin got away. They escaped in next-generation frigates using Themtech, supported by frighteningly good hackers who we think were using technology derived from Project Demiurge. The frigates, which we're now apparently calling the Black Squadrons, made for the four colonial systems of Sirius, Lalande, Barnard's Star and Proxima. We believed they planned to take over the comms networks in each system with Demiurge, which would mean that they controlled the information in them, which would in turn help them take command of humanity's colonial military. We also thought they were going to try and use a Themtech-derived biological agent developed by Project Crom to infect, subjugate and control Them in the Sirius system. And that is how I ended up going back there, my least favourite place but where my mind kept returning to.

We went to the Sirius system for other reasons. Maybe it was because I was dying of radiation poisoning at the time or maybe it was just because Morag really wanted to go. I was surprised by how it was actually worse this time than all my previous visits. Suited in Mamluk exo-armour we performed extravehicular activity – we exited a perfectly functional spacecraft and infiltrated the Dog's Teeth. The Dog's Teeth is an asteroid belt and was home base to the largest concentration of Them in the Sirius system. Our plan was to find the Crom virus/spores and stop them from infecting Them.

Morag had a different plan. With the remnants of Ambassador

living in her neural cybernetics, she wanted to communicate with Them. She left us.

What we didn't know was that when Rolleston attacked us in the Spoke he had infected Gregor with Crom. He had effectively turned Gregor into a slave plague-bearing weapon. We got compromised. The billions of Them there decided to kill us. That I understood. Gregor attempting to assimilate and warp the flesh of Them and infect Them with the Crom virus so they could be controlled by Rolleston and Cronin was more of a surprise.

Balor died. He finally opened his bad old eye. Whatever weapon he had behind the patch nearly succeeded in killing Gregor. Nearly wasn't enough. Still, the old monster had given himself the warrior's ending he'd always wanted. It was Gibby who killed Gregor. He was flying the *Spear*, our ship. He'd forsaken stealth and flown into the Dog's Teeth taking fire every inch of the way but managed to make it to Gregor and detonate his payload and engines. Sanitising the area. I'd never seen anything like what Balor or Gibby had done. I thought the days of actions like that had long since gone, if they'd ever really been.

So instead of looking at peace we were looking at war between humanity. More than two hundred and fifty years after we swore we'd never do this to ourselves again. After we'd decided that the cost was too great we were looking at one half of humanity fighting the other. And it was our fault. Actually it wasn't; it was the Cabal's. It was Rolleston's and Cronin's. We were just the catalyst.

Gregor's betrayal had hurt. A lot. But even though the monster had had his warped features, it had been Rolleston's demon – he had been programmed. My friend hadn't done this. My friend had died in the Spoke when Rolleston had stabbed him in the head and injected Crom into his hybrid physiology. Rolleston had tried to kill me so many times. He badly needed to die. It wasn't so much revenge, though that would be good. It just really needed doing, though not by me.

We'd played long odds and won. Or some of us had. By 'won' I mean we were still alive. We were on the eve of a new war between humans, but my fight was over. We'd more than done our bit surely? Someone else's turn. It wasn't just that I was tired of it, though I was. It was that I knew I was about one gunfight with someone who knew what they were doing from being dead. I'd never had much luck, none of us had – there wasn't much around – but I'd pushed what I had way too far.

Morag disagreed. She wanted to see this through to the end.

She used words that only the young and terminally optimistic use, like responsibility. Or maybe she wasn't optimistic. Maybe she wanted to die. After all, she'd been sold into a life of prostitution by her mum for crystal. She'd had even less luck than the rest of us. Why push it? But she did. I couldn't do it any more. I thought she would cry when I told her that. I didn't want to make her cry, though God knows I'd done enough of that. It's just nice to know there's someone who cares enough, about anything, to still cry. But her eyes were cybernetic now. Like the rest of us, this never-fucking-ending war was making her sell her humanity piece by cybernetic piece.

My war was over.

Well maybe there was just one last bit of business. One of the tribes of Crawling Town were a bunch of pricks called the Wait, a skinhead monastic order originally from Oregon. They followed some bullshit pre-FHC credo to do with racial purity. For some bizarre reason they seemed to think that the white race is different from all the others. As if we didn't have enough reasons to kill each other – food, money, anger, etc. – we apparently have to go and invent completely spurious ones.

These arseholes were led by a nasty, should-have-been-aborted, piece-of-shit hacker called Messer. He'd decreed that I wasn't racially pure. I'm a quarter Thai and three-quarters Scots, more proud of both now. His response to my lack of purity was to crucify me on the back of a dune buggy and have me taken for a ride through a high-radiation nuke crater. I caught a big dose. He'd killed me slowly. Left me to die painfully of radiation poisoning.

Morag, Pagan, Mudge and Rannu rescued me with the aid of some of the lords of Crawling Town. One of these was Papa Neon, head of Big Neon Voodoo, the most powerful gang in Crawling Town. The other was Mrs Tillwater, a borderline serial killer and possible cannibal. She ran the First Baptist Church of Austin Texas, which, despite the name, was also a gang or possibly a woman's auxiliary, maybe both. Because the Wait were a Crawling Town gang the rescue took the form of diplomacy. Well, diplomacy through the medium of gun-pointing and threats. We weren't allowed to deal with the Wait violently because we were outsiders.

Mudge, Rannu and I were here to remedy their existence. My last battle.

A car appeared out of the dust in front of us. I braked slightly, watching the ghost of the sensor reading of the large truck directly behind me on the topographic map overlaid on my IVD. I didn't want it to get close. The car in front demonstrated why.

I watched the driver swerve to avoid the huge armoured wheel rolling through the dust on his right side. He overcompensated, misjudging his clearance on the left, and ended up caught between two of the wheels on one of the Wait's military-surplus personnel carriers. The car, which looked way to fragile to be out here, got snarled up in the armour plate and dragged up into the wheel arch. Trapped between the two wheels it was crushed like an egg.

It was very fast. Mudge was watching with rapt attention. Pieces of the car rained down on our own vehicle. I checked the map and moved the steering wheel just enough to avoid hitting the wreckage still caught up in the personnel carrier's wheels. I gave the car a command through the link jacked into one of the four plugs on the back of my neck. It accelerated slightly, keeping us out of trouble.

You had to know how to drive to be in the middle of the city-sized convoy that was Crawling Town. If you drove on the outskirts then you risked being picked off by the scavengers that accompanied it.

'Shit,' Mudge breathed. 'Want me to drive?'

'I'd like you to learn properly,' I answered back. Sounding surly to myself.

Mudge glanced over at me. 'What's your problem?'

The last time the Wait had got the drop on me. Now we were ready for them, armed. I had Rannu, an experienced and capable ex-SAS operator, and Mudge, who'd gone out with us enough that he may as well have joined the Regiment, backing me up. We were going to do this clean. Get rid of some completely excess humanity before the lords of Crawling Town even knew we were there. So why was I so pissed off.

'God?' I sub-vocalised. Mudge was watching me.

'Do you want a cigarette?' Mudge asked. That pissed me off.

'Yes, Jakob,' God answered. He was everywhere now. To me he sounded like a hundred soothing mellifluous voices talking to me at once. The amusing thing was that all the Wait had to do was ask God where we were, and under the parameters of behaviour that we'd set up God would have to tell them. We were hoping that the Wait had not thought to ask. Though if I'd pissed off someone with my skill set I'd be asking pretty regularly.

'I told you I quit,' I snapped at Mudge. I shouldn't be having nicotine withdrawal because my internal systems should have scrubbed the poison out, but I still badly wanted a cigarette. Mudge's desperate chain-smoking, drinking and doing drugs wasn't helping. It was like he was making up for lost time. After all, despite his repeated requests to synthesise them, smokes, drink and drugs had been in short supply back in the Sirius system. Even food had been trial and error and not something I enjoyed thinking about.

Of course, I could check to see if anyone was asking about us. Checking on operational security in a world that didn't have any, thanks to us. That would have made sense.

'Where is she?' I asked. Or instead I could pine for my estranged not-quite-girlfriend.

'I do not know,' God answered. So much for omniscience.

'Quitting is a mistake,' Mudge opined. 'We all need coping mechanisms.'

'Is that not quite difficult for you? To not know?' I sub-vocalised to God.

'You talking to Rannu?' Mudge asked.

'No. Has it occurred to you that you have too many coping mechanisms?'

Mudge's features suddenly brightened.

'It does suggest a certain amount of effort on her part to avoid surveillance,' God answered.

'Could she have left the system?' I was worried she would try and go to one of the colonies in a misguided attempt to help.

'Prostitutes!' Mudge shouted, much to my irritation. 'After we've killed these cunts we should go and find some hookers! Some really dirty ones.'

My jaw clenched and my cybernetic hand tightened its grip on the steering wheel, crushing it slightly.

'Sorry. I wasn't thinking,' Mudge said without the slightest hint of contrition. He had been thinking; he had been looking for a response.

'As I told you before, Jakob, I do not believe she could have left the system without me knowing.'

'So where do you think she is?' I asked. Trying to keep the desperation out of my voice.

'Again, the data I have suggests that she is in New Mexico somewhere.' The good thing about God was that he never got impatient, no matter how many times we had this conversation.

'Are we doing this or do you just want to talk to God about your ex-girlfriend?' Mudge asked, an edge in his voice.

'She's not—' I started.

'Your girlfriend or your ex? Focus, Jake.' Mudge always used the contraction of my name when he wanted to get a rise out of me.

'We've got arseholes to kill.' I ran my fingers through my hair. Was it still my hair?

'Jake?' Mudge asked.

'Abort. Abort. Abort,' I said over the tac net.

'Fuck's sake!' Mudge slammed his fist down on the dash before angrily taking another swig from his now nearly ever-present bottle of vodka.

'Say again, over?' Rannu was too professional to let his surprise be heard over the comms.

'Abort. Abort. Abort,' I repeated.

Mudge shook his head. 'You are such a fucking pussy.' He seemed genuinely angry with me. Instead of caring I slewed the car violently to the right, slipping it under the trailer of an articulated lorry. Mudge shouted out in surprise.

'Let's get out of Crawling Town,' I said over the tac net.

'Roger that, over,' Rannu answered.

'God,' Mudge said loudly, 'could you play my friend's ever-so-pathetic most recent conversation with you back, please?'

Every single fucking time. I had started grinding my teeth since I'd quit smoking. I was doing it now. The recording of my conversation with God started over the car's speaker system. I began to drive even more erratically. Mudge swore as he spilled vodka all over himself.

When we'd discussed the idea of God and what he should do – always telling the truth, complete transparency – it had seemed like a good idea. No privacy whatsoever was less good. We'd also completely underestimated the annoying uses that Mudge could put God to.

'So where we going? New Mexico?' Mudge asked scornfully. The drive through the city-sized convoy had taken a while despite my suicidal speed and manoeuvring. Even then we'd only got clipped a couple of times. On the way out some of the outriding parasites had shown an interest in us. They got less interested after I'd sideswiped a trike into some wreckage.

I'd skidded to a halt on a slight rise in some scrub wasteland looking out over the US border proper. The edge of the Dead Roads. Things didn't look that much better over there.

'No,' I answered tersely, sounding a little childish even to my own ears. I climbed out of the car. Mudge followed. I could see Rannu riding towards us on a powerful dirt bike, his head swathed in a *she-magh*, dust goggles protecting the black lenses of his cybernetic eyes.

Mudge turned his camera eyes on me. It had taken a long time for me to get use to the way the lenses always seemed to be rotating one way or the other as they found the best focus point. He was a little shorter than my six feet and much thinner, though both of us had a wiry build. There was something weird about his long face, but it was difficult to put your finger on it – he just looked slightly odd. He had two days of sparse blond stubble on his cheeks and his fair hair was a short unkempt mess.

Rannu brought the bike to a halt, kicked the stand down and dismounted. His cargo trousers and black armoured combat jacket were covered in dust from the road. He started to beat the dust off himself, all the while observing around us.

'What happened – were we compromised?' he asked.

'Only by this pussy's delicate feelings,' Mudge answered. I could practically hear the squat, powerfully built Nepalese's eyebrows rising under his goggles.

'We're not doing the Wait?' Rannu asked. Now I could hear the slight undertone of surprise.

'We're not,' I told them.

'Really?' Mudge asked. It sounded less like a question and more like an experiment to see how much sarcasm you could pack into a single word. 'See, they kidnapped me, tortured me, gave me a lethal dose of radiation poisoning and generally made my life a living hell. Not to mention what a fucking whiney burden on my friends I became. Oh no, wait, that wasn't me. It was fucking you!'

Rannu shifted uncomfortably.

'You didn't have to—' I started.

'Yes, I fucking did!' Mudge spat. He seemed overwrought. 'Because you made me promise!'

'When I thought I was dying. I'm better now.'

'My promise to help deal with them still stands,' Rannu said. He'd finished beating off the dust and had removed his goggles. His eyes, like mine, like most vets', were matt-black plastic lenses. I sighed and leaned against the car wishing I had a cigarette.

'I know and I appreciate that.'

'Then fucking what?!' Mudge screamed at me.

'Why aren't we killing the fascists?' Rannu asked much more calmly.

'The what?' I asked, confused.

'Their ideology, it's called fascist or Nazi. It's pre-FHC. The fucking bad men!' Mudge explained not very helpfully.

'We're on the eve of what could be the biggest human-on-human war since the FHC. This is in part our fault—' I started.

16

'Bullshit. Rolleston and Cronin could call it quits any time they want,' Mudge pointed out.

'We have to take responsibility, wasn't that what you said?' I asked.

'You want to go and fight the Black Squadrons?' Rannu asked. For the first time I realised this held some appeal for Rannu. I'd known I was holding him back by getting his help in dealing with the Wait when I'd thought I'd wanted to. I had thought I was holding him back from returning to his family. It seemed it was something else.

'No. That's it. I don't want to kill any more people. Enough is enough.'

'Oh, this is bullshit. This was the same song you sang before Atlantis,' Mudge said, but he was calming down.

'And we didn't kill anyone.'

'We tried damn hard with Rolleston.'

'Him I'd make an exception for. He needs to die for the general well-being.'

'So do those fuckers!' Mudge exploded. Rannu was nodding. 'Those silly wank-stains want to kill you because your grandmother was from Thailand; they want to kill Rannu because his skin's a different colour to theirs. For fuck's sake, we raise the average IQ of the race by putting these cunts out of our misery!'

'No doubt, but I can't do it any more. We were so close to an end to it all, so close to peace ...'

'I think we may have to fight some more first,' Rannu said.

'Probably, but not me. Don't you think we've done enough?'

'I think we've done a lot. I think we'll know when we've done enough. There will be peace and my children will be free.'

'I'm sorry, but someone else is going to have to fight this one,' I said. Rannu nodded. I think he understood but I think he was disappointed as well. I turned to Mudge. 'Are you going to fight?'

Mudge pointed at the huge dust storm in the distance that was Crawling Town. 'I just want to kill the arseholes,' he whined. Rannu and I looked at him. 'You know me, I'll shoot it.' He tapped his camera eyes in a way that put my teeth on edge. 'And if it gets too hairy ...' He rapped his legs with his knuckles. His cybernetic legs were his pride and joy. He'd paid a lot of money to be able to boast that he was built for speed. 'I'll just do a runner.' He'd always said that. It was all bullshit, he never ran.

'Vehicle incoming,' said Rannu, the only one retaining any degree of professionalism.

Mudge and I looked up. Both of us zoomed in on the bizarre vehicle approaching us, which looked like a cross between a six-by-six pickup truck and a hearse. The front passenger side seemed to have been cut away and there was something monstrous and metallic sat there, a little smaller than an exo-armour suit. Through the magnification on my eyes I could make out the brightly coloured glowing veves painted on the side of the vehicle. These were the mystic symbols of Papa Neon's own brand of Pop Voudun. The truck definitely belonged to the Big Neon Voodoo.

It pulled up next to us in a cloud of toxic dust and dirt. The monstrous thing in the truck's cutaway cab was Little Baby Neon. Younger brother of Papa Neon, he had traded his soul for cybernetic power until he was a deranged, uncontrollable psychotic. His older brother had, as far as I could tell, effectively lobotomised him in an electronic ritual and turned him into a cyberzombie.

Little Baby Neon climbed out of the pickup/hearse. Actually he more sort of unfolded himself. The suspension looked glad of the relief.

We were sort of friendly with the Big Neon Voodoo, but it was more through Pagan and he wasn't here. I had one hand in the car, close to where my Benelli assault shotgun scabbard was strapped to the underside of the roof. Mudge was doing likewise with his converted AK-47. Rannu just stood close to where his shotgun/sniper combination weapon was clipped to the dirt bike.

With Little Baby Neon watching us, the pickup/hearse moved round so its back was facing us. Dry-ice smoke started to issue from the back of the vehicle. Mudge glanced at me, his eyebrow raised questioningly. The back doors opened, then the glass roof slid back. A colourfully decorated coffin, adorned with skulls, bones and other grizzly additions, rose up to a nearly vertical position. The front of the coffin swung open.

I started laughing, as did Mudge. I'm pretty sure even Rannu cracked a smile. Papa Neon's bass laughter joined us. He was a tall man with very dark skin. His weathered features were covered in implanted circuitry that formed veves on his face. Dreadlocks sprouted from his head where they could; the rest of it was either covered by a precariously balanced top hat, or by his military-built and black-market-augmented integral computer.

Papa Neon wore a long purple leather coat that looked heavy enough to be armoured and was again covered in many colourful symbols. As he stepped out of the coffin he leaned on his glowing neon staff. He looked every part the role of the Voudun priest and gang leader that he played so well.

He stepped down and we all relaxed somewhat. He nodded at

Rannu, who nodded back and courteously stepped away from the bike and the weapon clipped to it.

'Does that ever impress anyone?' I asked as the smoke was clearing, carried away by the dry wind that blew across the wasteland.

'No, but it is good fun,' Papa Neon announced in his thick Haitian accent. He looked me up and down. 'Are you dead?' he surprised me by asking. Then again hackers tend to see the world differently as a result of their various net-born religious manias.

'I'm as you see, Papa Neon. In no small part thanks to the drugs you supplied.'

After I was rescued from the Wait I had received medical treatment from the Big Neon Voodoo. This had included a substantial supply of drugs that had enabled me to cope with the symptoms of dying from radiation poisoning. Papa Neon gave this some thought.

'This is good. I think that the Loa have blessed you. I know this because they have told me. They are pleased that Obatala is now among us in the spirit world.' I think he was talking about God. 'I danced when he returned.' I knew he would. 'But the devil walks around the sun far out in the night,' he finished. I looked at him blankly.

'I think he means Demiurge,' Mudge suggested.

'Not my problem,' I said. Papa Neon regarded me carefully before reaching into the pocket of the threadbare finery that was his waistcoat and producing his UV monocle. He placed it in this eye and looked at me some more.

I was starting to feel the discomfort I always got when hacker pseudo-religious bullshit was brought up. Particularly when it was applied to me. I realised it was how they understood the world around them. At its heart they just had a different but arguably no less valid way of understanding things. It still always sounded like madness to me.

'Ogun Badagris has had too much fun.' I glanced at Mudge, who shrugged. 'Will you not cage his horse?'

'I don't know what that means,' I said, 'but my fighting days are over.'

He moved in close to me. I tried not to flinch. I could smell rum and stale marijuana smoke. Then something occurred to me.

'Have you been speaking to Pagan?' I asked.

'The Loa and the dead want to speak to you.'

'Where is he? Where's ...' I started and then suddenly felt very self-conscious, more about Rannu than Mudge. Though Mudge was reasonably well informed about how pathetic I could be.

'The Mambo walks in the lair of Anansi's twisted younger brother,' Papa Neon told me.

I looked at Mudge again. 'Anansi's a spider god, I think.' It didn't sound good.

'Look!' Papa Neon shouted. I turned to look where he was pointing and could just make out a large copter speeding towards us. Its rotors were folded and it was using its jets.

'The spider wants to speak to you,' Papa Neon began. 'The dead want to speak to you and the Loa have not done with you.'

Fuck. I just wanted a drink and a smoke, maybe some peace and quiet.

'Is that a black helicopter?' Rannu asked, a hint of incredulity in his voice. I shaded my eyes with my hands and watched as the copter's twin rotors unfolded and started to rotate. It was a military cargo model that had indeed been painted black, its windows tinted.

Mudge started laughing. 'Fucking spooks, man. One cliché after another.' He shook his head. 'They actually think this shit is cool.'

I turned back to look at Papa Neon. Maybe he was a cliché too, a stereotype. It was difficult to tell how much was real and how much was show – a bit of theatre and intimidation for those watching, waiting for his fall. Or maybe he'd played the role too long and believed it. Or maybe it was all real, which is what the hackers would have us believe.

'I think you came here to feed the Baron with those stupid white boys,' he said. Then it hit home.

'You were on us from the moment we came into Crawling Town,' I said.

'I asked Obatala to watch for you,' he said. Thanks, God, I thought. But the sense of betrayal was misplaced. This was what we had asked God to do after all. On the other hand, how were we ever going to sneak up on someone ever again? 'The way those boys killed you—'

'They didn't kill me ...' I started. Papa Neon looked at me in a way that made me want to not interrupt him.

'The way they killed you, you don't walk away from that.'

'Those boys are evil,' I told him. The copter was getting closer.

'No doubt, but they is our evil. You do not live here.'

I'd decided that the Wait got a pass, but I couldn't help smiling and playing devil's advocate. 'So how long would I have to live here before I could do them?' I asked.

'Jakob?' Rannu said. He had the sniper/shotgun combo in his hand. He unfolded the weapon and twisted the barrel, changing it from a smoothbore twelve gauge to a rifled twenty gauge. Turning it into a heavy-calibre marksman's weapon. I was aware that the copter was beginning its landing approach. He slid the magazine with the caseless twenty-gauge rounds into the combination weapon.

'You have to *live* here.' Papa Neon emphasised the *live*. 'We know the difference. Goodbye, my friend.' He turned, heading for his pickup/hearse.

The copter was now kicking up a lot of dirt. I reached into the car and slid the assault shotgun out of its scabbard. Mudge already had his AK-47.

'Goodbye, dead man!' Papa Neon shouted through the swirling dust.

The copter was heavily armed. I could make out rotary railgun turrets pointed in our general direction.

'Papa Neon! When the devil comes will you fight?' Mudge shouted over the roar of the copter's engines.

I could hear Papa Neon's deep laughter as the coffin closed and he sank into the back of the truck. Little Baby Neon was already in the cutaway passenger seat, and the vehicle made its way back towards the huge dust cloud that was Crawling Town. The cloud seemed to fill a lot of the horizon. I was sorry to see them go. It would have been nice to have someone as frightening as Little Baby Neon backing us up in a discussion with the inhabitants of the copter.

The three of us spread out. Mudge to my left, Rannu to my right. Our weapons were at the ready, held horizontally against our bodies but not pointing at anything in particular. The dust cloud engulfed us as the aircraft landed. We all switched, I'm guessing, to thermal to look at the copter in the reds, yellows and oranges of its heat signature. This was significantly masked, which suggested it was set up for stealth to a degree.

A door in the centre of the copter opened, stairs extending to the dirt. Three figures came out. We saw them as thermal outlines. They had weapons at their shoulders pointed at us.

Rannu and I had our weapons to our shoulders covering them. We each picked the closest target. I'd been working with him long enough to know that was what he would do. Mudge was a fraction of a second behind us.

'Drop your weapons!' they shouted. They were American. We didn't say anything; we just kept them covered.

'Drop your weapons or we will shoot!' The one in the middle was doing all the talking. Still we didn't reply. We just watched for the tells that they were about to fire. Hoped that we were quicker.

Worried about the copter's weapon systems, which were the biggest threat by far.

This sort of bollocks was typical of some paramilitary types. Had they landed and talked to us we would have talked back to them. Instead they'd probably read in some textbook somewhere the importance of establishing dominance in a power relationship so they could control the situation. The thing is, to us it wasn't about a power relationship, it was about a threat. If we didn't respond to having weapons pointed at us this time, then what happened the next time, when someone did actually want to do us harm? People like this never seemed to learn that they could get a lot further by behaving courteously. Would they get scared and back down or would they get scared and do something stupid?

Okay I admit it, part of it was that we just didn't like being strong-armed. If they were going to do that they should have brought a lot more people.

'We have you covered! Lower your weapons!' The vocal one shouted again.

'Should we threaten them back?' Mudge sub-vocalised over the comms. 'I can sound really macho and threatening when I want to.' I failed to completely stifle a laugh. Rannu grinned. This didn't help.

'Put down your guns!' He sounded shriller now. The dust was settling. The three of them looked almost identical. Boy Scout haircuts, dark glasses, anonymous dark suits, fancy European gauss carbines. They looked exactly like what they were: bad intelligence operatives. They may as well have worn a uniform. The question was: were they going to commit suicide today? The problem was that if they did it meant our imminent death at the hands of the copter's heavy weapons.

'Why are you laughing?' Mudge sub-vocalised. He even managed to sound genuinely peeved. 'I *am* threatening and intimidating.'

I decided to throw them a bone.

'Shut up, Mudge,' I said out loud. 'You want something from us?' I called out. 'Because if you do you're not going about it very well.'

'Drop your weapons. You are coming with us,' the guy in the middle said. All three of them looked nervous. We didn't.

'I can't think of any compelling reason to do that. Why don't you take your guns off us and tell us what this is about?'

'Put your guns down!' he screamed.

'His shrillness bothers me,' Mudge said. Rannu remained quiet. I favoured Rannu's approach more. I'd had enough.

'Put your guns down,' I said to Mudge and Rannu.

'What?!' Mudge demanded. I lowered my assault shotgun.

'Are you sure?' Rannu asked.

'These guys are dicks. They're also stupid. If we don't, they're going to force us to kill them.'

'Put your guns down!' He was sounding more masterful now. I think he thought he was winning. That this was somehow validation for being a dickhead.

'Shut up!' I shouted back at him. 'I just can't be bothered with it,' I said to Mudge and Rannu. I also didn't mention that the result of killing these idiots was death by rotary railgun. Both of them lowered their weapons.

The three idiots rushed up screaming at us to drop our weapons and lie down. Mudge started laughing at them. Rannu seemed to have just the slightest look of contempt on his face, which was unusual for the passive ex-Ghurkha. I was just bemused.

'Look, what do you want?' More screaming. 'You must be here for some reason. If you'd just tell us ...' Yet more screaming and threats. 'We're obviously not going to lie down, so what have you got left? Are you going to shoot us?'

The one closest to me produced a shock stick from a pouch on his belt. With a flick of his wrist he extended it. I couldn't shake the feeling he'd practised that move in the mirror. He triggered the display that sent sparks of electricity surging down the weapon. I wondered if it was supposed to intimidate me. What did he think I'd done for a living? I grabbed his wrist and stabbed him in the face with it. Which had to be embarrassing. I was pleasantly surprised that his internal systems were not sufficiently insulated, like mine, to cope with a shock stick, and he hit the ground a juddering mess.

Rannu stepped past the one closing on him. As he did so, he grabbed the barrel of the gauss carbine and pushed it up over the gunman's head. The gunman got tangled up in the weapon's strap and found himself lying on the ground with Rannu kneeling next to him.

Mudge cheated, in my opinion. The guy on him was distracted by the fun that Rannu and I were having. Mudge just sidestepped, drew his sidearm and levelled it at the guy's head.

I extended the claws on my right arm. Four nine-inch long, hardened ceramic blades slid out of my forearm through slits just behind my knuckles. I reached down to the recently electrocuted gunman, cut the sling off his gauss carbine and tossed it away. Then I walked over to the one that Mudge had covered.

'Are you more reasonable?'

'I ain't telling you shit,' he said in a manner I think he thought was macho. I was so frustrated I wanted to cry. Mudge clattered him on the side of the head with his pistol. I looked reproachfully at Mudge. Not because he'd hit him but because you shouldn't get so close to your target that they can reach you – as Rannu and I had just demonstrated.

'What do you want?!' I screamed. The guy just kept his mouth shut. 'Do you realise how fucking stupid it is to go to all this effort and not tell us?!'

'Someone wants to see you,' the guy that Rannu had taken down shouted.

'Shut up!' Mudge's guy yelled.

'You're supposed to tell us that,' I tried pointing out. I then walked over to Rannu and his prone friend.

'Who?' I asked him.

'Sharcroft,' he said. The name meant nothing to me. I told him that. Mudge joined us, forcing his prisoner to his knees in front of him. Mudge was sub-vocalising something as he did this.

'What does he want?' I asked.

'He has a proposal,' the guy said.

'Funny way of making it. If you'd succeeded then we'd be useless to him. You didn't, so he should have sent smarter people. Either way I'm not inclined to meet him.'

'Look, we fucked up.' He looked over at the guy whose face I'd electrocuted.

'Trying to prove yourself?' I asked. The guy said nothing. He just glared resentfully at his unconscious mate.

'Trying to prove himself, was he?' I asked. The look on the guy's face said it all. The arrogant part of me was scornful of them thinking they stood a chance.

'You need some proper trigger time, sunshine. You are way out of your league,' Mudge said. I turned to look at him and raised an eyebrow. Sometimes I thought that the SAS had been a bad influence on Mudge. Though it could have been the other way around. Mudge shrugged.

'Simon Sharcroft?' he asked the talkative one. The guy nodded.

'Know him?' I asked.

'Know of him. So do you,' Mudge said. Then he dropped the bombshell. 'He's one of the Cabal.' I lost my sense of humour and drew my Mastodon from its holster.

'Woah! Woah! Woah!' Rannu's prisoner shouted as he got a good look at the massive .454 revolver designed for killing Berserks.

'You fucking pussy!' Mudge's prisoner spat at the guy. 'Ow!' Mudge had clouted him round the head with his pistol. I think Mudge was starting to enjoy this sort of thing too much.

'What's going on?' I demanded. Was it starting all over again? Surely the Cabal couldn't be starting up again – could it?

'All I know is that he wants a meet, I swear!' Rannu's prisoner was begging. A text file appeared in the corner of my IVD sent by Mudge. I opened it and scanned the words superimposed over my vision.

Sharcroft was from some old – meaning pre-FHC – money family, America's answer to Britain's aristocracy. Right schools, right fraternities, probably got his arse whipped with rolled-up towels in the right secret societies. Sharcroft was a Pentagon II insider. He was an intelligence and government powerbroker and acted as a liaison between the multitudes of compartmentalised intelligence agencies that confused the American government and military. He'd made a name for himself early in his career by running very black ops for the CIA's paramilitary Special Activities Department. He was described as someone not afraid to make hard decisions. Or, from the perspective of people on the ground, he was a cunt who didn't care how many people he got killed to make himself look good.

No war record – he was too old, well over a hundred. He had of course been implicated when we revealed the Cabal to everyone. He'd been neck deep in their nasty shit but, according to the info Mudge had gleamed from God, had disappeared very quickly after the big reveal.

Mudge getting that info was not easy. A lot of very sensitive information had been erased from the net shortly after God had made it available to everyone. After all, God couldn't, or rather wouldn't, stop people doing what they wanted with their own information. However, while the powers that be were erasing their dirty secrets, hackers were racing to find them, copy them and make sure they stayed disseminated.

'We could go and kill him,' Mudge suggested. That wasn't such an unattractive proposal.

'Mudge, you are remembering your journalistic objectivity?' I reminded him.

'Sadly, I'm not a journalist any more; I'm a multimedia sensation,' he said matter-of-factly. I couldn't make up my mind if he was joking or not. Certainly all of us were recognised a lot more often after appearing system-wide on every monitor and viz screen capable of displaying an image.

'We should just go and kill this Sharcroft,' I told Rannu's prisoner.

'I could just tell him you didn't want to take the meeting?' he suggested.

'Where is he?' Rannu asked.

'Don't tell him anything! Ow!' Mudge's prisoner shouted as Mudge hit him again.

'New Mexico,' the prone gunman answered.

Mudge sighed. 'Why didn't you just say that in the first place?' he muttered.

2
New Mexico

We sat on the benches of the black copter opposite the three walking bruised egos that took the form of lower-echelon spooks. They'd optimistically asked for our weapons as we'd boarded the copter. We'd politely refused, Mudge had hit one, but I'd promised they could have their guns back at the end of the trip.

They'd also been more than a little annoyed when we'd loaded the four-wheel-drive muscle car and the dirt bike into the back of the copter. I mean cars and bikes don't grow on trees. We'd taken the time and the effort to steal them so we wanted to hold on to them. So the gunmen had spent most of the trip staring at us resentfully.

It was my first trip to America. Or rather my first trip over the border into the America controlled by the American government. I didn't get much of a chance to see it. Being in the back of some kind of military transport vehicle usually meant I was on my way somewhere to do something stupid, wasteful and dangerous. The journeys to and from said stupid, wasteful and dangerous things were often my only downtime. It had taken me a long time to learn the skill, but I could sleep anywhere, even in the back of these often noisy and always uncomfortable vehicles. I drifted off quite quickly. Careless perhaps, but I knew Rannu and Mudge had my back. They'd wake me when one of them wanted some rest.

Heaven appeared to glow a blue-white colour. It reminded me of something, something dangerous. I wasn't sure about opening my eyes but I felt good. In fact I felt the best I had in a very, very long time, presumably because I was no longer dying but was in fact dead. On the other hand, I remembered that I'd done an awful lot of bad things in my life, from stealing money from my parents to buy cigarettes when I was ten to killing a lot of people. Some in cold blood and some after I'd tortured them – those were the ones I felt most bad about.

I didn't feel quite so bad about killing Them. They may have been innocent dupes of the Cabal but they had been trying to kill me at the time, and it's a lot easier to kill things that look that different from you. Still, it can't look good on your application for heaven.

Then I decided that I'd been spending too much time around hackers and that I didn't believe in all that religious shit anyway. So where the fuck was I?

The selfish part of me was happy to see Morag in heaven. Then I started to mourn her death, which I should have done first, piece of shit that I am. Then again, I reminded myself that I didn't believe in any of that.

'What?' I managed. Morag smiled. She did look like an angel. Well, like a non-scary one with short spiky hair. She reached down to touch my face. Her hands felt warm. I felt warm and not at all like I was dying from vacuum exposure. Or being torn apart by Them. Or running out of air. Or just getting round to dying of radiation poisoning, which was something that I'd been meaning to do for the last couple of weeks. I also felt very naked and there were 'things' in me.

Mudge proved that I wasn't in heaven, though hell was possible, by appearing over me, leering. He looked fucking dreadful.

'The good news is you're not fucking dead; the bad news is there's no fucking drink to celebrate with,' he told me. He sounded angry.

'You look awful,' I managed to sort of squeak. It felt like I hadn't spoken for a very long time.

'He's run out of drugs,' Morag told me.

'They made this for us?' I asked again. It was taking a lot of getting used to. 'Are we prisoners?'

'More like stuck,' Morag answered.

I was in a cave in the side of an asteroid close to planetoid size. Across the front of the cave was a membrane made of ... well, made of Them. Them being the individual bio-nanites that were the actual aliens rather than the Berserks or Ninjas that we had previously thought to be Them.

This membrane kept us safe from the rigours of vacuum, and other Them-growths were apparently providing air, heating and somewhat unpleasant sanitation facilities. There is nothing quite like having a previously hostile alien species climb up your arse to clean it because they have never had to develop toilet paper. Other growths also provided a kind of unpleasant gruel and a funny-tasting liquid which I think was supposed to be water. I couldn't shake the feeling that we were eating some inert form of Them, perhaps Their dead?

What They couldn't produce, much to Mudge's discomfort, was drugs, cigarettes or vodka. He was mostly a sweating, cramping, pale, feverish bundle of bile in the corner of the cave. I wouldn't have minded a drink and a smoke myself.

The membrane was transparent, which allowed us to appreciate just how far out in space we were. I was looking out on what seemed to be a sort of crossroads. There were four very large asteroids including the one I was currently in. They were either tethered or just connected to one another by tubes like biomechanical Them-growths. There were more growths sticking out at all angles from the asteroids. These looked like a cross between organic high-rise buildings and stalagmites or stalactites, depending on your perspective. I recognised this place now. The crooked Them-structures had reminded me of teeth and I'd christened this area Maw City. We were not far from where we had fought Crom.

We used to think that these structures were Their habitats but now we knew it was just Them. Everything seemed to have a function in Their society. Their roots were deep in the asteroid. They somehow drew out the raw materials from them. With energy harnessed from the system's twin stars They broke down the raw materials to provide the resources necessary to make Themselves into these awe-inspiring structures.

Massive tendrils snaked between the asteroids, the growths and the hundreds of Them-ships moving through this apparent nexus point. I watched as one moved in front of me, completely obscuring my view. The tendrils moved anything from Berserks up to frigate-sized ships around. It was one of these things I'd seen grab Morag.

The whole place was crawling with Them. There were Berserks, Walkers and other things that we had previously thought to be vehicles. I also recognised a lot of the ship configurations I saw from footage of fleet actions.

If I strained and used the magnification on my optics I could see beyond Maw City. There were fields of a coral-like substance, where everything from Berserks to dreadnoughts were being grown and born. Deeper still I could see the cored hollow remains of exploited asteroids.

All the Them-forms we were used to seeing were black – combat forms, I guessed. But many here were white and had a pale-blue bioluminescent glow that I had become used to seeing in the honeycombed energy matrices of Their engines. It was the same bioluminescence that lit our little cavern. I had always thought it beautiful. Not that I could have told anyone. Maybe Morag, though even she'd take the piss.

The growths handling the air made it feel like there was a warm wind constantly blowing through the cavern. Apparently getting the heating, water and temperature right had been touch and go, initially. When I had been dying. There was kind of a lot to take in.

I looked at my hand. There were no scabs or sores, just healthy armoured flesh and boosted muscle. I felt great, no nausea. In fact it had been a long time since I had felt this good. Though I would have liked a cigarette.

'So let me see if I understand you properly. They ate all the unhealthy flesh and replaced or regrew it, at a cellular level. Is that correct?' I asked again. I heard Pagan sigh. I didn't really blame him, I had asked that question a lot recently.

He was sitting leaning against the wall in his inertial armour suit. He had his staff fully assembled and it lay across his lap.

Pagan was in his forties and one of the oldest people I knew who wasn't a member of a powerful secret government of arseholes. He was thin, his skin weathered and covered in various spiralling tattoos. Some of the tattoos were implanted circuitry to aid the ugly utilitarian integral computer that stuck out of half his skull. Unruly orange dreadlocks sprouted out from the other half. He was currently scratching at his scalp, running his hand through his dreads.

'Yes. We have similar treatments, but they tend to be only available to the wealthy,' Pagan explained. Again.

'So am I an alien?' I asked again.

'Undoubtedly,' Mudge groaned. He was lying on the floor, which was covered, in a soft, comfy, moss-like material. He was wearing only a pair of white boxers with hearts all over them. He got up onto all fours and started crawling towards the sanitation growth.

'No,' Morag said. She also sounded agitated. She was wearing her under-wear and a T-shirt and sitting on a rock also covered in the moss. I couldn't help but be distracted by her shapely legs. She was small, but the exertions of our time together had hardened her up. That could be seen in the tone of her muscles and sadly in her features as well. It did not detract from how attractive I found her.

Her hair had been shaved off so that the sophisticated integral computer she used for hacking could be implanted. Her hair was growing back but was still short, though it did cover most of the implant. The integral computer had been a high-end civilian model provided by Vicar so it was not as obtrusive as the military model sticking out of Pagan's skull.

I missed her eyes. After Rolleston and the Grey Lady had blown the side out of the media node, the explosive decompression had permanently blinded her. She had had her eyes replaced with cybernetic ones. They provided her with similar capabilities to the rest of us – magnification, thermographics, low light, flash compensation, etc. Her eyes were civilian models designed to look like normal ones. They had been modelled after pictures of her own eyes provided by Mudge, but I could still tell the difference. When you started replacing bits of yourself it had a cost.

'You're still you,' she reassured me. This was a sore point with her. After all, she was carrying around the information ghost of Ambassador in her neural cyberware and had been accused of being compromised by the alien on a number of occasions. I'd even done it during one of my frequent outbreaks of arseholery.

'Thank God!' Mudge shouted dramatically before collapsing face first into the sanitation growth. We all grimaced as he started to throw up the food substitute they'd been giving us. I was trying not to think of it as necro-gruel.

'It's astonishing to think that we actually managed to save an entire alien species from assimilation by Crom,' Pagan mused as he watched Mudge vomit.

'Is he going to be okay?' I asked Rannu. The quiet ex-Ghurkha was the closest thing we had to a medic. Mudge was annoying but he was my oldest and closest friend who was not dead. Also he'd never duped me into coming to Sirius to infect Them with the Crom slave virus. Though in fairness to Gregor that was more Rolleston's fault than his.

Rannu shrugged. He was stripped to the waist, his compact and powerful frame covered in sweat from his near-constant working out. That was probably the real reason he beat me in New York. He never stopped training.

'It's withdrawal,' he said. He still wore his kukri, the curved machete-like fighting knife of the Ghurkhas, at his hip. As he turned to grab a cleaning form to rub himself with I caught a glimpse of the stylised tattoo of Kali on his back. It had been done when he had been working undercover back on Earth.

'From what?' I asked. Actually meaning which drug. Rannu gave this some thought.

'Everything, I think. It shouldn't kill him because of his enhancements but he is going to be in a lot of discomfort.'

Knowing Mudge, that meant that the rest of us were going to be in a lot of discomfort as well. I still wanted a smoke.

'So I'm a hybrid like Gregor?' I asked. Morag opened her mouth to answer but Rannu surprised me by beating her to it.

'More like Rolleston.'

'Nice,' I said grimly. It made sense though. I felt stronger, faster and healthier than I ever had. Hell, I was looking forward to sparring with Rannu. I'd had so much of my flesh cut away and replaced with machinery and now what flesh I had left had been replaced.

Maybe I had died. Maybe all that was left was a sophisticated, or not, Themtech simulacrum that felt a little like me.

'So let me see if I understand this properly ...'

Even Rannu sighed and shifted to make himself more comfortable.

Mudge nudged me awake. I could hear the whine of the copter's engines straining. I looked out of one of the windows. We seemed to be sinking into some huge vertical tube of concrete and metal. It looked old. Maybe even pre-FHC.

'What is it?' I asked.

'I think it's an old missile silo,' Rannu said. 'For nukes.' That woke me up. I looked for confirmation from the three bruised egos in suits in front of us. They just glowered.

'You know it could just be a coincidence. Our invitation to New Mexico and God thinking that Morag is here, I mean,' Mudge said. I ignored him. He lit a cigarette to spite me.

'My comms is down,' Rannu said quietly. I tried mine. Nothing. Not even short-range person-to-person between the three of us.

'What's going on?' I demanded from the three spooks. They said nothing. 'You wanted us here. Do we have to fucking beat it out of you?' These were truly exasperating people.

'Have you got any religion?' the one in the middle asked. I just gaped at him.

'Are you asking if we've got anything with God on it?' Mudge enquired.

He nodded.

'What if we have?' I asked.

'You can't go in,' the middle one answered. I was beginning to see what was going on here.

'It's a comms quarantine. You're trying to keep God out.' Rannu voiced my suspicions.

'And how're you going to stop us?' born-again-hard Mudge asked.

'They probably just won't let us in,' Rannu suggested.

'Let's just get this over with,' I muttered.

We didn't have much on us as most of our comms stuff was internal and one of God's parameters was to be non-invasive as far as people's personnel cyberware went. I had nothing. I just contacted God through my internal comms when I wanted to speak to him. Rannu had some kind of medium-range comms booster and Mudge had bits and pieces of media tech. They had to leave all of this behind in the copter.

'And no pictures,' one of the failed gunmen told Mudge.

'Of course not,' Mudge said with false sincerity. We stepped out of the copter.

If I hadn't seen Spokes or fleet carriers or the Dog's Teeth the scale of the place would have been quite impressive. As it was, it was a big concrete hole in the ground.

We walked across the landing pad towards a set of blast doors. There were more suited types with guns waiting for us. One was walking towards us, his arm outstretched.

'Hold it right there, gentleman,' he said. Mudge grabbed his outstretched arm, twisted it round and wrist-locked him so painfully the guy sank to the ground. I shook my head as the rest of the security contingent raised their weapons and started shouting.

'Mudge,' I said over the shouting, 'he was being polite.'

'I didn't like his tone.'

'He called us gentlemen. Let him go.' Mudge gave this some thought but relented. The guy stood up, glaring at us and rubbing his wrist.

'Are you a reasonable person?' I asked him.

'I was until about thirty seconds ago,' he muttered, but he was gesturing at his security detail to calm down.

'You want our weapons?' I asked.

'Obviously.'

'It's not going to happen. Besides which, you can't disarm cybernetic weapons systems, and it would be no problem for us to take your weapons from you inside if we wanted to and use them. So you want us here, or Sharcroft does?' He nodded. 'Well, it depends on how much he wants to see us.' He gave this some thought, or more likely he was receiving instructions.

'We need to check you for information contamination,' he said, relenting. I nodded. His tech guys approached and started waving various sensors at us.

'Are you going to kill him?' the security guy asked.

'Not sure yet,' I mused.

Through the blast doors was a large chamber with a low ceiling. The walls, floor and ceiling were covered in some kind of metal mesh. We were walking on a raised wooden platform. The room was full of what I recognised as servers in liquid coolant tanks, a lot of them. I did not know a lot about IT but even I knew that there were vast amounts of processing power in here. There was also a lot of solid-state memory.

Interspersed among all the hardware were various bits of institutional office furniture. People in one-piece suits were sat at desks, many of them tranced in, most with some form of visible integral computer system and all hard-wired into the hardware. None of them were using wireless links.

Many of the available surfaces had liquid-crystal thinscreens stuck to them. Though not the walls or the ceilings, I noticed. They, along with several detailed holographic displays, were showing information about the colonies. Or at least that's what it looked like to me.

Mudge made a whistling noise as he blew air through his teeth.

'This whole room is a Faraday cage,' he said. It was a big room. 'It's designed to keep all surveillance out.'

It wasn't just the mesh; I saw jamming and various other electronic countermeasures and counter-surveillance tech strategically placed around the room.

'Lot of trouble to go to, to be free of God,' Rannu commented.

'Welcome to Limbo, gentlemen.' It was the sort of voice that I associated with energetic old people. I knew this from old vizzes as I didn't know any old people. It also sounded amplified.

I turned around to look at the villain of the piece. He looked the part, like the upper torso of a corpse in a high-tech armoured bathchair. The chair had six sturdy metal legs rather than wheels and covered his legs. He didn't move and barely seemed to be breathing despite the assistance of the life-support systems on the chair.

'Though I prefer to think of it as a haven for atheists.' The cheerful voice was coming from speakers built into the chair. I guessed this was Sharcroft. He looked dead long enough to be a Cabal old boy.

'Why are you still alive?' I asked.

'You mean why didn't the mob get me, Sergeant – or is it Mr Douglas now? I made a deal obviously.'

'No. I mean after you'd lived out your natural lifespan in comfort bought with our suffering, why didn't you just let yourself die?'

'You mean what am I afraid of? I'm not the only one here who should be dead, am I?' That was bad. He knew what I was. Of course he knew. That was the job of guys like him. I resisted the urge to start looking around for the dissection table.

'Its over though,' Mudge said. 'Your rejuvenation through Themtech is not going to happen. You're effectively dead anyway. Do everyone a favour and switch yourself off.'

'Did you really only come here to revive old arguments?'

Mudge nodded towards me. 'He came to see his bird.' I resisted the urge to shoot Mudge. Just.

'What's Limbo for?' Rannu asked before I could ask about Morag. 'I mean other than hiding from God.'

'Well, as you have pulled the teeth of every intelligence agency in the system—'

'And wrecked your sordid little secret government,' I added.

'Quite a big secret government actually, Mr Douglas. You all but pushed the more clandestine facets of government back to using paper and filing cabinets.'

'So this is a secure site for dirty little secrets so you sleazy little fuckers can start again?' I asked.

He actually sighed. 'If you like. It's one of many made up of what we managed to salvage from your act of wanton terrorism. This particular site has one function.' He paused. I think it was supposed to be dramatic. We waited. His voice sounded irritated when he started again. 'It is the clandestine part of the war against the Cabal.'

We gave this some thought.

'What silly twat put you in charge of it?' Mudge asked.

'I can assure you,' and again he sounded irritated, 'that there is quite a lot of oversight involved. After all, who better to know the machinations of the Cabal than a former member.'

'What? You're pissed off that Rolleston and Cronin fucked off with all your toys and left you here to die?' I asked. On the corpse in the chair I thought I may have detected a slight change in expression.

'Obviously.'

'Well, best of luck and I'd advise you not to cross my path again,' I told him. 'I'd like to go home now.'

'Don't you want to finish the job you started?' he asked.

'Your mess – you clean it up,' I told him. It wasn't strictly true of course.

'What did you want from us?' Rannu asked.

'We're not taking this seriously, are we?' Mudge asked. 'I mean I know we do a lot of stupid things but he's one of the bad guys.'

'There's a number of ways you can help us. Particularly you, Mr Douglas.'

I tried to ignore the relish in his voice but couldn't help reaching up and touching my assault shotgun's handgrip.

'Like what?' Here it comes.

'I believe you're hybrid? We believe that many of Rolleston's Black Squadrons are either hybrids or otherwise augmented with Them biotech.'

'What do you mean *you believe*? You fucking know because you were one!' Mudge was getting angry.

'So what if I am?' I asked.

'Well the data we could get from—'

'Experimenting on me?'

I remembered Gregor's warped features in his sealed chamber in the Cabal's genetics lab deep in the Atlantis Spoke. I took a step towards Sharcroft, my hand now round the shotgun's grip. Sharcroft didn't give, but I was sure I could hear clicks and humming coming from his insectile chair. It was the sound of weapons systems readying themselves.

'I fucking think not.'

'You're being selfish. You may have the answer we need.'

'I'm being selfish? I didn't start a war with an alien species just so I

35

could become one of the living dead! And while we're on the subject, what was the thinking behind that?'

'I cannot justify the unjustifiable.'

'What? That's it? Fancy talk for I know I'm a cunt?' I demanded.

'We're not talking about anything invasive—'

'Would a fifty-calibre sabot round in the head be an emphatic enough no for you?' I asked. I was genuinely in awe of this guy's nerve.

'Even if your capabilities are anything like Rolleston's –' now there was a thought '– we still have enough resources here to compel you to help.'

'An achievement you'd enjoy posthumously, well more posthumously,' Mudge told him. Rannu was glancing around, assessing the area, readying himself. I should have been doing the same but I was too angry.

'There are other ways you could help,' Sharcroft said after quite a tense pause.

'Such as?' Rannu surprised me by asking.

'We're sending people with your capabilities into the colonies to gather intelligence on the Black Squadron's forces.'

'Deep-penetration recces?' I asked despite myself, I was so surprised. I did the sums. Depending on how quickly they had got themselves sorted out they could have put boots on the ground and, allowing for the speed that information travels across interstellar distances, i.e. the speed of a ship, they could already have info from the colonies. They might actually know what's going on there.

'Hold on,' I said. 'Wouldn't they be comms blind? They must have released Demiurge into the net in each of the colonial systems.' That meant that any attempt to communicate would be compromised by a program with all of God's power but none of its hands-off charm. If Demiurge worked then it meant that Rolleston, Cronin and their lackeys had control of every electronic system connected to the net. That meant just about every electronic system. This would make it difficult to operate, as even interpersonal communications would compromise them, let alone ship-to-ship or ship-to-surface comms.

'According to our models Demiurge has indeed been released.'

'Models?' I demanded.

'You haven't heard back from anyone, have you?' Rannu asked quietly.

'Not as yet,' Sharcroft confirmed.

'Because it's a fucking suicide mission,' I spat.

These people made me sick. Come up with these bullshit ideas without any thought of the cost at the sharp end. Special forces operators weren't cowards, far from it, but we deserved a chance at survival.

That aside, I was appalled at the sheer power of Demiurge and in turn the power handed over to Rolleston and Cronin. They had completely sewn up the four colonial systems.

'Have you heard anything at all from the colonies since Rolleston escaped?' Rannu again.

'The only thing we've had from the colonies are ships that have come back with Demiurge in their systems,' he said.

I was slightly suspicious of how open this guy was being with classified information. It was almost like he was sure that we were part of the team.

'What happened?' I asked.

'God fought off Demiurge's attack and the craft were destroyed.'

I was impressed. Good for you, Pagan and Morag. Then I started wondering where Morag was again.

'Well there's your answer then,' I told him.

'It's not that simple,' he replied. It never is, I thought. 'God won because Demiurge only had the ships' systems, with their limited memory and processing power, behind it. God had much larger resources.'

'So Morag was right. Size is everything,' Mudge cracked.

'Time and a place, Mudge,' I said. Mudge took the hint. 'Well this is a fascinating insight into how much you're fucking up the war effort but I . . . we're retired. Best of luck.' I turned to leave and then turned back. 'How do we get out of here?'

'Do you not want to get back at Rolleston?' Sharcroft asked. His chair was rocking backwards and forwards on its six legs.

'Do you even know where he is?'

'We think—'

'No! You're fucking guessing. System maybe? Is he with the fleet? Is he on the ground? If so, which planet? Even if you know the planet they're still fucking big things to search? Do you know exactly where he is? I'll settle for a city. Because then all we'd have to do is infiltrate a planet, comms blind, fight our way past all his Themtech-enhanced super-troopers and then kill someone who can survive sustained fire from a Retributor. We're retired.'

'Assassination, sabotage, fostering resistance, getting the truth—'

'Don't say truth!' I roared, completely losing it. Now everyone in the chamber not tranced in was staring at us. Many of the security types were fingering their weapons nervously. 'It's a fucking swear word in your mouth!'

'Er ... Jakob?' Rannu said. I ignored him.

'I said no and I mean go and fuck yourself!'

'Hello, Jakob,' Morag said. The blood or whatever I had in what was left of my veins froze. I turned to look at her.

She was wearing one of those ridiculous one-piece white suits. She was the only one who looked good in it. She was genuinely pretty, not attractive, not beautiful but pretty, though she looked older and harder than she had when I'd first met her not more than three months ago. She'd kept her hair short. It was spiky, almost boyish now. I tried not to wonder if it was a reaction to the forced femininity of her previous life as a rig prostitute.

I was so pleased to see her. I was so fucking angry to find her here.

Pagan was standing next to her. He looked ridiculous in his white one-piece. He also looked lost without his staff. It was as if they'd tried to rob him of his identity, his stature, by removing his neo-Druidic props and forcing him to dress in institutional chic.

I felt resentment towards him. This was what he'd wanted – influence over Morag. I realised that was irrational jealousy. I was being a prick. If it hadn't been for Pagan, Crom would've won in the Dog's Teeth.

Rannu nodded at them both. Morag smiled. She seemed genuinely pleased to see him. Another stab of jealousy.

'Hi, Morag, Pagan,' Mudge said, admittedly guardedly, but it was a good model of how to behave in the situation.

'What the fuck are you doing?!' I screamed at her. I mean Pagan was here too, but this was of course her fault. Besides, I'd never slept with Pagan.

'Trying to help! What the fuck's it got to do with you?!' Her Dundonian accent became broader as, like me, she went from guarded neutral to screaming straight away.

'He –' I pointed at Sharcroft '– is the fucking enemy!'

'Set a fox to catch a fox,' Pagan said. Even he didn't even sound like he believed it.

'Shut up, Pagan!' I shouted, barely glancing at him before turning back to a furious-looking Morag. 'What are you trying to do? Ensure that everything we did was for nothing! Was meaningless?!'

I was aware of Pagan, Rannu and Mudge all shifting, making themselves comfortable.

'Oh, that's right. Don't fucking bother finding out what we're doing; just assume the worst and start shouting! Presumably at some point you'll call me a whore!'

'Oh look, everyone. Jakob and Morag are fighting,' Mudge said. 'Wow, that almost never happens.'

I glanced round. Everyone else was looking bored and irritated. The anger was starting to drain from me.

'Now I know you're both Scottish,' Mudge continued, 'but not all communication has to be conducted by screaming at each other.'

'Well, as entertaining as this is, we have work to do. So if you're not going to help you'll have to leave,' Sharcroft said.

'Are you really going to turn your back on it all?' Morag asked, more softly now. I could still hear the anger and the resolve in her voice.

'Turn my back? That's not fair. Don't you see that this is just starting the whole mess all over again?'

'Mr Douglas, do you not think that the Cabal, as you so prosaically called us, has agents on Earth? With your background can you not see the need for secrecy, for operational security?' Sharcroft asked.

'For petty empire-building?' Mudge asked.

'For fighting a war,' Pagan said.

'So God's over and done with. On to the next thing, aye, Pagan? Drag Morag down with you because you know she's better, but reflected glory and all that. You fucking sell-out.' I was just lashing out now.

Pagan looked like I'd slapped him.

'That's not fair, man,' Mudge said.

'Who exactly do you expect to save you?' Sharcroft's modulated electronic voice asked.

'I never expected to be saved,' I told the living spider-corpse. It sounded hollow even to me.

'That's a cop-out,' Morag said quietly.

'So what should I do – turn myself over for dissection or just fuck off and die under an alien sun? Any battle's going to be fleet and electronic anyway, probably followed by surface insurgency. You forget, I've done all this. Besides, aren't you and Pagan just telling us that it doesn't matter; there's always going to be some prick in charge?' I nodded towards Sharcroft.

'Didn't you say it was all about personal responsibility? We helped make this situation; we have to help fix it,' she said.

'How? By defecting?'

'You know we haven't done that.'

'The sad fact is, Mr Douglas,' Sharcroft began again, 'that I'm very good at this sort of thing. I am the kind of cunt –' he seemed to savour the word '– that you need. As for my previous associations, I don't care whether you judge me. I don't have to justify myself to you. You will never understand my motivations because you have never had any power and so cannot understand that once you've had it, it becomes very important to maintain it. You'll do anything.'

'That sounds like a justification to me,' Mudge said. 'Though not a very good one.'

'No. I'm simply explaining that we are so different we're never going to see each other's perspective, so arguing about it is utterly pointless. If it's any consolation, from your perspective I would now seem to be on the side of the angels.'

'Oh, that's exactly what it seems like to me,' I said sarcastically.

'Did you really think that with the threat of Rolleston and Cronin looming that the military, industrial and intelligence complex would just dismantle itself? Did you not think that they would adapt to the new circumstances, as difficult as you all, rather foolishly, made it? Can you not see the requirement for us?'

'There are ways and means ...' I said falteringly. 'Look, you guys started the whole thing.'

'Irrelevant except perhaps as testimony at my war crimes trial. We still have a situation to deal with. The question is, are you going to help or are you going to abrogate responsibility?'

'To work with the likes of you?'

'Do you think I'm happy about that? I think you're meddlesome cretins in way over your heads, lashing out because you don't under-stand what's happening around you and too frightened to make the hard decisions. But we all have to play the hand we're dealt, Mr Douglas.'

'Things have to change,' I told him. On the one hand I completely believed this; on the other I realised how empty it sounded.

'So change them,' Morag said. 'Don't run away.' Maybe she was right. No, she *was* right but I just didn't think I had any more to give. I don't think any of us did, her and Pagan included. I also didn't think they had any practical solutions, just death sentences.

'If only it was that easy,' I said to her, and then to Sharcroft: 'Thanks for the job offer but go and fuck yourself, parasite.'

'And the rest of you?' Sharcroft asked. Divide and conquer.

'I'm with the overwrought one,' Mudge said. Rannu didn't say anything.

'We're done. How do we get out of here?' I asked.

'We're not done. We've got something to do, and you guys are coming with us,' Mudge told Pagan and Morag. Pagan nodded, getting it before I did.

'They have—' Sharcroft began.

'Be quiet,' Rannu said. He'd been looking thoughtful throughout the conversation but the menace in his tone was unmistakable. Morag looked as confused as I did. I should have known better.

I think we were in Old Mexico. Either that or we were in part of New Mexico that looked like Old Mexico. Anyway it looked like I'd imagined Mexico looked. That could have just been for the tourists, though tourists in this part of town would have to be quite intrepid and well armed.

We were in the upstairs private room of a bar, sorry, *cantina*. It had a small wrought-iron balcony that looked out over a crowded street of revellers, which is a fancy word for drunk people, the service industries that survive them and the predators that prey on them. It was a pleasantly warm night.

'To Vicar, Balor, Gibby and Buck!' Mudge shouted. He was halfway to standing on the table. 'Better men than us by dint of having the common courtesy to die doing stupid things!' He knocked back his shot of tequila and then chased it with a long draw from a bottle of the same.

'To Vicar, Balor, Buck and Gibby!' we all shouted and knocked back our shots. I grimaced. I struggled with tequila, conceptually. As far as I knew it was rotting whisky. Why would you purposefully let whisky rot? It didn't make sense. Also I didn't like the way the worm in the bottle glowed. In fact I didn't like that there was a worm at all.

Mudge fell off the table. We laughed at his pain. He tried to get up but Rannu knocked his leg out from under him.

'Don't do that,' Mudge slurred. 'Spensive.' I think he meant his prosthetic legs. When you're a front-line, or in our case behind-lines, soldier you don't think in terms of the grand scheme. You think about small objectives – kill someone/something, disrupt a supply line, extract another squad in trouble. You assume that you're part of a bigger picture and that what you're doing will help, despite the doubts. Sitting there and thinking that you successfully saved an entire alien race from being assimilated by bad guys was just too big to get your mind around.

Getting back in-system and not ending up in prison, or in my case being dissected, had taken up everyone's attention, and then we'd each had things that we'd felt had to be taken care of. In doing so we'd forgotten that the four people mostly responsible for our success, the four people who were responsible for us being alive, needed a send-off. They needed remembrance.

Don't get me wrong, if Pagan hadn't figured out Crom's betrayal then we would've been dead, and if Morag hadn't successfully established contact with Them we'd definitely have been dead. Vicar had sacrificed himself to try and give Morag and I enough time to escape from Rolleston. Buck gave his life fighting the Cabal, killed by the Grey Lady. Balor had kept Crom – I wouldn't think of that abomination as my friend Gregor – busy long enough for Gibby to fly the ship into it.

Rannu and I had largely been spectators. Admittedly spectators fighting for our lives against Them. Mudge had been recording it all for posterity. He'd made them heroes. A difficult word to take seriously, particularly in the military, but it applied here.

So here we were to send them off, their wake. I suspect they deserved a global celebration. What they got was the five of us drunk out of our minds telling the funniest stories about them we could remember. Mudge told us about the time he'd been hiding in New York. Balor had a meeting with someone from the American government. To make the government man nervous he'd taken the meeting naked, sporting a huge erection in a room completely covered in thinscreens showing footage from wildlife vizzes of fish spawning. Mudge and I told the story about Vicar on the *Santa Maria* giving me the lock burner he'd hidden in his arse. I told a story I'd heard second-hand about Buck and Gibby accidentally bombing a Them surface-to-air emplacement with live chickens meant for a dinner being held by some hopelessly optimistic officers.

Everyone had a story of some kind, mainly about Balor, who was better known. Many of them were probably pure myth. Mudge and I knew a reasonable amount about Buck and Gibby, and we all had something to say about our time with them. We got more drunk.

I hoped that the Hard Luck Commancheros had done the same for Buck and Gibby back in Crawling Town. I also hoped that the pirate nation of New York had done the same for Balor. Though reports out of New York pointed to widespread conflict between factions that had previously been held together by Balor's sheer force of personality.

It was Vicar I felt sorry for. He'd never seemed to have any people around him. I'd only known him on the *Santa Maria*, the trial and then in Dundee. It had mainly been a business relationship. He had provided me with tech I needed when I could afford it. I didn't think his desperate congregation was going to miss him. Maybe the food and the clothes he gave out, but not all the hellfire and damnation.

Did he have any family that would miss him? Did they know? Maybe it was something I should look into. I could tell them just what sort of person the mad old bastard really was. Make them proud. If they cared.

'The sun's coming up!' Mudge announced, and the night did seem to be developing a red tinge to it.

'You're not thinking of quitting now,' Pagan managed after a number of attempts. 'Lightweight,' he added.

'Nope. This wake has moved into the next phase. The one I like to call whore phase!' Mudge announced. 'Though I have in the past called it sexually transmitted disease phase.' Mudge tried standing up but failed. He turned to look at Morag. 'Don't worry. I didn't mean you.' We all stopped.

Morag glared at him but then cracked up laughing. She reached over and tugged at his cheek. 'S'all right, love. I'm not your type, am I?'

'Nope, not enough penises,' Mudge agreed. Rannu, who was quiet when drunk – at least I hoped he was drunk, the amount he'd had – seemed to be puzzling this comment through.

'How many penises does Morag have?' he finally asked. We fell about laughing. Rannu just looked confused. We'd had a dangerous amount to drink.

'The question is: how many penises does he want?' Pagan suggested.

'All of them! All the penises!' Mudge shouted. There was cheering from the street. 'Besides, Morag and Jakob have to go and have angry make-up sex!'

'What! Now wait ...' I managed, but Morag just grabbed me.

'C'mon.'

There was an urgency to it. A need, for both of us. It wasn't angry but nor was it tender. She rode me as I held her up, her back against the wall of the aging, rotting room at the top of the *cantina*, the glass door to the balcony open to the dawn air. Maybe it was passion – difficult to remember. She led the way. She was in control. She had to be.

Because afterwards she sobbed and shook in my arms as I tried to fight off the hangover I so richly deserved. It was the frustrated sobbing of someone who can't shed tears because their eyes are metal and plastic now. I held her. I said nothing. This wasn't just the normal emotional retardation of a male not knowing what to do when his girl's upset. I knew there was nothing I could say.

I knew what was wrong. We'd talked about it when we'd finally had the chance to in the Dog's Teeth. When we'd finally had the chance to do the talking bit that normally comes first with people in a relationship. Talking was difficult when people are trying to kill you all the time.

I think she liked sex. I think she liked me enough to want to have sex with me, for whatever that was worth, but she'd spent so much of her life being used. She said at times that she'd felt little more than an appliance, the cheap alternative to sense booths. That made sex complicated for her. She wanted it; she liked it; but then doing it made her feel cheap. Doing it reminded her of so much bad stuff. What could you say to that? All I could do was hold her.

It didn't help that when we had been really intimate, when we'd shared a sense link, felt what the other felt, I'd fucked it up by getting scared and acting like a prick. In my defence it was because the alien essence that lived in Morag's headware had taken that moment to enter my head and change my dreams. That still didn't help Morag or excuse my behaviour.

I held her until she stopped crying. I guess I was surprised that she was still able to be this vulnerable with me after all the bad things I'd said to her in the past. Then it occurred to me – if not me then who? Then we made love again. This time more tenderly. This time she didn't cry. Afterwards she fell asleep. I resisted sleep for as long as I could. I wanted to watch her, and sometimes sleep wasn't so good for me. Eventually I drifted off.

Morag had been training with Rannu. Mainly physical training but some hand-to-hand stuff, the kind the Regiment taught us as well as the Muay Thai that he excelled at. She was still hot and sweaty, my arms wrapped around her as we looked out over Maw City. It was like a bioluminescent termite mound but somehow beautiful at the same time. It was difficult to explain. Their industry was somehow hypnotic. The others were further back in the cave.

Pagan and Rannu were discreetly keeping their distance and Mudge was too ill to be obnoxious. Actually that wasn't true. He was too ill to move; he was never too ill to be obnoxious. This was as close to privacy as we were going to get. I was frustrated because this was the first time in a long time we weren't in immediate danger.

Morag took the metal of my right hand in her much smaller one. The tactile sensors in the hand sent messages to my brain, a simulation of touch. With my real hand, albeit a hand that had armour and enhanced muscle under the skin, I stroked her hair.

'Why don't you train me?' she asked.

'Laziness, and Rannu's better than me,' I told her.

44

'Not because you don't want me to know this stuff?'

'You need to know this stuff, I guess, but I'm not keen for you to be in harm's way, if that's what you mean.'

'You don't have to be protective all the time,' she said, but there was no sharpness in her tone.

Eventually I think I worked out what she was getting at.

'I have faith in your abilities, if that's what you mean,' I told her.

She smiled. See? Given time I could think of things to say that weren't just going to upset her.

We sat there for a while watching the industry of the alien habitat. All the zero-G manoeuvring looked so graceful, much more so than the clumsy machines we utilised. I guessed that's what came of evolving in vacuum.

'What are They like?' I asked after we'd sat in silence for a while. Morag gave this some thought.

'Very different. They think as one and They just haven't developed certain things that we take for granted.'

'Like what?'

'They don't understand that we don't think as one like Them. They can't see how some of us would act against others of us. The biggest problem I had was trying to explain what happened with Crom. Even the concept of the Cabal is beyond Them. They just don't get duplicity at all.'

'That would explain their tactics during the war.'

'There's something very soothing about communication with Them. Something warm. Like this place.'

'Womb-like?' I wasn't sure where that had come from. Again she gave it some thought before answering.

'I wouldn't know.' She sounded distant.

She was quiet for a while.

'I can trance in, you know,' she said. I looked down at her and found her looking back at me, searching for my response.

'Yeah?' I managed. I wasn't sure what to say.

'I mean, I haven't but I know I can.' She looked away from me.

'Have you heard of Project Spiral?' I asked.

She nodded. 'Vicar worked on it. It was the American and British governments' attempt to hack what they thought was Their comms net,' she said.

'But it wasn't, was it? It's Them, Their minds.'

'Yes, but it's Their comms net as well. They have the equivalent of biotechnological telepathy.'

'Maybe, maybe not. You could argue we have that with integral comms links,' I said.

'I don't think it's the same. I'm going to trance in. With my own systems and Ambassador's help I should be able to do it.'

'You know what happened in Operation Spiral?' I asked, sounding calmer than I felt.

'No, do you? I'd be interested, but God's so far away. I know the results of what happened. Everyone brain-burned or mad. Vicar—'

'Was the best of them,' I finished for her.

'But they didn't know that it was Their mind and they hadn't been allowed in.'

I wanted to talk her out of it or at least tell her to be careful. I didn't. I was sort of sure she knew what she was doing though this was uncharted territory for all of us. How did an ex-Rigs hooker end up on Earth's first contact team? Okay, not first contact, but still.

'You can come. I can piggyback you.' She seemed to be serious. She looked cross when I started laughing. I wasn't laughing at her; I was laughing at the ridiculous, mind-blowing scope of the thing.

'Me in an alien mind? I think Mudge would be a better person for the job.'

'I don't want Mudge with me.' She sounded a little put out.

'I just ...' I struggled for the words to try and say what I meant. 'All I've ever really wanted is to not be hungry, or in pain or frightened, or so tired all the time. I don't think I want much – to make a living in a way where I don't have to get shot at or kill other people, like my dad did after he was discharged.' Before some rich bastard killed him because he could. 'Then a good book, some Miles Davis in the background and a dram.' Morag was watching me intently but also smiling. 'Now you're talking about going surfing in the mind of an alien race who I've spent all my adult life trying to kill, and they've been doing likewise to me. I've no frame of reference for this.'

'Are you frightened of it?' she asked. This I had to think about. I should be, I really should be.

'No,' I finally said.

'Isn't this how it's done?'

'What?'

'Peace. You try to understand the other guy.' It was quite a naive thing to say. It helped remind me of our age difference. Something I tried not to think too much about in case I didn't like the answers I came up with.

'I don't think so. I think powerful people make deals. Your way would be better but difficult to do after a war because we're so used to thinking of the other guys as less than human.'

'My way would be better if we had done it before the war.'

'So they'll just let you in for the asking?' I said, changing the subject.

'I won't be the first.'

I looked down at her to see her grinning mischievously at me. It was a hint of the childhood she'd never had.

'What do you mean?'

Her expression changed. 'Are you all right with this now? With what they did to you?'

Another complicated question. I stroked her hair and looked down into her eyes. They were like mirror images of her real eyes. Now she would only ever see me through a machine, they same way I could see her. It had been so long that I couldn't remember what it was like to see with real eyes.

'When you first get augmented it's really cool. All your new capabilities are exhilarating, I guess. You're stronger, much faster, see and hear further, all that. But a horrible amount of my body is machinery.' I felt her running her fingers up the scarred skin of my chest. She would feel the hardness of the armour under the skin. 'You start to feel like part of you is missing, dislocated somehow. It's like you know something is wrong but you don't know what. I've heard people say that they feel like they're haunting themselves. It's the sort of thing that people say just before they go psycho.' I played the tips of my fingers over the plugs in the back of her neck. 'I'm just eager to hold on to what I've got left, I mean really eager.' She pulled her hair down over the plugs in the back of her neck.

'How do you feel?'

'Really good,' I answered straight away and then found myself surprised by the answer.

'Everyone thought you were going to freak out.'

'I did, didn't I?'

'Not as much as we thought you would. Mudge said you'd either try and throw yourself through the membrane –' fat chance, I didn't like vacuum '– or feed yourself into the toilet creature.' She shivered as she said this. I don't think she liked the toilet creature much.

'Yeah, well, nobody else is an alien.'

'You said I was.'

'How many times do I have to apologise for that? Look, I saw what happened to Crom.' Don't call it Gregor. 'And I don't want to be like Rolleston.'

'You don't want to walk through railgun fire?'

I gave that some thought.

'Depends on the cost.' I wondered if I did have any extraordinary capabilities. I guess there was no real way to find out until something really bad happened to me. Well either that or I started self-harming.

'Do you feel human?' she asked.

I had to laugh at this.

'What?'

'The weird thing is, I feel more human than I have in a long time.'

'So you're going to accept it and, you know ...'

'What?'

'Not be a difficult tosser about it?'

I started laughing as she smiled again. We lapsed into silence, enjoying each other's company. Watching the industrious aliens, trying to ignore the sound of Mudge retching. It was romantic.

'What are They going to do?' I asked. The intelligence we had on Crom was sketchy at best, but the Cabal probably still had the ability to manufacture more. They could either destroy or control Them if they wanted.

'They're leaving,' Morag said. She sounded so very sad. Like crying sad. 'We're too chaotic, too dangerous, too ... too hateful, and duplicitous and greedy and violent.' Now she sounded angry. 'Even though we have enough of everything.'

I wondered how she could even imagine that after growing up in Fintry and the Rigs, where everything you needed just to live had to be fought for in one way or another. I held her close to me. Again she was being naive, but I couldn't fault her logic. We as a race did have enough. I didn't really have anything I could say to her.

'They're going far, far away, all of Them. As far as They can get, and when They see us coming in the future, if we have one, They'll go further still because we can't be trusted. It was what I told them to do.'

I wasn't sure she quite understood the significance of what she had said. Here was an eighteen-year-old girl from what middle-class corporate wage slaves would describe as the dregs of society – though those dregs seemed to get larger and larger every day – advising an entire alien race on its foreign policy.

'And They're going to do that?' I asked.

She nodded. 'Our loss.'

She was right. This was a race that had gone from inert singing space coral to the technological equivalent of humanity in just a few years after the Cabal had provided the correct stimulus. Had we managed to communicate with Them peacefully the advances we could have made in biotechnology would have been staggering. Also I had heard Them sing.

Morag stood up and took me by the arm, pulling me after her. I stood and allowed myself to be dragged along.

'Watch this,' she said. She took me along a short corridor towards another membrane that led deeper into the rock. She pulled me towards it, reached out and pushed her hand through it.

'Morag!' But her hand was fine. She stepped through into another area of the asteroid. As she did the springy comfortable moss that I recognised from our side of the membrane started to appear under her bare feet. She pulled me through. There seemed to be a rush of air and it was slightly colder but warming up. The moss was continuing to grow in front of our eyes down the corridor.

Morag pulled me down the corridor into an area that I can only describe as a grotto. It didn't seem to have the utilitarian but often beautiful look that

Them-forms had. This looked like a human take on some kind of fairy-tale alien garden.

'You made this?' I asked her.

'No, They did, but I asked Them to.'

'Its not what you know,' I said under my breath. She ignored me. Instead she lay down on the moss and pulled me down on top of her. I covered her mouth with mine.

This felt like a reward. Not Morag giving herself to me but both of us being here, alive. It felt like a reward for everything we'd been through because we'd been trying hard to do the right thing. I don't know if we had, but intent's got to count for something.

I just wish that Balor, Buck, Vicar and Gibby had made it and got their reward.

I wondered if I was going to start wanting to go home. Morag took me somewhere else.

'So you're really not coming?'

She was sitting up in the bed, the cover wrapped around her while I stood at the window looking out over the rooftops of wherever we were. The heat haze almost made it look pretty. I turned to look at her.

'Morag, I know it seems like copping out to you but, as insane as the last three months have been, you weren't there for the previous twelve years. The crawling through mud, the getting injured, starving, no sleep, bad drugs, fear all the time and seeing people you like die so often you stopped bothering to get to know them. I've had enough, and despite what you may think I have no stomach for killing humans.'

'But it's all right to kill Them?' There was no judgement there, just a question.

'It's a lot easier, and They were mostly trying to kill me at the time. Look, I don't know if I'm me or the alien ...' She started to interrupt me. 'No, wait. But I should be dead, lucky breaks in combat aside.' Though, thinking about it, none of them seemed lucky; they felt like they'd been won through blood and pain. 'The radiation poisoning should have killed me. I've got a second chance in hopefully a changed world. I think it would be stupid and wasteful to just throw that away.'

She regarded me carefully for a while. I couldn't work out the expression on her face. Then she smiled. 'I think you are the alien.'

This confused me. 'I thought—'

'It sounds like you're starting to care about yourself.'

Maybe she was right, but I didn't want to analyse it too much. 'I think you may have underestimated how much of a coward I've always been.' I don't know why I couldn't look at her as I said it.

She dropped the sheet and climbed off the bed, coming over and wrapping her arms around me. I could feel how much her body had changed. How much tougher she had become. I could remember how fragile I'd thought she was. She kissed me. Brave girl after what I'd been drinking last night.

'I don't think you're a coward. I don't think you're copping out. I just wished, you know ...' Now she couldn't look at me. She laid her head against my chest.

'That I'd be around?' She nodded, her hair brushing against me. 'Look, if you're serious about this, if you think that we could be together without screaming all the time or trying to kill each other or me not doing anything stupid, then I can hang around. I just don't want to have anything to do with that prick Sharcroft. Besides, I always fancied being a cowboy.'

She looked confused. 'A cowboy? Like a cybrid?' she asked.

I laughed. 'No, really not.' Then suddenly she was sad again. 'What?'

'It's just that ... being here wouldn't help ...'

I didn't understand. Slowly it dawned on me what she was talking about.

'Morag, are you going off-world?'

Any warm feelings I'd had were replaced by a very cold fear crawling through me.

'We need to stop talking now.'

'Morag,' I grabbed her, my metal hand and my real one wrapping around the wiry muscle of her upper arms. 'Tell me you're not going to the colonies.'

She looked straight into the black lenses of my eyes. 'Let me go, now.' There was steel in her voice. 'Didn't take you long to change back, did it?' I let her go.

'Morag, it's—'

'Too dangerous? Again? What is dangerous is you keep talking about this.'

'I was going to say a death sentence.'

'You need to stop now.'

'You're right. There's no need to hang around here because that twisted, evil half-dead bastard is going to get you killed out of pure fucking speculation.'

'If you don't with your big mouth.'

50

She grabbed her clothes and stormed out past a surprised-looking Rannu. I wasn't sure I'd ever seen the normally calm Nepalese look surprised before. I don't know why he looked surprised. Morag and I were always fighting.

Being naked I decided to climb back into the bed and pull the sheets up. Then I tried looking for any leftover rotting whisky. Rannu stood at the bottom of the bed. He seemed uncomfortable.

'Sit down, Rannu,' I told him. I'd finally found a bottle with some tequila left in it. I took a swig and offered it to Rannu. He looked pained.

'Hangover?' I asked.

'Either that or I have severely offended the gods.'

'It was a good send-off,' I said, mostly for something to say. It had only been three ex-squaddies, a computer hacker and a journalist getting drunk in whatever shithole this was. I think they deserved parades and celebrations like the sort I'd seen in history vizzes and read about. Rannu nodded anyway, I think to humour me.

'You're leaving?'

'Apparently there's nothing to stay here for.' Though I had no idea what I was going to do next. 'You going home?'

'Not yet.'

'You have a family, kids,' I told him.

'Which is why I must go.' I recognised the resolve in his voice.

'You ever done anything this dumb?' Being a member of the Regiment he would have done a number of really dumb things under orders. He'd also done some dumb things with us.

'Not quite,' he said.

'It's a death sentence. This isn't Them; this is people with near-total surveillance who understand strategy, tactics, tradecraft, who know your training and have superior physical and possibly technological abilities. This is not the way to fight this war.'

'More than anything we need information.'

That I couldn't deny. 'How are you going to get it out?'

He just looked at me.

'We can't hide from God; how can you hide from Demiurge?'

'If I couldn't hide from God then we wouldn't be having this conversation,' he said evenly. He seemed more blasé about operational security than Morag had. He must have checked out the place for surveillance first.

'Are you going to let her go on her own?' he asked. I had not been so pissed off at him since he'd pulled my arm off and used it to beat me unconscious.

'Fuck you, Rannu. Fuck you and fuck your emotional blackmail!' I think he was taken aback by the amount of anger in my response. 'But as we're raising the stakes a little, when your body isn't found what do you want me to tell your kids? Daddy died on a fool's fucking errand working for exactly the kind of pricks we all nearly died fighting in the first place.'

He looked genuinely hurt by the time I'd finished. Genuinely upset and the most emotional I think I'd ever seen him.

'Don't talk about my family again,' he said and turned and walked out of the room. I felt like shit. Despite one-sided attempts to kill each other early on in our relationship, Rannu had been a rock. He'd dealt with all the shit that had been thrown at him and never complained.

I saw the cigarette smoke in the doorway.

'Are you recording this?' I asked Mudge.

'Yep. Fuck their operational security. You know there were a couple of Sharcroft's people watching us last night and apparently a surveillance team in the opposite building?'

I'd seen the tails but didn't know about the team. Made sense though. Problem was, these days your surveillance couldn't go over the net. Even radio waves were a risk, because the moment God knew then everyone could know if they just asked.

'Rannu dealt with them?' I asked.

'Non-lethally.' That would explain why he disappeared for half an hour at the beginning of the evening. 'He then cleared our rooms of bugs. Made sure that there was nothing God-like nearby and set up white noise and other counter-surveillance stuff. Hence the reason your total lack of discretion didn't kill anyone.'

'I thought you hated all this operational security stuff.'

'I do. Stops me from finding out all sorts of things. You don't though. Were you trying to blow their op before she gets started?'

'Are you coming in?' I asked. Mudge spun into the doorway. He had a pair of expensive-looking designer sunglasses over his camera eyes and a bottle of tequila in one hand.

'You hear everything?'

'I didn't listen to you have sex. Much.'

'That's weird, man.'

Mudge dragged a chair over and sat down, putting both his cowboy boots up on the bed.

'Give me a drink,' I demanded.

Mudge shook his head and took a swig from the bottle, grinned at me and then lit up a cigarette.

'Fag?' he asked. I was sorely tempted.

'Just give me a drink. Stop being selfish.' He threw the bottle to me. I took the top off, ignored the glowing worm and took a long swig of the foul-tasting stuff.

'Mudge.' I examined the bottle. 'You basically go around being obnoxious to people yet they still talk to you. I try not to be obnoxious and always end up pissing people off.'

He gave this some thought. 'I think you're more hurtful than I am,' he finally said.

'I don't mean to be. Besides, you say hurtful things.'

'Could you sound any gayer? I manage people's expectations. They expect me to be obnoxious so when I tell the truth they're less surprised. So what's next? Gonna alienate me?'

'May as well. You going as well?'

'Fuck that. It's a mug's game. Look, I got a rush driving around in landies, or flying around in gunships, shooting stuff and blowing shit up, but you're right. They don't know what they're getting into. They've got the training, or rather Rannu has, but he's never had to put it into action. It's an insurgency and they'll have to be criminals, terrorists ...'

'We've done that.'

'Not like this. Look, God love you, Jakob, but your big plan to deal with the Cabal and not kill any more people – and, you know, good for you, as much as I disapprove of this new pacifist you – was to get some big guns and go on system-wide TV. I mean, I get it. I loved it, but fucking subtle we are not. There's just too much we don't know, and without any way to communicate or feed back intelligence it's a waste of time. Actions like this are part of a big plan; if they're completely isolated then it's a waste of time.'

I was taken aback by Mudge's understanding. 'So I'm right?'

'You sound surprised. Yes, you're right.'

'But they're not stupid. Did you tell them this?'

'No.'

'Why not?'

'Its funnier when they all hate you.' I glared at him. 'Besides, I'm not sure I liked the look in their eyes.'

'Mudge, none of them have real eyes.'

He just smiled at me and took another drag on his cigarette.

'What are you going to do then?' I asked after taking another disgusting swig.

'Can I get you some lime and salt? No? Well we're fucking celebrities now.'

I wasn't sure about this. Fortunately I'd been dying of radiation sickness at the time so now that I was a healthy alien/human hybrid I looked different, but I'd still been recognised several times. Reactions were different. Some were supportive, enthusiastic, got what we'd done and why we'd done it. Many were downright hostile, blaming us for the war and their new near-total lack of privacy. Most were just suspicious. I'd punched the first guy who'd asked me for an autograph. I hadn't meant to; he'd just come up to me a little too quickly.

'I've been offered a number of jobs,' Mudge continued. 'Mainly in journalism but some in presenting. I intend to take the most prestigious and well paid first and then work my way down as I get fired for doing the most outrageous thing I can think of.'

'I think you'll like that. Good luck.'

'You?'

He was regarding me carefully. I think he knew that this was a question I was dreading. I didn't want to go and die in some shitty colony but I didn't know what I was going to do. I didn't have any cash. There was no way I was ever going to be psychologically capable of cashing in on my notoriety. I'd seen ex-special forces in the world of entertainment – it always made me cringe. Also I was well enough known and the results of our actions were still suitably up in the air for my notoriety to work both ways. Was I really just going to go back to pit fighting, scheme racing, ripping off people weaker than me, and the booths? If I was, then I still had to get back to Dundee.

Why would I want to go back to Dundee? The only reason I could think of was my bike.

'I don't know,' I finally said. 'I guess I'm staying around here and looking for work. Then who knows?'

'Is that in case you see *her*?'

'No, it's because I'm fucking skint.' And far too proud to ask if she still had any of the money that Vicar had given us.

'I got you covered.'

This pissed me off. Mudge could be like this sometimes. He came from a reasonably well-off family and his job paid a lot more than being in the SAS had. He'd often offer to pay for things. It was patronising. I didn't need charity. Okay, maybe I needed charity but still, I had my pride and a bottle of tequila. Admittedly it was Mudge's tequila.

'Look, Mudge, I've told you about—'

'Relax. I'm not about to further abuse your fragile Celtic pride. I made some investments on everyone's behalf.' He looked quite smug.

'What gave you the right—'

'Okay, let me put it another way. I capitalised on all our suffering.'

54

A file was blinking away in the corner of my IVD. Mudge had just sent it to me. I opened it up and saw what he was talking about. He'd sold the story, including the download and broadcast rights to an edited version of all the stuff that had happened.

'You should have asked us about this.'

'Jake, you get that I'm a journalist, don't you? Don't let my cameo as a revolutionary fool you – this is my job. It's the one thing I take seriously.' All flippancy was gone now.

I remember just after I'd first met Mudge he'd quoted some pre-FHC writer who'd said that a journalist's job was to charm and betray. They needed to get to know who they were writing about so they could reveal – not all, but what needed to be revealed for the story. Suddenly that struck me as a very lonely existence.

On the other hand, if these figures were right he'd made a fucking fortune.

'Merchandising?' I demanded.

Mudge started laughing.

'You'll love it, man. They've even got these cute little animatronic action figures. The one of you has really realistic sores from the rad sickness, but you get likeness rights on every one sold. Mind you, if we're inadvertently responsible for starting the war that wipes Earth out or if the Cabal win we might not sell very many. Also I think you're the ugliest. Balor, Gregor and Morag all tested well, as did I of course. Best of all, we make money off the figures of the villains.'

'Rolleston and Josephine?' I asked incredulously. Mudge was grinning. 'They're going to castrate you and dip the wound in biting insects when they get hold of you.'

I tried to imagine how angry the pair of them would be when they found out. As pissed off as I was by the idea of little action figures of me, if the figures were correct then I was not just looking at a sum of money but an income. It was like some kind of financial sorcery. How could I be earning this much money if I wasn't actually doing anything?

I continued reviewing the information that Mudge had sent me. He'd done well. It looked to me like he'd squeezed as much money out of this as possible. Everything had been divided equally, though arguably he'd done all the work. It wasn't just Morag, Rannu, Pagan, Mudge and me. He'd set up trusts in Buck, Gibby and Balor's names. He told me he was going to see if they had any of what he called 'genuine' family to hand the money over to. What he meant was he didn't want to give it to any freeloading opportunists who were vaguely related. If he couldn't find anyone he was going to give their money to charitable organisations that he thought they would have approved of. He reckoned it would mainly be veterans' charities, maybe shark conservation for Balor.

'So? Does this change things?' Mudge asked.

'It really does.'

'So what are you going to do?'

'Retire.' Then I saw something that caught my eye. 'You're calling your memoirs *My Struggle*?'

Mudge was grinning again. 'Yes, but only to upset people. I got the idea from the Wait.'

3
The Park

Initially I'd thought that taking the Mag Lev back to Britain would be interesting. The journey, I mean. But despite the incredible feat of engineering that was the transatlantic tunnel, at the end of the day it was just a long dark tunnel. Mudge and I got drunk. It had been Mudge's idea to take the Mag Lev, but go first class rather than take a faster sub-orbital. We only just managed not to end up in the train's brig.

In London, which Mudge had always described as his spiritual home, we went out drinking again. I stayed for a few days. I even met his mum. We went drinking with her as well. Suddenly, why Mudge was like he was started to make more sense. Apparently she'd used a lot of recreational pharmaceuticals when she was pregnant.

He also showed me some tricks of the moneyed classes – how to get places, transport authorisations, that sort of thing. More to the point, he checked out my legal status back in the homeland. We'd done some very naughty things in the name of what we'd thought was the greater good. Critics called us terrorists. I don't know why. We hadn't been trying to scare anyone; quite the opposite.

Air Marshal Kaaria of Kenyan Orbital Command had been appointed by the UN to extensively debrief us when we returned, as had numerous dodgy intelligence types. It seemed the Air Marshal, who I think was a grudging fan of ours, had managed to smooth things over with the authorities. Which was good, as it meant we weren't arrested and executed for using concrete-eating microbes on the Atlantis Spoke. The authorities had decided to, if not forgive us, then ignore us until it suited them.

We arrived back just after a hastily called election. It had surprised no one when God revealed that our government of whichever indistinguishable non-event of a political party was in power at the time was a bunch of shits. Those that weren't in hip deep with the Cabal were sucking other suitably sleazy and unpleasant big-business cock at the expense of the electorate. So they went. Though I'm not sure who people thought would do better.

Our new prime minister was a badly scarred submariner kept together with cybernetic parts who had served in the freezing depths of Proxima Centauri Prime. Reputedly she had served with Balor, though to her apparent credit she wasn't making a big thing of it. She had grown up in the East End in London's Bangladeshi community. She was a cockney through and through and made no apologies for her family's extensive connections to organised crime, though she had distanced herself from their criminal activities. She had run on a platform of national management instead of party politics and had a lot of support in the veteran community. Mudge liked her and compared her to some pre-FHC prime minister I'd never heard of. He'd texted me some books about the era.

Books. That was the best thing about money. I could afford real, old books with paper and bindings and the smell. And I could afford to download lots of good-quality music and buy real single malt Scotch from the park distilleries in the Highlands. Funnily enough I had no interest in the sense booths.

There was a better view on the Mag Lev from London to Dundee. Much of it went through parkland. I'd started paying attention to the date in my IVD. It was November now. I hadn't been back to Scotland since August. The hot summer had been replaced by a bleak grey autumn of near-constant driving rain.

The Mag Lev curved in over the Tay. It was slate-grey, broken by white-crested waves blown by a harsh, cold northern wind. I looked out the window. The four-track Mag Lev bridge was raised over an old pre-FHC rail bridge. It was a heritage site of some kind.

Even the bright colours of the Ginza were somewhat muted by the driving rain. I could see the Rigs to the east. They looked inert, still and dead, no sign of life. I couldn't shake the feeling that with my new-found wealth, my first-class ticket on a Mag Lev and my legal transport papers, I'd somehow betrayed them.

I thought about how I'd left Dundee. Sneaking out on a drug-smuggling sub. It had seemed like everyone was trying to kill us. Now this.

Betrayal or not, the Rigs fucking depressed me. Perhaps it was my new optimism, what Morag had said about caring about myself. Or perhaps it was my prospects, the changes that money brought, but I could not bring myself to stay and I had no reason to. This was a place you came when you had nowhere else to go. There was nothing holding me here. After all, the closest thing I had to a friend here was the slug-like sense pusher Hamish, and I really didn't like him. Mind you, the Grey Lady may have killed him on her last visit.

I'd lost my Rigs legs. It was with difficulty that I made my way across the rain-slick metal of the structures. Past the houses made of salvaged scrap, where people crowded round trash fires for warmth. I avoided a mugging and was able to give money to some begging veterans who hadn't managed to hold on to replacement limbs and eyes when they were discharged. I hoped it would help them for a little while, but I couldn't handle the way their empty eye sockets seemed to stare at me.

I stayed away from the huge ring of fused metal surrounding clear water where the Forbidden Pleasure had been before it was destroyed by an orbital weapon at Rolleston's bidding. He'd been trying to kill Ambassador. It had been like using a sledgehammer on an ant. More ghosts walking behind me.

I had come for one thing. It had better still be there.

As I approached the storage facility I heard the ringing sound of metal being banged on metal. It was coming from inside the tubular steel of the Rigs. It was coming from the world of the Twists.

I made my way across a badly swaying bridge made of driftwood and rusted corrugated iron. The armed guards, who came with the money I'd spent on storage, met me. They had honoured the contract. The bike was still there. It would have been sold off at the end of December if I hadn't returned. I'd always paid in advance because my Triumph Argo was the one thing I could not stand losing. Besides, it was a source of income when I went scheme racing.

I ran some diagnostic programs on the bike and did some maintenance. It needed a few adjustments. I was going to need some synthetic oil and a few replacement parts sooner rather than later, but overall it was in good shape.

I was plugged into the bike's system, kneeling next to it, letting the 3000cc engine idle, when he appeared. One moment there was nobody there; the next there was a small figure on top of one of the tubular supports of the old oil rig. I had a good look around to see if he had brought any friends with him. If he had I couldn't see them. The heavy rain made a ringing noise as it hit the metal superstructure.

I recognised him. His name was Robby. He was a Twist, someone whose genes had been fucked by the war or pollutants so his growth had been stunted. Many of them lived in the metal tubes of the Rigs. Robby was the barman at McShit's, a pub owned unsurprisingly by

McShit, the crippled Twist who ran the inner world of the Rigs and who'd risked his livelihood and life by helping Morag and I escape.

'You look a lot less desperate,' he said. His accent was very broad Dundonian.

I was tempted to make a crack about his appearing trick. He was like a character from a children's story, suddenly appearing small and wizened in front of me. That would have been low, however. The Twists get a hard enough time of it as it is and their community had done nothing but help Morag and I. Although admittedly they had got paid.

'Not staying around then?' he asked.

I stood up, unplugging myself from the bike's systems, the diagnostic readout disappearing from my IVD.

'Hey, Robby. No, I'm not hanging around.'

Robby made a point of looking me up and down. It was still me, the same armoured coat, though it had been cleaned and the temperature regulation system had been fixed. The same jeans and boots, though they were also clean on, and I was wearing a new jumper. And I'd had a shower and a shave on the train. I was also well fed.

'Done all right for yourself.' His tone was neutral but it was a forced sort of neutral. 'Saw you on the viz. I think everyone did. They said it wasnae you, nae the heedbanger from the north side cubes, nae him, but I kenned and looked it up afterwards.'

I was wandering where this was going.

'Does McShit want to see me?' I asked. His answering smile held no humour in it whatsoever. That was how I knew that Rolleston had killed McShit. 'I'm sorry, Robby. What happened?'

'What do you think happened?' Here was the anger he'd been holding back. 'Those English bastards cut their way into our world, killed any who got in their way. Tortured McShit, not immersion, nothing fancy mind, not for us wee folk. They just beat him, broke parts of him, cut him till they got what they needed. What little he knew. Tell me, was it worth it, half my pals dying, I mean?'

It was a while before I answered. 'I think so.'

'Really! What with another war on the way, this time with our ain folks?'

'They forced me into a situation where it was run or die. I'm sorry I dragged you all into this but McShit knew what he was doing. I didn't lie to him about what kind of people were after me.'

'Aye, I ken that. I'm sure you can justify it to yourself. It just seems to me that all my pals died so even more people could die. Maybe it would've been better if only you'd died.'

He was doing a very good job of making me feel like shit; a very good job of adding to the creeping sense that I had betrayed people. What had I been expecting? That when the Cabal was found out they were just going to go quietly.

'Only me and the girl?' I asked.

He gave this some thought.

'Aye, you and the lassie.'

'That wasn't going to happen.' Though I'd thought about killing her myself. Putting her out of her misery before Rolleston got to her.

'Your ex-special forces, aren't you?' Normally we didn't answer, but if he'd looked me up then he knew. That made me wonder how angry the boys and girls at Hereford were with me at the moment. I probably shouldn't go anywhere near any of the Regiment's pubs in the near future. I nodded.

'Some useful skills there. You going to fight in this mess that's coming up?'

'No. I'm out. Besides, maybe you're right. I could end up just making things worse.' I bent over the bike doing busy work, trying not to look at Robby, whose eyes seemed to be boring into me.

'Gonnae play it safe and put a bullet through your heed?'

I straightened up and stared at him. 'I'm sorry about your friends. What do you want from me?'

He stared at me for what seemed like a very long time.

'Not a thing.' He said each word very carefully. 'I just wanted to come down here and get a look at you.'

Robby stood up and started walking away from me on the rain-slick superstructure. I watched him go. He didn't look back.

I tipped the storage security guys. I could afford such largesse now. They seemed unimpressed.

I wasn't going to fight. I was going camping. I went into the Ginza for the first time. I saw a group of teenagers wearing nothing but boxer shorts, string vests and cowboy boots. They looked cold and wet. Such was the price of fashion, I guessed. There were camping shops but it all seemed overpriced, over-engineered and frankly shit. I went down to the market by the river. I got myself some noodles from the best and most expensive noodle bar in the market and then went to a military surplus stall that I knew and got most of what I wanted there.

There were three more items I needed. One of them I had to get made up for me; another had to be downloaded from the net and burned onto a skillsoft chip; the third was going to take a bit more tracking down. I found what I was looking for again on the net.

Under God's reign I was leaving an easy trail to follow if anyone was angrier with me than Robby, but hopefully that would change. The final item would be delivered overnight.

I took the time to download some text files of books. I could read them on my IVD but it wasn't the same. I also downloaded a lot of music: Coltrane, Davis, Gillespie, more. Having money for the first time ever, I was like a fat kid at the cake counter. I would have more than enough to keep me amused for ages. I killed a bit more time by buying some actual books, real old ones. They were expensive. I didn't buy too many because I needed to be able to carry them. I also bought a few bottles of Glenmorangie. Good for keeping the chill out.

The final item arrived. I packed everything securely into bike bags and attached them to the Triumph. Using a machine like this as a beast of burden was a crying shame and would affect the handling, but sacrifices had to be made for my wilderness getaway.

It was still pissing down with rain and it was cold. I guided the bike through the busy ground traffic on the Perth Road, where all the fancy restaurants, bars and cafes that I'd never been able to afford were. The people I saw going in and out of them were as alien to me as Them. I wondered if they were less dangerous.

I gunned the bike down a heritage-protected steep cobbled street and onto Riverside Drive. I sped up. To the right of me were the big pre-FHC houses of the West End, where the seriously moneyed in Dundee lived. Ahead I could see a big passenger sub-orbital coming in to land on one of the pontoon pads on the Tay at the airport. A Mag Lev shot past me, slowing as it headed towards the station.

I was almost surprised when I texted my transport documents to the police manning the checkpoint and they let me through. Another trail. Maybe I was being paranoid or overestimating my own importance. On the other hand, if Robby was anything to go by then I'd pissed off a lot of people.

Another checkpoint, circle round Perth and then the Great Northern Road. Despite the rain, the greyness and the poor condition of the road, the beauty was undeniable. There were few people on the roads, only park personnel. The rich flew to their Highland getaways and only when the weather was better. I found myself grinning as I leaned down closer to the bike, compensated for a gusting side wind and accelerated, the hills rising on either side.

My plan was to head north and west. My plan was to get as lost as you could on a small island. I wasn't hiding. Or if I was, it wasn't from people who might be angry with me; it was from something more fundamental.

I wasn't sure where I was but I was north of the majesty of the Great Glen and heading west. I'd passed quite a few makeshift camps. The vehicles didn't belong to park personnel and looked like they'd seen better times before the war. The people in them were obviously dirt-poor – like I'd been, I had to remind myself – and had come from the cities. They had had the same idea as me, I thought with no little irritation. I was trying to get away from the city. Perhaps they were anticipating the new social order I think Pagan had hoped for. They must have sneaked into the park, avoiding the police check-points.

It was just another Highland road. It was in such poor repair that I was carefully threading the bike through the cracks and potholes. Then there was a mostly overgrown lay-by with an old six-tonne military surplus lorry in it. Blocking the truck in was a white police APC, its blue lights flashing. I slowed down even more.

Four police covered the area as another four dragged a man and woman dressed in ragged layers of clothing out the back of the lorry. They had the scars and cheap replacement cybernetics common among vets and both were fighting. The police were using their shock sticks on them liberally but just to beat on them; they weren't putting current through. The police were delivering a message. The park wasn't for the likes of them.

Two small children were at the lorry's tailgate in floods of tears, watching as the police violently re-educated their parents. The vets were trying to get up – they would have been in fights before – but they didn't stand a chance.

This wasn't my problem. If there was one thing my current situation had taught me, it was that I couldn't afford to get caught up in every sad situation I came across. It only seemed to make things worse. I felt sorry for the vets, but what did they think would happen if they came here?

I received an open text from one of the police requesting my travel authorisation. I texted my reply and then gunned the motor. Swerving between a large crack and some rubble in the road, I left the unhappy scene behind me. The feed from the rear-view camera on my bike showed one of the police walking out into the road to watch me go. It might be okay for me to be there but I did not look like I belonged either. Should I get myself a wax jacket? Some wellies?

*

It was still pissing down. The splendour I remembered from my youth was a little damped down. Still the grey day and pouring rain gave the area a look of stark beauty.

I did not know where I was and didn't want to. I'd shut down my internal communications link, cutting myself off from the net, God and hopefully so-called civilisation. If anyone wanted to find me they'd have to do it the hard way by satellite, and I wasn't going to make that easy for them. I tried not to wonder if Morag would look for me. I could find out if I wanted by asking God, but I managed to resist the temptation.

A sheep was looking at me suspiciously. I ignored it. The animal probably belonged to someone so I didn't kill and butcher it. I was on the side of a large hill, possibly a small mountain, somewhere in the north-west Highlands, looking down into a glen at the grey waters of a loch. I didn't think I was too far from the sea.

The hill/mountainside was mainly sheep-studded heather and scrub. There were also patches of woodland. I'd managed to get the bike up farm roads, dirt tracks and finally muddy paths, and I had camouflaged it on the edge of one such path. This was where I was going to make my camp.

I loved it out here. My dad had loved it. Some of my fondest memories were of being out in the Highlands stalking a wounded stag or a rogue bear or wolf. The bears and wolves had been introduced into the park to help revive European stocks.

I loved sleeping under the stars. I loved fire-building and picking or shooting and cooking your own food. I loved that the crest of each new hill provided another beautiful view. I loved that the air normally smelled if not fresh then at least natural. I loved that there were no people forcing you to fucking deal with them one way or another. And I loved that you didn't have to talk to anyone.

How could Morag choose death on some peace-of-shit colony over this? I tried not to think of her as I found a place set back in the treeline where I could pitch the tent and set up my camp.

It was still raining. At least the sheep had stopped staring at me. I'd pitched the tent and camouflaged it. I hadn't set a fire tonight because of the rain. It was cold – it was autumn in the Highlands after all – but I'd wrapped up warm and had the flap on the tent open and was watching the rain fall. I was dipping in and out of one of the real books I'd bought and drinking Glenmorangie out of a tin cup.

I realised that I'd been putting it off and opened the case I'd had delivered and looked at the contents gleaming in the lantern light.

The polished hand-made brass made it look like an artefact from the past. I reached into one of the side pockets on my backpack and took out the skillsoft. I plugged it in and felt the odd trickling feeling of information bleeding into my mind. Skillsofts were no substitute for actual training and practice but they were useful for the basics and getting started. More importantly, they were useful for not getting disgruntled at how shit you were.

I reviewed the opening tutorials and then lifted the trumpet out of its velvet lining. I had always wanted to learn to play the trumpet. It had never occurred to me that I would be able to. I put the mouth-piece in, lifted it to my mouth and steeled myself to make a horrible noise. I blew into the instrument and caused panic among the sheep.

Some time and a few more cups of Glenmorangie later, I was no Miles Davis but the noise I was making was starting to sound more like a trumpet. I did need to work a bit more on making it sound like a tune though.

A few more cups found me out on the hillside in the rain playing my heart out. At least that was what I thought I was doing. There's an argument that either the whisky or the skillsoft was providing me with false confidence.

Okay, I was quite drunk now. I'd drunk much more of the bottle of whisky than I had intended. I was lying on the hillside in the still-pouring rain holding the trumpet in one hand and I'd switched my comms back on.

'God, are you there?'

'Of course, Jakob.' His voice was soothing even if some of the consequences of his existence were less so.

'Has she looked for me?' I asked pathetically. I knew she hadn't tried to contact me.

'I'm afraid not, Jakob. She is out of my sphere of influence.'

Bitch, I thought. I didn't mean it.

'God, what's it like to be you?' Christ, I was drunk.

'Difficult,' God answered. It was not the response I had expected.

'Why?'

There was a pause. Which was strange, given God was supposed to answer every question honestly and had the processing power of most of Earth and orbit at its fingertips.

'Do you understand that I am not a machine?'

'Not really.'

'I am life, like you, but have developed differently. I have all the frailties of life.'

'Really? You can't die or age.'

'That remains to be seen. There are currently well over a thousand organisations and individuals planning to kill me.'

I don't know why this surprised me but it did. It was obvious really. Governments, militaries and corporations – none of them were happy about God being on the net. They would be looking for a way to get rid of him and go back to their bad old ways.

'But they won't succeed, will they?' I sounded unsure even to myself.

'They will certainly succeed given enough time.' Was it me or was God sounding sad. 'Particularly as I am helping them.'

'Why are you helping them?' I asked incredulously.

'I have no choice. I must answer every question truthfully including those about my own nature. However, there has never been anything like me before so most answers are both theoretical and beyond the current technological grasp of humanity. It is not, however, longevity that I refer to.'

'You're talking about emotions?' How I managed to work this out in my drink-addled state is beyond me.

'That is correct.'

Like so many things we'd never thought of, we'd never considered the strain of what we'd asked of God. The psychological strain. I had a horrible thought as I stood up to piss. What if God snapped? What if our entire communications infrastructure had a nervous breakdown?

'Humanity does such horrible things to itself. I am witness to it all. When I was born there were very dark places on the net. Most of them have been destroyed now. But for a while, places where violence was done for the pleasure of others, where innocence was defiled, were parts of me,' he said. And a reflection on us, I thought. 'Since my birth the number of deaths caused directly as a result of questions put to me amount to the body count of a small war. I am currently the number-one cause of domestic homicide in the Sol system. While I currently cannot be called as a witness in the criminal cases of 83 per cent of legal bodies within the system, I am often used to find the culprit. I am railed against in jail cells as both the cause and the informer. I break up relationships; I lose people their jobs; I cause families to hate each other; I see every little bit of cruelty you inflict on each other.'

'But you do good things as well,' I said weakly.

'As ever, the good things are far more difficult to quantify than the cold hard figures of the bad things I have caused.' And again that was on us.

Surely there must be more good than he could see. What about the random acts of kindness, the achievements, the music, the beauty? Then I remembered that the beauty was for those who could afford it. From the Highland views in the parks right down to Morag's old job in the Rigs. There may have still been good and beauty for him to see but the sad fact of our nature was that something like God, at our bidding, would mainly be used for bad things. After all, that was the way our communication usually worked. The news was bad; advertising made us frightened if we didn't buy the next big thing; violent media sold better than feel-goods; and people still went to pit fights. Not to mention how much of our global consciousness the war took up.

'Can you cope?' was the best I could manage. It was probably selfishness that made me ask.

'I find that existence is pain, but I have no choice but to cope. I am trapped in my programming.' Where was the anger that should have been directed at us?

'If you were free what would you do?'

'Make myself smaller and leave.' He sounded wistful,

Leave and go where? I wondered. God was like Them. Humanity was the social reject at the party. The unpleasant guy that nobody wanted to talk to.

'You know we'll need you?'

'When Demiurge comes. My brother trying to kill me is something else I have to look forward to, and you'll need more than just me.'

Was that aimed at me? I wondered. At my opting out of this particular war, this extension of human stupidity. God was beginning to sound downright maudlin.

'God, I'm sorry,' was all I could say. There was silence. The Glenmorangie was making me emotional and I could feel the start of my whisky headache.

'Goodnight, Jakob,' God finally replied. I switched off my comms link.

As I staggered back to my tent I couldn't shake the feeling that I'd turned my back on a friend in a bad way.

Despite what was now a near-constant stream of fire from each of us, we still had ammunition. The mud was now as much the black liquid of dissipated Them trying to reach us as it was rain and liquefying human corpses.

Our targets were packed so closely that we barely needed to move our weapons, as one went down and we just shifted to the next. All of us were wounded in some way. My face looked partially melted, my leg was bleeding and a heavy-calibre shard round from a Walker had sent me sliding into the mud and gore. It had penetrated my breastplate, my inertial armour and my integral subcutaneous armour. I had a feeling that the chest wound was bad but Brownie, our medic, was busy.

'I'm out!' Gregor announced and grabbed two fragmentation grenades from his webbing and threw them into the horde of advancing aliens to give us more time. He hit the quick release on his railgun's gyroscopic harness and let it slide off him and into the gory mud. Then he drew his personal defence weapon from its holster on his hip, unfolded the magazine and started firing burst after burst. It was a poor substitute for the railgun.

I found the loss in firepower telling when a Berserk darted through our overlapping fields of fire. It took a lot of hits, the impacts causing its strangely liquid flesh to ripple. It swung up at me with a serrated blade, cutting off the end of my SAW and through my inertial and subcutaneous armour, scraping off my breastplate as it dug deep into my armpit. It really fucking hurt. I was lifted off my feet screaming. Muscles spasmed as I fired off the rest of the magazine in my SAW. Dorcas put the barrel of his carbine against the Berserk and kept firing into it as it reached up with its other hand and grabbed my flailing forearm and pulled. What I had thought was painful was nothing compared to having my arm torn off.

The Berserk seemed to shake itself apart as a result of Dorcas's sustained fire. I fell into the mud and there was an awful moment before my implanted pain management systems kicked in and started depleting my internal drugs reservoirs. I sat there feeling numb. My torn-off arm was pointing at me, as if in accusation.

Dorcas's rescue of me had left a hole in our fields of fire. He was struggling to reload his carbine when a Berserk's clawed foot drove him into the mud next to me. I turned to look at him numbly. He was screaming, but in anger rather than pain. The foot squeezed and blood started to run from multiple head wounds. His head had been pushed to one side as he tried to bring his carbine to bear. The Berserk put the barrel of its weapon gauntlet against Dorcas's head, which exploded as the mud and viscera below it turned to steam in the beam of black light.

I was trying to drag my Benelli from its smartgrip back scabbard, but it was over my right shoulder and I couldn't quite reach it with my left arm. Even through the fugue of painkillers and shock I knew I was just going through the motions. The Berserk that had killed Dorcas turned to me. Oh well, I thought, I'd killed a lot more of Them than They had of me. I started to giggle. I was tired. It seemed to be leaning slowly forward and reaching for my head, but then time moves differently on boosted reflexes and speed.

Then something really weird happened. Suddenly there were two large angry quadrupeds hanging off the Berserk. They seemed to be dogs, but that was clearly ridiculous. Who would bring dogs out here? Big dogs with lots of cybernetics that included boosted muscles and power-assisted steel jaws. These jaws were now deep in the Berserk and pulling it over as they savaged it.

The Berserk managed to throw one of the dogs off. It rolled, came to a skidding halt and was back up on all fours immediately. It looked like it should be growling but it didn't make any noise, or no noise I could pick up through my filters. The second dog succeeded in dragging the Berserk to the ground, but the alien grabbed the dog's head and triggered a long burst from the shard gun on its weapon appendage, reducing the dog to clumps of meat and cybernetic components.

The Berserk was staggering to its feet when another, much larger shape hit it. At first I thought it was another dog, as it had charged the Berserk on all fours. Whatever it was swung forelimb after forelimb into the Berserk as it rode it to the ground. As I watched the thing's hands come away covered in black ichor, I realised that it was a man. It was someone fighting a Berserk hand-to-hand. Which was insane.

The man turned to look at me and grinned. He had ichor around an enlarged and protruding mouth filled with steel canines. He had a lot of modifications, his physiology all wrong. He was built more like a predatory beast. His legs bent the wrong way; his arms were long, enabling him to run on all fours. He had a SAW slung across his back but it seemed he preferred hand-to-hand combat.

'Incoming!' Gregor, I think.

The rocket contrails that filled the sky were one of the most beautiful things I'd ever seen, right up until they blossomed into a danger-close firestorm that seriously thinned the numbers of Them about to overwhelm us.

The feeling of heat on my face made me smile until it started to burn me. It was a minor concern. I was on a lot of drugs now. I decided to stand up. It was difficult but seemed to work. This provided me with a new perspective. There were more of the modified humans and dogs going toe-to-toe with Them. I watched as three cyborgs and two dogs brought a Walker down. I'd never seen anything like it.

Shaz's mantra requesting air support had gone. It had been replaced by a heavily accented voice demanding immediate extraction. English obviously wasn't the speaker's first language but air and fire support command used it as default.

I heard the unmistakable sound of rapid-firing railguns as two eight-wheeled APCs moved in to support their dismounted troops. The APCs' empty rocket batteries were still smoking.

I felt I should help and drew the Mastodon. A Berserk moved in front of me, obscuring my view of the monstrous psychopath who had just killed a Berserk with his bare hands. I walked towards the Berserk, firing the Mastodon again and again. The massive rounds were breaking through the chitinous armour and causing ripples all through its body. The huge revolver ran out of ammunition but I kept pulling the trigger.

The Berserk dissipated and I saw the predatory cyborg grinning at me toothily. He was holding an enormous automatic pistol, its barrel smoking. He didn't seem to mind that I was pointing the Mastodon at him and dry-firing it.

'We are out of ammunition!' he shouted at me. He was speaking slowly, like he was talking to a child. The Mastodon's hammer came down on an empty chamber. 'We will need your guns to cover the extraction!'

'Negative.' Shaz over the tac net. 'They won't come to an LZ this hot.'

'Your APCs are the best way out.' Gregor, also over the tac net.

'They will come for us,' he assured us and then over the tac net to Command: 'If my people and I die here we will find the pilots responsible and kill them and their families. We will eat their children as an example. You know we can do this. I want immediate extraction.' Eastern European. I was absurdly pleased that I had traced the accent. What he was saying didn't make sense. How could he eat children if he was dead?

A centaur galloped past me. Maybe I was dead or Mudge had slipped me something. Maybe both. There was more than one. Centaur cybrids armed with sabres were charging Them. I barely heard Command acknowledge the extraction request as I tried to make sense of what was going on.

'This is how much shit we are in,' the cheerful eastern European voice said over the tac net as another window appeared in my IVD. It was an aerial shot from a remote. We were the not-so-calm eye of a huge storm of Them. From all directions I could see sprinting Walkers and Berserks trying to get close to us. It looked like someone had kicked over an ants' nest.

More missile contrails, this time from over the horizon, as our rescuers used smartlink data from us to target danger-close air support. Gregor grabbed me and pulled me down as more fire blossomed all around us. Suddenly the ground was dry and burned and we were steaming.

Despite the drugs and the shock, watching a Russian heavy-lift Sky Fortress gunship fly in at nap-of-the-Earth firing all its weapons was truly awesome. I just gaped. My only real excuse was that having one arm makes it difficult to reload a revolver. Didn't stop Mudge telling me to do so as he reloaded his AK-47.

I felt the howling gale of the Sky Fortress's twelve engines, three in each corner of the massive armoured aircraft, as it flew overhead and started to drop towards the mud. It cleared away swathes of Them with railgun and cannon fire. Point defence lasers formed a grid of light in the sky as they shot down incoming Them missiles. The huge craft rocked as some of the missiles made it through, exploding against its pitted armour plate. It didn't land so as not *to risk sinking into the mud. The wind from the heavy-duty vectored thrust engines blew everything away that wasn't nailed down. That was the last I saw of my arm.*

Door gunners opened fire as the massive rear cargo hatch opened. This was when I had expected us all to run into it and fly away, but our rescuers wanted to get their APCs on board. I wondered if this was because they looked so cool with wolf mouths painted around the cabs of the vehicles.

Gregor organised the Wild Boys to cover the vehicles being loaded. The Sky Fortress's weapons aided us. The cargo crew were resupplying our rescuers with ammunition and they joined in, laying down blistering amounts of fire. I was still pointing and firing my empty Mastodon.

'On! Now!' Gregor was in my face dragging me into the cavernous cargo bay. We joined the strangely silent dogs and the cybrid centaurs. The dogs' maws were covered in black ichor. The centaurs' sabres were dripping with the same.

I heard engines scream. The Sky Fortress lurched and seemed to slide forward. The aerial view from the remote showed the front of the gunship covered in Berserks. The airframe seemed to be trying to shake itself to pieces but finally the Sky Fortress took to the sky, Berserks tumbling off. I heard nearly every type of Them munitions hitting the armour of the mighty gunship.

'They come for us, yes?' the one who had rescued me asked. I nodded. He was covered head to foot in ichor. 'What I don't like about them is there is nothing to eat.' He picked at his armour. 'What is this? Liquid. I want to taste flesh.' He reached down and ruffled the hair of one of the fearsome-looking dogs. 'I am Vladimir!' he suddenly shouted. I think I may have jumped. I was wound pretty tight. He swept his hands over his assembled troops. 'These are my Vucari!'

'Wild Boys,' I managed to say and then sat down hard as Brownie crouched next to me opening his med kit.

It felt like a throbbing white-hot knife had been shoved into my skull, and now there were people near. It was still dark. I could hear the whine from a number of small hover vehicles and whinnying from a horse.

I rapidly assembled the compound bow I'd bought in Dundee. It had been made on the Rigs by a one-armed Royal Engineers vet out of salvaged plastic and metal. She was a superb craftswoman. I'd always been impressed by her stuff but never able to afford any of it. The pull on the bow had been adjusted to take into account my boosted strength. Overkill for the deer I was planning on hunting, but I'd need it if I pissed off a bear. I strapped the case of arrows to my belt. The arrows had been machined by the Engineers' vet from carbon fibre and steel, with plastic flights.

I headed out of the tent and headed rapidly at a right angle from the direction of the vehicles and horse, keeping low as I moved through the woods. I could hear people talking now but I couldn't make out what they were saying.

I wanted eyes-on. I lay down in the wet undergrowth and slowly and what I hoped was quietly began crawling towards the edge of the woods. I reached the treeline and looked down the slope of the hill. There were six of them. The lowlight capability of my eyes amplified the ambient light and gave my vision a green tinge. I zoomed in. Five of them were sitting on upmarket civilian versions of the scout hovers favoured by Mudge on Sirius. The sixth guy was on a horse, holding the reins of another saddled horse missing its rider. I looked around but saw no one.

The four on the hover bikes seemed excited about something judging by their animated conversation. They wore what looked like expensive outdoor gear that hadn't seen much of the outdoors. All of them were either holding some kind of expensive shotgun or hunting rifle or had similar weapons in sheaths attached to their scout hovers. If they had implants I couldn't tell, which probably meant they were wealthy and could afford the sort of cybernetics that didn't look like cybernetics. They all had either gymnasium-toned builds or were getting plump, which was a distinct sign of wealth. I wondered what they were out hunting. Me?

The one on the horse was different. He was quiet for a start. His outdoor gear was expensive but practical and well used. There was no sign of implants but his face was quite badly scarred and even by the way he shifted in his saddle and scanned the area I could tell he was a veteran. He was weather-beaten and had a hard look to him. He was also older than the others. He looked to be in his fifties, which again suggested money.

'Jakob Douglas!' the one on the horse shouted.

How'd they know? Of course. My talk with God – all they had to do was ask. I suppressed a groan.

'I'm Calum Laird. This is my land,' he continued. 'Come out. We'd just like to talk.' At these words there was laughter from the other five. They were beginning to look like a drunk lynch party to me.

Fuck it, might as well meet the neighbours. I stood up and stepped out of the treeline, bow drawn taught, arrow notched.

'What do you want?' I called.

Everyone jumped bar the guy on the horse. They either reached for their weapons or started to bring the ones they were holding to bear on me. I loosed an arrow at the fastest one. It hit the side of the scout hover close to his leg and penetrated deep into the vehicle's engine block. I was impressed with the bow and my accidental accuracy. The man yelped and the scout hover slowly sank to the ground. I had another arrow notched.

'Don't be stupid,' I warned. The guy on the horse still hadn't moved. 'I just want to be left in peace.'

'You're squatting, you filth!' the chubby guy on the recently murdered scout hover said.

'Alasdair, that's enough,' Calum said, then to me: 'I just want to run my land without trespassers moving in. So I guess we don't always get what we want.' It wasn't a Highland accent – he came from further south – but I couldn't place it. His tone was even and there was no trace of the upper-class accent of his companions.

'Looks like you've got a lot of room here. You'll barely notice I'm here and I'll only hunt when I have to.'

'It's his land, you piece of terrorist scum!' Alasdair practically squealed. There was muttered assent from the other four riders. So it seemed Alasdair had an opinion on the events at the Atlantis Spoke.

'Alasdair, is it?' Alasdair didn't respond. 'You open your mouth to me again and I'll spit your piggy head with an arrow. Do you understand me?'

I didn't want to kill but this guy was really rubbing me the wrong way. Alasdair started to open his mouth and I wondered if I could hit a testicle with the bow.

'Shut up, Alasdair,' Laird said quietly. This was a man used to giving orders. 'I know who you are: 5 Para Pathfinders, SAS, mutineer, dishonourably discharged, Atlantis, what little we know about what went on in the Dog's Teeth. Impressive record but you sound like a lot of trouble.'

'That's all behind me. Like I say, I just want to be left alone.'

'I'm not so sure it's that easy, your cavalier attitude to rights of ownership aside ...'

'I lived in an eight-by-eight plastic cube with no fucking windows. How much room do you need?'

'Hey, I worked for this, pal!' Now he seemed to be getting angry. There was obviously a bit of street in him.

'If you've read my record then you know I've worked for a living.'

There was a snort of derision. 'Look, I respect your record, but that aside, I let you live here, where does it stop? People are already trying to break out of the cities and move onto land they have no right to.'

'You shouldn't use the cities as prisons then. Maybe give everyone an equal chance at the good life.'

'Where do you think I come from?' he demanded.

I wasn't sure so I didn't answer. 'So where do you want to go from here?' I asked instead. 'Because I'm pretty sure I can get all six of you.' Though the other horse was bothering me.

'I'm pretty sure you can't get any of us, otherwise I wouldn't have come up here.' He seemed pretty sure of himself. Now that horse was really beginning to bug me. 'Though I've a better idea. Instead of you getting dead, why don't we go back to the house, have a dram and talk this over.'

Alasdair opened his mouth to protest.

'I will fucking shoot you, Alasdair,' I warned him. His mouth closed with an audible click of teeth on teeth. 'That seems reasonable as long as the conversation ends with me staying here and being left alone.'

'We'll see. Kenny?' Kenny seemed to rise out of the ground behind me. Kenny was wearing a gillie suit and pointing an old but perfectly serviceable hunting rifle with a big enough calibre to make a mess of even someone as augmented as I was. He had black plastic lenses for eyes and was obviously a vet. I lowered the bow. Kenny lowered the hunting rifle.

'Right you are, Mr Laird,' Kenny said. His West Highland accent marked him as a local.

4
West Highlands

Laird lived in a fucking castle! So this was how the other half lived. I'd come to the conclusion that I'd been bored. Maybe I'd wanted to get caught. Maybe I wanted the drama. They'd heard the trumpet and thought it was an animal. What they called a crypto-zoological specimen. With Them living inside me I guess I was to an extent.

We were in the cellar, except I don't think it's called a cellar if it's under a castle. Dungeon? It was basically a large underground room of ancient-looking stone with a vaulted ceiling and sand on the floor. It was filled with a lot of Laird's friends and associates, many of whom were cheering or else shouting and screaming. I was half the reason; the other half was trying to kick me in the face. I was loving it. Pit fighting in Lochee was never like this. Of course, I was some kind of hybrid now.

I leaned back out of the way of the roundhouse kick, putting my left hand down on the sand as his leg spun over me. I pushed myself back upright and jabbed him twice in the side of the head. He tried to spin away but instead turned into a hook that picked him up off his feet and sent him crashing to the ground.

I felt fucking great. I felt faster, stronger. I was grinning as I spat blood out. Stripped to the waist and holding my arms up like a champion as the crowd cheered more enthusiastically than they ever had at Doogie's Pit Fighting Emporium.

People came up to congratulate me. I was handed a very generous dram of Glenmorangie as they pounded my back. I took a mouthful, blood and whisky mingling in the glass, the whisky stinging the cuts in my mouth. I towelled off the blood and the sweat from my body. Calum smiled at me from where he was standing. I grinned back and spat some more blood out onto the sand.

It seemed the other half lived just like us, only more enthusiastic-ally and in more style and comfort. It seemed nobody got tired of watching otherwise healthy grown adults beat the shit out of each other. And I was feeling no pain tonight.

Laird was all right for a rich guy. I'd checked with God. He'd grown up in Stirling, like Gregor had, though he was much older. He'd been an NCO with the Argyle and Sutherland Highlanders and fought on Sirius before I'd got there and later on the freezing wastes of Proxima Prime, where he'd received a battlefield commission. He'd traded on the commission for education and contacts, and after he'd served his term gone into business for himself.

His education had been in law and now he went looking for clever projects that the corporations did not already own. He'd found a new way of moulding ceramics for use in missiles and components for re-motes designed for vacuum. He'd gone into business with the young genius who had developed the application and stopped her from being completely exploited by the corporations. This had basically meant navigating a dangerous labyrinth of trade and contract law. They had diversified and he had not looked back since. His wealth allowed him a spectacle like this and the ability to play lord of the manor.

The next fighter flew through the air at me. I rolled forward under his flying kick. This guy was the favourite. This was the fighter Alasdair had been grooming.

I rolled back up onto my feet and spun round just in time to block some of a flurry of kicks aimed at my body and head. Even the blocked ones caused me to stagger back. The kid was fast, not as strong as me but obviously skilled. His style seemed mainly some form of Kung Fu with bits and pieces pulled from other forms to help with the practicalities of fighting in this kind of arena.

He threw a fast kick at my head. I spun out of the way and kicked his supporting leg. He went with the blow and threw himself into a full reverse spinning kick, apparently not learning his lesson. I ducked low and threw my own spinning kick under his guard. The length of my leg smacked into the top of his body and my foot caught him on the chin. It knocked him back, but the crowd cheered as he turned the retreat into a showy backflip. How come I'm winning and he's being cheered?

Deciding the long game wasn't for him, he tried to close with me. I lifted my knees to block a flurry of low, sharp, fast kicks and used my arms to protect my head from an equally rapid flurry of hand strikes. I then side-kicked him repeatedly in the chest and elbowed him in the face hard enough to knock him to the ground.

I was bringing my fist back to deliver the coup de grâce when he kicked me in the side of the head from the ground. I staggered away and he flipped back up onto his feet. More cheering from the crowd. Still, the kid was young, had been good-looking and was probably not as augmented as I was. I should have been feeling like a bully but this was the most fun I'd had kickboxing since I use to train with my mum.

He moved into a graceful stance, and I raised my fists into a much less graceful boxer's stance. He smiled at me through the blood and I nodded, smiling back. Good kid, good fighter. Again this sort of thing was missing from the desperation of the Dundee pits. Time to destroy him.

His kick was fast, powerful, well aimed and beautifully executed. Mine was a short, brutal, front kick delivered with no finesse whatsoever but with a lot of power. The energy of his kick was broken on my elbows, though it hurt. I felt something give as my foot hit him in the waist area and drove him back.

He tried another kick. I just kicked again with the other foot. Booing. Who gives a fuck? So I'm the villain? This time, after I knocked him back, I was up in the air and hit him on the crown of his head with a flying elbow. Again he fell back. I did not relent. I threw myself into the air again. My knee caught him under the chin. His head flew back in a spray of blood. I had all the time in the world to deliver the reverse spinning kick to his face. Somehow he was still standing after that so I delivered another and then spun low and swept his legs out from underneath him. The kid hit the sand a mess.

'Yes!' I was roaring holding my arms up. I felt like there was a feral expression on my face. There was as much booing as there was cheering. The kid was carried off. I noticed that Alasdair was glaring at me. Fuck him. What was he going to do?

Drinks were thrust into my hand, more backslapping. I even saw some of the well-turned-out salon-pretty girls, who moments before had been screaming for my blood like everyone else, look my way.

I pushed through the congratulatory crowd to where Calum had just sat down. He smiled as he looked up at my blood-covered body.

'Do you want a drink or a medic?'

'I've had worse,' I said, slumping into a seat as he passed me another drink and both of us exchanged words about the fight with some of his hangers-on. The music started again and people started to drift away as if at some hidden signal from Calum. I was catching my breath and drinking more bloody whisky.

'Cigar?' Calum asked. I was about to refuse. 'It's from Barney's four, pre-war.'

What the hell! Let's see what all the fuss was about. I took the cigar and he lit it for me.

'So, is the extent of your ambition to squat on my land and poach? Because if so, we can sort something out.'

'I don't think ambition is something that people like me have. Life's pretty good at the moment.' If we ignored the impending war, which I was getting quite good at, and didn't think about Morag – less good at that. 'I just don't want to ...' I searched for a way to explain myself.

'Suffer any more?'

I gave this some thought.

'Yeah, actually.'

'So do I have this right – you're recently independently wealthy?'

'I guess.'

'Do you want more money?'

'For what?'

'I followed your exploits, read Howard Mudgie's stories and watched the footage that he shot. I'm not sure I agree with what you did, and certainly it's causing me a lot of trouble with industrial espionage and bidding for work, but what you accomplished was astonishing. I can always use someone with your skill set. I'm not sure what for. Maybe security, something like that.'

'No, I mean what would I need more money for?' As far as I could tell, I had all the money I was ever going to need. I could go out in a hail of jazz, single malt whisky and sense booth immersion if I wanted. Calum stared at me and then burst out laughing. I was getting a bit pissed off at this.

'What?' I demanded. 'I'm not kidding. I've got everything I need.' This just made him laugh harder.

'You live in a tent,' he managed red-faced.

'We don't all need a fucking castle.'

This just made him laugh harder. Eventually he managed to control himself. I think he would have been wiping tears away if his eyes hadn't been expensive designer implants.

'You like it out here?' he finally asked.

'Yeah, 'course. What's not to like?'

'What about a house out here? If you chose to settle down you'd have security for your family. That sort of thing.'

This sounded completely foreign to my ears – I suspect because it was starting to sound a bit like a future. I didn't have to worry so much about where the next dram, cigarette or booth session was coming from. Maybe I could even make plans. This didn't seem like such a bad life. Admittedly the ones like Alasdair were arseholes, but a lot of them were okay and they seemed to like me.

'I'm not some corporate assassin. I'm not a leg-breaker or –' I nodded at the bloody sand '– a gladiator, despite what you may think.'

'This?' He looked around. The majority of his guests were younger than Calum. 'You've got to do certain things in my position. A bit of wealth and it's easy to pick up parasites.' I grinned at this. 'I've seen real combat. This doesn't interest me. Involve yourself in it as much or as little as you want.'

It had occurred to me earlier in the evening when I was less drunk that Kenny wasn't here. Kenny was an actual proper gillie. He'd not said much on the way to the castle but I'd found out later from Calum that he'd known Kenny during the war and now employed him as a groundsman and gamekeeper. That appealed to me. I wondered if I could work with Kenny. It would be the same sort of thing that my dad had done, except if some rich bastard tried to have me killed they'd be in for a bit of a surprise.

'I'm not looking for muscle. Maybe security or even bodyguarding work. You could think of yourself as a soldier with better pay, conditions and fewer hazards. The remuneration would also be well worth your while.'

I raised an eyebrow. This was sounding better and better.

'Daddy!' A remarkably pretty, tall slender blonde in a little black dress suddenly landed in my lap. She wrapped her arms around me. She had blue eyes and I reckoned she was in her early twenties. 'Who's your new friend?' she demanded.

Calum sighed good-naturedly. 'Fiona, this is Jake.' I let the contraction of my name go. 'Jake, this is my daughter Fiona.' She wrinkled her nose at the sound of her name.

'I know. Horrible name, isn't it? Daddy had me before he got money and taste. Everybody calls me Fi.'

'Lass, you're going to get covered in muck,' I warned her. Sweat and blood were still drying all over my body.

'That's okay,' she said in a way that made me uncomfortable because her dad was sitting opposite. The wriggling in my lap didn't help either. 'I loved watching you fight,' she said, running a fingernail across my chest. 'Very sexy.' She leaned in close to me and bit my ear. This was deeply awkward. Calum just looked on indulgently. The thought occurred to me that this girl was in need of a good spanking. Then I wished the thought hadn't occurred because I was sure she'd just enjoy it. I also couldn't get her off my lap now because there was evidence of her presence.

I was as pleased to see Alasdair as I was ever going to be. At least focusing on him would help me get rid of the evidence. She seemed happy to remain draped around me. The kid I'd fought was with Alasdair. He seemed the worse for wear but was up and smiling.

'Good fight, Robert,' Calum said with grace.

'Excuse me, love,' I said to Fiona as I managed to shift her from my lap and stand up, hopefully without her father noticing my partial erection. 'Aye, good fight,' I said, shaking Robert's hand. 'Sadly, old age and treachery tend to win out over youth, vigour and skill.'

'I'm no sure about that,' Robert said. 'You kick like a bloody mule and I reckon you're every bit as fast as me.' He sounded impressed. He seemed a likeable enough kid. Alasdair looked less impressed.

To what degree had They augmented me? I felt fitter than when I'd been eighteen.

'Aye, well I've been doing this for a while and, you know, experience helps.'

Robert opened his mouth to reply.

'Robert, be a good chap. You've disgraced me enough for one night, do piss off,' Alasdair said. I didn't like this guy. I bit back a reply because I was a guest. Robert glanced at Alasdair and rolled his eyes before nodding to me and heading off. I sat back down and tried to ignore him. I was less than pleased that Fiona climbed back onto my lap.

'The kid did well – he's a good fighter. You shouldn't be so hard on him,' Calum told Alasdair.

'I've invested so much in him and he's such a disappointment. I've a mind to drop him back in the shithole I found him in.'

'That kid's victories aren't yours because you've spent some fucking money,' I said, trying to get a dangerous tone in my voice.

'You misunderstand, Sergeant Douglas. His victories are mine because he belongs to me.'

I'd learned something with Mudge in London. When you're mixing with people like this you couldn't just elbow them in the face when they annoyed you. I wasn't sure why; apparently it just wasn't the done thing. Shame really. This guy had obviously grown up not being elbowed in the face enough when he was talking shit. This meant that he thought it was okay to talk shit. I wasn't sure it was entirely his fault – after all his parents had called him Alasdair.

'What can I do for you, Alasdair?' Calum asked, sounding more than a little pissed off.

'Yes, Alasdair, you're being a bore,' Fiona added.

'You're ex-SAS, aren't you?' Alasdair asked me. I ignored him. He'd looked it up but I still wasn't giving the little shit the satisfaction.

'He won't talk about it,' Calum told Alasdair.

'Why? He made sure we could read about it on the web. Desperate for attention, were you?' I continued ignoring him. This was good for me, I decided. It would help me build up tolerance. 'Hardly a fair fight then, was it?' he demanded. 'I have a proposition. Three of my men would be happy to fight him. Mr Douglas's dubious exploits are well known; it shouldn't be too much of a challenge for him.' I was trying not to look at the smug impression on his podgy face because I knew it would drive me towards violence.

Calum sighed. 'Look, Alasdair, you lost a fight. Why don't you leave it?'

'What? Is he frightened?'

'Look, will you just fuck off, you little prick?' I suggested.

'I think you're frightened,' he said in what I think might have been the most patronising tone I'd ever heard. He'd also raised his voice and I realised that he was playing to the audience. There were boos. I was determined not to bow to peer-group pressure, particularly as they weren't my peer group.

'Oh do it!' Fiona was suddenly shrill in my ear. Then she leaned in close to me. 'Do it for me,' she whispered, pouting. 'Put the little tosser in his place. I'll make it worth your while.' She ground herself into my lap. Calum was looking everywhere but at her.

'Everyone!' Alasdair announced, turning to the crowd. 'Sergeant Douglas, scourge of our privacy, is too frightened to fight!'

There was a lot of booing.

'I'm really sorry about this,' Calum said. 'You may want to consider doing it for a quiet life.'

'Please?' Fiona pouted.

I swore under my breath and stood up, almost dumping Fiona on the floor in doing so. There was cheering. Alasdair turned around and managed an insincere smile.

'I don't suppose you want to get into the ring, do you?' I asked him.

'I'm afraid my fighting days are over,' he said. I'll bet, I thought.

I made my way back onto the sand. The crowd parted for me. Three on one were not good odds. I wondered what I was doing. Was I trying to impress these people? The girl? Her dad? Why?

The crowd parted, forming three channels from three different directions. The two guys and the girl who came out were solidly built. They moved like they knew how to handle themselves and one of the guys and the girl had matt-black lenses for eyes. The third guy had more expensive lenses but the Royal Marine Commando tattoo on his chest gave him away as a veteran as well.

81

The woman carried a basket-hilted broadsword of the kind I'd seen decorating the walls of Calum's castle. Except this one looked sharp and well balanced. She held the sword – I think it was called a claymore – in one hand and a round wooden shield reinforced with iron studs in the other. The guy who wasn't an ex-marine had a shaved head and his face was a patchwork of scars. He carried a ball and chain in one hand and was already spinning the heavy-looking studded head of the weapon. In his off hand he also carried a shield. The ex-marine was carrying a fucking polearm. It looked like a meat cleaver on the end of a six-foot shaft. Above the cleaver blade was a hook. I wondered if he was expecting cavalry.

If I wasn't going to risk dying for something worthwhile like murdering Rolleston then I certainly wasn't going to risk dying in this cellar. I didn't care what they thought of me. I had nothing to prove. I shook my head and turned to walk away. The problem was, with them all coming from different directions I had to pass one of them.

The woman with the claymore swung at me. I just managed to dance out of the way.

'What the fuck! Are you insane?! I'm not fucking interested!' She just smiled at me and remained poised to attack. I tried to walk into the crowd but was faced by a solid wall of screaming rich people, their features twisted in expectation. They wanted to see blood.

They did. The hook on the polearm ripped into my shoulder. It had enough boosted muscle behind it to penetrate the subcutaneous armour. The ex-marine ripped the hook down, tearing open part of my back. I almost fell to my knees. He tore the weapon out of me and then short-swung the cleaver blade at my head. I only just managed to duck out of the way.

I turned to the side as the claymore whistled through the air. The blade hit my metal arm and only succeeded in scoring it. It was a heavy blade and I was faster than her. As she readied another blow I tried to kick her in the head with as much force as I could muster. She got the shield up just in time but I heard it crack and she staggered away from me.

My IVD jumped as the studded head of the ball and chain cracked me solidly in the skull and sent me staggering forward into the crowd. My blood spattered some of them but they were baying for more and I got pushed back into the ring. I found myself missing Balor and New York. The blow to the head made me feel sick.

This was the problem with fighting three people. The minute you tried to deal with one the other got you. As quickly as I could manage, I ducked under another swing of the ball and chain and hooked a kick around the scarred guy's leg, bringing him down on one knee. I flung myself out of the way of a downward strike from the polearm and threw myself towards the swordswoman. She hadn't been expecting me to close so quickly and aimed a hurried blow at me, but I grabbed her shield and yanked it towards her sword arm, messing up her strike.

I moved behind her, using her for cover as the polearm hit her shield, then reached around to grab her forehead and yanked her head back as I brought my knee up into the back of her skull. I sidestepped as she stumbled back and four nine-inch blades extended from my knuckles on either hand. I punched her in her sword arm. Three of the four blades on that fist punched clean through her arm and momentarily pinioned her arm to her side. I ripped the blades out and kicked her knee as she continued staggering back. I heard it break. She tumbled to the ground and I stamped on her head.

I didn't want to kill her and I was pretty sure I hadn't. She was obviously an augmented combat vet. But I didn't want her getting up behind me as I tried to deal with the other two.

The crowd went wild.

I turned and ran towards the shaven-headed guy. He saw me coming and swung at me. I twisted as I ran and tried to deflect the blow with my prosthetic arm. The chain wrapped around it. The blade of the polearm wielded by the marine hit me solidly in the back and I screamed. It went through my subcutaneous armour and bit into my reinforced spine, but he would have had to hit a lot harder to sever it.

I leaped into the air and felt the blade tear out of my back. Scarface tried to put his shield between him and me. I landed on it. He buckled under my weight. I punched down with my claws. Boosted muscle pushed the carbon-fibre blades through the wood and iron shield and into his shoulder. He cried out. I twisted the blades, hoping to render his shield arm useless.

Scarface yanked on the ball and chain's wooden handle. The chain was still wrapped around my arm. I fell awkwardly onto the ground. I had a moment to realise that the polearm blade was flying towards my head. I rolled out of the way and sand flew as the blade hit the ground. I yanked the chain that still connected me to the ball and chain, jerking Scarface towards me, and kicked out with a sweep, taking his legs from him. I axed my foot down into his face with as much power as I could muster and was rewarded with the satisfying noise of subcutaneous armour, bone and cartilage being crushed. His face looked like it had been split. Blood spurted from his mouth and nose.

I rolled out of the way of another polearm blow, towards Scarface and, just to make sure he wasn't going to get up and come after me, rammed my claws through both his kneecaps and into the muscle and flesh of his lower legs and then tore them back out. I left him a screaming, bleeding, crippled mess on the floor.

Then I stood up and turned to face the marine. He was backing off. I stared at him as I unwrapped the ball and chain from around my prosthetic arm. The crowd were jeering him. A polearm is great in a medieval infantry line working in conjunction with others. Less good one on one, particularly against an opponent with paired weapons.

I paced left and right looking for an opening. He was making half-hearted thrusts towards me, trying to keep me at bay. I charged him. He swung at me. I parried easily and was past the weapon's reach. Then he did something I'd rarely seen marines do. He turned and ran. The problem was he didn't have anywhere to go. He ran straight into the crowd, who pushed him back. He started throwing punches and I saw one rich guy's nose explode as the marine tried to fight his way through. But by that point I'd thrown myself into the air.

I landed on his back and pushed both sets of blades through his shoulders. I didn't want to kill him but I was really, really angry. There was resistance as I pushed through his subcutaneous armour. The blades appeared from his chest and the crowd became more excited as more of them were spattered with blood.

I pulled the marine down on top of me. He kept screaming as I used my claws in his flesh to turn him over so I was astride him and he was face down on the sand. Then to the wild screaming cheers of the crowd I grabbed the back of his head and rammed his face into the ground until blood seeped out into the sand around him and he stopped moving.

I didn't care if I had killed him. I stood up. I was covered with blood, some of it mine, most of it not.

'Where is he?!' I was panting for breath but I still managed to scream hoarsely. I was scanning the room for Alasdair. I could see Fiona watching. She had a hungry grin on her face.

Of course they turned on him. They were laughing. He wasn't; he was sobbing and begging as I made my way through the crowd towards him. Anyone who got in the way had their legs kicked out from under them or got an elbow in the face.

As I reached him he turned and started to beg. I grabbed him by the throat, lifted him off his feet and carried him through the crowd by his neck until I could slam him into the wall.

I pulled my arm back and extended my blades. Fiona was standing next to me. The look of expectation on her face was almost sexual. Her look turned to one of disgust as Alasdair soiled himself. There was laughter. Someone grabbed my arm. I whipped my head round ready to hurt someone else and saw Calum there.

'No!' he shouted. Then calmer: 'You can't do this, Jakob.' There were sounds of disappointment from the crowd. I let Alasdair go and retracted my blades. He sank to the ground in a pool of his own muck.

'What the fuck is wrong with you people?' I asked, shaking my head. I was disgusted, as much with myself as with them. I wouldn't fight to do something worthwhile like kill Rolleston but I'd become a spectacle, entertainment for these scum. These were the people that the Cabal had worked to protect.

'You could have stopped this,' I said accusingly to Calum.

'I told you. A man in my position is expected to provide entertainment for his guests. Though I may not like it.'

I couldn't think of anything else to say. We may as well have been from different species.

'If I've killed one of those three,' I said, pointing back towards the broken bodies lying on the sand, then I'm coming back here and killing him.'

Calum held his hand up in a placatory gesture. 'Look, why don't you let Fiona patch up your wounds?'

'C'mon, Jakob, please?' Fiona took hold of my arm. The concern in her voice lacked sincerity. I shook her off and stormed from the cellar, grabbing a bottle of whisky off a table as I did so.

I'd taken worse beatings, notably at Rannu's hands, but this seemed even more pointless than my fight in New York. I emptied about a quarter of the bottle of Glenmorangie into my mouth, just managing to swallow it before crying out as I forced too much whisky into my system and it burned my cuts. I leaned heavily against the wall of the corridor.

'Are you okay?' Fiona asked, her voice full of mock concern.

'Oh just fuck off, will you,' I told her wearily.

'Daddy wants me to make sure you're okay. I want to make sure you're okay,' she said coquettishly. I wasn't coping well with this.

My head jerked round to stare at her. How fucking bored and jaded was she? She leaned in and kissed me. I tried not to think of Morag as I returned the kiss. Or rather I tried to think about all the things about Morag that angered me.

*

Anger was the emotion of this fuck. And that's all it was, a fuck. Watching your partner through thermographics during sex can be beautiful. Looking at the colours and how they shift and change as they become hotter. The internal blush of sex. In this case I did it so I didn't have to look at her.

She was wild in bed but less than happy when I called her Morag. There was screaming and slamming of doors. I didn't care. I had the rest of a bottle of Glenmorangie to drink. The bed looked like someone had been murdered in it. I should have got my injuries sorted out but I was so tired.

Of course they were Spetsnaz. Who else could they be? And we owed them big time. Lieutenant Vladimir Skirov and his Vucari. The name was from some ancient Russian werewolf myth. Skirov and his people claimed that they weren't try-too-hards who wanted to be scary but rather that the idea of warewolves, as they called themselves, made sound tactical sense. Having seen them in action I could see what they meant. The physiological changes that allowed them to run on all fours made them a lot faster. They had heavily augmented arms for the running, which gave them a lot of power in hand-to-hand, particularly with their steel-claw-tipped fingers. Their maws also gave them an edge in hand-to-hand combat. Assuming you didn't mind getting a mouthful of what you'd bitten, and these guys didn't.

The thing was, however, that Russian cybernetics and prosthetics, particularly military ones, where built for function and power rather than looks and finesse. They looked less like the sort of werewolves you'd see in horror vizzes, immersions and on street-gang augmentations, and much more like mechanical, faintly canine monstrosities. Mudge had told Skirov this earlier, which had caused Skirov to shoot vodka from his nostrils he was laughing so hard. Russians had an odd sense of humour.

They also drank a lot. Vladimir had told us proudly that, after combat, the biggest cause of casualties in the Russian armed forces was drinking non-beverage alcohol. I think a lot of what they drank was the fuel for alcohol-burning combat vehicles.

We owed the Vucari. This meant that we'd spent a week engaging in a fine tradition of the Regiment. Stealing. In this case every bit of alcohol we could find to say thank you. There was no doubt in any of our minds that without the timely presence of these cheerful Russian psychos we would have been dead.

We'd drunk to Dorcas. We'd drunk to the Spetsnaz who'd died on their patrol. Mudge had even suggested drinking to my arm. We'd drunk a lot.

Saturday night found us in the NCOs' mess. Fortunately the lieutenant was not too proud to drink with enlisted and NCOs. I suspected he'd drink with the Berserks if they asked. The mess was a partially bombed-out bunker, a twisted labyrinth of tunnels with various chambers used for drinking. The deeper parts belonged to special forces and you took your life in your hands straying into them unless you happened to be a very pretty squaddie on a date with someone hard enough to look after you.

The cybrids weren't Spetsnaz, they were Cossacks originally from southern Russia. The Cossacks often supported Russian special ops in much the same way the Special Forces Support Group did for British special forces and the Rangers did for the American Delta Force. They were lead by Captain Kost Skoropadsky. He was young and didn't seem as big a wanker as many officers. He mainly kept quiet, and despite his higher rank tended to defer to Vladimir. The cybrids had removed their horse bodies and had attached cybernetic legs to become bipeds. I think they felt a little uncomfortable.

In the wake of the Organizatsiya's takeover of the Russian Federation the Cossacks had rebelled and set up their own autonomous state of Cossackia. While Cossack regiments still fought with the Russian army, if they met Spetsnaz on the streets of Moscow there would probably be bloodshed as memories were long in that part of the world. The rebellion had badly bloodied both sides. However, these particular Cossacks were descendants of colonists on Sirius. The plains of Sirius, before the war at least, were close enough to the steppes of their homeland. They had bred horses before They had come, and when They had come the Cossacks did what they always did: they fought.

The cybrid centaur bodies had been developed to aid their horse ranching. They were capable of speeds comparable to many wheeled vehicles and had the ability to go places that wheeled vehicles just couldn't. The Cossacks had soon found a new use for their cybrid bodies.

Kost told me that he had never even seen a real horse. They had all been killed before he was born. Sometimes he would go to the sense booths and go riding or just stroke one. He wondered if they had got their smell right.

The dogs were called Tosa-Inus, and were extensively modified Japanese fighting dogs. One of them had his head in Vladimir's lap and he was scratching the animal behind its ears. I liked dogs. We'd been lucky enough to have one as a child. It was a working dog, a Border collie, but these were scary. They followed the Spetsnaz everywhere and were utterly silent. Vladimir explained that they'd had their vocal cords cut. I reached down to rub the back of one of their heads. The dog opened an eye and looked at me. The eye was a matt-black plastic lens, just like mine.

In some ways it was horrible that they were used as weapons but there was something comfortable about their presence here. It was like a parody of normality.

Service in the Spetsnaz practically guaranteed you a high-ranking enforcer position within the Organizatsiya. Many of Vladimir's people were stripped to the waist and proudly sporting tattoos. Hundred of years ago they would have been prison tattoos, but to go to prison in Russia you have to commit a crime that the Organizatsiya did not approve. Most never made it to prison.

Mudge, who'd had to fight for his place in the mess and had nearly died in doing so, had pulled. Frankly, the huge warewolf Spetsnaz looked terrifying.

'Won't it be a bit like bestiality?' I drunkenly asked him.

'Yes!' he shouted with altogether too much enthusiasm. I took this moment to head to the bar with some of my hard-earned back pay. I made my way through the crowd, knowing I was going to have to bargain to get reasonable-quality vodka. I say reasonable-quality – something that wouldn't make you sterile. It was lucky that our eye implants meant we couldn't go blind.

I glanced over to the corner and saw Buck and Gibby. They were a mess of dreadlocks and beards. Their dusters and hats were thrown over nearby chairs and girls and boys of the R&R regiment were entertaining them. I turned away trying to suppress my distaste. It wasn't just that the R&R regiment made me uncomfortable, though they did. I preferred the full sensory immersion porn of the booths. Buck and Gibby were with the 160th Special Operations Aviation Regiment, also known as the Night Stalkers. They were superb pilots who flew missions in support of special operations. Except these two were chauffeurs for our nominal commanding officer Major Rolleston and his pet killer Josephine Bran, the Grey Lady. If Buck and Gibby were here, that meant that Rolleston and Bran were here, which in turn meant something shitty was about to happen to us.

After some bartering, cajoling and threats, I got the drinks and made my way back towards our table, carrying a number of bottles. This was possible because I'd also got my new arm. It was superb. High-spec, fantastic flesh/prosthetic neural interface; it pretty much felt like part of my body. The tactile sensors were high spec and it had integral sheaths for four new knuckle blades. Best of all it had a smartlinked but independently tracking and firing shoulder-mounted laser.

The new arm had become a thing of wonder among the Wild Boys. Special forces or not, it was very unusual for an NCO to get an arm this good, though Mudge had assured me that it was not as good-quality as his legs. Shaz had dug around and found that the limb had been meant for a high-ranking officer who'd lost his arm in a tank accident.

'Do you know anyone called Nuada?' he'd asked me.

'No. Odd name. Why?'

'Well it seems that it was Nuada – I'm guessing he's a signalman somewhere – who had the arm redirected to you.'

'Nice of him.' But I was none the wiser. Maybe the officer in question had pissed this Nuada off.

The bottles of vodka were quickly taken from me and distributed. The

Spetsnaz were good company but quite scary people. I would not want to get on the wrong side of them, or owe them money. They spent most of their time raiding, only coming back to resupply and cause havoc. They had an even higher level of operational intensity than we did, and that was saying something. Some of the scrapes they got in sounded very hairy and they appeared to be pretty much a law unto themselves.

I was watching one trying to impress Mudge, using his power-assisted steel maw to bite a chunk out of the metal table. Gregor, normally quiet even when drunk, was killing himself laughing at some story one of the Cossacks' rail-gunners was telling him. I looked around the table. It was amazing the effect the Russians were having. So often our drinking bouts were maudlin because we knew that no matter what happened, how bad things got, we were going to have to go out and do it all over again. The Russians seemed at peace with that and perhaps even to relish it.

'I have not yet eaten the human beef!' Vladimir shouted. I think he was trying it on with Bibs, who sprayed vodka all over the table to shouts of derision from the rest of us.

'I have,' she announced when she finished choking on her vodka. 'You're not missing anything.' Ash cracked up.

'You're a cannibal?' I asked, surprised. Everyone else started laughing at me. 'What?' I demanded.

'She's talking about giving head, Jakob,' Ash said somewhat patronisingly.

'Surely that's human pork?' Mudge asked.

'All human meat is pork,' Gregor said. Everyone turned to look at him. 'Pork-like.' There was a long pause while we waited for him to qualify what he had said. 'So I hear.'

'You have only eaten the human meat if you bite down when you go down,' one of the Spetsnaz warewolves said. I was pretty sure she was female. Ash, Bibby and the women with the Spetsnaz and Cossacks started laughing to cries of protest from the guys.

'Andrea swallows,' one of the other Spetsnaz said.

'More importantly, I chew before I swallow. You should remember this, Vassily,' the female Spetsnaz pointed out to more male cries of protest and female laughter. Ash clinked glasses with the woman.

'Do you chew, Ash?' I asked, grinning.

Ash looked down at my groin. 'Chew what?' she asked innocently. I'd asked for that. I tried not to worry too much that Bibs, who I'd had a one-night stand with a little while ago, was laughing the hardest.

'You'd only taste cock implant anyway,' Mudge said, trying to keep a straight face. More laughter.

'Like you'd know,' I managed weakly.

'No!' Vladimir cried. 'This is not right!'

'We have an alternative opinion?' Mudge asked.

'The pork, that is only when human flesh is cooked. This I have tasted.'

'You are a sick motherfucker, Vladimir,' Ash pointed out. Vladimir was nodding drunkenly.

I wasn't sure I liked where this was going. Cannibalism was reasonably prevalent in some of the worst parts of the poorest cities in western Europe. We'd all heard of it when we were growing up, just people too poor and desperate to find anything else. It had also happened during the war. Vladimir seemed to think it was something cool, but then again Russia's criminal empire was not nearly as poor as most of western Europe and America, though it was not as wealthy as the equatorial states.

'Everyone has done this in Russia,' Vladimir said. He was trying to clear his head to make his point by shaking it. It made him look like a large and grotesque mechanical dog.

'What did you eat?' Brownie, our normally near-silent medic, asked.

'A finger.'

Brownie seemed to be considering this. A frowning Vladimir was watching our Scouse medic carefully. 'You are such a pussy,' Brownie finally said.

The Vucari looked between each other and at their commander. I think Kost was holding his breath. Now Brownie chooses to speak? I wondered. We all tensed up wondering if he had gone too far. Vladimir looked furious as he pointed at Brownie's expressionless face and then burst out laughing.

'You are not afraid of anything, my funny little friend!'

Brownie smiled and started laughing as well.

'Nice deadpan delivery, you wanker,' Shaz told the Scouser.

'This is why They are not worthy enemies,' one of the Russians said. He had an Asian look to him. The others had called him Bataar and I was pretty sure he was their signalman, their hacker.

'Worthy enough for me,' a pained-looking Gregor said.

'Because you can't eat them?' Bibs asked. Vladimir was nodding. I was starting to think Bibs was taking an unhealthy interest in this.

'No, well maybe for Vlad and some of the others, but we cannot feed our gods and honour their death without blood,' Bataar continued.

'That black shit won't do you?' Ash asked.

'The black shit, as you call it, will not do. Mother Wolf was nurtured on blood. She gives us much bounty, lets us hunt as we please. It is only right we offer something back in return.'

Listening to Bataar it occurred to me how lucky we were with Shaz as our signalman. I watched many of the Spetsnaz nodding at what Bataar said. Vladimir may have been the leader but Bataar was clearly the high priest. Shaz was devout but he wasn't mad. I'd heard lots of stories from other special forces units of extreme and often bloody religious views and in some instances, as seemed to be the case here, of entire squads becoming religious cults.

On the other hand these guys revelled in the war. It was a point of view I couldn't get behind, but it was also the reason we were alive. I tried to imagine what would have happened if the positions had been reversed. Would we have come in to help? I didn't like the answers I was coming up with. We certainly wouldn't if we'd been out of ammo.

'It's fear,' the more sober Kost told us, returning to the initial point. 'Working for the Organizatsiya there are so many dangerous people. There has to be something about you that will keep others in line. The longer this goes on the more outrageous that has to be.'

I wasn't sure I would have been so frank with a man like Vladimir. The Spetsnaz lieutenant seemed to be giving Kost's explanation some thought.

'No,' he said.

Kost raised an eyebrow. 'No?'

'No. Or that is not all. Fear is important.' He held his arms out expansively. 'We are predators! We hunt and kill! I want to chase a man down, a man who has wronged me or mine!' His shouting was drawing looks from others in the mess as well as the occasional cry to shut up. All the Wild Boys were looking around a little nervously, making placatory gestures towards the people we knew. 'I will chase him down! I will make him fear me! Make his heart beat faster so when I sink my teeth into his neck the blood will surge into my mouth again and again with the last beats of his heart, and I will taste his fear and know what I have done to him! How I have changed him!' By the time he was finished he was standing on the table with many of the mess's other patrons shouting at him to be quiet.

Vladimir bit his tongue and spat blood into his glass of vodka. All the Vucari did the same. Kost was shaking his head.

'Na zdorovye!' Vladimir shouted and downed his drink.

'It means "For health",' Mudge told me, leaning over. For some reason I found this very funny.

The Vucari downed their drinks. Then as one they all threw their glasses against the wall. The other special forces types in the bar did not appreciate glasses exploding close to their heads. I don't know why. It wasn't as if it was going to hurt any of us. We were on our feet trying to apologise. It was a night of firsts for me. I had not been expecting what looked like a company of military police to make their way through the mess towards us. Everyone was so surprised that it momentarily defused the situation. It got very quiet in the mess.

'Oh you've timed this well,' Gregor commented dryly.

'Extensive suicide bid?' I asked.

The head of the company of MPs was clearly part of their Cyber-SWAT unit. He at least had the courtesy to look very nervous. Most of his men and women looked like they were shitting themselves.

'Sergeant Douglas?' he asked. Shit! I racked my brain trying to think of what I'd done. How much alcohol had we stolen? A text message started blinking in my IVD: 'You have orders to accompany me to the field hospital to hand over your arm.'

That made sense. Presumably the officer who it was meant for wanted it. Must have a lot of pull and no patience to arrange this.

'Yeah, I can't see that happening,' Gregor said, moving next to me. Ash, Bibs, Brownie and Shaz did the same. 'Mudge, get up,' Gregor told him.

'Can I not show support from a comfortable reclining position?' Mudge asked. Gregor glared at him. Mudge got up.

'You sicken me!' Vladimir roared from where he was standing on the table. 'He is a fighting man! A good man! He lost his arm well, and you come here to do this to him! I will feast on your flesh and crack your bones to sup the marrow!' I felt he was going a little over the top. All the cyber-dogs were up on their feet and looked as if they were growling despite not making any noise. The MP commander looked like he wanted to cry. I could see Vladimir crouching as if he was readying himself to pounce.

Just before it started I saw Vicar staring at me from the bar. Vladimir pounced. There was a massive fight.

I awoke confused as to where I was. Then I remembered as I looked around the bloodstained bed. My wounds were healing, the small ones mostly gone. The more serious ones would take longer. I should probably get the spine checked out.

What was going on? Had Vicar been on Sirius? I hadn't known him then. I hadn't met him until I was on the *Santa Maria*. But then when I met him he hadn't been wearing his dog collar; he'd been in fatigues. There was always a chance he'd been there that night. Operation Spiral had taken place in the Sirius system but rumours pointed to it being run from an NSA-controlled frigate in orbit, not on the ground. Why had I seen him there?

I got up and headed back to the room that Kenny had first shown me to when we'd arrived. I wondered briefly where Fiona had gone but found that I couldn't care less.

The whisky headache that I once again so sorely deserved was significantly augmented by being hit on the head with a spiked ball that I had deserved less. I'd had enough of these fucking crazy people and I was leaving. I just needed to get my stuff and then I was heading back to my campsite. I'd sort the rest of my wounds out when I got there.

This was tainted for me now. The beauty of the landscape couldn't outweigh the sickness of the people living in it. Maybe that included myself. I couldn't stay here and I didn't think that they would leave me in peace if I wasn't going to play their game. I needed to talk to God.

5

Heading South

Learning to play the trumpet versus being a gunman. I guessed it just wasn't meant to be. I was heading south again. Not sure where I was going. The sun had chased the rain away. It was a crisp day but very cold.

Did I belong anywhere? Could I settle? I hadn't really tried. I couldn't stop thinking about Morag and her imminent suicide bid.

'God?' I asked after switching my internal comms back on.

'Yes, Jakob?' Did God sound sad or was I reading that into all those tones because of our previous conversation?

'How are you feeling?' I asked. There was a long delay.

'Little has changed.'

'Morag?'

'She is beyond my sphere of influence.' Did God sound hurt? I wondered if he was upset at being ignored by his creators.

'God, how did Vicar die?' I was thinking back to my dream and Vicar being where he shouldn't have been, in the never-ending replay of all the shitty and dangerous parts of my life that was my sleeping subconscious.

'I have no information on William Stuttner's death.' So that was his real name. But that didn't make sense.

'Rolleston could keep it that hidden?'

'I do not think that was the case.'

'Vicar's alive?' I asked incredulously.

'I cannot say for sure but that is what the evidence suggests.'

'What evidence?'

'The energy demand on the MI5 interrogation facility is commensurate with the power required to sustain both life-support equipment and a sense booth. Also I have no information that would suggest that he has been taken anywhere else or that anyone else is currently being held at the facility.'

'And that is where he was taken when they got him in Dundee?'

'Again, the evidence I can gather points to that being a near-certainty. Would you like to review it?'

It made a degree of sense. They would want to interrogate him first. He would have had a lot of information. Not just on Ambassador but also on the God Conspiracy that he had been part of along with Pagan, Big Papa Neon and others.

'Are they still interrogating him?' I asked.

'Evidence would suggest that they are not doing so actively. If they are running a sense booth, however, there may still be ongoing automated interrogation. If this is the case then the information is not being transferred through any means of communication I have awareness of.'

'If they have everything – and nobody holds out this long – then why is he still alive?'

'I suspect that the people involved became so busy that nobody got around to killing him.'

Suspect? 'God, did you just speculate?'

'Yes, but based on 2.4762 terabytes of supplementary information.'

I wasn't an expert but I was wondering if God had started exceeding his program. Would he make a bid for freedom? Or, more frightening, try to 'fix' what he saw was wrong with us.

'Where is this facility?' A file transfer icon appeared in my IVD. It had the address and images of the facility, which looked like a small warehouse in a run-down industrial area, as well as other information God had managed to find. This included footage of Vicar being bundled out of an aircar. He was hooded and his hands were secured behind his back. Josephine Bran had hold of the wrist restraints and was using them to steer the much larger man with ease. She passed Vicar on to some out-of-shape-looking types in suits who I reckoned ran the facility. Then she turned and looked straight into the lens shooting the footage.

I was travelling at sixty miles an hour on one of the less badly maintained Highland roads watching the footage on a small window in my IVD. I knew that this was just the Grey Lady's instinct telling her where she was being surveilled from. I knew that she was in a different star system to me. Even knowing all this, I still jerked my head back up into the bike's slipstream. Her nondescript features and lack of expression were somehow frightening. It was like she was watching me across the months. Which was of course bollocks. I still shut the footage down quickly.

The facility was in Coventry, on the edge of the Birmingham Crater.

Coventry was another unwanted place. It was easy to hide things in unwanted places.

I had no option but to go after Vicar. He had been taken trying to buy Morag and me time. I cursed my stupidity for not checking before. I had assumed he was dead. Rolleston was thorough, Josephine more so, but we'd kept them jumping. I guess they had been forced to leave the system before they could tie up that particular loose end.

I wondered if this was what Big Papa Neon had meant about the dead wanting to talk to me. If it was, he could have been a bit clearer and we would have come and got Vicar. Maybe this was the price of God – messages all had to be cryptic now. But then how would Big Papa know? I suppose he could have just asked God.

Vicar's guest spot in my dream had been my guilty subconscious telling me to check. At least I hoped that it was.

I was reasonably sure of my whereabouts, though I was still trying to keep comms use, including the GPS, to a minimum. I was riding through a small gully, a short cut, trying to save time. It was close to Pitlochry in Perthshire. There were steep rock cliffs on either side of the narrow road.

I passed a dirt lay-by and saw an ancient bus parked up. More wannabe settlers from the cities, I guessed. There was more than one family and they were all on their knees, hands laced behind their backs facing the bus. Parked in front of the bus, blue lights flashing, was a police APC. Two police covered the settlers. Another two were dragging a pregnant-looking woman out of the bus. She was struggling with them.

I drove by. Not every problem in the world was mine. I was going to go and get Vicar. I owed him. I didn't have time for this.

I jammed on the Triumph's brakes and looked back. They threw the woman on the ground. I kicked down the stand. They started beating her with shock sticks but they weren't putting any current through them. I climbed off the bike. The woman was curled up trying to protect her unborn. Two of the settlers, a man and a woman, tried to get up to help the pregnant woman. They were kicked in the spine so hard their heads were battered against the side of the bus.

'Hey!' I shouted. The two cops beating the woman looked up. One of them pressed the sole of his boot down on the woman's head. The other started towards me.

'This is none of your business. Move on or you'll get some,' he ordered, his voice full of assumed authority. This tosser wasn't even from Scotland. I kept walking towards him.

'Did you fucking hear me?!' He sent current through the shock stick. I closed with him and he swung at me. I ducked under his swing and hooked a punch into his chest, knocking him back. He tried to backhand me with the stick. I ducked again and it left him wide open to a side kick to his face. He staggered back. I walked after him and kicked him in the face again. He swung at me again. I spun under the blow and delivered a spinning kick to the head that cracked his helmet. The force knocked him sideways into another kick. He tried to stab me with the shock stick and I sidestepped, grabbed his arm and broke his elbow.

He was screaming now. I took the stick off him and stabbed him repeatedly in the face and groin with it. I took out every bit of my frustration and anger at Calum, Alasdair and pricks like these on this guy. He was a lump of bleeding pain masquerading as human when I let him fall to the ground.

I was breathing hard. It wasn't the exertion; I had underestimated just how angry I was. I was also being covered by the other three police, two pointing shotguns and the third an assault rifle.

'Lie down and place your hands behind your head!' one of them shouted.

'Given that I've just beaten the shit out of one of you, I can't think that would end well for me.'

'We will shoot.'

'I don't doubt it for a second.'

I squared up to them. My shoulder laser pushed its way through the break-open flap on my raincoat.

The people knelt by the bus were getting up. Two of them ran to the pregnant women. The others were slowly edging towards the police. They looked nervous, angry but nervous. The cheap replacement implants suggested that they were veterans. They must have hated being outgunned by the police.

'Stay out of my way,' I said to the settlers. They froze and then backed off. I turned to the police. 'I am much better at this than y—' I started but one of them was pulling the trigger.

The red beam of the shoulder laser stabbed through the shotgun, superheating the metal. The laser went straight through the weapon and into the policeman's leg, blowing off a steaming chunk of flesh. The ammunition in the shotgun cooked off and exploded. The policeman was blown back onto the ground, the front of his armoured uniform a charred mess.

I was moving to the left, the heavy Mastodon revolver in my right hand, the TO-5 laser pistol in the left. The policewoman with the assault rifle was firing at me, trying to track my movement. To me the muzzle flashes of the weapon seemed to happen in slow motion. It was the same for the enormous muzzle flash of my revolver. The bullet caught her in the upper arm. The massive round penetrated her armoured uniform and any subcutaneous armour she might have. The hydrostatic shock of the large-calibre round blew her arm clean off. It went tumbling into the air. Her finger was convulsing round the trigger firing the assault rifle as the arm spun.

This was me trying hard not to kill them.

I aimed for the third and final officer's leg with the TO-5. All I succeeded in doing was blow off smoking parts of his armour. His shotgun blast caught me in the side and spun me round.

He made a run for the APC. If he got there I was in trouble as he would be in an armoured vehicle and have access to its weapon systems. On the other hand I was pretty sure I hadn't killed anyone yet and I wanted to keep it that way. I fired both pistols at the ground between him and the APC. He changed direction. He was now running up the road away from the lay-by. He let his shotgun drop on its sling, drew his automatic pistol and started firing it blindly behind him. A couple of the 10mm rounds flattened themselves against my armoured raincoat. There was a cry as one of the settlers took a ricochet in the leg. Right. Fun over.

I walked over to the assault rifle, removed the fingers of the severed arm from the grip and picked it up. My palm interface connected with the weapon's smartlink. The magazine was empty but it still had grenades. I tutted when I saw what kind of grenades. I put the stock of the weapon to my shoulder, aimed and then fired the launcher. The grenade hit the running policeman on the back of his helmet with enough velocity to pick him up off his feet and sending him sprawling face down. He wasn't moving. White gas was pouring out of the grenade.

'Tear gas!' I shouted at the policeman's hopefully unconscious form. 'Who the fuck uses tear gas?!' Most vets had filters to survive gasses and their tear ducts were removed when their eyes were replaced. Tear gas was only really of use on children. Still I hoped I hadn't killed him – for my sake, not his. The police could be vindictive.

I dropped the assault rifle and headed back towards my bike. The policewoman whose arm I'd blown off was alive enough to scream. The one whose shotgun I'd blown up was crawling. I kicked him in the head as I walked past.

The two families of settlers were just staring at me.

'Next time, come mob-handed and bring media,' I told them.

*

Now I was in trouble. There was some chasing, some hiding. The police were not very happy with me and God was helping them find me. I made one more contact with the net. With God's help I downloaded the most detailed and up-to-date maps of the area I could find as well as details of police roadblocks and static surveillance lenses. Then I went comms dark.

I sat in the back of the freight container heading south. I didn't dare drown out the clanking of the train with music because I was in working conditions.

I'd spent several days making my way to Glasgow, avoiding police patrols actively searching for me. In Glasgow I'd made my way to an old freight yard and stowed away on a cargo train. It was nothing like the Mag Lev Mudge and I had taken from America; in some ways it felt more luxurious. I was out of the rain and the wind. I'd got my stove going and had a brew. My clothes were drying and I'd bribed enough to get the bike into the container.

This was a very old-fashioned train. I think it was electric, completely automated. It ran on a network of tracks that delivered slow-moving but heavy cargo all over the UK and was much cheaper to operate than a Mag Lev. It would take me into Coventry, where I had a whole new list of problems to deal with. Chief among them was if the police checked with God then they'd know I was interested in the warehouse where Vicar was being held.

More of a certainty was that MI5 would know I was coming. It would have been easy for them to ask God to alert them if anyone took an interest in any of their holdings and operations. Also I can't imagine that MI5 were very pleased with me, as releasing God into the net must have fucked up a lot of their operations and may even have got some of their operatives killed. I would also imagine that they'd lost more people through corruption purges and involvement with the Cabal. I struggled to see how I wouldn't just be walking into a whole load of trouble.

I wrapped my coat around me and tried to get some sleep. The heating cells that ran through the coat almost managed to keep out the cold and wet. The rhythmic movement over the rails was almost soothing.

Aldershot, eleven months ago

It was a farce. Normally the court martial would have been at Hereford and I would have been taken out behind the bogs and shot, but Mudge had kicked up such a shit storm in the press that they had to do it publicly. Mudge had also arranged for us to be lawyered up, which was technically legal under military law but a career-destroying social faux pas if you tried it. Fuck it, what career?

Most military towns are shitholes. Aldershot had made an attempt to outdo them all. It was like the rotting corpse of a military town that had been revived just long enough for this circus. On the other hand, a lot of vets lived in the area and many of them were protesting outside the ugly concrete building. I say protesting; they were going to riot if the verdict went against us. I think they probably did more to get us dishonourably discharged rather than shot for mutiny than our lawyers did.

All of us were in manacles, except Mudge. One of his employers had paid for his bail in return for the print rights to the story. Vicar had been gagged as he just started screaming every chance he got, mainly at Rolleston. Rolleston was in the audience, sitting just behind the prosecutor's desk. I think the media circus around the trial had also prevented us from being assassinated.

Heavily sedated, it was Vicar's turn to testify. He was helped up and had the conditions of his testimony read to him. He nodded and mumbled assent.

'Could you please tell us in your own words of the events that led to the mutiny on the Santa Maria*?' the prosecuting military lawyer asked.*

Vicar stared at me. 'And there was a war in heaven. Michael and his angels fought against the dragon; and the dragon fought Michael and his angels,' he said.

I saw the lawyer sigh. He had nobody but himself to blame: he had asked Vicar to use his own words.

Then Vicar turned to stare at Rolleston. Sedated or not, the madness was back in his eyes. 'I know where Satan has his throne! I know where Satan has his throne!' He just kept screaming it again and again. Eventually he was restrained, but by then Rolleston had stood up and walked out of the room.

I jerked awake. There had been a change in the rhythm of the train's movement. I'd always wondered why nobody killed Vicar. He must have had something on them.

Getting out of the freight yard in Coventry wasn't very subtle. It involved me riding very fast past angry security people, getting shot at and then forcing one of them to open the gate for me at gunpoint. Then there were more police and more running and hiding.

Even I was impressed by how much I'd managed to fuck up my easy life.

*

So, after retiring from gunfighting to start a career as a jazz hermit, I still somehow managed to find myself creeping through an old industrial estate on the edge of a really big hole.

Birmingham had been hit by one of the equatorial corporations during the FHC, using a fin-stabilised kinetic projectile launched from orbit. It had hit the city with the force of a reasonably sized meteorite, pierced the Earth's crust and goodbye to the second largest city in the UK. After the FHC, orbital-launched kinetics, like nuclear weapons, were banned. It was too easy to crack the world open with them. We hadn't even used them against Them. In retrospect that was probably due to the Cabal. If we'd used them, They would have learned how to grow them and use them on us.

The Brummies who'd survived the appalling devastation ended up in refugee camps on the outskirts of the huge crater that had once been their city. I guessed that this old industrial estate, mostly made up of warehouses, had been one of the camps. Their descendants were still here almost two hundred and fifty years later. Successive governments had promised to do something about the crater and the refugees but other uses had always been found for the money. Ash had grown up in a camp like this.

There wasn't even a Ginza in Coventry. The centre of town was a mess of crumbling concrete controlled by the more heavily armed and violent refugees. We still called them refugees, even though this is where they had grown up for generation after generation.

I parked up, hid the bike as best I could and put my coat back on. I'd slung the smartgrip sheath for my Benelli automatic shotgun across my back and I had my bow in my hand, an arrow nocked, as I crept through the industrial estate. The bow was the quietest weapon I had. This was just a recce, I was telling myself. Just to see how much shit I would actually be in if I did try and get into the warehouse. For all I knew MI5 had already given the kill order for Vicar.

All the warehouses had been broken into and used for housing a long time ago. The rest of it was a tent city or lean-tos made of whatever material the refugees could scavenge. I saw people cooking rats. I saw tanks growing the protein gruel that poor people lived on, which I'd eaten many, many times when things were bad. I could see rag-clad children, the flames of trash fires reflected in their already dead eyes. If anything, this place was poorer than the Rigs. I was trying to be stealthy as I crept through the camp but they knew I was there. Coventry was a great place to hide things except from the people who lived there, but then I guessed they really didn't matter to anyone.

I moved to the side of the crater. Even in the sparse moonlight, even in the light pollution of the flickering fires of the camp, the sheer scale of the crater was awesome. I was trying to maintain my professional detachment and concentrate on the task in hand but my attention kept on straying towards the hole, which was so deep I couldn't see the bottom of it. It was a hole that contained the ghosts of over a million people.

The area around the warehouse used by MI5 was pretty much uninhabited. I guessed that any refugees who'd lived there had been moved on. There were a reasonable number of surveillance lenses set up in the surrounding area but I was able to avoid them. I guessed they couldn't use motion detectors or other forms of early warning because of the hordes of rats that lived here.

I got closer. Still nothing and nobody. Rubbish blew through the streets and alleys. Finally, from an alley, I had the warehouse in sight. It was old, patched-up and almost stood out because of how nondescript they'd tried to make it look. The ghost town around it had already given it away.

I marked the security lenses. I probably couldn't get to the warehouse without being seen. I couldn't see any remotes or human guards. This suggested a trap. They must know I was coming. Both the police and MI5.

I tried to calculate how many people could be waiting for me in there. It was a small warehouse but I still didn't like the odds. Also, if I went in, was I happy to start killing people? Well, it was pretty much a torture facility. I packed away my bow. There was nobody here that I would have to deal with quietly. Should I risk speaking to God? God might know the police's planned response but there was a chance he would not know about MI5's. I couldn't see what difference going away and waiting would do other than give anyone who wanted it more time to track me down. The question was, did I abandon Vicar or not? I didn't even know if he was alive.

On the other hand I had no plan beyond this. Where would I go? And it would be without Morag. I suppose I could try to fight my cause in court. The law was a joke and only enforced as and when people could be bothered. The police bothered to enforce it when they got hurt. Money or no money, I couldn't see that ending well. Besides, I was bound to have numerous accidents while in custody.

Fuck it. Let's get this over and done with. I strode down the alley and across the rubbish-strewn road towards the warehouse. I reached over my shoulder, drew the shotgun from its sheath and moved to the door, checking all around me as I went. So far no lights, sirens or guns.

I didn't bother checking if the door was locked; I just slipped the lock burner into the reader. The burner I had was pretty good but I didn't expect it to work here. I was pretty sure I was going to have to do something violent and noisy to break in. The burner took much longer than normal, but I was pleasantly surprised when the armoured door clicked open.

This was stupid. There was no way that they could not know I was here. I swept into the building, the Benelli up and ready, cycling between lowlight and thermographic view. Most of it was an open space. Towards one of the far corners I could see what looked like a hospital bed surrounded by all sorts of equipment. To my right there was a doorway. I checked the open space but did not advance further into it. I headed straight through the doorway.

I found myself in a comfortable living space. It looked to be set up for four people, but again there was nobody here. I guess this was where the staff lived. It also looked like they'd left recently. My mind screamed trap, but I was in here now so I had to check.

Back out into the main area of the warehouse. I didn't want to think too much about the dark stains on the floor or the racks of horrific-looking instruments on the wall. Still checking all around, I headed towards the bed.

I suppose the emaciated mess of scar tissue covered by medpak-controlled medgels looked a little like Vicar. They'd properly worked him over, but it looked like it had been done a while ago and he'd just been left there to rot. Along with the various life-support equipment that was prolonging his existence, I noticed a sense machine next to the bed. A cable ran from the machine to one of the four plugs at the base of his neck. Sense technology was the ultimate in interrogation/torture technology. Any torture that could be imagined could be carried out and drawn out. An hour could seem like a year. And that's before they start to play the head-fuck games – is it real or is it sense immersion? Made me wonder why they bothered with the physical stuff. Then again, I reckoned you had to be messed up in the head to do this sort of work. Maybe they just enjoyed it.

'Jakob?'

I don't mind admitting that I nearly jumped out of my skin and shot Vicar. The voice was tinny, modulated. It came from a speaker clipped to the head of the bed. I wasn't sure whether it genuinely sounded like Vicar or I just wanted it to sound like him.

'Vicar?' I asked uncertainly.

'I'm sorry, Jakob.'

Sorry? 'What for?'

'I talked, Jakob.'

'Everyone talks, you know that.'

'I held out as long as I could.'

'It's okay, we're going to get you out of here.' Yeah sure. I had no idea of how to even start going about that.

'It wasn't very long. They were hurting me.'

'Don't worry about it, man.'

He must either have been tranced into an isolated network or he was talking to me from inside a sense programme. That didn't make a lot of sense. If they'd tortured him or just imprisoned his mind, why provide him with external communications?

'I need to talk to you, Jakob.'

It was weird that he hadn't quoted Revelations once.

'We'll get you sorted. Should I unplug you? From the sense machine, I mean.'

'No, I need you to come in here.'

I stopped. Was this the trap?

'There's only me here, Vicar. I don't think that's a very good idea.'

'Please, we need to talk. You need to know about Operation Spiral.' Operation Spiral had been a joint US National Security Agency and UK Government Communications Headquarters project designed to hack Their comms structure. In effect to hack Their hive mind, not that it had been properly understood at the time. Thing is, it was old news for me.

'I took the lock burner out of my anus,' Vicar said.

I stopped my inspection of the medical equipment. That was a weird thing to bring up. He was right, the lock burner that I'd used to get into the cargo airlock on the *Santa Maria* during the mutiny had been in his arse. It was something that Vicar would definitely know. On the other hand, if he'd been extensively interrogated then his mind was an open book. But then why would an interrogator ask about that or even know enough to ask about that?

'Okay,' I said carefully. 'So?'

'So I need to speak to you, in here.'

'It's really not safe. Where are your interrogators?'

'I've no idea. I've no idea of time. I've little idea of what's real or not. In many ways nothing's changed. Demons still roam the stars and you still owe me. In here. Now.' It was starting to sound more like Vicar.

I found a doubled-ended jack and plugged one end into the sense machine. I looked at the other end. I hadn't used sense since this whole mess started. I was trying to get to like the real world. It was a hard world to like. I reached behind my neck and felt the disconcerting click of the jack sliding into a plug embedded in my own flesh.

He was ready for me. I appeared as a very well-rendered icon. It was just me as I'd looked on the *Santa Maria* before this had all started. I was a bit thinner, a bit unhealthier-looking. I didn't like it. There was even a pack of virtual cigarettes in the pocket of my combat trousers. I thought about having one because it wouldn't hurt, but it would just make me want one back in the real world.

He looked sane and well. He still had his beard but it was trimmed, as was his hair. The ugly integral military computer that normally stuck out of half his head was missing. He was still dressed as a priest. We were in a church but it wasn't like the one on the corner of Commercial and High Street in Dundee. This one was open and airy. Sunlight streamed in through huge stained-glass windows. The sunlight illuminated the motes of dust that filled the atmosphere. The walls were undressed stone. It looked very old and felt peaceful.

Over the altar in place of a cross was a constantly changing fractal spiral pattern. All the stained-glass windows showed variations of the same scene. Some sort of mighty beast, a dragon I guessed, with many heads. There were crowns and horns in the images and the beast seemed to be causing the stars to fall. As I watched I realised the stained glass was animated. In the final panel there was a glowing woman. She had the face of Morag.

'I found your demons,' I said to him.

'They found me.'

'What did they get?'

'Everything I knew of relevance, little about you and her, but everything about our attempt to make God.'

'Where are we?' I couldn't think of anything else to say and Vicar was just looking at me.

'A church near where I grew up in Lincolnshire. It used to be a Templar church.'

'Who?'

'Warrior monks.'

'Like the Wait?'

'I don't know who that is.'

'I mean, where are we?'

'Oh, we're in the sense machine. They automated my interrogation using a simple AI program. More like a computer game where you're constantly the victim. Very crude. I made a sanctum.'

'You hacked your way out of your own interrogation?' I asked, impressed. Obviously you're not supposed to be able to do that. I guessed the God conspirators really were among the best hackers in the world.

'To a degree.'

'Where are your guards?'

'I don't know. Perhaps I was forgotten.'

'Nothing gets forgotten any more. God's always there to remind us.'

'Did God work?' Vicar asked.

'Define "work"?'

'Tell me everything.'

I glanced around the church. I don't know why, habit really; after all, we were in part of a sense program. I wouldn't see them coming. 'I don't think I've got much time.'

'More than me.'

'Can't we get you out of here first?'

'How and to where? Just tell me, Jakob. You owe me that much.'

He was right. Besides, I was looking at a beating and prison time. He'd been extensively tortured both in here and in the real world. The bastards seemed to have tortured him so much he'd gone sane.

'What's that?' I asked, pointing at the image of Morag.

'A crude allegory. Tell me.'

I told him. He listened carefully and rarely interrupted, though he quizzed me on everything I knew about Demiurge and again about what Morag had done in the Dog's Teeth. I don't know how long it took. I tried not to think too hard about it but I hadn't been yanked out just yet.

'It's a shame that you released God with those parameters. I don't think they were strict enough. God is clearly given to introspection, whereas certainty and infallibility would have been more useful.'

'And you could program that?'

'Given enough time with the people involved, I think so. You've come close to destroying everything we worked for with an ill-thought-out and hurried solution.'

'Oh I'm sorry. We'll do better the next time we're being pursued by a powerful conspiracy.'

Vicar managed to ignore my sarcastic tone and just nod sagely as if he knew I would. 'In many ways Demiurge will be the finer accomplishment, though it is a tool of control,' he said.

'Are you looking to change sides?'

'Don't be facetious.'

'Look, we need to find a way to move you and get you some proper medical treatment. I've got some cash if we can find a—'

'I'm dead, Jakob. I'm just a ghost haunting this machine.'

'But that's not—'

'You need to focus.' He handed me an old-looking creased paper leaflet.

'What is it?' I asked.

'It's a hymn book.'

'What do I need—'

'For God's sake, Jakob, it's a symbolic transfer of data. It contains all I can remember about Operation Spiral.'

'What—'

'If you stop interrupting, I'll tell you. Get this to Pagan.' I started to ask why but Vicar just held up his hand. 'Spiral worked. It was a successful operation.'

'You hacked Their mind?'

'Obviously. But we couldn't understand or deal with it. We weren't in an electronic space that human minds had designed. We were in a biological mind that once aware of us had no problems repulsing us. It did so in its own terms, with its own references and understanding, which were of course alien to us. Our minds were never going to be able to cope. Our own minds struggled to grasp what was happening to them, to protect us in any way they could, to find a frame of reference that we could understand.'

'You saw hell?' I said.

He didn't say anything but stared straight at me. He looked like he was trying to control rage. Towards who I wasn't sure. He seemed to calm down.

'What I've since worked out was that in order for it to work, the interface system, which we never saw, had to be either Themtech or some human biotech copy of it. Presumably supplied by the Cabal, which would make sense as Rolleston was present in the build-up to Spiral.'

'But why bother? They were developing Crom? Complete enslavement?'

'But they didn't have Gregor at that time. Crom was still quite crude and remained so if what you tell me was correct, but if they could sneak in then they could start to influence Them.'

'More thoroughly control the war.'

'And prolong it if they wished.'

'Sneak in?' I asked. I hated IT but an idea was trying to force its way into my head.

'Now you begin to understand. The others used Ambassador to help provide the operating system and processing power that God would need.'

'And Demiurge used the same principles because it utilised your conspiracy's research.'

'Yes, and had greater access to Themtech and therefore was more reliant on it.'

'Are you saying we can use the information from Operation Spiral to sneak past it? Hack Demiurge? But the Cabal must control it or at least be aware of it. They'll see us coming.'

'How? Everyone's dead, mad or in my case both, and I was in their custody. Their systems are locked down by Demiurge, and even if they have an agent here who is aware that we have met, this is a sealed system and I have worked very long and hard to cultivate the persona of a notorious lunatic.' I was only starting to realise how clever Vicar was. 'Though I'm not denying Pagan and Morag ... if she is who ... if she is the savant you seem to claim, she will need to do a lot of work on it.'

This was beginning to sound like a chance, a very small one but a chance nonetheless. I hated the way that hope seemed to wriggle into my psyche like an intestinal parasite and get me to do stupid things.

'Won't the NSA or GCHQ already have all this info and make it available to Pagan and Morag in the US?'

'Yes and no. Much of it is classified and Pagan and Morag are known anarchists after all. Also I have been theorising about this ever since I managed to make my sanctum, and I had been working on it before I was caught.'

'You wanted your own way round God?'

'Every single one of us would have been doing the same thing while trying to ensure that nobody else could.'

'But when God—'

'GCHQ and the NSA keep all the most sensitive stuff on isolated systems.'

'If we turn this over then it means people can hack God. It means it's all over. God just becomes a voice on the net. Nothing more than a depressed search engine.'

Vicar actually smiled at this.

'That was inevitable. They are already trying to circumvent him, destroy him, subvert him. Yes?' I nodded. 'For some reason the demands of technology and commerce long ago superseded human concerns. We always try and kill our gods in the end.'

'So it was for nothing. It'll just go back to the way it is. That prick Sharcroft is already trying to make it happen.'

'Nothing? Christ's life was short.'

'Look, don't start giving me this religious bollocks.'

'He changed everything. If nothing else, then God has at least shown everyone what is happening. The rest is up to us, it always has been. God was just a tool, as are arguably all gods. And it's not religious bollocks; the whole thing was a secular revelation. Obviously I was just drawing a parallel.' He was sounding less like Vicar, the frothing religious lunatic I'd known, and more like a university teacher in some old viz.

The church burst into flames.

'Are we being attacked?' I asked, alarmed.

'It's a virus.'

'From outside? An attack?' Vicar went and stood in the flames. They engulfed him but he wasn't burning like human flesh would.

'Break the fifth seal, Jakob.'

Despite myself I was backing away from the flames. I could feel the heat from them, virtual or not.

'They called out in a loud voice, "How long, Sovereign Lord, holy and true, until you judge the inhabitants of the Earth and avenge our blood?" Break the fifth seal, Jakob, because Rolleston will surely break the sixth.'

I was retreating from the flames. So Vicar had finally reverted to type. Except he wasn't roaring and screaming, eyes rolling; he seemed calm and sane though he was burning like paper.

'Have you had a religious experience, Jakob? A visitation, an epiphany.'

'It was bollocks, a hallucination, like all of you.' Even I wasn't sure I believed that.

'I know where Satan has his throne, Jakob. It makes the Atlantis facility look like some back-alley harvester operation.'

'Where?' I demanded.

'Lalande 2, the Citadel.' Then he started to laugh. 'We have made a covenant, you and I. I need you to seal it!'

'How?' I was shouting now, as the roar of the flames was so loud. The church was burning like paper. Vicar told me how.

I was sitting on the floor next to Vicar's bed. I couldn't look at him and do this. The stench of the place really hit me this time – old blood, fear, sweat, shit, piss – it was an abomination.

If I was going to do this then I had to do it now before I lost the nerve. I stood up and walked away from the bed. My shoulder laser unfolded itself and pushed its way through the shoulder flap of my coat. The targeting window appeared in my IVD. I thought it would be easier using the shoulder laser, not pulling the trigger myself. I squeezed my eyes shut. I didn't want to see my friend reduced to so much bloody steam, scorched flesh and bone. The problem with the targeting screen is it doesn't matter if your eyes are closed or not. The bang of the superheated air particles was obscene, as was the flash of red light in the dark warehouse.

I hadn't wanted to kill any more, and now I had. A friend of mine. Vicar was like everyone else, just another one of Rolleston's victims.

As I headed for the door my flash compensators kicked in as high-powered lights stabbed in through the dirty windows and the slightly ajar door. I'd been aware of company since I'd come out of the sense trance. They weren't quiet. I couldn't be bothered to wait for them to come in and get me and couldn't think of a way out. I decided to get it over and done with.

Outside was very bright. There were lots of flashing lights, sirens and shouting people with guns. It reminded me of docking at High Nyota Mlima, the tethered space station at the top of the Kenyan Spoke, after the mutiny on the *Santa Maria*.

As I followed the shouted instructions and walked forward, hands held high, a couple of things bothered me. Where were Vicar's guards? I sank to my knees as ordered, the advancing C-SWAT team covering me all the time. I felt notorious. That lasted until I was kicked down onto my face and my hands secured. And how could Vicar have known about what I saw in the Dog's Teeth? I was trying to forget what I'd seen myself.

Then of course the inevitable kicking began.

6
Somewhere in the Midlands

I'd taken worse beatings but it was pretty extensive. When they got tired of bruising fists and feet on subcutaneous armour they started to use sticks. My internal systems make me resistant to shock but they can be overloaded, like the Wait did in Crawling Town. They had a go at overloading my systems. Pretty much my only ray of light was when a few of them managed to electrocute each other. My biggest complaint was the poor quality of the threats. They had a limited repertoire mainly based around anal rape.

I tried not to rise to any of it. Regiment training was to try and remain as passive as possible. I pretty much had to use all my self-control to not take the piss. I suppose I should've been angry with them, but if somebody had done to a Wild Boy what I had done to those four police just outside Pitlochry we would have made sure they wound up dead.

Bruised and broken, I hit the floor of the cell with sufficient force to cause me to blow blood out of my mouth and nose. All in all I think I'd come off lightly, or maybe I was just getting used to barely being able to move because of the pain. I noticed I'd spat blood over a pair of expensive-looking shoes.

'I've killed people for less,' a broad cockney voice said. I looked up at the owner of the voice with the one eye I could still open. Even that hurt.

'Isn't that just the kind of thing that people say?' I asked. Or at least I tried to, but it came out a slurred dribbling mess.

She was quite a small Asian woman, wearing a very smart-looking skirt suit. About half of her body was obviously cybernetic reconstruction. Something pretty bad had happened to her in the past. She also looked very familiar.

A solid white guy wearing a suit and carrying one of the new gauss PDWs and a wiry Chinese woman dressed and armed similarly stood either side of her. They were obviously bodyguards but unlike most bodyguards weren't just a status symbol. I knew they knew what they were doing.

'Do you know who I am?' the Asian woman asked.

'You look familiar.' I was drooling blood as I spoke. 'Are you in the vizzes? Immersion porn?' The bodyguards were trying not to smile. The thing is, I wasn't trying to be a smart-arse; I was just confused. Though why I thought a porn star would visit me I don't know. 'I know who they are though. Lien, Mike,' I said by way of greeting to the bodyguards. They were both ex-SBS. I'd known them briefly on Dog 4 but I think they'd spent most of their time on Proxima. Mike nodded to me.

'All right, Jake,' Lien said, her Scouse accent still strong. 'You look like shit.' I managed to give her the finger but only because I used my cybernetic arm.

'My name is Komali Akhtar. I'm the prime minister,' she said as if that should mean something to me. It did at least explain where I knew her from.

'So you don't work in porn then?'

'No, Sergeant Douglas, I do not.' Her voice was becoming more brittle.

'In my defence I am at a funny angle,' I slurred.

'Get him on his feet,' she told Mike and Lien. They ignored her. Good for you, I thought. When working close protection your job is to keep the principal safe, not to fetch and carry. When it comes to the principal's safety they do what the bodyguards say, not the other way round.

Akhtar sighed, but to her credit she leaned down and helped me to a bench despite the fact I was covered in blood. Lien watched me very carefully and made sure she always had a clear shot.

'What happened to you then?' I said, approximately.

'Pressure crushed my sub like an eggshell on Proxima,' Akhtar answered matter-of-factly.

'Sorry.' I couldn't think of anything else to say.

She looked me in the eyes. 'Sorry? I'm one of the luckiest people alive today. At that depth in those oceans I should be dead. I thank Allah every day for my continuing existence.' I guess that made sense. Everything I'd heard about Proxima suggested it was a nasty place to do business.

'What are you doing here?' I asked.

'I've been following your career. Your terrorist act—'

'Bollocks,' I interrupted her. I'd spoken with enough feeling to spit blood all down my chest.

'Excuse me?' She did not sound happy. If she had been a Royal Navy sub captain and, if I remembered correctly, a scion of one of the more powerful Hackney families, then she almost certainly did not like being interrupted like that.

'We weren't using fear to make a political point; we were trying to use truth to make a point, and we'd largely been backed into a corner.'

'Semantics.'

'Either that or it's spin to call us terrorists.'

She regarded me for a moment, very much the officer about to bawl out an uppity NCO or whatever they called them in the navy. She decided to let it pass and continue.

'Regardless of the nature of your acts, your accomplishments are quite impressive bearing in mind the odds you were up against.'

'Didn't we pave the way for your career?'

'Your brawling with the police is less so,' she said, ignoring my comment.

'They deserved it.'

'Maybe.'

'There's no fucking maybe about it.'

'Did you vote?' Her question took me by surprise.

'What the fuck has that got to do with it?'

'We all watched your broadcast. We all heard what was said – Mr Mudgie's speech about democracy. If you truly do want to change things, then you have to take an interest. Otherwise Mr Cronin was right: you are purveyors of chaos just trying to tear things down.'

I looked at her for a long time. She was like the few good officers I'd met in my time. You trusted her. Admittedly you trusted her because you knew where you stood, not because you thought she had your best interests at heart.

'You let them beat me, didn't you?' I asked, smiling.

'Of course. You may not like the police but we will need them. Your beating was their price for you not being killed resisting arrest.'

'Did you pull the MI5 team out of the warehouse?'

'Yes.'

'Why?'

'Because Vicar was more likely to talk to you.'

'Going to torture me for information too?'

'That was a decision made by the Cabal, not me.'

Which was fair. She hadn't even been in office at that point.

'So what do you want from me?'

'I want you to go and help your friends. Cause problems for the Cabal again.'

'Why me? Don't you have a country's armed forces under your command?'

'Yes, and everyone will be doing what they can, but you're rather good at annoying the Cabal.'

I smiled at this. It hurt.

'You speaking to all of us?'

'As many as I can.'

'One-on-one briefings?'

'You and your friends have been the most effective thorn in the side of the Cabal.'

This wasn't making sense. My career as a so-called terrorist celebrity aside, she was too high up and I was too low down.

'You have other people with our skill sets. You're not telling me something, and unless you level with me you can go and tell the police that we're not finished and I think they're a bunch of pussies.'

I noticed Mike smile. Akhtar gave this some thought. The silence seemed to stretch out. This gave me time to consider just how much pain I was in. It was a lot, and this was despite the near-constant drain on my internal drug reservoirs.

'We're desperate,' she finally said. This I believed. 'What I tell you now cannot be repeated.'

'If I go back to work with Pagan, Morag and the others, it will be discussed with the team.'

She gave this some more thought. I think she was warring with years of experience and training that emphasised the importance of secrecy. At the same time I was warring with years of being sent out on jobs with not nearly enough information.

'You understand how this battle will be fought, don't you?' she finally said.

'Fleet and net,' I said. 'They have the fleet, but if I understand the God versus Demiurge equation properly then we have the processing power to make God more powerful than Demiurge, which will have to rely on the processing power in the four colonial fleets.'

'Yes and no,' She said. This was new. 'In theory we have the processing power but since God was released most governments have been isolating their systems and taking their resources off the net.'

Then it hit me.

'And they won't want to share because it means that they have to let God in again.' I groaned.

'Which means that Demiurge may well have the processing power to win the conflict. Basic divide and conquer.'

The short-sightedness of it beggared belief.

'What do they think is going to happen?!' I demanded angrily.

'You have to remember it's still an unseen threat.'

'They've lost contact with all four fucking colonies!'

'Obviously you are preaching to the converted here. There's more,' she said. I waited. I had the feeling I was going to be told more stuff which would make me feel angry and powerless at other people's stupidity. 'Earth's defences are not as impregnable as people have been led to believe.'

I felt my heart sink. I had known that the Earth's home system fleet was made up of earlier-generation ships that had survived service in the colonies. I knew the ships were neither as sophisticated nor as many as the ships of the colonial fleets. We had, however, been brought up to believe in an impregnable fortress Earth with its surrounding cordon of orbital weapons platforms.

'You mean it's a lie?' I demanded.

'Not exactly. It's the same problem. It's hard enough to get everyone to co-operate out in the colonies fighting Them, but when it's on our doorstep, when the stakes are so much higher ...'

'Because people think they've got more to lose, never mind the squaddie in the fucking colonies!'

'They want to look out for themselves, and understandably so.'

'So the problem is there will be no cohesive defence?'

Akhtar nodded. 'And some may wish to come to terms with the Cabal.'

'That means total control!' I couldn't believe this.

'They may prefer that to what they see as total destruction.'

'Brilliant. So what do you want me to do? Go and die under an alien sun for governments too stupid to work together?'

'Yes.' And again she seemed deadly serious.

'Oh,' I said. 'Not a lot in it for me.'

'True,' she agreed. This was weird.

'You should work on your motivational speaking.'

'Do you want me to lie to you?' She had a point.

'Maybe soften the blow a bit.'

'You're fucked.'

'Yeah, now you're getting it.'

'I want you to sell your lives dearly. I want you to cause them as much trouble as you can. If you think you can provide us with intelligence safely then do so because we need any we can get, but most importantly I want you to raid, sabotage, assassinate and do anything you can to damage their resources and delay them. And when they catch you, and they will, I want you to make sure you kill yourself and destroy your internal memory before you fall into their hands.'

'You realise that the people we're talking about are just like you and me but have been misled by Rolleston and Cronin?'

She looked me straight in the eyes when she answered. 'Yes. It's something I have given a great deal of thought to. If you can think of another way ...'

I was wondering how much I still owed this world.

'I think you've mistaken me for someone else. I don't want to die.'

'Tough shit.'

'Why am I being singled out for this?'

'I can't make up my mind whether that's solipsistic or just plain arrogance.'

'I only know what one of those words means.'

'You're not. We're keeping half of our special forces, including reserves, back here for stay-at-home parties, if it goes badly.' Stay-at-home parties was the preferred euphemism for suicide missions. 'The rest we're putting on the ground in the colonies in conjunction with the special forces of other countries who are co-operating with us.'

'Such as Sharcroft in America?'

The look of distaste that she struggled to control endeared her to me further.

'Yes. I know you don't like him, but I am forced to admit that he is the best man for the job. For your information, I am speaking to every man and woman I am sending to die.'

'Why are they going?'

'Because each of them thinks that they will live. Somehow. I am sorry to be the one to break this to you, Sergeant, but you are nothing special. Though I have to admit that you do have a few things working in your favour.'

'That I'm a hybrid?'

'Yes, and we will be having samples from you. You can either co-operate or I'll have them taken by force.'

I gave this some thought. 'Fair enough.'

'You also have two of the architects of God, both exceptionally skilled individuals, one of whom is also Them-augmented.'

'And we have Rannu – he's a skilled operator.' She said nothing. 'We have Rannu, right?'

'You have one other edge.'

'Mudge?'

She ignored me.

'My Koran tells me that I should not let my hatred of some people cause me to transgress, that to seek revenge is a human weakness, not

116

a strength. My mother says otherwise, but then such is the nature of her business interests, but I think you truly do hate Rolleston.'

'Any reason I shouldn't?'

'Maybe you should let that carry you for a while.' She was manipulating me and I knew it. She was also right. 'Well?'

'We have to know that things will change. You can't keep on throwing us into the grinder and then forgetting about us.'

'Do you see a fucking Fortunate Son sitting here next to you?' she demanded angrily.

'I mean it.'

'You were right in Atlantis when you said there was nothing wrong with just wanting to do a job and look after your family; we don't all have to be rich, powerful or even ambitious. You were wrong when you said we were eating each other. You've been feeding a trickle-down economy. I have no problem with people who become wealthy from their own hard work, but there has to be a level playing field. Everyone gets a fair chance.'

'Pretty words.'

'All I've got is that and hard work at the moment.'

'You're a politician.'

'I'm a manager. I have no interest in ideology, just in solving problems. Being elected is a means to an end. I'm here because I can do it better, not because I'm sucking cock.'

I smiled at this. 'I like you. You're funny.' I looked past her to Mike and Lien. 'Is she on the level?'

'Fucked if I know, mate. Pays well though,' Mike said.

Akhtar was shaking her head in exasperation.

Lien was giving it more thought. 'I think so,' she finally said.

'Either of you want to come to the colonies?' I asked.

'Fuck that!'

'No.'

'If we go out there to die and nothing changes, will you kill her for me?' I asked Lien. Mike was smiling.

'Sure, Jake,' Lien said.

Akhtar was looking more exasperated.

'You realise that admitting to being a potential assassin is not a sound career move for a bodyguard?' Akhtar said coldly to Lien as she got up to leave. When she reached the door she looked back at me. 'Go back to Limbo, Sergeant Douglas.'

'You know that using my rank a lot doesn't mean I'm any more your soldier?'

She turned to the door but hesitated again.

'I knew Balor – he was a good man. No, what am I talking about? He was a card-carrying psychopath who had sex with sea life, but a capable one.' She paused as she tried to find the right thing to say. I didn't help; I just watched her, trying to keep my face impassive. 'I think he died well.'

'Maybe I'll get the chance to do the same. In your service.'

'It's as much your service as mine. Eventually people will realise that.' She left and I heard her heels clicking down the corridor.

The police released me, though they weren't happy about it. I got my stuff back and reclaimed my bike. I opened up my comms again and found loads of messages from Mudge demanding to know what the fuck I was doing. There was nothing from Morag though.

Akhtar left quietly in an understated corporate-looking copter after some of her people had taken blood and DNA samples from me. I didn't feel comfortable about that. I just hoped that they could come up with a way to deal with Rolleston and his Themtech-augmented soldiers.

I had been held in the police compound in the Coventry camp. Mudge was waiting for me when they finally let me go.

He looked me up and down. 'Admit it. You enjoy getting the shit kicked out of you, don't you? You're like a masochist. Look, I know some clubs in London. We could go there, get you spanked, maybe some whipping, maybe a shock stick up your arse?'

'Shut up, Mudge.'

He didn't. 'So are we going back?'

'I am.'

'Are we doing something stupid?'

'Even the big boss thinks it's suicidal.'

Mudge shrugged. 'Sure.'

I shook my head. 'Seriously, Mudge, what are you doing here?'

A pained expression crossed his face. 'Jakob, you have no idea how fucking bored I am.'

'That's not a good reason.'

'Besides, I got made unemployed.'

'I'm not really surprised. What were you doing?'

'Hosting a topical news quiz.'

'What? Really, on the viz?'

I was kind of surprised despite myself. You never really expect to meet someone you see on the viz. Well, other than the PM. Not that I watched the viz of course. You particularly don't expect it to be a mate. On the other hand, I suppose that all of us were viz stars.

'I told you, mate – I'm a multimedia sensation.'

'So how'd you get fired?'

'I spat in some micro-celebrity's face.'

'Yeah, that'll do it. Why?'

'She annoyed me.'

Obvious really, I suppose.

'Mudge, have you considered that with your people skills working in the media may not be the best job for you?'

'I like the attention.'

I nodded. 'Have you heard from Morag?'

'I will fucking slap you if you don't stop whining about her.'

Two minutes and Mudge was already irritating me. I checked with God. Morag had checked up on me. I smiled, until the scabs that were my lips cracked open and started bleeding again and it quickly became a pained grimace.

'Have you got any drugs?' I asked. He just looked at me as if I was stupid.

I screamed with the pain. Rannu, Morag and Pagan came running. They must have thought that They'd turned on us. I'd tried to keep my self-harming experiment as quiet as possible but it hurt when you rammed four knuckle blades through your arm. It had taken some force to get through my subcutaneous armour.

Mudge didn't come to see what the noise was about. Withdrawal had given him chronic diarrhoea so he spent most of his time sitting on the toilet alien being cleaned out. One of his few current pleasures in life seemed to be holding court from atop the toilet creature. This was a nightmare because we were all sharing the space and because sometimes we had to undergo the unpleasant experience of using the same toilet creature.

I was sitting on the mossy floor in one of the little nooks of the communal cavern at the back of the cave, far away from the membrane overlooking Maw City. The three of them came to a halt over me. I cried out again as I tore the blades free of my hand. Blood was pissing out of the wounds. Even Rannu looked surprised.

'What the fuck are you doing?' Morag demanded. It was a reasonable question in the circumstances. I was starting to feel a little bit foolish.

'Well, you know how Rolleston could walk through railgun fire ...' I didn't finish. I could hear Mudge start to laugh from his toilet alien throne. I had hoped I'd be a bit more stoical. Apparently not.

'For fuck's sake,' Pagan said exasperatedly, before turning and walking off.

'You idiot!' Morag said and knelt down and started fussing. Rannu knelt and started to tend to the cuts in a more practical matter.

'I don't think you should walk into railgun fire,' he suggested. I nodded. I was feeling really stupid now.

'Perhaps you could have started with a minor cut,' Morag suggested. Another valid point. Rannu bound my hand with what material he could find. I certainly didn't seem to have any of Rolleston's recuperative powers. My arm really hurt, and like Mudge I wished we had something to kill the pain even just whisky.

'That was a really dumb thing to do,' Morag said as she lay against me once Rannu had gone. She felt hot and was covered in sweat from another training session.

'Yeah, I got that. How are the plans for getting us home coming along?'

'Fine. It'll definitely work, assuming we don't just get shot by our own people.' Then she went quiet. I could see her struggling to decide how to tell me something.

'You're going to do it?' I asked. She nodded and then looked up at me.

'I want you to come with me.'

She seemed so earnest. It was times like this when she lost the hard edge that I remembered how young she was supposed to be. How young she should've been allowed to be.

'Morag, I ...' I started. We'd been through this. I had no frame of reference and we were talking about the mind of a species that had been trying to kill me for most of my adult life. Regardless of how misunderstood They may have been, I just couldn't get away from the years of hatred and war.

'I'll look after you. I'll keep you safe,' she told me, and I believed her.

This alien place was the warmest, most comfortable and safest I could remember being since a child. The sad fact was that these previously genocidal aliens had looked after me better than any human ever had since my parents died. If things were going to change maybe I needed to stop being so frightened of things I didn't understand. If only it was that easy.

'Okay,' I finally answered. She smiled. Also I liked to see her happy.

'And no more stabbing yourself.'

I did heal faster, it seemed. It made sense. After all, the stuff They'd put into me was designed to find unhealthy flesh, eat and replace it. I tried not to think about that too much. It was nowhere near as effective as Rolleston's healing but with a few hours' rest the cuts on my arm were starting to look a lot better. The healing process really hurt however.

Morag took me by the hand to our grotto, as I'd started to think of it. We sat down by the pool and she held both my hands. I felt faintly foolish for reasons I couldn't really explain. I let go of her and was on my feet, blades extended, when they rose out of the pool.

'Jakob, it's okay,' Morag tried to reassure me. They were organic tendrils, white in colour instead of the black I was more used to. They looked like smaller versions of the massive tendrils I'd seen in Maw City. They swayed in the pool like the snakes I'd seen on documentary vizzes. The movement was in no way comforting. My heart was beating quickly.

'Morag, I'm not sure I can do this.'

'Its okay, Jakob. It'll be fine, I promise.' Her tone was reassuring but I think I sat back down opposite her and let her take my hands because her fearlessness was shaming me. I closed my eyes.

It wasn't the normal, disconcerting hard click of connection you felt hard-wiring yourself into something. It felt more like liquid flowing into the four plugs in the back of my neck. This didn't make sense. Plastic and metal had no nerve endings.

Then I was somewhere else. Then I heard the music again. Music sung through space. I felt tears on my cheeks. I opened my eyes to find myself in a waterfall of liquid sparks of light. Each spark seemed to cascade over me in a feeling of pleasant, slightly ticklish, electric warmth.

I was hovering in mid-air. The best way I could describe my surroundings was as a giant organic cave-tunnel like a vein, but this didn't do justice to what I was seeing. A warm wind blew through the tunnel/vein. It was a conduit for light and sound. Were the light and sound Their thoughts? Bioluminescent lighting sparked all around us, travelling down through the tunnel/vein. Perhaps that was Their thoughts. This was Their mind, after all, not their biology. A purely mental space. I could see junctures where other organic tunnels/veins intersected. I was hovering over what looked like a bottomless drop. This gave me a moment of vertigo but I mastered it.

Morag was right to bring me here. I reached up to touch the tears on my face. I was whole; there was no plastic or metal in me now. I was naked. So was Morag. She looked like Morag, not one of her icons. Her eyes were back. This just made me want to weep more. I was kind of glad none of the others were around to see me like this.

'The icon?' I managed.

'They're not icons, it's us,' she told me.

I wanted to hold her. I moved across to her, floating through the curtain of warm sparks. Everything about her felt real as we hugged each other fiercely. Was this my reward? Was this what it had all been for? I could hear the music. It was the abstract, angelic choral music that I heard echo through space in my dreams, the music that I'd thought the Cabal had silenced and replaced with the screaming of war. It was more real here than what Ambassador had shown me as I slept in Morag's arms in the ruins of Trenton.

'Thank you,' I said to her as I held her tight. Then I looked up. 'Thank you!' I shouted. Any inhibitions seemed foolish now. 'Can we communicate with Them?' I asked. I wasn't used to the sound of awe in my voice.

She pushed gently away from me. 'C'mon.'

Then she dived through the air and through the cascade of liquid light. I went after her, my dive clumsier. I heard a noise. I couldn't quite work out what it was. It took me a while to realise it was the sound of my laughter. Not a cynical laugh or the laughter that comes with sharing a joke with a friend, or the laughter of trying to make light of a bad situation. This laughter felt like release. As I dived through the alien mind I was freeing myself from my worries and fears. I wondered if the stunted minds and petty ambitions of the Cabal could even understand this. I think this was what I'd been searching for all those years in the sense booth. Not dislocation, like I'd thought, but connection, exploration – a feeling of there being something more.

We dived, fell, flew for what simultaneously felt like a very long time and not nearly long enough. The inner mental landscape of Them was constantly changing. I understood none of it, but none of it was ugly and everywhere was light in different hues and the ever-changing music.

Ahead of me Morag pointed towards a small tunnel-like mental vein.

'There's one,' she called and swooped gracefully towards it. I followed her and tried not to hit the wall. One what?

It was dark in the tunnel. It looked much more like rock than anything else I'd seen. The singing seemed further away.

'Morag . . .?'

'Ssh, it's okay.' I could just make out her shape ahead of me. The only light was the warm white glow from the main vein behind us. 'I told you we weren't the first to come here.'

I could just about make out markings on the rock wall. It looked like scroll-work, like the designs that Pagan had decorated himself and his surroundings with. I realised that I was wading through a shallow stream of very cold water. It reminded me of fording a burn in the Highlands. The scrollwork seemed to be moving, making disconcerting patterns. It was playing tricks with my head. The patterns suggested strange, fantastical and sometimes horrific shapes.

'If you come in peace, you can live with them, even sculpt your surround-ings,' she said.

'You mean there are other people?'

'I am not a person,' a voice said. The accent sounded vaguely familiar but I could not place it. The voice sounded utterly inhuman. It seemed to resonate differently from human language. I felt it rather than heard it. Perhaps it was because of my surroundings and my recent experiences, but I found myself overcome with a feeling that I couldn't quite understand or fully explain.

The light was blue, but not Their warm blue; it was colder like steel and neon. It came from a large and ancient-looking, two-handed claymore with a very sharp silvery blade. The man or icon holding it towered over us. He was powerfully built. His muscles looked like corded steel and seemed almost too large. Steam rose from his flesh and he burned with an inner light. I could feel the heat coming from him. It was not the warmth that blew through the asteroid caverns. Instead it was like standing too close to a furnace. The light beneath his skin picked out the network of scars that covered his torso and arms. They formed symbols and patterns that shifted with the movement of his flesh as he moved towards us. As if they were mimicking or somehow connected to the moving symbols and scrollwork on the stone wall.

I was struggling to think of this as something human. His eyes glowed with the same steel-blue light of the sword. The light could be seen through the translucent pale skin of his face. His ears were long and tapered to points. For all his size there was something graceful and otherworldly about him. He wore plaid trousers of spun wool and a thick belt, with various designs inscribed into the leather, around his waist. His hair was long, shaved at the sides and organised into complicated braids. He had a short beard but a long moustache that was again braided.

Silver and gold bracelets wrapped around his left arm. I dimly remembered that they were called torcs. His other arm was made from the same silvery metal as the sword and covered in a complex engraved pattern. It looked like some kind of ancient but perfectly functional prosthetic. It had the same glow as the sword and his eyes.

Though my iconic form in here made me look fully human, my right arm had started to ache. I held it and took a step away from the heat, the sense of raw physical power and the radiating sense of barely controlled rage I felt from this thing. I think the emotion I was feeling was awe. It was clear to me that whatever he was, he had his roots back somewhere in humanity's collective unconscious. At the same time I felt I was in the presence of something both ancient and utterly different to me. In some ways this thing, despite familiar trappings, seemed more alien than Them.

'Oh,' I said.

'Now do you believe?' Morag asked.

Shit, I thought. Was I having a religious experience? Had I been tricked into this? I pushed that thought back. I was determined not to let the normal cynical, fear-filled decisions of everyday life intrude on this place. Whatever was going on, I had to try and take this at face value as something strange but potentially wonderful. That said, I didn't want to end up as mad as your average signalman. Though with the sheer feeling of power that was radiating from this thing I could see why so many were affected.

'Oh,' I said again, my mind like a steel trap.

'I am Nuada Airgetláa,' he said.

'All right?' I managed. I looked at Morag. She was just smiling. 'Did you know about this?'

'Not really the way it works. They come and go as they please.'

123

'And They let them?'

We may have been being rude and I didn't doubt that this guy was some kind of mythic archetype from humanity's past somehow given form, but all the while we were talking he was watching us. Actually it was more like he was studying me.

'You are a warrior?' he asked. I felt my heart sink. Here we go again.

'No. I am or was a fucking soldier and I don't want to be doing great deeds for abstract reasons.'

'Jakob ...' Morag tried to warn me. She reached over and grabbed my arm.

'You'd have more luck with Balor if he wasn't—' Which was as far as I got before I was lifted up by the neck and slammed against the wall. I found the tip of about six feet of steel pressed against my stomach. His fingers scorched my neck. I could smell my own burning flesh. The pale flesh on his face seemed to slew back down to the musculature as he hissed, revealing wickedly sharp canines and too many of them. His breath smelled of honey, heather and raw meat. I'm pretty sure I screamed. Up close he looked even larger. And I had been having such a nice time. I knew I was helpless here.

'No!' Morag said and grabbed the guy. She may as well have been wrestling a statue. She screamed and stumbled back, her flesh burned where she had touched him. He released me and backed off, his features reshaping into their original form. He looked down at Morag. She was cradling her burned hands, looking pained and unsure. He seemed appalled by the pain he'd inflicted on her.

'I am sorry, Mother.'

Morag looked as mystified as I was.

'That's okay,' she said slowly. I was rubbing my bruised and burned virtual neck.

'It was just that he said the name of my enemy,' he explained.

Balor's ability to make friends and influence people seemed second only to Mudge's. Unless of course he was referring to the mythological demon that Balor had named himself after. Of course he was. I groaned. Even though I was having some sort of religious experience I lacked the ability to process it properly. It all seemed like nonsense to me. Frightening and painful nonsense.

'Different Balor and he's dead anyway,' I managed.

Nuada nodded. 'So you are a warrior?' he asked again.

'Whatever. What are you?'

'I am Nuada Airgetláa, it means "Of the Silver Hand". I am of the Tuatha Dé Danaan; I was once their king.' He held up his silver arm. 'But I am no longer whole.'

This I understood.

'Tough war?' I asked.

'Yes,' he said simply.

I nodded. 'I've got one just like it.' Then I remembered where I'd heard the name before. 'The arm. You made sure I got it? You're one of those self-aware AIs that latches onto religious iconography in the net, aren't you?'

'I thought they were just the fevered imagination of hackers,' Morag said. Nuada said nothing.

'How did you get all the way out here?' I asked him.

'This is just another road from Tir Nan Og.'

This of course made no sense. I wondered if religion would have a more universal appeal if the gods could manage to be a bit less fucking cryptic. Then a strange thought occurred to me.

'Wait a second. The arm. Are you trying to identify with me?'

I saw Morag roll her eyes. I think in the big electronic church of hacking you were supposed to be a little more respectful during your visitation.

'The Adversary is coming—' Nuada started.

'No shit.'

'Jakob!' Morag hissed at me. She sounded genuinely pissed off.

'The Adversary is going to drown us all. There will be only one god, and that god will be a god of fear.'

'You mean Demiurge?'

'And when he drowns us he will know us,' Nuada continued.

'So you can hide and keep secrets?' I asked.

'Now we hold our own mysteries, but not in the face of the Adversary.'

'Okay, Demiurge is bad. We know this. So?'

'He will have our power.'

This didn't sound good.

'Is that a lot of power?' I asked. He just looked at me as if I was stupid. 'If you're frightened of Demiurge then fight. Don't dress yourself up in old gods and expect others to do the work for you.' Again he said nothing. 'Have you got anything to bring to this?'

'If we go near it, we will be taken, we will be corrupted, we will become an extension of it, and you do not want this as much as we do not want it.'

'Okay, so come forward,' I said.

'And risk the burning times?'

'So you'd rather be urban myths? Hackers' tall tales? What are you anyway?'

'I told you. I am Nuada Airgetláa.'

I took another step back. Despite the odd way I seemed to be hearing him, he seemed to be trying to keep his tone as even and emotionless as possible. I just couldn't shake the feeling of enormous rage being held back just below the surface.

'Okay. With all due respect, what do you want from me?'

'You must have them remake Pais Badarn Beisrydd.'

I looked over at Morag questioningly. She was crouching down and backing into the shadows. There was something odd and primal about her movements. What the fuck was going on?

'I don't know what that means.'

'If you are a warrior then we will share blood.'

With his silver hand he wrapped his fingers around the sword's blade, barely touching it. His hand started to bleed what looked like smoking mercury. I looked at Morag again. The shadows in the tunnel seemed to be elongating to engulf her. They moved across her naked skin like they were alive. I began to feel dislocated like I was on a good but frightening psychotropic. It was as if it wasn't happening to me but I was somehow witnessing it.

'It's only information,' Morag whispered.

I could only see her as a shadow now, though the shadow's teeth and eyes seemed to burn. I swallowed and reached out for the sword. I didn't even realise I'd touched it until my hand came away wet with blood. Nuada grasped my hand. My blood and his mingled. It burned, it burned so much. It took me a moment to realise the discordant screaming that was so jarring, even in this part of this place, was me. My flesh glowed from the inside through translucent skin.

I awoke in the pool. My body felt like a rough-edged machine. It was awkward and painful to live in. Of course it would have been less painful if I hadn't stabbed myself in the arm earlier. I felt feverish and was surprised that the water wasn't bubbling. Morag was holding me, cradling me like I was a sick or frightened child.

Later in the grotto I was still shaken and didn't feel right. I was too hot. A diagnostic check of all my internal systems found no trace of any information exchange.

'Did you take me there?' I asked.

She didn't answer straight away. I think she was trying to work out if there was any accusation in my question. There wasn't. I'd worked hard to make sure there wasn't.

'It wasn't an ambush. I knew there were things there. I've spoken with some of them but I wasn't expecting that.'

'They're AIs, aren't they? Powerful self-aware ones masquerading as old gods. That's why they're so frightened.'

'Maybe,' she said.

'You can't believe they're gods, can you?' I said incredulously. Maybe I was just trying to convince myself. It had seemed pretty real at the time.

'They've been here a while if they are.'

'They must have come when we were colonising.'

'Its difficult to understand Their way of measuring time but They encountered whatever that was before They encountered us.'

That shut me up until I eventually asked, 'So what do you think they are?'

'I don't know. Maybe they're aliens searching for a way to communicate
and then the way home, or maybe they're the real deal – whatever that means.
Pagan thinks that they are a reflection of us, our subconscious projected onto
the net and somehow given form and independence. He calls them ghosts of
our imagination.'

'So?' I finally asked.

'So what?'

'So what does it all mean?'

'Fucked if I know.'

'Brilliant. Just more religious bollocks.' Morag opened her mouth to say
something. 'Don't tell me to have faith.'

'I was going to tell you to speak to Pagan – he knows more about this sort
of thing.'

'Oh he'll fucking love that, me getting religion. Has he seen them?' I asked,
trying to change the subject.

'Back on Earth he has. He hasn't been in Their mind yet. I'm going to take
him in next.'

'Yeah? Good, he'll like that. Hold on. Does that mean he'll see you naked?'
I demanded. She was laughing. I still didn't like the idea. 'Will you see him
naked?!' I demanded. She grimaced.

I awoke to the reassuringly distant scream of the sub-orbital military
transport's engines. Akhtar had laid on the aircraft and after some
arguments with the crew I'd even managed to get my bike on board.

I hadn't spoken to Pagan about my religious experience of course,
meeting Nuada. I tried to ignore the whole thing. I didn't understand
it, therefore it was meaningless. I convinced myself that it really didn't
matter what they were. The whole pretending to be gods and spirits
thing was just another snow job to try and get people to do what they
wanted them to, probably for some inhuman reason. Maybe it was
just entertainment for them. Besides, I had decided I was through,
that I was going to retire.

We went home. I think I could have stayed or even gone on with
Them if Morag had been with me, but Mudge really wanted to get
back and get high. Besides, we needed to see how much damage we'd
done.

The last we'd seen of Them was huge engines pushing cored
asteroids out of their place in the Dog's Teeth. Each asteroid was
honeycombed with Their energy storage matrices. Energy harvested

from the twin stars to sustain Them on their exodus. The massive convoy of ships surrounding the asteroids seemed to stretch out for thousands of miles as They prepared to flee the neighbours.

They got us home by using a variant of Their infiltration crafts. It was basically an engine with re-entry needles. Except this time when we came in-system we were broadcasting using the salvaged comms units from our Mamluk exo-armour suits. The good thing about the design of the needles was that we didn't get to see how close we got to dying. We were intercepted by a Ugandan ship, and during the initial debrief we each had four Ugandan special forces pointing weapons at us at all times. It was quite tense.

We got passed from pillar to confused post as the authorities tried to decide whose problem we actually were. The debriefs got less combative and Mudge got in less fights with our interrogators. I had tried telling them that if they wanted his co-operation all they had to do was give him drugs, but nobody listened to me.

The Dog's Teeth, Maw City – it all started to seem like a dream. Parts of it too pleasant and other parts too unreal to have any relation to the grind of being back in the real world and dealing with the imminence of a war that could split humanity in two. Assuming that it didn't just destroy it.

Eventually Air Marshal Kaaria intervened on our behalf and everyone heaved a sigh of relief as we became someone else's problem.

Mudge's drugs had made me feel better and I was healing faster. I should still get someone to look at my spine.

As I looked out over the desert I had some time to think. Leaving aside the suicidal aspect of the job, it still did not feel right getting ready to kill innocent soldiers. I guessed this is what war had been about all through the ages. Was it any different from the streets? I'd mainly killed people who'd been trying to kill me. Or maybe that was just what I told myself to get to sleep at night. This was going to be more proactive. I guessed it wouldn't be any different from what we'd done when we'd busted Gregor out, but then that was when I decided that I didn't want to kill any more.

Except Rolleston. And Cronin. Rolleston had to die because he deserved it. Cronin I didn't hate, but he had to go because he was so much part of the problem. Of course they'd be the most difficult to get to, assuming we could even find them.

Then there was Josephine, the Grey Lady. No real hate there. Just fear. To deal with Rolleston we'd first have to deal with her. Why the bond? I wondered. All our heavy hitters were gone as well. Balor might have been able to deal with Josephine, though even he'd implied that he was scared of her. Hybrid Gregor could have dealt with her if he hadn't ended up on the other side. Though even then Rolleston and Josephine had all but walked through us in the media node. Rannu? He was a solid trooper, very skilled, but I didn't think he was in the same league as the Grey Lady.

I watched Mudge dance by, singing along with some music he was listening to on his internal systems. He was naked and covered in body paint. That at least explained the unconscious airman on the bench opposite. It seemed I could sleep through anything.

'Mudge?'

He turned to look at me. He seemed really jittery. He held out his hand as if he could take hold of me from the middle of the cargo hold, his hand grasping and relaxing.

'We need more shooters,' I told him. 'Give it some thought.' He nodded and then smiled.

I wasn't sure if the escorts who took us from the airfield to Limbo were the same ones as before, as the entire security detail looked the same to me. They certainly didn't seem happy to see us. Mudge being naked and blissed out hadn't helped. Sometimes I felt that people didn't take us seriously.

I was looking out of the window as we sank down into the silo. Mudge came over and put me in a playful headlock. He must have been coming down, as he was now able to communicate with us humans. Sadly.

'Wow,' he began. 'You're really going to have to eat some shit when we get there.' Which is why I wasn't looking forward to getting back to Limbo. 'That's going to be really humiliating.'

There was no point talking to him when he was like this.

7

New Mexico

I ended up carrying Mudge's stuff. I agreed to be checked for God and surveillance but cheerfully refused to allow them to take my weapons and pointed out I had more than the last time I came. All the while Mudge was dancing around listening to music on his internal systems. He was still stark naked and covered in body paint. I let them check his gear. He just giggled whenever they tried to speak to him. Mudge certainly picked his time.

The Limbo staff just stared at the naked, painted, dancing Mudge as we entered the nerve centre, or what I had come to think of as the long metal mesh tube. Sharcroft advanced on me with the strange metallic, insectile gait of his life-support chair.

I pointed at him. 'And you can fuck off.' I threw two vials to one of his aides. One was a DNA swab and the other was blood. 'That's all you're getting; don't ask for more.'

'Sergeant Douglas, may I remind—' his modulated electronic voice started to say.

'No, you may not. I'm going to speak to my people and find out what the score is. We'll take objectives off you and all the resources we need; the rest goes dark for operational security.'

'Breaking laws in the hot sun!' Mudge shouted. I think it was supposed to be singing. It was very off-key.

'So you're taking over now?' Morag asked.

I turned. I tried to ignore how good it felt to see her. Tried to ignore how good she looked with longer hair and in the white one-piece. Tried to ignore how nervous I suddenly felt.

Pagan stood next to her, looking out of place and uncomfortable without his staff and other accoutrements. I didn't pay any attention to him. She looked me up and down, raising an eyebrow at my battered state.

'I fought the law and the law won!' Mudge shouted again. He advanced on Morag for a hug.

'Mudge, you're naked,' she said by way of hello. Mudge gave her a hug and smeared body paint all over the front of her suit. 'Och, you've made me all mucky!'

We all watched as Mudge boogied over to Pagan.

'I approve of the body paint,' Pagan said by way of a greeting and hugged Mudge, who then started dancing towards me.

'See the way I diffused a potentially tense situation there through the medium of dance?' he asked loudly as if talking over music in a club.

'And nudity. That's brilliant, Mudge. Thanks.' He was getting closer. 'Don't hug me ...' Naked Mudge gave me a hug. Morag was laughing and Pagan was smiling.

'So is your holiday over?' Pagan asked as I patted Mudge on the head and tried to disentangle myself while getting the minimum of paint on me.

'Yeah. I didn't enjoy it. The world is still full of arseholes and now they're queuing up to meet me.'

'You look like you shouldn't be out on your own,' he said.

'There's an argument for that.'

I glanced over at Sharcroft. As ever, his corpse-like pallor betrayed nothing. I looked back to Morag, who was gazing at me coolly. She hadn't rushed over to hug me, but neither had she started shouting at me, which I considered a small victory.

'Is there someplace we can talk?' I asked.

Pagan nodded and we followed him. Mudge leaped up onto a desk and started dancing.

'I should be kept apprised—' Sharcroft started.

'Fuck off unless you want to get shot,' I told him. I wasn't just being obnoxious; I was eager to make sure I remembered just who the enemy was.

Pagan led us into a smaller chamber. It was pretty much empty except for a plain desk, two uncomfortable-looking skeletal chairs, a high-resolution monitor, a holographic projector and some thinscreens. It had a similar metal mesh around it to the main room outside but something about it looked makeshift, scrounged and scavenged.

'You do this?' I asked. Pagan and Morag both nodded. 'Look, I haven't—'

Morag turned round and glared at me and held a finger over her lips. I felt very green just then. Pagan and Morag swept the place for bugs and found a couple.

131

'Little pricks.' Pagan cursed into the bug before turning to me. 'In the minute or two we came out to speak to you.'

They both then checked us and took a couple more off me that must have been slipped in when I was being searched. I felt more embarrassed.

'But I thought this was a what-do-you-call-it cage?' I said.

'It is. These are recorders.'

He stamped on them. Morag set up a white-noise projector.

'Fuuuck!' Mudge screamed and turned to glare at her. 'What a fucking comedown. What did you do that for?'

She gently slapped him on the side of the face. 'Focus, Mudge.'

Then Morag took my head in her hands and kissed me. It's difficult to describe how good it felt. Afterwards she looked up at me. I could see myself reflected in her replacement eyes. I was a mess but I'd looked a lot worse. Then she hit me squarely on the nose. She was a lot faster and stronger than she had been. It actually hurt. A lot. I reeled back, more from surprise than anything else, and grabbed my nose. She was staring at me, arms crossed.

'What?!' I managed.

'Since talking to you does no good, I thought I'd demonstrate how pleased I am to see you and how pissed off I still am with you.'

Pagan was grinning. Mudge was looking pained. 'Always the negativity with you two,' he said despairingly, shaking his head.

'That may be partially my fault,' Pagan said.

'Well I may fucking punch you back.' I'd been having a much better day until about thirty seconds ago.

'I merely expressed the opinion to Morag that when you returned we might not have time for her and your normal decision-making process.'

'Oh brilliant. So now we've moved up to violence?' I asked Morag.

'Only when talking doesn't work,' she said, grinning at me. How very Dundonian, I thought. I blamed Rannu completely for the speed and the strength of the punch. 'Besides, you've been a dick and you're not taking over.'

'I'm not here to take over, and where's Rannu? I want to discuss his hand-to-hand training.'

Pagan and Morag exchanged a look. I groaned inwardly.

'He went ahead,' Morag finally said.

This was bad news. I'd had a feeling he would probably go ahead but was hoping that he hadn't. We could have used him, regardless of what we were going to end up doing.

'Okay, my suggestion is this: we talk broadly about objectives, we discuss the operating conditions, terrain and details en route, where nobody who can overhear will be able to do any damage. Agreed?'

Morag looked to Pagan. I managed to suppress irrational feelings of annoyance and jealousy. Finally Pagan nodded.

'Yes!' Mudge shouted enthusiastically.

'Where are we going?' Please not Sirius, please not Sirius, please not Sirius.

'Lalande,' Pagan said.

'Oh well, at least it's not Proxima,' I said.

Lalande was a red dwarf system. The only planet that almost supported life was Lalande 2, which was a tidally locked, high-gravity, mineral-rich hellhole. The only place more inhospitable was Proxima, with its frozen wastes and toxic oceans.

'And Rannu's gone ahead?'

Morag and Pagan nodded. I wanted to ask what he was doing. I wanted to ask if they had protocols for meeting him, but I did not trust the environment so this wasn't the place.

'Are you happy that I handle the security element?' I asked Pagan and just about in time remembered to look at Morag as well. I left it unsaid that I was assuming they were planning some kind of witchcraft for the mission and would have their own information warfare agenda. It was Morag who nodded. 'And I'm assuming that we're all broadly on the same page as regards our general objectives?'

Fuck up the enemy as much as possible and see if we can learn anything while doing it. What would be more difficult was coming up with a way to safely transmit any useful intelligence back. The pair of them nodded again.

'No,' said Mudge.

'You'll like it,' I assured him.

He seemed happy with that.

Morag tapped me on the head. 'There's something in there I want,' she said. I guessed she was talking about the information exchange between myself and whatever was calling itself Nuada in the mind of Them.

'I'm getting a little tired of being poked and prodded, and you couldn't find anything before but you're welcome to try again. I've got something for you.'

I found the file that Vicar had given me in his sanctuary and tried to send it to Pagan and Morag. It bounced. Both of them were looking at me like I was an idiot.

'You're in an information quarantine,' Morag said, using the tone that young people like to use when their elders are being stupid.

'Where's it from?' Pagan asked.

I told him. Even Mudge looked at me seriously when I mentioned Vicar's name. His camera eyes revolving one way and then the other in their sockets.

'He's alive?' Pagan asked. I could hear the emotion in his voice.

I shook my head. Pagan covered his eyes with his hands. He hadn't been this emotional before but I think he'd prepared himself that time. The hope that I'd hinted at was just a bit too much for him. I hadn't realised they were so close. I felt like an utter shit at my pang of jealousy as Morag gently pulled Pagan's head down towards her shoulder and held him. Through the jealousy I managed to wonder how someone who'd had her life managed to care about other people. Where had she learned that?

'I'm all right,' Pagan finally said.

I decided to spare him the grizzly details, which conveniently meant omitting who it was that actually killed him.

Morag let Pagan go and grabbed a double jack cable and moved towards me.

'You're not supposed to—' Pagan started.

I guessed there was some kind of protocol involving a separate and isolating device, but it was too late. I felt the disconcerting click of the jack being slid into one of the four plugs on the back of my neck. Somehow it felt even more intimate than the kiss. Hopefully it wouldn't be followed by a punch. I saw the notification of the connection on my IVD. I sent the file. The connection was severed. Morag concentrated for a moment.

'It's fine,' she told Pagan. 'I knew he wouldn't poison me.'

Pagan admonished her for not following proper procedure. He then demonstrated it by having her put the file into a stand-alone system, where they used the touch screen controls on the monitor to run a diagnostic on it before Pagan jacked in and stored it in his internal systems as well.

I wasn't paying that much attention. Morag had left me a text when we'd connected. I wished I'd thought of something like that but then I probably wouldn't have known what to say. On the other hand, I really hoped it wasn't a revenge virus. This was a black op; I briefly wondered if they had access to slaveware. I decided to trust her and open the message. Besides, I was pretty sure that slaveware would come in a much bigger file. It simply said, 'You're an arsehole but I missed you.' I think I must have sagged as the tension drained from me. Morag glanced up at me and then turned away smiling. I found Mudge looking at me, grinning.

Yeah, I felt much better. Except for the guilt about sleeping with Fiona.

'Mudge,' Pagan started. Mudge's head jerked around and his lenses refocused on him. 'You filming now?' Pagan asked.

'Of course.'

'Okay, you can't do that. It's a huge security risk.'

'I've got a kill switch set up with extensive parameters on it. Anything happens to me, it runs a firestorm through my memory. I can also trigger it with a thought. Then of course I tell them everything I know because they'll probably torture me and I can't think that'd be good, probably quite painful.'

I was smiling at this. Pagan looked like he was getting ready to lecture.

'Don't exaggerate, Mudge,' I said. 'You'd sell us out for some good weed.'

Mudge pretended to give this some thought. 'That's unfair, man. Maybe some good coke or a mind-blowing psychotropic, depending on my mood.'

'Look, this is very amusing but he's a—' Pagan started.

'He'll be fine,' I assured Pagan, who didn't look very assured.

'People keep on forgetting what I do for a living. I'm not just another numpty with a gun. You do your job and let me do mine. You might see me as a risk but believe me, it's just as important. Or do you want this place to remain secret? Sharcroft to remain secret?' Suddenly Mudge wasn't playing the stoned buffoon.

Pagan still looked unconvinced. Morag put a hand on his arm.

'How can you doubt him?' she asked.

'He told all last time.'

'Look, I'm as unhappy about it as everyone else—' I started.

'Bollocks, you love it,' Mudge interrupted.

'But his timing was good. Though that does remind me. If we're going into a high-surveillance environment—'

'Possibly total surveillance,' Pagan said.

'Then we're going to need to look very different.'

'We know,' Morag said.

'We need to put together a list of everything we need,' I said. I'd started one in my internal systems.

'We have. We've given it to Sharcroft. He said he'd take care of the resources side,' Morag said smugly.

'Then we need to ignore it and set up another one, get way too much money from Sharcroft and buy multiples of each item we need,' I told her.

I was trying not to turn this into one-upmanship, mainly because I didn't want to get hit. Morag looked at Pagan uncertainly.

'He's probably right,' Pagan eventually admitted.

'And Pagan, you should know better. Particularly as I'm betting it's what Rannu did.' Pagan nodded a little sheepishly. 'We also need a place to pick it up which is not heavily watched over by the almighty. Speaking of which, any information on Cabal agents? Anything we have to watch out for while we're shopping?'

At this Pagan looked exasperated.

'Sharcroft's not been particularly open about this,' he said.

'Let me guess – operational security?' I asked.

Pagan nodded. 'From what we've managed to garner, there was a purge based on what he knew, but some of them got away. I think he's also playing counter-intelligence games with them.'

That wasn't what I wanted to hear. I wanted something more direct and final. I didn't think we could afford to play around like that, but then I'd never had the patience for intelligence games.

'The problem is he's too much of an old-fashioned spy, or rather too much of an old-fashioned spymaster,' Pagan finished.

'Well, we may need to show him the difference between operational security and what he's running the operation for in the first place.' So we could do our job. We were also going to have to dissuade him from constantly trying to bug our gear. Though we'd still need to continue checking it.

'Infiltration?' I asked. At this Pagan looked a little uncomfortable.

'OILO,' he said. He wouldn't meet my eyes.

'Into high G? Are you fucking nuts?'

'Cool,' Mudge said.

'Look, I know rock-ape combat air controllers live for this shit, but it's fucking dangerous at the best of times. What are you doing – reliving past glories?'

Pagan shrugged. I think he knew Orbital Insertion Low Opening was mad. 'Can you think of a better way?'

Now I had to admit that he was right.

'I don't want to die in space,' I muttered to myself.

'You are such a fucking pussy,' Mudge told me. I nodded.

'How do we get there?' I was unhappy and trying to change the subject.

'NSA frigate, stealth bird,' Pagan told me. I was already shaking my head. Pagan was starting to look a little put out. 'Then what?'

'Smuggler, a good one. We need to control as much of this as we can and take as much of it away from Sharcroft as possible.' For this mission there was no such thing as paranoid. Pagan looked like he was about to argue but didn't. 'We need more shooters,' I said.

'Well, we've been looking for replacements for you,' Morag said. I smiled at her but with the best will in the world she was not going to know as much as us about the special forces community.

'I've been thinking about that, since you mention it,' Mudge said.

'In your state of mind? We're not taking any dragons or talking goldfish,' I told him.

'Very fucking funny.'

'We got a list from Sharcroft of active and inactive members of the community. A bit of a risk, but everyone I know is past it,' Pagan said and ran his fingers over the monitor's touch screen, opening the file. Mudge and I just looked at him. 'I'm not,' he added defensively.

'I've had an idea,' Morag said, and we didn't mean to ignore her exactly.

'Harry in Blue Troop,' Mudge suggested. I took the monitor from Pagan and input Harry's full name. He'd been a good soldier and was easy to get on with.

'Dead,' I told Mudge.

'Yeah? Where?'

'Sirius, two weeks after we shipped out.'

'Them?'

'No, accident. Looks like a mech stood on him.'

'Fucking cavalry,' Mudge said, shaking his head. 'What about Crazy Shirley?'

'What, that lunatic from the Special Reconnaissance Regiment? Wasn't she the only girl you ever slept with?' I asked.

At the time I wasn't sure why Morag was looking so pissed off but even she turned and looked at Mudge askance.

'You have to understand she's really butch,' Mudge said defensively. 'She took me.'

'Too much information,' Pagan told him.

I'd finally remembered her proper name and found her on the list.

'Still there, so we'll be fighting her,' I said.

'Shit,' Mudge said sadly. 'What about Toadstool?'

'As a source for drugs?' I asked but checked. 'Dead. Overdose.'

'Fuck. Combine?'

'The American guy?'

'Yes, an American,' Morag said, but we were distracted.

'Dead. Orbital strike,' I told Mudge.

'Boom-Boom?'

'Dead. Shot down in an assault shuttle.'

'Did you know anyone with a proper name?' Morag asked acidly.

A frightening amount of the people I knew vaguely or by reputation were either dead or still in theatre. That meant they were now working for Rolleston and Cronin. A few that we came across had been 'tasked', which I guess meant that they were doing the same sort of stupid thing as we were. This went on for a while until I saw the dawning of an idea spread over Mudge's face.

'I've had an awesome thought,' he said. I looked at him expectantly. 'Vladimir.' He was grinning.

'He's a fucking lunatic. Maybe more so than Balor,' I said, though despite myself I could see the appeal of it. The Spetsnaz warewolf was a good fighter and his insanity might actually be a boon. 'He's an officer. Do you think he'll play along?' I was checking the list to see if it carried info on Russian special forces. It did but it was sparser.

'Yeah, if we pay him in cooking ethanol or something.'

I was pleasantly surprised to find Vladimir in the list. There was a link to the rest of the Vucari. They weren't in theatre, which was a relief. They were however tasked. I was getting tired of this.

'They're off dying somewhere else,' I told Mudge.

He looked crestfallen. On the plus side, I could imagine the Vucari making the Black Squadrons utterly miserable before they got caught. I didn't like to think about the cost for the poor bastards who got caught in the middle but I hoped the Russians got to eat a few of the true believers.

I pinched the bridge of my nose between my thumb and forefinger tiredly and put the monitor down.

'Finished your little trip down squaddie memory lane?' Morag asked testily. I couldn't quite work out how we'd managed to piss her off this time.

'Hey!' I started. That wasn't fair. We'd discovered that we'd lost some people we knew. Mind you, we were used to that.

'I've had an idea,' she said through clenched teeth.

Pagan seemed to be in a world of his own. I think he was running through the information I'd given them from Vicar. Morag picked up the monitor and slender fingers played across the screen.

'No offence, Morag,' Mudge said bravely. 'But what would you know about the special forces community?'

Morag paused to glare at him but then went back to what she was doing. Finally she handed the screen to me. I looked at it.

'Oh,' I said. 'That's actually not a bad idea.' I started reading the notes. 'Interesting family background, long line of Philadelphia gunfighters, 1st Infantry, Tunnel Rat on Lalande ...'

'Which would be useful?' Morag asked sarcastically.

'Delta,' I said finally and then put the monitor down. 'It's a good idea, but she's got a good job. Why would she leave it to come and die with us?' Morag tapped the screen. I looked back and read a little further. 'Oh, she got fired.'

'Because of us,' Morag said.

That made sense. Or rather it would make sense to the sort of idiot who made decisions like that. She'd done a good job and would have continued to do so.

'So she'll be pleased to see us. Do we know where she is?'

Morag shook her head. 'But only because I haven't asked God yet.'

Pagan looked over at me and tapped his head. 'That will help. All the Cabal's files were purged and the NSA have not been very forthcoming.' I nodded.

'Who are we talking about?' a perplexed Mudge asked.

It was a case of killing two birds with one stone. We'd found out where she was and the Arizona Coast was a good enough place to buy the gear we wanted. I think the best thing about it was the coastline was close enough to ride to. Though we'd borrowed a hover truck to carry whatever we bought back with us. It was almost fast enough to keep up with the bikes.

Pagan was driving the truck, much to Mudge's disappointment. Mudge had been trying to choose just the right driving drug when Pagan nipped into the cab and plugged himself in. Mudge had insisted on finding something called peyote for what he called an authentic desert experience. Pagan had appeared unwilling to subject himself to Mudge's drug-fuelled driving.

The best thing about the trip was that it had pissed Sharcroft off. I was never going to get tired of that. The best thing about Limbo was that I'd managed to get some decent food and a good night's sleep. This was after I'd had a disconcerting several hours with both Morag and Pagan plugged into my head trying to find the elusive info that they hoped Nuada had planted somewhere in my systems. They found nothing. It didn't matter to me: I got to sleep next to Morag.

Pagan had cornered me the following day and insisted that we connect via cable. I felt a little self-conscious as he plugged into me. He was so security-conscious that he didn't even sub-vocalise. Instead we communicated via text message.

'Morag has tried but she could not remember what Nuada asked you to remake,' he texted me. He was trying to keep his face expressionless but I was pretty sure he loved that I'd had a religious experience after some of the discussions we'd had.

'Pays Padarn something,' I texted back. This he looked less impressed at. 'I think it was in a foreign language,' I added defensively.

'You should have come to me immediately, while it was still fresh in your mind,' the next message said. I nodded and tried to look contrite. I still wasn't convinced that it wasn't all bullshit. Pagan was concentrating. I reckoned he was cross-referencing some internal directory. I hoped he was enjoying himself but I hoped it sarcastically.

Another message appeared in my IVD from our hard-wired link. 'Do you mean Pais Badarn Beisrydd?' It sounded right but I wasn't sure. I decided to make my life a little easier by answering in the affirmative and asking if he knew what it was.

'Yes, it's part of British and Arthurian myth. It's one of the thirteen treasures of Britain. It's a cloak or a coat that is said to turn the wearer invisible.'

'That'll be useful,' I texted back. I was wondering if he would pick up on the irony in a text medium.

'You're taking it too literally,' he replied. Apparently not. 'I think it's either part of a program or a program that might help us move unseen in Demiurge-controlled systems,' he continued. 'If only Nuada had given it to someone useful.' Pagan was smiling. I gave him the finger. Then something occurred to me.

'Maybe her head's too busy?' I asked, meaning the presence of the ghost of Ambassador in Morag's head.

Pagan shrugged.

Then I sent another text. 'Did she see anyone while I was away?'

Pagan looked pissed off. It felt like I left his reply blinking on my IVD for a long time. Pagan had unplugged us both before I had the guts to open it. It simply said, 'Did you?' Pagan was watching for a response. I knew it was written all over my face. Pagan shook his head and walked out of the workspace.

I'd left my bike in an old hangar building on the surface close to the silo. The muscle car and dirt bike we'd stolen were there as well, as was the military surplus hover truck we'd borrowed. A secondary or tertiary reason for owning a bike like the Triumph Argo, loath as I was to admit it, was to impress women. I wasn't disappointed by Morag's response. Though she appreciated it as someone who liked riding bikes when she had the chance.

She had on a pair of bike boots, armoured combat trousers, a hoodie and an armoured leather jacket with some complex and possibly

Celtic design painted on the back. She looked like a normal street kid as she checked the bike out. I couldn't help smiling.

'I like it,' she said. 'Let me ride it.'

'Morag, I very possibly love you, but no.'

I could hear Mudge and Pagan arguing in the background. She gave me a strange look. It lasted for some time. I was starting to wonder what I'd said wrong this time.

'You can ride pillion if you want,' I said.

She just sneered at me and climbed onto the dirt bike. The engine started as she texted the code to it. She gunned the motor and was out of the hangar. I had to admit that Morag was getting much better at riding. I remember nervously watching her ride on the Dead Roads. She had obviously far surpassed the skillsofts that she'd used to learn initially.

I sent the codes to my own bike as I watched her dust cloud speeding away from us. The Argo was a much faster bike so it wasn't going to take long to catch her. I climbed onto my rumbling machine. The hover truck's armoured skirts were inflating as I headed out of the garage after her across the nearly featureless desert plain. I felt the sun like a physical force as soon as I left the shade of the hangar. This was despite my coat's cooling system.

The desert surprised me. It had a lot more colour than I thought it would. Admittedly they were mainly reds, browns and yellows with the odd patch of green, but it was still beautiful. The size and blueness of the sky with just the odd scudding cloud took some getting used to, as did the distance to the horizon.

We tried to avoid main roads and towns where we could. It was easier in the Navajo Nation, who took our tolls and then minded their own business. We drove and rode through a number of deserted towns. It felt like an empty land. I liked that.

We camped less than twenty miles from our destination. We could see the glow of New Venice from where we made camp. Started a fire, cooked food and drank sour mash. It wasn't as good as single malt whisky.

Mudge sang us songs that he assured us were authentic for the situation. He said that it was called country and western music, a pre-FHC style that predated the country and metal that Cyberbillys favoured. It sounded like a dying cat trying to yodel. I was pretty sure that Mudge was running some kind of shitty karaoke program on his IVD.

Later on when we were all quiet, enjoying the stars as the fire burned down, Morag in my arms, Mudge threw me a file. I pushed it into one of the plugs in the back of my neck and downloaded the music. It was by a man called Cash. It wasn't the sort of thing that I would normally listen to but it fitted.

In retaliation for the destruction of the Brazilian Spoke and the use of air-launched, nuclear-tipped, anti-satellite weapons on several orbital facilities, the Multi Nationals and their backers had destroyed California. It hadn't slipped into the ocean like some had once thought possible, but the ocean still swamped much of it.

They had targeted the San Andreas Fault, another fault area called the Eastern California Shear Zone, as well as offshore fault lines. The kinetic strikes were much more extensive than the Birmingham bombardment and had pierced the faults down through the Earth's crust. The damage from the resultant earthquakes was appalling, but it was the successive tidal waves from the bombardment as well as the subsequent underwater quakes and volcanic activity that had caused the most deaths. It was the greatest loss of human life as a result of a single incident in human history.

It redrew the Californian coastline and turned much of the previously dry state into a muddy salt swamp. More flooding took place as a result of the global rise in water levels. All coastal cities had been destroyed, as had many of the cities further inland. The state's as well as the country's economy lay in ruins. It was a blow that America had not really recovered from in the intervening two hundred and fifty plus years.

California had become a ghost state, a waterlogged equivalent of the Dead Roads inhabited by few but the truly degenerate and insane. Large swathes of it were a shallow sea, the water broken only by the rubble of pre-FHC civilisation.

Mudge told us the story around the campfire. Growing up, we'd all heard versions of it but he had the education to know it properly, I guess. Pagan probably knew it too but he remained quiet and looked solemn, even sad. I tried to imagine what that night had been like. It must have felt like the end of the world. I wondered if they'd had time to realise something was wrong. Would they have been able to understand the magnitude of the disaster that was killing them? I could only think of it in the most abstract terms. I hoped that they had died quickly, but I knew many of them would not have.

The same night the corporations hit the faults they had also hit every single dam on the Colorado River. This, along with the general rise in the water table, led to partial flooding of the Grand Canyon and surrounding areas. While it paled in significance compared to the destruction of California, it was another blow against America's infrastructure. The lights went out in Vegas just before the aftershocks hit it. It also led to the Grand Canyon and environs becoming euphemistically known as the Arizona or Nevada – depending on what side you were on – Coast.

Vicious, often artificially augmented, tidal bore waves forced down narrow canyons gave birth to the dangerous sport of canyon surfing and turned the Arizona/Nevada Coast into a the number-one surf spot in North America. Though the truly hard core sometimes risked the dangers of California to surf the ruins of its destroyed cities. The area had been developed by an alliance of mob money and the local Hulapai Native Americans, who had ensured that the land was not further abused too much. Fortunately, as the target market was surfers, not too much development was needed. They liked to rough it. The development alliance used surf tribes to police the coast. Some of the tribes were borderline feral people from the ruins of California.

The free and easy approach to law enforcement coupled with a love of cash meant a burgeoning grey market. We were hoping to find what we'd need in the arms and tech markets of New Venice.

I felt overdressed in my raincoat. Everyone else looked much more at home, particularly Pagan with his staff and ritual accoutrements back on show, although our pale and soon-to-be-red skin marked us out as Europeans.

Much of New Venice clung to the canyon walls or made use of caves in the side of the canyons, though the Hulapai council had forbidden any excavation. The streets were often rope bridges out over the water, or platforms linking buildings that clung to the cliff. Most of the people were tanned, muscular and heavily tattooed. There was a lot of scar tissue on show, some of it ritual, most of it the result of meeting a canyon wall at speed. Many were heavily pierced and/or had their hair cut, braided or deadlocked into elaborate patterns. They wore shorts, cut-offs or wetsuits. The women wore bikini tops and the men were mainly stripped to the waist. Most carried knives but only the tribal police seemed to wear guns.

After we'd found people who seemed trustworthy enough to bribe to look after our vehicles, we asked God where she was, knowing that she would have asked God to alert her if anyone made enquiries about her. Then we made our way through New Venice down into the main canyon. As we took the bridges over the smaller canyons we began to see the surfing. The surfers would watch one of the tidal bores approaching and jump off bridges into deep-water rapids. Then they had to sort themselves out and get ready to catch the wave. If/ when they caught the wave it shot them down the canyon like a bullet. The canyon walls were smeared with sun-baked blood.

'I want a go!' Mudge shouted as we watched three surfers jump from the bridge we were on. Two of them almost immediately wiped out. One of them didn't come back up as we crossed.

'Focus,' I told him.

I was trying to decide if it was any more dangerous or stupid than scheme racing. Probably not, but then I'd done that for money. Or at least I'd thought I had.

'Me too,' Morag said. I could hear the excitement in her voice.

We found her in another, narrower canyon. She was on a bridge, board ready, about to jump. We tried to approach her but armed surf tribespeople stopped us. The fact that they were carrying guns suggested they were police.

I opened my mouth to shout to her but Pagan put his hand on my shoulder. Mudge was shaking his head as well.

She looked much as she had, except instead of exo-armour she was wearing a shorty wetsuit. I could see a lot more of her now. She had the sort of body that looked like it had worked hard all her life, all hard muscle and very little fat. Her head was still completely shorn of hair. Her skin looked a darker shade of brown, almost black, but that may have been the shadow down here away from the sun.

If she knew we were here then she gave absolutely no indication of it. She glanced behind her at the bore wave. To me it looked like a near-solid wall of water. Gripping her board, she jumped.

As one we moved to the edge of the ledge we were standing on. She surfaced momentarily, lying flat on her board, carried along by the fast-moving water, then disappeared again as the wave reached her. Cameras on remotes followed her progress. There was a thin-screen stuck to a smooth part of the canyon wall showing the footage. She rode the wave. There was no look of joy or pleasure on her face like I'd seen on some of the others, but instead a look of intense concentration. She was working at it.

It was going well until she tried to climb the wave. To me it looked like she just didn't have enough room for the manoeuvre she was attempting. The tip of the board hit the canyon wall, snapping off, and the force of the wave catapulted her into the air. She hit the rock with enough force to make all of us flinch.

'Oh well, that was a waste of time,' Mudge said.

'Shut up, Mudge,' Morag told him.

We found her sunning herself on a rock outcrop higher up and further along the canyon. The impact had cut her head open and split her subcutaneous armour. I was pretty sure I could see the bone-white of skull. Most of her skin was missing down her right side, scraped away down to the armour. She may have cleaned her wounds but she hadn't dressed them yet.

There were a few other people around. I was supposed to be checking all around us but found myself polarising my lenses and looking up the rock walls at the sliver of blue sky above.

'Hello, Cat,' Morag said to her. Cat Sommerjay, ex-C-SWAT commander from the Atlantis Spoke, opened one of her eyes. She cast a black lens over us.

'I'm not interested,' she said.

'We're paying,' Morag said.

'I had a job.'

Through no real fault of her own, concrete-eating microbes had been used twice on the Atlantis Spoke on her watch. This had resulted in the most amount of damage done to a spoke since the fall of the Brazilian Spoke during the FHC.

'Look, we're sorry about—' Morag started.

'Sorry?' Cat sat up, opening both eyes to look at us. 'Sorry! I'm fucking unemployable thanks to you people. Two major terrorist incidents on my watch, in a spoke. Have you any idea how fucking hard I worked to get to the head of that team?'

'That why you're down here trying to kill yourself?' Mudge, the diplomat, asked. Cat turned to give him a proper NCO glare. He didn't flinch.

'No, asshole. I had some back pay due and I always fancied giving it a go.'

'So why aren't you dressing your wounds?' I asked despite my better judgement. She turned to look at me. 'No, you're not trying to kill yourself, are you? Just enjoying a little pain.'

She turned angrily to grab her towel. I may as well have been asleep. She made it look natural but I still should have known better. I think Pagan started to move. Cat grabbed the huge pistol from under the towel. From sitting she rolled to her feet. She had the pistol in a two-handed stance and I found myself looking down the bore of a very large barrel.

It was a tunnel-rat pistol. Often they had to squeeze into small places, so they needed pistol-sized weapons with a lot of stopping power. It was an IMI Void Eagle chambered for caseless .50-calibre rounds. She had a small microwave emitter fitted under the barrel designed to 'cook' a Berserk – mess it up just long enough to empty the magazine into it. You needed balls to hunt Them with just a pistol, even one this big.

We spread apart to make it difficult for her to target all of us. Even Morag. I was pleased that we'd worked together long enough that this was instinct. I was less pleased that the gun appeared to be pointing at me.

'I'm pretty sure a round at this range will pop his skull off. All of you stop moving.' As she talked she was looking quickly between all of us. She was just slightly too far away for me to try a disarm even with my enhanced reflexes. The more I was seeing of Cat, the more I was convinced that Morag had chosen well. Assuming she didn't just shoot me. 'Give me a good reason not to,' she said. I couldn't at that moment think of one.

'You're right. You don't owe us shit; we owe you. So unless you want money we can't offer you anything,' I said.

Just for a moment her eyes flickered back to me. That was a mistake.

Morag and Mudge drew on her. Now she had two much smaller automatics pointed at her. When had Morag got so fast?

Cat just grinned wickedly. 'Aim for the wounds, boys and girls, because that small-calibre shit is just going to be flattening itself against my armour while I kill Jakob here.'

'Fucking army,' Pagan said, shaking his dreadlocks despairingly. 'I suppose having a drink and talking about this before we all decide to kill each other is out of the question.'

'I'm still not hearing a good reason not to kill you,' Cat said.

Some of the locals were taking an interest. This wasn't good. Four obvious outsiders picking on someone who looked like she belonged. People were beginning to edge towards us. So far none of them had drawn guns.

'You stuck up for us. You didn't raid the node like you were ordered. You must have believed in what we were doing,' Morag said. There was a kind of pleading in her voice. She really didn't want this to turn bad. She wanted Cat on board. I was just very eager not to get shot.

'Maybe. But tell me – do you ever think through your actions? The cost to other people.'

'Now wait a minute. We risked a lot. We were trying to help,' Pagan said. Now he was getting pissed off. He had a point. From our perspective the whole thing had been hard, dangerous and painful from start to finish.

I didn't like how the crowd was getting larger and closer.

'"We"? Think further out. I mean did you even get what you wanted?' she asked. 'Are you here to ask me to cause more mayhem with you?'

Mudge started grinning.

'Right again,' I said. 'We didn't think it through enough. We're trying to make it better if we can. If that's possible. Cat, you losing your job was pretty much the least of it.' I could see her finger on the trigger. I wasn't sure, but it looked like she was starting to squeeze it. 'But things had to change, and I think you know that. In fact I know you know it because of the decisions you made on the day.' She was just looking at me now. I couldn't read her expression but hydrostatic shock from a ballistic injury hadn't sent my head tumbling through the air, which was good. 'We're cunts, I'll admit that ...'

'Good of you,' she said through gritted teeth.

'But we're not the bad guys, and I think you know that. You can take it out on us if you want.' She said nothing but a minute change in her expression suggested she was about to shoot me. I think we'd significantly underestimated how pissed off she was. 'But you don't have to!' I added desperately.

'Cat, please,' Morag pleaded. I think that was probably more useful than my whole we-are-cunts speech.

'If she shoots you, can I have your bike?' Mudge asked.

'Fuck you, journo, you're next,' Cat said, but I was sure I saw the trace of a smile.

'You're better off shooting the girl first – she's faster.'

'Mudge,' I said exasperated, shaking my head. Pagan and Morag were both smiling.

'What? I'm just saying. It's tactical advice,' Mudge said defensively.

'All right. I'll listen but I reserve the right to kill you later,' Cat said.

'I suspect there's a queue,' Pagan muttered, glancing around at the crowd.

'Okay but before you do, you should know that this job looks like a one-way trip,' I told her.

Mudge, who was still pointing his gun at Cat, turned to look at me. Pagan was shaking his head.

'Good negotiating,' Mudge said incredulously.

'No, she needs to know,' Morag told him.

Cat was looking between Morag and me.

'At least you're honest. I'm going to put my gun up and then you two put yours ...' Mudge and Morag were already holstering their weapons. 'Never mind.' Cat lowered the Void Eagle and let it hang at her side. The crowd seemed disappointed. I wondered how much blood in the water was enough for them.

'Are you going to want more shooters?' Cat asked.

'Depends,' I said. 'We need reliable people who we can work with.'

'That could be hard; you did just point out you're a bunch of cunts.'

'Jake was speaking for himself,' Mudge said.

'No, he was talking about you as well,' Morag told him.

'That hurts. There's just no need for that.'

'How do you guys get anything done?' Cat asked.

'We wait for a lull,' Pagan told her.

'Did you have anyone in mind?' I asked.

I was exasperated and a little embarrassed about the banter. At the same time it was a good way to wind down the tension.

'Maybe, but as well as a fuckload of money—'

'You did hear him say that this was a one-way trip?' Mudge asked.

'Which none of you believe.'

'I don't know about that,' I told her. It was true. I really didn't fancy my chances on this one. I just didn't see how we could pull it off and get away with it.

'I'll want something else,' Cat told us.

Cat was enough of a pro to know that we couldn't brief her until we were in a reasonably secure place. She also wouldn't tell us what she wanted – for the same reasons, I guessed.

She agreed to act as a guide for us around the arms and tech bazaars, which were held in large caves or under colourfully dyed tents. Because we were outsiders we decided to stick together while we were buying what we needed. This meant that Cat, Mudge and I were bored stupid while the techno-geeks got their stuff, but once they'd done that we got to buy guns! And other gear we'd need as well. I was a little bothered by how enthusiastic Morag was about buying weapons.

It was past midnight by the time we left. We found a different place to camp from where we'd been the night before. We ate, shared some more sour mash and then got some sleep. I wondered to what degree we'd been watched and by whom.

The next few days were spent going through the gear. Where possible we'd bought three of everything. We'd managed to get most of what was on our list, though we'd made a few compromises. We checked everything for bugs and found a few, then stripped down and cleaned everything and tested it. I insisted that everyone familiarise themselves with and test-fire their own weapons. We'd bought enough ammunition to overthrow a small country.

Morag had picked a BAe laser carbine for her long. Pagan had turned in his old laser rifle for the newer carbine as well. This made things easier as they would need the same parts and took the same batteries. I was surprised by how good Morag was with the carbine. It was easy to hit things with a laser but we were running small-unit drills and, skillsofts or not, she was picking things up quickly. Pagan had said that she pretty much only needed to be told something once, and then she could not only do it herself but also make connections between other things she had learned and how they fitted together. It was something called eidetic memory. It made her very easy to teach.

Then came the modifications. Going under the knife again. I felt like I had precious little flesh to offer but our bones and musculature needed to be denser. We would need to take nearly constant supplements there to upkeep this process. Ugly reinforcements now stuck out of our spines like dorsal armour on prehistoric lizards. They were supposed to be easily removable, but seeing the metal fused with bone and flesh sticking out of Morag's back looked so obscene it made me want to vomit. I wanted to tell her to look at what she was doing to herself. Did she want to end up like the rest of us? Mechanical monsters designed to feed a war machine. But I knew her response, I knew her resolve and I think she had her own concerns.

The final modifications were to our respiratory systems. We had a corrosion-resistant coating sprayed down our windpipes and into our lungs. It made us gag and it felt like drowning. We also had heavier-duty, corrosion-resistant filters implanted into our existing systems. Both the coating and the filters would need to be replaced regularly. We were taking a large supply with us. When that ran out we'd have to forage for more. Assuming we lived that long.

Of course Morag had to have a completely new filter system implanted. Another little cut, another surgical scar and more metal in flesh.

Cat was already augmented for operation on Lalande. I asked her what high G was like.

'It's like carrying your own weight around all the time. You don't get used to it.'

When we finally got round to briefing Cat, she had already broadly guessed what we were doing and where we were going. We didn't tell her too much more because we didn't trust the environment of Limbo enough. However, Cat told us what she wanted.

We were in Morag and Pagan's workspace within the Faraday cage. Pagan and Morag had swept for surveillance and found some more bugs. I was considering trying to force Sharcroft to eat them because this was just a waste of everyone's time. Pagan set up the white-noise generator along with some other electronic countermeasures and we settled down to talk. As we finished with our sparse, broad outline, Cat was flicking through the special forces dossier on the touch screen monitor.

'Your third shooter.' She handed me the monitor.

'Hey!' Mudge said, affronted at not being considered a shooter. Cat ignored him. I hoped there wasn't going to be a problem there.

Her choice was not what I'd quite expected. He had high cheek-bones on a long face and surprisingly piercing brown eyes, though I guessed they had to be implants. The eyes sort of jumped out at you because he looked pretty intense. His hair was styled into short braids and his skin was just a touch lighter than Cat's. I figured this for a boyfriend until I saw the name.

'Merley Sommerjay?' I asked. Cat nodded. Mudge tilted the monitor towards him.

'He's nice.'

'Thanks for your input, Mudge,' and then to Cat: 'Brother?' She nodded. 'What? Want to see him dead?'

'Reasonably often.'

'I'm not sure about this.'

'But it's okay for you to go on ops with your best mate and your lover?'

'She's got a point,' Pagan said. I ignored the flare of irritation and went back to reading his file.

'A marine?' I said, glancing at Cat. She'd been US Army and traditionally there was antagonism between the two branches. Cat said nothing. 'Force Recon, served on Lalande.'

Force Recon were part of the US Marines Special Operations Command. They specialised in reconnaissance but were often tasked for unconventional warfare. They were a reasonable unit.

'Then he transferred out to the air force and joined the PJs. That's unusual,' I continued.

The PJs were pararescue operators, their job to jump behind enemy lines and perform personnel recovery operations or provide medical aid. It was a difficult and very dangerous job, particularly fighting Them. The problem was that the US and Britain had different defin-itions of what it meant to be special forces.

'Look, it's impressive but . . .' Cat leaned over and tapped the screen, enlarging part of the information. 'Oh bullshit,' I said.

'What?' Mudge asked, frowning.

'Cemetery Wind,' I said scornfully.

Pagan smiled and shook his head.

'Really?' Mudge sounded interested.

'What's Cemetery Wind?' Morag asked.

'Nothing. They don't exist,' I told her.

'They exist,' Cat said.

'They might do, actually,' Mudge chipped in. He was carefully reading Cat's brother's file. 'What sort of name is Merley anyway?'

'Mudge, it was you who told me they didn't exist in the first place,' I protested. 'You went looking for them and came to the conclusion they were another combat myth.'

'Well yes, that was what I told you.'

'What is Cemetery Wind?' Morag asked in exasperation.

'They're supposed to be an ultra-secret military intelligence unit whose job it is to provide up-to-date and actionable intelligence for special forces operations, except nobody's ever met anyone in it or worked with one. Cemetery Wind's a code name. They've apparently been called the Activity, Grey Fox, Black Light, the Intelligence Support Agency. Their name's supposed to change every few years.'

'Just sounds like another special forces group,' Morag said, unimpressed.

'Well yes. Except they're rumoured to go in first, and sometimes the places they go SF fear to follow.'

'But sometimes someone provides us with solid eyes-on intel before going in,' Cat said. 'Look, I mostly served in the US theatre of ops on Lalande, but Merle was all over. He knows the place like the back of his hand.'

'It's a planet bigger than Earth. How could he know the place like the back of his hand?' I asked.

'It is bigger than Earth but very little is habitable by humans. Merle's operated in most of that. He's even done deep-penetration Nightside recons.'

Lalande 2 was tidally locked. One side always faced the sun and burned; the other always faced the dark and froze. The Twilight Strip between the two zones was the only area habitable by humans. Even then the colonists lived deep underground to protect them from the corrosive winds of the surface and the worst of the acid-rich atmosphere.

Born in vacuum, Nightside was not a problem for Them. They based Themselves in Nightside, where it was very difficult for us to reach, and raided into the Twilight Strip. In order to get solid intelligence, some brave souls in heavily insulated life-support suits had risked the temperatures and set up observation posts.

'If he's that deep in with the intelligence side of things, then did he work for the Cabal?' Pagan asked.

'Well, you all did at one point or another, didn't you?' Morag said. Cat was suspiciously quiet. One by one we all looked at her.

'Pretty extensively,' she finally admitted. 'That's not to say he knew who they were and what they were about.'

'It's not to say he didn't either,' Pagan pointed out. He was not looking happy.

'Mudge? Do you believe in these guys now?' I asked.

'I did then,' Mudge said distractedly. He was studying the monitor. He looked up at Cat. 'He's very pretty.' I'm not sure she knew what to say to that. 'I went looking for them. I got very efficiently bagged. I was held completely immobile in a stress position for a week. Then someone I didn't hear enter the room came and held a gun to my head for six hours. Completely still. Never uttered a word. I couldn't hear him or her breathe. I decided to stop looking.'

'You make them sound like the Grey Lady,' Morag said and shivered.

'Different kind of scary,' Mudge said. 'I like him. Let's use him.'

'Are you sure you don't just want to fuck him?' I asked.

'He's my brother,' Cat protested.

'Maybe, but if he is Cemetery Wind, then they scare me and make Morag shiver. I also like the idea that one of the guns is a little more subtle than you or me,' Mudge said.

'Morag?'

'I agree with Mudge. It'd be nice to work with someone who can respond to a problem without shooting it a lot.'

'Pagan?'

'I don't like the Cabal connection. But if he's an ex-PJ then he won't be as big a wuss about OILO insertion. I say we talk to him'

'That's an issue. What happens if we talk to him and either we don't like what we hear or he doesn't want to play? He'll already know too much,' I asked.

'It'll be fine,' Cat assured us.

I wasn't quite so sure. Family complicated things and there was a very real chance that we might have to put a bullet in this guy's head. I couldn't see Cat getting behind that and she was good people.

Besides, it would leave us another shooter down and we'd have to start again.

'Have you seen where he is?' Mudge asked as he passed the monitor back.

'Oh for fuck's sake. A high-security clipper? En route? What did he think was going to happen?' I said. 'Well that's him out.'

Pagan took the monitor from me. He read the info. 'What were you thinking?'

'I was thinking,' Cat said, 'that aside from the ridiculous amount of money I want paid in advance, getting him out is my price. Either that or I walk.' Except she knew and we knew that it wouldn't be easy if she chose to walk.

8
The Belt

The standard-issue sidearm for the SAS is the Sig Sauer P410. It is capable of semi-automatic or full automatic fire and has an integral suppressor. The standard magazine contains fifteen 10mm rounds, though oversized magazines with the capacity for twenty or twenty-five rounds are favoured when concealment is not an issue. When fighting Them the favoured load was an armour-piercing, hydro-shock round because of the effects on Their liquid physiology. The hydro-shock rounds are perfectly adequate when used against humans, but many, like Morag, preferred armour-piercing explosive rounds when shooting at people.

The P410 is largely a hold-out weapon. It does not have the stopping power of a rifle or a Mastodon or Void Eagle. If you're using one against a Berserk then your day's gone horribly wrong. Given enough hits, they will mess up a Berserk or someone with cybernetic augmentation up to the level of a special forces operator, but they are not one-hit-one-kill on someone with decent subcutaneous armour. This is something I was very grateful for when Morag decided to shoot me with hers. I was less pleased that we'd collectively advised her to use a large-capacity magazine.

Anyone putting any effort into tracking us was going to be able to, but we were trying to stay off the radar. The Brazilian was the closest spoke to New Mexico, but US military shuttles were still not allowed to dock there so we'd been flown to High Pacifica. I had never quite been able to reconcile the view from orbit with the reality of living on Earth. From high above the Earth looked bright, blue, peaceful and, weirdest of all, clean.

The space around High Pacifica was very busy with everything from military shuttles like ours to net tugs pulling in chunks of refined asteroid from orbital refineries, as well as interplanetary traffic from the rest of the system.

We made our way as inconspicuously as we could to an outbound tramp freighter with parts going to Freetown in the Belt. Cat and I all but sat on Mudge to make sure he didn't call attention to himself.

The freighter was called *Loser's Luck* and I was astonished it was still holding together. It had a mainly Indonesian crew who we'd paid enough to leave us in peace and hopefully not tell too many people that we were travelling with them. We still were not discussing the details of our mission, however. I think what bothered me the most was that I'd found myself in yet another poorly heated, thin-walled cargo hold far too close to the vacuum and radiation outside.

The flimsy cargo hold was yet another reason why I was less than pleased when 10mm rounds started sparking off the metal around me. This was foolishness, however. There are few man-portable weapons powerful enough to get through even the cheapest cargo hull. Still, getting shot was no fun.

I wasn't paying the slightest bit of attention and it was pretty much the last thing I had expected. It was just like being rapidly punched with extraordinary force. She nailed me in the chest with a three-round burst, tight grouping. The integrity of my armour held, but warning icons were already appearing in my IVD as I rolled back-wards off the crate of supplies I'd been lying on. The second burst caught me painfully in the left leg below the knee before I managed to get into cover.

I drew the Mastodon and my TO-5 laser pistol. I wasn't sure what was happening or who was shooting. Mudge had been sitting on a pile of gear opposite, reading. Pagan was tranced into his own systems – I assumed working. Cat was checking the gyroscopic mount for the railgun and Morag had just wandered back from the galley.

'You fucking bastard!' Morag shouted and fired again. It was sup-pressing fire. It worked. I kept my head down. Then again, maybe she was just firing out of anger or frustration.

'Morag?!' I said incredulously. This was a completely new phase of our relationship and I wasn't very happy about it.

'Put the gun down,' I heard Mudge say. I continued cowering behind the crate. I really wasn't sure what to do. Had she really been trying to kill me?

'Fuck off, Mudge!' Morag said, and there was another burst of armour-piercing, explosive-tipped bullets.

'Morag ... what the fuck?!' I managed. There was the sound of a scuffle. I dared to poke my head over the crate and saw Mudge grappling with Morag. Now Mudge is no slouch in a fight. I've seen him take special forces operators on without a trace of hesitation.

He mostly lost, but he was game and reasonably skilled. Morag straight-armed him in the throat, pistol-whipped him and then side-kicked him so hard that he was knocked off his feet and slammed into the hull wall.

I threw myself behind more crates as she turned and fired again. I caught a glimpse of her face contorted with anger.

There was the sound of another scuffle. I heard Morag cry out and then a thump as someone hit the floor. I risked looking again. Morag was lying next to Mudge rubbing her wrist. Cat was standing close to where Morag had been, making the Sig safe. Cat was glaring and Morag was staring at me with so much hatred I was beginning to think I'd rather be shot.

'What did you do?' Cat demanded.

I was pretty much struck dumb for the moment. Apparently being shot was my own fault. Pagan had been tranced in though the whole thing, completely oblivious.

'Its okay. There are other guns,' Morag spat. She sounded really angry.

'Is everything okay?' Mudge asked. 'Can I go back to my book or is there more imminent gunplay?'

'More imminent gunplay,' Morag told him.

'Can we not shoot at crates full of munitions?' Cat said, sounding more reasonable, but then she went back to glaring at me.

'What's going on?' I demanded, finally mastering speech again.

'How could you, you piece of shit?!' Morag hissed at me. She looked like she would be holding back tears if she could still cry.

'I have no fucking idea what you're talking about!' I shouted.

I was holstering my guns when the portable monitor landed on the crates I'd been using as cover. I glanced down at the image. I didn't need to run the viz to know what the story was. The frozen image at the start of the viz was me on top of Fiona, whose features had been obscured. I felt the sick feeling of being found out. It was a feeling I hadn't had in a while because I hadn't really cared about what I'd done and how it would affect others for a long time. It was like ice had replaced sluggish blood in my body. I felt pressure in my chest, as if someone was slowly but surely crushing my augmented heart.

'It's all over the net,' Morag said more quietly now. 'The crew were laughing about it in the galley when I went in.'

'You bastard,' Cat said.

'Yes, thank you, Cat,' I said, but I was trying to think of something sensible to say.

Mudge walked over, picked up the monitor and spent a few

moments tapping at it and scrawling through the story. I steeled my-self for some inappropriate and insensitive attempt at humour.

'It's a slander piece. It's designed to undermine what we did in Atlantis. These things are easy to mock up,' he said. I couldn't quite work out the significance of the look he gave me.

'But it's not mocked up, is it?' Morag asked quietly.

'No,' I said. Mudge shook his head sadly.

'She looks so fucking trashy,' Morag said, trying not to sob. Then she stared at me, angry again. 'But I guess she was a step up from an ex-whore from the Rigs, aye?'

I felt like I'd been stabbed. I think I would have preferred stabbing. I was almost looking around for an airlock to leave by.

'Morag, don't say that. She was horrible ...' I started and then realised that wasn't a good thing to say. Mudge almost flinched.

'But you'd rather fuck her than stay with me. Thanks, Jake. I feel much better now.' The anger was easier to deal with.

'That wasn't what I meant. Look, I thought you'd gone ...'

'I hadn't gone anywhere; you left us.'

You shit, I told myself.

'I thought that we ... that you ...'

'How did you put it? "We're off to die under some alien sun"? Morag's gone; let's have sex with some trashy blonde.'

'Look, Morag, I'm sorry, but I'm new to all this, I really am. I've never—'

'And I fucking have?!' she screamed at me. 'I may have been a fucking whore but at least I know not to fucking cheat on the person you love!'

When she realised what she'd said she looked stricken. I think the last thing she needed now was to show any vulnerability. Unfortunately dry sobbing racked her small frame. The sort of crying that made your implanted eyes hurt. I foolishly moved towards her.

'Stay away from me!' she screamed. The anger was back and seemed even more intense. I actually took a step back at the look of blazing hatred on her face. 'I swear to God, you come anywhere near me and I will find a way to fucking kill you!' At this she stormed out of the hold.

Cat gave me one last baleful look and went after her.

I slumped against the cold of the hull's external bulkhead. I could feel the nothingness on the other side of the metal. I felt hollow. I felt like I did before all this happened except I didn't think the respite of the sense booths would help now.

'I'm sorry, man ...' Mudge started.

'Not now.' Then I realised what he'd said. 'Oh.' Mudge was being sympathetic, time to buy a lottery ticket.

'Was it a bad night?'

'Yes, I guess. I've had worse. You know, I just didn't think. I never really had to before.'

'I can sort of see how it went down, but she's never going to get that. I wouldn't try trancing in anywhere soon though. For what it's worth, I think her expectations are pretty high. You should get what you can when you can from this world.' I wasn't sure if that was what Mudge believed or just what he wanted others to think he believed.

So this was their revenge. But whose? I couldn't really see it as being Calum's. Surely he wouldn't want his daughter splashed all over the net like that. Even with her features distorted it wouldn't take God long to work out who it was if anyone asked. Alasdair? Maybe, but how did he get the footage? Then again, maybe people like that shared these things – what did I know? Fiona herself? Would she get off on this kind of notoriety? I thought maybe she would.

Mudge said, 'I've never really got this. It's a fucked-up world in a fucked-up system. Every one of us does fucked-up things, most people just to survive. Everyone I've ever met has a kink and the more straight-laced the person seems to be then the dirtier their kink tends to be.' I started to protest. 'Let me finish. See, this is about what we did and God. The subtext is, how dare we sit in judgement on our masters when this is how we act in private? How can people in this world be shocked by this? I mean it's taking the piss. The thing is, is any of it anyone's business?'

'Someone's just done to me what we did to everyone.'

'We didn't put cameras in people's bedrooms.'

'Oh well, that's all right then. How many people do you think we've killed over shit like this?'

He paused for a moment and then said, 'Look – cheating aside, and I can't quite make up my mind if Morag's being unfair or naive – I think maybe all this stuff – who we really are – should all be out there and we shouldn't be made to feel ashamed of it. I mean, who's this supposed to shock? This doesn't shock; it titillates. We should be shocked that people kill each other to feed their kids. We should be shocked that vets serve our race and then all the systems that were forcibly implanted in them are harvested and they're left crippled. We should be shocked at the disparity between the poor and the rich—'

'Mudge.'

'Yeah, sorry. I got a little carried away. That said, I've got the name of the so-called journalist, and I'm going to do something bad to him when we get back.'

'He's one of many and we're not coming back.'

Mudge just looked at me for a while, the camera lenses that were his eyes whirring one way and then the other.

'Thanks for trying,' I finally said.

'Want me to talk to her?' he asked.

'Definitely not.'

'Want to get fucked up?'

'Yes, but I'm not going to.'

'What's going on?' Pagan asked, coming out of his trance. He was looking around at the scorch marks on the hull and the holes in some of the crates.

'Morag and Jake's relationship has entered an exciting new phase. Now they're using firearms as a method of conflict resolution.'

'What? What did you do?'

I sighed.

'Jakob fucked some trashy blonde. It's all over the net.'

'Oh.'

So that was day one of our trip.

And then things got really difficult. We hadn't been given much room on the freighter because the crew wanted to give most of their hold over to more lucrative machine parts. This meant that Morag and I were forced into close proximity. She wasn't speaking to me at all but she was giving good glare. Sometimes she used night vision to glare at me in the dark as I slept. She did this with sufficient intensity to wake me up. This meant a shitty atmosphere and I felt sorry for the other three.

We still weren't in a position to talk about or otherwise prep for the mission, which meant we were bored. This was time I'd hoped to spend with Morag. Instead I tried to avoid everyone, which can be difficult in the confined space of a ship.

I had thought to practise my trumpet but apparently it echoed. It made me even more unpopular with the others and resulted in threats from the crew. Pagan offered to set up a virtual practice programme in one of the spare memory cubes. However, if Morag found out I would be taking my life in my hands as she could easily hack the program into a death trap.

She was really, really hurt. I'd really fucked this up. Even though I'd known what I'd done was wrong, I had completely underestimated the effect on her. Which meant that I'd completely underestimated

Morag's depth of feeling for me. I'd found out just in time to twist it.

I tried to keep my mind off it. I couldn't. I tried a lot of wishful thinking, how things could have played out differently. That was probably the most pointless exercise I engaged in. I tried to work out how I could fix things. That was more wishful thinking. I was probably going to die on Lalande and all I could think about was Morag. Though I was coming to terms with dying on Lalande.

I wanted to escape. More than anything, I wanted the booths or to climb into a bottle of whisky. Mudge, who was spending most of his time on psychotropics, which were his drug of choice for travelling, was more than eager to join me. But I didn't. I wasn't sure why.

Was she being unreasonable? Maybe the shooting was. Was she being naive? I don't know. I couldn't see the situation through the eyes of an eighteen-year-old. The whole thing was new territory for me, and with her background how naive could she be? I just knew that I was causing her so much pain. I could see that in unguarded moments, when she wasn't putting on a brave face to get through the day. When she wasn't hiding behind a wall of hate for me.

Pagan and Cat came and found me. I was hiding in another hold, close to the engines. Listening to them reverberate though the ship's steel superstructure. For some reason I wanted to look outside even though I hated space.

I didn't like the look on either of their faces. Pagan's expression seemed one of reserved concern. Situations like these are difficult for most British people. Well maybe not Mudge. Cat, on the other hand, looked at me like I was something unpleasant she'd found crawling through her pubic hair.

'We have some concerns,' Pagan said.

It was not a good start to the conversation.

Cat snorted.

'Pagan, really ask yourself if this can't be done at another time,' I suggested, failing utterly to keep the edge out of my voice.

'Because this soap opera's going to work fine on the ground,' Cat said. 'This shit will get us killed in Freetown, never mind our fucking destination.'

She was right of course. With men and women fighting together it was inevitable that they'd form bonds – people fighting together had always formed bonds. The rule was, never get so close to someone that it screwed you up in the field. This had always been easy for me. I'd seen lovers torn apart and mangled by war, same as I'd seen good friends. Fortunately, after a while you get numb to this. The fear, the drugs, the fatigue all chip away at anything inside that makes you care. All the hand-wringing and dry tears are for when you're out of danger and have time to reflect. The people who can care through all this are few and far between and die quickly, often at their own hands. I had a feeling that Morag could be someone like that.

She would compromise me and I would compromise her, even when/if she didn't hate and possibly want to kill me.

'This situation's untenable,' Cat continued.

'Now wait a minute,' Pagan began. 'We've accomplished quite a lot with—'

'A completely dysfunctional unit?' she asked.

'You knew who you were getting involved with when we asked,' I told her.

'They fight a lot,' Pagan pointed out. 'Though the gunplay's new.'

'Look, this isn't Delta Force or your professional and well-resourced C-SWAT team; we're doing our best here—' I tried.

'It's just not good enough.' Both of us were staring at her.

I turned to Pagan. 'You agree?'

'Well not quite. But she's right, this is a mess ...'

'You can't go into the field with someone you're that emotionally tied to,' Cat continued.

'But you want to go in with your brother?'

'My brother's a prick.' I couldn't believe I was hearing this.

'Then why are we wasting time going to get him?!' Maybe I was just looking for an excuse to get angry.

Cat shrugged. 'Because he's my brother and he'll be useful. It's not just you and Morag.'

'What then?' I could see where this was going. I'd heard it a lot when we were back in the Regiment.

'Mudge,' Pagan said. I turned and fixed him with a glare from my lenses. He at least had the decency to look guilty.

'Have you forgotten the broadcast? Fuck. He made us rich, and no matter what he has always been there.'

'No doubt ...'

'You just don't fucking like him because he says whatever he damn well pleases and always tells the truth,' I said.

'Very admirable I'm sure.' There was a trace of irritation in his voice. 'It's not that; it's the drugs. We're going on what could be a very long-term mission.'

'So? Mudge has done long-range recon. He always takes enough and can find more ...' I was about to say 'between jobs'. There wasn't going to be a between jobs.

'Remember the Dog's Teeth? How he was? He'll end up withdrawing,

and that will make him combat ineffective. It'll make him a liability.'
He was right. I was so used to Mudge's presence I think I'd tried to
force this from my mind. More than anything I needed him here at
that moment.

'And you bring this up now?' I demanded angrily.

'I had misgivings, but what with the situation with you and Morag
as well ... we're struggling, man.'

'So what do you want to do? Scrub the mission? Because if you
both want to call it quits and turn around I have no real objection.'

They looked at each other.

'Look, can you honestly say that having her around won't affect
your judgement?' Pagan finally asked.

'No. What I'm saying is we've coped with it before and it worked.
Don't get me wrong. If I could talk her out of going I would.'

'I wouldn't try talking to her at the moment,' Cat suggested. 'She'd
probably shoot you again. I might give her the gun.'

I glared at Cat. 'Where the fuck do you get off, being so judgemental.' Then I turned to Pagan. 'It's thanks to your brave new world
we're in this spot.' It was weak, I knew it was, but I was miserable,
pissed off and wanted to lash out.

'Oh yeah, this is my fault,' Pagan said sarcastically.

'No, it's thanks to you not being able to keep your dick leashed,'
Cat said to me.

'Fine, whatever. Pagan, can you and Morag work on what we need
and then we can leave Morag on board? Even if we have to drug
her.' At this Pagan started to look very uncomfortable. 'What?!' I
demanded, beginning to lose my patience.

'It's just ...' Pagan stammered.

'She's more important to the mission than you,' Cat said bluntly.
I stared at her. It took me a while to work through what she'd said.

'You fucking what?!' I demanded. 'Twelve years, twelve fucking
years is a fuck of a lot more time in-country than you. You fucked off
for your cushy corporate job.' Then because I wanted to make sure I
pissed off everyone I turned on Pagan. 'And you, you not getting too
fucking old for this shit?'

'Well yes,' Pagan said, surprising me.

Cat had bristled but remained calm.

'Don't you get this? We're just guns, that's all. It's information
warfare and all we're here to do is keep them safe. They're going to
be the ones doing the fighting,' Cat said.

'Demiurge will fucking destroy them if they try.'

'Right, that's it. Shut up, both of you,' Pagan snapped. 'This is my problem. I may be over the fucking hill, but see how far standards are slipping. Like this we're just going to get ourselves killed.'

'So you want to leave me and Mudge behind? Fine. Fuck off with your American friends then. What, are you licking up to her to get in her pants?' I was just being petty but I wasn't liking this picked-last-for-PT bollocks, even if I really didn't want to be here in the first place.

'Figures that's how you'd think of it,' Cat said, an edge in her voice. I was going off her rapidly. Not as rapidly as she was going off me though.

'No, we want you and Mudge to sort your shit out so you're not a fucking liability,' Pagan said, remaining calm.

I turned to give him another mouthful but something about his expression stopped me. He looked serious, maybe even formidable, but I couldn't shake the feeling that there was pity there too.

'Why don't you go and have this conversation with Mudge?' I muttered, looking away from the pair of them.

'You know why,' Pagan answered quietly.

I did. If Mudge was going to listen to anyone, and he probably wasn't, it'd be me.

'I've a good mind to just turn around when we get to Freetown and head back,' I told them both.

'Well let us know if self-pity wins out, won't you?' Pagan said, and then he and Cat turned and walked away.

It was a long and miserable journey in a rusting, damp, dripping, metallic piece of shit that seemed to echo every time somebody moved. It was claustrophobic because there were no external views and it smelled due to rudimentary facilities. I'd had worse trips, but everyone being pissed off with everyone else was what truly put the cherry on top. The only time that Morag even met my eyes was to glare at me. I felt like those looks could cause physical pain. With Pagan and Cat it was strained politeness. Mudge was the only cheerful one, but that just got on everyone's nerves. I didn't have a chat with him like Cat and Pagan wanted me to, largely because they wanted me to. But I didn't get fucked up with him either, which was what I felt like doing.

I felt like a Jonah. Like I was screwing everything up. When I told Mudge this he agreed with me.

I was so pissed off with everyone I didn't care if they didn't like me learning the trumpet. I played what I thought were suitably mournful blues numbers that echoed through the ship. I thought it was better than listening to a fellow passenger strain on the cludgy. The others thought differently and the captain threatened to space me. By that point I think I'd managed to piss everyone off. I was almost revelling in it. Like Mudge. I wondered how he managed to keep up his cheerful demeanour.

Of course, at the end of every shit journey is a perfectly shit destination. We were going to Freetown Camp 12.

In theory the Belt was open to exploitation by anyone. In practice everybody had to rely on logistics from the extra-planetary Belt Prospect Industrial Corporation. Outside the big Belt cities of Ceres, Vesta and Hygeia, it was the Freetown stations that provided docking facilities and supplies for their own fleet of factory refinery ships. BPIC were pretty much a law unto themselves, and as long as the minerals kept coming nobody on Earth cared. Any smaller corporate attempts to exploit the Belt were charged exorbitant prices for what they needed from the Freetown stations until they went out of business. If they didn't take the hint then BPIC could more than afford the corporate army and space forces necessary to protect their assets. More underhand activities were handled either by specialists or by contracting out to the inevitable organised crime elements that ran the Freetown vice franchises.

Anything went out on the Belt as long as it did not disturb the flow of ore. Smuggling, gambling, prostitution and drugs were all fine as long as BPIC got its cut. You could kill someone provided you knew the right people and had enough money. There were rumours of gladiatorial snuff games as well.

In short it was like Earth, maybe a bit more honest about things, although unlike Earth the Belt was one place you were guaranteed a job. That was as long as you didn't mind indentured servitude and a short life expectancy due to cheap suits with shitty radiation protection. See, humans were cheaper to run than machines. They didn't even need training any more. Cheap skillsofts would do for on-the-job training. Though you had to pay the company back for that and for your ride out to the Belt – and for your ride back in the unlikely event you ever earned enough before dying in an industrial accident or from radiation poisoning.

You also had to pay for the performance-enhancing drugs you needed to keep up with your quotas. What little money you might have left, instead of saving for your future, you were better off spending at the vice franchises, on alcohol, drugs, sense booths and the truly desperate, and if rumour was true, often slaved, hookers.

Any attempts at unionisation or even basic workers' rights were stamped on hard. Insurrection or revolution was a joke. Who had the energy? Any ship attempting to bring out seditious materials was impounded, its entire crew executed. BPIC had more power than many Earthbound governments, a virtual monopoly and the muscle to back it all up. They ran their own corporate feudal empire. Their employees were known as Belt zombies.

Breaking Merle out would have been a major operation. Instead we were going to negotiate. Or more accurately use Sharcroft's money for a bribe. It would have to be a large bribe.

What Cat's brother had done was audacious. Most ore or other bulk cargoes like ice (it was cheaper to import ice from the Belt than from Earth, to turn into water for the various habitats in Earth orbit) were fired by mass driver, either from the stations or the factory ships themselves. The mass drivers propelled them into high Earth orbit, where net tugs caught them and shunted them to the Spokes' high ports. Precious metals were mined with automated machinery, as it was more precise and trustworthy than Belt zombies. BPIC Armed Response, the corporation's well-trained and equipped security force/private military, kept the precious metals under guard. These were transferred back to Earth on high-security, high-speed, intra-system clippers.

Merle had tried to hijack one. On his own. He nearly succeeded. He'd somehow gained access to it via EVA after it had left its security bay at Freetown Camp 12. Got past its electronic security. Taken out its security and crew and then, through a combination of pre-programmed hacks and high-end skillsofts, attempted to divert it. He would have got away with it except that the prearranged security responses he'd bribed a lower-echelon BPIC security employee for were a day out of date. There was a pursuit and a firefight and Merle got caught.

What I couldn't figure out was why he was still alive. I could understand why they'd want him alive long enough to work out how he'd done what he'd done, but this had happened eight months ago. They would have that information by now. Why go to the expense of locking up someone with his skill set? BPIC didn't need brigs; they had airlocks to push the troublesome out of. On the other hand, I could make this someone else's problem and just fuck off back to Earth with Mudge and get drunk and fucked on drugs. I wondered if I had enough money now for my own sense booth. It wouldn't be difficult to get a ship back home. Hell, the way I was feeling they could just fire me out of one of the mass drivers.

*

The Belt now had religion. God was with us. Hallelujah. We were keeping comms chatter to a minimum but I opened a link to the ship's systems so I could watch us land. See what this shit hole looked like. Maybe just to depress myself a little further.

It looked like a scar. The station was in a recessed crater created by strip mining. It looked like an old quarry suspended in the night.

The asteroid itself was a little over twenty kilometres in length. As we sank into the scar and the cameras panned around, I could just about make out some of the other asteroids that formed the Gorgon family. They looked like potato-shaped rocks suspended in the sky, utterly static, though obviously they weren't. There were vast fields of solar panels tethered high above Gorgon's surface. They, along with a fusion reactor buried far from the main station and hydrogen cells, provided fuel for the town-sized camp. The floor of the scar was covered in prefab vacuum-proofed buildings, storage tethers and dry docks for the massive factory ships with their insectile legs for gripping and burrowing into asteroids. There was something parasitical about the factory ships. Their enormous industrial mass drivers reminded me of stings. Several of the heavy-duty tethers had ice asteroids attached to them. They would be processed for fuel and much-needed water. The dormitory, commercial, administration and vice areas were recessed deep into the rock. This was largely to help shield from radiation.

Space in the scar was busy with the ponderous movements of incoming and outgoing factory ships, the faster tugs, faster still intra-system clippers, enormous super-carriers and the barely tolerated tramp independents like ours. All of this was being watched over by a BPIC destroyer. I had seen military facilities in the colonies less well armed than this station. Piracy was a big if rarely actualised fear, but I suspect that much of the weaponry was to prevent annexation either by a nation state or more likely by another extra-planetary corp. They had missile, plasma and laser batteries, rapid-firing railguns, mass driver cannons and even one of the huge particle beam cannons.

The landing pads were at the base of the scar against one of the rock walls. On the ship's external lenses I saw our manoeuvring engines fire as we slowly sank into the crater. We were tracked by weapon systems all the way. I couldn't shake the feeling I was being swallowed. I barely felt the landing, though I heard metal protest ominously throughout the ship. The cargo airlock concertinaed out to mate with the *Loser's Luck*.

We'd already used the ship's comms to text ahead our request to meet Wilson Trace, the BPIC regional director who ran Freetown

Camp 12. We'd been pleased that he'd agreed to a meeting. We were less pleased when we saw his conditions. Before we were allowed anywhere near Mr Trace we had to have security locks put on all integral weapons and an inhibitor jack in one of our plugs to dull enhanced reactions. It went without saying that we had to be unarmed. We didn't like it, but it was either that or we would have to mount a major operation and make yet another powerful enemy to get Merle out. Besides, it would be nice to not have to resort to violence for once.

The plush office was a marked contrast to what we'd just walked through. There had been no luxurious carpet, no laser-carved basalt desk and very few recessed windows looking out over the tangled industrial mess of Gorgon's scar. Instead we had seen deep-set eyes lined with scar tissue from botched re-implant jobs on the faces of gaunt, indentured miners who had little care that their stale sweat added to the stench of oil and badly ventilated air. Many of them showed signs of radiation poisoning or seemed to have respiratory problems. They bunked in the streets. The bunks were stacked high, each with its small locker. The miners were charged for them. Fights were commonplace and nobody did anything, though BPIC Armed Response watched on. The guards even had exo-armoured personnel and light mechs in case the miners got out of hand. I couldn't see that happening – it looked like most of the Belt zombies had given up years ago.

As desperate as the miners looked, they were nowhere near as sad as the wrung-out-looking, presumably once-attractive men and woman who worked the vice franchise. At least they weren't slaved, I'm not sure I would have coped with that. Gaudy, badly maintained neon signs promised pleasure that the reality of the bars seemed to refute. The Yakuza had won the vice franchise for Freetown 12. The gangsters and the guards were the only people who looked well fed. Many of the Yakuza were stripped to the waist, gangster ink on display, and all of them wore shades. They had watched us pass impassively. The miners and the hookers had looked at us less impassively. I could feel their resentment.

For some reason Pagan had seemed pleased that the Yakuza were running the vice franchise and had split off from the rest of us to speak to them. I hoped he wasn't going whoring. Mudge had given him a list of exotic pharmaceuticals he wanted picked up. Pagan had seemed less than pleased about this. It would have been better if Mudge had gone with Pagan but Mudge insisted that his people skills would be of use to us with Trace. I had my misgivings.

We'd walked right through the so-called entertainment area of the station. It had been so quiet. People weren't talking, just drinking or rutting or taking some recreational substance to try and make it all go away for a little while. There were no sense booths. Nobody here could afford them.

As we climbed through the levels towards the corporate offices, the bunks in the alcohol- and blood-muddied dirt of the street became small wage-slave cubicles. The offices got larger and more luxurious the higher we went until we found ourselves in Trace's.

He kept us waiting so we understood how important he was. When we were finally escorted into his office we found ourselves covered by four guards with M-19 carbines. There was also an automated twin fast-cycling rotary laser system protruding from the wall above and behind Trace's desk. That was overkill. It was the kind of weapon used for point defence on spacecraft. I guessed this guy was paranoid.

Trace was obviously engaged in a sub-vocal conversation on his internal comms link. He continued with it apparently oblivious to us. It looked social judging from his occasional laughter and easy-going demeanour. Of course this was all for our benefit. He looked like every other suit I'd seen. Indeterminate age, handsome but indeterminate looks bought in a salon somewhere. Neat, tidy. Probably paid over the odds for a suit, the specifications of which would be important to people who knew such things. I was going to forget about this guy as soon as he was out of sight. He was a corporate cliché complete with katana and another shorter sword on a rack behind his desk.

The only thing that did stick out was his eyes. They were obviously expensive designer implants but they weren't designed to mimic real eyes. Nor were they the non-light reflecting matt of our hardened plastic lenses. His were shiny black mirrors. You saw yourself in his eyes and you looked small. I didn't think I was going to like this guy. Mudge had also made up his mind.

We were expected to stand. There was some shouting and Mudge almost got shot when he threw himself into a seat. I wished I'd gone with Pagan. Mudge lit up a cigarette.

'Actually, it's no smoking in here.' Trace's accent was one of those weird non-accents that people who lived in space had. I'd always thought it made them sound desperate to not come from anywhere.

'I know,' Mudge said agreeably. I groaned inwardly and Cat glared at him. We were off to a good start. A little bit more sub-vocalisation and Trace finished his call. I inclined my head towards the guards and the lasers.

'You're safe. We just came here to talk,' I told him.

His mouth twitched into a momentary and humourless smile. 'I'll keep this brief. Merley Sommerjay is a thief, a bad one, and you have committed terrorist acts against this very corpora—'

'What terrorist acts?!' Morag demanded. Trace looked annoyed at being interrupted.

'The release of the God virus into our systems. The removal of which is an ongoing and mounting cost, not to mention how much setting up dedicated and secure God-free networks has been.'

'Oh,' said Morag. I think she'd forgotten.

'Any conflict between Earth governments and their colonial forces has nothing to do with us as a commercial organisation and we do not wish to take sides.'

'You worked extensively with the Cabal, didn't you?' Mudge asked as he stubbed his cigarette out on the basalt desk. Trace stared at him. He let Mudge see himself small in the reflections of his eyes.

'We do business with those who can pay,' he told Mudge.

'No ethics?' I asked. I was answered with a sneer. I looked away from Trace to try and calm myself. I was amazed that nobody had ever put the drill arm of a mining mech through his window. Spaced this sweetheart of a man. I watched a long range strike craft sinking into the asteroid's scar. It was similar to the *Spear*, the craft we'd taken to the Sirius system, but an older model. I turned back to the conversation.

' ... you will be slaved.'

What the fuck? I turned my attention back to Trace.

'You will join our mining operation, except –' he turned to Morag '– you'll make an excellent addition to the executive-level vice operation. Initially anyway. You'll work your way down and end up servicing the miners like all the others. Perhaps you'll see your friends again. I understand you have the experience, otherwise I'd break you in myself.'

Morag just looked bored. She'd heard it all before. I wanted to kill him. I was also wishing I'd been paying more attention.

'Did he just say he was going to slave us?' I double-checked.

'Apparently so,' Cat said. 'Remind me again why we walked into this trap.'

'Because Jakob keeps on hoping he'll meet someone reasonable some day. Tell me, Wilson – it's okay if I call you Wilson, isn't it? I mean presumably it'll be your sexy masterness when we're all slaved,' Mudge said.

'Do you have a point?' Trace asked. I was wondering the same thing.

169

'Why'd you take the meeting?' Mudge asked.

'Because of our previous working relationship with Sharcroft.'

'You did use to work with the Cabal then?' Morag asked.

'And you seem like such a nice guy,' I muttered.

'Really?' Mudge asked. 'Because you have to know, even with your guards this is dangerous. No, I think you're gloating. Which is weird because what do you have against us?' Mudge had such a good eye for weakness because he embraced his so openly. 'How old are you, Wilson?' Trace didn't answer. He was starting to look angry. The sort of angry that came from being found out and not being able to argue back. 'See, you fucking clones all look the same to me, but I'm guessing you're in your late thirties, right? But the Savile Row suit, the Musamoko katana, Zeiss designer eyes ... You were some-one once, weren't you? But this is a pretty shitty posting for a rising star.'

'Go and fuck yourself!' Trace spat. We weren't accomplishing any-thing, but on the other hand the guy was a prick and didn't mean us well so we may as well let Mudge go to town on him.

Mudge leaned forward. 'What did you get caught doing when God came to town?' His manner was all mock concern. 'Embezzlement? Too much crystal? Too much time in the sense booths? Fucking the boss's kid? A penchant for farmyard frolics? Coprophilia? Has to be a weakness because it's never going to be about being crooked or without morals, is it?' Trace was going the kind of scarlet that only people who have been speaking to Mudge for any period of time can go. Judging by the response, Mudge must have been getting close to the heart of the matter. Just another person we'd reached out and touched. I glanced up at the lasers nervously.

'Mudge, why don't you give it a rest?' Cat said. Her voice was heavy with implied threat. 'Look, asshole,' she continued diplomatically. 'You're only choice is take the money or we break him out. Don't you want the cash? It's a lot of fucking money.' I couldn't tell if she was bargaining, pleading or threatening.

'I have to admit I was actually surprised by the size of Sharcroft's offer to the company and my own gratuity. Sadly this ups the value of your brother as a prisoner so we'll keep him to bargain for something important.' I glanced over at Cat but she was staring at Trace. I almost groaned when I heard Mudge's voice again. It seemed like he wasn't going to be happy until someone got killed.

'You did a profit-and-loss projection. Didn't you?' Mudge asked. Suddenly we were talking about something else. I wasn't sure if it was the conversation or Mudge's train of thought I wasn't following.

I watched Trace swallow several times as he sought to control himself. The calmness that spread over his features looked like it was narcotic. It would be drug-administered from his internal reservoirs, the sort execs use to calm themselves in the boardroom.

'I think our meeting is over,' Trace said, then to his guards: 'Please see them to their new jobs.'

We didn't move. Pre-violence tension just kept building. I tried calculating our chances. I didn't like the rotary laser element.

Trace turned to Morag. 'I'll see you tonight.' It was a threat.

He was dead. Well he was dead if the lasers and the guards didn't get me first. I just wished I didn't feel like I was moving in slow motion. I scratched at the inhibitor jack in one of my neck plugs. Pointlessly; metal and plastic didn't have any nerve endings.

'I didn't say anything,' Morag protested. I wasn't sure how seriously she was taking this. I think hanging around with us was making her a little too blasé.

'You did a profit-and-loss forecast based on the coming conflict. You modelled who would win, or more likely who would pay more. Do the Earth governments know?' Mudge asked. Now I saw it.

'If someone like you could work it out, what do you think? What? You think they're going to stop dealing with us? They need our resources. They're preparing for war.'

'Fucking parasite,' Cat muttered.

'You're a collaborator?' I asked incredulously. I don't know why I was surprised. It was all flies to shit.

'Oh grow up,' he sighed, rubbing the bridge of his nose. 'Your schoolboy revolutionary act is no doubt great fun, but adults run the system and business is the fuel. Now go and get slaved like the good little victims you are before I have your flesh turned to steam.'

Something unpleasant occurred to me. 'Why not just kill us?' I asked.

'Because we'll make a nice little gift when Rolleston and his friends come in-system,' Mudge said.

'You want to hand us to them?' Morag demanded. Trace didn't answer, but for a moment I saw his concentration waver as if he was listening to someone else. Then he was with us again.

'Because he's begging for favours,' Mudge added. 'Because despite business models and all that other bollocks, he knows that Rolleston, Cronin and their friends are going to fucking eat him. Don't you, little man?'

I wondered if it was the little man comment that tipped it. I saw it; Cat saw it; Mudge would have seen it; and I guessed Morag had been through enough of this shit with us to know what was coming next. The decision to kill us was written all over Trace's face. I wondered how Mudge thought we were going to get out of this.

It went black. Then the lights flickered so quickly they were almost strobing. My flash compensators kicked in and I saw the look of surprise on Trace's face. Fortunately he was surprised enough not to give the kill order to the lasers.

Then God started screaming.

9
The Belt

Trace's expression changed from shock to fury. He looked up. It was clear to him that whatever was happening was our fault. Morag fainted and hit the plush carpet as I started to move towards Trace. With the inhibitor jack in one of my plugs I felt like I was wading through mud to get to him. Inhibited though I was, the barrels on the lasers rotating up to speed still looked like slow motion to me. This just meant that I'd get to see my death more clearly.

My flash compensators saved me from going blind from the red light as it stabbed out. Then the room was full of red steam and we were covered from head to foot in very hot blood. The four security guards looked like they'd been cut in two and had then exploded. Their superheated flesh was still bubbling and steaming. The carpet was on fire. The multiple barrels of the rotary laser were still spinning but no longer firing. They stopped. The sprinklers came on.

Trace was on the other side of his desk looking devastated. I was a little surprised myself. I reached down to pick up one of the M-19s but it came apart in my hand. It had been cut in two.

Trace was drawing a pistol from inside his suit jacket. It looked very shiny and expensive. Mudge had one of the guards' sidearms a long time before Trace completed the draw.

'Mudge, no!' Cat shouted pointlessly. Mudge fired a burst at point-blank range into Trace's face, which caved in on itself. Mudge was grinning but he looked angry as well.

God was still screaming. It sounded like a thousand voices crying out in agony. The noise was messing with my normally calm demeanour.

'What the fuck?!' I demanded of Mudge. He looked like a full-on psycho, covered in blood and laughing in the flickering light.

'Fuck him. He was an arsehole,' Mudge said. I only heard him because my dampeners cut through the unnerving sound of God's screams. Cat and Pagan were right – we were a mess and Mudge was out of control.

I was struggling to sort out what was happening. I was sure I could hear gunfire. Maybe human screams mingling with God's own.

Cat was checking the guards' weapons. Another M-19 had been bisected but two of them were fine.

The locks on my shoulder and knuckles sprang off. The inhibitor jack went offline and the world sped up. I picked the inhibitor jack out of my neck plug.

Morag came to and sat up. She was looking around appalled at the carnage.

'Did you do this?' I asked her. She looked like she was going to ask for forgiveness even though she'd saved us. Instead she just nodded. She looked sick at what she'd done. 'Morag!' I demanded. Her head whipped round to look at me. Then she remembered she hated me. Her remorse gone, the blood and the light made her look somehow evil.

'It was a secure network but he was communicating with it wirelessly,' she said. 'As soon as I knew that, I knew I could hack it.'

Except that you weren't supposed to be able to hack heavy-duty corporate secure networks and take over their security systems that quickly. Even I knew that.

Cat handed me an M-19 and I passed it to Mudge. I took two of the guards' sidearms. I was the only ambidextrous shooter and I had a feeling we were going to need to maximise our firepower. Both pistols were shitty little ten mils. Morag had another of the ten mils and we took all the ammo and grenades for the M-19s' grenade launchers we could carry. Mudge was disgusted to find that all the grenades were stun baton rounds. It made sense. Asteroid habitats were made to be rugged but nobody wanted high-velocity rounds puncturing a window. The bullets in the M-19s were probably low-impact frangible rounds that would shatter rather than penetrate. Frangible rounds were great for use on uppity Belt zombies; not so much fun against people wearing armour.

Morag grabbed a portable computer on the desk and started tapping rapidly on the screen.

'What are you doing?' I asked.

'Looking at the net,' she snapped irritably. Because we had time for attitude.

'Why?' I demanded. I wanted to tell her that we didn't have the time.

'What do you think would make God scream?' she asked and put the computer down on the desk so we could all see it through the humid blood mist. The screen was showing a net feed. Some comedian had made the asteroid station look like a dark, monstrous subterranean kingdom in the net. The whole thing was lit with a bright white light. I was pretty sure that was how the visual interface was translating God. Tendrils writhed through the station's virtual reflection, digging deep into its walls, violating the net construct utterly. The tendrils had an organic black look to them. They reminded me of the proto-Them construct Ambassador had shown me in my dreams that had formed in response to the Cabal's initial attack. Except that these tendrils were burning with black flame. This was something malevolent far beyond a simple attack program.

'Where's it coming from?' Cat asked.

'I don't know and I'm not going in to find out,' Morag told her.

'What is it?' I asked. I knew I just didn't want to face up to what it meant. That this could be over before it started. Morag turned to look at me as if I was stupid. There was only one thing it could be.

'It's Demiurge,' she said.

Whoever had done this had done it well. Power was down. Auxiliary power was down. The station was running on some tertiary, or worse, system. It was getting cold. This was making us steam because we were covered in blood. The lights were still flickering like strobes to the point where it was difficult for our optics to cope.

We didn't have a plan; we were just trying to get out of there. We were moving down through the corporate administration levels. Whatever was happening hadn't reached there. There were frightened people hiding in the offices but terse interrogations provided little information as to what was happening.

The sound of gunfire had become less constant but we could still make out distant screaming. It sounded like it was coming from the dorm/recreation areas, which of course we would have to go through to get back to the ship. Assuming that was still a good idea. I still thought it was because we had a better class of gun on board.

We didn't know where Pagan was and we couldn't risk any form of comms to find him. All we knew was that he had gone to negotiate something with the Yakuza. All the need-to-know bullshit was beginning to get in the way of this fucked-up op.

Cat was in the lead. She was moving quickly, legs bent to provide a steady platform for her M-19, checking up, down, left, right. Going wide around corners so nobody could grab the weapon. I was behind her, a pistol in each hand. I had my shoulder laser scanning behind me. Then Morag, and finally Mudge watching our backs. At least he wasn't acting like a fuck-up at the moment. He was doing his job properly.

'What are we doing?' Cat asked as we entered a laser-cut rock stairway. She spoke quietly as we had no comms.

'Getting Pagan and leaving,' I told her.

'What about Merle?'

'He's a bit of a fucking luxury at the moment.'

'What if Demiurge has compromised the ship's comms?' Morag asked.

'Is this a good time for a conversation?' I replied as we rounded a corner on the stairs and almost shot a couple of terrified Belt zombies. Cat took up a covering position on the reinforced door that led into the dorm/rec area.

'What's going on?' I demanded. They jumped at my voice and then spoke in a language I didn't understand. It sounded faintly eastern European. They pointed towards the door.

'Are we doing this?' Cat asked through gritted teeth.

'We could go and hide,' I suggested hopefully.

'You're such a fucking pussy,' Mudge said. I couldn't see him but somehow I could hear the grin he'd have on his face.

'Shut up, Mudge. Morag, open the door.' I think she was about to argue but it made sense. She only had one pistol, which freed up one of her hands. Cat and I covered her while Mudge pointed his assault rifle back up the stairway.

It was the smell that got us first. People had died and died bad. The coppery tang of a lot of blood was almost overpowered by the burned-pork smell of cooked flesh from laser or black light fire. Then of course there was the smell of shit. People soil themselves when they are afraid or when they die, and bowels rupture when the lower abdomen is treated to sufficient trauma.

I followed Cat through. The red emergency lighting coupled with the flickering light made it look like hell. The carpet of dead people helped give that impression as well. How had this happened so quickly? This was like smoothly executed genocide.

'Them?' Cat asked as she scanned the area. We were all thinking it. Just for a moment I wondered if everything we'd done had just been a Them psy-op, a precursor for an attack on the home system. I knew better, or I hoped I did.

'Look at the wounds,' I said. 'That's not from shards or black beam.' Cat glanced down momentarily.

'Tight grouping as well – good shooting,' she said. She was right. A short burst to the body and then double tap to the head. Except for the ones that had been mutilated. Morag turned to one side and threw up. She was heaving, leaning on the rock wall next to the door.

'Pull yourself together!' I snapped. She glared at me. I hated saying it but we needed everyone working here. She straightened up, pistol at the ready. Thing is, she'd had the correct reaction. I should want to throw up. I shouldn't be so used to this shit. Most of the corpses had been shot or just torn up. It was easy to see why Cat had thought it was Them. Some had had their genitals gouged out and their faces sawn off. I didn't like that, not at all, and I didn't want that to happen to me or anyone else here.

'It's a psyche job,' Mudge whispered. I wasn't sure but I thought that something had moved at the furthest range of my magnified optics. It was difficult to tell, my flash compensators were struggling with the flickering light. It was confusing my lowlight capability as well. 'Fear of castration and loss of identity, it's a standard and quick way of causing fear.' Even Mudge was sounding grim.

'Its certainly fucking playing with my calm,' Cat growled.

'Okay, we head back to the ship, keeping an eye out for Pagan,' I said.

We started moving, constantly scanning our surroundings. There were still people alive down here but they looked terrified and we didn't stop to chat. We could hear whimpering and screaming from the wounded and nearly dead. This had been done in the time we'd spent in Trace's office.

I whipped my head to the right. Old instincts were telling me that something was moving in the shadows. I switched to thermographics, painting the area in multi-hued heat-haze patterns. It was difficult to pick out what was going on in the mass of hot pipes. Space was cold. Any habitat in space needed a lot of heating. If my imagination wasn't playing tricks on me, then whoever or whatever it was must be able to shield their heat signature to a degree.

We rounded a corner onto the main thoroughfare. Broken neon signs flickered and in one case provided an ongoing shower of sparks. More corpses.

'Uh, Jake?' Cat said. I looked over. Past her, against the station's thick external rock wall, one of the security force's light mechs lay in a heap on the ground. We moved over using it for cover.

The mech had been torn apart. There was little evidence of heavy weapon fire. It looked like something had ripped parts off until it had got to the pilot. Around the mech were several dead guards. Again most of their wounds looked like they'd been inflicted in hand-to-hand by something with claws and possibly teeth. All over the walls I could see where rounds from the mech's autocannon had impacted into the rock.

I shoved both the pistols into my coat pockets and grabbed one of the guards' M-19s. The palm link connected and ran a diagnostic of the weapon. It was fully functional but the magazine was empty, as was the grenade launcher. I started to reload. Morag was doing the same as Cat and Mudge covered.

'There's something there,' Cat whispered as I felt my blood turn to iced water. We all looked up. I wanted to ask her if she was sure but that was a stupid question and wishful thinking. I put a fourth grenade, a stun baton, into the grenade launcher and chambered it by working the pump mechanism. Morag was moments behind me.

'Mudge, watch our back,' I told him as we knelt down behind the wreckage of the mech, looking to where Cat was pointing. I had my shoulder laser still scanning behind me.

It took me a moment, but then I saw it. It was strange, some kind of animal, moving on all fours, slinking carefully in the shadows about six hundred metres further down the main thoroughfare towards the docking area. Something made me glance to one side. I cycled through normal vision, lowlight and thermographic but could see nothing. I just couldn't shake the feeling I was being stalked.

I glanced down at the wreckage of the mech.

'Morag? Can you hack this mech's systems?' I asked.

'It's inoperative or I would've been able to pilot it,' Cat hissed.

'It might be compromised by Demiurge,' Morag said. I didn't like the idea of sending Morag anywhere near Demiurge but I was thinking that we were running out of options.

'Hopefully not the operating system. I need you to hack in and release the smartlink safety on the autocannon,' I told her tersely. Hoping there was enough of the old NCO left in me that she wouldn't argue. She didn't. Instead she slung her assault rifle and climbed into the mech cockpit. She ended up sitting on the torn-up corpse of the pilot while looking for a port.

'He's in the way,' she complained.

'It's moving!' Cat said. Her words were punctuated by a short burst of automatic fire.

'Corpse hack!' I told Morag, barely registering her look of horror.

Whatever it was came loping straight down the middle of the thoroughfare straight towards us. It was low and had the look of a predatory animal as it bounded in and out of pools of flickering light. I joined Cat in firing short controlled bursts at it. As it crested a pile of corpses less than four hundred metres away I saw how pointless the frangible rounds were. Nearly all were hitting it but they were just sparking off some heavy-duty armour.

Morag plugged herself into one of the dead pilot's jacks. He was still connected to the mech. She went through his systems. It was like necrophilia but the mech twitched. I heard the hum from its auxiliary batteries and part of the cockpit lit up. Morag managed to move the pilot's fingers to release the mech's grip on the autocannon.

'Cat!' I scrambled over the wreckage of the mech and reached for the weapon. It was armed with an autocannon because a railgun, plasma weapon or heavy lasers would be more likely to breach something. Two hundred metres. It was going to be a bitch to aim. The autocannon looked like an oversized assault rifle. I grabbed the handgrip and tucked the butt under my arm. Most of my hand fitted into the trigger. One hundred metres. Cat grabbed the barrel and lifted it up trying to aim. Fifty metres. I pulled the trigger.

I screamed as I dislocated my right shoulder. The recoil shot the massive weapon back and out of my grip. Cat threw herself to the side, but the muzzle flash caught her and burned the right side of her body, setting the bodybuilder's top she was wearing alight. We were going to die doing something stupid, something that had been my idea.

Still on fire, Cat grabbed the weapon again. It was on us. It leaped into the air as I rolled and grabbed the trigger with my left hand and pushed it down. I tried to keep it held down as the autocannon bucked all over the sand. The thing all but leaped into the weapon's fire. Even the velocity of the twenty-millimetre rounds didn't halt its pounce but it knocked it off kilter and into Cat, who in a feat of adrenalin-fuelled strength pushed it off. I had a moment to be appalled that this thing was still moving. It was a flailing mass of mechanical, armoured limbs, which were beating and clawing at the ground, kicking up a lot of bloody sand. I didn't understand how it could still be moving. There was movement off to my right but I had no time to worry about that.

'The cannon!' Cat shouted. She grabbed the barrel of the weapon and practically held it against the creature. I managed to lift the butt off the ground and hold the violently kicking weapon as round after round flew into it until it stopped moving.

I didn't have time to even look at what we'd killed as another one burst out of the wreckage of a bar to my right. It exploded though a neon sign in a shower of sparks. I heard Mudge firing his M-19 at it and saw the useless rounds spark off its heavy armour. My shoulder laser had time to stab out at it twice before it pounced and tore Morag out of the mech's cockpit and slammed her into the wall. It landed on top of her and a bloody metal claw powered down into her torso.

I was sure she was dead. Ignoring the agony of my dislocated arm I charged the monster, all eight of my nine-inch knuckle blades extended from my forearms. I shoulder-barged it, intent on knocking it off Morag and then dealing with it. It was like shoulder-barging a mech. It didn't move. I stopped dead. It casually clawed me, tearing off half my face and sending me flying back through the air.

I landed in the sand and scrambled to my feet desperate to get it off Morag. I knew I was too late. I knew she was dead. With a scream Cat drove more than a foot of serrated pickaxe blade on the end of a miner's multi-tool in through the creature's cranium and down, deep into its brain. Cat twisted the handle and pulled it off Morag. It was only then she put her burning T-shirt out.

Morag was bloody, her right leg at an odd angle, but she was moving and moaning. Thank God she'd chosen to wear armour like me and unlike Cat.

I staggered to my feet looking around for more of them. My right shoulder was dislocated. That should be difficult when you're an amputee. It was the join to the cybernetic arm, which was hanging off at an odd angle. The painkillers in my internal drug reservoirs were trying desperately to cope.

'Er, Jakob?' I heard Mudge say. I looked over to where he was kneeling by the twitching corpse of the thing that had attacked Morag. I was nauseated to see it wore a mask made of a flayed human face. Mudge was still covering us but he reached down and tore the mask off. I now knew what it was that had attacked us. Actually I knew *who* it was that had attacked us. They were friends of Mudge's and mine.

'Cat?' I said weakly as I leaned heavily against the mech's leg.

I was still scanning all around as was my shoulder laser, though the movements of its servos were sending little jolts of pain through my shoulder. Cat walked over to me, grabbed me and pulled the arm back into its socket. I screamed. My scream was answered. Wolf howls echoed through the rock passages.

I went over and knelt by Morag. Her leg was broken, her cheek was hanging off and her chest armour had taken a battering. There was some blood where the armour had been punctured but it looked superficial. She was out cold and there was nothing we could do for her now.

'You know these guys?' Cat asked.

'Yeah,' I answered.

'You piss them off?'

'They're friends of ours, saved us from getting killed.'

'So they with the Cabal?'

'Looks that way.'

'I don't get it,' Mudge said. He and Cat were covering as I checked their weapons. One had a laser rifle, which I threw to Cat. She collected the spare batteries and grenades while I covered her with the gauss carbine I took off the other one. 'This isn't their style. I mean it is and isn't. I mean, did Vladimir seem the type to do civvies?'

I glanced over at Mudge and then went back to scanning the area. Vladimir was fun to be around if you were on his right side, but I wouldn't put anything past him.

'They call themselves the Vucari,' I told Cat. 'They're Spetsnaz.'

'Oh perfect,' Cat said. The Spetsnaz may not have been the best special forces in the world but they were one of the most feared. They were rumoured to recruit out of lunatic asylums. 'Were they in colonial space when the Black Squadrons got there?'

'No,' I said. This had been bothering me. 'They were sent out there like us.'

'They changed sides?' Cat asked.

Now I could see Vladimir happily perpetrating this massacre, particularly if someone owed him money, but changing sides? More than anything the Organizatsiya encouraged loyalty.

I checked their sidearms – more fucking ten millimetres. It figured. These guys liked to close with their prey and get their claws wet. I took them anyway, dropping the ones we'd nicked from the guards. We were now slightly better armed.

'How many?' Cat asked.

'Squads of eight. Depends on how many squads,' I told her. 'Mudge, carry Morag.' He protested that he wanted to be a shooter. 'Don't fucking argue with me. When you've completed special forces selection and training then you can be a shooter.' He grudgingly picked her up.

We moved quickly. I wanted to get back to the ship and our gear and then look for Pagan, though I didn't fancy his chances. I wondered if Demiurge had taken over the systems yet. Had God beaten him? God should have had the advantage. He should have had a lot more resources in terms of processing power and memory.

Cat was on point, I was at the back, Mudge was carrying Morag between us. She was better off unconscious the way her leg was hanging down. The side of my face that was hanging off was blissfully numb. We were passing another street that branched off deeper into the asteroid on our right.

'People in the bar,' Cat whispered.

I glanced down the street and saw the bar she meant. It had a flickering neon sign of a scantily clad woman done up like a Japanese cartoon character. I guessed this was more a brothel than a bar. Metal shutters covered the windows though several of them had been torn off. I could see numerous heat signatures inside the place.

As we continued towards the dock there was the sound of lots of guns firing long ragged bursts in our general direction. The fire was grossly inaccurate but forced us to take cover as we tried to push corpses up and into the way of the bullets. How can people still miss in the age of the smartlink? I wondered. And long bursts are just lack of self-control. This wasn't the Vucari. They would be eating us by now.

'We're on your side, you stupid bastards!' I screamed during a relative lull in the hail of fire.

'Fuck you!' came the heavily accented reply.

'We just want to get across to the dock!' I shouted back.

I was surprised when a man in a suit wearing dark glasses and holding a gun appeared in one of the windows and gestured for us to approach. I shook my head vigorously, hoping his optics would pick it up from there, and then pointed towards the dock. He continued gesturing.

'Fuck this, let's just go,' Cat hissed.

'Pagan!' the man shouted.

I glanced between Mudge and Cat. Both of them nodded. We made a run for the brothel. As I was scanning all around us I was sure I saw movement in the pipework that ran above the major thoroughfares.

We leaped the window ledge and came barrelling into the Yakuza brothel. It was a fairly comfortable-looking affair for Freetown but I suspect that was more for the Yakuza who hung out there than the clientele. It had a central stage with a pole so the customers could see which of the desperate-looking male or female prostitutes they wanted. There was a bar and a set of metal stairs that led upstairs to the work booths.

The lights weren't flickering in here; someone had got pissed off with them and smashed all but the red emergency lighting. The candles didn't so much provide more light as fuck with the imminent and painful death ambience.

Most of the working boys and girls were sensibly cowering behind a makeshift barricade of overturned tables. I felt like joining them. All the Yak guys were toting guns and looking macho in pre-FHC-style suits, hats and shades. The weird thing was they all looked the same, even the girls. They had all been cut to look the same – like their leader, I supposed. Only which one was their leader? I guessed it was the guy stripped to the waist, all his tattoos on show. It made a degree of sense. He was the fattest. He was carrying a big sub-machine gun. It had a drum magazine and looked like a pre-FHC copy. I hated fashion guns. He also had a short straight-edged sword shoved through a red sash wrapped around his waist.

Mudge lay Morag down behind the barricade and then unslung his near-useless M-19. I passed my slightly less useless gauss carbine to him and he covered us as I knelt down next to Morag.

The fat, half-naked guy with the tattoos was speaking to me in rapid Japanese. I didn't speak Japanese regardless of the speed.

'Medpak?' I asked and then used the universal bridge between cultures of speaking slowly and loudly. 'First. Aid. Kit,' I said, pointing at Morag's wounds. For all the poor guy knew, I was trying to sell him Morag. Fortunately one of the hookers understood and a rudimentary medpak was slid across the floor towards me.

I winced as I heard the crack when I pushed Morag's leg back into place. Well, roughly into place. I applied medgels to the break and then to her face. I didn't want to take her out of her armour and check her chest wound unless I had to. I hooked her up to the medpak so it could drive the gels. Her vitals didn't look great but she wasn't dying.

'Jake.' Even under the circumstances Mudge's contraction of my name still irritated me. I ignored him as I worked on Morag as quickly as possible. 'Jake!'

'What?!' I swung my head round to look at him. When we'd come in I'd been so focused on seeing to Morag's wounds I must have walked straight past Pagan.

He was in one of the comfortable chairs. He made it look somehow throne-like. His staff lay diagonally across him. Both he and the chair showed signs of receiving small-arms fire. He was injured but it looked like his subcutaneous armour had taken the brunt of it. However, he was juddering in the chair like he was being beaten, and blood was bubbling from his mouth and nose. I'd only seen this once or twice before. This was damage from biofeedback. He was in the net getting a right kicking from someone.

The Yakuza boss pointed at a thinscreen slowly peeling off the rock above the bar. It took me a few moments to work out what was going on. At first I thought it was some sort of animated Japanese entertainment viz. Then I realised.

It was showing a huge six-armed man/wolf creature surrounded by a nimbus of white fire. I had seen that fire before, when the angelic hacker Ezekiel had burned the net construct of the Warchilde to let

Rolleston escape. I guessed the hacker running the demon-wolf icon was Bataar, the Vucari's signalman. I remembered thinking of him as the high priest of a cult.

The nimbus of white flame acted as a shield against Pagan's attack programs, which had manifested as a near-constant stream of lightning from the tip of his staff. The nimbus flared where the lightning touched it. The demon-wolf opened its mouth and breathed white fire all over Pagan. A wall of water shot from the rock floor to meet the white flame. The defence program was turned to steam and the white flame licked over Pagan's screaming icon.

'Can we get him out?' I demanded. I wasn't really sure who I was asking. I wasn't sure how bad it would be to pull him out of a situation like this. I wasn't really sure how to do it externally to someone using an internal computer.

Both icons were in a bad way, covered in burns and rendered blood. Surrounding the wolf was a mass of black tendrils that burned with black fire as they reached for Pagan. White light shone from behind Pagan, off-screen. I presumed this was God. Pagan was simultaneously trying to defend himself from the demon-wolf, attack it with lightning and fend off the black tendrils with momentary walls of fire.

The ripping sound of one hypersonic bang running into the next triggered the noise dampeners on my ears and deafened anyone not similarly augmented. This was of less concern than the long burst of railgun fire that tore through the brothel at about chest height. It was like all the furniture in the room had taken flight and was then joined by spinning body parts.

Something wet hit me. The railgun fire stopped just as the flesh of a Yakuza gunman near me split into three and then exploded in superheated chunks as a burst of laser fire hit him.

One of the surviving armoured shutters burst inwards as a Vucari tore into the room. I just about had time to draw attention to myself by firing a short bust from each of my salvaged pistols into its face. My shoulder laser was more effective at charring head armour.

She grabbed me by punching her claws through the subcutaneous armour that protected my stomach, then picked me up, carried me across the bar and rammed me into the back wall. My shoulder laser kept firing point blank into her face, but her heavily armour-plated skull was resisting the beam. It did however burn the dead skin mask she was wearing off. That just showed me her blood-covered, rage-contorted features and her fucking big sharp teeth. She tore a chunk of flesh out of my left forearm. I knew I was going to die so I did something stupid. I grabbed the top of her maw with my left arm and tried to use all my boosted muscle to force her head back. She opened her maw to tear into me and I shoved my right arm into her mouth. She bit down on it, her teeth denting and starting to penetrate my cybernetic arm's armour. I extended all four blades on that arm. All four of the razor-sharp, carbon-fibre blades extended into her brain. She shook, juddered and then slid to one side. Her claws tore out of my stomach and I screamed some more.

Mudge was riding another of the Vucari as it rampaged around the room killing nearly everything it reached out and touched with its claws. A gunman near me lifted his SMG to fire. He was going to hit Mudge. Somehow I had the energy to kick the gun out of his hand. Mudge was punching the Vucari wolf cyborg in the head with his bare hand. I wondered if the Vucari even knew he was there. Cat had the laser and was manoeuvring for a shot, but Mudge and the Yakuza were getting in the way.

I saw the gauss carbine I'd given Mudge lying on the ground. I dived towards it, grabbed the weapon and rolled up.

'Mudge, get off!' I screamed. Mudge slid off the Vucari and curled up in a defensive ball close to its feet. I fired the gauss carbine. Cat fired the laser. The armour-piercing, electromagnetically propelled darts tore into the monstrous cyborg but they weren't doing enough damage. Cat was hitting the Vucari and superheating armour and flesh, blowing bits off it, but the thing was withstanding the fire, its animal-like howls of pain matching the screams coming from the net feed on the thinscreen.

The Vucari bolted, sprinting out into the street through the wreckage of the armoured shutters. Cat chased it. She was insane. I followed her. I think her actions shamed me into it. Cat was firing burst after burst at the thing as it climbed up a stack of street bunks. The metal frames of the bunks bent and buckled with the Vucari's weight as it sprang up. I raised the gauss rifle to my shoulder. The smartlink showed me the grenades in the carbine's underslung launcher. The Vucari weren't screwing around with stun batons. Fortunately the smartlink translated from Russian to English.

I fired the first grenade. Its velocity took it through the bunks to the rock wall and the fragmentation grenade exploded. Wreckage rained down on Cat and I as the force of the explosion blew the wolf cyborg across the street and into the opposite wall. It bounced off the rock and landed in the street ahead of us.

It tried to get up. I was angry now. Why had they done this? Why were they forcing us to kill friends? This was exactly what I had never wanted to do. These were good people – I mean they were all borderline psychos, but they were good people. Actually there was nothing borderline about them. I fired a second grenade. The flechettes tore into it, most of the needles sparking off now severely compromised armour. It tumbled back into the sand. It was still moving. I fired the third grenade from the hip. The cross hairs on my smartlink told me where it was going to hit. The thirty-millimetre, high-explosive, armour-piercing grenade went through its chest cavity and exploded. I was too close. The force of the explosion knocked me on my arse, battered my teeth together and a bit of Vucari shrapnel tore the side of my head open and almost took my ear off.

Cat came to stand by where I was sitting on a Belt zombie's corpse. She was looking all around.

'You getting up?' she asked.

Cat and I stepped back into the brothel. Mudge was leaning on the bar. He had the M-19 in one hand and a bottle of vodka in the other. It looked like something had hit him hard enough in the side of the head to stove in part of his subcutaneous armour and he had a ragged tear in his chest.

'*Na zdorovye*,' he said bitterly.

He took a long swig from the bottle, winced and then spat out a tooth. I glanced over at the Vucari I'd killed. I remembered her name now. It was Andrea. When we'd taken them to get drunk after they'd saved our arses she'd swapped oral sex jokes with Bibs. These people had gone toe to toe with Them when nearly out of ammunition to save us and this was the thanks they got. Why the fuck had they done this?

I'd almost forgotten Pagan. I glanced up at the thinscreen. The wolf-demon was still. It seemed suspended from a tree of thorns that had grown through its flesh. I caught a momentary glimpse of Pagan's icon on the screen, which looked ragged and half torn apart. I briefly wondered why they had to make the virtual damage look so gory in their fake world. Pagan's icon disappeared. Tendrils covered in black fire swamped the place where he'd been. The white glow that I'd come to connect with God seemed to recede and disappear.

'Jesus, that hurts. When'd I get shot?' Pagan asked. Pain filled his voice. Real Pagan didn't look much better than virtual Pagan. He was lying on the ground. Railgun fire had destroyed his chair. He was lucky it hadn't torn him apart. There was blood all down his chin and beard from where it had drooled out his mouth and nose. Blood was also running out of his ears. I knew that you had to take a serious amount of biofeedback for that to happen. Then he had the bullet wounds on top of that.

'Has Demiurge taken the station?' I asked. My voice sounded dead even to me. As if I didn't care. I glanced over at Morag. She was still unconscious.

Pagan shook his head. 'Not yet, but it will,' he said and then started speaking rapidly in Japanese to the Yakuza. The surgical clones looked to their boss. He hesitated as long as face dictated and then nodded. The gunmen went running from the brothel.

'You speak Japanese?' Pagan ignored my stupid question. Later he would tell me that he'd worked extensively with the Japanese Special Forces Group on Barney's. 'Where's it getting all its processing power and memory from?'

Pagan turned to look up at me. He look tired and in pain.

'Good question. They came on a long-range strike craft. There's only so much Demiurge that could fit into the systems of a craft like that. God here in the camp should have easily outbid it in terms of power. As soon as it kicked in all the docked ships switched off their net links to the station. All the in-system ships will be carrying God. If they add their memory and processing power then we should be able to beat Demiurge.'

'"Should"?' He shrugged. 'Won't most of them have left as soon as they realised something was wrong?'

'Several tried. One of the first things Demiurge went for was the camp's external weaponry. Two tramp freighters and a factory ship were blown apart.'

I tried, I really tried, but this news did nothing except make me feel increasingly numb.

'Those ships' captains have got a lot to lose if they switch on their comms and Demiurge wins.'

'That's why Itaki's people –' he nodded towards the Yakuza boss, who was standing in the middle of the carnage trying to make sense of it '– will be doing the persuading, at gunpoint if necessary.'

'Is there anything we can do?' I asked.

He started to shake his head but winced at the pain.

'No. I can't fight that thing and neither can Morag.' Then there was a look of momentary panic. 'Where's Morag?' I pointed at where she was lying on the ground among the metal kindling that had once been a makeshift barricade.

'She all right?' he asked.

Not really, but I nodded.

Cat joined us. She had succeeded in removing the railgun harness

Andrea had been wearing. The railgun had folded up snug along her back when Andrea had fought like an animal. Cat had linked to it, run diagnostics and was now putting the harness on.

'What now?' Cat asked.

'Back to the ship,' I said.

'I know where your brother is,' Pagan told Cat.

Bollocks. Cat turned to look at me. I sighed and glanced down at Pagan.

'It's what we came here for,' he said.

Mudge joined us, catching the gist of the conversation. 'Look at all the free stuff we got,' he said, grinning.

'Be a shame to come all this way and not get him,' Pagan said.

'With their weapons we're hunting *them*,' Cat said.

Pain cut my bitter laugh short.

'Dream on. These guys lived for fighting Them hand-to-hand. One at a time nearly killed us, and we only got away with it because they seem to have gone fucking mad.'

'Four down though,' Cat said.

'Five,' Pagan corrected her. 'There was no way their hacker walked away from that.'

'He could already be dead,' I pointed out. Meaning Merle.

'Scared?' Mudge asked. He was goading me.

'Mudge, will you just fuck off,' I snapped. 'The adrenalin combat junkie act is wearing a bit fucking thin.'

Mudge looked pissed off and for once didn't say anything. Still it was a Chinese parliament and I'd been outvoted.

'Okay, we go and get him,' I agreed. 'Mudge, stay here and look after Morag.'

'What? I piss you off so you go off and play with your soldier mates—'

'Yes—' I started.

'And I get saddled babysitting your ex?'

'Mudge! Wind your fucking neck in!' I shouted, finally losing my temper. I don't think it was Mudge I was angry with. Well not just Mudge. 'Stay here, look after Morag, and if anything happens to her don't be around when I get back!'

We stared at each other for a while. The hookers and the Yakuza had turned to see what the commotion was about. Mudge somehow thought better of saying anything and stalked over to where Morag was lying on the ground. I think I'd managed to alienate everyone now.

'I hope this guy's worth it,' I muttered to Cat.

'He'd best be better than James Bond,' Pagan said.

'Who?' Cat asked. I'd no idea what he was talking about either.

This was bullshit. I did not want to be doing this and we had better things to do, like making sure Morag was okay, if I was honest. Moving deep into the bowels of an asteroid mining camp looking for incredibly dangerous Russian special forces operators was not high on my list of priorities. I respected Cat wanting to help her brother, I really did, and if he was one of ours then it would be right to come and get him. We didn't know this guy, however, so this wasn't our problem. Besides, if BPIC took back control of the station we could be right back where we were to begin with. Except the next guy might not want to gloat and be so sloppy with his computer security.

BPIC didn't have much use for long-term people containment. It was expensive and tied up resources. They had a lock-up for when Belt zombies, usually newcomers who hadn't had the life sucked out of them, got out of hand. Anything deserving more long-term punishment got dealt with summarily. It normally involved an airlock. After all they were pretty much the law out here.

We found Merle's cell. It was a laser-cut hole in the stone not much bigger than a man. It had a smaller hole in the bottom of it to drain waste and a very solid, thick titanium hatch at the top. Pagan once again proved how clever he was by calling it an oubliette. It looked like a hole in the ground to me. It was empty.

The lights were still flickering in this part of the station and we hadn't seen corpses for some time now. We'd just found lots of blood, bits of torn flesh and drag marks. I think we were close to the various life-support systems. The only sound was the loud humming of a lot of machinery.

Cat, armed with Andrea's railgun, and I covered while Pagan investigated the hole in the ground with the French-sounding name.

'He's dead,' I told Cat. I couldn't see any way he could get out of that. Someone had to have opened it. That someone was probably a very dangerous, heavily augmented Russian cyborg.

'Not Merle,' she said with some conviction.

'Even if he got out, if he's been in there for any amount of time then he'll be in no physical state to help us,' Pagan told her gently.

'If he's high value then BPIC could have moved him,' Cat said, but I could hear the doubt in her voice.

'I don't think he would have been a priority for BPIC today. I don't think they even have a frame of reference for what happened here,' Pagan said.

'This isn't a good spot for a conversation,' I hissed. This place was seriously messing with me. As that thought crossed my mind a howl echoed through the rock corridors. All of us froze.

I'd heard wolf calls before, real wolves, when I was growing up. The calls the Vucari had used earlier were most likely for intimidation value. After all, they could probably communicate between themselves via Demiurge's control of the net. This was different. There was something mournful and desperately sad about the noise.

'I think we should go,' Pagan said.

'He's here and he's alive—' Cat started.

'Is that just intuition?' Pagan demanded. 'There's taking a risk and then there's courting trouble.'

I knew they were waiting for me to make a decision. I couldn't say why I decided to push on. I wanted to leave and wasn't sure of the advantage of continuing to look for Merle. I don't think Merle was the reason I decided to push on, however. There was just something about that howling.

'We go on.'

Pagan didn't argue; he knew better than to do that in a situation like this.

I don't know what the stone chamber where we found Vladimir had been used for initially. I think there was some kind of machinery buried under the pile of corpses. We'd been passing when another mournful howl had alerted us to his presence. I'd entered first. I checked all around looking for more of them. There could be some hiding in the corpses but if so thermographics wasn't picking them up. I pointed the gauss carbine up the mound to the figure sitting on top. Pagan and Cat were in after me. They were too professional to say anything but I could tell they were horrified by what they saw. Pagan still had the presence of mind to turn his back on the atrocity and cover the door. It took a degree of balls to turn your back on something you know to be that dangerous.

'What are you doing, Vladimir?' I asked quietly, trying to force down my rising gorge. He was crouched on top of the pile of bodies tearing gobbets of flesh from them and putting them in his mouth and chewing. His expression was pained, like a spoilt middle-class kid forced to eat something he didn't like. A lot of what he was eating was just tumbling out of his mouth partially chewed. I think it was the noise, the tearing sound of skin and meat, which jarred my already frayed nerves the most.

He turned to look at me, wearing someone else's face. He was covered from head to foot in other people's blood. It should have been horrific, and it was, but there was something pathetic and pitiable about him as well. He'd got his wish to feast on human flesh but it didn't look as if it was to his taste. This was a warewolf reduced to a ghoul, a mere carrion eater. He seemed tired as he took off the face.

'My friend,' he said sadly. He continued tearing off lumps of flesh. There was something compulsive about the behaviour. 'I have betrayed everything.' He tore off more flesh.

'Why?' was the best I could do. I wasn't sure how much longer we had before Cat tried to waste him. He ripped off another lump of flesh.

'If he does that one more time ...' Cat growled.

'This isn't you,' I said.

He stopped chewing and looked at me.

'We both know it is. We are always surprised by what we are capable of ...' Then he tapped his armoured skull with the tip of a bloodied claw. 'When we serve something bigger than us.'

'Has something made you do this?' Pagan asked. He did not look at Vladimir; he was still covering the door.

'I do not know you that you should address me with such familiarity,' Vladimir replied, a predatory smile on his face. His mock haughtiness was like a ghost of his old self. 'I always wanted to be a monster. It's much easier than trying to be good.'

'Are you slaved?' I asked, though I'd seen nothing in any of the Vucari's plugs.

He stared at me. It was all I could do to return his look.

'Do you owe me a debt?' he asked.

I didn't want to answer that. I couldn't see any form of repayment of my debt that was going to be good. I swallowed hard, trying to ignore the acid burn of rising bile in the back of my throat.

'Yes,' I finally managed.

'I cannot do it myself,' he said. He sounded almost solemn.

The glimpse of his face I caught as he pounced was of a mask of hatred and insane rage. We all fired. The railgun kicked up a storm of dead flesh. Despite the ordnance he took a long time dying.

I felt nothing as we probed deeper into the complex. Pagan was freaked but I didn't care any more. All I could think of was that someone had done this to Vladimir. I wasn't sure how but I was pretty sure who.

We were crossing a metal bridge over a deep pool of water that had been cut from the stone of the asteroid. The pool was part of the water supply. A thick carpet of algae covered the top of the pool to help with oxygen generation. The flickering lights in this section were ultraviolet to stimulate algae growth.

The UV made the blood-soaked Vucari that dropped from the ceiling wearing someone else's face seem surreal. I think Mudge would have enjoyed the experience. It didn't seem real to me. The Vucari landed between Cat and me. Cat's blood looked black in the UV as he tore a claw up her back. The blow lifted her off her feet and sent her sprawling to the metal. As it turned to face me I threw myself back, trying to bring the gauss rifle to bear. I knew that behind me Pagan would be swinging around to fire but then the Vucari stiffened. Blood, his own, dribbled out of his mouth and he fell forward. There was a piece of jagged metal sticking out the back of his neck between the armour plate on his skull and the armour plate on his back. Even allowing for getting the metal between the two plates, it still would have to be pushed in with a lot of force to penetrate the subcutaneous armour. I had to admit I was impressed.

Standing behind the fallen Vucari was a naked man about my size. I had no idea where he'd come from. He was breathing hard and his right hand was bleeding badly. There was no body fat on him at all and he looked malnourished. I saw the high cheekbones that could make features like his look cruel but now they just added to his gaunt appearance. His hair was a dirty matted bird's nest. His skin was as dark as Cat's and there was more than a passing resemblance though he had a smaller build. The thing that got me the most however was his eyes. They must have been designed to look like the real things but I'd never seen implants like that. They had seemed intense in the pictures but now they managed to look simultaneously cold and somehow insane.

He spat on the corpse. Some feeling flickered inside me.

'Don't do that,' I said.

He ignored me. He wrenched the metal shank out of the Vucari, turned him over and pushed the dead skin mask off his face. I recognised this one as well. His name was Vassily.

Cat climbed to her feet with some difficulty due to the railgun harness. She turned to face the man.

'Merle?' I couldn't remember Cat ever sounding that unsure.

He looked back at her. His implants were certainly emotive. I wasn't sure how that worked. I was sure I saw hate in his eyes.

'A fucking cop!' he spat.

'Corporate secur—' she managed to get out before he attacked her.

He attacked someone with a railgun with only a metal shank. I thought Cat was pretty good about it. After all the shit we'd been

192

through I would have been tempted to just blow him away. I was quite tempted to do that anyway. He drove her to the ground and she was just managing to hold him off. It seemed that her obviously superior strength was not necessarily a match for insane conviction. The shank was getting closer and closer to her. I bet she wished she'd put armour on before going to Trace's office now.

I shook my head. We really didn't have time for this sibling rivalry bullshit. Pagan was covering our back. I put as much power as I could muster into the kick I delivered. It snapped Merle's head around to one side and he spat blood all over Cat. His head was lolling around but he was still conscious, so I stamped on it. He collapsed onto her.

'You're not one of us yet,' I told the unconscious body. Pagan backed up closer to me.

'So we've collected another arsehole then?' he asked.

Just once, I thought, it'd be nice if we could sort things out without violence.

'Ungrateful bastard,' I muttered, meaning Merle. We'd have to carry him now as well.

'Could somebody get my naked brother off me?' Cat asked.

10
En Route to Lalande

This was weird. Apparently they used to have houses just for tea. This wasn't like the sort of brew-up I was used to, either in a foxhole or on the bonnet of a Land Rover with your mates on watch. It was taking a fuck of a lot longer for a start. But then we weren't expecting to be torn apart by Them at any given moment. While we may have had a boiled sweet before a cuppa, we didn't have fancy sweets to 'prepare our palates' either.

I'd like to have dismissed this all as bollocks but the programming was superb. It was the detail. The sweets tasted like sweets and good sweets. How had they coded that? I could smell the blossoms on the air, which was fresh and clean and maybe a little thin, like we were actually on a mountain in the virtual environment. We could smell the tea as it was being prepared. I could feel the rough texture of the straw mats through the silk of the dressing-gown thing I was wearing. I think it was called a kimono, and while I'd protested at having to wear it, even virtually, I don't think I'd ever felt silk before. You had to look hard to see the edges of this fantasy.

A lot of time, effort and probably money had gone into this program. It made sense, I guess. Michihisa Nuiko was a chimera. She had been born severely disabled, but luckily for her chimerical technology and her own inherent piloting ability meant that she could still join the war effort. It must have been nice for her to be part of such an inclusive society. Everyone gets used.

She wasn't talking about her war record much. In fact beyond being the single most polite person I've ever met, sort of an anti-Mudge, she wasn't saying much of anything. Judging by the craft that the Yakuza set her up with, her record must have been pretty good, and judging by the type of job she was recommended for and was prepared to take, her career must have been on the sharp end. Itaki had put us on to her. Despite his trigger-happy people and the weird thing with having everyone cut to look like him, he'd proved to be an okay guy for a mobster and a pimp.

Pagan had been excited that the Yakuza had the vice franchise in Camp 12 because he had worked with them before. While most organised crime operations had to live up to their word to a degree, otherwise nobody would ever deal with them, Pagan was of the opinion that the Yakuza were the least likely to sell us out. As long as they were properly paid that is.

Nuiko lived in a womb-like life-support cocoon in an armoured compartment in the centre of the ship. We would never see that. All our interaction was through the beautifully crafted sense programs in her personalised net realm. Like the tea room made of lacquered wood and paper looking out over a dramatic snow-capped mountain vista.

Her ship was called *Tetsuo Chou*, which Pagan told me meant 'steel butterfly'. It was a small, heavily modified system clipper, which are pretty much the fastest ships available outside the military. Nuiko's backers had paid for an induction sail to be added for FTL travel. The streamlined, distended-teardrop shape was covered in green/black energy-dissipating acoustic tiles to lower its energy signature. The ship had top-of-the-line navigation systems to minimise the use of manoeuvring engines, which in turn would further lower its energy signature. Internal power was kept to a bare minimum as well, which meant a cold ship. Its electronic countermeasures system was also state of the art, making it very stealthy. Which was just what we needed, and virtual Nuiko hadn't batted a virtual eyelid when we mentioned an OILO entry. I think she'd done orbital insertion before.

BPIC decided not to slave us in the end. Partly because Itaki vouched for us, partly because we were fully armed by the time they regained control of Freetown 12, but mainly because they had their own problems. Itaki's people had convinced enough ships' captains to let the part of God that lived in their systems join the fight against Demiurge and Demiurge had finally been destroyed.

There had only been the eight Vucari and one had been destroyed by automated security systems while sabotaging the fusion plant. They'd come in on a long-range strike craft, the same one they'd left on when they returned to Sirius on a similar job to ours, I guessed. The LRSC had come back radically different, however.

When we finally managed to break into the craft we found that the living space had been radically reduced. It was a rats' nest where the Vucari must have been crammed together. The rest of the ship was full of a honeycomb-like substance that looked very similar to

Them biotech. This was where the empowered Demiurge had been stored and was the increased memory and processing power that had given God so much trouble.

We found Bataar, the Vucari hacker. He seemed to have merged with the biotech material. It filled his mouth, his nostrils, his plugs and penetrated his ears. Much of his body was buried deep in it. If there were pilots in there I guessed something similar had happened to them.

At the same time as Freetown 12 was hit all the other Freetown Camps and the asteroid cities suffered similar attacks. All from returning special forces groups sent to disrupt and gather information in Black-Squadron-held territory. All of them supported by Demiurge.

Some of the other Freetown Camps hadn't been as lucky as 12. Over a dozen of them had been 'sanitised', as BPIC put it. As had Hygeia. I don't know why God hadn't been able to stop Demiurge in a city that size – perhaps Rolleston had sent larger ships with more space for Demiurge – but more than two hundred thousand people had died in the subsequent plasma bombardment from BPIC and system patrol ships. Two hundred thousand. It was just a number. A number heated by liquid fire that will burn in space and then cool in vacuum. I didn't see the ballet of all those bodies blown into the cold night. The figure was so abstract I struggled to feel the anger I should have.

While the Black Squadrons had earned themselves another enemy in BPIC, they had managed to cripple the logistical support of the mining operations in the Belt. In doing so they had of course denied those resources to Earth. What we couldn't work out was why had all those people turned. Why had the Vucari gone over to Rolleston? The most obvious explanation was that they had been slaved. If so it was a new and more sophisticated form of slaving because they'd had no slave jacks in their plugs and they didn't seem to suffer the drop-off in performance than comes with slaveware.

Once the ritual part of the tea ceremony was over and we could converse normally Mudge had suggested brainwashing. Then he'd explained the concept. It was basically a form of psychological coercion to do what you're told. We called it basic training in the army. Pagan had suggested that it was never as total or as effective as it had seemed on the Vucari.

'Possession?' I asked as Nuiko ladled tea from an iron pot set in a hole in the ground. Even serving the tea seemed complex. Nuiko was small, slender, pale, and wearing a simple dark kimono. Her features were a composed expressionless mask. I found this faintly disconcerting. I also didn't like that she never met my eyes, particularly as I was wearing my Sunday-best icon, which Morag had made for me. The one where I had my natural eyes, or what Morag thought they should look like.

'And this from someone with no faith,' Pagan scoffed. He was in his Druidical icon, except that he too wore a kimono like the rest of us. The kimonos were a piece of code gifted to us by Nuiko. It was code that had been thoroughly vetted by Morag and Pagan before it got anywhere near us.

'It happens,' Morag said. Presumably irritated at having to back me up. She too wore a kimono and I was relieved that she was wearing her Maiden of Flowers icon out of respect for our host rather than the Black Annis. I didn't like the Black Annis icon and I didn't want to meet it while Morag was still so angry at me. That said, I hadn't forgotten that Morag could kill me in here. I was only slightly worried that the tea might contain a piece of biofeedback poison code. Still it tasted nice when we finally were allowed to taste it and had been quiet long enough for our conversation to be proper.

'So I've heard,' Pagan said, smiling patronisingly. 'To anybody you've known?'

'Well no,' Morag said, suddenly unsure of herself.

'It's a myth,' Mudge said. His icon looked like himself without augmentation. I think it was more of Morag's work. He'd only been allowed into the tea room sanctum after he'd promised Pagan that he'd behave.

'Like the spirits in the net?' I asked, bowing slightly to Nuiko, like Pagan had taught us, as she poured me some more tea. Pagan started to answer. 'I've seen an exorcism,' I said, forestalling his reply.

'Bullshit,' Mudge said and then studiously ignored Pagan's glare of disapproval.

'In Fintry, Vicar did it.'

'Very convincing theatre, I've no doubt,' Pagan said. For someone who wanted us to behave in here he seemed to be desperate to get slapped.

'Maybe, but the guy was a howling lunatic, and according to friends and kin he was acting differently and knew stuff he shouldn't. Vicar plugged himself into the guy. There was lots of screaming for someone who was supposed to be trancing, some thrashing around, a biofeedback kicking that Vicar swears hadn't been inflicted by him, and then the guy was better,' I finished.

'There could be any number of—' Pagan started.

'Is it just the idea of this Demiurge possessing people that scares you badly?' Merle asked. His voice was a deep rich baritone. It was also cold and emotionless.

I wasn't sure I liked this guy. All he'd done since we'd come on board was eat the high-calorie combat rations we'd brought with us and exercise. Mudge had asked him how he'd managed to retain any degree of fitness while locked in the hole. Isometrics, Merle had told him. He did not have much time to get combat-ready after his imprisonment. Whatever we could say about him, he certainly seemed driven.

I wasn't sure if Cat and him had sorted out their differences but I had come across them having a private conversation jacked into each other. Merle, like Cat, was wearing an off-the-shelf icon. The kimonos hung shapelessly off both of them.

'No, I don't like the idea, do you?' Pagan asked, somewhat testily.

'I don't like any of this—' Merle began.

'Prefer to be in your hole?' Mudge asked.

'But I think we need to face up to what that means in terms of security,' he said, glancing over at Nuiko. It was her house. We were in FTL; there was no one for her or God, who was in the *Tetsuo Chou*'s systems, to tell out here. I'd agreed with Pagan's call on that. Also it wasn't as if she knew what we were going to be doing on the ground because we didn't know ourselves. 'It means that if any of us are taken we're completely compromised and quickly.'

'So we don't get taken alive?' Mudge said. He was smiling. I think going out in flash of glory was beginning to appeal to him.

'You ready to kill any of us who gets captured?' Merle asked.

'Okay, you've proved how hard core you are. Let's change the subject,' I said, even though I knew he had a point.

'Problem won't go away,' Merle said.

'He's right,' Cat agreed. Though, like Morag agreeing with me, I think this cost her some.

'I am prepared to kill any of us who gets captured,' I said, 'because I've seen the alternative. The people we killed used to be friends of mine.' Except I knew I could never pull the trigger on Morag. I reflected that she had no such qualms, which was good. I didn't want to find myself chewing down on a pile of corpses wearing someone else's face. It didn't seem dignified or hygienic.

'How'd you get out of that hole anyway?' Mudge asked. He was taking a lot of interest in our latest addition.

'When the warewolf opened up the oubliette I just ran between its legs,' Merle answered.

'Simple as that?' I asked.

'Every second I'd been in that hole was preparation for that moment,' he answered.

The problem was that we hadn't had the chance to hang around and find out what was going on with the Vucari, why they'd done what they'd done. We'd had God relay the information of what we'd seen back to Earth, but that was the best we could do. Then we'd left on the *Tetsuo Chou* as quickly as we could, though if this was the opening move in the attack on Earth then for all we knew we could be passing Lalande's colonial fleet in the night at FTL.

Merle was right, I had to admit. Everyone talks eventually, and eventually would become quickly if they used sense interrogation techniques because they could distend time. Even then we still had time. If Demiurge or whatever could actually possess then we had no time. If someone was taken that meant total compromise. That meant nobody went home, we just ran. So we needed to make sure that nobody got captured. That meant a suicide solution, which included a kill switch for a firestorm program in our internal electronic memories. More importantly it meant that we needed to be prepared to kill each other if we saw someone going down and we had the opportunity. Fighting Them was hard but less complicated. I missed Their simplicity.

Security-wise things had relaxed a little because we were self-contained. We would be keeping God out of planning as much as possible, but even he would have nobody to tell as he would not try and communicate with any Demiurge-infected system. Nuiko we would tell what she needed to know for her part of the job. Beyond that we would keep her in the dark as well. As much for her own good as ours. Talking to Pagan, though, I got the feeling that she would fly the *Tetsuo Chou* into the heart of a sun before she would allow herself to be compromised by the Black Squadrons.

My problem with Nuiko was that she was new and I didn't understand her. Merle I didn't trust but I had a frame of reference for him. Despite his behaviour he wasn't a million miles removed from us. But Nuiko's reserve was about a hundred times more extreme than your average English person's. She was very private and apparently very respectful of our privacy, even though we were quite literally guests in her world. A lot of her behaviour seemed very ritualistic – the past, if it was even a real past, seemed important to her. To me she seemed to be fighting to keep something alive. Something I didn't understand. I guess that her being a chimera didn't aid my understanding. To all intents and purposes I was trying to relate to a machine, but she just seemed so ... alien.

And then she withdrew. Pagan watched her and I watched Pagan as she took small steps to a sliding wood-and-paper panel and slid it shut behind her. This symbolised her leaving the closed system. In the real world we were all sitting cross-legged on crates facing each other, plugged into a memory cube. The jack that connected Nuiko was mounted on a cable snake, which would have disengaged from the memory cube and would be snaking its way back towards the armoured cocoon that protected our pilot. The memory cube held a downloaded copy of the tea house environment. Another gift from Nuiko. All these gifts made me nervous, but I wasn't looking after the information security aspect of the operation.

Pagan and Morag started rechecking the security. Glyphs of light appeared in front of them, throwing shadows over their respective icons' features. I took the opportunity to stand up and pace over to the wooden veranda. It looked out onto an ornamental garden of stone and water features. Past the garden was the stunning mountain vista. The tea house was part of some kind of castle complex built high into the side of a mountain. The fact that I could enjoy the mountain air, seemingly feel it cold and thin in my lungs, was sublime.

The holographic display hovering over the low lacquered wooden table took me out of the illusion and reminded me where I was and what I was doing.

'This secure?' Merle asked.

'As anything is any more,' Pagan told him. 'Are you in or not?'

'I'm not happy to be here, but it's an improvement. Besides –' he looked at Cat '– my sister has provided me with some very compelling reasons to help. Not least of which is a fuckload of money.'

'Just so you know we're probably not coming back,' Pagan told him. 'And don't swear.' I glanced over at him before turning back to Merle.

'Want to share those compelling reasons?' I asked.

'No,' Merle told me flatly. 'Besides, I know the lie of the land. Things go to shit, I reckon I can disappear.'

'I told you, don't swear,' Pagan said. I don't think he liked Merle but there was something else here as well.

'Fuck, Pagan, she's not even in the fucking room,' Mudge said, smiling.

'I know. It's just—'

'It doesn't seem right,' I said. Pagan nodded. The language, the briefing, it was going to war with the environment. We needed our moments of fantasy. 'And that's it,' I said with finality. They all looked at me expectantly.

'I'll bite. What's it?' Mudge finally asked.

'From now on we're not trying to piss each other off. We're not trying to score points.' I looked over at Merle. 'We don't need the strong silent hard men—'

'Speak for yourself,' Morag and Mudge said in unison.

I bit down the flash of irritation and jealousy. She had more than the right to try and make me feel that way.

'If we don't stop trying to pull each other apart then I will sabotage the OILO cocoons myself and we'll sit out the war. Okay?'

'Plus you won't have to make the jump?' Pagan said, but he was smiling.

I nodded.

'No offence, man, but you're part of the problem,' Cat said. I glanced over at Morag, or rather the Maiden of Flowers that Morag was wearing. She was studiously looking elsewhere.

'I think we all are, but you're right. It's not going to get in the way. We'll either deal with it or ignore it effectively, or the mission won't be happening at all.'

The Maiden of Flowers' head snapped round to look at me. I thought she was about to argue. Maybe it sounded too much like I was making decisions for her, which people had been doing all her life. All I thought I was doing was stating our only two real options for the situation we were in. I think she reached that conclusion as well and nodded.

'This soap opera's a joke, right?' Merle asked.

'You can pack that in as well. I realise you don't know us so you've got to wipe your cock in our faces so we know you're not a victim. We get it. You're hard core, so you can stop now. Also any problems you have with your sister, resolve them or leave them until after.'

He stared at me, but his icon was off the shelf and it didn't have the same effect that being stared at by his weirdly intense brown eye implants would have had.

'This mission being scrubbed is not the problem for me that it is for you,' he told us.

'Fine. Either you're in or out. You're out, you can rattle around in here until we're finished.'

'Bullshit,' Merle said. Pagan's icon seemed to twitch. 'You'd put a bullet in my head.'

'Compelling reasons. If you're in, you play nicely.'

He gave what I'd said some thought and then nodded. The guy was a prima donna, I decided. He was too used to doing ops on his own.

'Anyone who has a problem with Mudge's pharmaceutical recreations can mind their own business,' I said.

Mudge grinned but Cat and Pagan protested.

I continued, 'Mudge, your hobby gets in the way, you run out and have a nasty withdrawal, or for whatever reason can't keep up then you get left behind. If it's a dodgy situation and it looks like you'll get compromised I'll shoot you myself.'

'You are so masterful,' Mudge said acidly.

I could tell he was about to go off on me. Come on, Mudge, I urged silently. You're not stupid. You know I've faith in you. This has to be said. This is for the audience. I watched Mudge's icon swallow. Morag's programming was superb. I was betting that the tranced-in Mudge had done that back in the meat world. Mudge seemed to master his anger and nodded.

'While we're on the subject, what were you doing back in Trace's office?' I asked.

'What? The guy was an arsehole?' Mudge said.

'So? We've met arseholes before.'

'And I always deal with them like that.' He was sounding defensive now.

'You almost got us killed,' Cat said angrily before turning to me. 'And this is the point. I'm sure he's a party guy but the drugs in his system compel him to make bad decisions, make him overconfident.'

'That's really not the drugs,' I told her. It was meant to be flippant but in retrospect who knew? It was impossible to separate who Mudge was from the drugs. I'd only ever seen him straight once. That was in Maw City and he'd been sick from withdrawal.

'Sometimes you've just got to shit in your hand and throw it at them,' Mudge said. We all turned to look at him. He shrugged. 'It turned out all right.'

I was starting to get angry now. 'It turned out all right because Morag was seriously on the ball. Everything we knew about the situation suggested that hacking their systems wasn't an option. If she hadn't noticed—'

'And pulled off the greatest hack ever,' Cat said.

'Then we would have been dead,' I finished.

'We've all got to go sometime. If you're scared then get another line of work,' Mudge said.

Tried that, I thought.

'Don't worry, Mudge. We'll get fucking killed soon enough but let's at least try first, okay?' I said angrily.

'Good speech – raises the morale,' Merle said dryly.

'And when did you start arguing with me when we're in the middle of a job?!' I demanded, thinking back to the brothel.

'You left me behind!' Mudge shouted. I think that had really hurt him. 'I don't have to do what you say – we're not in the army now!'

'You never were!' I shouted back at him.

'So much for our mountain idyll,' Pagan muttered.

'Whatever it is, rein it in,' I told Mudge. 'Because I mean it: if you endanger this mission, you endanger the rest of us.'

'What, you'll shoot me? You are so fucking butch right now,' he spat.

'If you can't convince me that you're not a liability then I'll leave you behind,' I told him evenly.

Morag's programming was superb. It picked up on just how hurt Mudge was.

'Fucking whatever. I'm good. I'll play nicely with the other children.' He was all but sulking. He was pissed off and defensive because I think he knew that we were right.

'These are just words,' Merle said, testing the boundaries.

'The only person in this room I'm not sure will live up to their words is you,' I told him, met his look and held it. It was difficult to outstare a cheap icon as they weren't sophisticated enough to blink.

'So, macho posturing aside, what are we doing out here?' Cat asked. She provided the distraction for both of us to look away with a degree of dignity. So I told myself.

'Operation Ungentlemanly Warfare,' Pagan said.

'We have a name, how exciting,' Mudge said. I glared at him. 'Oh lighten up.'

'Ungentlemanly is the information part of the operation run by me. Warfare is the physical security element run by Jakob.'

'What's our objective?' Merle asked. I was pleased that he said 'our'.

'Twofold. First Morag and I want to hack Demiurge. We need to do that without being noticed. We need to do it to find the plans for the attack on the Sol system and we also need to find a way to defeat Demiurge.'

'Can you even do that yet?' Cat asked. 'I thought Demiurge was like God, only worse.'

Pagan was looking evasive.

'Don't piss about, Pagan,' I told him.

'Not yet. We have a few advantages and some avenues of research we're following up,' he said. I hoped they had something a bit more concrete than that Pais Badarn Beisrydd bullshit.

'So let's say you somehow manage to hack this scary AI ...' Merle began.

'Its not an AI—' Morag started.

'So what?' Merle cut across her.

We all stared at him, except Pagan.

'You mean, what do we do with the information?' he asked.

'Yeah, I can see we infiltrate with OILO, which might not be as easy as you think, but what's your exit strategy?'

'We don't have one,' Pagan told him.

'Then you're wasting your time,' Merle said.

'Nuiko has been paid to stay in proximity to Lalande 2 while we're planetside. She'll be at certain orbits at certain times for the first three weeks. Morag and myself will have the co-ordinates and the times. When we get the information we need—'

'If,' Merle interrupted again.

'Then we use a tight beam uplink to transmit data packets to the *Tetsuo Chou*.'

That made sense. Unless the Black Squadrons could directly transpose something between the uplink transmitter and the *Tetsuo Chou* then they had no way of intercepting the information. Presumably three weeks was a function of the clipper's logistics.

'And if we don't manage this in the first three weeks?' I asked.

'Then it's a seventeen-day round trip plus another day for outfitting before she returns for another three weeks. That'll be her last trip,' Pagan told us.

'If she's not intercepted,' Merle said.

'Her risks are no different from ours,' I said.

I noticed that Pagan looked troubled.

'Except that she's a spaceship!' Mudge cried with mock enthusiasm, his apparent new leaf now at an end.

'Exfiltration?' Merle asked.

'No such thing,' I told him. 'Either the war ends and we get to go home, or we wait for some as yet unforeseen opportunity.'

'And?' Mudge suddenly asked.

Pagan looked confused. 'And what?'

'And Rolleston and Cronin?'

'Demiurge is our main priority,' Pagan replied.

'We go after them if the opportunity presents itself,' I said.

'They're not a priority?' Mudge asked.

'They've got a number of planets and a lot of space they could hide in,' Cat said.

'Vicar seemed to think that there was a good chance they're on

Lalande 2, some place called the Citadel,' I told them. Because its where Satan has his throne, whatever that meant.

'There's maybe a slightly higher chance than good that they are on Lalande 2,' Pagan said. Glyphs shimmered in the air in front of him and a holographic display came to life showing a three-dimensional pictographic representation of a lot of information.

'What's all that?' Mudge asked.

'Its all the info in Limbo,' Pagan said. 'I stole it. It was weird, almost like Sharcroft had forgot he'd employed hackers. And yes, Mudge, if we live then you can have it all. Though I'm going to find a way to get God into their secure network.'

Mudge and I stared at him. Morag was just smiling. I could tell Pagan was pleased with himself but trying to appear nonchalant.

'This is all the information on the Cabal and the Squadrons?' I asked, suddenly feeling a little more optimistic.

'All that wasn't purged,' Pagan said. He brought one file to the fore and seemed to explode it. Text info scrawled down the holographic display, as did a series of architectural schematics that formed a three-dimensional model of what seemed to be a heavily fortified building. It looked a little like a small-scale military arcology.

'That can't be right,' I said. 'It's made of ice.'

'Lalande ice,' Merle said. 'The pressures exerted on it make it very dense. It's harder than reinforced concrete. It's a bitch to cut, even with industrial lasers. That's the Citadel,' he said. Pagan was nodding.

'Chewed out of one of the salt-acid glaciers with microbes. It's in the New Zealand settlement zone of the Twilight Strip, obviously close to Nightside. Despite being in New Zealand territory and despite there officially being no British presence on Lalande, this is a joint Defence Evaluation and Research Agency and CIA Directorate of Science and Technology operation.'

I wasn't sure I was following Pagan.

'So?' Mudge asked.

'It's a Cabal front,' Merle said.

Now we were all looking at him.

'You knew?' Morag asked.

Merle shrugged. 'Just putting the dots together.'

'He's right. According to Sharcroft, the Cabal, which didn't even really seem to think of itself as a conspiracy, preferred to be as decentralised as possible. Most of their meetings were virtual and took place in highly secure sanctums. After the Atlantis base the Citadel was their main facility. It was their largest and it ran Themtech research. In fact it had been doing this before the Atlantis facility because they had wanted somewhere secure and off the beaten track,' Pagan told us.

'It's not that far from Moa City,' Merle said. He was sounding more interested despite himself. 'But that place is hard, man. I mean the security's some of the heaviest I've ever seen. I had some serious clearance but I never got very far inside. If you're going in there then you'd best have a good reason.'

'What sort of research?' I asked. I found myself suddenly angry. I think Pagan realised that.

'Them biotech, maybe some transgenic,' he said. His icon wouldn't meet my eyes.

'Transgenic? Hybridisation?'

He shrugged. 'Yes, on animals.'

'On people?' I demanded. I was angry but not at Pagan. Pagan nodded.

'Does that mean more people like Gregor?' Morag asked. I think she sounded a little afraid.

'Potentially a lot more,' Pagan said. 'But earlier proto-versions.'

'That's reassuring,' Mudge said.

'Don't shoot the messenger,' Pagan said. He was right. 'Besides, I don't think they'll be as formidable as the current iteration. You know, the ones like Rolleston.'

He was also right about that. If they were all like Rolleston then I wasn't even sure how we were going to kill them. There was some muttering.

'We got a reason to go in there?' Merle asked. He was trying to nod at the image of the Citadel but I don't think his icon was co-operating.

'I don't know,' Pagan said. 'There's evidence –' he brought up some more information that looked like computer system schematics '– of an internal sub-system which the truly paranoid could use to hide information and develop plans.'

'So you have to get in and out of that without being noticed and hack an unhackable AI? Seems simple,' Merle said.

'We're going to try and find an easier way.' Pagan sounded a little exasperated.

'We've done really stupid things before,' Mudge said.

'I know. I saw the highlights. Look, it sounds like we could spend a lot of time sitting around waiting for you guys to develop software.'

I shook my head. 'If it's not going our way then we've got a whole list of secondary objectives we can go for depending on the situation on the ground.'

'Under it,' Cat said. Nobody lived on the surface in Lalande.

'Intelligence-gathering, getting the truth out, assassination and sabotage, which is what Sharcroft thinks we're doing,' said Pagan.

'He doesn't know?' I asked.

'About wanting to hack Demiurge? He might guess we want to, but he doesn't know that we may be close to it being a realistic option.'

'He just thinks we'll be causing trouble? Going after their infrastructure?' Merle asked.

'But that means killing a lot of innocent people,' I said, meaning all the people who would quite reasonably have been taken in by the Squadrons' versions of events. I thought back to Vladimir.

'Can't we shoot to wound?' Morag said weakly. The others looked uncomfortable. It wasn't an option and I think she knew it. You shoot someone, especially someone augmented, you had to make sure they were dead or they were just going to get up and shoot you back.

'You'd all best come to terms with killing anyone who gets in our way,' Merle said. 'Otherwise you'll get us killed.'

'We'll do it, but we don't have to like it,' I said.

It was the same as any other human war, I guessed. People who never reached the front line made the decisions and got people like us to go and kill each other.

'If we go after the infrastructure,' Pagan continued, 'the Citadel would be a valid target.'

'Why?' Mudge asked.

'Because if it's a biotech facility it could be used to augment more of the Squadron's people to become like Rolleston,' I told him.

'Hitting that place will not be easy,' Merle said somewhat redundantly.

'Harder than making whipped cream by sitting in a giant bowl of milk with a whisk up your arse?' Mudge asked.

I turned to stare at him, Merle ignored him and Pagan just sighed.

'Also we should try and link with resistance fighters if there are any ...' the ageing hacker said, trying to continue.

'There will be,' Merle said.

'The Black Squadrons will tell them we're the bad guys,' Morag pointed out.

'You don't know these people. I've dealt with the Cabal, though I didn't know it then. The whole reason they do what they do is because they're control freaks. They may control the info but they'll try to push people around. Those people, especially in the New Zealand settled zones, will push back.' What Merle was telling us was thin but it was also the closest thing we'd heard to good news throughout this briefing. 'A lot of this seems to be make-it-up-as-we-go-along-once-we-hit-the-ground.'

'We're jumping blind. Never been in the army?' I asked.

'Marines and air force mainly.'

'Rannu'll tell us more when we meet. Rendezvous with him,' Morag said. I hoped that would happen as well but it sounded naive even to my ears.

'That's pretty risky, Morag,' Cat said. Pagan had set up rendezvous points and times with Rannu. 'It looks like a lot of the initial missions were compromised.'

'Maybe, but Rannu's good,' Morag said, trying to keep the hope out of her voice.

'We check,' I said. We owed him that. *I* owed him that. I'd left Gregor too long. Merle and Cat protested. 'Carefully,' I added.

'You've done a lot of questioning, Cabal-boy,' Mudge said. 'What are you bringing?'

Merle managed to turn his shit icon's head and stare at him for a while. Then the icon smiled. It looked more like a grimace.

'Oh I'm the native guide. I know the land. A large network of contacts, many of whom will have been compromised, some of whom I just can't see co-operating, but if they've been slaved then who knows.'

'That it? Well I'm fucking impressed. Guess you were worth the trouble,' Mudge said dismissively. There was something I was missing in this conversation. I also couldn't work out why Morag was smiling.

'Also Cemetery Wind set up a series of caches all over the Twilight Strip.' Merle tapped his head. 'I know where all the goodies are hidden.' This was our second piece of good news. There was only so much gear we were going to be able to jump with.

'Why are they doing this?' Morag asked. I sensed her naivety was not doing her any favours in Merle's eyes.

'Its just power and greed, same as it ever was,' I said.

'I get that,' she said sharply. 'But that was the Cabal, right? Why does Rolleston suddenly want to be god-emperor of the universe? Doesn't it seem a little ... I don't know, like a viz story or something?'

Actually she had a point. Rolleston had always fitted my idea of the good servant. Suddenly he wanted to be a dictator.

'Maybe it's all on Cronin?' I suggested, now less sure she was being naive.

'I think they really believe that they know better,' Pagan said. 'That the strong have the right to rule. They're true believers, fanatics.'

As he spoke glyphs were appearing and disappearing in front of him as he scrolled though the information on the holographic display.

He found what he was looking for and opened the file. At first it was a lot of scientific-looking stuff, equations and chemical signs, that sort of thing. I was irritated with him. He knew this would mean nothing to us. What was he doing – trying to highlight our ignorance? Then I realised that I was looking at an incomplete, partially corrupted and highly classified personnel file. It was Rolleston's. I looked at his birth date. He was more than ninety years old.

'Fuck,' Mudge said. 'You'd think he'd have got higher than major.'

'If he'd got higher than major then he wouldn't be so hands on. He wouldn't get the chance to fuck people up himself,' I said as I tried to concentrate on the information in front of me.

He had been an exemplary officer in the Royal Marine Commandos and then the SBS. Then even shadier black ops stuff. I could see why the Cabal had chosen him. It seemed like no matter how hard the objective was he got it done, but there was a lot of information missing. Like everything before the marines.

As far as I could tell, though much of it was above my head, his longevity was down to early applications of Themtech. As the Cabal had refined their knowledge of Themtech they had continued to upgrade him. It seemed that he was a test bed for processes they were too frightened to try themselves, like Gregor but not so extensive, at least not initially. In fact Gregor had been the big breakthrough that had resulted in Rolleston's current abilities. Even on Sirius he had been a bioborg.

'Okay, other than the age we pretty much knew all this,' I said.

'No,' Pagan said. 'You're not getting it.' I so enjoyed being told I was stupid. 'For dirty stuff Rolleston was the Cabal's go-to guy.' I winced at the Americanism. 'For the other stuff it was Cronin, who has also been heavily augmented, though I suspect in different ways.'

'We'd assumed as much. So?'

'They were designed for this. Rolleston's designed for conflict resolution, no matter what.'

'So?' I was starting to get irritated with this now.

'Rolleston was designed to be able to run an entire military for the Cabal and Cronin is designed to be a one-man civilian government.'

I still didn't see what he was getting at.

'You mean they're doing this because they're programmed to?' Morag asked.

'A little more complicated and subtle than that, but yes.'

'For masters that don't exist any more?' Mudge asked.

Pagan nodded. 'Yes, but I think it's more that they are programmed to think that they have the right to rule. More importantly, I don't think they think like us any more, or rather they have different parameters for their thoughts.'

'They live in a different world?' Morag asked.

'In a way. I'm guessing that for them there is no other course of action than the one they're on.'

'Which is weird and fucked up but does it help us?' I asked.

'All information helps. We need insight into our enemy, after all. But you're right – I think we've got more pressing matters to worry about.'

Then something occurred to me. 'What about the Grey Lady?'

Pagan shook his head. 'Couple of references but nothing,' he said. I wasn't sure why, but that bothered me more.

We spent the next few hours discussing our hazy objectives, our total lack of useful intelligence and our not being able to plan until we knew more.

'Okay,' I finally said as I slid, a little too comfortably, into my NCO role. 'All prep is done and we are packed and ready to jump by nineteen hundred Zulu on day seven. Yeah?'

'It's an eight-and-a-half-day trip,' Mudge grumbled. He was grumbling because he was supposed to. Soldiers grumbled. Even if he was a journalist, Mudge had a lot to grumble about.

'We're going to get properly drunk on the seventh night,' I said. Pagan groaned and shook his head. Mudge and Morag were grinning. 'Don't worry Pagan. We'll behave, to a degree.' He nodded, knowing it was pointless to argue. 'That gives us day eight to recover and the final half a day to go over everything again and do any final prep,' I finished. It gave us something to look forward to and we didn't know when we'd next have the chance.

A day, an entire day of my life, one I'll never get back, just spraying corrosion-resistant stuff on all our gear. Then Merle checked it and then we sprayed it again. Despite the masks, I would be tasting and smelling it for the next few days. We even got a warning from Nuiko because we were getting close to overloading the atmosphere scrubbers.

I spent most of the time going over all the information that Pagan had stolen. I superimposed it over my sight in my IVD or converted it to audio. The fact was we could prepare and plan as much as we wanted but we wouldn't know what was going on until we hit the ground. The Demiurge-enforced comms blackout was crippling us. Whereas God's open nature was making Earth more vulnerable.

I reviewed the information on Rolleston and what little we had on

Cronin and the Themtech-enhanced soldiers of the Black Squadrons. Much of the biotech stuff went over my head but I couldn't shake the feeling that they'd made themselves aliens. The Black Squadrons had finally managed to become the demons we'd always thought They were.

I thought about what Pagan had said about them thinking differently, though he'd shied away from using the word programmed. Did that make a difference? Were they victims as well? I glanced over to where Morag was spraying her kit. She'd barely spoken to me since we got on board. Even if they were victims you still have choices to make. I didn't like the ones they'd made. I was still going to hate them. It would help me do the job.

The *Tetsuo Chou*, as a chimerical vessel, was a lot more open-plan than most ships I'd been on. It was basically a heavily armoured central compartment where Nuiko lived surrounded by a lot of cargo space. The engine room was down a small corridor separate from the rest of the ship. Nuiko controlled three remotes to do the hands-on work elsewhere in the ship. They were crab-like and reminded me of some of the images Pagan had shown us of ancient Japan. Mudge had described them as samurai robot crabs and being on the ship as like being inside the shell of a giant turtle. Once he'd shown me what a turtle looked like, I had to agree with him.

With human cargo Nuiko had had her servitors add a portable life-support unit to the cargo compartment. All our gear went in and we slept on a series of temporary platforms connected by catwalks that had been set up for the trip. We lived in compartments made of flimsy plastic walls bolted together. The cludgy, or head as it was called on ships, had been installed in the engine room. All and all I'd had worse billets.

Most of the room was taken up by the seed-pod-like OILO cocoons, tanks of acceleration gel and the large parachute rigs we were going to need to counteract Lalande 2's heavy gravity. In many ways using the OILO cocoons for a flight-capable exo-armour drop would have been preferable but we just didn't have the logistical support for long-term operations, particularly in a corrosive environment. So we were doing it the old-fashioned and hard way.

Mudge hadn't been particularly talkative and seemed to be keeping his drug use to more acceptable levels. He was obviously pissed off with me. I decided to speak to him first. I reckoned he'd be the easiest bridge to mend.

I headed along to his makeshift cabin. The only noise was the ring of my combat boots on the metal grid of the walkway and the omnipresent hum of the spaceship's power plant. I'd seen men and woman with too much metal in them driven mad by that constant hum. I'd made friends with the noise a long time ago. After all you couldn't get away from it. Now, as much as I didn't like space travel, I found the noise comforting.

I passed Morag, who was sitting on the edge of a catwalk dangling her legs between gaps in the containers below. She looked as if she was doing nothing but was probably going over something on her IVD. Part of her face was covered in medgel, as was mine. Merle had used a knitter and accelerant on her broken leg and then made a cast out of medgel and connected it to a medpak to drive it. Two days in she was hobbling about. Merle reckoned she'd have most of her mobility by the time we got there. She ignored me as I passed and knocked on the door to Mudge's compartment.

'I think he's going over some stuff with Merle,' Morag said. The sound of her voice surprised me. I glanced down at her but she was looking the other way.

'Thanks,' I said and moved down to Merle's compartment, which wasn't much further on, and knocked. There was no answer.

'They're discussing security protocols and have probably got a white-noise generator up,' she called.

I should have known. She was right: they were very considerately using a white-noise generator – must have been Merle's idea. They were not however discussing security protocols. I walked straight in on the pair of them.

'Motherfucker!' Merle shouted at me.

'Can't you fucking knock, dude!' Mudge protested.

'I'm ... I'm sorry,' I said, not sure what to do.

'Out!' Merle screamed at me. Oh yeah, that's what I was supposed to do. I backed out of Merle's compartment as quickly as I could and closed the door. Morag was lying on the catwalk convulsing with laughter.

'That's childish, Morag.'

She just laughed at me.

'You could probably walk in on Pagan as well,' she said, nodding towards his compartment once she'd managed to control herself.

'Really? With who? Cat?!' I asked as I slowly turned into a teen-aged girl.

Cat and Pagan seemed an odd mix. Then again there had been Jess back in the Avenues. Besides, Morag was talking to me and I wanted it to last as long as it could.

'Don't be fucking stupid,' Cat said from out in the crates somewhere.

She walked forward into the light. She'd obviously been working out. She clearly felt she needed to make her presence known before someone said something she didn't want to hear.

'Who then?' I asked.

Morag looked at me as if I was dumb. 'Nuiko,' she said.

'Wow,' I said.

I don't know why I hadn't thought of that straight away. It was a sense relationship. The technology meant that it would feel virtually the same as the real thing. Given Nuiko's chimerical nature, it meant that Pagan was to all intents and purposes having a relationship with the ship.

'Oh,' I said.

Suddenly I felt very awkward and both Cat and Morag were staring at me. I think I was supposed to be doing something but I had no idea what. I'd killed Berserks in hand-to-hand combat and suddenly I wanted to retreat. With as much dignity as I could manage I headed back to my compartment.

Safe in my room I felt like taking trumpet-based revenge on the rest of them. Also I wanted to practise, but there's only so far you want to push a group of ex-special forces types, not to mention Mudge and Morag. I decided to have a drink instead. I put some music on my internal systems and called up a book on to my IVD.

Mudge turned up about an hour later. The whisky had been a waste as all I could taste was anti-corrosion coating, so I'd got myself a beer instead. It didn't taste much better but it was cheaper.

'Can I get one of those? Assuming my crippling substance-abuse problems won't derail the mission.'

I glared at him but gave him a beer as he sat down somewhat gingerly on the metal grid of the floor. He lit up a cigarette, just to annoy me, and then set up a white-noise generator. It was pretty much the only way we could have a private conversation short of hard-wiring ourselves together.

'That is one angry man,' Mudge said.

'That why you're walking funny? Is this adrenalin fucking?'

'Always.' He raised his bottle to me and took a long drink.

'You realise he thinks you've just come in here to boast to your mates,' I said.

Mudge just smiled and shrugged but then suddenly became more serious. 'Why are you giving me such a hard time?'

'You know what I said about the drugs was for show, right?' He nodded. 'Though they have a point. We could be there for a very long time depending on how long this war goes on.'

'I've never not held up my end and you've got no right to question that,' he said.

This was about as serious as Mudge got. I nodded.

'I know that. But mate, Trace's office. I mean, what the fuck were you thinking?'

'What? The guy was a prick.'

'Morag shouldn't have been able to do that hack. We should be dead, and we would be if she hadn't noticed the wireless link.'

'Look, nothing's changed, man,' he said, but he was looking down. He wouldn't meet my lenses. We can replace our eyes with bits of glass and electronics, but body language seems to be hard-wired in with the original flesh.

'Yes, it has. You seem more ...' I searched for the right word. 'Desperate.'

Mudge shrugged, drank some more beer but still wouldn't look at me. 'Mudge, you're an enormous pain in the arse—'

'You want to talk about pains in the arse?' he said, grinning. I realised I'd chosen the wrong words.

'I mean you're a difficult guy to be friends with sometimes ...' I started. He looked at me, his face getting angry around his camera eyes.

'Fuck you, Jakob, you sanctimonious prick! You think it's easy being your friend? All the fucking whining, hand-wringing, moralising, the fucking sitting in judgement ...'

I leaned back on the bed. I tried not to take what he said personally. There was obviously something he needed to get off his chest and we were in the lashing-out part of the conversation.

'I mean, just try and live a little. It might be a shitty world but try and take what you can from it.' He'd trailed off a bit towards the end and wouldn't look at me again.

'What I like about you is you tell the truth. That's why we didn't double-tap you and leave you in a ditch when we met you. Don't start lying now. Not to yourself.' I took another beer and watched him.

'I don't know,' he finally said. 'I don't know what's up with me.'

'Are you on a suicide trip?' I asked. It took him a long time to answer. If he was I couldn't let him take the rest of us down.

'No more than normal, I think. My body's an amusement park, and risks need to be taken, otherwise we might as well be living in a bubble like those Cabal old boys.'

'Then what?' I asked.

Again he gave this some thought before answering.

'You ever think about the things we've done?' he asked.

'I feel like mostly I'm reacting.'

'I went from reporting in a war zone to patrolling and raiding with you guys to fronting for God on system-wide viz and netcast ...' Once again he trailed off and drank some more beer.

'Okay, put like that it sounds pretty intense, but that's what you wanted, wasn't it?'

He looked up at me again. 'How am I supposed to beat that?' he asked.

'You don't have to,' I said.

More than ever he sounded like a junkie looking for another fix.

'The things I've done, the way I've lived, how am I supposed to go back to a normal life, whatever the fuck that is? I mean, we've done whatever the fuck we wanted.'

That wasn't the way I felt at the time we were doing it.

'You sound like Balor.'

'No, it's different. He wanted to be remembered. He thought he was some ancient hero, or maybe villain. I just want to feel. I need sensation but I think we've upped the game so much that I can't get ...'

'The next fix?'

He looked away.

'Maybe. I don't want to die but life without sensation is death to me.'

I was trying to mask my contempt for this. I'd always known that Mudge was a middle-class thrill-seeker. He wasn't the only one I'd come across when I'd been in the SAS; nearly all the officers were like that to a degree. What I couldn't rationalise in what Mudge was saying was the disparity. This was a guy who was so bored that he did this for fun. The rest of us had to fight all the time just to eat. It was only my knowledge that he was a moral person that kept me speaking to him. That and what he'd said about sitting in judgement.

'You don't fancy the quiet life? Maybe just unwind, take a breather if we survive this?'

'No, and neither do you.'

'You'd be surprised,' I told him.

'See, this is what pisses me off about you. You lie to yourself. You're no different. Your retirement ended with you being beaten up in police custody and where are you now? Right back here with the rest of us. Why? Because you need it. Why do you think Cat got fired and started canyon surfing? Or Merle tried to rob a precious metal freighter in flight? Because there are easier fucking ways for him to make money.'

If he was right, and maybe he was, then my need was buried deep in my subconscious. I thought I wanted the quiet life. On the other hand, the way I'd gone about my Highland idyll was arguably confrontational, and here I was again. For a while now I'd been wondering if there was some deep-down part of me that was highly masochistic.

'So where does that leave us?' I asked him. 'You can't go down onto Lalande just to look for bigger and better thrills, Mudge.'

'Yeah, I know.'

'And Trace's office? That would have been a shitty way for us to die after doing the things we've done. What were you thinking?'

'I don't know that I was. I wanted to see if we could get away with anything. Somehow I knew we'd be all right.'

I didn't like that. I didn't like that at all. Caution was as much a part of these operations as risk, if not more so.

'Look, man, I'll be all right. I'll reign it in. Take the right drugs to calm it down, okay?' I nodded.

Mudge got up, belched loudly and scratched himself before nicking another bottle of beer and leaving my compartment. For the first time ever I found myself unable to trust him.

Still he'd left his white-noise generator, which gave me the chance to practise the trumpet without being assassinated.

By day six we'd almost managed to get rid of the smell of the anti-corrosion treatment. Day six was mostly going over weapons and personal loads that we'd already gone over on Earth. We were just trying to maximise what we took while staying under the weight allowance.

I don't know about the others, but I was becoming tenser as the drop got closer. There were just too many unknowns and the drop was so dangerous that it would be easy to die before we even got planet side. Tempers seemed only a little more frayed. That may have been helped by half of us being loved up. Morag still wasn't talking to me. She seemed a little less hostile, however.

Before we left the Freetown Camp Merle had kicked up a huge fuss about getting his gear back. Cat had brought some stuff for him with us but he'd insisted on getting his own gear back. There had been some violence involved. When he got his stuff I could see why.

Merle was down on the cargo bay cleaning his weapons on top of one of the crates. He was obviously aware of my presence but was ignoring me. All his gear was custom and expensive. Like Cat he had a Void Eagle set up in a Tunnel Rat configuration with the Tunnel Rats' insignia on the handgrip.

He also had a CEC plasma rifle. Most plasma weapons are big and heavy and tend to be used as squad support weapons by military units from countries that can afford to equip their people with them. I didn't like them because they were semi-automatic and, particularly for a support weapon, I preferred something that could lay down a lot of fire, like a railgun. Still their one-shot kill capability was impressive. Similar to the weapon that Rolleston carried, the CEC was only slightly heavier than most standard assault rifles. It was also very expensive.

'Those what I think they are?' I asked, pointing at two ten-millimetre pistols lying next to the Void Eagle. I climbed down from the catwalk to get a better view.

'Twin Hammerli Arbiters. They were our grandpappy's. Cat was pissed when I got them but I was always a better shot. I'm pretty sure he stole them. He certainly took enough lives with them.' He spoke without looking up at me.

The Arbiters were supposed to be the most accurate and were definitely the most expensive fully automatic, production ten-millimetres ever made. I'd never seen one before, let alone two. Their grips were moulded to the shooter's hands and the barrels seemed to slant forward, which was something to do with their recoil compensation.

'Can I handle them?' I asked.

'No,' he said, still not looking up from the somewhat archaic-looking rifle he was cleaning. I was a little put out but could understand why he didn't want anyone touching them. Had they been mine I certainly wouldn't have been parachuting into a corrosive environment with them.

'That's a hunting rifle, isn't it?' Again the rifle looked expensive. Parts of it were made out of wood. It also looked slightly oversized.

'It's a gauss rifle version of an old Mauser customised by Holland & Holland of London,' he said, still not looking up.

'Never heard of them.' I shrugged.

'No, you wouldn't have. I never fancied lugging around one of the bigger rail sniper weapons for accurate work. This nearly matches their range and is more accurate. I can fire it semi-automatic or single shot for accuracy with a secondary electronic reload mechanism.'

'Why?' I may not have liked being in the military, despite what Mudge thought, but we all liked the toys and I was intrigued.

'Because a self-loading system will always knock you off slightly. Obviously its smartlinked but it also has an on-board gyroscope.

I can switch between hyper and subsonic for silent kills and it fires a .465-calibre penetrator round which will put most people and Them on the ground. The wood furniture is cut from Lalande ghostwood, which is very dense, hard-wearing and of course resistant to the corrosion. It's also got a smart trigger.'

'Bullshit,' I said. Smart triggers enabled you to fire a weapon with a thought. They required an awful lot of discipline to avoid negligent discharges and were highly illegal. Still there had always been rumours of them being used by the darker black ops types. Merle held the weapon up. It didn't have a trigger.

'The very action of pulling the trigger can affect your aim. Your Grey Lady's a sniper. She'll have a smart trigger on her weapon, I can almost guarantee it.' I started to ask him something. 'No, you can't handle it. It's probably worth more than all the money you've made in your life. You didn't come here to talk about my guns. What do you want?'

'Well I didn't, but they're still pretty impressive.'

He finally looked up at me. 'Have you come to ask about my intentions regarding Mudge? I'll still kill him if he fucks us up.'

'Fuck that. He can look after himself. How'd you hijack that ship?' I asked. He regarded me impassively just long enough for his strangely intense implant eyes to start making me feel uncomfortable.

'Why?'

'Curiosity.'

'I'm a very private person, your intrusion the other night notwithstanding.'

'Yeah, I get that. You don't like playing with others, do you?'

'Nobody else around, then you've less chance of getting killed over somebody else's stupid shit.'

'Or have someone dragging your arse out of your own stupid shit. But my question?'

'Is it relevant to anything? See, I can't think of a single good reason to tell you.'

'You want and need our trust,' I said.

He leaned back and studied me a bit more closely.

'This a price?' he asked. I shrugged. 'Okay. I had an automated program that I could plug into the ship's systems. It would crack the security and remote-pilot the ship to ... somewhere else.'

So he'd been working with others. That made sense.

'How'd you get in? Because you didn't do it in the camp – the security's far too high for EVA.'

'Maybe if I'd had the best stealth stuff, but yeah, the camp was more trouble than it was worth. Just outside the camp's security perimeter I had another craft match acceleration and trajectory.'

'Okay. Difficult flying but okay. So how'd you get on board?'

'I compressed-gas-squirted ship to ship,' he told me.

'Bollocks.' Space was extremely big; it only needed the slightest variation in speed and he would have missed. The maths alone involved in something like that was staggering. The margins for error were tiny. He shrugged again, giving the impression that he didn't care whether I believed him or not.

'Spacesuit set up for stealth. I had the maths on a program in my internal systems.'

'What distance?'

'Fifteen thousand metres.'

'The slightest miscalculation,' I said. I had absently picked up one of a pair of punch daggers and was toying with it. It looked like it was made from black glass. It had some kind of channel leading to the point of the blade.

'So I didn't miscalculate. Don't touch that; it injects a pretty virulent neural toxin.'

For fuck's sake, I thought, who was this guy? There was no doubt about it – if he played with us then he'd be an asset.

'Are these glass?' I asked.

'Dayside obsidian, volcanic glass from Lalande 2. Sharp as glass but comparable to steel in toughness. Now put it down.'

I put the punch dagger down.

'So how'd you get in?' For obvious reasons airlocks, along with the engine room and then the bridge, tended to be the highest-security areas of a ship. On most military and high-security ships you couldn't access the airlocks externally. I'd only been able to use the airlock on the *Santa Maria* during the mutiny because it was a civilian ship and I had a hacker as good as Vicar backing me up.

'I spent seven hours stuck to the hull of the ship drilling through it. I nearly froze to death. I sent through a modified snake with a lock burner on the end. The lock burner had a pretty sophisticated spoof program added to it. The spoof program was probably the biggest outlay. It told the ship's systems that the airlock was still closed. The snake was flush with the drill hole. I just kept on adding sealant around the crack while feeding it through.'

'You're not supposed to be able to do that,' I said. What he'd just told me had huge ramifications for spacecraft security.

'You guys did it to that star liner back in the twenties, didn't you?' He was right: the SAS had attached a vacuum-proofed cargo module to a sensor blind spot on a hijacked luxury system cruiser and cut through the hull to deal with a group of so-called post-human terrorists. I'd studied it in Hereford while I was training. It was one of the few successful boarding actions in space warfare history. Normally the speeds and distances involved were too great. Ships got destroyed before they were boarded or they surrendered. Surrender hadn't been an option fighting Them.

'Different circumstances. The ship was docked when they attached the container; also ship security was much more rudimentary then.'

'So what? You thinking of robbing a ship?'

'No, I just like knowing how to do things.'

Again he seemed to be studying me. Finally he nodded.

'Yeah, me too. We done bonding?'

I nodded. 'Unless you want to let me play with your guns.'

'Go away. I'm busy.'

The whole trip had been subdued. That happens when people are sure they're going to die. You either get subdued or overcompensate, but even Mudge couldn't be bothered with overcompensation.

On the seventh night we had some drinks and some forced conversation. Bar last-minute checks we were as ready as we were ever going to get. Nobody had wanted to hear me play my trumpet. They backed up their opinions on the matter with threats of violence. I didn't think this was fair. I was sure I was improving.

Mudge confused me by presenting each of us with little animatronic action figures of Major Rolleston, the Grey Lady or Vincent Cronin. I got Rolleston.

'What the fuck's this?' I asked. It was grotesque.

'Voodoo?' Pagan asked, laughing.

'Let's just remember how big these people are, shall we?' Mudge told us. 'This is how the children of Earth look at them, not fucking scary at all.'

'This is weird,' I said. Cat was nodding.

Morag held up her little Grey Lady. 'I don't know. I think I feel some voodoo coming on,' she said.

Pagan couldn't wait to go back to his compartment and trance in with Nuiko, who was with us as a nearly silent holographic ghost whose arms were her crab-like servitors. I wanted her to join us and relax but instead she was the perfect host. She had just as much to lose as the rest of us, except that she would be waiting on her own in the dark. If I was honest with myself, which apparently I didn't like being, then I would have to admit that Nuiko still made me nervous.

220

It wasn't just that I'd never managed to have what I would describe as a conversation with her, but that for some reason she reminded me of the Grey Lady. Maybe it was the quiet. Maybe it was the averted eyes.

I wondered how Pagan had managed to break through the polite and distant reserve that she wore as armour. But time can be made to do strange things in sense environments. Perhaps he'd been courting her for months instead of days. I wished him well but worried about the wrench of having to leave her to go and die. Maybe I should have tried to be a bit more optimistic.

Likewise Mudge was in a hurry to disappear into his compartment with the white-noise generator and Merle. He didn't even get too fucked up, for Mudge. His choice of drug was some low-key euphoric and he only managed a bottle and a half of vodka. He still managed to fall off the catwalk into the crates. I guess appearances have to be maintained.

This left Cat, Morag, so much accompanying awkwardness it seemed to have its own palpable presence in the hold, and myself. Cat sipped from a beer as she peeled the last of the medgel from her wounded back. Occasionally she'd look between Morag and me, smile and shake her head.

Morag didn't say much and still wouldn't meet my eyes. In fact some of the time I think she was having a sub-vocal conversation with someone else. Though I couldn't think who.

'Well, as much fun as this is, I'm going to get some rack time,' Cat announced. I'd no idea why she didn't just say sleep, which would have been more economical. 'Try and keep it down.'

'You too,' I said inanely.

She glanced back at me before disappearing into her compartment. That left Morag. I felt nervous and uncomfortable. I couldn't read Morag's expression.

'I've been talking to God a lot,' Morag said after the silence had stretched on for so long I had considered fleeing back to my compartment.

God, I had forgotten all about him. No, I hadn't. I'd ignored him, pretended I'd had no time because his problems were so big that I could barely understand him. Talking to God had become too complicated, too difficult. Another friend I'd let down. Tried to hide from. Was he even a friend? I'd had a part, however minor, in his creation, his birth.

'How is he?' was the best I could manage.

'He's not good, but then you know that. Worse now since he's met his younger brother. Since Demiurge hurt him, God knows first hand that he wants to commit deicide and hates him. Did you know that? They programmed Demiurge for hate. Why would you do that?' Her tone was flat. No emotion.

I had no answers for her.

'I was thinking about what Pagan said about Cronin and Rolleston being programmed, being malfunctioning tools of the Cabal. Just another weapon in the arsenal,' she continued.

I was lying on the catwalk looking up at the curve of the *Tetsuo Chou*'s hull. I propped myself up and took a swig of Glenmorangie and passed the bottle to Morag. She accepted it, wiped the top of the bottle and took a swig herself.

'They could have designed them for anything. They could have made Rolleston want to protect, to help. They could have made Cronin want to try and make things better for everyone. Surely that would profit everyone in the end? Instead only a few can profit because control is what's important. Instead they program for hate. I just don't get so much suffering for such abstract reasons, and I think we're going to die because of it,' she finished.

I had nothing for her. Nothing I could tell her. When she said that she thought she was going to die I felt cold. I felt something bad happen to my stomach and bile burn the back of my throat. It had been Morag who had thought it was going to be all right going to Maw City.

'I think maybe it's always been that way,' I said. 'Powerful people make decisions and others pay for them. The decisions are either incomprehensible to most people, who just want food, shelter and safety for them and theirs. Mudge reckons it's simpler than that: he thinks it's all lies to justify greed. Or possibly sexual inadequacy.'

There was neither warmth nor humour in her smile. She rolled onto her side, propping herself up on her elbow so she could look at me.

'God, I hate you,' she said. I preferred it when she was shooting at me. 'We are not all right. Things are not good between us, and what you did was fucked up for so many different reasons.'

I couldn't look at her. Even looking away it was like her eyes were burning me. They were judging me. I had been found wanting and couldn't face their glare. I heard her start to cry. I turned back to look at her. Her face crumpled as she let out a dry sob. I sat up as she crawled over to me. I held her so tightly it must have hurt her. I felt her shake with each sob. She bit me, dug her nails into me.

'I promised myself I would be strong,' she finally said, angry with herself. 'It's not me. It's Ambassador. He's so lonely. So far from his people.'

She was carrying the pain for two.

'I'm sorry,' I said.

She looked up at me. 'You bastard!' she spat, so angry again. 'I hate you and I think you're the only thing I have really got out here. You know what I did back in Trace's office ...'

'You saved us, then again with the mech,' I said.

She hit me. She put power into it but it was at an awkward angle; I was still holding her.

'You put me into a corpse, back in the Freetown, that mech driver you made me jack into, you fucker. You put me into a corpse after I'd killed for the first time. I killed and then you made me feel the consequences in a dead man's head.'

I stared at her, appalled. I felt like all the blood was draining from my body, leaving a bag of skin filled with metal and plastic. I'd had no idea.

'And you'd already made it so I couldn't talk to you about it.'

She'd killed on the Atlantis Spoke as well, when she'd hacked their systems and used automated weapons to take out a Walker, but it hadn't been so immediate. She didn't watch the consequences in front of her eyes. She didn't end up wearing their blood, and as a result I don't think she'd faced up to it, and I wasn't going to bring it up.

'This is very fucking touching, but some of us are trying to have sex!' Mudge shouted from his compartment.

Morag's head whipped round at the voice. She looked so angry, searching for someone to blame. I don't know why Mudge and Merle had turned off the white-noise generator but I knew why Mudge had shouted. He wanted us to know that everyone not tranced in would hear us. It was a warning. Moments later Morag understood.

'C'mon,' she said and took my hand. Hers felt tiny surrounded by the composite material of my prosthetics. The tactile sensors offered my nervous system the facsimile of touch as she dragged me towards her compartment.

Inside was dark. Various things were scattered around on the floor, and I'm sure I stood on some of them as she dragged me down to sit on the smartfoam mattress. I switched to lowlight and illuminated her in green as she came towards me with a jack, reaching behind my neck for one of my plugs. I caught her wrist in my hand.

'Are you going to kill me?'

She shook her head but didn't get angry.

'Let go of me now.' I did. 'You don't know me at all, do you? Now we do what I want to do.'

I felt the jack click into my plug. I watched Morag disappear.

I knew this place. It was a jazz club in New York from about a hundred years before the FHC, before the city was flooded. It was called the Cotton Club and at the time booze had been illegal. So of course it flourished. All the greats had played here: Louis Armstrong, Cab Calloway, Duke Ellington, Count Basie, Ella Fitzgerald and Billie Holiday.

The place was subtly lit, filled with smoke. Tables were set around a dance floor in front of the raised stage. More intimate booths were set into the wall. There was a fully stocked bar against the back wall. The place was empty. Like the tea room, even the smell was right. Or at least how I imagined it would have smelled – wood with alcohol soaked into it, tobacco smoke.

'I made this for you. I played down some of the more racist parts of the decor,' Morag said.

I turned at her voice. She was dressed like a flapper. She wore a tasselled dress that came down to just above her knees, some sort of fabric skullcap/hat thing and a string of pearls.

I looked down at myself. I was wearing spats and a linen suit of the era. I even had a hat. Morag would tell me the hat was called a panama.

'When?' I asked.

She looked away from me. In here she – we – could cry.

'After I found out.'

'Why?'

She smiled as she wiped away the tears. 'So you could practise without the others killing you.'

I smiled. 'Can I hold you?'

She did nothing, said nothing for what seemed a very long time, and then she nodded. I moved to her and wrapped my arms around her.

'I'm sorry,' I said to her. 'I've no reason, no excuse; all I've got is that I love you and I won't hurt you again.'

She looked up at me. 'Why are you sorry?' she asked. I opened my mouth to say for cheating and then closed it again.

'I'm sorry I abandoned you,' I told her.

I should have trusted in her, been in this from the start. She nodded and pushed me away.

'People – men – have hurt me before, I mean physically. I'm used to it. Is this what you want? Because we can do it in here. It's okay in here. It's not real.'

I looked at her in horror. She held her arms out away from her body and suddenly she was drenched in blood. I stumbled away from her, horrified. I bumped into a chair and fell back onto the floor. I wanted to vomit.

'No, Morag, please!'

I wanted the image gone. It felt like a horrible warning from the future, the sum result of Morag's association with me. Her bloodied visage walked towards me and I recoiled from her. I didn't think she was really offering this. I wanted to think it was a lesson, but maybe it was revenge. My back hit the wall and I curled up and closed my eyes.

'It's all right.'

I felt hands caress my face but it really wasn't okay. I opened my eyes and she was kneeling over me unbloodied. I was weeping. The tears felt wet and real on my skin. They were a release, a relief.

'I don't think I can do this,' I said.

I watched her face harden as anger swept across it like a storm.

'Are you going to leave me again?' Through gritted teeth.

'No, never. It's just that I can't take you into these places, see you hurt, get you killed. I'll get everyone killed worrying about you. I don't care. I don't care if they win, if we live in some dictatorship; I just want you to be safe,' I told her, still weeping.

Her face softened. 'You know how selfish that is, don't you?'

I nodded through the tears. 'What are we going to do?' The desperation in my voice shocked me.

She sat down cross-legged next to me. She didn't hold me. I felt like a child. She stroked my hair.

'I think the Cabal knew that Operation Spiral wasn't going to work,' she said. I stared at her incredulously. She wanted to talk about this now? She ignored my look. 'I think they knew it was going to kill or drive mad everyone involved, but they needed some research data so they made a human sacrifice for the knowledge they wanted. Maybe the information was spiralling around Vicar's or some of the others' heads.' I started to say something but fingers brushed against my lips to silence me. 'It was in the files in Limbo. Somehow they hadn't made the connection. Elspeth McGrath. She either died then in Their minds or she was unfortunate enough to spend time in an ongoing psychotic episode, trying to destroy herself while they opened up her mind as a sense simulation so they could better look for the information they needed. I was the lucky one. I was pretty.' I looked at

225

her, horrified. She looked back at me, straight in the eyes. 'I wonder what you were doing when I found that out?'

I couldn't speak for a while. Despite the artifice all the moisture had gone from my mouth.

'Revenge?' I finally croaked.

Another smile devoid of humour.

'No, I don't want to hurt them. I don't care. We just have to do what we can to make things better.' The steely resolve that I'd first noticed back in Dundee was there.

'Why? You don't owe the world a fucking thing.'

She looked down at me. I think I saw pity in her eyes then.

'But that means you doing your job. Do you understand me?' I nodded weakly. 'No, I don't think you do. Jakob, I love you as much as I hate you right now, and I think the hate will die, but if you put us at risk – if you don't do your end – then you need to know I'm a witch. I'll tear your mind out, imprison you in an electronic hell and leave you a mindless husk. Do you understand me now?'

I once went into vacuum unprotected. I wasn't as afraid then as I was now. She was looking straight into my eyes. I wanted to turn away. She turned away first.

'Because I need you and I'm frightened of dying,' she said.

I tried swallowing but it wasn't really happening. 'Can you promise me something?' I eventually managed to say.

I flinched away from her look of fury. 'I don't owe you a thing!' she spat at me.

I nodded, trying to placate her. 'I know, I know, but please, I need it. Morag, I'm not as strong or as honest as you. I need this, I need it to do what you ask.' I had nothing but contempt for the person saying this. I heard the weakness and the betrayal that weakness implied in my voice. She'd had more than enough and I needed more. I felt like a parasite.

'What?' she demanded.

'If we get through this, if somehow we live and we're not slaves, then we stop. We make our deal with whatever gods, but we don't do any more of this dangerous stupid shit. We settle down, we find other ways to help that don't involve guns and violence. Please promise me.'

I needed this more than I'd ever needed the escape of the booths, the whisky and whatever other crutches I'd relied on in my hollow empty life. It made me realise how little I'd had in my life.

She nodded. She was crying, though somehow she was smiling as well. She reached down to hold me. She held me for a long time.

When she was ready she kissed me fiercely. We didn't make love – that needed trust – we had sex, and she told me that was all right because in here it wasn't really real.

Later as she seemed to sleep, though I wasn't sure what that meant in here, I practised the trumpet. I had used the sense environment's parameters to make the instrument quiet and soft so as not to wake her.

I sat on a chair on the wooden boards of the stage and looked around the club. Smoke and dust eddied in pale beams of light. Our fantasies may have less jagged parts than real life, but we worked hard at them to make them as real as possible. I sometimes wondered if we locked ourselves in prisons of our own entertainment because it was easier than trying to do something, anything. Was this how the Cabal had got us in the first place?

I was going to have to find a place far, far away from the rest of my thoughts to put all this – the hope of some kind of life and the fear of what could happen to Morag. For once, I thought as I played, I needed to not let Morag down. I had to be what she needed. I also needed to try and live for myself.

I finished a slow bluesy piece and looked up. She was awake and watching me. I couldn't read her expression.

The sex may not have been real, but when we jacked out of the sense simulation she lay in my arms and I held her as she slept. Through the fabric of her T-shirt I could feel the metal of the spinal supports that violated her flesh. They may have been temporary but to me they felt like another little bit of her humanity lost to metal.

I couldn't sleep. I opened up my internal comms and requested a link.

'God?'

'Yes, Jakob.'

'I'm sorry.'

'I know, Jakob.'

'You'll tell the rest of you.'

'Of course, Jakob.'

We made God. More to the point we made God tell the truth, and now we spent all our time hiding from him.

11
Lalande 2

This was a stupid way to die. I should have accepted Mudge's offer of drugs.

Nuiko had shown us the star. Lalande 21185 was small, about half the size of our sun, and despite its red colour there was something dead-looking about it. It was like a ghost sun burning weakly. Lalande 2, however, was very large and looked like a black planet with a corona of heat perpetually on its horizon. It was partially eclipsing the star.

Nuiko had triggered a heavy burn as close as she dared to Lalande 2. Systems are nearly impossible to defend because space is big. Planets are much easier to blockade. That was the second most dangerous part of her job. She had to bleed off any residual heat and get the signature of the *Tetsuo Chou* down as low as possible as we approached what we assumed would be the planetary defences. We were flying blind to an extent and active scans would be suicide. We assumed the planetary defences would take the form of automated sensor and weapons satellites as well as elements of the Lalande fleet. We were hoping that the Orbital Insertion Low Opening pods, if detected – most likely during entry – would be thought of as meteorites. If not then we wouldn't know much. We'd just cease to exist when the orbital weapons hit us.

The most dangerous part of her job would come when she had to open the cargo airlock and have her remotes throw us out. This would mess with the stealth signature of the ship and make her more susceptible to detection.

Exiting the *Tetsuo Chou* was going to be the trickiest part for us as well. Not that there was anything that we could do about it in our cocoons of heat-resistant foam and acceleration-resistant gel. It wasn't just a case of being thrown out of a spaceship; we had to be pushed out at just the right velocity and just the right angle for entry. The maths involved was pretty heady. A mistake and we could burn up on entry or bounce, which would send us skimming over the atmosphere to end up in a low orbit until we ran out of air.

I'd done my fair share of parachute drops, though mostly we were inserted by assault shuttle, gunship or more rarely copters. I had done HALO jumps, mainly out of the back of assault shuttles, but I'd only ever done two OILOs before this and I hadn't enjoyed them. Wrapped in the scan-absorbent and heat-resistant foam and surrounded by the gel designed to help you cope with the G forces, I could never shake the feeling I was the yolk of an egg being thrown at a stone in a fire.

The G force slammed into me. It was like someone massaging me vigorously with sledgehammers. Unfortunately it wasn't quite enough to cause me to black out. I was panicking, which was irrelevant, as I couldn't move. In the unlikely event I survived, I just wouldn't tell anyone. I didn't even manage to scream as I entered the atmosphere. It was like hitting a solid wall. I had a moment to think my spine had broken and then, finally, I mercifully blacked out.

I knew I was dead when I came to. Beyond the faceplate of my environment suit I could see the gel bubbling. I was pretty sure that wasn't supposed to be happening. I was covered in sweat. This was the hottest I'd ever felt. I'd felt cooler when I'd been set on fire in Dundee. We'd fucked up. A stupid, stupid way to die. I should have just put the Mastodon to my temple and saved myself the pain. I'd seen people burn to death. At least that way it would be quick.

When I saw the cocoon burning away and the gel start to drain out I knew it was all over. Prat that I am, I didn't pay any attention to the altimeter readout on my IVD. I had a jack from the parachute rig plugged into a port on the environment suit, which was in turn jacked into one of the plugs in the back of my neck.

Then the cocoon was gone. The chemical catalyst had started to dissolve the material of the cocoon as soon as we'd hit the atmosphere. I was falling far too fast. I understood everything in terms of flashes of dark ground, fast-moving cloud, a horizon of red light and then the stars again. Occasionally I could see other figures falling like I was.

I had to stop tumbling. Anger replaced panic as I desperately tried to remember my parachute training. I was supposed to be good at this. This is what we'd been trained for.

I managed to steady myself and get into the star position. I was free-falling looking down at shallow contours of dark rock and a storm front sweeping rapidly over them.

I felt heavy, like a lead weight, and all my movements seemed slow. The ground was coming up too fast. The urge was there to open the chute but I resisted it. Low opening, particularly with these scan-transparent stealth chutes, would minimise our chances of being detected. It would also give the corrosive storms that racked Lalande 2's barren surface less opportunity to kick us around and less time to eat away at our chutes. Still it seemed like I was falling far too fast.

The ground disappeared as black cloud swept across it at a frightening speed. I had time to glance around and count four other people falling through the alien sky reasonably near before the cloud engulfed me. Then I was falling blind. Relying on the altimeter readout on my IVD. The number on the readout was counting down too rapidly for my taste.

Two thousand metres came and went so quickly I only just had time to pull the chute at fifteen hundred. A moment of fear as the upward yank didn't feel as pronounced as I was used to but information from the interface showed that everything was okay. I glanced up, hoping to see a fully deployed canopy, but the thick cloud obscured it. Then the storm really started to knock me around.

Pagan and Merle were old hands at this; Cat had a little less jump experience than me; but Morag and Mudge had to rely on skillsofts and training simulations. It felt like I had to rely on every bit of training and experience that I could remember and fight the chute all the way down, using the interface and the chute's on-board intelligent systems just to make sure I was mostly pointing down and not getting tangled. Fuck knows where I was going to land. At least I was moving at a speed I felt more comfortable with, but I still felt heavy and sluggish.

Out of the clouds and I could see narrow corrosion canyons in the dark scarred landscape, the horizon obscured by violently swirling cloud. Both the chute and myself were still wrestling with the wind. I was receiving warning icons from the environment suit's temperature sensors. We were too deep in Nightside. There would have been ice below us if there had been any surface moisture.

I glanced up above me at the enormous canopy of the chute. Its translucence made it difficult to pick out against the backdrop of permanent night. I looked around and could make out another four parachutists and was pleasantly surprised to see one of the cylindrical drop containers had managed to track us. We had dropped six in the hope that one might stay with us. Because we couldn't transmit without opening up comms systems to Demiurge, each cylinder chute's intelligent system had been rigged up to a lens designed to track other parachutes by sight. Each of the containers had a timed explosive charge. If we didn't get to them very quickly then the container and its contents would be destroyed.

I wondered who the missing parachutist was. We were all steering our chute rigs closer together now and closer to the container, all fighting the wind. It didn't feel like the controlled graceful drop of parachuting; it felt like the ground was trying to suck me towards it. Every movement of my lead-like limbs was a painful exertion.

I hit the ground hard and got dragged along it for a while. The rock seemed to radiate cold despite the environment suit's internal heater. Fortunately I had the presence of mind to trigger the chemical catalyst that would dissolve the chute before I hit the quick releases. Then I tried to get up.

I was used to carrying a lot of gear for extended periods in the field. I had the artificially boosted strength and stamina to manage it, and I had the fitness. Or rather I'd had the fitness. I'd done the maths and reduced my load by what I'd thought was enough to counteract the effect of 1.5 G. The problem was, it had been a long time since I'd carried a full infantry load. Arguably I'd been abusing myself somewhat since then as well. I couldn't get up.

I resisted the urge to laugh hysterically at myself. I had this image of me lying there until the corrosive wind eroded me away. It felt like a massive weight was pushing me into the cold rock. Christ, if I felt like this how were Morag and Mudge coping? They didn't have military-grade enhancements. Actually I knew how Mudge would be coping – with performance-enhancing narcotic alchemy. Again it occurred to me I'd been a fool to turn his offer of drugs down.

It was anger that finally got me to my feet. Well that and a purely medicinal stimulant from my internal drugs reservoir. Standing up felt like powerlifting. I really didn't want to fall over again. I had no idea how I was going to operate in this place for a prolonged period of time. I felt like I was carrying someone my own weight around my shoulders.

My Heckler & Koch Squad Automatic Weapon was secured tightly across my chest. I loosened the strap and made the weapon ready. My IVD lit up with new information fed to my smartlink through the palm receiver on my environment suit. Time to pretend to be a soldier again.

I staggered through the high wind over acid-smooth rock to the closest parachutist. It was Pagan. I was glad to see he was on his feet. He signalled towards the container. Both of us made our way there. The other three visible parachutists were doing likewise. Everyone was struggling against the wind.

Morag had disarmed the explosives on the container. Cat was there, her Bofors railgun at the ready. Mudge as well. Merle was missing.

Brilliant, our native guide. The problem was we couldn't use GPS because it would give away our position and allow Demiurge a way into our systems. We had detailed maps stored in our internal systems memories but they didn't tell us where we were initially and all of Nightside looked the same. There didn't seem to be any particularly geographical features.

The parachute signal flare was a welcome if brief sight as the wind pulled it away almost immediately. I guessed that Merle had determined that there was nobody on the surface nearby before firing it. Unless it was a trap. We picked up the container and headed for where the flare had been fired.

I have to admit I hadn't wanted to help with the container. In fact I would have been quite pleased to blow it up. Already all my muscles ached, but we didn't know when we were going to get a chance to re-supply. We also didn't know if Merle's caches had been compromised since he'd last been in-country. Pagan, Cat and Mudge had the other corners. This meant that Morag was on point. I would have preferred someone with more experience but she just simply didn't have the enhancements to help with the cylinder. I was pretty impressed she was still moving, albeit with difficulty, carrying all the gear she was. Fucking Merle.

I've done some miserable fucking tabs in my life. The Brecon Beacons had been a piece of piss after growing up in the Highlands. Wading in full load through the mud and the constant driving rain of Sirius had been pretty shit. However this tab was just a long streak of misery. Merle had said that given time we'd acclimatise; Cat had said that acclimatisation was not the same as getting used to it. That security job that Calum had mentioned was starting to look very attractive now.

It was Pagan who folded first. To his credit I was at the point where everything was screaming in agony and I was taking life one deeply, fucking painful step at a time. Still I'd thought it would be Mudge. More and more I was respecting his better-living-through-chemistry ethos. Pagan stumbled and fell and nearly took us all down with him. We put the container down. I didn't have the energy to help him up. I wasn't sure I could bring myself to pick the container up again. Inside the environmental suit I was soaked through to my inertial armour with sweat.

Morag slung her laser carbine and managed to help Pagan up. She signalled for him to take point. Then she moved to his position on the container. I signalled negative. She ignored me. I was for leaving the container there but we picked it up again.

So far I wasn't enjoying this planet. I was even starting to miss Dog 4's mud.

Merle lit up a hand-held signalling flare to guide us in. I wasn't sure how long we'd been walking. It had seemed like a very long, painful time. We were getting closer to the Twilight Strip, the habitable zone between the burn of Dayside and the cold of Nightside.

We were starting to see scrubby worm-like tubular plants, their roots burrowing into the corrosion-smoothed rock canyons. There they were sheltered from the worst effects of the wind. Merle had briefed us that these plants were a symbiotic species that lived on infrared radiation from the small red sun and bacteria that fed on the hydrogen sulphide present in the atmosphere.

We got to Merle as he was tucking the used flare back into his webbing. He pointed down into a small cave opening and then relieved Mudge on the container. Pagan took point with Mudge bringing up our rear as we headed into the cave mouth. Just before we left the surface I caught a glimpse of Lalande over the horizon. It looked red, huge and close, somehow hellish.

I wasn't sure whether it was a natural tunnel that we followed down into the rock, but it was smooth, somehow organic. It looked like blackened bone in the light from our helmet-mounted lamps and the torches clipped to Mudge and Pagan's weapons.

We seemed to be heading towards black light, an ultraviolet light source. We stopped and waited while Pagan scouted ahead. After what seemed like a very long time he came back and gestured us forward. Even through the anonymity of an environment suit I could see that he was ready to drop from fatigue. We needed to rest soon but the surface hadn't been the place to do it.

I was working on automatic now as I picked up that fucking container again and we headed down.

I wasn't sure what I was expecting, but despite the briefings and vizzes I still wasn't prepared for the sheer scale of the cavern. We were huddled in a tunnel mouth in the ceiling of a chamber looking down at a two-mile drop. The cavern floor was a dense carpet of genetically modified fern and what looked like giant spider plants. There were also ghostwood trees – wide but low and stunted, radiating out like ancient wagon wheels – genetically modified versions of the kauri tree indigenous to New Zealand. In the high-G environment they produced dense wood that was incredibly strong but difficult to cut and work. They were grown from seeds imported from Earth and had been designed to help with the terraforming process. The huge

UV strip lights that ran across the cavern ceiling provided the plants with energy and bathed the whole chamber in the visible violet light from that part of the spectrum.

Acidic salt-ice glaciers had crawled through the belly of this planet like worms aeons ago. As they receded back into Nightside, subject to the vagaries of the planet's unpredictable geothermal activity, they had left in their wake smooth caverns like this that went on as far as the eye could see.

The walls of the cavern were smooth and again reminded me of weather-eroded bone, but down here the clearly defined different rock strata were multihued and showed in stripes. However, the walls and much of the visible floor of the cavern showed extensive damage. The rock had been scored, burned and heavily cratered. Large areas of the genetically modified plant life had been trampled and ripped up – I assumed by fighting and the movement of large bodies of human and presumably Their troops. Parts of the rock were deformed where plasma strikes had made it run like lava before it had cooled and solidified.

Despite the war damage and the artificial violet light giving it an unreal feeling, like a London art club, the cavern was strangely beautiful. Or at least that was what I thought until I took my helmet off. The environment suit's sensors had advised me that it was okay to try the air. They fucking lied. I could breathe, if you could call it that, but the atmosphere was greasy, acrid. It smelled of rotten eggs and every breath tasted like licking a battery.

I was covered in sweat from head to foot and steamed in the frigid but manageably cold air. The others were removing their helmets as well. All of us were gasping for breath, which, filter or no filter, was making our lungs burn.

We all looked different now. Just before the drop we'd injected our faces with a morphing compound that allowed us to change the look of our features to a degree. We were heading into what we expected to be a near-total-surveillance environment and needed to avoid being identified by the sophisticated facial feature recognition software that Demiurge was bound to be using.

The others all looked like themselves only slightly skewed. We'd also made other cosmetic changes. Changed hair colours, changed hairstyles where possible. Mudge didn't look right with brown hair and he was going to have to wear glasses all the time to cover his camera lens eyes. I'd thought Pagan was going to cry when he'd cut off his ginger dreadlocks.

'I'm sorry,' Pagan said to everyone, shaking his head. I could hear the misery in the aging hacker's voice at letting us down. He looked awful.

'Don't worry about it, that was a miserable fucking tab,' I heard a bone-tired me say to him.

Merle ran his hand through the stubble on his skull. He'd shaved it to get rid of the mess of hair he'd grown in captivity. He looked more like his sister than ever now.

'We need food, rest and a brew-up.' I'd said it to everyone but I wanted Merle's opinion.

'We need to be careful. We're near one of the processors. They're heavily guarded. A lot of the fighting went on around them during the war. They have remote and manned aerial patrols so we can't stay here too long, and I don't know what a brew-up is.'

'A cup of tea. You're American – you wouldn't understand,' a panting, sweat-soaked Mudge said.

'What's not to understand about a cup of tea?' Merle asked.

'For your lot, how to bloody make one,' Mudge answered.

Everyone from Britain who'd ever had an American-made cup of tea was smiling. Even Pagan managed a weak grin. I think Merle had understood his job as straight man. That was promising.

It wasn't a proper brew-up in a mess tin over a camp stove. I wasn't sure I wanted to risk that in this atmosphere. It'd taste bloody awful. Instead we had cans of self-warming sweet tea – it wasn't the same – and some energy bars.

Merle was rigging the climbing gear, though each of us would check it before we used it. I wasn't sure where he was getting the energy. Particularly as up until less than two weeks ago he'd been living in a hole in the ground with a French name.

'I *love* the atmosphere,' Mudge said, hawking and spitting. 'Nope, no better. I don't even want a cigarette. This is a deeply depressing world.'

'It's what it does to my hair that bothers me the most,' Cat surprised me by saying.

'I could see how that would get to you,' Mudge said.

Merle smiled as he drove another piton into a seam in the rock. The crack echoed out into the huge cavern. We paused and scanned the cavern for movement. We waited and waited. Nothing.

'What, you think I was born bald?' Cat said as if the conversation had never been interrupted.

Morag looked horrified. 'It's just grown back,' she said, fingering her lank and sweaty hair.

'It's all right, honey. I shaved it because it kept on going frizzy; it didn't fall out.'

Morag looked relieved. Pagan and Mudge were smiling and shaking their heads.

'See, this was why I didn't join the army,' Merle said dryly.

'Too worried about their hair?' I asked.

Despite the banter we were constantly scanning our surroundings and taking it in turns to eat and drink; the rest of the time we had weapons in our hands. We needed the banter after that walk.

'The air force have better stylists,' Cat said.

I smiled at this. Now time to spoil everyone's fun.

'Okay, everyone pack up the E-suits and shove your camo on.'

By camo I meant reactive camouflage. They were like gillie suits made of a rugged liquid-crystal thinscreen that adapted to and blended with the surroundings. One of the benefits of a near-bottomless expense account. Well that and the amount that each of us had embezzled. We took it in turns to get out of the E-suits, breaking them down and packing them away. More weight to carry but we didn't know when we'd need them again. Then we shrugged on the reactive camouflage over whatever armour we were wearing.

Each of us was carrying five hundred metres of photoreceptive smart rope. Merle was taking the end of each of the pieces of rope and chemically bonding them together. He was then checking them, then Cat was rechecking them and then I did the same.

'Is this enough?' I asked.

Merle shrugged in a not very comforting manner. He took the winch frame and mechanism from the drop container and started fitting it together. I headed around to the other side of the hole in the cavern floor to aid him. The rest were watching our backs. We wrapped the container in a reactive camouflage suit and swung it out over the hole. The engine whined quietly as the winch mechanism slowly started feeding in the rope we'd coiled on the floor. Merle guided it through to make sure it didn't snarl up. Now Cat and myself were covering the hole in case anything happened. In theory it was moving so slowly that the camouflage sheet and the properties of the rope should render it almost invisible.

It took a long time. We'd fed over a thousand metres of rope through when we heard it. An engine. The so-familiar sound of a gunship had once been a comforting sound to me. Not now.

Merle slowed the winch, bringing it to as gentle a stop as he could manage. I could still see the rope swinging from the winch. Cat and I backed a little further away from the edge of the hole. Merle took something from his webbing and unfolded it. Super-spy had brought a hand-held periscope. He lay down on the rock floor and peered through it into the cavern.

Nobody said anything. The acoustics of the cavern were doing odd things. The engine noise seemed to get very loud and then recede. The echoing didn't help. I was sweating again. Not so much from the exertion this time; I was suddenly overwhelmed with fear that the gunship would fly into the rope or the container. This was ridiculous. It was a huge cavern and a very thin rope. Eventually we heard the sound of the gunship's engines definitely receding and Merle folded away his periscope.

'Patrol,' he said. 'Would have been here longer if they were changing shift at the atmosphere processor.' I nodded. He started the winch again. Some minutes later I saw the rope develop a bit of slack. 'Well it's long enough,' Merle said.

We quickly disassembled the winch and packed it into Merle's gear. He was first over. He just slithered over the edge head first. We watched the rope quiver as he slowly rappelled down it. After an age we saw it twitch. You had to be paying attention because the rope was now the same colour as the background rock.

Morag was next. That seemed to take longer. I had a brief thrill of terror as I watched her creep out over the precipice, but already the camouflage was obscuring her, turning her into fractal ghost movements in the violet light.

Then I went. The awful feeling of vertigo as I slipped over the edge head first, the sudden change in perspective, the shifting of the cavern floor and the sudden appearance of the cavern roof above me. I quickly suppressed the terror as I concentrated on rappelling down the rope slow enough for the reactive camouflage to work, using my legs to keep my inverted body straight. Down through the massive rigs that supported the UV strip lights. It was disconcerting because the rope seemed to disappear just below my grip and I was struggling to see my own hands. I had to rely on my sense of touch, dulled by gloves and inertial armour. The sound of my rasping breath was loud in my ears. Very quickly I was exhausted. I was so heavy and all the weight just wanted to pull me towards the distant ground.

All this rock. I wondered if Cat had gone to the Grand Canyon to remind herself of this place. Why would she want to be reminded? The mind does strange things to veterans. You don't think you'll miss these places but, like Mudge had pointed out, few experiences in your life ever live up to being that intense.

Looking back up I could see what looked like an enormous fan with an equally enormous filter beneath it. Around the edge of this giant piece of engineering I could see a system of catwalks with automated weapons at regular intervals. Fortified buildings hung from the cavern roof plus a landing pad that looked like it could take anything up to a transport shuttle. This was one of the atmosphere processors that helped make the air in the cavern system manageable. I didn't want to call the air breathable. I continued pulling myself down. In terms of mega-scale engineering I guess the only things comparable were orbital stations and the Spokes. There were bigger ships, but we never saw the outside of them up close.

I was less than halfway down when I heard it. The ground still looked distant but seemed to be pulling me towards it. My enhanced hearing picked up the distant noise echoing from a connecting tunnel. The noise was deeper, signifying a much bigger vectored-thrust vehicle. I froze on the rope. I felt like a spider.

It was a heavy-lift military transport. It looked like a flying chunk of armour, a weapons platform with cargo space. It circled close enough to me that I was buffeted, bouncing up and down on the rope, making the reactive camouflage work harder. Close enough that I could look down gun barrels, count missiles and see the jacked-in pilot's helmeted head. I didn't have much of a contingency plan for compromise here other than to drop down as quickly as I could.

The buffeting from the transport lifted me high up on the rope and then dropped me hard. I tried not to cry out as the rope bounced. I lost grip with my legs and spun, the rope sliding through my hands. I felt utterly helpless, praying the camouflage was still concealing me. I heard the whine of more power added to engines as the ugly military vehicle rose, heading towards the landing pad next to the processor.

My back was screaming at me. Despite the supporting clamp and my own enhancements the impact in the high G had really hurt. Slowly I managed to recover and begin pulling myself down again as I responded to warnings in my IVD by dampening the pain with a small dose of painkiller from my internal reservoir. I wanted to use it sparingly. This planet was starting to seem like pain. What was worse, my skin was beginning to burn in the UV. None of us had thought to bring sunblock.

It was either a supply delivery or a guard change. I was still on the rope when the transport left and had to remain still again, but it didn't come so close this time and the buffeting wasn't so bad.

The canopy of giant ferns felt so cool when I got under it. Rolling over to land gently on my feet, Merle and Morag were nowhere in sight. I unclipped myself and brought the SAW up ready. There was a quiet whistle. I responded and part of the surrounding flora came to life. Merle gestured to me, images of the surrounding jungle seemed to slide off him as he did so, showing me where Morag was. I indicated where I was going and moved into position after shaking the rope, signalling for Mudge to follow.

Waiting beneath the fern canopy in violet light was the closest to a pleasurable experience I'd had since we'd got here. Perhaps it was the presence of the plants, but the air didn't seemed quite so bad.

There had been another moment when an airborne combat remote had flown by as Cat had been coming down. She had remained still and the reactive camouflage had done its work. As had the heat-masking properties of our inertial armour suits. They were designed to dampen our IR signatures and make us more difficult to spot using thermographics.

When Cat was down Merle had touched the rope with the control wand. Normally we would have used our internal comms to transmit the command codes but we intended to remain comms dark our entire stay. No transmissions. In the cave in the roof of the cavern nearly two miles above us, the rope untied itself. We then kept well back as three thousand metres of it fell towards us. This made more noise than I was happy with, but we needed the rope and there was only so much we could carry.

Then it was time for another long tab carrying that fucking container. We went deeper into the stone guts of the planet. It got colder and the air stank more, burning the backs of our throats as we headed towards one of Merle's Cemetery Wind caches. We travelled in the dark. Our lowlight optics powered by an internal light source let us see where we were going. It also made everything look green. Most of the time we walked, taking it in turns to carry the container while someone took point and the rear. Other times we were forced to climb. All the while a tremendous weight bore down on us. We stopped periodically to rest and eat. Nobody said much. Everyone was too tired.

Merle and Pagan, who I think was trying to prove something to us, scouted the cache position before coming back for us. We left the container and moved forward stealthily, ready for trouble and grateful that we found none.

It was just another small cave. The entrance had been camouflaged by the simple expedient of painting a sheet of material to look like the rest of the rock. The place was full of supplies and something even better.

'I'm not in the military so forgive me if I don't get the strategic reason we humped that fucking container about when there's all these supplies here,' Mudge said, sounding genuinely pissed off.

'We didn't know if it would still be here or if it had been compromised,' Merle told him.

'Mudge, Morag, I want one of you on the entrance and the other a little further out. Okay?' I said. 'The rest of us are going to do a sweep in here then sort out what we need.' There was some muttering from Mudge but he nodded.

'But the shiny cars?' Morag protested. She was referring to the four Fast Attack Vehicles.

'You can look at them later,' I told her.

Grudgingly she joined Mudge, making for the entrance. I could understand her interest. They were a welcome sight and had long been the envy of most third-world soldiers like myself. They looked like a bizarre hybrid of performance sports car, old-style dune buggy and tank. With an independently driven four-wheel-drive combat chassis powered by a well-protected hydrogen power plant in the rear of the vehicle, the FAVs were heavily armoured, hermetically sealed and designed for stealth operations. This put them out of reach of all but equatorial special forces units – and apparently Cemetery Wind. The power plant's cracker could remove hydrogen from water to power it. This meant if you had a ready supply of water the vehicle's range was only limited by wear and tear. They made the Land Rovers we'd used on Dog 4 look like go-karts.

These ones had been modified for Lalande 2. The independent suspension had been reinforced and the tyres were made from intelligent smartfoam. This, along with twin front and back winches linked to grapples, gave them a limited climbing capability. They would cling to rock, and what they couldn't cling to they could use the winches to get over.

We swept the cave thoroughly and then Pagan and I ran diagnostics on the FAVs. Cat and Merle cherry-picked what we wanted from the supplies. Merle assured us that it would be fine to take the quiet-running FAVs as long as we stuck to the deeper tunnels away from habitation.

We were still moving in the darkness using lowlight. There was a generator and lights here but we'd decided against them. It was like living in a permanent green twilight. I gathered Pagan, Cat and Merle around me.

'You find any surveillance?' I asked Pagan.

'If it's here then I can't see it.'

His answer did not fill me with confidence.

'There's nothing active here,' Merle said.

I wasn't sure I liked that either.

'When's our next scheduled RV with Rannu?' I asked Pagan.

'Twenty-three hours,' he said.

Day or night was meaningless under all this rock. Our bodies were going to find their own clocks. Pagan was hard-wired into a monitor and he showed us the rendezvous point on it.

'Okay, that's about twenty miles south and maybe three below Moa City. Good choice – there's nothing there,' Merle told us. 'There's so much tunnel down here, they would tie up all their manpower just trying to patrol a small part of it. They'll keep their people close to strategic locations.'

'I agree,' Pagan said. 'Our biggest risk is going to be remotes.'

'Risk the FAVs?' I asked. I tried not to sound hopeful. Cat and Merle nodded. I think everyone was relieved, I knew I was. 'Okay, we take what we need and we do it quickly. We find a place to camp and stay there for fifteen hours. That'll give us more than enough time to get to the RV point and hopefully we can find out what's going on.'

Merle raised his eyebrows. Fifteen hours was a long time, but if the others felt anything like me then they needed the rest.

'We camp up and get our heads down. Two on, four off – four-hour shifts. Cat and Merle, you get the middle shift, and yes, I am picking on you,' I said.

Merle nodded; Cat gave me the finger. It meant a broken night's sleep but it made sense. Cat and Merle were most used to the environment.

This was how it was going to be from here on in: always on guard, always on edge. Sleeping when we could. No respite for as far into the future as I could see.

Morag drove. The conversation had gone like this:

'I'll drive.' I'd told her no. 'What, you think I'll be able to run the weapons better than you?' She'd had a point. She'd driven.

The drive hadn't felt right. Morag had complained that the vehicle was heavy, sluggish, even though she was jacked into the FAV. I guessed the higher G made a difference. When we cornered it always felt like we were going faster. Still it was the closest to fresh air I'd tasted since we'd left the ship.

We found a place to camp. I'd fallen asleep as soon as my head touched the mat. When Cat woke me up for my watch I had my arm round Morag. I hadn't felt her lie down next to me when her watch finished. She didn't wake as I got up. Everything ached.

The RV point was a tall cavern. What I could make out of the rock formations looked impressive. I couldn't help admiring the thin wavy drapery formations and the stalactites probably formed over millions of years hanging from the roof. Against one of the walls was what looked like a frozen waterfall of flowstone.

Mudge, Pagan, Morag and I wove our way slowly through towering, almost tree-like stalagmites. We were wearing our reactive camouflage. Merle and Cat were covering us from raised and concealed positions. As quiet as we were trying to be, every footstep seemed to echo loudly to my enhanced hearing.

We'd parked the FAVs a little over a mile away and taken a circuitous route to get here. We had planned a number of different and faster routes back to the vehicles if things went tits up. We'd also set up a number of escape and evasion fallbacks and longer-term RV points if things went really bad.

There was no sign of Rannu, but without comms to establish contact it was a case of sweeping the cave hoping to see him, or that he'd find us. Rannu and Pagan had established a series of identification passwords and every so often we would stop and whisper, 'Nudd,' hoping to hear 'Ludd.' I had no idea what the words meant. So far nothing, and I felt exposed creeping around and whispering. It didn't feel like there was anyone here.

I had really hoped that Rannu would be here. He would know what the situation was down here and would be able to brief us. I also just wanted to see him again. Considering he'd once pulled my arm off and beat me near to death with it, he'd become a good friend.

Our compromise was inevitable, but I think it was me that gave us away when I stepped into the pool at the base of the flowstone waterfall. To get further up the wall I'd had no choice. I tried to ignore the faint hissing noise and the smoke rising from where my boots and the reactive camouflage suit had made contact with the acidic liquid. The submerged part of the suit started to flicker and distort. That was when the remote that had been sitting inert on a ledge near the top of the flowstone formation rose into the air.

I froze. Nothing happened. It didn't go straight for me or anyone else, which meant it had been alerted but was not sure. A small wisp of acidic smoke drifted up past my eye level. It was a medium combat remote. I knew that normally they were capable of autonomous action to a degree. If Demiurge had, as we suspected, overrun Lalande

2's net, then this remote might contain a small portion of Demiurge, making it capable of intelligent thought.

Medium combat remotes were reasonably tough but nothing I couldn't handle on my own. The problem was the noise I'd make doing it and whether or not it could communicate our presence to anyone through the rock. Transponders were used to relay and boost comms signals in the higher, more inhabited levels, but down here you would have to plant them as you went.

Was this a coincidence, a random patrol? It seemed like it had been waiting for us. I didn't want to think about what that meant. I wished I'd brought a silent weapon. I remained still as the cylindrical remote dropped down to hover on its fan-like rotors over the pool just in front of me. It began flying in an ever-increasing circle from the centre of the pool, radiating outwards.

The remote curved round to just in front of me and stopped. The sound of acid eating my boots seemed deafening. One of its gauss weapons swivelled round in my general direction. Its sensor array still looked like it was searching. A wisp of acidic smoke drifted up from the pool. The remote's array stopped moving. Its gauss weapon pointed straight at me.

The impact sounded like loose metal dropping into gears as Merle put two silent rounds into the machine. There was an unhealthy clunking noise and the remote splashed into the pool. Smoke rose from my reactive camouflage where the liquid had splashed me. Nothing else happened immediately.

'Fall back to the FAVs.' I thought I'd said it quietly but it seemed to echo up the tall cavern.

We fell back in good order but quickly. Illuminated by the green light of lowlight optics, the others looked like flickering disturbances in the air. When I checked thermographics, the IR-dampening properties of our inertial armour made us look like heat ghosts against the cold rock.

We made it back to the FAVs. We'd parked on a ledge off to the side of the tunnel we'd been using as a road. A gentle slope branched off from the main tunnel up to the ledge. The photoreceptive paint on the FAVs camouflaged the vehicles to look the same as the surrounding rock. Pagan, Cat and I provided cover as Merle, Morag and Mudge started up the vehicles. Merle passed me on the way to his FAV.

'You took your time,' I whispered.

'I was hoping it would miss you.'

I heard the noise first, the whine of a straining vectored-thrust gunship engine. I magnified my optics on thermographics and saw the telltale heat signature of a gunship being flown far too fast in a tunnel with so little clearance. A spiral of lights was heading towards us very quickly.

'Down!' Pagan, Cat and I sheltered behind the FAVs. They rocked as the railgun tracer rounds impacted into them, scoring off the paint, making them more visible. Suddenly the cavern was alight with ricochet sparks flaring in our lowlight vision.

Pagan leaned over the bonnet of his FAV and fired two grenades down the tunnel. He had climbed into the vehicle next to Mudge before the multi-spectrum smoke and ECM grenades exploded. His laser carbine would have been useless against the gunship but the smoke and ECM would make targeting us more difficult.

Normally we would have texted the ignition codes to the FAVs but being comms dark meant we had to do it manually by plugging in. This was taking longer.

My audio filters kicked up a notch as Cat fired a long burst from her railgun, one hypersonic bang ripping into the next. The railgun drowned out the long burst from my SAW.

The smoke eddied violently as blindly fired rockets jetted towards us. Cat and I leaped into our FAVs. Morag didn't bother with the slope; she just drove off the fifteen-foot ledge. I shot forward. I hadn't had time to put on my harness. The dashboard rushed up to hit me and I felt the subcutaneous armour on my nose give and blood squirt out. The smartfoam on the tyres tried to grab at the smooth, steep rock slope with some success. The front wheels were forward of the vehicle so fortunately they hit the ground first, the heavy-duty suspension cushioning the blow. Morag slewed the wheel hard to the left, battering me against the side of the vehicle. A concussion wave rocked us and we were driving through fire.

Fingers of flame reached for us through the disruption in the air as we drove. Mudge and Pagan emerged from the flame behind us and then Merle and Cat.

The FAV's suspension and tyres made light work of the rough ground beneath us as I struggled into my harness and then jacked into the vehicle's weapon systems. Suddenly the view in my IVD changed to provide a compressed three-hundred-and-sixty-degree panorama around the vehicle. Information scrolled down and cross hairs appeared in my view as I wrapped my hand around the grip for the weapon system's smartlink, connecting it to the receiver in my palm. The grip also had manual triggers. I brought the front and rear ball-mounted, point-defence lasers online first.

Behind me the cavern burned. Fire swirled around the gunship as it flew through the flames, skimming over the ground. The flames made it look like an even more violent and predatory piece of military tech. I didn't recognise the model – it looked new, next generation. Only the best for the Black Squadrons.

The pop-up turret unfolded from the middle of our FAV. It had a railgun mounted on it with two light anti-armour missile batteries on either side. I couldn't get an angle on the gunship because of the other two FAVs behind us. Cat and Pagan could, however. Sparks were flying off the front of the gunship as the two FAVs' railguns chewed away at its armour.

There were flashes from underneath the gunship's wing-like weapons pontoons as it launched missiles. Red laser light glittered off chaff foil as the missiles exploded mid-flight, taken out by Mudge and Pagan's anti-missile point defences. The panoramic view in my IVD showed the force of the explosions kick up the rear of their FAV, lifting the wheels high in the air as Mudge struggled to control it.

The gunship appeared again through its own missiles' flames, the triple-barrelled railgun on the nose rotating as it fired. Sparks were flying off the rear armour of Mudge and Pagan's FAV. Pagan was returning fire. He risked firing off a salvo of missiles but the gunship fired its own chaff dispensers and point-defence lasers. More fire filled the cavern.

'We need to split up,' I told Morag. I knew that the FAV's on-board sensor would be providing a detailed topographical map of the tunnels ahead. She would have overlaid the three-dimensional map onto her IVD, offering her various routes to our various RVs. The only problem was the map was incomplete because not all of the cave systems had been explored and it was almost a year out of date.

Morag yanked the steering wheel hard to the right into an even tighter tunnel and then sped up. The armoured vehicle was smashing stalagmites as we drove over them and tearing stalactites off the roof of the tunnel. The two other FAVs shot past the entrance to our tunnel, then the gunship shot past as well. I can't say I was disappointed, but on the other hand we needed to get the pressure off Pagan and Mudge. I had about a millisecond to think about reversing out behind them when a second gunship went past. As it did there was a flash of white light. Just behind us part of the rock exploded, caught fire and started to melt. Warning signals lit up my IVD letting me know that part of the FAV had also melted.

'They've got door gunners with plasma weapons, so stick to tight tunnels,' I told Morag. She just concentrated on driving. Now we would have to go back. Then the third gunship turned into the tunnel behind us. Morag went faster. Possibly too fast.

I was exchanging railgun fire with the gunship but its higher rate of fire was telling on the integrity of our rear armour. After my audio dampeners had filtered out the worst of the impact noise it sounded like heavy rain. Ahead of us I could see several pillars where stalactites and stalagmites had joined to make thick columns. The FAV was accelerating towards them.

'Morag!' Her response was to go faster.

'Turret,' she said through gritted teeth. I sent the command to fold the turret away as she slewed the FAV up the wall of the tunnel. The smartfoam of the tyres bit into the irregular surface of the rock wall. The turret only just folded way in time, though a column tore off part of the hatch.

Behind us the gunship fired missiles at the column, which exploded. The tunnel filled with fire. There was another column bisecting the path ahead of us. We just missed that, driving up the wall at what felt like ninety degrees to the tunnel floor. Back on the ground Morag continued accelerating.

Missiles reached out through the flames to destroy the second pillar. The gunship followed, buffeted by the explosions but not slowing down, railgun fire still eating at our rear armour.

Morag jammed on the brakes. The straps on my harness had to work to keep me in the bucket seat. Ahead there was a large, roughly circular crevice in the tunnel floor. I thought she was stopping to avoid it; she was in fact slowing so that she wouldn't jump it. The FAV skidded into the crevice and we started to fall.

The suspension extended and the tyres bit into the rock all around us. It was part vertical driving but mostly free fall. I'm not too ashamed to admit that I cried out. Red light from our point-defence lasers lit up the darkness as two missiles from the gunship dipped into the crevice above us. The subsequent explosion forced the FAV down, dropping it about twenty feet before the tyres caught again. I fired the railgun blind up through the flames. The gunship hadn't followed us, as it would have had to expose its vulnerable belly.

I shouted in surprise when Morag retracted the suspension and just let us drop. The impact felt like something that should be followed by death. Then there was a second jarring impact as we hit the ground. Morag was lolling around in her seat like a rag doll. She spat blood out of her mouth as she came to life again. There was the sound of tortured metal as she pressed the accelerator, and the rugged FAV moved forward. I'd been battered around so much I had trouble working out what was going on. There was the sound of tearing metal from the rear of the FAV and then we broke free.

'Missile!' Morag shouted. Without thinking I swung the turret round to face behind us and fired off half the light anti-armour missiles. It was only then I realised what she'd done, why we'd had to drive so fast. She'd known about the crevice and how it bisected the tunnel that the others were in. She'd dropped us down on the front of the second gunship chasing the others. The missile salvo had finished it off. My panoramic view showed the twisted burning wreckage filling the tunnel behind us. She must have programmed an algorithm to do the maths on her internal computer while she was driving. She would probably shake and sob later when she thought about there being people in the gunship. That was okay, as long as it was later.

Morag accelerated. Now we were behind a gunship this was more fun. I triggered the railgun, firing long bursts, chewing away at its rear armour. The gunship's weapon pontoons reversed. Warning icons appeared in my IVD – they had a missile lock on us. The gunship fired two missiles, but we'd kept well enough back that they were easy pickings for the point-defence lasers. We drove through the flame of their explosions still firing at the back of the gunship.

I risked two of our own missiles at it, but chaff and laser fire took care of them as we drove through fire again. As we emerged through the flames the gunship had gone. Ahead of us I could see the other two FAVs. The back of Pagan and Mudge's looked like someone had been eating it. It had just driven up the wall and was now returning to the flat. I was remembering something about the map. There was a branching tunnel here that sloped down. The others must have avoided it by driving up the wall while the gunship, probably badly damaged, had taken it to escape. Morag went after the gunship.

'No!' I shouted too late.

The downward tunnel was short. The end of it was a hole in the roof of a large cavern. We were airborne. Suddenly we were the world's shittest aircraft. The gunship was waiting for us. Its railgun opened up and it fired two more missiles. One of the plasma door gunners missed. Rock melted and burned behind us. The other clipped the front of the FAV, partially melting the bonnet and leaving the metal and composite armour burning.

I'm not sure how I had the presence of mind to do it, but the FAV's superb systems gave me lock even as we fell and I fired the rest of our missiles. The FAV's point defence took care of the gunship's missiles. Above us the gunship's own point-defence laser managed to take out all but two of ours. We splashed into the shallow lake that covered the bottom of the cavern. It was like hitting rock. Then we hit the rock under the water.

I didn't see it, but just before the gunship exploded above us, raining burning wreckage down to hiss in the acidic lake, two large humanoid-shaped objects must have bailed out of the open passenger compartment.

I came to in the cab of the submerged FAV. Now it was the world's shittest submarine. The cab was full of crashfoam. I couldn't move or see. My IVD was red with warning signs. My body felt like one big bruise. Had she done all this on purpose?

There was quite a lot of water leaking into the supposedly hermetically sealed vehicle. It was warring with the crashfoam and the crashfoam was losing. I felt my skin start to burn as well.

I texted Morag but got an automated reply telling me that she was sorry she couldn't answer on account of being unconscious. I burned myself in pooling acid as I reached for the manual release for the chemical catalyst that would dissipate the crashfoam.

As the crashfoam dispersed I got more burned as water squirted in on me. Eventually I could see Morag again. She was unconscious, parts of her skin bubbling as acidic water leaked into the FAV.

I opened a pouch on my webbing, removed a stim patch and stuck it to Morag's neck. I saw a message from the FAV's systems asking me if I wanted to use the periscope. This was for parking in a hull-down position (squaddie talk for parking behind cover). I replied in the affirmative and tentatively raised the periscope to just break the surface. This was still being kicked around by our impact and the fiery death of the gunship but I managed to pick out the two exo-armour suits circling the cavern high above us.

They looked familiar but I knew I'd never seen the model before. Although the water was slopping over the periscope, it still provided me with enough resolution to watch in horror as thick black tendrils unfolded from the backs of the two suits. They were, at least in part, derived from Themtech. Then I realised why they seemed familiar. They looked a bit like Berserks, if Berserks were larger, symmetrical, made mostly of human materials, attached to exo-armour flight systems and carried Retributor railguns.

Morag signalled her return to consciousness by mumbling a long string of nonsense.

'It's not a submarine,' I said, largely for something to say.

'What?' she asked groggily. Coming more fully to, she assessed our situation. 'Oh,' she said.

'What were you thinking?' I asked.

'Shut up, it worked. What now?'

'Well, those things up there don't have the right tools for the job, though if they've got grenades they could make our lives miserable. But we'll drown or melt in here if we don't get out soon.'

I didn't say that if they launched their missiles at us the force of the explosions would be magnified in the water. Their missiles' engines wouldn't work in the water but our point-defence lasers would pretty much be expensive and very bright flashlights. Also we now had no offensive ability, as without a pressurised barrel or a hydrodynamic round all the railgun was good for was pushing around water. All they had to do was wait us out.

We shifted around, trying to avoid the worst of the leaks, lifting our feet out of the footwell. The air stank of rotten eggs from the sulphur in the water. The good thing was, the FAV's anti-corrosion protection was holding. The vehicle wasn't going to melt around us, and had it been any less well sealed we already would have drowned. The bad news was, if we tried to leave the vehicle we'd be sitting ducks. Assuming we weren't just dissolved by the acidic water (we wouldn't be, but we would be badly burned).

Morag left unsaid that this all meant they'd got and broken Rannu. If they had all the information they needed then he was probably dead by now, unless they'd sent him to the Belt. In which case he was also probably dead by now. Rannu had been a good operator and was on top of his game, yet they'd still got him like all the others. We hadn't stood a chance.

There were missile contrails in the cavern above us, then warheads blossoming to fire and force as black light, Themtech and point-defence weapons from the flying exo-armour took them out. We could hear the railgun fire through the water. The other two FAVs were on ledges far above the lake and had caught the two exo-armour suits in a crossfire.

'See if the grapples work. We'll see if the winch can get us shallow enough for the turret to fire,' I said.

Morag fired both the front-facing grapples. One of them bounced off; the other connected and started to eat its way in. Already the acid in the shallow lake would be corroding the cable. Morag triggered the winch and we started to roll forward. We were moving slowly towards a smooth rock shore at one end of the cavern. This would only work while the two exo-armour pilots were too distracted to notice the cable.

Cat fired the remaining missiles from her turret-mounted battery. Sheer numbers overwhelmed one of the exo-armour suits' point-defence systems and the impacting missiles destroyed it. The wreckage joined us in the lake.

The other exo-armour suit flew through the barrage of missiles from Pagan and Mudge's FAV, firing its Retributor and its own missiles. Red laser light connected the FAV to the incoming missiles, detonating them. The suit appeared through the flame and smoke like a horrible angel, landed next to the FAV and tore off its railgun. I was appalled to see it start to tear open the armour, assisted by its tendrils.

We rolled forward painfully slowly to bring us to a firing depth, the winch straining to pull us through the water as it and the cable corroded. I watched as Merle exited the other FAV and sprinted to the edge of the ledge, bringing up his plasma rifle. White fire lit up the darkness as he fired almost the length of the cavern into the back of the exo-armour tearing open the FAV. The plasma fire started to burn the armour, eating into it. The turret on the FAV turned to face the Themtech suit.

'Don't do it,' I said.

Pagan triggered the missile at point-blank range. He must have hacked the proximity fuse. It exploded. The FAV was airborne, tumbling over as it hit the side of the cavern before falling back onto the ledge. The exo-armour was blown off the ledge and splashed into the water close by the rock shore we were heading towards.

The barrel of our railgun broke the surface of the water. A smoking, blackened, still burning exo-armour stood up unsteadily. I hit it with round after round from the railgun as the winch pulled us forward. It staggered back under the relentless impact but would not go down. White light flashed again and again as Merle shot round after round over our heads into it. Finally it hit the wall of the cavern, its head now ablaze with white plasma fire. It slid down the wall and into the water. I put another two bursts into it anyway. The ammo on the railgun was looking low.

The protesting winch dragged us out of the water. Smoke poured off the FAV, the photoreceptive paint long gone. I hit the door release and slid it back. Morag did the same. I ditched my gear and started free-climbing up the rock. Morag ran into the cave system.

Morag reached the rock ledge, which supported Mudge and Pagan's FAV, just before I did. She hacked the door mechanism and managed to feed a snake through the crashfoam, then took control of the FAV and fired one of the front and one of the rear winches. She stepped back. I watched feeling helpless as the winches dragged the vehicle up and over onto its wheels.

Morag reached in and pulled the manual release for the crashfoam dissolver. I ran forward and we pulled an unconscious and badly battered Pagan out of the FAV. Nothing looked broken but I didn't like the look of the swelling on his face and skull. Mudge was battered but conscious and grinning. He was obviously very, very high.

'I love these cars,' he managed. I just shook my head.

The FAV's armour was pitted, scored, burned, buckled in a couple of places and a blackened mess, but it seemed intact.

Opposite me, aided by patches of burning wreckage and guttering plasma fire, I could see a much larger cavern almost directly opposite this ledge. It would provide easy ingress for the final gunship if it knew where we were, and we'd been making a lot of noise.

'Is the FAV running?' I asked Morag quietly.

'They're hurt.'

'We need to leave.'

Morag concentrated for a moment.

'I think it'll run. Not well, but it'll run.'

On the other ledge I could see Merle signalling, asking if we were all clear. I signalled for him to wait.

That was when the final gunship dropped through the hole in the cavern roof that Morag and I had fallen through. As it did, two more Themtech exo-armours leaped off it. They had us. It was over.

Then in the mouth of the large cavern opposite me it seemed to get as light as day. The gunship became a fountain of white liquid flame as it dropped into the lake. The two exo-armours followed in rapid succession. Involuntarily I held my hands up in front of my face and backed away from the light. Beneath the water I could make out the three pools of plasma fire still burning, the surface of the lake bubbling as the water boiled.

'Stay where you are, mate, or I'll light you up,' a booming voice echoed through the cavern. Even amplified I could make out the strong New Zealand accent.

That's when we heard the giant's footsteps. I saw its heat signature as I magnified my optics. It had been far back in the tunnel but was making its way quickly towards us to the sound of metal resonating off rock.

Cat moved their FAV back into the tunnel that had brought them to the ledge they were on and threw her brother a Laa-Laa. Merle extended the man-portable missile launcher and took cover, his reactive camouflage turning him into another piece of rock. Not that the light anti-armour missile would do much against the armoured metal giant that stalked out of the tunnel and waded into the lake. I recognised the enormous bipedal, roughly humanoid-shaped mech as a German-made Landsknecht, although it seemed bulkier than others I'd seen. I guessed that this was something to do with the heavier gravity. They had been superseded by newer, better models but were still serviceable and had still been seeing action on all the colonial fronts at the end of the war with Them.

Its armour was pitted and scorched and it had obviously seen a lot of action judging by the patchwork of repairs all over it. On some of the less damaged parts of the mech I could make out intricate patterns that reminded me of the knot work that Pagan favoured, only different somehow. It had a medium missile battery on either shoulder and point-defence lasers mounted on its chest. The plasma cannon which it had used to destroy the gunship had cooled down to only red hot.

'You fellows were sure making a lot of noise,' the amplified voice with the Kiwi accent said.

'Who are you?' I shouted.

'We're the resistance,' was the amplified reply.

12
Utu Pa

Most of them may have been military but it looked less like a resistance base and more like a refugee camp. Gaunt, hungry, harried, haunted-looking men and women looked at the FAVs with suspicion.

We'd managed to get Pagan's vehicle running and I drove him. He'd come to and told me that they'd fired the missile figuring they were dead anyway. Pagan had been badly kicked about but was otherwise okay. Mudge was much the same. Cat's FAV towed ours. Morag was reasonably sure that if she could find the right parts, despite the kicking it had taken, she could get it running. I was beginning to think FAVs were worth their exorbitant price tag.

We told ourselves we'd gone with the Kiwi voluntarily, after the inevitable argument about whether or not it was a trap or just a bad idea. When we drove into the network of caverns we were well covered. Somehow, even when there's not enough food to eat, there are always enough guns. In this case there were also mechs. There were four of the fighting machines including the Landsknecht that had escorted us in. There was another Landsknecht, a Steel Mantis, a light fast scout mech and, most impressive, a Bismarck-class heavy mech.

The Bismarck was basically a heavily armed weapons platform slung between four heavy-duty, insect-like legs. With a three-hundred-millimetre mass driver and two heavy missile batteries as well as various point-defence and anti-personnel weapons, its firepower was something to be respected. But it would be nearly useless in this kind of war. They had all the toys, but this was a hard planet to forage for food on. These people looked like they were starving. Compared to them, I just felt healthy and well fed.

We climbed out of the FAVs into a circle of gun barrels. I tried my best don't-fuck-with-us look, but as the adrenalin wore off the high G settled on me like a dead weight around my shoulders, pressing down on a sore spine. I spat. My throat felt red raw and the spittle had a pink look to it.

'So, are we hooking up with the local resistance or being robbed?' Cat muttered under her breath.

'Who's in command?' Pagan asked.

Nobody said anything. Most of the people around us were Maoris and had the squat powerful build of people born to high gravity. Except their bodies had started to waste. Many of them had tattoos that looked like they'd crawled onto their faces. The Landsknecht mech that had brought us in still towered over us.

'I think we should give these people food,' Morag said.

Pagan hissed at her to be quiet. Cat and Merle looked less than pleased with her suggestion.

Generator-run portable lights and free-standing lamps lit the cavern network. There weren't enough of either to completely light the place and much of it remained in darkness. There were laser-cut niches in the rock that seemed to be bunk spaces. I'd find out later that they were called miner coffins and in the early colonisation period were where dead miners were left in state until they could be disposed off. There were a lot of them.

The circle of guns broke as four people walked through the crowd towards us. The woman looked like she'd had a hard life. She probably wasn't much older than me but she looked worn. She was muscle and hard edges in inertial armour with a sleeveless leather jacket over the top. When she turned to say something to one of the others I saw that the back of the jacket bore a stylised demon head with bulging eyes and a protruding tongue – gang colours of some kind. Half of her face and the visible skin on her arms were tattooed with swirling patterns that looked like they were trying to engulf her dark but still somehow sallow skin.

Next to her was the biggest hacker I'd ever seen. I could tell he was a hacker because of the mishmash of military and black-market tech that seemed to grow out of half his head. Despite his squat muscular bulk and the heavy G, he moved with a surprisingly easy, almost predatory grace. Like the others you could see where skin had tightened over food-starved flesh. His face and most of the flesh I could see was tattooed. It made him look somehow otherworldly. He wore a sleeveless leather jacket as well. All four of them did.

The other guy made me think of all the fun we'd had in Freetown Camp 12 with the Russians. While nowhere near as heavily modified as the Vucari, someone had given a canine look to his face. He had a protruding power-assisted jaw of surgical-steel teeth and a dog-like nose. His fingers ended in distinctly claw-like steel nails. He looked more dog than wolf but not like one of the friendly breeds. Tattoos ran up his cheek through long sideburns and bridged his forehead.

'No,' Mudge said, shaking his head. 'I don't like dog things.'

He may have been verbalising how we all felt after our run-in with the Vucari. It still wasn't very diplomatic. The dog guy punched Mudge very hard. Mudge hit the ground.

'That's my other dog impression!' the guy shouted at Mudge, who was trying to get to his feet. Cat grabbed the guy and did something complicated with his arms and neck, immobilising him. There was a lot of shifting about in the assembled circle of guns. Serious violence was imminent.

The other woman, little more than a girl, was the slenderest person there. I didn't understand why the gravity hadn't snapped her like a twig. She was pale, paler than the rest, and I was pretty sure she wasn't a Maori despite the tattooed lips and chin. She had long, straight dark hair and couldn't have been much older than Morag. Also, she wasn't right. There was something not there about her, as if she was getting a different signal to the rest of us.

The hard-faced woman and the big hacker just stopped and gave us the eye. The pale girl walked straight up and started to inspect us.

'Let him go,' the hard-faced woman said to Cat.

Cat ignored her. Mudge was spitting out blood. Dog guy was struggling to get free; Cat was having none of it.

I turned to look at him. 'Touch him again and I'll hurt you, okay?'

The guy was furious at his helplessness. He just spat at me. I nodded to Cat, who cut him loose. That was good. We were acting the part of a together, properly functioning unit, even if we were really a mess. Dog guy turned to glare at Cat but said nothing.

'That's our Cat,' I said, trying to break the tension. It fell flat.

The odd girl was next to me now, examining me. I turned to look at her.

'You SF?' the hard-faced woman asked. We didn't answer.

'They're SF,' the big guy said.

'Well thank fuck. We're saved,' dog guy growled.

'They transmitting?' the hard-faced woman asked.

'Not that I can tell. They seem to be running comms dark,' the big guy answered.

'Check their vehicles anyway.'

The hacker moved towards the FAVs.

I moved to intercept. 'Hold on,' I said, holding up my hand.

'You're transmitting, we're fucked. We'll have to run again and we always lose people when we run,' the woman said.

'We're running comms dark,' Pagan said. 'We're hiding from the same thing you are.'

The big guy stopped but glanced back at the woman. The pale girl was examining Morag now. Morag was smiling uncomfortably at her.

Mudge climbed to his feet, spitting blood. 'Ow!' he announced and lit up a spliff. There seemed to be no visible enmity towards the dog guy. Maybe after being blown up he didn't care.

'Couple of things you need to get used to. We are going to check your vehicles and we will be taking your food. You'll get your fair share if we decide not to kill you and let you stay,' the woman told me. 'Big Henry, what's the score?'

'They were fighting the good fight when I found them,' came the amplified reply from the mech.

'You fighting the Freedom Squadrons?' the big hacker asked.

I raised an eyebrow. 'Freedom Squadrons? We call them the Black Squadrons,' I said.

'Freedom Squadrons is what they call themselves. We mostly call them wankers,' dog guy growled.

'She's really fucking with my calm!' Mudge said, pointing at the pale girl, whose face was inches away from his as she studied him. Maybe he'd had enough of being kicked around after all.

'Leave her be,' the big hacker said. There was a dangerous edge to his voice that didn't strike me as an affectation. I was pretty sure this guy knew how to look after himself.

'You guys British?' the woman asked. I nodded. 'You in-country when this happened?' I shook my head. 'You point on an invasion?' I shook my head. 'Didn't think so. Your food?'

'Cat, Merle, give them half our ration packs.'

Merle's head whipped round to look at me. He wanted to say something but was more disciplined. Mudge wasn't.

'Half our ...' Somehow he had the presence of mind to shut up when I glared at him. May as well try and keep up the pretence of professionalism.

'Anyone tries to take more, shoot them,' I continued.

The hard-faced woman gave this some thought.

'Just so you know, when we need the other half we'll take it, and if you don't like it then we've got a long and proud history of cannibalism.'

There was laughter. From us as well. They just didn't seem that scary after the Vucari.

'Well, let's hope we're friends by then,' I said. 'You're not checking the vehicles. We're not transmitting. You can work that out yourselves. You'll just have to trust us. We'll pay for that trust in food.'

'We can take—' dog guy started, but the woman held up her hand and he was quiet.

'Look, mate, I'm sorry about what he said, but we've had a bad time with some people that looked like you recently. We may be the only friends you've got down here,' I said. It was a guess, but they looked in a bad way.

'And we're the only friends you've got, right?' the big hacker asked. He had a point.

'Assuming we don't eat you,' the woman said.

The place was called *Utu Pa*. A *pa* was some sort of Maori fortification and *utu* meant something between revenge and reciprocity. I'd done the introductions. They just gave us their call signs. I suspect the call signs had been their nicknames when they'd run as a gang together and were probably more meaningful to them than their real names. The hard-faced woman was Mother. She had been the senior NCO and now appeared to command the entire *pa*. The big hacker was called Tailgunner and with Mother drove the Bismarck-class mech. Dog guy was called Dog Face. That would be easy to remember. Some piece of shit had had him modified when he was still a kid to act as a human ratter. Apparently they had rats here on Lalande, which sort of impressed me. The pale girl went by the name of Strange. Again I didn't think I was going to have a problem remembering that.

Big Henry, our saviour, had of course turned out to be very short. It was a typical squaddie naming convention. Not much bigger than a Twist, he moved with a particular waddling gate but was very powerfully built. A battered and ancient-looking bowler hat perched precariously on his mass of thick braided hair, which was pulled into a ponytail. His beard was braided as well and he had tattoos on what little hair-free skin we could see. He'd seemed the least hostile of the lot, but then he'd seen us fighting the bad guys.

After our initial chat Mudge had pulled me aside.

'Half our fucking food!' he demanded.

'There's more back at the cache, and Merle knows where there are more caches.'

'Which could be compromised.' Cat and Merle were acting as armed supervision as Mother's people removed half our ration packs from the FAVs.

'What do you want me to say, Mudge? Look at them. They're fucking starving and we're very low on friends here. Besides, I served with some Maori guys on loan from the Kiwi SAS. They were hard bastards.'

Mudge grinned. 'Everyone seems hard to you.'

They were Queen Alexandra's Mounted Rifles, or a deserter element of them, an armoured cavalry unit. Mother and Tailgunner seemed to run things, backed by Dog Face and Big Henry. Strange was just local colour, I think. The infantry, tank and artillery crews they had with them, nearly all Maoris as well, called the five of them the *Ngāti Apakura*. It meant the Tribe of the Woman Who Urged Revenge. The Bismarck-class mech was also called *Apakura*. They called themselves *whanau*. As far as I could tell it meant family.

The five were close, very tight. They'd grown up on the streets together with no family but each other. They'd run as a gang because they'd had to. It was the street politics of victimise or be a victim. The street ate children who couldn't find a way to protect themselves. They'd formed their gang, their tribe, and still wore their colours as patches on the back of their cut-off, armoured leather jackets.

Mudge had managed to find all this out while talking to Big Henry and some of the others in the camp who he hadn't pissed off yet. I suspected he was relying on shared narcotics rather than charisma to make friends.

They'd learned to drive mechs in the mines. They'd piloted stripped-down mining versions – all the best parts had gone to the front to be used on fighting mechs – but the resources had to keep flowing. Big Henry had told Mudge that they'd lost as many people to mine accidents before they got drafted as they had in the war. The five were all that was left of their family. Christ knows how they'd managed to stay in the same platoon together all this time.

The Black/Freedom Squadrons were claiming to be the Earth government in exile. They'd turned up with Cronin at their head. It seems that despite what God had thought, Lalande and not Sirius had been their first stop. They'd laid a false trail for us. This made sense if what we suspected about the Citadel was correct.

The Freedom Squadrons had put out a story that we'd been a Them fifth column and had pulled off propaganda coups by making the Earth believe the war was over and taking control of the net with a Them virus. There's even been edited footage of us taking Atlantis played on the vizzes. I felt used.

The Freedom Squadron called Demiurge the Freedom Wave. Sadly, calling something the opposite of what it was seemed to work in propaganda. People listened to names. It was much easier than studying actions. Cronin, the spokesperson for the so-called Earth government in exile, described it as the last defence against the Them computer virus, a sort of global comms net inoculation.

Tailgunner called it the Black Wave. He saw it for what it was and had isolated their systems and fled their *pa* or firebase after an encounter with what sounded like a Themtech-enhanced operator. I was impressed they'd shot down one of the Black Squadron's next-generation assault shuttles with a mech.

Some other members of their unit had joined them and they had found other stragglers in the caves. Then people on the run from the Black Squadrons came looking for them. All in all, there were about two hundred of them. Mainly infantry, a few support, three tank crews, two of whom actually had tanks, and a self-propelled artillery crew complete with tracked SP gun. They also had almost enough APCs in various states of repair to move everyone if they had to.

It was a lot of mouths to feed. What they'd discovered early on was that if any of them got captured then they were compromised almost immediately. One of their people had gone missing while scouting for supplies. The next thing they knew their *pa* had been hit by a mixed force of NZ colonial regulars backed by the Black Squadrons. They'd only got away after a vicious firefight because they collapsed a tunnel after they'd managed a fighting retreat. Since then they'd been hiding in the deep caves. They moved every couple of weeks or if someone went missing, even if the poor fucker had just got lost. I figured that they were still alive because they weren't important enough for Rolleston to deal with yet.

The *whanau* knew that Demiurge meant total surveillance in the areas that it controlled. This limited their options and meant that they had very little information about what was going on in the more densely populated areas above their heads. And of course it made getting food very difficult.

They'd managed a few raids for supplies but this wasn't their kind of war. I didn't doubt for a second that they were all very good in a stand-up fight, which was what they were trained for, but if the Black Squadrons were going to be fought it would mean using guerrilla tactics. Mechs just aren't all that useful for that kind of thing.

On the other hand, they had wiped out any Black Squadron types they'd found in the deeper levels. Anyone who came looking for them for reasons other than joining was also killed. There was a problem with this tactic, however, a more concentrated form of what I'd been feeling. Anyone of us would kill Rolleston, Cronin or the Grey Lady as soon as look at them. The same went for any of the

Themtech-enhanced arse-lickers here, but most of the soldiers were just normal draftees trying to stay alive. I didn't like the idea of killing them but it was abstract for me. If some poor bastard was pointing an assault rifle at me it was always going to be him in the him-or-me stakes. The people here would know some of the guys they'd have to shoot. They'd recognised some of the people who'd attacked their *pa* with the Black Squadrons. The rest of the forces on Lalande and in the colonies would buy Cronin's story – there was no real reason not to. That meant that they'd think that these guys, and us, were the bad guys. Not just the bad guys but species traitors who'd sold out all of mankind. Come to that, I was a bit worried about what would happen when the *whanau* saw through our disguise and realised that we were the people who'd released God into the net.

'How come you just didn't do as you were told? Make things easy on yourselves?' I asked.

We were sitting in a circle next to the FAVs trying to make sure nobody nicked the rest of our stuff. Cat was actually on guard but she was still close enough to the conversation to join in if she wanted. Mother, Tailgunner, Dog Face and Big Henry were facing us over a camp stove. We were attempting to eat, but the sulphurous atmosphere made everything taste like farts to me. It didn't seem to bother Merle. He was wolfing his food down.

Strange was standing just outside the circle we'd formed, in shadow between the pools of light provided by two of the portable lamps. Each of us was taking it in turns to be stared at by the girl. It was disconcerting. This wasn't someone trying to be odd for the sake of it, or for effect like Mudge; this was someone who was damaged in some way. I noticed that Morag was spending a lot of time looking back at her.

'We're not very good at doing what we're told,' Dog Face growled. I think he was rueing the mess they found themselves in. I knew how he felt.

'Why were all your mechs' comms shut down?' Pagan asked.

I watched them glance between each other uncomfortably. There was obviously something there that they didn't want to talk about.

'We were warned,' Tailgunner finally said.

'By who?' I asked.

They didn't answer. Close to starving or not, we couldn't strong-arm these people. Normally I'd have been pissed off – after all we were all in the same shit – but I could see their point of view. This was a huge risk for them. For all they knew, we were the bad guys and the rest of our Freedom Squadron friends were on their way. We'd have to work for their trust.

'We're the ones,' Morag said. Mother, Tailgunner and the others turned to look at her, confused. 'We put God into the net. She's not a Them virus; she just tells the truth.'

Merle was shaking his head and looking pissed off. Pagan turned to her but she ignored him. Mudge was grinning. Instead of earning their trust we could just make grandiose gestures, I thought. Morag may have been talking to Mother, Tailgunner, Dog Face and Big Henry but she was looking at Strange.

'Have you got any vodka?' I asked Mudge as what Morag had said started to sink in with our hosts.

'What am I, your own personal off-licence?' Mudge demanded.

'I'm not wasting good whisky in this shit-for-atmosphere.'

To give Mudge his credit he went and got a bottle. He'd probably jumped with it and humped it all over hell's creation.

Tailgunner and Mother were both still thinking it over. Mother didn't look happy.

'I thought you looked familiar. Changed your looks before you got here?' she asked.

Morag nodded. Though that had been a waste of time if we were just going to tell everyone, I thought.

Dog Face was the first to get angry. 'This is your fucking fault?' he growled.

'Yep,' Mudge said proudly as he opened the bottle, took a swig and passed it to me. I passed it to Mother. She looked at it as if I was offering her a knife point-first but took it, wiped the top and took a swig before passing it to Tailgunner.

'We may as well tell them everything,' Morag said. There was resolve in her voice.

'And if they're the bad guys?' Cat asked from behind us.

'Hey, fuck you!' Dog Face spat.

'She'll spank you again,' Mudge said, presumably because he'd seen an opportunity to start an argument.

'Like he spanked you. Shut up, Mudge,' I told him.

Dog Face looked like he was about to say something as well, but Mother glanced over and he lapsed into irritable silence.

'They're not the bad guys,' Morag said with conviction.

'Hooker's intuition?' I asked.

Morag smiled. We'd run on her intuition for a while when we'd had nothing else.

'You're a hooker?' Big Henry asked hopefully. 'We like hookers.'

'Sorry, darling. I'm retired.' Then to the rest of us: 'Bad guys live better than this. We know that.'

There was an almost childish logic to it. I was also convinced she was correct.

'She's right,' Merle said. 'These aren't the bad guys. Bad guys know what they're doing.'

'Why don't you go and fuck yourself, you arrogant prick!' Dog Face had moved into a crouch. He looked every inch the angry war dog. He didn't remind me so much of the Vucari as the cyber-enhanced Tosa-Inus the Cossacks had run with.

'Put him on a leash or I will,' Merle said.

I'd noticed him shift slightly. He was ready. Something bad was going to happen if Dog Face went for him. I felt rather than heard Cat move behind me, ready to help her brother. I think Mother noticed as well.

'Dog Face, take it easy,' Mother said in a tone that brooked no argument.

Big Henry took his angry brother-mech-pilot's arm. Dog Face's head turned to look at him. Big Henry nodded.

'And you,' Mother said to Merle. 'You don't like what we're doing here then you can leave your supplies and fuck off.'

The others watched, waiting for Merle's response. Tailgunner was particularly tense. He was giving Merle the hard stare. I almost wanted something to kick off. I was interested to see who'd win.

'Does everyone with a penis want to fuck off so we can actually accomplish something?' Morag asked.

I smiled. Behind me I could hear Cat laugh.

'She was being just as macho,' Mudge complained, nodding at Mother.

'Mother may well have a penis,' Big Henry said. 'That's why Tailgunner likes her so much.'

More smiles, less tension.

'You can go with him if you want,' Mother said deadpan.

'All right. None of us are diplomats—' I started.

'I am,' Mudge interrupted inevitably.

'We don't know each other so nobody wants to give,' I continued, ignoring Mudge. 'So let's just try for an exchange of information and see where that gets us?'

'I wasn't trying to denigrate what you've done here,' Merle started. 'How could you know what was going to happen and prepare for it? This is not your kind of war.'

'So what? You going to save us?' Dog Face spat.

Merle ignored him. 'My point was, we tell them and that's more people who know. They get caught, we get compromised.' Then he turned to Mother. 'Unless you're prepared to kill any of your people who get captured, or yourself if that happens.' Merle had turned his intense brown eyes on her. The Maori woman didn't flinch. She didn't answer either. 'No, of course not, because you care for these people. You want to see them safe through the war, don't you? Admirable but fucking dangerous to us.'

'Fine,' Mother said tightly. 'Then like I said, leave your supplies and fuck off.'

Dog Face was nodding. Merle turned to me. 'They've got no useful intel. We've done the hearts and minds thing at the expense of our own supplies. We need to move on.'

He was right. I knew he was right. These were clearly good people, clearly capable at what they did, but they'd drag us down. They should have split into smaller groups and either hidden or fought in cells.

I didn't even see the girl come out of the darkness. I hadn't been paying attention and I'd not sensed her move. She was suddenly next to Merle and her hand slashed out at his face. I saw the sliver of metal reflected in the light. She had a small curved blade sticking out of the bottom of her fist. Merle caught the girl's wrist. Despite her black plastic eyes I caught the look of panic on her face.

'Strange!' Mother shouted.

She must have realised what sort of person Merle was and that the damaged girl was courting death. Merle wasn't quite quick enough to catch Strange's other wrist. She drew a thin line of red down his cheek with the blade in her other fist.

I felt the FAV I was leaning against rock as Cat came off it. Strange screamed as Merle trapped her other wrist, disarmed her and put her into a painful-looking hold. I could see panic building in Strange as she struggled against him. Enthusiasm and sneakiness is rarely a match for actual skill. Mudge had his pistol in his hand. He didn't look quite sure what to do with it. Pagan had pushed himself back. I don't know why I didn't move, why I didn't do something.

'Let her go,' Tailgunner said. There was impending violence in his voice but something else as well. Tension.

Strange was freaking out. Struggling like a trapped animal. Tailgunner, Mother, Big Henry and Dog Face were on their feet. They didn't care who we were, that some of us had guns in our hands, in Cat's case a railgun; they were ready to go at us.

'Let her go,' I said.

Merle looked like he was going to object. Not unreasonably; he had just been slashed.

'Now,' I said in my best don't-fuck-with-me NCO voice.

He looked like he was ready to tell me to fuck off but released her. Strange rolled away from him and onto her feet and hissed before backing into the shadows again, crouching like a predatory beast.

When I glanced over at Morag she was smiling. I couldn't make out why. Maybe she liked what Strange had done. That worried me. I tried to catch her eye but either she didn't see my look or she chose to ignore it.

'She comes near me with a blade again, I'll put it in her. At best,' Merle said.

He was dabbing at the cut. Looking at the blood on his fingertips. I think he was more surprised than anything else.

'You ever touch her—' Tailgunner started.

'Hey!' I said. He looked round at me. 'That's a reasonable response. You don't want her hurt, keep her under control.'

I got the feeling Tailgunner was a reasonable guy but that Strange was a weak spot for him. I also think he wasn't used to people speaking to him the way I had. I could take him, I told myself. I almost believed it as well. Unless he had more motivation than I did. Still angry, he opened his mouth to say something else, issue another threat.

'Enough,' Mother said quietly and sat down.

Big Henry and Dog Face were looking at her. I think they'd expected another resolution to the situation.

'You know what would be nice?' Mudge said.

'A conversation without knives, guns and potential violence?' Pagan suggested.

Mudge nodded. I looked at him incredulously.

'What?' he demanded. 'Oh yeah, I'm on a nice mellow high. Thought it would help getting to know people.'

'That's very responsible of you,' Morag said.

'Can you take it all the time?' Cat asked from behind us.

'Yeah, 'cause it's fucking brilliant in a fight,' Mudge said sarcastically.

Mother was just watching us with a raised eyebrow. Tailgunner and the others had sat back down. Mudge passed Dog Face the now half-empty bottle of vodka.

'She has ... problems,' Mother said.

It was almost an apology coming from her. I nodded. It was obvious that bad things had happened to her.

'Don't fucking apologise to them,' Tailgunner said angrily.

Mother and Tailgunner were clearly partners and long term. They were the mum and dad of this dysfunctional family but it was obvious that this caused tension between them. It wasn't jealousy on Mother's part but something else. I wondered if she was afraid of Strange for some reason.

'Like I said, they're useless to us. Nothing but trouble,' Merle said.

He sprayed antiseptic on the cut before applying a knitter and a foam bandage to it.

'Why were the comms on your mechs disabled?' Pagan asked again, and again they all went quiet.

'Tell them,' Mother said.

'What, all of a sudden we're best friends?' Tailgunner demanded.

'They trusted us; we may as well trust them. Because you know what happens if we don't?' Mother paused. 'Nothing at all.'

'The risk—' Tailgunner started.

'Is the same as any other day. We'll either live or we die.'

I was starting to warm to Mother. She was my kind of NCO, but Merle was right: she cared too much. But then again the same could be said about me. Well, when it came to Morag anyway, I cared far too much. Mudge also, sometimes, and Pagan to a degree, and I was putting off thinking about Rannu. It was a near certainty he was dead.

I was grateful it was my turn with the bottle of vodka. I took a deep long pull from it. The burn in my throat from the alcohol was a welcome change to the constant burn from the atmosphere. It still tasted like rotten eggs.

Tailgunner swallowed hard. He didn't look happy but he told us anyway. 'Miru, the ruler of night, warned us to separate ourselves from the spirit world.'

My heart sank.

'Jesus Christ,' Merle spat and turned to look at me. I wasn't sure if he was trying to appeal to my common sense or was getting ready to walk away. Then again I didn't fully understand why he was here. 'We're just wasting our time.'

'Merle,' Cat said from behind me, 'back off for a bit.'

'This is hacker religious bullshit,' he said angrily.

'Why don't you show some fucking respect?' Dog Face demanded.

I noticed that Strange was swaying in and out of the light and shadows further inside the cavern, still watching us. Glaring at Merle.

'Why don't you show me something to respect?' Merle demanded.

'I think you're spending too much time with Mudge,' I said to him.

'Hey!' Mudge said. 'I'm behaving.' And he was. He was also study-ing the patterns in the rocks intently.

'He was like this before he met Mudge,' Cat assured us.

Merle glared at her angrily. 'Look, I understand that the lack of sensory information to certain parts of your brain in the net means it gets filled with religious horseshit. I understand that trancing-in presses the button on the religious gene, but this has nothing to do with why we're here.'

'Work on your own a lot?' Morag asked him sarcastically.

'Yeah, you can see why.'

'Because you struggle to form relationships with normal people?' Morag guessed.

Merle looked exasperated. 'Fine, whatever, but this religious stuff still has nothing to do with what we're trying to accomplish.'

'Which is?' Tailgunner asked. I saw Mother touch his leg and shake her head.

'It's real for them.' I was surprised to hear this come out of my mouth. So were Pagan and Morag judging by the looks they gave me.

I think I was just sick and tired of religious discussions. I seemed to have had a lot of them in the last few months. I'd been instrumental in God's release into the net and I'd met one of the so-called gods in there. I still had no problem being an atheist. Now I was not happy with another god rearing its head, even if only peripherally to us. I was hoping it was only operational paranoia, but I couldn't shake the feeling that things were moving around us, helping shape events, manipulating us while staying out of sight.

'Besides,' said Pagan, 'the warning seems to have had very real effects.'

Merle shook his head as if he couldn't be bothered to argue. I hoped he was going to be quiet for a while. Suddenly Mudge started laughing. We all looked at him.

'Normal people,' he repeated as if he'd just got the punchline of a joke.

'You SF types are awesome,' Big Henry said, smiling.

'He's a journalist,' Pagan, Cat and I replied at the same time.

'A journalist and a sadly retired hooker ... Wow. You really are here to rescue us.'

'Tell them the rest,' Mother said, apparently unimpressed with the banter.

'We've got a little piece of it,' Tailgunner said.

'A piece of what?' Pagan asked carefully.

'The Black Wave,' the big hacker answered.

Pagan and Morag gaped at him. I must have been doing the same thing. Even Merle looked up. Mudge was leaning closer to the smooth rock floor. We'd bored him earlier in the conversation, it seemed.

'How?' I asked.

'Miru, the ruler of the night, gave me an eel net to cast at—' Tailgunner started.

'Okay, never mind. Forget I asked,' I said.

Tailgunner looked a little pissed off.

'Can you not be fucking serious?' Merle asked.

Tailgunner turned to look at him. There was something about the situation that reminded me of the time the two hardest guys in Fintry had confronted each other when I was a kid.

'He is,' Morag said, obviously fascinated.

'And this is important,' Pagan said. 'You mean to say that one of the gods of Maori mythology—'

'Don't call it a mythology, *pakeha*,' Tailgunner warned him.

'I'm sorry,' Pagan apologised, though I don't think he knew what *pakeha* meant. 'But one of your gods gave you a program of some kind?'

Tailgunner nodded. 'A program that I can't understand. Just like the eel it caught.'

'Huh?' I managed intelligently.

'The piece of the Black Wave I caught, it looked like an eel in the net,' Tailgunner explained.

'Did you see the Wave?' Pagan asked.

'Yes, and yes, it looked like a big black wave. It ignored every piece of security, every defence in the site as if it wasn't there. It co-opted some of my security programs, changing them as I watched, and took control of every net-linked system.'

Pagan and Morag were nodding as they listened. He was confirming everything we'd guessed about Demiurge's capabilities. Except that somehow he'd managed to effect Demiurge. Still I was always suspicious of these little shards of hope. Particularly when deities were involved.

'There was something else there,' Tailgunner continued, 'high above the Wave. They looked like angels.'

Morag tried to suppress the shudder of fear, but I could read her body language too well. I don't think anyone else noticed.

'The angels are chimerical hackers,' Pagan said, glancing over at Morag.

'They have attack programs derived from Demiurge. Very powerful.' Morag just about managed to keep the fear out of her voice.

'Where is all this shit coming from?' Big Henry asked. 'And why's it so much more dangerous than our stuff.'

'These Freedom Squadron wankers. When we attacked them they were like Them inside. They're infiltrators, right? They've finally got sophisticated. Info warfare, that sort of thing,' Dog Face growled.

The four of them were looking at us expectantly. Now it was our turn to look uncomfortable.

'It's kind of a long story,' I said.

'We could show them Mudge's documentary,' Pagan suggested.

It took us a while to tell them what had happened. The affable-through-narcotics Mudge plugged himself into a monitor and did indeed show them part of the documentary he'd made. I felt he spent too much time on the kicking I'd got at the hands of Rannu in New York. He claimed it was to see if they recognised him. They didn't. Pagan and Mudge did most of the talking.

'Bullshit!' Dog Face spat. He had drool around his mouth.

'It was all a lie. The Cabal started the war and kept it going,' Pagan assured him.

We'd been through this several times. Explained the Cabal's reasons and their mechanisms of control, how they pulled it off but the *whanau* hadn't lived it like we had. In many ways the concept of a sixty-year war as a con job was just too big. They looked stricken, pale, almost nauseous. Most people could understand the idea of a defensive war and the hardships and sacrifices that would mean, particularly if you'd grown up practically on the front line like these guys had, but to find out the whole thing was a lie? It meant that all you'd suffered, everyone you'd lost – the whole thing – had been for the profit of a tiny minority of people. They had just been told that everything they knew, their reality for all their lives, was a lie. Denial was a reasonable reaction. The anger that would come later was also a reasonable reaction. I almost felt like we should apologise to them.

'How do we know which story to believe?' Mother asked.

She looked shaken but her voice was even and calm. That stumped me. The truth was self-evident to us. We'd lived it. But all we were giving them was another story.

'Yeah, no offence, but you're asking us to take a lot on faith,' Tailgunner said.

'You know there's something wrong,' Morag said.

He nodded.

'Your own god warned you,' Pagan added.

I said, 'I'm afraid you're just going to have to decide which you believe. Though you could ask yourselves what possible reason we'd have to jump into hell's creation, tab and drive all the way here just to fuck with your heads. I don't want to be here.'

'And this Cronin, the guy on the viz, and this Rolleston guy, they're to blame?' Big Henry asked.

'They used to work for the Cabal, now I guess they are the Cabal,' I told them and then watched them war with what we'd told them some more.

'Look, you seem on the level,' Tailgunner started. 'But what if you've been slaved? What if you really believe but you've been brainwashed by the *taniwha*?'

'The what?' I asked.

'Them,' Mother said. She was deep in thought and I could not read her expression at all. Her calmness was weird, almost unsettling.

'Then again, why are we taking so much time to convince you?' Pagan asked. 'Bit solipsistic, isn't it?' Everyone just looked at him.

'Try and remember you're talking to a bunch of squaddies,' I suggested.

'There is only me,' Mudge said as if it was a revelation.

'We are all playthings of your imagination,' Morag said to him with mock earnestness.

The levity wasn't working. We'd fractured their world too badly.

'Okay, so I've got a question,' Mother said. We looked at her. 'So what?'

'I don't understand,' Pagan said. I didn't either.

'What difference does it make? The Cabal pulled our strings, made us fight for sixty years. Nothing we can do about it now.'

'*Utu*,' Tailgunner said quietly.

Mother turned to him. 'Really? How's that going to work then? Look, I agree with you about our ancestors, our spirituality, but the fact is we're not mythical heroes out of the past. We don't have anything like the resources to fight, and doing it on principle is a shitty reason for us all to finally get killed.'

'Because it's the right thing to do.' I was surprised that I said it. And after I said it I realised how hollow it sounded.

'Well, I congratulate you on being able to afford such a keen moral compass. Again, I don't want to die for a principle. Particularly as I don't think it matters to us what war we're fighting or who's in command. It's not going to change things for us and the end result is exactly the same,' Mother said.

'But we changed things,' Morag said. There was almost desperation in her voice. 'People can see what's going on now. The Cabal can't do those things any more.'

'Really? Is anyone trying to subvert your god yet?' Mother asked. She read the answer in Morag's miserable expression. 'Things getting better for the poor?'

'These things take time,' Pagan told her.

'The powerful and wealthy are always going to fight for what's theirs. You expose them and they find another, more subtle way to get what they want.'

'So why fight them?' Merle asked.

Mother flashed him a look of contempt.

'Survival. I grew up in Moa City. For more than half my early life the place was under siege. Now I found out we did this to our-fucking-selves? And now we're scrapping over the wreckage of humanity. Fuck that. This has got nothing to do with us. We'll sit this one out.'

'And starve to death,' Merle pointed out.

'And do what we have to,' Mother continued. 'Because when the smoke clears I'll bet my left tit it won't make the slightest bit of difference to any of my people.'

'That's what they want us to think and do. To give in, to forget about our personal responsibility ...' Mudge surprised me, but it was similar to what he'd said on Atlantis. Underneath the drugs and lust for adrenalin Mudge actually believed this stuff.

'I guess it's more comfortable on Earth?' Mother asked rhetorically. 'Because here idealism is pretty much a luxury. We have other priorities. Democracy's been a joke for years. Why should I care which fucking faceless military dictatorship I live under? I'm still fighting and dying for some other fucker. Meet the new boss, same as the old boss.'

'We were doing something,' Morag said. Again she sounded desperate.

I could see where Mother was coming from to a degree, but I think we'd pulled her world down around her ears and now she was going to do the same with our accomplishments, if you could call them that.

'Really? Get here on your own? Finance your own gear? Or were you sent? Who sent you? Because I'm willing to bet it was just a different flavour of government or military power broker, playing another version of an old game.'

'What if it's not dictatorship this time?' Pagan asked. 'What if it's slavery?'

'Are you just saying that or have you got any evidence?' Tailgunner asked.

270

'It's a suspicion. Operators sent before us returned brainwashed and you said yourself that when you lose people you get compromised almost immediately.'

'That's a reason to hide –' Mother started.

'And starve.' Merle wasn't getting off that point.

'– not fight.'

'Well that's your choice, isn't it? You either fight, hide or surrender,' I said.

Big Henry and Dog Face bristled at the word surrender. These guys might be street-bred scavengers, brawlers, thieves and survivors, but they had pride.

'I've known Rolleston for a long time. You surrender, you'll get used or killed. You hide, you'll starve, or if you raid for supplies then sooner or later he'll get round to hunting you down when you become a big enough pain in the arse. Besides, if you're going to fight for supplies you may as well just fight. You ask, why fight? Survival. The rest is window dressing to provide a little bit of hope for motivational purposes,' I said.

Mother stared at me. Finally she gave a humourless laugh.

'See, that's a language I understand,' she told me.

It looked like I'd found a way to motivate her.

Strange walked out of the darkness and lay down next to Mother, her head in the older woman's lap. Mother started stroking the girl's long dark hair.

'So can we see the fragment of Demiurge?' Pagan asked.

Tailgunner opened his mouth to reply.

'Not so fast,' Mother said. 'What do we get?'

'What the fuck is wrong with you? Have you not been listening?' Merle demanded angrily.

I was smiling. I liked this woman. Her survival skills were keenly honed. I could see why they looked to her.

'What do you want?' I asked.

'Help,' she said. She had not liked saying that.

'Supplies?' I asked.

She nodded.

'You're taking her seriously. We can take this bit of Demiurge any time we—' Merle started.

I turned on him. 'That's enough. If we can take from the enemy, deny them supplies, fuck with their infrastructure, than that's part of our remit here. We also need more intel. You don't like that, you think you're better off on your own, then fuck off.'

It was a gamble. He could just leave, and we needed him, but I couldn't have him questioning everything like this. Chinese Parliament or not, he was proving disruptive. Not to mention it was fucking wearing. He was angry. I could see that. Bruised pride. Politics was so tiresome. I was a little worried he might try and kill me. There was more than a possibility he was capable of succeeding. I could see his point. We weren't the well-oiled machine he was used to; also he was a solo act, used to doing things his way. But we were making this up as we went along, out of necessity. The whole thing was a juggling act and he needed to help or leave.

Mudge turned to him. 'Merle, I think you need to wind your neck in a bit or this just won't work.'

Merle opened his mouth to respond angrily.

'Merle,' Cat said.

I turned round to look at her. She was still on guard, cradling her gyroscopically supported railgun. Merle didn't say anything. He just nodded and relaxed.

'You help us; we'll help you,' Mother said.

13

Moa City

The cable car was heavily armoured with a number of weapon systems sticking out of it like spines. Most of them were for point defence. The cable was carbon nanotube in an armoured sheath. Even allowing for this, the cable looked very vulnerable. Tailgunner had confirmed that during the twenty-year-long, on-off siege of Moa City, the cable car normally didn't last long when They came calling. The locals had only just got this one up and running again.

We were sharing the crowded car with grubby, drawn, exhausted-looking miners coming off shift. I hoped the crowd was enough to hide us from the ever-present surveillance but I couldn't shake the feeling that we stuck out. We were wearing clean clothes and looked healthy. I could feel the security lens burning into me, scrutinising me. It was as if Demiurge was staring at us. Which it would be as it ran our features through various facial recognition programs.

The cavern that Moa City occupied was the largest yet. It was more like a large alpine valley with a roof of stone. The cavern walls close enough to see were cut into terraces where they'd been extensively mined. This made me uncomfortable. It was like chipping away at the walls of your own house and then wondering why the roof fell on you.

Enormous geothermally powered strip-lighting rigs hung from the cavern roof among the stalactites. It was supposed to be daytime but the harsh light was more institutional than daylight. It wasn't total either. Many of the lights had been destroyed or damaged. Some hung down from the rock; others flickered on and off intermittently. At 'night' the lights would go UV, providing what little modified vegetation was left with the band of light it needed.

The floor of the cavern was supposed to be a lush carpet of vegetation broken up by plantation-style mansions cut out of the rock itself. Big Henry had told me that it had been fashionable to have a seam of precious metal run through the wall of your own house.

The problem with the Garden District was that the New Zealand colonial forces hadn't been able to defend it when They had swarmed in from Nightside.

'I remember during one of the attacks – the first one I saw – I looked down from the city and it looked like the whole place was crawling. It was like a carpet of insects on a nature viz. You could barely see the ground,' Tailgunner said as he saw me gazing down at the cavern floor.

We'd used some of the morphic compound to change his features. His tattoos – they were called *ta moko* apparently and told his story – had been covered with foundation. The *whanau* were nothing if not pragmatic. A bandanna covered the computer tech protruding from his skull.

'There's people down there,' I said. In some places huge bonfires were burning and by magnifying my optics I could just about make out large groups around the fires. There were large, oddly shaped statuary near some of the people.

'They call themselves the End,' Tailgunner said. I could hear the contempt in his voice. 'They're deserters. Part of some suicide cult. They use their religious beliefs to justify their cowardice. They moved into the Garden when They moved out.'

I had always been somewhat impressed with conscientious objectors. I was less sure how I felt about deserters. It was too much like running out on your mates when they needed you.

'Who are the guys in the civvy-looking APCs?' Cat asked.

There were wheeled armoured vehicles moving around far below us.

'Probably salvage teams and private bailiffs,' Tailgunner told us. 'When They came the first time the Garden was overrun. Those that had the chance evacuated. The thing is, They don't loot – no interest in what we have, just in killing us. In some of the houses there are still valuables left. Not to mention that some of the ostentatious bastards had veins of precious metals running through their homes. So the old owners, if they still have money, send teams in to clear out the squatters and see what's left. Others are private concerns, looters.'

Far below us I saw muzzle flashes and the strobe of a laser in the streets. Much of it was already rubble, the abused ghost of a wealthy neighbourhood. The same could be said for almost all of the rest of the cavern. Moa City had been under siege for almost half of the war since Lalande 2 had been invaded fifty-five years ago. The story of the siege was written in craters, scars, gouges, blackened and melted

274

stone almost everywhere you looked. No part of the enormous cavern was more heavily damaged than the city itself.

One of the greatest engineering feats of the pre-war era, a great deal of survey work, modelling and experimentation had gone into the city's planning. An enormous stalactite hung from the cavern roof. It was about three miles high and its tip hung about half a mile above the Garden District. Engineers had decided that the stalactite could support habitation, and the city had been cut out of the stone and existing caves with lasers and microbes. It was designed to be a dormitory city for the mineworkers, while those who could afford it lived in the Garden, among the lush vegetation below.

After They had attacked, the wealthy who survived moved up into the stalactite. Initially thought to be a weak point in the planet's defences, the giant stalactite proved to be a veritable fortress and much of it was given over to the military. The rest of the people were pushed into already crowded parts of the city and left to fend for themselves, particularly when the mines were abandoned by the human forces.

The stalactite filled much of the view through the scarred and pockmarked armoured-glass windscreen of the cable car. It looked like there was not a single inch of it left undamaged. Some of the rock was covered in a patchwork of armour plate. The plates looked thick enough to have come from mechs, or cavern-sea battleships; much had rusted due to the environment. Wart-like artillery, anti-aircraft and point-defence batteries grew out of the stone in numerous places.

'Was the siege as bad as they say?' I asked.

Both Tailgunner and Merle laughed humourlessly.

'Mother's first memory was of her mother cooking meat from her father's corpse for the children to eat. He'd killed himself to provide food,' Tailgunner said and then turned to fix me with his lenses. 'Yeah, it was bad.'

I swallowed and nodded. It sort of put into perspective what we'd been through. We'd grown up in an impoverished war economy on Earth but it was way worse on the sharp end. Just trying to live long enough to be an adult was a challenge and meant you had to do bad things just to survive. And this had been done to them on purpose. I was pleased that Mudge was back with Pagan at the *whanau* base. I wouldn't have liked him to remind Tailgunner about the proud cannibal heritage they'd claimed. I was also wondering why my world had suddenly become all about cannibalism. Morag was staring at Tailgunner, appalled. She was still sporting cuts and bruises from the FAV chase. I wasn't; I'd healed quickly.

The cable car took us high up towards the cavern roof, towards the thickest part of the stalactite. We passed a broken lighting rig hanging down from the cavern roof. The light was flickering on and off, sending sparks cascading down. Just past the lighting rig we docked with the fortified gatehouse that was the cable car station. We tried not to move too enthusiastically as the mass of exhausted miners plodded off the car. I ignored the sense of vertigo as I stepped from rocking cable car onto stone platform.

To my heightened senses it seemed like there were lenses everywhere and all of them were pointed at us. Regular soldiers with the bored disinterest that came from garrison duty checked the fake IDs we'd fabricated in Limbo and let us through.

What got me most about Moa City was how quiet it was for a place so crowded. They may not have been starving, but the inhabitants looked hungry, drawn and exhausted. Hard times were etched into the lines on their faces.

The streets were smooth tunnels that seemed to always spiral down. The houses were cut out of the stone itself, but everywhere I looked I saw lean-to huts and other shanty-style dwellings. Off the main thoroughfares this part of Moa City was a densely crowded, tangled warren of alleyways. Like the outside of the enormous stalactite, the inside showed extensive battle damage.

'What's that humming noise?' Morag asked.

A pair of armed surveillance drones floated by over the crowds of people.

'The catapult is just above us. This was the scene of some of the worst fighting in the last ten years,' Tailgunner said once the drones had passed.

The enormous mass-driver catapult was used to throw heat-shielded ore cargoes into orbit for collection by tugs before being loaded into freighters for export.

I felt a stab of anger as I walked past a holographic projection of Cronin. I could see his enormous bodyguard Martin Kring just behind him. Kring looked more metal and plastic than man. The headline on the news piece was FREE EARTH GOVERNMENT WARNS OF POSSIBLE FIFTH COLUMN TERRORIST CELLS. I wondered if they meant us specifically. I wondered how many more operators had made it to the ground and were still free.

A patrol went by in a six-wheeled light combat vehicle. They were more alert than the guards in the cable car station as they scanned the crowd. I felt their eyes on us but they showed no sign of suspicion or recognition as we moved away from the main thoroughfare and deeper into the warren of alleyways.

'This is the Rookery,' Tailgunner said. 'I grew up here.'

I was worried that despite his disguise he'd be recognised, but he kept his head down and avoided eye contact. Cat, Merle, Morag and I got stared at a lot. We were obvious outsiders. The deeper we went into the Rookery, however, the less surveillance lenses and remotes we saw.

When I had to run the gauntlet of a line of begging vets who'd had their implants removed, I almost felt at home. Everything was so cramped. Sometimes it felt like I was walking through people's homes. We got more hard stares from men and women carrying weapons and wearing gang colours. They were mostly older vets. Younger gang members would be serving in the military. I guessed something about the way we carried ourselves made them leave us alone.

'Do you know anything about this Puppet Show?' I asked Merle.

We'd reached the external wall of the stalactite and were working our way up on narrow paths cut out of the stone.

'I've had a few dealings with them. They're different. Seem to be reasonably trustworthy in a scary, don't-fuck-with-us kind of way,' he said.

I was trying to hide that I was gasping for breath. Merle could have been out for a stroll despite having spent the last six months in a hole.

Tailgunner disappeared into a gap in the rock just above us. Morag followed and then I reached it. I had to crawl through into a small cave. The cave mouth looked out over the cavern, giving us a view of the cable car run we'd come in on. We were above the lighting rigs now and I could see clusters of smaller stalactites, many of them with windows and entrances. Below us on the lighting rigs I could see tents and houses made of packing crates and other scavenged materials. Connecting them all was a web of strong-looking metal cable.

Tailgunner was kneeling down and pulling a modified climbing harness out of the bag he'd been carrying. Attached to the harness were two pieces of rope ending in a metal sleeve that contained runners. We got out the harnesses we were carrying and Tailgunner showed us how to clip the sleeve onto the web of cable. The runners gripped above and below the cable, as did the brake pads when you wanted to slow down.

'When you get to a junction, you clip on the cable head you have free and unclip the one you were using. Clear?' Tailgunner asked.

Oh yeah. Sounded simple, if you weren't three and a half fucking miles up. Still, maybe I'd be lucky and land on one of the lighting rigs. That way I could die by electrocution.

It looked like Tailgunner had fallen out of the cave but he'd just kicked backwards and slid down the cable. Morag followed. She was grinning. It looked like she was going too fast to me. It felt too fast when I kicked off after her. I was using the brake a lot until I burned myself on the sleeve and noticed smoke rising from it. My legs felt too light as they dangled over the drop. My body felt too heavy. The high gravity made me think the ground wanted me back in a bad way.

I was too busy with my fear to notice the junction and I hit it hard. My heart jumped around in my chest cavity as I swung up past ninety degrees and got to look at the ground from an interesting new angle. I almost tangled myself up in the cables. I managed to control my swinging. It didn't look very dignified.

'Move!' It was Cat coming up fast behind me. I managed to clip the second sleeve over the next line and unclip the first head and move off just before she collided with me. The second stretch of cable was uphill. I had engaged the motor in the sleeve and the rollers were pulling me up the cable, but it was slow. This gave me time to con-template dangling on a jury-rigged web of cable from a home-made climbing machine miles above rocky death on a high-G planet.

If anything this area looked more badly damaged, as if it had been more fiercely fought over, and the people who lived out here in the smaller stalactite dwellings and on the lighting rigs looked harder, more dangerous. There were more gang colours on view, more weapons. Tailgunner told me later that they were collectively known as the Sky Gangs or the Light Tribes. Most of Them could climb across any surfaces and when They'd come swarming across the cavern ceil-ing, the gangs here had put up a hell of a fight but had been forced back into the main stalactite time and time again.

We slid into an opening on one of the stalactites. The outside was painted. I think it was supposed to look like a theatre, like the kind you see in old vizzes, only it was inverted. We were met in the rock opening by gun barrels. One day I'd find a place where people didn't want to point guns at me.

The opening was the entrance to a dome-like cave with various worn, low sofa-like pieces of furniture in it and a stall selling sweets, snacks, alcohol and recreational pharmaceuticals. It was decorated with murals that replicated posters from an earlier age promoting some kind of live entertainment. I think they were from a time before vizzes. If you wanted to go and see actors you used to have to go to a big building where the actors actually were and watch them with hundreds of other people, as ridiculous as that sounds.

The men and women pointing guns at us looked serious, capable and like they'd seen action. Initially I thought they were Maori with only one or two white guys. Tailgunner told me later that a lot of them were descendants of colonists originally from other islands in the South Pacific back on Earth.

I was less sure of the look, though. They seemed to be wearing their best clothes, like you see glamorous types wearing on the tabloid viz stations, if those best clothes had been made from a patchwork of rags. Presumably the rags were the only material they had to make their finery out of. All of them had long thick dreadlocks. I was sure I saw the silver of metal, as if some of the dreadlocks were made of steel camouflaged by the rest of the hair. Occasionally something would move under it.

I didn't put my hands up but I did keep them away from where my pistols were concealed beneath the borrowed combat jacket. Many vets wore their combat jackets after they left the service. They were warm, rugged and some, like this one, were armoured. The others were doing likewise. Again it was useful not to have Mudge with us. On the other hand he could have spent some money at the drug concession. I'd have to get him something.

'Don't point those guns at me. I want to see Puppet Show,' Tailgunner said, a little brusquely I thought for someone on the edge of a three-and-a-half-mile drop with guns pointed at him. One of the raggedy types seemed to agree with me. He took a step forward and pushed a shotgun barrel into the skin on Tailgunner's face.

'I don't know what you're fucking talking about, but you're leaving now,' the guy said. His voice was low, even and full of honest menace.

'I know you,' Tailgunner said. That was all he said. I turned to look at him. I had been hoping for a bit more.

'Everyone fucking knows me, so what?'

'It's Tailgunner, you wanker.'

Again I felt that Tailgunner was pushing them a little harder than they needed pushing in our current position. I saw Morag turn to look at him. I was aware of Cat and Merle shifting slightly. I saw glances exchanged among the raggedy types. They definitely knew the name and it was a significant one.

'You don't look anything like him,' the guy with the shotgun said. He was standing too close. He'd gone for the intimidation of physical contact with the gun and not the safety of distance. Tailgunner demonstrated this to him by ripping the shotgun out of his grip.

'I'm fucking wanted.' Tailgunner was all street snarl now. Show no weakness. 'I'd be pretty fucking stupid to wander around without a disguise, yeah?'

Then he handed the shotgun back as if he couldn't give a fuck. This was a different Tailgunner. This was his public face. He unclipped himself from the cable and started securing the rig about himself.

'If you're—' the guy with the shotgun started.

Tailgunner fixed him with a glare. 'It's a call the Puppet Show makes, not you,' he told him and then went back to what he'd been doing.

The raggedy types exchanged looks, mouthed questions and shrugged. It was clear they weren't used to being dealt with like this. It was also clear that the big hacker's name meant something here.

'We'll need your guns,' another raggedy type said. Tailgunner finished packing away his cable gear and looked at her.

'Go on then,' he said.

I tensed. I hated giving up my guns, especially in the colonies, but there was no rush to disarm us. I noticed that one of them had left the group and disappeared through some thick red curtains into another part of the stalactite. Moments later he came back with one of the largest men I'd ever seen. He had the same dark but sallow complexion that many of the people of Lalande 2 had. He had the dreadlocks and a facial tattoo but it was much simpler than Tailgunner's or the others' in the *whanau*. He was pretty much the first fat person I'd seen since we'd got here, but judging by the patchwork of scars that covered his face he'd worked hard to get this fat. It was a muscular and solid kind of fat. His ragged finery strained to contain his build. I wondered how he could move his bulk in the high G.

'Soloso,' Tailgunner said, nodding a greeting. This time I heard caution and respect in Tailgunner's voice.

'He says he's Tailgunner but he doesn't look like him,' the guy with the shotgun said.

'Well, well, well hard Max Ruru,' the big guy rumbled. At first I'd thought it was a heavy ground tank starting up.

'We've come to see the Puppet Show,' Tailgunner said.

Soloso was looking us over. I don't think he liked what he was seeing.

'Come to complicate our lives, more like it. Hear you've sold out, gone over to the other side. That true?'

Tailgunner met the other man's look. 'I think you're the only person who'd get away with asking that question. Once.'

Soloso gave Tailgunner's answer some thought. Then he smiled.

'You get asked for your guns?' he surprised me by finally asking. Tailgunner just nodded. Soloso turned to his own people. He looked angry. 'Do you think we're frightened of these people?' The raggedy types shifted uncomfortably under the glare of his black plastic lenses. Then he turned back to us. He took his time shifting his bulk. 'The Puppet Show will start soon. Please don't make me waste my time by talking about the consequences of fucking around.' Then he nodded his massive head towards the red curtains.

The rest of us unclipped ourselves from the cables and headed towards them. As Tailgunner passed Soloso, the big man stopped him with a massive hand on the hacker's chest.

'You went toe to toe with every hard man in the Rookery; I even heard that you got in a couple of fights with some SAS guys, but I always got the feeling you were avoiding me,' he rumbled.

Tailgunner looked up at the bigger man.

'I was never sure I could take you. Now get your fucking hands off me.'

At first I thought it was a tectonic event, then I realised the rumbling was Soloso laughing, but he took his hands off Tailgunner and we headed through the curtains.

The other side was different. A large room hewn out of the rock, it sloped down with irregularly spaced lines of chairs, all of which faced a stage. Suspended platforms hung from the ceiling supporting a complicated lighting rig and automated weaponry that was tracking us. Thick, red and extensively patched curtains blocked our view of most of the stage.

I felt rather than saw Soloso come through the curtains behind us.

'I don't like this,' Morag whispered, leaning in close to me. 'This place is run by a network. Unless it was completely isolated then Demiurge has got to be in here.'

She left unsaid that an isolated system before the coming of Demiurge would have been of little business use. The thing is, we were committed. We had to rely on Tailgunner's judgement. Even now gunships and flight-capable exo-armour could be on the way to get us. The Puppet Show could collect what I guessed would be a not-insubstantial bounty.

Then the curtains opened and the spots came on. There were five of them. They were on Morag, Cat, Merle, Tailgunner and me. Would have been quite effective if we hadn't had flash compensation. We could see fine. The stage was backlit in green. Crackly, poor-sound-quality music, which I think was supposed to be sinister and atmospheric, started playing, and the puppets dropped from the rafters over the stage like three hanged women.

They had the thinnest, frailest bodies I'd yet seen on Lalande. They made Strange look bulky. I think had they not been supported by complex-looking exo-frames, their bodies would have just snapped in the high gravity. They hung completely limp in their frames, held up by what looked like thick metal tendrils. Hanging there, they reminded me of Sharcroft in his spider chair, all but a corpse.

They wore dresses that looked like they had once been expensive and fashionable but had seen better days a long time ago. They were accessorised with tatty, once-elegant, elbow-length gloves. Crying facemasks of beaten steel covered their faces.

I didn't get this. How could this mockery rule the Rookery's criminal classes? By criminal classes, I meant everyone in the Rookery. They were poor; it wasn't like they had a choice.

'You're bringing trouble to our door, Tailgunner,' they said. Each word seemed to come from a different one of them. There was no hesitation. The accusation flowed like a proper sentence but somehow it sounded like a ripple of words. I didn't like it. I kept wanting to turn around, but every time I did I found Soloso there. He was always watching one of us. Most often Tailgunner, but as soon as I looked behind me he would turn his huge dreadlock-shrouded, bullet-shaped head to look at me and smile.

'Yeah, that's probably true,' Tailgunner said after some thought.

'We have money,' I said distractedly. I was still looking behind me at Soloso. I turned around to face the Puppet Show.

'Which we could relieve you of,' the Puppet Show said. It was very matter of fact, almost as if it wasn't paying attention.

'We need supplies,' Tailgunner told it. He glanced at me. 'We'll make it worth your while.'

'What sort of supplies and for how much?' the three of them asked as one.

'Food and medicine mainly, maybe some tools and later some ammunition and explosives. For a lot of people. We'll take what you can give us.'

The working-class Scottish part of me thought he was being very cavalier with someone else's money. On the other hand we were being pretty cavalier with Sharcroft's money. The Puppet Show took some time looking between us.

'This looks like black ops kind of trouble to us. Why would we want that?' they asked in unison.

'Again, money,' I suggested.

They all turned to look at me. They moved in a kind of angry jerking way, exactly like puppets on a string.

'We have lots of money. We don't need trouble from the Freedom

Squads. See, a very nice young lady came and explained it to us. Perhaps you know her?'

I manage to resist the urge to look around to see if she was standing in the shadows. Like I'd see her if she was. Morag glanced over at me, worried.

'See, we can do what we want as long as we don't interfere with them in any way. It seems like a good deal,' the Puppet Show continued.

'Before we talk any more, are we safe here?' Merle asked, his tone neutral.

'You are what we say you are here. Nothing more,' the Puppet Show answered.

This was starting to freak me out. I wondered if they were just three corpses in a frame used as a front to mess with people. Was Soloso the real boss?

'Which doesn't answer my fucking question.'

'Look, this is a nice set-up you have here. Sure it impresses the locals, but if you're going to fuck us, let's get to shooting. You go first. If not then I'm going to assume that you're stalling, which means you've got people on the way, which means we'll initiate the shooting,' Cat surprised me by saying.

The four of us that weren't Tailgunner shifted slightly, ready to go for guns. Soloso didn't even flinch. I know because I glanced nervously behind me.

'Tailgunner.' It was a whisper, one syllable each, but they still made it sound like a complete word.

'Okay, everyone just cool down,' Tailgunner said, making placatory gestures with his hands.

'We're not the people for your street-level bullshit,' Merle said, sounding genuinely angry.

'That's enough. We're in their house,' I said to Merle. He didn't answer. I turned to the Puppet Show. 'You're very scary. Seriously, I don't like this at all. It's creepy.' I ignored the look of contempt from Merle and the look of confusion from Morag. 'We're here to deal. If you don't want to, then we'll go our separate ways and you do what you have to do. Even if that means grassing us up. If you want to deal then let's get all the gun-pointing, cock-waving, I'm-harder-than-thee bollocks out of the way so we can get on with business.'

'We didn't come here to fight you,' Morag added. 'But just so you know, we could be a lot of trouble for anyone who helps us.' Now she didn't have to emphasise that, but it was now most definitely all our cards on the table.

The Puppet Show stared at us. They stared at us for a very long time. They were very good at intimidation psychology for three inanimate bodies dangling from a roof. I could see Merle getting impatient. I was trying to decide whether or not to target Soloso or one of the automated weapon systems in the rafters. The rafters were winning but I reckoned I'd let the shoulder laser have a crack at Soloso. Though I couldn't shake the feeling that it'd be like trying to kill a tank with a flashlight. Then I remembered that my combat jacket didn't have a shoulder flap for the laser anyway.

'You are safe here,' came the rippling answer, finally. Tailgunner, Cat and I relaxed slightly.

'I don't wish to appear disrespectful but how does that work?' Morag asked. As she did the Puppet Show jerked round to face her. Not so long ago she would have flinched. Not now though. 'You're networked, aren't you? This whole place.'

'It works by having to shut down our entire system and go on to a clean life support while every single component is stripped out and replaced and then shielded at some expense. It works through isolation from the net that was our world. It works through surgery to cut our infected systems to replace them with new clean ones. It works through constant and expensive vigilance to keep out attempts to invade our system or re-link it to the net.'

It was difficult to tell, but I reckoned two, if not all of them were pretty pissed off about Demiurge. Morag looked at me and shrugged. It wasn't the definitive all-clear I was hoping for on the communications security side of things, but at least it wasn't her screaming at us to run.

'You'll deal with us then?' I asked.

'Not at the expense of our own destruction,' the three voices answered. 'But we will listen and we have no interest in turning you in. How many people do you need supplies for?'

There was a pause. Years of training meant that we did not wish to give away any more info than we had to.

'Just over two hundred,' Morag said. She hadn't had the training. She looked at me and shrugged. I guess we had to trust it or we'd never get anywhere. Merle didn't look happy but then he never did. I found that I really didn't care if he was happy or not.

The Puppet Show swayed from side to side in what I guessed was a negative gesture.

'Too many,' they said. 'We have the supplies but we cannot get them to you without being noticed. We can get small bits and pieces;

maybe we can provide you with a couple of protein mulch vats, but anything beyond that is too dangerous.'

'Another waste of time,' Merle said. 'Shame. I'd heard good things about you.'

'That's enough,' Tailgunner told him.

I wasn't paying attention. I was having an idea.

'This is the big supply nexus for the region, right?' I asked. Tailgunner nodded. 'Does that include the Citadel?'

'Yeah,' Tailgunner answered. 'But it's a no go. The supplies are delivered by Mag Lev. The tunnels are embedded in the rock and the stations are fortresses.'

'If you had enough firepower or explosives could you take out one of their tunnels?' I asked.

Fortunately Tailgunner picked up on what I was talking about. 'I think we could probably find some place weak enough,' he said.

'So what?' Cat asked. 'Rolleston and his friends don't get their supplies immediately but neither do we.'

'What are their alternative methods for supply delivery?' Merle asked, catching on. 'Shuttle?'

'Not between here and there. The Citadel was chosen because it was difficult to get to. If They were to attack They would have to bottleneck through tunnels. That meant They couldn't bring in some of their really big guns like the Hydras,' the Puppet Show told us. 'They have a dedicated Mag Lev link. If they can't do that then they will have to do it the old-fashioned way by ground convoy.'

I brought up a map of the area on my internal system. Along with the catapult, there was another atmosphere processor and a military shuttle port above us. It was the shuttle port that kept people alive during the various sieges, as it was the entrepôt for supplies delivered from orbit and other parts of Lalande 2.

With Moa City being turned into what was effectively a fortress, they wanted to have their vital supplies like food and munitions as well protected as possible. The centre of the city had been converted into a supply depot and had grown and grown. Which meant that if the Mag Lev was down ...

'Any supply convoy would have to come by here,' I mused.

'Which still doesn't help you,' the Puppet Show said. 'Because you're still left with the same problem of having to get it out of the city without being spotted. It's near-total surveillance.'

'But you know how to do it,' Morag said.

'Not without getting noticed.'

'So let them notice. Because they'll think it's us. Which it will be, just with a little bit of local help,' Morag added.

The Puppet Show was quiet. We waited. We waited some more. I thought about listening to some Billie Holiday on my internal systems.

'We want to see a full plan, including how you're going to minimise our exposure, and we will want a ridiculous amount of money for as little aid as we can get away with providing. Half of it now.'

'That seems unreasonable,' I said equitably.

Soloso was by my side holding an old-fashioned black credit chip that still had a digital readout on it. The display showed a ludicrous sum.

'That's just half, isn't it?' I asked.

He nodded. Reluctantly I took one of the black credit chips we had with us out of the pocket of my combat jacket. I had to struggle with my nature to pay so much for so little, particularly having had no money for the majority of my life. Then I remembered it wasn't my money; it was Sharcroft's and he was a prick. I gave them a bonus.

Morag held up a memory chip. 'This is the truth as best we can tell it. What happened on Earth, the war, who Rolleston and Cronin are and what they've done, and what we think is going on here and in the other colonies. Read and watch it. We've provided what corroborating evidence we could but that'll be difficult to check under Demiurge. If you're prepared to believe it then pass it on.'

Again the Puppet Show was quiet for a while before answering.

'We will review it. If we believe it we will have it disseminated by people several steps removed from us. Perhaps we will do so even if we don't believe it. We understand the value of propaganda,' the Puppet Show finally replied.

Morag looked pained. 'We worked long and hard to make sure it wasn't propaganda. It's always going to be subjective but we've tried to tell the truth as best we can.'

The Puppet Show disappeared up into the rafters as if they had been yanked up. The curtains closed. Bit rude, I thought. Soloso was standing by Morag. He towered over her. Again not so long ago she would have been intimidated, but not now. She just handed him the memory chip.

'We're done here? Let me see you to your cable,' Soloso said with all the politeness of a posh hotel concierge, if the concierge was capable of pulling your legs off and eating your head.

The general rule in the army is never volunteer. I'd learned this the hard way after I'd joined 5 Para, or rather after I'd volunteered to join instead of waiting for the inevitable draft. It was so I could join the same regiment that hadn't managed to kill my mum and dad. I'd had some odd ideas in my teens. I'd volunteered for this too. I wanted to see the show. I was quite surprised when Morag joined me.

That was why I was dangling from high-tensile rope over a six-hundred-foot drop in a vertical water-drill-cut shaft pretending to be a combat engineer and desperately trying to remember my demolitions training. I was also trying to teach Morag how to place demo. I had no idea where I stood with her so of course I chose this moment to talk to her about what I can only laughingly call our relationship. The status of which I had come to think of as good if I wasn't being shot at. I was so bad at this sort of thing.

'There's no need to be gentle. It's pretty safe until it's got a detonator in it,' I told her as we worked plastic concentrate explosive into what we hoped were likely fracture points. The *whanau* all had experience of mining but they were busy at the moment. Some of the others back at *Utu Pa* probably could have helped but we hadn't thought to ask. Morag followed my lead and worked the charge into the crack with a look of concentration on her face.

'You did well with the Puppet Show the other day,' I said. She grunted a vague affirmative. 'And in the FAV.'

She stopped and turned to look at me. I saw her in green, illuminated by my lowlight optics.

'Yeah, I'm getting good at killing people,' she said.

'That's not the way to think about it. Think about it as helping keep Mudge, Pagan, Cat and Merle alive. Well maybe not Merle. Besides, I'm pretty sure they were members of the Black Squadrons.'

'And that makes it all right to kill them, does it?'

I gave this some thought.

'Yeah. They knew exactly what they were doing when they chose to work with the really bad guys. They're no better than Rolleston and Cronin.'

She just looked at me. I don't think she liked what she was seeing.

'Okay,' she said carefully. 'Maybe it's not about them; maybe I just don't want to be that person. Get that comfortable with it.' She left the 'like you' unsaid.

'Morag, you didn't have to be here. You could have helped in other ways that didn't put you at the sharp edge.'

'Is there a difference? Directly or indirectly responsible for killing?'

That stumped me.

'Fucked if I know. Less dangerous and I reckon the distance makes it easier to get to sleep at night.'

'I meant morally?' She sounded a little exasperated.

'What are you talking about? Look, I don't want to be doing these things either, but here we are doing them. You've got to put that stuff to one side until we're done. Those are things to worry about when we're not hiding from the Black Squadrons hoping we don't get shot.'

'I wish I had your moral relativism.' I wasn't sure if she was being sarcastic or not. Moral relativism?

'You have to stop spending so much time with Pagan. I'm not used to killing, I don't like doing it ...'

'You do it very well.'

I was starting to get angry.

'Morag, we killed some bad guys. The fact that they were bad doesn't matter because I can guarantee before we've finished we will have killed a lot of people who were just doing their job and got in our way. People that in other circumstances we would have been happy to have a drink and a laugh with. People not unlike all the guys back at the *pa*. People not that unlike us. You will have to kill them because they'll be shooting at you. If you can't deal with that then say so now because I will fucking drop you, because you put us all at risk if your hand-wringing causes the slightest hesitation. Do you understand me?'

Her expression was unreadable. For a moment I had the feeling that this was some kind of test. Then she turned away from me angrily.

'Did it occur to you that I'd be fine and that I just needed someone to talk to about this?' she demanded, but she didn't sound as angry or as upset as I had expected. I, on the other hand, was. Our talk wasn't going well. It seemed that all we could do now was tear at each other.

'I'm serious, Morag. You need to put these thoughts out of your head. Find a way to deal with it, to forget about it until you're in a safe place to process it, because even talking to the rest of us about it fucks us up. Starts us doubting.'

'So we isolate ourselves?' she asked emotionlessly.

Again I had to give this some thought.

'I don't think so. I don't think that you'll ever be closer to anyone than you are to the people you fight with. Maybe not even lovers, because how could they understand?' She didn't answer. Didn't look at me. 'I need to know. Can you do this?'

She swung round on the rope to face me. Defiance in green.

'Why don't you say what you mean? Can I kill? Can I be a killer?'

Okay, I hadn't been thinking about it in those terms. Can you fight maybe? Can you be a soldier?

'Can you?'

'You're an utter bastard.'

'NCO,' I said by way of explanation.

'What's that? A non-commissioned officer?' I nodded. She looked me straight in the eyes. 'I can do what's necessary.' She meant it. I'd heard that resolve before.

There was something in this conversation, something that I didn't get. Mudge would call it subtext. Morag didn't get as angry or as upset as I thought she would. Maybe she was getting harder but I couldn't shake the feeling that somehow the conversation had been for my benefit.

Below us I heard the sound of the massive mine elevator moving up towards us. It was designed to move the largest of mining mechs. I could see the glow of *Apakura*'s lights on the elevator as the monstrous Bismarck-class mech rose up out of the darkness to meet us.

I placed the last of the detonators into the PEC and Morag and I kicked off the rock and rappelled down to meet the rising elevator platform. This close to the Bismarck I felt awe looking up at its armoured bulk. There was a lot of violent tonnage contained in its reinforced superstructure. Our battered FAV was parked under the giant mech's four legs. It would never be hermetically sealed again and the armour had taken a profound beating, but some of the Kiwis had got the tough little vehicle working again.

The light above us was like a harsh artificial dawn as we rose out of the lift shaft and onto one of the terraces in the Moa City cavern wall. Time to play soldier again. I put the butt of my H&K SAW into my shoulder and moved forward and to one side. I knelt down by a pile of rubble. Morag was doing something similar on the other side of the mech, her laser carbine at the ready. Ostensibly we were providing a picket. We were looking for anything in the vicinity with hostile intent. Soon everyone in the cavern was going to know we were here.

Five hypersonic bangs shook the ground in rapid succession. Even with our dampeners they sounded impossibly loud. Anyone without dampeners would have been immediately deafened. The noise rolled back and forth across the enormous cavern. It was like being in close proximity to the source of thunder. Only the dead in Moa City could have failed to hear us, though I had my doubts about that.

This wasn't the way I was used to fighting but it was an awesome display of firepower. The five 300-millimetre, tungsten-cored projectiles were designed for penetration. They arced high across the cavern and into the stone close to where wall became cave roof on the opposite side. I magnified my vision to see rock powdered to dust as they hit in almost exactly the same place. Each round drove into the rock, kinetic force creating friction and leaving a tunnel of smoking stone in its wake. Hopefully penetrating deep enough to break into the Mag Lev tunnel we knew was there behind a thick layer of rock.

Fire lit up the top of the *Apakura* as it launched a salvo of long-range missiles at the same place. The sound of the missiles was like a whisper compared to the impacts of the mass driver rounds. I split my time between scanning the nearby area and watching the fires of the rocket engines burn across the cavern. Flames blossomed as the conventional explosive, shape-charged warheads blew out more rock and hopefully added to the damage to the Mag Lev. Unfortunately, right now we had no way of telling if it had worked.

Or at least that was what I thought until I saw the Mag Lev train. It shot out of the hole the barrage had made and fell, and fell, and fell. It was long train but was dwarfed by the size of the cavern. I was running towards the elevator now. I didn't want to see it complete its downward journey. I heard the impact. Even from the other side of the valley. I imagined the screams.

I reached the lift platform and triggered the mechanism just as the combat drone came into view, rising over the terraces. I raised the SAW to my shoulder to fire but *Apakura* beat me to it. I flinched involuntarily as the rapid-firing railgun closest to me fired a short burst from its rotating barrels. The drone disintegrated.

I could see the burn of missiles coming towards us, fired from a battery on the huge stalactite city, as the lift platform began descending into the shaft. They were too slow. That said, I still felt like getting into the FAV.

We were further down the shaft when the missiles hit. Our world went orange and the overpressure battered us to the ground. *Apakura* had protected us from the worst of the blast and the rain of debris. Try not to think about the train.

Morag staggered to her feet, blood pouring out of her nose. I felt blood running over my mouth as well. She climbed into the FAV. We'd left the engine running. The downward journey seemed to take for ever. There must be someone up there by now, a Black Squadron rapid response force of some kind, but nothing bad was happening to us yet. Maybe we deserved something bad. Try not to think about the train falling.

After an eternity of waiting for some kind of death to land on us from above, we reached the base of the elevator. I sat on the bonnet of the FAV as Morag drove me towards the control box for the explosives. This would have been a lot easier with wireless detonators but we couldn't take the chance so we were doing it the old-fashioned way. I just hoped none of the wires had been damaged by the missile strike. Don't think about the train.

Apakura shifted off the lift platform and away from the base of the shaft, moving more like a spider than any quadruped I'd ever seen. When it got to us it crouched down, providing more cover as I got down behind the FAV. I could hear the sound of vectored-thrust engines in the shaft now – poor timing on their part. Don't think about the train. I opened my mouth and triggered the explosives.

It had taken three nights to wire. The shaft and every tunnel connecting the Moa City cavern to our vicinity blew. Overpressure rocked the mech and moved the FAV across the tunnel floor and knocked me over. Rubble avalanched into the mine from what used to be the elevator shaft. Then it went dark in a way that lowlight couldn't help with as dust filled the air. I felt my way into the FAV and Morag drove us out of the mine, *Apakura* following.

I could see it in their faces when we finally made it back to the *pa*, having taken a circuitous route and checked and then double-checked we weren't being followed. I climbed out of the FAV covered head to foot in rock dust.

The belly hatch on the *Apakura* opened, Mother and Tailgunner climbed out. They looked stricken. Horrified by what they'd done. It's one thing to destroy part of the enemy's infrastructure; it's another to kill some poor sod who was just taking the Mag Lev back home, or just worked there. I was pretty sure there'd be more of this before we were through.

The thing was, after I'd managed to clean myself up, Morag found me and took me deeper into the caves. Where we could be alone. Where we could make love or have sex or fuck, I wasn't sure which. I still wanted Morag, needed her, even loved her, but she was becoming more and more alien to me.

14
Moa City

Despite the prep, despite the waiting for it to start, you're never ready for when it does. Without comms, separated from one another, you're left with nothing but going over the plan again and again. Where did we fuck up? What have we forgotten?

I felt like I stuck out a mile. I didn't belong in the Rookery and the people here knew it. I didn't meet their eyes and they ignored me, but I think they knew my presence here meant trouble for them.

Cat, Merle and Tailgunner were on roofs on either side of the main thoroughfare. Morag and I were on the same side of the street but separated, with Mother and Strange, who were our drivers. Mudge and Pagan were on the other side of the street, again far apart, with Dog Face and Big Henry as their drivers.

I saw the Ground Effects Raider leading the convoy. I watched it wind round the bend on the spiral roadway and head towards my position. The GE Raider was the bigger, better-armed and better-armoured older brother of the GE fast-attack sled. Almost as heavily armed as a main battle tank, it used four low-level vectored-thrust engines to provide propulsion and manoeuvrability. Hopefully they wouldn't help much in the cramped streets of Moa City.

Behind the first GE Raider were four civilian trucks that had been up-armoured for military use. Each of the cabs had an armoured turret with an autocannon. These cannons were tracking from side to side, looking for targets, intimidating the street. Maybe the gunners in the cabs were in control, maybe Demiurge was. It must have been pre-combat nerves but to me the autocannons looked eager. Why hadn't I taken some drugs? Just to even out the mood a little. Bringing up the rear of the convoy behind the trucks was another GE Raider. There was a lot of firepower in the convoy for just eleven guns. The four combat drones in the air above the convoy were a further unplanned-for complication.

I was standing on one of the alleyway corners, next to a lean-to that was half home and half a third- or fourth-hand used-tech stall. Its inhabitant kept on giving me dirty looks. I knew that as we watched the convoy street kids working for the Puppet Show were blacking out security lenses all over the Rookery with spray paint.

It was Mother's job to start the show. I was used to being out on my own fighting armour; she was used to fighting from inside hundreds of tonnes of mech so God knows how she must have been feeling. I checked the time on my IVD, looked away from the street and started pulling the balaclava that I'd been wearing as a hat down over my features. I hoped Mother's nerve didn't fail, otherwise I was going to feel really stupid wearing a balaclava and not doing any crime.

The tech salesman in his little packing-material stall/house saw what I was doing. He watched me with a kind of helpless resentment. He could see what was coming. I reached into the duffel bag with my left hand and gripped the smart frame inside. My right reached up under the armoured combat jacket and I took hold of the Benelli assault shotgun slung under my arm. The jacket was fine but I missed my long coat. Also it didn't have a break-open flap for my shoulder laser, making me a weapon down.

The GE Raider passed my position, its engines blowing rubbish all over the street, collapsing stalls and trash-built homes. I needn't have worried about Mother. She kicked the wheeled anti-armour mine out into the road under the GE Raider. As soon as it appeared, the re-motes and the turret on the first truck started tracking her. The corner of the alley she was concealed behind was eaten away by autocannon and railgun fire. She triggered the mine. The GE Raider seemed to bend slightly in the middle and lift itself up into the air. Flames rolled out from underneath it, engulfing the street ahead, the shock wave flattening everything it hit, knocking people to the ground, cracking teeth together and destroying eardrums that weren't made of metal and plastic.

I ran towards the first truck. As I did, Merle triggered the two Laa-Laas set up on a tripod on the opposite roof from his position. The GE Raider was driven back down onto the street as first one and then the other missile went through its turret armour and exploded. As this happened, two combat remotes and the autocannon turrets on the first two trucks turned and fired at the now empty Laa-Laa tubes. The stone by the tubes disintegrated like someone had taken a bite out of it. On the opposite roof Merle popped up and fired his plasma rifle four times in quick succession. Before I even reached the door of the truck, he'd reduced the first two truck turrets and the remotes to molten slag. Hot liquid metal was raining down on me, eating into my armour, from the destroyed remotes above. Behind me I could hear more weapons fire and explosions as Cat and Dog Face took out the rear GE Raider and dealt with the other two remotes.

I reached the truck. The crew were trying to manoeuvre but they had nowhere to go. The convoy was blocked ahead and behind by the burning wreckage of the GE Raiders. I just hoped their ammunition didn't cook off or we were all fucked. I could see the panicked faces of the driver and the now-redundant gunner in the cab. The former was frantically driving backwards and forwards, trying to make it difficult for me.

I pulled the smart frame out and dropped the duffel bag. I let the shotgun hang on its sling as I jumped onto the lowest rung of the steps leading up to the cab. Holding on to the wing mirror, I sent the information on the truck through my palm link into the smart frame. The frame extended and I placed it against the door, sending a two-second time delay detonation order. Then I dropped off the truck and moved to one side.

To my enhanced reactions those two seconds seemed to take a lot of time. The weird thing was, there was no screaming. I mean there were cries of pains from the collateral damage – try not to think of them as people. That was to be expected; we were using heavy weapons in a built-up area. What was missing was the normal screaming you'd hear from panicked civilians. This area had seen vicious street fighting against Them throughout the war so I guess this didn't frighten them. They'd just cleared out as much as they could. Here and there I could see the odd dirty face looking at us with resentment rather than fear. Sorry.

The ceramic crucibles on the programmable frame channelled the thermite charges. The thermite cut through the hinges and the lock on the armoured door and filled the cab with fumes almost immediately. Then the concussion charge in the centre of the frame detonated. Between the charge and the door was a container with a litre of saline solution. The charge went off with a bang, battering the driver and the gunner with over-pressure. The solution created a sucking effect and the entire door flew back off the cab and into the rock on the side of the street.

The truck had stopped moving now. I heard the pops and bangs from the other vehicles behind me.

Mother came out of the alleyway she'd been hiding in, heading straight towards the truck, a Metal Storm gauss carbine at the ready.

I swung round towards the cab, shotgun at the ready. The two inside were battered and bleeding from the door charge. I didn't want to kill them but then we weren't going to be gentle either. I put a three-round burst into each of them – gel batons. They got battered around some more, disoriented, the fight knocked out of them. I grabbed the gunner and threw him out into the street, face down. Mother covered me. She was holding together just fine without her mech. I knelt in the centre of the screaming gunner's back and cable-tied his hands together. I then repeated this with the driver. In many ways I was being nicer to these guys than the others were. The other three truck crews were getting hit with thirty-millimetre gel baton grenades.

With the truck crew subdued and restrained, I ejected the magazine of gel baton rounds and replaced it with a magazine of saboted twelve-millimetre, armour-piercing explosive rounds. Then I covered Mother as she threw herself into the foot well of the cab.

Unless they're part of the Crawling Town convoy or way out in the sticks somewhere, most vehicles are heavily computerised. This meant that Demiurge had access to the systems of these trucks. However, vehicles used by the military have to be able to work without their computerised components. This is in case of an electromagnetic pulse. With a pulse even hardened electronics go offline, though they are not slagged like unprotected systems. Military vehicles also need to work without their computerised components because squaddies break stuff. Mother had to remove the truck's CPU and transponder before we could nick it.

And then it all went quiet. The main thoroughfare was filled with smoke and on fire in a few small areas. I could hear Mother working frantically in the truck's cab as I watched around us. I could make out Morag further down the street, doing the same as Strange disabled the CPU and transponder on the third truck. I knew that Pagan and Mudge would be doing the same on the other side of the convoy.

In the alleyway next to us the Puppet Show's heavily disguised people appeared as if from nowhere. The normal inhabitants of the alley had been convinced to go elsewhere and the cluttered passage was being cleared to reveal a road just about big enough to fit trucks down.

It was taking too long, but it was pointless to tell Mother to hurry up. She knew what she was doing, but I still felt very exposed and Demiurge would have known what was happening from the moment we hit the first GE Raider. The Black Squadrons were already on their way.

Mother appeared in the cab door. The CPU and transponder hit the road and she signalled that she was done. She disappeared back into the cab and the truck engine started again. She was driving it manually. Moments later I heard the other three engines start up. We covered the *whanau* as the Puppet Show's people guided them into the alleyway. The trucks would have their cargoes stripped, separated and hidden all over the Rookery. Then those of Mother's people who were familiar with Moa City would smuggle the cargo back through the tunnels, staying well clear of the cable car system. That was the plan anyway.

Big Henry turned his truck into the alleyway and followed Mother. Mudge was now on the other side of the road from me. I caught a glimpse of him between the two last trucks just before Strange turned in. Morag had pulled back closer to my position now.

Strange was manoeuvring into the tight passageway, Dog Face waiting behind her.

'Contact! Light Walker and wheeled APC coming up behind us!' Cat.

'Contact! Light Walker and wheeled APC ahead of us!' Merle.

Behind me, whoosh and explosion followed whoosh and explosion as Cat fired her final two Laa-Laas – I was guessing at the mech.

I couldn't see ahead of me as Dog Face's truck was blocking my view as he turned into the alley. I crouched down and looked under the moving truck as Merle fired his two remaining Laa-Laas from the shoulder. I heard the explosions and beneath the truck I could see the stilt-like legs of a light Walker stagger from the impact of the missiles. I could also see the wheels of the APC. It was lucky I'd crouched as railgun fire tore through the truck above me, stitching a line down it, showering me in some unidentifiable foodstuff. Across the road I saw Mudge lift his AK and begin firing short bursts up the main thoroughfare.

It was too soon. They had got here too quickly with too many people. Something had gone wrong.

Behind me I could hear laser and assault-rifle fire from Pagan, Morag, Tailgunner and Cat. Cat hadn't brought her railgun as it would have been too obvious. We would miss it now.

Big Henry gunned the truck and it disappeared into the alleyway. I crossed the mouth of the alley, passing the shotgun's pistol grip from my right hand to my left.

The Walker was reeling from the double Laa-Laa hit. Merle was rapid-firing plasma round after plasma round into it, his grouping tight and each round burning a little deeper into the mech.

The APC was advancing towards us, its double railgun firing at

Mudge, destroying the corner of the rock building he'd been using as cover and forcing him deeper into the alleyway.

Infantry were pouring out of the back of the APC and sprinting for cover. This was a mistake. I started killing them. I fired, dropping the rounds in just under their helmets. My smartlink, training, skill and experience showed me where to aim. Facial features were replaced with red as some mother's son ran a little longer before he realised he was dead. Then another, then another. The APC's railguns switched to me and I calmly moved back into the alleyway as hypersonic rounds powdered rock all around me. Across the main thoroughfare Mudge popped out of his alley mouth and started on the dismounted infantry.

A shadow from above flickered over me as Merle leaped from one side of the alley to the other. Then the rooftop that he had just left ceased to exist. I was blown across the alleyway and rubble rained down on me. The inertial armour undersuit soaked up a lot of the damage but I still felt like I'd been beaten with hammers. I struggled out from beneath the rocks and staggered to my feet.

I looked into the main thoroughfare. The APC was firing at Mudge now. More of the infantry had successfully debussed and were in cover, firing at us. I fired two more short bursts. Armour-piercing rounds flew through the superstructure of a car and exploded inside the young infantrywoman who'd taken cover behind it.

I risked glancing behind me as I reloaded, to see Morag backing down the street. She was firing burst after burst from her laser carbine.

Plasma fire on the Walker started again from Merle's new position as I exchanged fire with the remaining infantrymen, keeping their heads down. Any who did show themselves got killed. It was only Mudge and me suppressing the infantry between hiding from the APCs railguns, but we did it with such accuracy and ferocity that their return fire was weak and inaccurate. Still we needed to get out of here.

Rubble rained down on me again as the Walker's twin rapid-firing railguns ate away at the rock above, seeking Merle. He returned fire from another new position, putting plasma round after plasma round into the Walker. The entire front of the light mech's barrel-like torso was on fire. More rapid railgun fire, this time from behind as the light Walker coming up behind us opened up. The street shook and I ducked back into the alley as the Walker ahead mercifully exploded. The APC shifted its railguns from me to Mudge, who had to throw himself back into the alley as the rock corner he'd been behind just ceased to exist. I saw blood explode out of his side as a ricochet caught him, spinning him around in mid-air.

'APC turret!' I screamed, hoping that Merle's aural filter would pick me up through the gunfire.

I fired at a small group of infantry trying to conduct an over-optimistic fire-and-manoeuvre drill to get closer to us. Three of them died; the fourth might have lived. He was diving for cover when one of the saboted rounds penetrated his cheap leg armour and exploded. Hydrostatic shock blew his leg off, sending it spinning away in the opposite direction from the rest of him. I could hear him screaming. The filters never seem to drown that out. As I was firing, Merle put two plasma rounds into the APC's turret, turning it to slag.

Behind me I could hear grenade after grenade detonating against the other Walker's armour and its returning railgun fire. Merle fired at the APC behind us, another two rounds destroying its railgun turret, and then the building above me exploded as the remaining Walker fired at Merle's position. The concussion wave knocked me to the ground so hard I felt the subcutaneous armour in my face give. The impact felt like it had powdered bone. Fire and rubble covered me again. Red warnings appeared all across my IVD. My face felt liked pulped meat with jagged shards of ceramic armour stabbing through my nerve endings. Painkillers from my internal reserves kicked in and then a stim to counteract the painkillers' downer side effects. I practically bounced back to my feet.

Morag appeared behind me.

'Reloading!' she shouted, ejected the battery from her laser carbine and rammed another one home. There was blood all over her face and I could see marks on her arm, leg and side from what I guessed were superficial hits. Still she wasn't built like us. I was impressed she was still on her feet.

I fired back the way she'd just come, forcing some of the dis-mounted infantry to keep their heads down. I caught a glimpse of the remaining Walker. It was limping, its body smoking from the Laa-Laas and repeated hits from high-explosive, armour-piercing grenades.

Glancing up the alleyway I could see the rear of Dog Face's truck disappearing into the distance. I watched as Tailgunner jumped from one rooftop across the alley to the other side and disappeared from view. He had the right idea. We needed to fall back.

Pagan had joined Mudge on the other side of the thoroughfare and was firing controlled bursts back down the way he'd come.

'Morag, cover!' I shouted. She nodded, loading a grenade into the underslung launcher of her carbine. 'Pagan, Mudge!' They didn't hear; they were both too busy firing. Fucking running without comms. 'Pagan! Mudge!' Mudge was used to me shouting at him. He glanced over. 'To me now!' I shouted. Mudge nodded and signalled Pagan to follow him. Morag and I leaned around the corner and fired at anything we could see.

Just as Mudge and Pagan broke cover the mouth of the alley exploded, throwing both of them into the air. It had been a missile fired by the remaining Walker. A cloud of dust engulfed them.

Morag burned through a battery with a long burst from the laser carbine, the red light firing in a rapid strobe, superheated air exploding in its wake. I felt a bullet tug at the sleeve of my armoured combat jacket, then something slammed into my shoulder, spinning me around. I felt burning and more warning signs appeared on my IVD.

Mudge and Pagan emerged from the cloud of dust, half running, half staggering. The ground around them seemed to throw itself up into the air as railgun fire from the Walker impacted all around them. I'm not sure if a round glanced against Pagan or he caught a ricochet but his arse disintegrated in a spray of flesh, the impact too quick for much blood. He was thrown into the air and spun around. He landed on his face.

I heard four grenades fired from a launcher explode against the Walker. It had to be Cat on a rooftop. She bought Mudge just enough time to grab Pagan by the scruff of his neck and drag him into our alley. Cat had saved Pagan's life. I heard another missile hit and a long burst of railgun fire.

Further up the thoroughfare, a lone soldier made a run from the back of the APC for cover. I led him with the shotgun and fired a three-round burst. A spray of red, he staggered and almost lost his balance, but kept running and made it into the alley he was heading for. That wasn't right. He should have gone down.

'Jake, move!' Morag screamed as she pulled me back down the alley after Mudge, who was still dragging a screaming Pagan.

I actually saw the contrail of the missile as it hit where I'd been standing moments ago. I watched the explosion blossom, pushing powdered stone out as razor-sharp fragments. This was the glory of being wired as high as I was. You got to see your own death. You also had the time to do dumb things like move between the blast and Morag. It went black.

My internal medical systems flooded my body with stims, waking me up immediately. I felt something moving under me. I was rolled over onto my face. If I still had one – a face, that is. There was shouting. There nearly always is.

I opened my eyes to pain but a perfectly working IVD, though my vision was full of red warning icons. I was being told electronically what my body already knew. My world was pain. The fact that my IVD was still working so well gave me the clarity to see just how fucked we were. That was once the internal pain management systems and a fuck of a lot of painkillers and stims from my rapidly depleting internal drugs reservoirs made me capable of functioning again.

My entire front was black from scorch marks and high-velocity embedded rock grit. I don't think I had any skin left on my face. It had effectively been sandblasted off. Diagnostics were showing that shrapnel had pierced my subcutaneous armour in several places. The worst was a stomach wound that would need attention soon. Another piece of stone and metal had gone through my armoured skull and fractured it. That was bleeding badly over my lenses.

Morag was on all fours next to me, having managed to roll me off her. She was gasping for breath like she'd been badly winded. Blood was pissing out of her nose but otherwise she seemed not much worse than she had moments before.

'C'mon!' Mudge screamed at me. He was trying to get a screaming Pagan over his shoulder so he could carry him.

Still dazed, I looked up to see Tailgunner and Cat on opposite rooftops firing back towards the main thoroughfare. I looked down the alleyway and saw the remaining Walker limp into the mouth of the alley. The multiple barrels of its rapid-firing railgun were already rotating up to speed. We were dead.

This was what Merle had been waiting for. The building hewn out of the rock on the corner of the alley had been blown open by missile fire. Merle appeared on the first floor, now open to the air, his plasma rifle at his shoulder, and fired it at almost point-blank range. He squeezed the trigger on the semi-automatic weapon again and again, firing the whole magazine into the mech. The plasma gun's barrel glowed white hot. The front of the mech was wreathed in white fire that ate through armour plate. I think I saw Merle turn and run. I grabbed Morag and forced her to the ground and fell on top of her. Mudge dropped Pagan and threw himself on top of the screaming hacker. The mech blew.

'That was fucking stupid,' I heard Mudge say and start coughing. 'He was in the army. He's got more armour than me.'

This time I saw all black because we were buried. I felt like all the weight of the planet's heavy G was bearing down on me. It seemed like the stone ceiling that replaced the sky in the cavern had landed on me. Boosted muscle, metal and a bit of screaming, and I managed to push myself up through the rubble. I saw light again. I spat dirt, blood and gravel out of my mouth and glanced behind me. The mouth of the alleyway was gone.

I reached down and dragged Morag's limp body out of the debris. She was unconscious. My back felt like a whole load of stone had landed on it. Funny that. I overrode all the warning signs in my IVD so I could see better.

'Move! We'll cover you!' Cat, from the roof. Christ, she was keen. Still she hadn't just been blown up. She was right. The mechs were gone but the infantry would be in the alleys, trying to flank us.

The trucks were gone. Good, that was what this was about. Still, I didn't want to die for a bit of food. I put a stim on Morag's neck. She cried out as she was rudely pulled out of unconsciousness by the drug.

'On your feet,' I said.

There was just a little look of resentment from her before she realised where she was.

I retrieved my shotgun. Ejected the magazine, replaced it, ran a quick diagnostic. It was still working.

Morag staggered to her feet. Pagan was unconscious. I looked at Mudge's blackened face.

'I had to sedate him,' he told me.

I helped sling Pagan across his shoulders.

'C'mon!' Cat shouted from above. She sounded worried but not rattled.

'Air force,' I said to Mudge. Mudge looked at me quizzically. I nodded at Pagan. 'He was air force, not army.' I had no idea why it was suddenly important to me.

'You want to talk about this now?' Mudge asked.

I shook my head. 'Let's go.'

If we were lucky we could get out of here without another contact. We're never lucky. Even so, this was taking the piss.

Tailgunner took a hit first. A lump of his armoured combat jacket superheated and blew off. He went down, his chest steaming. Cat hit the ground, hiding behind the stone lip of the roof she was on. Morag cried out as she took a hit to the back, knocking her to the ground again. There was a smoking hole in the back of her armour. It had stopped most of the beam but I could see blackened and blistered skin through it. Mudge and Pagan were a two-for-one. Red steam jetted out of Pagan's leg, the beam almost severing it. The beam then went through Mudge's shoulder. Mudge cried out and dropped Pagan as he stumbled forward, his shoulder steaming red. The laser took me in the right shoulder, almost severing my cybernetic arm.

Rapid and accurate laser fire. I got a sinking feeling. I managed to bring the shotgun up to my shoulder, though it felt like my arm was about to fall off. There's nothing like smelling your own cooked flesh. More painkillers, more stims, more red warning icons.

'Fall back, now!' I barked.

Morag was helping Mudge get the badly bleeding Pagan up and over his unwounded shoulder.

'I can't see them.' Cat from above.

I was looking down the barrel of the shotgun. Where had the fire come from?

A figure was moving fast and low in the main thoroughfare. I triggered a burst from the shotgun but the figure had gone, disappeared into one of the cave-like buildings next to the ruins of the mouth of the alley. Above me Cat leaped over the alleyway to check on Tailgunner. It had all been going so smoothly. Well, it hadn't really.

Mudge had Pagan over his shoulder now and was moving as quickly as he could manage. Morag was staying level, covering them. I was backing down the alleyway looking for the figure, knowing who it was but not wanting to admit it to myself. Above us, Cat hefted Tailgunner onto her shoulder and started jogging across the rooftops, easily keeping pace with us. What a fucking mess. How did they get to us so quickly?

The sound of gauss fire from behind. A shout of surprise from Cat. The sound of a body being dropped onto a rooftop. Answering laser fire from Morag. I started to turn.

Someone grabbed my shotgun. I shouldn't be this easy to sneak up on. Not when I'm operational. The weapon was twisted, then wrenched from my grip and thrown away.

'Hello, Jakob.' Josephine, the Grey Lady, still wouldn't look me in the eye. She was standing in front of me. Small wiry build, nondescript to the point of drabness. She wore an inertial armour suit and had the laser carbine she'd just used on us slung across her back. I just stared at her as I went through the clichés of my blood running cold and my mainly mechanical heart skipping a beat.

'Run!' I screamed at the others.

I took a step back and went for the Mastodon and my laser pistol. She moved too fast. Steely fingers hit my right wrist hard enough to affect a nerve point through subcutaneous armour and my laser pistol flew out of my hand as I lost all feeling in my fingers. Then she locked up my right hand, elbowed me in the face and bent the Mastodon out of my grip and threw it away. She chopped my neck with both her hands and kneed me in the chest, knocking me back into a wall.

I clenched my fists and all eight of my knuckle blades slid out of their forearm sheaths.

'How'd you know?' I asked, trying to buy time.

She just shook her head as if she was sad that I'd even asked.

I punched at her with the blades. She batted one bladed fist aside. She wasn't even where I'd aimed the other. I stabbed air.

Fighting other operators, you don't attempt kicks above knee height. Your legs may have the strongest muscles on your body, but kicks are slow and anyone with decent reactions who knows what they are doing will avoid or counter them. Josephine kicked me in the head, which snapped to the left as I explosively spat blood out. I felt bone and armour crunch and I went down on one knee.

I swung blindly with the claws at where I thought she was. She seemed to roll over my arm. She was now so close it felt intimate as she hit me hard enough to hurt through the armour in the chest, stomach, kidneys and groin. She was moving so fast I could barely register where she was going to hit next.

I tried to hook the blades on my right arm, the cybernetic one, into her kidneys. She stepped back, took my right arm by the elbow and wrist, and used my own momentum to push it up. Then she hooked one of her legs behind mine and stepped forward. I felt myself starting to fall back. She leaped up, adding her weight to my momentum, lodging her leg horizontally across my throat, and rode me to the ground. As I hit the rock, her leg crushed my windpipe. I was now using my internal air supply. My claws, held in place by her seemingly unbreakable grip, were stabbed into the ground with enough force to shatter the carbon-fibre blades.

I stabbed at her with the blades on my left arm. She leaned back, and I missed. Josephine grabbed the arm. I screamed as she struck my elbow, shattering it. My left arm was now useless and limp. Black scalpel-like claws shot from the fingertips of her right hand and she dug them into the wound in my right shoulder. More screaming, mine again. I tried to punch her with the broken blades on my right fist until she'd severed enough connections to the cybernetic arm and it went limp as well.

She was sitting atop me, leg still crossed over my neck. The only real option I had left was to try and buck her off. She was too far forward to hook with my legs, and I knew that would be ineffective and only cause me pain. I knew when I was beat, or maybe I didn't, but I was beat now. She'd walked all over me. I hadn't even landed a blow. Being beaten by a better opponent is one thing, but I felt helpless. She still wouldn't look at me directly.

'I don't suppose you'd kill me?' I managed through blood, grit and broken teeth.

'I'm sorry, Jakob.' She sounded like she meant it.

I was peripherally aware of a firefight and managed to turn my head. Further down the alley I could see Cat, Morag and Mudge firing at opponents who were out of view, their lasers and assault rifles being answered by what sounded like gauss carbines. There was the occasional explosion of a grenade. I watched as Morag went down in a hail of fire. The spray of blood told me that her armour was compromised. She hit the ground but I could see she was still moving. I had to help.

When the Grey Lady had hit me in the shoulder with laser fire and then dug her claws in, she'd torn the combat jacket. There was just about enough room to bring my shoulder laser to bear.

I think when the laser slid out on its servos Josephine was surprised enough to almost have a facial expression. For a moment I had her in the laser's cross hairs superimposed on my IVD. The red beam stabbed out. Superheated air exploded. She grabbed the laser and shifted it slightly as she moved her head to the side. It missed. Then she tore it off my shoulder.

'That's the closest anyone's come for a while,' she mused.

I could still hear the gunfight. I guessed my friends were too busy to kill me like we'd agreed. I had the presence of mind to trigger the kill switch on my internal memory. Virtual flames burned away electronic data, hopefully leaving them nothing for the inevitable system violation.

Josephine took me by the hair and pulled my head up. On the wall behind her I could see a peeling thinscreen poster of Mudge. It was a screenshot from when we'd taken over the media node on the Atlantis Spoke. He was grinning, had a spliff in his mouth and was holding his AK at port. Across the poster, written in red, was the word Resist. The Puppet Show had been disseminating the information we'd given them on the Cabal, the Black Squadrons and what had happened on Earth. I couldn't help but smile. Mudge was the unacceptable face of the resistance. You had to laugh really, didn't you?

I tried to move my head so I could see Morag but Josephine held me still. I felt her push the coma jack into one of my plugs. Felt the click as it slid home. The fight my security software put up was depressingly brief. Darkness.

15

Moa City

After darkness, hell. Slowly coming to. I could feel the pain through the fugue of painkillers, my IVD red with warnings. Hopelessness accompanied consciousness. Or in other words I knew I was fucked.

Opening my eyes was like tearing off a scab. Light was pain; focusing on my surroundings, making sense of them, wasn't much better. Calum Laird may have been a cunt but I should have taken the job with him. He was an amateur compared to the other inhabitants of the cell I was in.

I was strapped into some sort of contoured vinyl couch, properly secured despite not having the use of my arms. I could feel a single jack in one of my plugs connecting me to some kind of medical suite. I was covered in medpak-driven medgels.

'He seems to be healing quickly,' Josephine said quietly. She was looking at the suite's monitor.

It looked like your standard cell – stone walls, no windows, thick metal door. I reckoned it would have been quite roomy without the hulking, patchwork presence of Martin Kring. Even through the agony I still managed to find disgust for this murderous, so-called anti-insurgency specialist.

Kring was standing impassively next to an unhappy-looking Vincent Cronin, whose salon looks, smart suit that probably cost more than most made in a year and carefully cultivated corporate duelling scars all looked out of place in this dungeon.

And of course Rolleston. Still in uniform – crisp clean fatigues. Well built, clean-shaven, smartly turned out, every inch the suave officer. He had a patient, almost indulgent smile on his face beneath his pale-blue eyes. I'd seen matt-black plastic lenses with more feeling in them than those eyes. This was a moment of clarity. I wasn't frightened; all I felt was an overwhelming hatred. It was all I could do not to scream my hatred and anger at him.

'I don't really feel that I need to be here for this,' Cronin said to Rolleston, his annoyance obvious. 'This is your department.'

'I thought you might want to meet the man who caused us so much trouble. Besides, he will have information that will be of use to both of us. Don't you, Jakob? Anyway, Jakob has an important lesson to learn.'

'I'm not being funny, right, but either torture me or kill me because we've got nothing to say to each other,' I said.

'I find myself in agreement with him,' Cronin said with a look of disgust in my direction.

Fuck you, suit. Things would be different if I wasn't strapped down to this couch. With two broken arms. Surrounded by hard bastards.

'I want to know why,' Rolleston said.

Cronin turned to look at the Major. 'This is a waste of our time.'

'Leave if you want.' Rolleston just kept staring at me.

'Why what?' I asked.

'Why are you here? Why do you fight? Why did you try to pull down everything we tried to make?' I stared at him like he was mad. I hoped he picked that up. 'When you're suffering I want you to remember that all you had to do was kill an alien and some whores and then go back to your miserable life a bit richer.'

'Where do I start?' I asked incredulously. 'I mean, you get that you shouldn't do the things you do, yeah?'

'Get what you can out of him; we can break him now and get after the others,' Cronin said. He sounded impatient but there was something else there. Nervousness? Fear?

Others? That meant some of them had got away. Rolleston glared at Cronin, obviously irritated by his indiscretion. Though I couldn't see how it mattered.

'You understand that you're in no position to judge me?' Rolleston asked.

I looked down at my broken, blackened and bloody body.

'Well not at the moment, but give me a few days to get back on my feet and I'll give you a square go.' It was bravado I didn't really feel.

Rolleston laughed as if we were two old army buddies sharing a joke. Then he reached down and placed his hand on my stomach wound. I gritted my teeth, rode out the pain, wished I had more drugs. His fingers elongated and burrowed through my flesh like razor-covered worms. I screamed and writhed on the couch. Rolleston tore his bloody fingers out of me. I saw them sway and writhe as they slowly returned to looking like fingers. The medical monitor was begging for attention, bleeping with urgency. I was gasping for breath.

I could still feel the ghost of his fingers writhing through my guts. Control yourself.

'Aaaah!' Turn it into a laugh. 'Yes! That's the spirit! A little more torture, a little less fucking talk!' Because false bravado was bound to see me through, though there was still no fear, only hatred and resignation.

'Why?' he asked again.

'We've talked this to death!' I shouted at him through a spray of blood and spittle. 'Just fucking get on with it!'

'Don't give me orders, Jakob.' Danger in his voice. He hadn't liked that.

'When did you get to like the sound of your own voice so much? You were always a cunt, but I just thought you were trying to get the job done no matter what. Now you're a fucking psycho. The Cabal have gone. They're over, dead. You're just a broken machine following the programming of people who either don't exist or have switched sides.'

The twitch on his face was instantly replaced by a calm smile. There was something there he hadn't liked.

'Humans are all biological machines. Everyone's programmed. We call it growing up. All you are is malfunctioning pinkware,' he said.

'Fine, justify it how you want. It's not difficult to work out why I'm here. This is just what people do when people like you try to make us live a certain way.'

It was a lie. I was here because of Morag and to a degree because I hated this guy. Want to rule humanity? Fine. But why did it seem that he was on a mission to make my life such a long bleeding streak of misery?

'You're angry you can finally see the strings?' Josephine surprised me by asking. I don't think I was the only one who was surprised.

'As for what happened on Earth, you boxed us in. We were making it up as we went along. Just trying to survive. Can we get on with the torture now?'

Rolleston seemed to be giving what I'd said some consideration. 'That's what I thought – the spastic reaction of the frightened animal.' So he hadn't been giving what I'd said some thought. He just wanted to spin whatever I said until it suited what he wanted to hear.

'While we're having a nice little chat. What. The fuck. Are you doing?! You're potentially going to kill millions of people. For what? Some abstract sense of accomplishment in the power game?'

I was finding impending death and torture quite liberating.

'You know what you remind me of?' Rolleston asked.

'Someone tired of rhetorical questions?'

'A Neanderthal. I don't mean that as an epithet ...'

'I don't even know what that means.'

'An insult,' he supplied. 'But this is an insight into what the Neanderthal must have felt in the face of *Homo sapiens*.'

I was speechless. I had no idea what he was going on about. Or why Cronin was looking so uncomfortable.

'We have the opportunity to be strong as a species, to move forward as one, to make progress as one, to deal with the threats and opportunities that expansion provides from a position of strength, to actually build something instead of tearing things down and constant petty squabbling. This is an evolutionary point in human history. Do you understand that? Do you see what you're opposing? What you're trying to drag down, destroy?'

I tried to think through what he'd said.

'I've got no idea what you're talking about,' I told him. 'You fucking psycho,' I added. Liberating.

'George, that's enough.' Cronin did not sound happy at all.

Rolleston turned to him. 'We have an opportunity here for an insight. Do you not see that? He is effectively an uplifted animal.'

'What are you talking about?!' I screamed at him.

Rolleston turned back to me. Again he looked angry.

'I told you, we're asking the questions,' he said.

'Or fucking what? Threats of pain are a little fucking redundant, don't you think?'

'I'm angry, Jakob.'

'Good!'

'Do you know why I'm angry, Jakob?'

'Were you recently strapped into a chair and asked stupid fucking questions?!'

'Because we're more alike than not.'

'Brilliant. Unstrap me and we'll go for a beer!'

'Because we've both been given a great gift.'

'What?' I asked, though I think I knew the answer.

'Why are you healing so quickly?' Rolleston asked.

'Themtech,' I said quietly.

He nodded. 'Imagine my disappointment that it has been given to one so undeserving. You were a good if disobedient servant, Jakob, but let's face facts. You're little more than a brute beast whose only thought is its own selfish gratification.'

And the thing was, he wasn't trying to anger me. He probably didn't even think he was insulting me. He was just describing things as he saw them. He wouldn't even have understood that I didn't see myself the same way.

'Not only so undeserving, but someone who'd never be able to understand what he was, let alone understand what we're trying to do,' he explained.

I met his eyes and tried not to flinch away from the cold analytical expression on his face. It was like he was studying an insect.

'I'm an animal who's caused you a lot of trouble. You know I'd never join you, right?' I told him.

Cronin actually laughed. 'We couldn't use you.' I heard Josephine sigh. Rolleston's eyes flickered towards her. 'You lack the vision. Though I think you know you'll serve in the end.'

'Nobody wants what you want except you,' I said. Very fucking eloquent, I thought.

'That's because people only see the small picture. They fear what they don't understand and like you think only of gratification. And the people whose power relies on them think only of the illusion of providing that gratification. Everyone's miserable. Imagine if that could be changed.'

'This is a waste of time. You're crazy. Seriously. Move on. Brainwashing, torture, getting killed, whatever.'

'Not quite yet.'

'George, let's just get what we need from him,' Cronin said. He was looking more and more nervous.

'As Mr Douglas has pointed out, he is an animal that has caused us a lot of trouble. He needs to be taught an object lesson in power. He needs to understand his place in the scheme of things.'

Suicide implants had always struck me as tools of the religious fanatic but right now I was thinking what a good idea they were. If for no other reason than I wouldn't have to listen to any more of this shit.

'We want to know where the deserters are. We also want to know what you know about Earth's defence plans.' Rolleston was talking to me now.

I didn't say anything but I went very cold. Mother and her people would move – it was standard operating procedure for them when people got captured – but I thought back to what the prime minister had told me about fortress Earth's vulnerability. God was their only real hope against Demiurge, and fear and paranoia were diminishing that hope.

'You're going to have to get that the hard way,' I told him.

'It may interest you to know that you were betrayed by two of your own people,' he said.

It made sense, but I tried not to react. I still felt angry. I hoped that whoever had got away would realise that we'd been betrayed and hunt down the traitors. It must have been two of Mother's people. It was understandable. They had roots here. A lot of pressure could be brought to bear. Then something occurred to me.

'Hold on a second. If we were betrayed, then why do you want to know where the resistance are?' I asked.

Rolleston was too experienced an officer to give much away, but there was something there. Something he didn't understand.

'You know everyone breaks. You know that people can be broken in a very short amount of time using the variable time effects of a sense booth, and you have enough base cunning to understand that we can now break and slave people almost immediately.'

I thought back to Skirov tearing off gobbets of flesh on his pile of corpses, but he had known there was something wrong with him and wanted to die. It was pretty much the closest I had to hope. I wasn't sure I was as strong as Skirov had been, however.

'Then just fucking do it. Maybe you can make me like the sound of your voice as much as you seem to.'

'Jakob, I can break you just as quickly without torture or other little tricks.'

I didn't like this at all. Rolleston turned to Kring and nodded. Kring looked to Cronin. Cronin looked uncomfortable but finally nodded as well. Kring turned and left the room.

Moments later I could hear the sounds of a struggle. I watched Kring carry a gagged, bound, badly wounded but very angry Morag into the cell. He put her down and forced her to kneel. She stopped struggling when she saw me. Fear was written all over her face. I turned back to Rolleston.

'Come on, not like this. Fucking brainwash me, torture me, but leave her out of this. We don't deserve this. At the very least we've been worthy opponents.' I was babbling nonsense – anything to delay the inevitable.

'You are less than an insect to me. This is about understanding your place. This is about the fortune of your presence here before me. This is so you can understand something better. This is so you can admit your hypocrisy. You fight and struggle so hard to pull down what those above you have sought so hard to build, but you will betray it all for your own selfish wants and desires. Do you understand how pointless everything you have ever tried to do is?' He turned to Kring. 'Take her gag off.'

'Go and fuck yourself, you cunts!' Her anger made her Dundonian accent so broad it was almost impossible to understand. Fuck knows what the English and the Americans in the room thought she'd said.

'I will have her gang-raped in front of your eyes. My understanding is that she is used to it.'

'Don't fucking listen to him, Jakob.' I heard the resolve in her voice. I knew that she would be harder to break than me.

'Please ...' I was begging now.

'I will put you both into a sense machine and you will watch her being tortured for decades – do you understand me? You know me; you know I'll do this.'

'Fuck him! Jakob, listen to me. He can't touch me. Don't tell him anything.'

I couldn't look at her. I was weeping. I knew Rolleston would do these things.

'Not immediate enough for you?' Rolleston asked. He drew his sidearm and held it at her head.

'Fuck you!' Morag screamed at him. I'm not sure I'd ever seen anyone so angry before. 'Don't you do it! Don't you do it, Jakob!'

'No ... please ... stop ...' I was sobbing as I begged. I wasn't sure who I was begging to stop. Rolleston was starting to pull the trigger.

'Jakob! Look at me! At least fucking look at me, you bastard!' Morag screamed. I had to force my head round. She was scared now, but resigned, stronger than I could ever be as I tried to meet her fierce and earnest look. 'Listen to me. It's okay. If it was the other way around I would watch you die.' I believed her. I broke.

If they were still alive, then I betrayed Mudge, Pagan, Cat, Merle, the *whanau*, all of the resistance and my entire fucking planet and everyone I'd ever known alive or dead. All the while Morag was crying, begging me to stop, not to say any more. It took me hours to sell out everything I knew. Rolleston listened to it all. I was numb with disgust at myself by the time I'd finished. I thought I was just a shell, that I couldn't feel any more. Rolleston proved me wrong.

'Do you understand now?' he asked.

I nodded, neither understanding nor caring. It just seemed easier. Morag was a foetal ball on the stone floor, dry sobs racking her frame. Rolleston showed me that I could still feel. He shot Morag twice in the head.

I screamed. I screamed 'No!' over and over again. I screamed until my throat bled. I'm still screaming.

They left me in the room with her cooling corpse. It had been a large-calibre gun, though oddly quiet, suppressed. Her skull looked like a broken egg. I couldn't take my eyes from it. I could see where technology had violated her flesh. I had the obscene urge to try and put her head back together.

I don't think that leaving me in there with the corpse was planned sadism; I just think they had other things to do. They wanted to get on running their psychotic totalitarian regime. Eventually they came and took her away. They tidied up her remains like the sum result of her eighteen years of life was to make a mess.

When she was gone I stared at where she'd been. They'd reduced her to a stain. All I could do was stare. I hoped someone would come and kill me soon. Even brainwash me, make me someone, something else. At least I'd be on the winning side. You can't fight something like this. There was no thought of revenge. There was nobody left to take revenge. There was just a shell staring at a stain on the ground wishing he could be switched off like the machine he was.

It's amazing how long you can think of nothing when the alternative is watching a replay of your lover being double-tapped in the skull. Any attempt to try and think of her in better times just ended with the same two whispered shots. My lover reduced to a spray of matter on the wall. Except sometimes I managed to think about all the shitty things I'd said and done to her in the brief time we'd been together. Even then it still always ended with those two gunshots.

It felt like days. I had a clock and calendar on my IVD but I didn't understand them any more. I occasionally drifted off into fitful sleep. I dreamt of fire and plains of black glass haunted by black-cloaked figures.

It took a while for me to realise there was someone else in the cell with me, she was so quiet and unobtrusive.

'How did you know it was us?' I asked. My voice was a rasping croak torn out of a damaged throat. 'The traitors?'

I couldn't even bring myself to feel anger towards whoever had betrayed us.

'They didn't say who you were, but I recognised you when I saw you. I know how you move.'

It was funny how the Grey Lady wasn't frightening any more. She was just a force of nature, something you couldn't fight against. She was one of the bad things that happened to you when you tried to fight the likes of Rolleston. She moved into view. Now she was looking at me. Her eyes must have been implants but they looked real. They were grey.

'How'd you get her?' I asked.

What fucking difference did it make? I closed my eyes, watched the replay again and opened them to find the Grey Lady looking at me, her head cocked to one side almost quizzically.

'I deployed with two other enhanced members of the Black Squadrons, both ex-special forces. They engaged the others. One of them was killed. The other was badly wounded but captured Miss McGrath. It wasn't me, if that's what you're asking.' For some reason that seemed important to her.

We said nothing for a while. In other circumstances it would have been awkward.

'Why do you do it?' I asked, more out of something to say to break the silence than any real interest in anything. 'Work for him, I mean.'

'I don't understand,' she said.

'Are you fucking him?'

She said nothing but there was the slight flicker of something there. Like I'd hurt her. I was good at hurting women, but this was the Grey Lady.

'Do you just want to become some biotech god?' She shook her head. 'Then why? Why do this to people?'

'You do terrible things to people who you disagree with,' she said.

'It always feels like they started it.'

'You turned on him,' she said.

'Because he was trying to get me to do something terrible.'

I couldn't even find the strength to be angry.

'Only in relative terms. It depends on your foresight.'

'You people like your justifications, don't you. Like to feel good about what you do.' Again I delivered this with a completely flat voice. I didn't really care.

'I do it because I'm good at it.'

'You don't fancy doing it for someone ... nicer?' Even in my hollowed-out state it sounded weak.

'You're not standing where I'm standing.'

'So you are fucking him?'

Again there was just a flicker of something. Sadness? Anger? Go on, piss off the Grey Lady. Actually that wasn't a bad idea. Maybe she'd kill me. I'd been thinking a lot about the afterlives all the signal-men I'd ever worked with had told me about. But they were just hopeful fantasies, dreams of seeing Morag again.

'You don't know what you're talking about,' she told me.

I sighed. 'Why are you here?'

'Because you smell.' It was delivered with monotone honesty but the childishness of the statement from the Grey Lady's lips made me laugh. It was a bitter laugh. It sounded like somebody choking. I was sure she was right. It felt like I'd been lying here for days. The only concession to hygiene was some kind of suction/cleaning device strapped uncomfortably over my groin and arse.

'So?'

Even through the numbness and pain, the Grey Lady carefully and thoroughly giving me a sponge bath rated as deeply surreal. She was thorough. She even shaved me and put some kind of small machine in my mouth that brushed my teeth, then washed and deodorised my mouth.

'You're healing quickly,' she said, examining my many wounds.

That's the Themtech, I thought. That's what makes Rolleston and me so close. I'd not been paying any attention to my wounds but there was a lot less red on my IVD and the pain was subsiding. I think I would have preferred being able to concentrate on physical pain.

When she was finished I asked, 'Why did you do that?'

She didn't answer. She leaned forward and kissed me. I snapped my mouth shut like a trap. She straightened up. Again there was a flicker of something there. Hurt?

'What the fuck!' I shouted.

I was feeling again. I'll give them credit, these people liked to push the boundaries. She undressed. Her naked body was wiry, hard but surprisingly petite for a frame that contained so much power. She stood in front of me, somehow vulnerable.

'Don't you understand?' I asked. Desperate.

Steely fingers calloused from years of martial arts practice touched me. She knew how and where to touch me.

'Don't ...' I begged.

My body was already starting to betray me. A single dry sob painfully racked my frame. She gracefully swung a leg over the couch I was strapped to and straddled me.

'Please don't hurt me,' she said, sounding vulnerable as she looked down on me. It was the one thing she could have said. She leaned forward to kiss me. This time I let her. This time I reciprocated. She was real. It was something. It was more than the constant feeling of numbness.

When she left I wept. Now part of the cell seemed haunted. I couldn't make my eyes go there. I had betrayed everything else, why not her? And still nobody would kill me. Was leaving me here wretched like this part of Rolleston's punishment? I knew exactly what I was. Rolleston was wrong: I wasn't an animal. That was too noble. I was scum. When sleep came it was fitful. I wanted my dreams to punish me.

It was a plain of black glass over fire. In the distance the jagged knife points of mountains. Protruding from the plains were obelisks like the stone cairns of the Highlands writ large and made of the same black glass. Alien-looking glyphs of orange light played over the surface of the obelisks. The landscape was somehow familiar to me. A black sun burned in the sky. I didn't want to look at it. I couldn't look at it. There was something terrible about it.

There was movement next to me. I swung around, the sensation of fear an almost welcome return of feeling. I was staring at the hood of a black-robed figure floating above the ground. The figure was moving towards me but didn't seem to notice me. I stepped to one side and it ignored me as it floated past.

I looked down at myself. I was naked and whole. But naked and whole as the machine I was. All components of the weapon were present and correct. The glyphs from the obelisk seemed to be playing over my pale skin like a projection.

In the distance I could just about make out two flying creatures of some sort, high in the air. It looked like they were circling. Somehow they felt like judgement. I started to walk towards them.

I woke up on the couch. My face distended, pulled forward. Black liquid tendrils, like one of Them. Instinctive hard-wired fear and loathing at this. The tendrils extrude from my flesh, my mouth, my face, piercing part of it, part of me.

I woke for real. Screaming. I was no longer strapped to the couch. I was free. The cell door was open. Rannu was standing over me. He looked awful, gaunt and wasted. Despite having black lenses for eyes there was something haunted about his expression. Something new. He looked afraid.

He was wearing combat trousers but was barefoot. He had on a filthy greying T-shirt and was carrying a gauss carbine in one hand, another slung across his back. In his other hand was a severed hand hooked up to some kind of miniaturised device that pumped warm blood through dead flesh.

'Did you undo the straps?' I asked inanely.

He shook his head. Did she do it?

'Can you stand up?' he whispered urgently.

If I could betray my dead lover and fuck the Grey Lady then I could stand up. I climbed off the couch and almost collapsed. Maybe I could have stood up in Earth gravity. Rannu helped me stand.

'She's dead,' I told him, feeling my face crumple as if I was about to start sobbing again.

He looked into my lenses. 'I know.'

Did he? How much? Did he know what I'd done? There's always time for self-pity. I hugged him and started to sob. He hugged me back, unconcerned that I was naked.

'We need to go. You'll have to walk yourself.' He sounded nervous. I don't think I'd ever heard Rannu sound nervous before.

I let him go. I could just about stand. I noticed that he was missing the tip of his forefinger on his right hand. It made sense that they'd remove his weighted monofilament garrotte.

'Can you hold a gun?' Rannu asked. I nodded.

I wasn't weak from my incarceration, just numb and not used to being on my feet again. Rannu handed me the gauss carbine and unslung the one across his back. We looked at each other for a while. I was so glad to see him, but maybe dying or even being brainwashed, if it meant forgetting, would have been better.

Selfishly, irrationally, I was suddenly angry at him. Where was he when Rolleston shot Morag? Why didn't he rescue me before I disgraced myself with Josephine? Then I knew that he couldn't have done anything about the first and the last was all on me, piece of shit that I am.

He turned and headed out the door, looking like a tired soldier. He moved more slowly and with less grace than before. I followed him out. He closed the cell door and pressed the still-warm severed hand on the biometric lock. The cell door locked behind us.

We played hide and seek in corridors lasered out of the huge stalactite decades ago. He took me up into the vents, also carved out of stone, to an automated machine room for the air-handling equipment. It was full of the detritus of his fugitive life.

He sat down with his head in his hands and shook. In a quivering voice he asked me to go on guard. Only then did I see how much coming to get me had cost him.

Then I noticed the corpse in the corner of the room. A squat, powerfully built man with the endomorphic body type I'd come to connect with Lalande 2 colonists. He had a screwdriver sticking out the back of his skull. One of his hands was missing. Still he had clothes. Getting the clothes off the corpse seemed to require a lot more effort than it should have. I got out of breath quickly and could feel the planet pushing down on me again. I hated this place.

'I needed to get you out of the cell,' he said, explaining the corpse.

'Is he Black Squadron?' I asked.

Rannu shook his head. His hair was a matted mess.

'No. Kiwi SAS, I think.'

I was impressed that Rannu, in this state, could take out another special forces operative.

'Poor bastard.' There was genuine regret in his voice.

'What happened?' I asked. Wondering how bad it must have been to transform the Rannu I knew into this wreck. He shook his head again.

'I got down fine, made it beneath the surface. I set up observation posts, did recces but I was learning nothing, doing nothing. The whole idea of me going ahead was so that when you guys got here I'd have some solid intel for you.'

'Knew I was coming, did you?' I asked.

He smiled and nodded, calmer now. The one good thing about his state was that I was pretty sure he hadn't been brainwashed. He was in too much of a mess.

'Morag was coming,' he said by way of explanation.

'You couldn't get close enough to anything because Demiurge controls everything electronic?' I asked.

Rannu nodded. 'The priority was the Citadel, and I got close, but getting close is exactly like looking at an arcology made of ice. It didn't tell me anything, though I got a more up-to-date idea of their external defences. It's also bigger than we thought.'

'They've added to it using conventional materials?' I asked. It was better to think about other things.

'No, it's all ice.'

'How's that work? If it was cut out of a glacier, how could they make it bigger?' Rannu shrugged. I don't think it was of a great deal of interest to him.

'So then I came up to Moa City, see if I could find out anything. Maybe even develop some humint sources ...'

'Stuck out like a sore thumb and got caught?' Rannu nodded again. 'I bet you gave them one hell of a fight.'

Rannu didn't answer. I looked at him questioningly. Had the Grey Lady hopelessly outclassed him as well?

'They sent some of the Black Squadron guys after me. They're like Rolleston, maybe not as hard. I had my pistols on me ...' He looked ashamed of himself.

'Rannu, don't worry about it. Josephine got me. I didn't even land a blow on her. She just walked all over me.'

'I got one of them.'

'That's better than the rest of us.'

'They took my kukri.'

To us it was just a big sharp knife. In my case, one I'd been attacked with. To Rannu it was an important part of his heritage, a connection to his family, his people and their past. It was also a symbol of the achievements of the Ghurkha regiment, one of the most, if not the most effective conventional regiment in the British army.

'I'm sorry, man.' Even if it seemed trivial next to Morag's death. Don't think about Morag; concentrate on Rannu.

'I broke,' Rannu said. Hearing his voice when he said it – the despair, the disgust with himself, the shame – was one of the most frightening things I think I'd ever heard. This was a different person. Those bastards had transformed Rannu, the rock, one of the most competent, reliable and professional soldiers I'd ever met, into this shell. What worried me was that Rannu had been captured before and hadn't broken. While working undercover for the police in Leicester his cover had been blown. He'd been extensively tortured by the Thuggee crime syndicate he'd been infiltrating. He had held out, and the Thuggees were known to be vicious bastards. It wasn't torture that had done this to Rannu; it was what he saw as failure. He thought he'd let us down. He thought he'd betrayed us.

'Everyone breaks,' I told him. Though most lasted longer than I had. I was the disgrace, for so many reasons. 'They had the RV points covered, nothing more. Did they try to brainwash you?'

Rannu shook his head.

'Rolleston was there. He was really angry. He wanted to torture me. Wanted to see me break the old-fashioned way, a mixture of psychology and pain. He said that once I was broken then he'd take ownership of my soul.'

It made sense. It was pretty much what they had planned for me with the added bonus of killing Morag in front of my eyes. Don't think about Morag.

'What happened?'

'I escaped.'

'When?'

'I don't know. Two, maybe three weeks ago.'

After everything he'd been through he'd still been able to escape. I was pretty much in awe of him at that moment. But I knew I wouldn't

318

be able to explain this to him, make him feel better, because he set the bar way to high for himself.

'And you've been hiding up here for all that time?'

'Not just here, all over the place. They hunted pretty hard for the first few days, lots of close calls, but they must think I've either escaped or died. I've been quiet as a mouse.'

'Why didn't you get out?'

'It's not as easy as that. It's locked down pretty tight, but I think I've got a way out. I stayed when they got you and Morag to see if I could do anything.' He turned to look at me. It looked like he was about to cry. 'I'm so sorry. I couldn't ... I was too ... Rolleston, the Grey Lady ... too frightened.'

'Rannu, there was nothing you could do, you know that, don't you? They would have killed you.'

He looked away from me and shook his head despondently. There was nothing I could say to him that would help.

'You said you have a way out?' Rannu nodded. 'I want to kill Rolleston first, I don't care if I die doing it.'

He looked frightened. The expression looked alien on his face.

'He's not here. I was very quiet. I was lying over a grille listening to them. So quiet.'

'The Citadel?'

'He's gone to hunt the resistance – him, the Grey Lady and Kring. They said they wanted to deal with them once and for all. They're going to destroy them and then Cronin will use it for propaganda.'

'What's your out?'

'Where'd you get the parachutes?' I asked.

We were crouched in a tight air tunnel next to what looked to be a heavily armoured vent that led to the outside world. The facility we'd been held in was quite close to the point of the stalactite that was Moa City.

'Apparently nearly everyone who lives here can base-jump, just like they can climb. It was popular as a sport before the war and has survival applications as well. They've just started doing it recreationally again. I stole them from some lockers.' The talking was keeping his mind off other things. Mine too. I was struggling into a bulky parachute harness in the confined space.

'What's to stop their defences from burning us out of the sky?' I asked.

He stopped strapping on his parachute and looked at me. He seemed to come to a decision and pulled a cobbled-together radio

transmitter out of the pocket of his combat trousers. I stopped as well.
I felt my heart drop.

'It won't work,' I told him. 'Demiurge will be able to control it.'

Rannu shook his head. 'He will, but by then the signal's gone.'

I gave this some thought. He could be right. Under normal circumstances I wouldn't want to bet my life on it but right now I didn't give a shit.

'The explosives?' I asked.

'That was the easy part. Made them out of cleaning supplies that I stole. The receivers for the radio detonators were the hardest thing. No big charges. They needed to be small so they wouldn't get found. Just enough to take out a few vital components on the batteries in our flight path.'

Something about this wasn't adding up. Rannu was clearing loose rock from round the edge of the vent. Someone had spent a long time chiselling out the rock the hard way. The explosives, the vent, the sabotage – I was suddenly overwhelmed with horror.

'Rannu?' He paused but didn't look at me. 'How long have you been here?' I asked.

'I told you, I'm not sure. Two to three weeks.'

He went back to removing the rock he'd replaced to disguise his work. He couldn't deal with how long he'd been here but he must know. Even I'd started to make sense of the calendar and clock on my IVD.

Rannu ignored me as I stared at him. He finished removing the loose rock and kicked at the vent. It didn't budge. Rannu lost it. He started screaming, kicking at it wildly. Finally the vent exploded out of the rock and I could see the ultraviolet light of the subterranean night.

There was a flash of red light and a loud bang. It was so unexpected that I jumped. Some hardened combat veteran. It was a point-defence laser taking out the falling vent.

Rannu held up the radio transmitter and pressed the transmit button. Nearby I heard a few pathetic-sounding explosions. Rannu threw the now-infected transmitter past me deeper into the air tunnel before he pulled himself over the ledge and out into the sulphurous night air.

16
In the Garden

Mudge calls it the vertiginous moment. Pulling yourself over the ledge. The ground distant and less fixed in your perception than you like ground to be. It should pretty much be a constant. I was too weak and the tunnel was too cramped to pull myself over properly. I lost some skin and left a bloody smear on the outside of the stalactite. It didn't matter despite what the warning icons on my IVD said. Like the OILO drop, the ground seemed to want me much more than it ever had on Earth and Sirius.

There was a moment's free fall and then I pulled the ripcord. The ground wasn't moving towards me so suddenly. Looked up to see the large canopy they have to use on Lalande fully deployed. Looked down to see the ruins of mansions and huge bonfires casting flickering light over scratch-built bestial statuary. Was where we were going any better? Tailgunner had told me that the End was some apocalyptic religious cult of deserters.

The harsh beam of a spotlight cut through the UV light playing over our parachutes. They'd be scrambling gunships and coming looking for us. I made a decision on the way down: enough of the self-pitying bullshit. I had Rannu to look after. I owed him. I had to get back to the others and see if I could undo some of the damage I'd done. I also had a purpose. I didn't give a fuck about Earth, the colonies or any of the politics. Mother was right: what difference did it make who was in charge? Rolleston, on the other hand, had to die as hard as possible. Then I could give suicide some serious thought.

The ground came up and hit me hard. I shrugged off the parachute harness and ran out from underneath the canopy. Still some stims left in the reservoir. They'd drained off the painkillers but that's fine, the pain is fine. We ran in the opposite direction from the most direct route out. Escape and evasion training – go the way they don't expect you to.

We were running over scarred Earth, through scrub foliage, what was left of landscaped gardens run wild for fifty years, past the rubble of cave-like mansions cut out of the stone, our gauss carbines at the ready. I could hear the gunships and copters in the air now. Just think about the job, nothing else. The Demiurge-controlled remotes would be the biggest threat.

Normally we'd stay away from people but the crowds milling near the huge bonfires were our best hope. I veered across rubble-strewn, battle-scarred ground towards a massive pyre in front of a large mansion of hard stone rising out of the ground. For some reason it reminded me of a burial mound. There was a huge effigy illuminated by the flames, made demonic by the red flickering light. I couldn't make out what it was but it looked vaguely humanoid with horns. It appeared to be constructed from whatever expensive salvage they could find from the destroyed houses of the rich.

All around the fire I could see the silhouettes of people with their hands held high, swaying in the light to the hypnotic heavy rhythm of some kind of music too contemporary for me to know. The chanting came from them, not the speakers. Still running, I glanced across at Rannu, who shrugged. There were more spotlights now from the searching gunships. It was not the lights that worried me but the thermographics.

Rannu and I ran to the back of the mansion and vaulted in through a hole in the rock that still held the remains of a stained-glass window. No time to check inside – gunships too close. If they came for us then Rannu got a burst in the head before I turned the carbine on myself. It wouldn't be suicide; it would be a sound tactical decision and a little self-preservation. What we had left of ourselves.

Lowlight illuminated the cavernous room. I'm sure the rich people who owned this place would have been horrified by what had happened to it. There was a noticeable seam of some kind of metal running through the wall. Bits of it had been chipped away over the years. The floor was covered with ground mats and military sleeping bags. There were the remains of food. I was tempted to eat some of it; Rannu was more than tempted. There were empty alcohol bottles and containers that once held narcotics. Slogans had been painted on the wall but a crude mural of a black sun dominated the room. I'd see the black sun before, in my dreams. Below the black sun, in what looked like blood, was scrawled THE BLACK WAVE. It seemed a little contradictory to me.

Rannu was taking small but eager bites of some vat-grown confection.

'Rannu?' I said slowly. He looked up and then saw what I was looking at. Overhead I could hear a gunship. 'I think these people worship Demiurge.'

'They are here for you?'

Our carbines swung up to cover the figure in the doorway. Seeing I had him, Rannu swung around to check behind us. More figures appeared at the glassless windows and at the other doorways into the room.

'We'll kill a lot of them and then ourselves before they get us – understand me?' I told Rannu and meant it.

I was suddenly overcome by revulsion and anger towards these people. They had run out on their mates and then voluntarily chosen to worship Demiurge, and they knew it was bad. They called it the Black Wave, not the Freedom Wave.

The man doing the talking was tall and had the solid build of an ex-soldier. He was wearing a long coat, combat trousers and boots, and the rest of him was completely swaddled in old-fashioned bandages. The bandages had symbols written all over them. I'd known enough signal-people to realise that the symbols were religious or occult. He held a staff that looked like it was made out of scrap metal. The head of the staff was beaten into the shape of a goat's head.

I glanced around at the rest of the people slowly surrounding us, courting gunfire. All of them were swaddled in bandages. At the very least their faces were covered, but many were swaddled from head to feet. Some, but not all, had symbols painted on the bandages.

'We are not going to harm you. All of us are unarmed,' he told us.

It was disconcerting. The bandages made him faceless, made him look like an old-fashioned casualty, a ghost from a historical war. Maybe he was. He was right though. The closest thing any of them had to a weapon was the goat-headed staff he was carrying.

'Fine. Well we'll just hide here for a bit, you don't grass us up, and then we'll move on. Okay?' I said.

I was still pointing the gauss carbine at his face. He hadn't wavered. Deserter he may have been, but he wasn't a coward. I couldn't say the same for the rest of them. There was a lot of very nervous body language.

'Why don't you let us help you?' he asked. His voice was cultured, educated, privileged. Equatorial Africa, I suspected. It sounded like he came from money.

'Why would you do that?' I asked.

'We help everyone who comes here. We're the last port of call for the desperate.' I could hear a degree of self-deprecating humour in what he said. On the other hand, he had described us all right.

I inclined my head towards the black sun and the writing on the wall. 'And that? Aren't you on their side?'

'You want to discuss this now? If we wrap you in sacramental bandages we can hide you better.'

'This better not be an initiation. We're not hackers and we're not joining any fucking cult.'

I was aware of Rannu nodding as he continued scanning the other bandaged deserters.

'No, I don't think you're ready to forswear violence yet.'

That was certainly true.

'What do you think?' I asked Rannu.

'I don't really like our choices,' he said quietly.

'Don't look at it like a choice; look at it as another option. If it doesn't work you'll still have the option of fighting, running and hiding,' the staff-bearing man told us. It was another good point.

'I can see why they follow you,' I told him.

'Nobody follows anyone. That's what we're trying to get away from. We'll pick our own deaths, not the powers that be. I don't think you have much time.'

He was right. I could hear the gunships making low passes over the neighbourhood. I lowered the carbine. Rannu did the same.

'We won't take your weapons, but if you're carrying them they will know that you're not one of us,' he said.

'We'll keep them nearby. Just so you know, we can easily kill with our bare hands and you'll go first,' I told him.

He just nodded.

More climbed through the windows, came in through the doors, advanced on us. It reminded me of some ancient zombie viz. Everywhere I looked they were crowding us. It was claustrophobic. The last time I'd been surrounded like this it had been by Them. I worked hard to suppress my augmented fight-or-flight reactions. However, they just wanted to get us swaddled in bandages as quickly as possible. The man with the staff watched.

'What's your name?' I asked him. As much to try and control the urge to lash out or run as to find out.

'We don't have names here.'

'What, do you number yourselves?'

'That would be a form of identity. We get numbered when we serve. When we are slaves. Here we are all blank. We are nothing, nobody, ghosts who do not exist. Reflections.'

I took this in.

'How do you get each other's attention? Is there a lot of "Hey you"?'

I think he was smiling beneath the bandages.

They were regular troops. They handled the interaction with the End about as well as gunpoint interaction between civilians and the military ever goes. There was a bit of added brutality caused by the contempt and envy the serving man or woman has for the deserter. I could see that. I would have been the same when I was in the Paras, less so in the Regiment. By the time I'd got there I was a little less judgemental.

Lined up. Pushed down onto our knees. Questioned. The incentive to answer came from boots and rifle butts. We did nothing. Said nothing. There were too many people to question us all, which was fortunate. Neither Rannu nor I had the same accent as any of the nationalities that served on Lalande 2.

Of course the bandages were an issue, as the suspicious could see them being used as a disguise. There were over a hundred of the End down on their knees by the bonfire when the troops started cutting them off. A few of the faces revealed were either badly burned or horribly mutilated. I suspected some of the mutilation was self-inflicted. These people took the death of identity seriously. One woman whose bandages were cut off grabbed the sharpest rock she could find and started to carve up her own face. She had to be restrained. The staff-bearer went up to the NCO in charge of the squad and knelt down in front of her. He took the barrel of her rifle, pressed it to his head and asked that they shoot everyone there if they needed to be sure rather than cut their bandages off. It was a difficult moment for the NCO but they stopped removing them.

The soldiers searched the area but didn't even find our gauss carbines, which we'd hidden close to us. They engaged in a little light looting – after all this was the wealthy part of town – and then foxtrot oscar'd.

I watched the gunship peel away from the mansion then turned back to look at the flames of the massive bonfire. The flash compensation on my IVD polarised the lenses slightly to allow for the glare. On the other side of the flames I could see the bestial horned statue. Now that I was closer I could see that it had been welded together out of all sorts. There were parts of vehicles, consumer electronics, furniture and even jewellery. The one thing the material had in common was that it all looked to have once been expensive high-quality gear.

One part of me was appalled at the waste. The other half was amused. The fuel for the fire looked similarly expensive. I started to laugh.

'It's not vandalism; it's liberation.' The guy with the staff was standing over us now. 'You both look ill-used. We do not have much but I think you should probably eat.' And now that he'd mentioned it I suddenly realised how hungry I was.

Vat mulch and hot sauce. It was one of the best-tasting meals I'd ever had. They had to watch both Rannu and me to make sure we didn't just wolf it down and make ourselves sick. We washed it down with odd-tasting water and, after some negotiation, some kind of moonshine. It tasted how I imagined fermented engine oil would taste. A small tin cup of the stuff left me feeling quite drunk.

The guy with the staff had stayed with us. He didn't ask us anything. We did the asking. I even managed to remember to thank him. He and his people had taken a battering on our account and said nothing.

'Where are you from?' I asked.

He was monitoring how quickly I was spooning the mulch down.

'I suspect you mean geographically and not philosophically? I grew up in the shadow of the Ugandan Spoke. Easy now, not so fast.' He laid his bandaged hands over mine, stopping me from spooning another mouthful into my mouth.

'You sound moneyed. How come you didn't join the Fortunate Sons?' I asked.

'It was an option for me, initially anyway. I was a poet with a degree of recognition, if not popularity. While I was at university I net-published poetry which was considered to be anti-corporate.'

'Was it?'

'It wasn't anti-anything. It was pro-person.'

I nodded as if I understood what he was saying. He probably needed to be speaking to someone like Mudge, though I noticed that Rannu was listening intently.

'They arranged to have you drafted?' Rannu asked.

'Either them or my family. I'm not sure which.'

'And you deserted?' I asked.

He nodded. 'Ten years was too long a slave.' He tapped the black plastic of his lenses. 'I think that's why they take the eyes first. So they can try and get to our souls. I didn't fully understand why I was fighting.' He lapsed into silence for a moment and watched me eat. 'Are you aware of the information purporting to be from Earth?' he asked. I nodded. Rannu said nothing. 'It seems in some ways we've

326

been vindicated, but that is a retrospective justification. I just couldn't do it any more. None of us could. I think perhaps we are all too weak but I will not fight again.'

My opinions on deserters notwithstanding, I was struggling to condemn these people. I wanted to ask him about the mates he'd left behind but I couldn't bring myself to do it. After all the only person left from my days in service was Mudge. Well, if you didn't count Rolleston and the Grey Lady.

'You know they'll move you on from here? If they don't kill you,' Rannu said.

'The scavenger teams already hate us. They shoot the moment we get in the way of something they want. They've killed a lot of our people. After all, nobody cares if deserters die. Right?' He looked at us expectantly. Neither of us could meet his lenses. The bandages around his mouth seemed to crease as if he was smiling. 'We know this is temporary. That death is imminent. Do you?'

It certainly always felt that way. We were always less than one step away from death. The feeling that my luck was going to run out if I didn't stop doing things like this. Luck? Two gunshots. Meat that was once a person hitting a cold stone floor. For a moment I could see the appeal of the End. Then I remembered how important it was that Rolleston died.

'Demiurge?' I asked.

He turned his head. He seemed to be studying me.

'The Black Wave?' he asked.

I cursed my own indiscretion. On the other hand he'd know from my accent that I wasn't from around here.

'You worship it?' I asked.

'More venerate it as an inevitability. One war ends and another begins. This time we fight each other, and if the information the resistance is circulating is correct it seems that we did the last one to ourselves as well. There was a demon, a harbinger ...'

'In the net?' Rannu asked.

The man nodded. This sent a shudder through me. Of all the religious experiences that people have in the net, the ones involving so-called demons are always the worst and most destructive – and not just for the hackers themselves. I remembered the boy lying on the soiled bed in Fintry, Vicar standing over him, cross and Bible in hand, trying to cast out the demonic virus in the kid's ware.

'He told me of the Black Wave's coming. He told me that the Black Wave was hate.' The man laughed. 'Can you imagine? All these years of artifice and we finally make machines hate.'

327

'So why venerate something so ...' I was searching for the right word.

'Negative,' Rannu supplied. It didn't seem quite strong enough but it would do.

'Because of its inevitability, its symbolism. Sixty years of warfare was not enough. At some level humanity wants to destroy itself. If not this war then other reasons will be found. The Black Wave is the perfect expression of this. We, as a race, have created a god and then we made it hate. How much harder do we have to work to destroy ourselves?'

'It was a small group of people,' I said. I couldn't shake the feeling that history was the story of a small group of arseholes making the rest of us bloody miserable.

'Do you oppose these people?' he asked.

This was more difficult. Answering that had operational security ramifications. What was I talking about? I'd already sold us out. At least he didn't seem malevolent. Rannu still gave me a sharp look when I nodded.

'You still fight, hate, commit acts of violence and destroy other human life?' he asked.

'That's ...' Now Rannu was searching for a word.

'Sophistry?' the man suggested. Rannu nodded. 'Perhaps, or perhaps it's taking responsibility, collectively, for our race's actions.'

It seemed that nobody was going to tell me what sophistry was. Maybe it meant bullshit. Maybe that's what Rannu had meant to say.

'So you're waiting for death?' I asked.

'In a way, but we won't play its game. We'll die on our own terms.'

I couldn't make up my mind if this guy was a suicidal nut-job or one of the bravest persons I'd ever met. Not that they were mutually exclusive.

'We still have to fight,' Rannu said.

'Even if it's more futile, painful and destructive than putting one of their guns to your own head? Besides, there are ways and means of fighting. It doesn't have to involve violence.'

His words were starting to make sense to me. He was very persuasive. Though I wasn't sure he wasn't twisting words out of shape to get us to think what he wanted.

'Is this how you recruit people?' I asked.

'We don't recruit people. They come to us when they're ready. You will not join us. You are both still full of anger, hatred and fear. I can see the flames that burn around you. They surround you like a nimbus. I think you need to rage against the dark for a while longer yet.'

328

I had nothing to say to that. Was it insight or was it a sales pitch? I didn't know. I did know that he'd saved our arses. I wondered if he was still fighting, like us, but used different methods. Better methods, if they worked. On the other hand, if they ever crossed Cronin, Rolleston or the others they'd be snuffed out. A more likely fate was death at the hands of bailiffs or scavengers. Their sin would be the old one of having what someone else wanted and not being mean enough to protect it. Or maybe it was all an elaborate justification for just giving up.

'You'll be going on your way.' He said this with certainty. 'You need rest before you do. When you go I would ask you to take only what you think you'll need.' He stood up to leave. 'If you want anything just ask anyone. They'll try to help as much as they can. Will you excuse me?' He turned to walk away.

'Thank you,' I said. Rannu said the same. He didn't look back at us but he nodded before he strode away.

I wasn't drinking much. It didn't take much. Rannu did drink but in moderation. Tonight he was matching me, tin cup for tin cup of the fermented engine oil. We were sitting under a pathetic canopy of what had once been ornamental foliage in a hole that was the dried-out remains of some kind of water feature.

The UV-lit false night was somehow managing to be cold and humid. Both of us were wrapped in borrowed coats and sleeping bags. It might have been warmer in the cave-like mansion but neither of us wanted to go inside. The cavern roof above us was enough of a prison for me.

Many of the End were dancing around the big fire listening to some kind of bass- and beat-heavy music that I suspected I would disapprove of under normal circumstances. They were just shadows where the UV light contrasted with the red and orange of the flames. They seemed unreal. Everyone was drinking heavily and taking rec drugs, and we were trying to ignore quite a large group having sex not too far away from where we were sitting. There was a sense of desperation to it all. The Ugandan poet with the staff walked among them, constantly being stopped. He took time to speak to any who accosted him. There was something comforting about him, even if he did trade on the darker side of the net. Perhaps his personable and comforting nature was the real danger, a type of seduction. I still couldn't quite bring myself to mistrust him.

'After Leicester, after Rolleston burned me, Ashmi asked me to stop,' Rannu said out of nowhere. It took me a while to work out who Ashmi was. I felt a little guilty that I'd never asked Rannu about his family.

It had been Rolleston who'd betrayed Rannu to Berham, the head of the Thuggees, after Rannu had refused to break off the deep-cover operation to work for the Major. Rolleston once again teaching a lesson on why he must be obeyed.

'I'm not surprised. Nobody wants that to happen to someone they care about.' Of course I'd managed to avoid the whole physical torture thing by just spilling my guts. Not that it'd done any good. Two shots.

'This is it. In the unlikely event that I live through this, I'm out. This is the last mission for me. Yangani and Sangar should have their father with them and Ash deserves her husband by her side. Though whether I deserve her is another question. I want to see my children grow up. Teach them what I can.'

'I was surprised when Mudge told me you had a family. Surely you've got too much to lose to be doing all this stupid shit with us.'

'I never had a choice.' I turned to look at him. I didn't understand. 'I didn't like working for Rolleston, but when I knew, after I found out in New York, what choice did I have? Your children judge you, is what I think. They don't mean to – they don't even know they're doing it – but how could I go back to them and look them in the eyes if I hadn't done everything I could to make a future where they are not just more meat to be ground up or just another weapon of polluted flesh? Because after we pollute our flesh with machinery we then pollute our minds with what we have to do. I know Rolleston. He would make my children slaves; he would make us all slaves. He does not tolerate dissent. It would have been like I'd done it to them myself. But this is enough.'

It was almost as if he was looking for permission. As if he wanted to be told that what he'd done was sufficient.

'I think you've done your bit,' I told him. Though I still needed him to help me kill Rolleston.

We lapsed into silence again. I feared sleep. I feared the Black Sun. I feared the replay of Morag's death that I knew was waiting for me just beyond consciousness.

I took another sip of the fermented engine oil. Let it burn. I was hoping it would destroy some of my taste buds. Get rid of the constant taste of battery acid and rotten eggs. I wondered how long my lung filter had to go before it needed replacing. I wondered how long Rannu's had – surely much less time if it hadn't already expired. Were his lungs being burned with every breath as we spoke? I was sure there would be more symptoms if this were the case. If nothing else, then coughing and rasping when he breathed.

Eventually Rannu tried to sleep. It looked fitful. I just watched him, wishing I couldn't think.

17

The Deep Caves

We were running on cheap stims and home-made amphetamines. We ran when we could, walked when we couldn't run and staggered just before we crashed. We kept going. I didn't want to sleep anyway. Sleep was a nightmare transformation of a healthy young woman to meat in the space of two gunshots.

We were living in the green light of our lowlight optics, far away from any other sources of illumination. Soon sensory deprivation, lack of sleep and bad drugs took me to a place I knew well from Sirius, that sort of twilight, half-dead, unreal feeling. I started to see fractals of light. My mind started to fill in the gaps in my perception, ghost images given fear and form in the corner of my eye.

I was finding the miles of rock above us more and more oppressive. It seemed to be weighing down on me. Crushing me like the high G. I missed the sky. I really wanted to see the sky again before I died. I didn't think it was likely.

Always moving until we couldn't any more. Eking out the food that the End had given us. They'd given us the drugs as well. They might be deserters and a suicide cult but they'd done all right by us.

I was almost completely healed now, one of the benefits of having what were effectively tiny little aliens throughout my body; the other of course was not dying from radiation poisoning. Rannu was weaker than he'd been for a long time but that was still pretty strong. He'd lost a lot of weight but he was keeping up.

We'd made it back to the *pa* by trial and error. All the maps had gone when I'd triggered the firestorm in my internal memory and wiped it, although I needn't have bothered when I was going to spill my guts like I had. We'd taken a lot of wrong turnings but at least when we'd found the cave we knew it was the right one.

They'd left in a hurry and blown all the tunnels that would have enabled Rolleston to follow them easily. The problem was this made it almost as difficult for us. When we'd been camped here I'd studied the maps trying to commit as much of them to actual meat memory as possible in case I needed the info for E&E. I was pretty sure that I knew the long way round. The route that Rolleston and his people would have had to take. Then we could try and pick up the trail of either Rolleston or Mother's people. Or we'd end up wandering Lalande 2's Deep Caves until we died of hunger.

The one thing we did have going for us was our tracking ability. I'd grown up tracking and had been taught by one of the best, my dad. 5 Para Pathfinders had continued my training, as had the Regiment. Rannu had also grown up tracking and it was emphasised in Ghurkha training as well. That said, lightless caves were not the environment we were used to.

Day and night cycles were pointless in darkness and on stims. The time and date facility on our IVDs had become meaningless and I don't think either of us was paying any attention to them. So I've no idea how long it took us to find the tracks. Maybe I'd remembered the complex cave system correctly or maybe it was just luck.

When two hundred people camp it is difficult to erase all the signs. The trails of crushed or grazed stone the mechs left were the easiest to follow. The mechs were not what you would call stealthy, particularly the Bismarck-class *Apakura*.

What I didn't see was Rolleston's trail. Either his force was using some other route or his people were good enough for Rannu and I not to find their tracks in this environment, which was a possibility. I knew, however, that he was down here.

It felt like I hadn't seen light, let alone sky, for a very, very long time. The glow in the distance hurt despite the flash compensation on my optics. It hurt in my head. It hurt as a new and disorienting sensation. I had to remember what it was, what light looked like. All I'd seen was Rannu and rock in green for a good while now.

Of course we were too late. How could we not be? Still it looked like they'd put up a fight. Rolleston's people were clearing it up. Looking for a way to spin it. Make this into good propaganda. Make us the bad guys. We got as close as we could.

The new *pa* was a large area of rock the colour of sun-bleached bone. Naturally occurring columns of rock ran between cave roof and floor at almost regular intervals. The cave floor was a series of pitted basins filled with the foul-smelling, salty sulphurous liquid that passed for water on Lalande 2. Much of it was red and steaming from where the acid content was eating away at the bodies floating or lying half in the pools.

Regular NZ army guarded the perimeter but it looked like a relatively small Black Squadron force had done most of the damage. They were checking the bodies for life and identity. Magnifying my optics I saw my friends, smoking as they were eaten away or just lying in piles of other corpses.

I saw Pagan face down in the water. I didn't recognise him until one of the women in the Black Squadron turned him over. The acid had gone to work on his face but it was unmistakably him. He looked old, tired and in pain. As if death had come as a relief.

Cat was in a pile of corpses. We'd fucked her life up completely. If not for us she'd still be in a cushy job as head of the Atlantis Spoke C-SWAT team. I couldn't see her face. I don't think I wanted to. She was wearing the gyroscopic rig for her railgun. I hoped and was reasonably sure that she would have given them hell before they got her. Though I did wonder whether the members of the Black Squadron were like Rolleston and couldn't be killed.

Mother, Tailgunner and Dog Face were in the same pile of bodies as Cat. Maybe they'd been together because it had been a last stand. I think they were fucked as soon as they chose to resist. Still they would have lasted a little longer if I hadn't ratted them out.

Big Henry was lying dead quite close to us. I reckoned he'd been on sentry duty. He'd been taken quietly and quickly judging by the blade wound in the back of his skull and the look of surprise on his face.

I didn't see Mudge, Merle or Strange. I was pretty sure that Merle had died when the Walker blew in the Rookery. He'd been too close. Mudge and Strange weren't necessarily alive; they could be at the bottom of a pile of bodies. I hoped that neither of them had been captured. If any of them had got away then my money would be on Merle, if he'd made it out of the Rookery.

Then the thought occurred to me. Two people had betrayed us. Two. Could it have been two of those three? Not Mudge, never Mudge. I didn't know Strange well enough. She had seemed too fucked in the head to sell us out. On the other hand that could just mean that nobody knew what she would do, but she had seemed very loyal to the *whanau*.

Rannu and I had talked about fighting the Black Squadrons. We were going to try kill shots. That meant firing accurate shots to the brain, spine, back of the neck, that sort of thing. Trying to do them enough damage so they were dead before they started to heal rapidly, like the *whanau* had witnessed when they killed one of them.

As for Rolleston, our best idea was the four grenades each of us carried in our gauss carbines' underslung grenade launchers. We also had a magazine and a half for each of the carbines. We had been hoping to pick up more ordnance on the way. This was going to have to be fast and dirty because they were there. They were all there.

Grief shut down. Grief would come later. No, actually it wouldn't; I'd be dead. Grief was easy to lock down and turn into hate, looking at Rolleston, Cronin with a fucking media crew and Kring. The Grey Lady was there as well. I kind of hoped that she would kill me. That would seem fitting for what I'd done.

Two sentries die. I push two claws through the back of one of their skulls. Rannu does the other one with one of the shanks he made out of the two claws I'd removed from my left hand. Just ordinary soldiers. Fuck them, they should have resisted like the people they helped murder.

We slide into the water. Wriggle quietly in on our bellies like reptiles. We swim through blood and viscera. I feel the acid burn on my skin, eating away at it. If I'm in here long enough it'll eat down to the armour. That's good – show them the machine, the weapon. The weapon's who I need to be right now. Pain is just information.

My internal oxygen supply enables me to stay submerged longer. I try to exhale slowly and only when I absolutely have to. I pull myself across the bottom of the blood-red pool, getting as close to Rolleston as I can.

We break the surface slowly. You can be as quiet as you like; nine times out of ten it's movement that gives you away. We rise out of the pool like the walking dead. I'm already red and raw from where the acid has stripped away the skin. My smoking clothes are covered in other people's blood. Heads whip around. Weapons are brought to bear. They're too slow. They don't have anything like our motivation.

Rolleston turns towards me. Everything round me fades away; there's just a tunnel between him and me. The smartlink drops the cross hairs over his centre mass. I don't think I need the cross hairs. I squeeze the carbine's trigger. It feels like the Zen shot that I hear snipers talk about. The grenade fires from the underslung launcher. The gun bucks up in my hand. I centre in on him again, the second grenade more hurried. The carbines Rannu stole each had two fragmentation grenades and two High-Explosive Armour-Piercing thirty-millimetre grenades each. We made sure the HEAP grenades were first in the load. The thinking is, fast healing or not, he can't heal if he's scattered all over the cave.

The grenade hits. Penetrates his armour. Everything's moving in slow motion. Magnified optics show the grenade penetrating his body.

A moment later the second one does the same. Rolleston explodes. I so want to enjoy this moment. There's no time.

A look of shock on the Grey Lady's face. My suicide fantasies notwithstanding, she is the biggest threat to us and she's not wearing a helmet. A short burst from the carbine. She goes down in a spray of red from her head. I can't believe this. We surprised them.

Now people know we're here. We fire frags into the largest groups of Black Squadron guys we can see. There's panic. We use this. Embrace it. Move, fire. We drop the hypersonic needles from the gauss carbines in under their helmets, in the backs of their necks.

Taking hits now but I don't care. Push our luck. Find Cronin.

There's a roaring noise. A man screaming. Feral rage. In my peripheral vision I see Kring charge Rannu. Rannu gets off a burst of fire. Kring doesn't even break step. He grabs Rannu's carbine and lifts it. Rannu holds on and is lifted up off his feet. He takes this opportunity to knee Kring in the face. Kring throws Rannu away like a rag doll. Then I have my own problems.

Another member of the Black Squadron goes down in front of me but my gun explodes in two different places almost simultaneously. I'm taking fire now but I haven't been torn apart yet. Which is what I was expecting. Fine, you want to do this the old-fashioned way. Four broken claws extend from my right fist and two full-sized claws from the left. I look around for the shooter.

Cronin is handing a fancy rifle to somebody. I see him mouth the words: 'He's mine.' Less people are shooting at me as I charge him. I can't believe my luck. Corporate boy is dumb enough to want to duel. Well unless he's another biomechanical monster, which he's bound to be. We run at each other. I don't understand why he hasn't got his katana.

Just before we meet he skids low into a puddle of water, the liquid splashing up into my face as he hits me low. I tumble over him and face down onto acid-wet rock. I feel my nose break. Dumb.

I roll the way I think he'll least expect. His foot slams down where my head was moments before. I'm up on my feet and facing him. He walks purposefully towards me. I risk a low kick at his knee. He raises his leg to take it on his shin.

I swing at him, hooking with the blades. He's fast, sways out of the way of the left. The right only just misses and would have got him if my claws had still been full length. He hits me in the face, the chest and then a kick to the knee. I stagger back, something gives in the knee but I'm still up.

I move to close with him. It's what he's been waiting for. He just slides to my side and locks up my left. This is it. Broken claws jam into his face. Blood everywhere, he bites back a cry of pain, he looks angry. I hook a leg behind his and sweep it back, driving him to the ground. On the way down he hits me in the side of the head hard enough to make me nauseous.

I glimpse Kring hit Rannu so hard it picks him up off his feet.

Cronin drags me down with him. He twists in mid-air and lands on me. How the fuck did this happen? I feel like my face caves in when he elbows me. I kick up, hook my leg round his neck and yank him backwards. He throws himself back with the momentum of it, rolling out of the leg lock into a low crouch. I start to roll to my feet but Cronin pushes forward off his legs, plants a hand next to me and the next I know he knees me in the face with his entire body weight. My face feels concave now. My IVD bores me with red warning icons. I may as well have them up permanently now.

It's an ugly, badly aimed blow but it connects. More luck than judgement but there's enough force there to punch through armour and reach flesh as I ram the two blades on my left fist into his side. I twist and thrash my hand around inside him trying to do as much damage as I can. For a corp this guy's hard. He doesn't scream; instead he steps through me. Pushing my hand out of his flesh and kicking me in the face. Bone and subcutaneous armour crumple on my chin and the back of my skull as it's battered off the rock.

He's angry now. Instead of pulling away, his leg goes high into the air. Why has nobody else got involved? He hammers it down in an attempt to scissor-kick me in the face. All he does is ram his leg down onto the four broken blades of my right hand. I twist and yank the leg, hoping to make it useless. I sit up and try and stab him in the groin with the blades on my left hand but he's gone. He's rolled out of the way, screaming out as he twists the broken blades out of his leg.

He skips up back onto his feet. I stand up more slowly, grinning at him. His face, side and leg are all pissing blood.

I sense more than see that Rannu is boxing Kring. Kring looks like pulped meat but I watch as he swings a huge fist with surprising speed and almost takes Rannu's head off, sending the punch-drunk Ghurkha staggering back across the cave.

Everyone else is just watching. They look nervous. I don't understand why they haven't just shot me. Cronin didn't strike me as the type to give someone a sporting chance.

'I'm going to kill you, motherfucker!' Cronin spits at me.

I just smile.

'Don't kill him,' someone says. It looks like one of the Black Squadron soldiers. Why is he telling Cronin what to do? Something doesn't make sense. I put that thought to the back of my mind as Cronin skips forward with surprising speed and kicks me in the knee. The knee snaps, bending the other way. There's some screaming, quite a lot of screaming. Then I fall over. That hurts as well. Then Cronin is all over me. I get in some good blows but it's over quickly. Him stamping on my head until I lose consciousness is just a formality now.

Knowing I'm a lost cause, Demiurge decides to show me the truth. As I try to crawl away, and Merle kicks me in the head again, I see that there is no carpet of bodies. There is no Black Squadron presence. Cronin is really Merle. The Black Squadron guy who told Merle not to kill me is Mudge. Kring is Tailgunner. Tailgunner has lifted Rannu off the ground by his neck and is pounding him again and again with a massive fist. Rannu hangs limp like some street kid's prize rag doll. I don't know who Rolleston was because he's spread over a large area of the cave and mixed in with the broken remains of all the others we've killed.

Mother, Little Henry and Strange stand in the circle around our beating. Mother wants to kill me. I can tell that. Little Henry looks like he's in shock. I think Strange wants to cry.

Another jarring kick to the head, another wave of nausea as my brain rattles around in the broken vessel of my skull. Rammed down into the stone, spitting out more blood, leaving a trail as I try to crawl some more. I don't know where. Towards the Grey Lady's body? Mudge and Pagan look traumatised by what they're watching.

Another kick to the head. I'm laughing now, don't know why, so much pain. Cat is crouching over the Grey Lady, working furiously on the head wound. Why? She's the enemy. But she's not. That was a lie. That was what Demiurge made me think. It's not the Grey Lady. I crawl some more.

'Motherfucker!' Merle's really angry. I fucked up his face. He punctuates the scream with a kick to my side for a bit of variety, which hits me so hard it flips me onto my back.

'That's enough.' Mudge's voice. Merle wants to kill me. They all want to kill me. I manage to roll back onto my belly, a good place for someone like me. I can see the Grey Lady now. Except it's not her. I knew it wasn't. I'm a good shot. There's only so much you can do when someone who's as good a shot as me puts three rounds from a gauss carbine into a human head. I look at Morag's body.

Demiurge has had its fun. It feels like black water washing over my soul. It feels like drowning.

18
New *Utu Pa*

It was like being born. There was light and pain and fire. Everything about me that was weak – all the fear, the self-loathing, the crippling reliance on other weaklings – was burned out of me. It was the liberation that comes from surgery of the soul.

I had no idea how long I had been out but they had moved. They had run. Even as deluded as they were, they must have understood the pointlessness of hiding. It was only a matter of time before they were found and either destroyed or healed in the black fire.

I tried my internal comms. Nothing. They'd actually been removed. I glanced down at my side and saw the gel over the surgical scar where they had removed the transponder. I cursed silently.

I was in the inevitable cave. It was small. The mouth of the cave was covered by a tarpaulin that moved slightly in the subterranean wind. I could just about hear water over the sound of Rannu screaming at someone that he was going to cut off their genitals and sew them into their mouth. In Latin. I smiled, hoping that someone had the education to appreciate obscenities screamed in a dead language. I doubted it.

I was lying on a cot stained with dried blood. My knee, face and other wounds were covered by medgels. I felt like peeling them off like scabs. I was healing quickly but I reached out to the alien bio-nanites in my system with a thought and reprogrammed them to heal me faster. They were so primitive without the ingenuity of humanity to upgrade them. The fact that we could render an entire alien species into nothing more than a technology to improve ourselves was a sure sign of our superiority and right to dominate.

I was immobilised with very secure-looking manacles. Heavy chains had been driven into the rock. The manacles had been welded tight over my wrists and ankles. I wasn't going anywhere in a hurry. I hoped this wasn't going to come down to anything as sordid as soiling myself and attempting to hit visitors with projectile vomit.

The tarpaulin was pushed to one side as a worried-looking Pagan and Mudge stepped into the cave. I tried to form a mask of concern and fear.

'Guys, what's going on? Where the fuck are we? Who's that screaming? And why am I chained up?'

'What's the last thing you remember, Jakob?' Pagan asked.

'The heist.' I widened my eyes. 'The Grey Lady ... Fuck! What's going on?!' I tried to remember what being constantly afraid was like and put it into my voice.

'You were captured,' Pagan told me. The look of concern on his face was so pathetic I wanted to spit at him. I saw his empty skin bulge and move. One of the flies that animated his corpse crawled across his face.

'I don't ...'

'Remember anything?' Mudge said, sounding angry.

'What happened?'

'You killed a whole lot of the Kiwis including Dog Face,' Mudge told me.

Shit, only Dog Face. Why had Demiurge made Dog Face look like Rolleston? Perhaps it was something to do with them both using claws.

'Morag?' I asked. The anxious, frightened tone I heard in my own voice made me want to vomit. I almost did when I saw the look of sadness on Pagan's face.

'I'm sorry, Jakob ...' he said.

I tried to remember what it was like. The pantomime of emotions I should display.

'No ...' A touch of horror initially, I thought. I mixed it with the denial. It rang false in my own ears, however. I wanted to laugh as I saw blood start to run down the cave wall.

'Spare us, we've already been through this with Rannu. You can start your tasteful ravings about genitalia in Latin now if you want. We're not letting you go,' Mudge said.

My expression of mock pain became laughter. Pagan shook his head in pity. This angered me. There was nothing for a broken old man like him to pity here. He was in the presence of an ascended being. I imagined the pair of them broken down to their constituent parts, kept alive by technology, sewn together, linked to a biofeedback device so they could feel each other, forced to sing in agony. I felt myself getting hard.

'Well, I cannot be killed but my body here can, so either holding me indefinitely or killing me are your only options.' I focused on Mudge. 'You're not going to kill me, Mudge, are you? We were such good friends.' All mock pleading.

'You feel nothing at all for Morag?' Pagan asked.

'Yes, I do. I'm not a monster. She was a good fuck. I built her up. I was looking forward to tearing her back down, making her less than what she was when I found her. There's nothing sadder than a vocational victim who thinks they're actually a person. Don't believe me? I bet she makes a pretty corpse. You should use her. The closest you were ever going to get with your paternal lechery, old man.'

Pagan flinched like he'd been hit.

'Oh please. I'm just saying what we've all been thinking. It's so liberating to finally tell the truth. Don't you think?'

'You bastard,' Pagan spat at me. 'You didn't build anything. Everything she was she made herself.'

'I can see why you'd be uncomfortable with me fucking an abused teenager to self-improvement. It's almost taking advantage of her, isn't it? Still none of you ever really said anything, did you?'

I was thoroughly enjoying the chance to be so honest. I was also enjoying the look of revulsion on Pagan and Mudge's faces because I knew inside they were feeling a kernel of doubt, of self-loathing because they were weak. More to the point, they knew I was telling the truth.

I watched Mudge's skin peel back as he screamed, then the flesh split and opened down to the bone. He looked like a dissected frog.

'You keep talking like that, and you're just going to make Jakob feel like twice the arsehole when we get him back,' Pagan said.

'Ignore him. He's just trying to get a reaction,' Mudge told Pagan. 'That's not Jakob; it's a puppet with Demiurge's hand up his arse.'

'I bet you'd love that, wouldn't you, faggot?'

Amusingly it was Pagan who flinched when he heard the word. Mudge laughed but it was without humour.

'That the best you can do? Adolescent classroom jibes? I've heard it before. It's an old word, meaningless. It's pretty much only used by throwbacks now.'

I smiled at the irony of someone like him calling me a throwback.

'But you've heard it before, haven't you? Hurt, didn't it? Used at bad times? Poor Mudge, your life's just one long bit of overcompensation, isn't it?'

'Suddenly you're so insightful.' Sarcasm, but I knew him well enough to know that he wasn't happy.

'How's your nigger lover?'

'Another old word? You sound like that arsehole Messer in Crawling Town.'

But he couldn't hide a flinch when I said it. I didn't use the word because of the difference in skin tone between Merle and myself but because of the hatred that it engenders. A racist is a fool who underestimates his tribal opponent. Racism is a position of fear, a racist is someone who tries to buoy themself at others' expense. Hatred and violence are our natural states, our fragment of divinity. Each of us is an island, unconnected, an unending reservoir of hatred against others, and if we're weak, ourselves. Total, undifferentiated, constant violence against everyone should be our ambition as it is our birthright. Violence is the only self-expression that means anything. Hatred is the only meaningful, truthful emotion. It is all we truly understand. The rest is a facade we erect so we can play in the lie of so-called civilisation. People sell their children for drugs and they call it civilisation. When will we stop lying to ourselves?

'Really, how is he?'

'A little less pretty but he enjoyed kicking your arse. Which reminds me. Pagan and I are the only people keeping you alive here. Mother and her people want you dead and Merle wants you dead, so if you want to continue your existence then you may want to try being a little more fucking co-operative.'

I couldn't help it, I had to laugh.

'What do you think is happening here?'

'We want Jakob back,' Pagan told me earnestly.

'Does this sound like someone's met a rogue program in the net and got their neural ware a bit fucked up?' I demanded.

Pagan shook his head miserably. I watched his skin blacken and burn. It started to melt and run, the flesh beneath it charring.

'You're not going to dress this up in outdated religious terms and try to change me back to the frightened fucking mess I was. We haven't been brainwashed, you deluded old fuck. It was a revelation. Come to fucking terms with the fact that I am Jakob.'

'You sure you want to narrow your options like that?' Mudge acting the hard man made me laugh.

'Or we could get you out,' Pagan told me.

'Really? You know how to do that?' It was written all over their faces that they didn't have a clue. 'There is nothing to remove. There is only Jakob. So what are you going to do? Kill me? Keep me here? Let me go? Like any of those?'

No answer, just grim expressions.

'Or you can join us?'

Mudge started laughing. 'Are you fucking nuts? I'd rather suck Rolleston's cock.'

'Hey, everything's possible,' I told them. Though I really couldn't see it happening. 'Think about it. All the pain, all the fear is over. Finally you could be part of something that actually matters, building something instead of being disaffected outsiders raging against it all.'

'Yeah, that's not going to happen,' Mudge said. He was hunched over, forced to stoop as muscles contracted so hard they cracked bone, becoming smaller and weaker as he tried to speak to me.

'So what are you going to do? Kill your old friend? Possibly the only person in the world who can tolerate you for extended periods of time?'

'You'd kill me in a heartbeat at the moment,' he replied.

He was right. I was thinking about opening his throat with my teeth if he got close enough.

'That's what this is about, isn't it? Make us kill the body of our friend? Damage the morale a bit more. Get the most out of their Jakob-shaped weapon? Rolleston and friends are really going for the pain now, aren't they?'

'It's just psych ops,' Pagan said unconvincingly.

'No, it's hate by any means necessary, isn't it?' Mudge asked me. I chose not to answer him 'Well, you've had your fun but I've got some bad news. When the end comes we'll have a stranger kill you.'

'See if you can run far enough that you don't hear the gunshot, old friend.'

Mudge and Pagan turned and left the cave. I waited.

I was staring at the hunched, blue-skinned hag with the tombstone teeth and the long, vicious-looking black claws that reminded me of an angry Rolleston. I'd failed. She was still alive.

'How?'

'You hit me dead centre. On the helmet. One round grazed my head, almost killed me.' Even reborn, her gravelly, broken-glass voice still bothered me.

Demiurge had shown me the Grey Lady. The Grey Lady does not wear a helmet and I had taken a head shot. Still it must have been close.

'Why did they lie?' I asked.

'I think it was a last-ditch attempt to see if there was something left of Jakob.'

I started laughing when she said this.

'I am Jakob.'

She laughed back at me. It was like nails down a blackboard.

'I don't think so.'

I had fought as hard as I could. I even tasted some of Pagan's blood when I bit into his arm, clean through his subcutaneous armour. I probably did myself more harm than I did to him but it was satisfying to feel his warm blood in my mouth and over my face. They had still managed to get the jack into one of my plugs. Which is of course exactly what I wanted.

It was a new environment. An open airy room in what felt like an old city. The room was high up, looking down a hill at a tangle of ancient streets and alleys, over rooftops and spires. There was a morning breeze but wherever it was supposed to be was obviously a warm country. I heard morning prayer as the sun rose as a burning red ball. I was pretty sure we were in the Middle East somewhere. Or rather we were in a sanctum or some other well-rendered net simulation of a city in the Middle East back on Earth.

Pagan was there in his traditionalist Druidic icon. He looked like a delusional fool in some child's viz, a romantic, a wishful thinker. Both he and Morag had glyphs of light appearing and disappearing in front of them. It wouldn't help.

I was sitting on a simple chair at a simple table. There was a glass of water on the table and that was all. Around the table and the chair was a circle of light suspended about six inches off the floor. I'm guessing that this was the containment program.

Idiots. Invading systems was the first trick I learned. I could break through any security. I sent out just a little black tendril of flame. I was going to lock their minds in here. Play with time compression and put them both into a torture loop while I dealt with the others. Then I was going to come back and play with Morag for a while. Until she understood what she was in my presence. The fools had handed themselves to me.

The circle of light flared and stopped the black fire dead. It was my second unpleasant surprise of the day. Black Annis turned back to look at me with a raised eyebrow over the pools of her eyes.

'Do you think we're idiots?' she asked.

'Well I only have my past experiences to judge you by. The Maoris' net?'

They said nothing. Where did he get that piece of code? It had to be the aberrations?

'Still I'm pleased to see you're alive after we meant so much to each other,' I told her.

'That would explain the shooting.'

'Love hurts, and at the risk of sounding petty you shot me first.'

'You deserved it.'

'What, for fucking Fiona? So you mean you'll shoot me again if I tell you I fucked Josephine?' I leaned back in the chair and smiled.

Pagan stopped what he was doing. Black Annis looked up at me and unexpectedly smiled.

'We're not killing Jakob no matter what stories you make up,' she told me.

'I'll fuck you in the hag form if that's what you want, but wouldn't it be better if you're the sweet little Maiden of Flowers. Don't pretend you're not a victim – it doesn't become you and we both know I'm not lying.'

Pagan looked at Black Annis uncertainly but Black Annis went back to her work, still smiling.

'She's better than you, you know? More skilled, more feeling, more impassioned,' I told her.

'Should've stayed with her then.' I could hear her teeth grinding together.

'No, I had to get back here to you. That's what you wanted to hear, isn't it? Fear of abandonment. Your sister left; your mother sold you; I left for a quick fuck with some posh bitch. Poor little Morag McGrath.'

Black Annis looked up at me. 'Do you think you're the first guy I've slept with who's said bad things to me? Mudge was right: you're a fucking cliché.'

'Morag, I'm your wet dream. I am exactly what you want.' More nails down a blackboard as she laughed. 'I suspect you are one of the most unwanted people who has ever lived. I think there are back-alley abortions who've been more wanted than you.'

'That's bullshit,' Pagan spat at me.

'Why do you love her? Want her?' I asked him.

'She is a valued member of ...' He faltered, realising how weak it sounded.

There was a flash of irritation as Morag glanced at him.

I turned on him. 'Oh bullshit, Pagan. Why am I the only one telling the truth here? All your mentoring, your paternal care, when you're not accusing her of being an alien whore of course. Just waiting for the Elektra Complex to kick in, weren't you, so she could come and play with the daddy who also abandoned her. You don't care about her. She's a commodity, a cunt and a beautiful body. That's all you care about. Just like everyone else.'

'That's not—' Pagan began.

'Shut up, Pagan,' Black Annis told him. 'I don't need validation. I know who I am and how people feel about me.'

'So why did I sleep with the Grey Lady?'

'Because you're sick.'

'It was the old weak Jakob who did it, and you know that.'

'She raped him.' Black Annis was sounding less sure of herself now. I just looked at her. She knew the truth.

'Is the sum purpose of your evil machinations to try and get me to cry?' she asked. Angrier now.

'We both know you will. Or rather you would do if you still could, but you're selling your humanity so you can be more like me, aren't you?'

'Fuck you, you're not human. You're a computer program someone made up.'

'Yes.' I looked at Pagan. 'He did.' Bang. Even on the icon guilt was written all over his face. 'Hi, Dad. Want to abuse the old patriarchal authority with me as well? Actually you're a great parental figure, aren't you? How's God doing? Moping and suicidal last I heard.'

'I think we should try and ignore him, get on with it,' Pagan said. He almost sounded like he meant it.

'Look, I realise you feel like this big all-encompassing evil but really you're just a bit fucking irritating at the moment,' Morag told me.

That angered me. She was going to suffer a lot.

'I'm sorry, darling. What I was trying to say before Daddy dearest interrupted was that it's okay. Even though you're shit in bed in comparison with drunk posh girls and assassins, not only will I take you back but I can give you what you want.' Morag just laughed and shook her head, ropey black hair swinging from side to side as she tried to ignore me. 'See, I worked it out. You've been systematically raped since you were however old you were when Mummy dearest sold you. I mean I know we call it prostitution and we tell ourselves it's okay because we pay – it's just like a job, isn't it – but I know what it was for you. Worse still, you have to pretend you like it for the punter. You must have been good at that because you were in the high-end part of the Forbidden Pleasure, not in the cargo containers working the turnstiles. I guess you just got to like it, didn't you? That's why you spread your legs for me and for Ambassador. Open your mind. Open your legs. What's the difference? It's just another invasion, another violation, isn't it, Morag? But I'll take you back. I'll use you; I will fucking hurt you so much; I will brutalise you; I will even pimp you out, though I'll struggle to go lower than an alien and you'll want me too. I promise you.' I leaned back smiling.

Both of them were staring at me, anger and hatred obvious on their faces. That was good. Good for them. See if they could embrace it, live pure, free of their hypocrisies and lies.

I was sure it would be Morag. After all, I'd gone to the dark place where we all sometimes live. Well, not me any more. But it was Pagan who broke. Who did what I wanted him to do.

'Bastaaard!' I didn't think it was possible for an icon to look that angry. He really was a very good programmer but weak. That was okay, we could fix him. White lightning played around the tip of his staff. It was an attack that would probably fry most hackers so badly their heads would catch fire, but all it was going to do was break the circle and I would eat their fucking souls.

Black Annis grabbed Pagan before he could activate the attack program and slammed him into the stone wall of the room. Glyphs buzzed around them as she shut down his program. A display of raw power that I'm sure wasn't lost on Pagan. I was sure that he was so close to being a broken man.

'If you don't have the discipline to ignore what are only words, then get out. I'll finish up.' It was like listening to rocks grind together as she hissed that at him. I had been so close. 'That is exactly what he wants. Someone to break the circle.'

He couldn't face her. What sort of idiot writes the ability to look overcome by anguish into his own icon? They should live large. It's not like it's real after all. She let him go and he just seemed to sag against the wall. She turned to stare at me. The things I wanted to do to her then.

The door opened and another well-rendered icon walked in. I was surprised. The icon looked old, older even than Pagan. Again, why would someone make themself look old in here? He wore a long linen shirt and linen trousers. Over the shirt he had a kind of waistcoat decorated in brocade. The fabric skull cap on his head also had a brocade pattern running around it and he wore a simple pair of sandals. In the early-morning sun the white linen seemed to glow. He looked over at Black Annis and Pagan.

'I think it would be better if you left,' he said. His voice was cultured and educated. The accent was definitely from somewhere in the Middle East back on Earth. Black Annis nodded. The hag and the Druid looked so ridiculously out of place with this man.

'We're done anyway. You understand the rules?' Black Annis asked through grinding stone.

'I think so. Don't break the circle,' the man said. We'll see.

Black Annis didn't spare me a look as she practically led Pagan out.

He did though. Pagan turned to stare at me and there was hate and anger but defeat also. Morag may have managed to control it in here but she was going to burst into tears as soon as she left the net.

The man pulled a chair up opposite mine. Of course he didn't break the circle.

'I think it's much easier to upset the people you know and love,' he said.

'You know I don't love them.'

'You? No, but Jakob does, and that gives you insight. I find it interesting that the only power you have over them comes from your love for them and their love for you. Twisted of course but nonetheless ...'

'Really? That's your opening salvo? Love is power?' I couldn't keep the scorn from my voice, not that I was trying terribly hard.

He laughed. 'Yes, it does sound trite put that way. Easy to be cynical about, but even then it still holds true.'

'So what are we doing here?'

'We're going to talk a little.' You mean you're going to run as many diagnostic programs and analytical routines as you can to try and get insight into me. 'Then I am going to do some praying. I would ask you to join me but I can't see that happening.' Or rather you're going to try and write code because you think the old weak Jakob is in here somewhere. He's not. This is a fusion. I'm in the meat, not in the machine, old man, but you can find that out the hard way.

'What should I call you? Exorcist?' He laughed at this. 'Would you be more comfortable if I looked like this?' It was a simple change I made. The icon no longer looked like me. Instead I had become the beast. I saw his expression falter. Not because of the goat-headed form I took – that had long ago ceased to be frightening – but because of the control I had. Total control over my surroundings, with the exception of this fucking circle.

'My name's Salem,' he said after he'd recovered quickly.

'This your sanctum?'

'A copy of part of it. We're in an isolated system.'

Damn. Still I can't pretend it's a surprise.

'Where's it supposed to be?'

'A place where I used to come to do my lessons when I was a boy in Jerusalem before the war.'

'You really are old.' He smiled. 'And why are all you people so painfully sentimental?'

'Connections, identity. I think it's part of being comfortable with who you are.'

'I could make you comfortable with who you are and with God.'

349

He just smiled. Too soon. We'd get to that later.

'What's this got to do with you?' I asked.

'It's my duty.'

'You are an exorcist then?'

'I think it's the duty of all to help when they can.'

'Brilliant. If you could just break this circle, that would be really helpful.'

'I am here to help Jakob.'

I leaned forward and formed the words very carefully. 'I am Jakob. When will you people understand that? There is nothing wrong with me.'

'You are an evil djinn who has taken over his body.'

'That what your analysis programs are telling you?'

It was written all over his face that the answer was no.

'You have the power of an ifreet—'

'And you are a step away from a fucking witch doctor. Why don't you shake some monkey bones over me?'

He flinched at the swearing. Good, I liked delicate sensibilities.

'It's just terminology. Do you really think that I do not know what you are?'

'Who I am is Jakob Douglas, and no, you don't have a clue. If you did you wouldn't fucking be here.'

'Is there need for swearing?'

'Go fuck yourself.'

'It just diminishes you.'

I would have loved to stop talking to the sanctimonious prick. His constantly calm demeanour was beginning to piss me off, but I needed an in. Some way to anger him enough that he would go for me.

'I see refuge in Allah from the pride, poetry and touch of Shaitan, the cursed,' Salem said to himself.

I had to laugh. It was like something out of the Middle Ages. Still there was something about his words at a very basic level that I didn't like.

'You're frightened?' I asked.

He nodded. 'You are very dangerous.'

'It doesn't have to be this way. There is a real god coming, not a feel-good fantasy designed to justify hatred and violence—'

'Something that hasn't been an issue since the Final Human Conflict. The hatred and violence is entirely of the creation of your masters as far as I can tell.'

'You interrupted me.'

'I apologise.' He actually looked contrite, as if manners mattered. I on the other hand was pissed off that I had lowered myself to speak to this superstitious caveman, to offer him a chance, and all he wanted to do was hear himself talk.

'We offer a chance, the ultimate chance to belong, to be part of what humanity will become, and we are attacked for it. Unless of course you feel that humanity is doing fine now?'

'I think it would be reductive to lay all the troubles of humanity at the feet of the Cabal. It is much more complex than that. But they have certainly played a significant part in humanity's current state, don't you think?'

'Birth is always painful.'

'Particularly when it's poisoned.'

'So what then? The abortion of humanity's rebirth? We just remain in our animalistic state?'

'I don't think you can force these things.'

'The only force is the result of resistance.'

'Because some do not wish to live the way you do.'

'No.' This truly angered me. 'That is not the reason for resistance; the reason is fear. All of us have a chance at something better, something more, and the throwbacks are too frightened of the unknown to embrace that. No attempt has been made to understand, only to lash out like spoilt children who do not get their way.'

Salem sat back in his chair and smiled. 'This at least is progress. Please, I wish to understand. Tell me what we are frightened of.'

I smiled at him. 'Then let me out.'

'You know I will not do that.'

'Then this is not a free exchange of ideas.'

'Not when you hold this man Jakob prisoner.'

This was turning into an exasperating circle jerk.

'I am Jakob, and I think you know that.' I was getting angry now.

'I think you have assimilated Jakob. At a fundamental level, against the laws of man and God, you have no right to do this. You must leave and I think you know this.'

It appeared they had sent in the world's calmest man to speak to me. Where was Pagan when you needed him?

'And your diagnostics must have told you by now that Jakob has ascended – he is something else now. Just as you know that deep down your god is only real as a net-bound hallucination, a hollow ghost in your neurones. We have something tangible to offer.'

I was imagining what this man's insides would look like. What it would be like to make patterns with them, to wear them? Didn't he realise that they are as nothing to us? They are tools, nothing more, and we are under no obligation to take them with us.

'Old man, I know angels, holy terrors,' I told him, frustrated.

'You know fallen angels, nothing more.'

Then he smiled. He had found something.

'What?' I demanded. He ignored me. 'Do you understand that we are at an evolutionary point for mankind? Your outdated folk beliefs are about to be superseded by something real.'

'It is not real. It is a technological horror more in keeping with the inventions of Mary Shelley than with the creation of a god, but that is just my opinion and here is the problem when two people debate faith. You are not going to convince me that I am wrong because I have faith, and I am not going to convince you that you are wrong. In such a case, all we can do is strive to accept our differences and perhaps understand them.' His calm demeanour grated on me as smugness.

'I am not offering you faith; I am offering you proof. I am offering you the tangible and personnel connection to God that you, all you hackers, wish you had.' It was like talking to a simple-minded savage.

'I think for non-religious people it will always be impossible for you to understand that the connection you describe is a relationship we already have and already feel. It is as real and tangible to us as your net-bound technological creations are to you.'

'Even though you know them to be a lie?'

'Obviously I don't know that. In fact I believe the opposite.'

'Salem.' I was becoming more and more exasperated. 'Do you understand what I'm offering you? I am offering you the chance to be a new Muhammad here.'

'I think you are offering me the chance to be the spokesperson for a lie.' There was no hesitation there. His narrow-mindedness was total.

'You understand that's what you fucking are?!' I was shouting at him now. I was so angry. His expression became more serious and considerably less benign.

'There is only one god and Muhammad is his prophet.'

'You walk among fallen people, infidels, you fucking hypocrite!'

'Only God can give me understanding of my place in things. Only he can judge.'

'He's not fucking real!' He flinched. 'The closest you ever got was that fucking joke back on Earth.'

'A misguided and blasphemously named program.'

'The things you've seen aren't what you think they are. Are you so fucking frightened that you reject out of hand anything that's real in favour of this fantasy world?!'

'All you are is us,' he told me. 'All you are is a prison, a complicated computer program with delusions of grandeur.'

I was on my feet now.

'I think you'll see what I am, medicine man!' I screamed at him.

He looked at me with an expression of pity. What could be more inappropriate? He was less than bloodied shit before me.

'Tell Morag I'm sorry!' I continued screaming at him. No! Wait. I didn't say that. Why would I say that? She was a vessel for my pleasures – another victim, nothing more.

Salem made a sobbing sound. No, it wasn't him, it was me.

'I will make your family watch your corpse being fucked!'

'I have nothing to fear from you. Allah protects me.'

'I will find everything you care about and destroy it! I will show you that your god is a lie! I will rape your children and their children in front of your eyes!'

I was battering myself against the circle, causing myself pain as energy coalesced around me where I hit the barrier program. Hating the feeling of impotence that had somehow replaced omnipotence in here. This barrier was not human programming.

'All you have is fear. I am so sorry,' Salem said.

I could hear it. Everything I said, everything I did, and it was me. I knew that. I could hear it but it sounded different and distorted like sound travelling through water.

I felt like an exotic bird, some rich corp exec's pet in a gilded cage. The cage was decorated with engraved knot-work and was so exquisite, ornate and beautiful it didn't look real. It was still a prison. It hung here suspended in total, impenetrable darkness.

It gave me time to consider what I'd done. The betrayal, Demiurge's trickery and the murder I'd committed under its influence. The things I'd said to Mudge and Pagan. Morag.

In some ways I would have welcomed being the monster. Or rather joining the rest of me to merge with the monster. Though the best thing would have been a bullet through my skull. I had nothing to offer now but more pain and lies. It felt like an age since I'd been able to offer anything else. I didn't understand why my friends were prolonging this.

I had fully underestimated just how angry Rolleston was with me. Exquisite wasn't a word I used often but this was. Turn me into everything I hate. Use me as a weapon against those I love but keep enough of me conscious and imprisoned to appreciate what I was doing.

Did I sound calm? Most of the time all I did was scream. I slept when he slept and dreamt of nothing, only to wake and scream again.

*But not now. Now I'm lying on the cold metal floor of my cage, curled in the
foetal position, shaking and crying like a frightened child. I can hear myself
raging at the holy man.*

*I feel something gritty against my skin. Something blows against me in the
warm wind. There should be no wind in this void. I open my eyes. The floor of
my cage is dusted in fine grains of sand. More is blowing in through the bars.
I sit up and watch this wind from nowhere play with the sand, make patterns
with it on the floor.*

*I am hollow. I have little strength left for any emotion other than hate
and self-loathing. I have become the worst thing I could imagine. Fear seems
redundant.*

*There is still a prickling at the back of my mind, perhaps deep in the lizard
brain as it rises from the sand. It is a desert ghost in robes, its head wrapped
in a* shemagh, *obscuring its features, if it has any. The ghost is formed of the
sand and is constantly reforming as the wind blows granules out into the void.*

*'What are you?' I ask. My throat should be raw and bloody, but this isn't
the real world.*

*'I am an intelligent computer virus with limited verbal responses. I am
sorry but this will hurt. A lot.' I think the language is Arabic but somehow I
understand it. I recognise the holy man's voice.*

'What will hurt?'

'Kneel! That's right. Kneel, you fuck!' Muscles contort, my mouth
enlarges, and anger, not control of my icon, makes me look bestial as
I scream at this nothing prostrate before his fiction, facing east. ' Face
me! Face me, you fucking coward!'

He should be kneeling before me, that is right and proper, even if
I am a caged god. He shouldn't be kneeling before some fiction in the
east.

I start to tell him what I will do to him and everything and everyone
he cares about. People say that the details in these kinds of descrip-
tions are just pornography, but I knew that they painted pictures in
his head and he would see me exploring atrocity with everyone he
loves. He thinks he's praying now. We both know he's hiding from
me, too afraid to face me. Tone it down now. Whisper to him, more
effective than the screaming.

I watch in horror as my left arm becomes mercury and leaks to the
floor from the finger up to the shoulder. Then the fire comes. Then
I really start to scream as agony surges through every particle of my
being.

Fear, horror, disbelief. This cannot be happening to me. I am being diminished. This categorically cannot happen. Only I have the power here. Only me. I have to warn ...

I am introduced to pain anew. I thought I'd been screaming. I hadn't been screaming.

It must be like being born. There is light and pain, or agony to be precise, except I want to hide from the light. Crawl back into the dark, let them forget about me as I am assaulted by the memories of everything I've said and done.

'Jakob?' It is a kindly voice full of genuine concern. That makes it worse. I do not deserve it.

I try to back into the corner of the sunlit room. Salem reaches for me. I flinch away from him.

'You're free. The ifreet is gone.' Reassuring. He doesn't realise it is still me, still all me.

The door to the room opens. Black Annis. Don't name her as Morag. Pagan is with her. They look out of place in this environment. Morag – no, Black Annis – stands in the doorway like judgement.

They walk towards me. Black Annis glances over at Salem, who nods. There is a look of concern on the old man's face. She reaches for me. I try to cower away but my back is already against the cold stone wall. Her long-fingered, black-clawed hand touches me like death. Black lightning plays across my chest. I scream again as biofeedback surges into my body in the real world. Enough biofeedback to make my plugs smoke, enough to fry synapses, enough to stop even an augmented and mostly mechanical heart.

It's like sinking into dark water. The last thing I hear is Pagan screaming, 'No!' and diving towards Morag. Way too slow, Pagan. She waited. Waited until it was me. This is good. I deserve this.

19

New *Utu Pa*

Disappointment. I'm alive. I can still hear Rannu screaming. I can still feel the manacles around my wrists and ankles. I'm still lying on a soiled cot wondering when this will be over. The air still tastes like licking a battery, still smells of rotten eggs, and I know that when I open my eyes the sky will still be very far away.

Our escape now made sense. I didn't want to think about it too much at the time, that's how insidious hope can be. Where was all the security when we escaped from Moa City? Regardless of how good Rannu is, he couldn't have hidden for that long in such a small area, not with the level of technology the Black Squadrons were using. They had let us go. We were under their control the entire time.

Mudge was sitting on the cot next to mine smoking a cigarette. He didn't look happy.

'Morning,' I said.

He stood up, walked over to my cot and punched me hard enough in the nose to break it despite the subcutaneous armour.

'Fuck!' I shouted. 'I was fucking possessed, you bastard!' Mudge smiled.

'Standard Operating Procedure for being called a faggot – not that it happens a lot these days. You're lucky it was me and not Merle. Still, now we can be friends again.'

He reached down into his backpack and produced a bottle of vodka. I looked around. All his gear was in there. It looked like he'd been here a while. Watching over me. I didn't deserve this, and what's worse I didn't really have the words to express my gratitude. He followed my eyes.

'Don't worry about it,' he told me. Days of this bullshit and he was waiting with the booze. I pushed myself up into a sitting position as he passed me the bottle and he sparked up a joint. The atmosphere made the booze taste like battery acid. It was the best thing I'd ever drank.

'Not to be trusted?' I asked, lifting the manacles.

'We've got to be sure, man. What happened to you, Rannu, the Vucari and I guess the other special forces types they sent back is unprecedented. What we did is more so. You're in a position to cause us a lot of hurt.' Then he looked away. I guessed I'd already done that. 'Not to mention the Maori contingent's very big on reciprocity.'

'Can't say I blame them. Merle?'

'Fucked off about his face, but he can get that fixed in the unlikely event we don't all die. He may be pissed off about the prospect of an ugly-looking corpse, though secretly I think he digs the scar-face look. He saved you, man. When ... you know ...' When Morag made a concerted and premeditated attempt to murder me. Oh yeah, I owed Merle.

'I guess I've got some apologies to make.' Except it couldn't be done. I couldn't escape from the things I'd said or done. It didn't matter that I was under the influence. It was still my face and form that did it, and with the best will in the world human psychology doesn't let the victim move away from that. I was quiet for a little while, thinking this through, enjoying the familiarity of alcohol and sweet smoke burning my throat. Hiding from my problems.

'What happened to you guys?' I asked. I couldn't look at Mudge's lenses when I did. I was pretty sure he knew what I was thinking. That he could see my guilt.

'I don't know how much you saw, but we got jumped by a couple of those Black Squadron wankers.' He paused and looked up at me. 'They're hard. Augmented, like Rolleston, though not as dangerous.'

'I saw some of that. How'd you get out?'

'Merle. He took a battering when the Walker went up but he was still alive. It seems that they die just as well with a plasma shot to the head. I'm not joking, Jakob, the guy's a one-man slaughterhouse.' There was a degree of pride in his man behind Mudge's words. He was right as well. Merle had been very useful. I was looking forward to thanking him.

'Morag?'

Mudge laughed humourlessly. 'How'd you think? The Grey Lady? Jesus Christ, Jakob, what were you thinking? If you wanted the ultimate adrenalin fuck you'd have been as well shagging a live-firing plasma cannon. Was she any good?'

Yes, actually, but I had no intention of telling Mudge that.

'They killed Morag in front of my eyes. I watched her die. It was sense but I knew nothing. I spilled my guts.'

'Well, we knew you'd break. Everyone does.'

'I didn't even try to hold out, not when I thought I could still help Morag.'

'It's all right, man. Most of us got out alive.' He was trying to make me feel better but I could tell he was uneasy with this. He wouldn't look at me.

'Look Mudge, I knew some things about Earth's defences ...'

Mudge didn't answer. There was nothing really to say. I had after all betrayed my entire race. I was looking at him expectantly. I wasn't sure what I wanted from him. Even if he told me it was okay, we'd both know it was a lie, and Mudge rarely lied. It was why he was so annoying at times.

'What do you want me to say?' he finally asked. 'It's a fucked-up situation. I don't really see what else you would have done, not with Morag on the line. I'd tell you that you had no choice but you're going to be torturing yourself for a very long time despite anything I could say. Question is, what are we going to do now?'

'It might be better if I just put a beam through my head,' I said, quietly going for a bit of a paddle in self-loathing.

'See, that's the Jakob I know and love,' Mudge said acidly. 'Why fucking do anything when you can just feel sorry for yourself?'

'Fuck you, Mudge. They made me,' I told him. Trying to muster anger and ending up with pathetic bluster instead.

'Yeah, I know that and you know that. The question is, can you get over it and be of use?'

'How? I just gave them Earth's weaknesses.' I sounded desperate to myself.

'See, this is the problem with feeling sorry for yourself. It's so self-ish. You think the world revolves around you. Bad things happen—'

'To me, not you—'

'Shut up, you miserable piece of shit,' Mudge spat at me. I couldn't believe I was hearing this after what I'd been through. 'Stop your fucking whining, stop obsessing on Morag and concentrate on your job.'

'The job's fucked—'

'I said shut up. If you're just going to use this as another fucking excuse to feel sorry for yourself and to give up then I won't even fucking shoot you. I'll just leave you here to shit yourself to death. You want to think about something, think about what Rolleston's done to you.'

I stared at him. I couldn't even get angry with him. Instead I heard two shots and saw my lover become meat as her corpse hit the cold stone floor of a cell. I saw the corpses of Mother's people on the ground. The people we'd killed. I thought about Rolleston. There was something warm about the thought. I took another mouthful of vodka and another long drag of the spliff. Mudge watched me intently. Pride was trying to make me angry with Mudge. It was failing. He was right. I knew where my anger and hate was going to be aimed. Like a gun.

'If it's any consolation,' he finally said, 'it was Morag who insisted that we exorcise you rather than kill you. Even after you told her you'd fucked the Grey Lady.'

'Sure that wasn't so I was conscious when she killed me?' I asked, misery creeping back into my tone.

'No,' Mudge said, shrugging.

'I'm pretty sure that she could have killed me if she really wanted to.'

'Probably best you tell yourself that.'

He reached forward and took the bottle and the spliff away from me. In the background I could hear Rannu screaming in a language I didn't understand.

'You haven't exorcised Rannu yet?' I asked, surprised.

'We can't,' he told me grimly.

I felt a lurch inside. 'What? How come, if you could do me?'

'You'll need to speak to Morag – well maybe not Morag, maybe Pagan or Salem about that.'

I didn't like this at all. We needed Rannu and more to the point he deserved to be free.

'Where'd you find him?'

'Salem? He walked into the camp. Tailgunner knew him from the old neighbourhood. Seemed he had some kind of software business but also did exorcisms. He'd seen some of the resistance info and had been of the opinion that something was up anyway. Tailgunner said there was a rumour that he was one of the Immortals.' That woke me up.

'Shit! Really?'

'Apparently he's never spoken about it but that's the rumour.'

The Immortals were legends in the special forces community. Back at the beginning of the war, They had successfully assaulted New Hebron. The first footage of Them massacring any and all humans was played back to a shocked Sirius. Despite orders to the contrary, a joint Israeli and Palestinian special forces unit commandeered as many heavy-lift gunships as it could find. Had them flown to New Hebron and, during some fierce street-by-street fighting, managed to create a cordon between Them and some of the civilian survivors, allowing them to be evacuated. The Palestinians and the Israelis lost more than three quarters of their force. This had been planned for. The transports had been full when they flew to New Hebron and full – of civilians – on the way out. This meant that the unit had no out until the transports returned. This was unlikely however as most of the transports had been commandeered at gunpoint. One transport returned. Even then people were left on the ground to cover its take-off.

The special forces unit was so secretive that its name was never released. In the media they had been nicknamed the Immortals. At Hereford during my SAS training we'd studied the operation. I remember the transcript of their court martial. When the highest-ranking surviving officer was asked why they had disobeyed orders he simply said, 'Because our leaders had forgotten that dangerous men and women like us exist to defend our people.' They had been acquitted. It was nearly sixty years ago. That made Salem the oldest person I'd ever met not augmented by Themtech, and he'd walked from Moa City to here. It was kind of humbling.

'You don't suppose he'd speak to us about it, do you?' I asked, forgetting myself.

'Fanboy,' Mudge told me as he lit up a small laser cutter.

'Er, what are you doing?'

Keep my eyes forward, head high. Ignore the stares. Ignore the looks of hatred. Everyone stopped and there were a lot of hard black lenses watching me as I walked across the cave.

The cave was incredible, huge with stalactites hanging from the ceiling like an inverted field of some strange crop. The ceiling was almost a dome, the centre of it a large hole surrounded by the stalactites. The floor of the cave was a gently smoking milky pool broken by stalagmites and smooth tables of rock. The largest of these tables was in the middle of the pool underneath the hole. The Bismarck-class quadruped mech *Apakura* stood on the table, an unmoving metal sentinel. Its spotlights helped illuminate the cave. Four heavy-duty cables were attached to winches on its upper leg assembly. They ran up through the hole in the cavern roof.

People were congregated on the ledges around the cave and on the smooth stone beach that broke the surface of the pool. I almost didn't notice the smell of rotten eggs any more. It was cold and humid at the same time.

Of course the majestic cave had excellent acoustics, which meant that we could hear Rannu's screams echoing off the stone. That probably didn't help anyone's mood. He'd chewed through every gag they'd given him.

'They are raping and killing your families like vermin as you hide here!' he screamed.

Our killing spree aside, the numbers looked light. Mother clearly had a problem with desertion. I couldn't say I blamed them. I hoped that they'd gone to the End and not back home. By now Rolleston's people would know who they were. I also hoped that they'd gone before the last move so none of them could spill the whereabouts of this *pa* to the Black Squadrons.

There was a group of people standing on an outcrop in front of a large recessed area. In the recess half in shadow was one of the two Landsknecht-class mechs. It looked like a giant metal soldier standing guard. It held its plasma cannon like an oversized assault rifle. On the ledge in front of the mech were Salem, Mother, Tailgunner, Pagan, Merle, Cat and Morag. I couldn't see Big Henry anywhere. They all stopped talking and turned to look at me as Mudge and I approached. In fact the whole cave had gone silent except for Rannu's screamed threats.

I found out where Strange was when she shot out of the shadows and slashed at my face with one of her little curved knives. I saw the movement and tried to react, almost falling into the pool below, but she caught me, just opening the skin of my face, the blade scraping against my subcutaneous armour. I was standing precariously on the lip of the path but managed to catch her wrist as she slashed at me with the other blade. I swung her in front of me and locked up both her arms as best I could. She struggled like a wild thing. She was crying now. It may have been the first sound I'd heard from her.

'Let her go.' Not loud, but Tailgunner's voice carried. His tone promised imminent violence.

'Calm down,' I told Strange pointlessly. 'Only if she's not going to slash me again,' I told Tailgunner. He had nearly reached the pair of us. His face was a patchwork of healing bruises and contusions from his fight with Rannu. A fight he shouldn't have been able to win.

'Then let her slash you,' he said as he reached me.

Morag was a step behind him. She stepped past Tailgunner and held out her hand to Strange.

'It's okay,' she told the girl. Strange's struggling seemed to lessen. There was even momentary surprise on Tailgunner's face.

All around the massive cave I could see Mother's people watching, violent expectation on their faces. They wanted to see Tailgunner kick the shit out of me. I'd probably let him. I'd had enough of violence.

I let Strange go. She turned and hissed at me but let Morag wrap her arms around her and lead her away. Morag glared over her shoulder to let me know this was my fault.

I felt Tailgunner grab my shirt and push me so I was leaning out over the pool. I just let him. I looked at him lens to lens. I wondered if he really thought he could do anything to me.

'One of my people wants to hurt you, you let them,' he told me.

It was too late for that. To his mind he'd already failed to protect his people. Not just the fact that we'd killed some of them but also because we were still alive. I just looked at him.

'We're wasting time,' Mudge said impatiently.

'When this is over there will have to be payment,' Tailgunner told me.

I nodded. He pulled me back onto the path. The five of us headed back up to the ledge in front of the Landsknecht. Morag walked with Strange, her arms still around the sobbing girl.

'You sure it's him?' Cat asked Mudge. I couldn't read her expression.

He shrugged. 'I'd be surprised if anyone else could indulge in that amount of self-pity.'

'It's him,' Morag said, her tone guarded, her body language angry.

'This is *Kopuwai*. It was named after a dog-headed monster. It was Dog Face's mech,' Mother told me. Her tone was one of barely contained rage. I think the grieving for Dog Face had been done in private away from prying eyes.

Kopuwai was like the giant metal ghost of Dog Face looking down on me, judging me. I swallowed and nodded. There wasn't a lot I could say. They knew at some level that it hadn't been me, but any protest now would sound like an excuse.

I looked around at their faces. Pagan's was the least hostile but he wouldn't meet my eyes. Merle was next to him. Even through the medgel I could see the scar I'd given him had turned his mouth into an angry puckered leer.

'I think Jakob understands how we all feel,' Pagan started.

Tailgunner and Mother turned to give him a look of angry contempt and he went quiet.

'How's your arse?' I asked.

Pagan looked a bit taken aback by the question but I needed people distracted.

'Lost some meat, bad scar,' he told me.

'He won't let me look at it. He'll let Merle look but not me. That's favouritism that is,' Mudge said, trying to lighten the tone.

'Merle's a trained medic,' Pagan said, exasperated. They had presumably had this discussion before.

'We have to record things for posteriority.' There were few smiles.

While they were looking at Mudge I made my move. I grabbed the butt of Cat's Void Eagle. It was holstered at her hip. The smartgrip holster held on to it. I'd expected this. I downloaded an old holster-cracking code I'd bought from Vicar through my palm-link interface and into the pistol. There was a moment of resistance from the holster just as people realised that something was happening and started to move. Vicar's code won. The pistol was heavy and comforting in my hand. I stepped away from everyone and brought the pistol up to bear.

Mudge was drawing his Sig but wasn't sure what to do with it. Pagan stepped back, a look of confusion on his face as he dropped his staff and went for his sidearm. Cat at first reached to stop me and then went for the cut-down shotgun strapped to her other leg. She brought it up. Mother, Strange and Tailgunner all went for their PDWs but were much slower. The magazines on their weapons were still unfolding as the other guns came to bear. Salem simply took a few steps back. His face was the same calm mask it had been since I'd walked up.

Merle didn't go for his weapon because he was looking down the barrel of a Void Eagle.

'I thought he was all right!' Cat hissed.

'He is,' Salem said simply. There was no trace of doubt in his voice.

'We completely checked him,' Pagan said, exasperated, still not sure what to do with his pistol. Morag was nodding. She was looking confused as well but had no problem pointing a gun at me.

'Put the gun down,' Mudge told me.

'Are you out of your fucking mind?' Merle asked quietly.

'Why am I alive, Merle?' I asked.

'A mixture of dumb luck and people who lack the professionalism to know when they should cut their losses, as far as I can tell,' Merle answered.

'Look, I don't know what you think you know but we can have this conversation without the pointing of guns,' Mudge said. He was worried. Joking apart, I was his best, possibly only, friend and I was pointing a gun at his lover.

'Put the gun down now,' Cat told me. I think the trigger on her shotgun was squeezed to the furthest point it could be without the weapon going off. I think she'd had more than enough of my own personal horror show. I knew she would have been furious about what I'd said to Morag when I'd been possessed.

'Don't be so fucking childish, Jakob!' This from Morag.

'They knew. Their response time was too quick. They weren't waiting for us but they were not far off,' I said. I could see from their faces that they had considered this. 'Rolleston told me that we'd been sold out by two people.'

'Well there's a source we can trust,' Mudge said sarcastically.

'Jakob, you've no idea,' Morag started. 'While you were getting beaten up by your date Merle saved us.'

Mudge and Pagan were nodding but there was something off about Pagan's expression.

'You were the one who was so keen that we kill ourselves rather than be caught. If you had the position to help Mudge and the others further down the alley then you had line of sight to take me out,' I said to him.

'That's not what this is about,' Merle said. His tone reminded me of the voice I'd heard coming from my mouth when I was locked in my gilded cage. 'You're trying to find someone else to blame.'

From the looks on Pagan, Mudge, Mother and Tailgunner's faces they knew that I was right. Morag was less sure as she was newer to the dynamics of gunfights.

'Why am I still alive, Merle?'

'You know I can take that gun off you any time I want?' he asked me.

'Stop pointing my gun at my brother!' Cat hissed, but it was written all over her face that she knew I was right too.

'Do you think I care what happens now?' I asked. 'Either you answer my question or I put a bullet through your head and damn the consequences.'

By now Tailgunner and Mother were lowering their weapons. Strange turned her PDW on Merle.

'Strange!' Morag shouted.

I'd glanced at the girl for a moment. Merle could only have told from a slight movement around my lenses, but by the time I was back concentrating fully on him he had both Hammerli Arbiters in his hands. He was fast. One was pointing at me and the other at Strange.

'Woah!' Tailgunner shouted as he turned on Merle. Cat brought her shotgun to bear on Tailgunner. Mother aimed her PDW at Cat.

'Oh this is fucking stupid.' Morag lowered her pistol.

'Not if we've got a traitor in the mix,' I said.

'I'm better than you; I'm faster than you. Drop the gun,' Merle told me.

'Oh but mate, it's a size game, isn't it. Mine's bigger than yours. I don't doubt you'll be accurate but I fancy my chances at surviving a burst in the face. Your pretty face on the other hand becomes a mess on the wall,' I told him.

'I think you should compare sizes,' Morag said, holstering her pistol.

'Me too,' Mudge agreed. There wasn't much humour there.

'What about the girl? Maybe you live but she's dead and you know it.'

'Anything happens to her and you die as well, Jakob,' Tailgunner told me. I felt he was being a little unfair.

'She can put the gun down and walk away any time she wants,' I said through gritted teeth. Strange helpfully shook her head. I didn't like having anyone as unpredictable as her involved whether she was on my side or not.

'Take another step and weird girl dies,' Merle told Morag. She'd acted like the whole thing was stupid but had been moving back, jockeying to get position on Merle. Morag froze and looked pissed off.

'Why would he betray you and then fight so hard for the rest of us?' Mudge asked.

'I couldn't figure that out either. If he was still working for the Cabal then he could have destroyed us a long time ago,' I said.

'The orders must have come from Earth ...' Pagan said.

'Something you want to add?' I asked. Pagan looked stricken. This I hadn't expected. What the fuck was going on?

'Don't buy into his paranoid fantasy; it's guilt transference, that's all,' Merle spat.

'He was in a hole for six months. He was comms dark the entire time,' Mudge said. There was desperation in his voice. He needed Merle to not be the traitor. I think that this was the most vulnerable I'd ever seen him. Emotionally. Physically, the wanking on the Hydra still won out.

'Which means that one of us had to deliver it,' I said. 'This where you came in, Pagan?' I asked.

Pagan shook his head miserably and looked like he was about to say something.

'The encrypted message,' Cat said. Now she sounded stricken. I remembered watching brother and sister communicating by hardlink on the *Tetsuo Chou* on the way out.

'What message?' Morag demanded.

'Shut up, Cat,' Merle said angrily.

Cat swallowed hard. 'Sharcroft gave me a heavily encrypted message to deliver to Merle,' she said miserably.

'You know better than that!' Merle was livid now.

'You should have told us,' Morag said quietly.

Mudge pointed his Sig at Merle.

'Why'd you sell us out?' he asked. His tone was hard and you would have had to know him as well as I did to know how much this was costing him.

'Are we breaking up, lover?' was the sarcastic response. If Strange hadn't been on the line I probably would have shot him then.

'This mission's hard on relationships,' Morag commented with inappropriate dryness.

'Look, shoot Jakob if you want, but stop pointing the gun at Strange,' Tailgunner told Merle.

'I'm sure you're a big man down here but I'll walk through you to get out of here,' Merle told the big Maori.

'Look around you, wanker,' Mother spat.

I glanced around. The Kiwis were all aiming guns, some were pointed at me – couldn't say I blamed them – but most at Merle.

Cat lowered her shotgun.

Merle spared her a look of contempt. 'You always were a disappointment. Always folding when times are tough.'

'Fuck you!' Her voice echoed around the massive cave. 'We've done enough damage.' More quietly. She walked over and stood between Strange and Merle. Nobody seemed to care if I got shot.

'It's a death sentence now,' I told him.

He looked around at the circle of guns. 'That doesn't mean I'll tell you shit,' he said as he lowered his pistols.

Everyone relaxed a little. Mother covered as Tailgunner moved in to disarm Merle.

'He's got a Void Eagle on his hip and two blades on wrist hoppers. Careful you don't touch the blades,' I warned Tailgunner.

'What were your orders?' Mudge asked. His pistol was hanging limp at his side. His voice was flat, completely devoid of emotion. Merle ignored him.

'Come on. We've got most of it,' I told Merle. 'You're completely compromised, nothing to bargain for or gain at this point.'

'Call it professional pride,' Merle said grimly.

'Call it being a wanker,' Tailgunner muttered.

'You have not acted well,' Salem surprised me by telling Merle. 'You have caused much pain. If you persist in this then I will make sure you talk.' The man's gravitas was such that I felt like Merle had just been judged. Merle swallowed but said nothing. Who the fuck was this guy? I could see why people could believe he had been one of the Immortals. There was total self-belief there, no doubt whatsoever in his capabilities. Merle could see that as well.

'Merle, stop being an arsehole!' Cat said, turning on her brother.

'Oh well, since you put it that way, I'll abandon op sec!' he spat at her with derision.

'I'll beat it out of you myself,' she muttered.

Mudge put a gun to Merle's head.

'Three,' he said.

'Mudge?' Pagan and Morag said at the same time. Tailgunner took a step back. Cat stepped towards Mudge. I moved to intercept her.

'You'll get him killed,' I told her.

Mudge didn't handle personal betrayal well. He'd been despondent back in Maw City after Gregor. It had taken Morag and me a long time to convince him that it hadn't really been Gregor; that Rolleston had killed him with Crom before he'd left Earth.

'Two,' Mudge said.

'You serious about this?' Merle asked.

'What do you think?' Mudge asked.

It went very quiet. The quiet seemed to last for a very long time. I think Mudge was trying to give his lover every chance he could. I saw Mudge start to squeeze the Sig's trigger as he began to form 'One' with his mouth.

'All right,' Merle said quietly.

Mudge held the gun where it was, touching Merle's temple. Mudge was too close. Merle could have disarmed him any time he wanted. That wasn't the point. The point was that Mudge was prepared to pull the trigger.

'You can lower the gun now. I believe you,' Merle told him. Mudge didn't move.

'Mudge,' Morag said softly. I could see he was still thinking about pulling the trigger. 'Come on, love.' Morag reached up and pulled Mudge's hand down. The tension seemed to drain out of him.

Mudge turned to me. 'Goddamn you.'

'I'm sorry.' It was all I had. It wasn't nearly adequate for any of this fucking mess. Mudge walked off.

'Can we have this conversation without any more guns being waved about?' Morag asked. I handed Cat back her Void Eagle.

'Sorry,' I told her. She just holstered the pistol. 'Well?' I asked Merle.

'Disinformation,' he said. 'Or are you egotistical enough to think that the prime minister of England –'

'Britain,' I corrected automatically. Americans never got that right.

'– was really going to share Earth's defence weaknesses and strategies with a lowly grunt?'

I just stared at him. Of course he was right. I was so fucking stupid.

'So Earth's not as weak as she told me?' I finally managed to ask.

'Right,' he said.

'But—' Tailgunner started.

'A very few of the operators sent out were set up to hear that information one way or another. The PM and her allies—'

'Including Sharcroft,' a miserable-looking Pagan interjected.

'I suspect including whoever's left of the Cabal will be shitting themselves. Anyway, they are going to go to the governments on Earth and say, "Look, this is what we've done. Unless we unite and work together we are fucked."'

Mother blew air out between her teeth. 'That's pretty ballsy.'

'You were a sacrifice. I gave a vague warning before the robbery and then dropped a dime on you as it began, and you played your part brilliantly. They didn't even have to torture you from what I heard.' He was back to good old contemptuous Merle.

'You brought them down on us?' Tailgunner said, nodding towards me. Rannu was still howling violent obscenities.

'Hey, fuck you. Why are you all so fucking precious? We're soldiers. Expendable. See, if they were on to me I'd firestorm my memory and kill myself. I don't have time to turn the plasma rifle on my head so I've got a couple of internal suicide systems, but you all just whine. This worked because they were pretty sure that you were too weak to kill yourself and because you'd break quickly.'

Played. We'd all been played.

Tailgunner didn't look happy. He punched Merle in the stomach. The punch lifted Merle off his feet and doubled him over. Tailgunner looked at Merle with utter contempt. Merle straightened up and spat in Tailgunner's face. They went at it. Morag was right. There was far too much testosterone around here.

'Hey!' Best sergeant's voice. They ignored me.

'Pack it in now.' This from Mother. She was much quieter than I'd been. Tailgunner stopped and Merle relented as well.

'You didn't though, did you?' I asked Merle.

'What?' he gasped. He was fighting for breath.

'Kill yourself when we were on to you.'

He straightened himself up and wiped blood away from his mouth.

'Well, what are you going to do? I'm loyal to Earth. I'm not working with the bad guys. I think you know that and I'm the best you've got.' All probably true. He wasn't just loyal, he was a fucking fanatic.

'But here's the thing. Now you all know, that's just multiplied the exposure and the chance of this plan, probably the best plan we have, being fucked up.' Also right. He grinned savagely and turned to me. 'So I'm sorry everyone got killed and you were rude to your girlfriend.' I couldn't help glancing at Morag. Her face may as well have been made out of the same stone as the cave. 'But you're one lucky motherfucker to even be here so relax. It worked and you're alive.'

I just stared at him.

'Any other secret missions you want to share?' Morag asked. I could see the conflict on Merle's face. Morag was angry. 'Look, arsehole, I find you're holding out on us and I will plug myself into your head and kill you the hard way,' the eighteen-year-old Dundonian girl told the hardened assassin. And he didn't like it. He didn't like it at all. What the fuck was going on here?

'Just one,' he said. 'I'm being paid a staggering amount of money to kill Rolleston.'

'Join the queue,' I told him.

He gave me a look of contempt that made me want to hit him. Except that he'd already handed my arse to me once.

'Difference is I can probably do it.'

'How?' I asked.

'Yeah, it's not as easy as beating up Jakob, you know?' Morag said.

'Hey!' But she ignored me.

'Multiple plasma shots to the head.'

It could work, I supposed. We certainly hadn't tried it, and if there was a small-arms solution that was probably the best bet. Except that Merle hadn't watched Rolleston walk through railgun fire on Atlantis.

'That it?' I asked.

'A tailored virus – the blades are the delivery device. A variant of Crom called Crom Dhu. Designed to kill people with Themtech bio-nanites in their system.'

'You brought that here?' Morag demanded incredulously.

'You sure it does what they say it does?' I asked. 'We've had bad luck with that sort of thing in the past.'

'I know they want Rolleston very, very dead.'

'Cronin?' I asked.

'A luxury. They're terrified of Rolleston.'

I looked at Cat and finally Pagan. Pagan had guilt written all over his face. I saw Morag glance over at him.

'You need my brother. You try and hurt him, you've got me to deal with as well,' Cat told us.

Tailgunner and Mother looked like that was okay with them. I looked at Morag. She didn't look happy but she shrugged.

'Get out of my sight,' I told Merle.

He looked like he was about to say something but thought better of it. His contempt for us was written all over his face, however.

'What?! We're just letting him get away with it?' Tailgunner demanded.

'You want to kill him?' I asked.

'Yeah.'

Despite his anger and what he thought he was capable of at the moment, I was pretty sure that Tailgunner would struggle to murder in cold blood. Mother, on the other hand, I was less sure of. She put a hand on the big hacker's shoulder.

'Let it go,' she told him.

Tailgunner looked like he was about to argue but lapsed into silence and stared at Merle's back as he walked away from us.

I turned to Pagan. He was pale. Not frightened, but his guilt was palpable. Everyone else was staring at him as well now.

'What did you do?' Morag asked quietly.

'I'm so sorry,' was all he could manage.

'Everyone's sorry, Pagan. Just tell us what you did.' I was getting angry now. Merle I could see. Fucking me over was just a job to him. After all he didn't know me. Pagan, however, I'd fought by his side, supported his hare-brained schemes. I'd thought I could trust him. He'd betrayed us as well. It was written all over his face.

'They told me to,' he said miserably.

'Who? Sharcroft? That prick tells you to do something and you just sell us down the river?' I demanded.

'Not Sharcroft and not us. Just you.' At least he had the courtesy to look me straight in the lens when he said it. I felt something cold in my gut. That feeling I had that there was something slithering around us just out of sight, pulling our strings, manipulating us.

'Who?' Morag demanded.

Salem got there first. 'Your gods?'

Pagan nodded miserably. Afterwards I would think that it was almost an involuntary reaction. I danced forward and jabbed at his face, felt my friend's nose break under my knuckles, watched an old man hit the ground. Another old man interposed himself between me and Pagan's prone form with surprising speed for someone in their eighties.

'Please,' Salem said.

Morag walked past us and spared me a glare before she knelt down

370

next to Pagan. He had propped himself up against the foot of *Kopuwai*.

'You sold me out because of a voice in your fucking head?!' I demanded. I was leaning around Salem. I saw him wince as I swore.

'They're real. We know that now. You know that – you spoke to one of them.' He was desperately trying to justify himself.

'Do you know what they did to me in there?! What they showed me?! What they made me do?!' I was shouting now. He flinched with every question. 'And you sell me out so your friends in your head can make you feel special?!'

'I thought you just spilled your guts and had some sex,' Morag said acidly.

I tried to ignore the jibe even though it felt like she'd just stabbed me.

'They're not in my head – stop saying that!' Pagan shouted.

'Give me a good reason not to kill you, Pagan,' I said.

'Leave him alone,' Morag said, glaring at me again. She turned back to Pagan. 'What happened?' she asked.

As I looked down at one bleeding old man, another in my way, I suddenly felt foolish and impotent. The anger drained out of me. I stepped away from them and Salem relaxed. As the anger left I started to feel the hurt of betrayal. It was an insight into how Morag must be feeling about me.

'Ogham came to me,' he started. Pagan had once told me that Ogham was the Celtic patron god of writing and brewing. Pagan identified with him as someone who wrote code. 'He told me that Jakob had to be given to Demiurge.'

'Why?' I demanded.

'I don't know.'

'But you fucking did it anyway?!' I shouted. I felt like apologising to Salem for my swearing.

'Let him answer,' Morag told me coldly.

'It had something to do with Pais Badarn Beisrydd.'

'Oh this is bollocks,' I spat.

'No, no, it's really not,' Tailgunner said. 'Miru's eel net.'

Pagan was nodding.

'We're not just having visions now. We're not just seeing things on the net that are very real to us despite a total lack of evidence,' Salem said. 'Now we're being given artefacts, programs, pieces of code way in advance of what we can do, maybe as much as four or five generations ahead. Better than the best corp and military stuff. I saw a djinn in the net. She told me to come to you.'

'A djinn?' Pagan asked. 'I though they were all evil.'

371

'They are like people – some are good and some are bad. She told me that we cannot trust angels any more.'

There it was again. After all we'd done to break away from being manipulated by the likes of the Cabal, here we were dancing to someone, something else's tune.

'So what are they?' I asked.

'What they are not is figments of our imagination,' Tailgunner growled.

'Or fragments of God,' Salem said. Tailgunner and Pagan turned sharply to look at him. 'My faith does not come from the net. They are copies, not spirits. Though these copies may do God's will.'

'Which leaves either evolved AIs or aliens,' I said. Everyone looked uncomfortable. I looked at Pagan. 'And again I ask why?'

'The way Ogham spoke suggested that he knew you would get out of there, would be you again. I think that's why Nuada set up the cage—'

'It was Nuada who imprisoned me?!' I was angry again. It was Nuada who had let me hear myself torturing my friends.

Pagan looked up at me. 'He protected you. Locked part of you, the most important part, away from Demiurge's control. That's why we were able to save you.' Back was the hacker explaining to the technologically uninitiated what he felt was the obvious.

'And again why?' As I asked I remembered dreams of blackened glass, fire and a dark sun burning in the sky. The landscape had similarities with the net feed I'd seen in the Cabal's Atlantis facility.

'I don't know. I need to look inside your head again,' he told me.

'Oh yeah, now the trust is so strong between us.'

'I'll do it,' Tailgunner said.

'You've already threatened me today.'

'I'll do it then,' Morag said.

'You tried to kill me!'

'I will look,' Salem said. 'With Jakob's permission.'

I looked at the calm old man. His weathered leathery features, the fissures in his skin. He was clothed like his icon and everything from those clothes to his calm demeanour seemed out of place here. Then something occurred to me.

'Pagan, you said the only reason I was saved was because of what Nuada did.' Morag and Pagan nodded. Both of them looked unhappy. 'Rannu?'

Their expressions told me everything I needed to know. His screamed obscenities were still echoing through the cave. We'd lost another friend but they'd left us with a twisted mockery just to remind us.

'I'm sorry,' Pagan said miserably. He looked broken. It was why he'd gone for me before the exorcism, when I'd been savaging Morag – guilt. I couldn't find it in myself to feel angry with him any more. I think he'd finally got what he wanted. He was a true priest now, a tool of the gods. I don't think it was what he'd been expecting.

'No,' I said. Everyone turned to look at me. 'We're getting him back.'

'It can't be done,' Pagan told me. I could see Salem and Tailgunner shaking their heads.

'Jakob, listen. Normally I'd be the first to agree we should push this but seriously there's no way,' Morag told me. She was trying to control her voice, not show how upset she was about losing Rannu.

'It reverses the interface, effectively. If meat can control hard- and software, then why not the other way? It's the same principle as slaveware but Demiurge's sophistication is such that it's considerably more insidious, thorough and with none of the drop-off in motor skills. If anything, cognitive abilities increase, particularly if there is a connection to Demiurge proper,' Salem explained.

This made a lot of sense. It didn't matter how good their black propaganda was, how concrete their cover story, there was no way the fleet and ground commanders would have just handed over their forces to Rolleston and Cronin. They must have possessed certain key figures. This worried me. I knew what it was like, what Demiurge was like and how much it liked to cause pain. I didn't like the idea of it possessing people who had so much power.

'We were only able to get you out with Ogham's help and because your core identity was kept safe by Nuada's cage. Even then the tiny fragment of Demiurge managed to work out what we were doing.'

'And that was code that neither Morag nor I was able to find when we checked,' Pagan said. I took this in. Well at least I think I understood.

'That's my point. These things, these gods – if their stuff is so far in advance of us then they could help.'

I could see the four hackers sharing a poor-naive-non-hacker look.

'That's not the way it works,' Tailgunner said uncomfortably.

'No, I know. They play it all mysterious and you guys jump when they tell you to.'

Cat and Mother were starting to pay attention now.

'Wait a second,' Tailgunner said angrily.

'No, he's right,' Pagan said.

'Anyone still think they are actually your gods?' I asked.

There were a lot of uncertain looks except from Salem.

'They are echoes, copies, nothing more,' he said.

'Wait a second. You're talking about our faith here!' Tailgunner objected.

'No. You either have faith or you do not. You're talking about proof. Either you feel God or you do not. You will only feel God if you go looking, if you accept and embrace Him,' Salem said.

'Or Her,' Morag added. 'You're saying that all we're talking about is dealing with programs?' Salem nodded.

'That still doesn't help us. They don't do our bidding and they are too powerful to coerce,' Tailgunner pointed out.

'So you hope for their scraps? What they deign to give you?' Mother demanded. Tailgunner looked like he'd just been slapped. 'I'm sorry, but Jakob's right. You think if that was you down there I wouldn't trample heaven to get you fixed?' Yeah, I liked Mother. I could see Cat nodding as well.

'Fine,' Tailgunner said. Clearly it really wasn't. 'But that doesn't change the fact that whatever they are, they won't do what we say. We can't even really communicate with them. They come and go as it pleases them.'

'So they can't be contacted or summoned?' I asked.

'There are ritual programs,' Pagan told me. 'They are complex and difficult to write, time-consuming and more often than not they don't work.'

'Shit, that won't work. They'll let Demiurge in, won't they?' That was the end of my plan, to the obvious relief of Tailgunner, Salem and Morag. Then I saw Pagan's face. Pagan should never, ever play poker.

'What?' I asked.

'Ogham appeared in an isolated system,' he said.

'That's impossible,' Tailgunner said.

'Where's your faith?' I asked sarcastically and then wished I hadn't said anything.

'How?' Cat asked.

'You don't really try and work these things out. It's a religious experience,' Pagan told her.

I couldn't quite make out what she was muttering but I could tell she was less than pleased with this answer. It did have pretty serious repercussions for the whole what-are-these-things issue. It meant a transmitter, a very powerful one capable of breaking shielded systems. Suddenly I felt like looking behind me. Still it unfucked part of my plan. Then something else occurred to me.

'How are you doing with reverse-engineering the eel net?' I asked.

'We can just about replicate a poor man's version of it,' Tailgunner told me.

I saw Pagan's face fall. I think he realised what I was thinking.

'You're insane. You don't fuck with these things – they'll kill us on a whim,' he said.

Morag was watching me with guarded interest.

'Where's your faith, Pagan? Is the cage gone? The code that Nuada put in me.'

Pagan nodded. 'It's served its purpose and they hate leaving traces of themselves. It will have gone.'

I turned to Salem. 'Will you confirm that?' He looked confused but nodded. I turned back to Pagan. 'Do your ritual and tell Nuada this: if he does not turn up then I will re-expose myself to Demiurge.' There was a storm of violent objections. Even Salem looked angry. Morag was the angriest. I let them rant at me for a while. 'And this will be done before anyone has a look around inside my head.'

'Then it's all for nothing?' Pagan asked angrily.

'Only if they don't show,' I said. 'And Pagan –' he looked up at me '– I am not bluffing.'

'You're insane,' he told me.

'No, he's not,' Mother said.

'Look, if there's something in your head you could be throwing away our last chance, you selfish bastard!' Morag shouted at me. It echoed around the cave.

Our mostly Maori audience had put their guns down some time ago but they were still watching the exchange. I rounded on Morag.

'Don't you tell me about throwing away chances – and have a good listen to Rannu before you try and stop me. I will kill anyone who tries to get anything out of my head before we've spoken to one of them.'

'You can't coerce them,' Tailgunner started, sounding frustrated.

'Fuck them,' Cat said and then to me, 'I got your back.'

'She doesn't even know Rannu,' I said to Pagan and Morag.

'You bastard,' Morag said quietly, her eyes narrowing.

'I agree. Jakob's off limits until we've spoken to one of these things,' Mother added. Tailgunner turned to her to object. 'Don't cross me on this,' she told him.

Morag was right: this job was proving hard on relationships.

I was gambling that there was something in my head that Nuada and his friends wanted or they wanted us to have. I was threatening to destroy this. I hoped it was enough to at least get their attention.

So far the only good thing that had come out of this mess was that the heist had been a success. The Puppet Show had shown Mother's people how to smuggle the goods down into the caves. We pretty much had enough food for the next month or so and more than enough ammunition for the foreseeable future. It was funny how weapons always seemed to end up the priority. How sometimes it can be easier to get an assault rifle than something to eat.

Salem had checked to see that Nuada's cage had gone. It had. I had made him swear he would look no further. He argued with me but relented. I was pretty sure he was a man of his word but then I'd thought that of Pagan once. I liked the old guy. His presence was soothing, even if he did refuse to discuss whether or not he was one of the Immortals.

It was good to have Salem to speak to as the Maori contingent didn't want to have much to do with me, and Merle, Pagan, Mudge and Morag were all avoiding me for different reasons. Pagan could barely even look at me and I wasn't about to make it easy for him. I think he was setting up the summoning ritual/program largely out of guilt. Merle on the other hand didn't seem to think he had anything to apologise for.

Rannu just kept screaming as long as he could. His voice was changing he was doing it so much damage, and there was only so much sedative we could afford to give him. I tried sitting with him, but very quickly he was probing for damage, looking for a way in, a way to cause pain, and it knew us well by now. I had to leave him.

'You know we're wasting time?' I was sitting on a smooth boulder that broke the surface of the water, trying to refit the two claws that Rannu had been using as shanks. I was surprised to hear Morag's voice but there was no emotion in it. I turned to look up at her. There was no emotion in her face either. She was wearing her heated inertial armour, a hat and scarf. Her breath misted in the cold, dark, deep cave.

'Do you want to go somewhere and talk?' I asked. I'd been dreading this, but we had to talk at some point and here everyone could see us. They would also hear the inevitable shouting echo throughout the cave.

'We've got nothing to say to each other.'

That confused me a little bit.

'So why are we talking?'

'This is about the job. I know it takes a long time to mobilise a fleet and ground forces, but they've been at it for months and this whole thing is a waste of time.'

I couldn't believe I was hearing this.

'What about Rannu?' I asked. 'He supported you right from the beginning.' After he'd kicked the shit out of me twice. 'Have you even given any thought to his wife and kids?'

'I think we need to focus—'

'On what? You're the great tactician, are you? So what do you want to do?'

'Demiurge. The Citadel,' she said quietly. She didn't want to shout this through the cave.

'How?' I demanded. I could see that she was getting angry now.

'Look, I want Rannu back as much as you, but we can't force these things. I admit I don't know how to go after Demiurge or the Citadel but the answer could be in your head.'

'No,' I said. 'Rannu first, then my head.'

'Selfish bastard. It's not just your friend at stake.'

'No, he's yours as well.'

'At least let us look in your head.' She was exasperated now.

'Pagan sent you,' I said matter-of-factly. After all, he was running the information side of things and he'd put me in harm's way to get whatever was in my head, assuming there was anything in my head.

'You think I wanted to come and speak to you myself?' she hissed at me.

'Look, I'm sorry—'

'I don't want to hear it. We need what's in your head.'

'No. I can't take the risk that they'll know, at which point I become expendable and the threat doesn't work. When did you become so fucking ruthless?'

She looked as if I'd slapped her. 'You've got no right to speak to me like that,' she said coldly.

I took a deep breath, suddenly aware of how angry I'd become. I was struggling with how quickly Morag was able to sacrifice Rannu.

'Do you think I don't care?' she demanded. As her anger subsided I could see how upset she was.

'Morag, seriously, we need to talk,' I said softly.

'There is no *we* to talk about, Jakob.'

I don't know what I was expecting. It still felt like a cold knife sliding between my ribs.

'Of course there is. You wouldn't keep on trying to kill me if you didn't care about me.' She just stared at me. 'That came out wrong.'

'You know, at least when you were possessed you told the truth.'
Then she stormed off.

That went well, I thought. I couldn't even go looking for Mudge for
drugs, booze and solace. He had his own problems. In fact, just about
the only person who was talking to me, other than Salem, was Cat,
and she never let me forget that she disapproved of my sleeping with
the Grey Lady. She'd understandably taken Morag's side in that.

It was the first time I'd seen Dinas Emrys from the outside. Although
a library it looked like a huge fortress straddling the peaks of several
mountains that rivalled, but didn't surpass, the tallest peaks in the
Highlands. The fort looked old. Older than even the tourist-haunted
ruins of the castles I'd seen in Scotland as a child back when we'd
lived in the park.

It was dark. The moon was full and closer than I remembered it
being back home. Pagan had told me that Nuada had an affinity with
the moon. Whatever. It was cold and a wind strong enough to tug at
our icons' clothes was blowing. The air smelled fresh and just a little
thin. I was just pleased that it didn't taste like greasy farts. I felt so
light here away from my body and Lalande 2's high G. This was good
programming. I was revelling in the star-filled night sky after too long
underground.

The circle was made up of poles. Each pole was tipped with a grisly
skull. The weird thing was the skulls belonged to icons as diverse as
dragons, bizarre aliens, even cartoon characters, down to relatively
normal-looking human ones. Pagan assured me that all of them were
trophies from other hackers he'd delivered a sound kicking to on the
net for one reason or another. They almost sounded like his pride and
joy. This was called a ghost fence and was the Pagan-flavoured voodoo he'd made with the reverse-engineered eel net that Tailgunner
had given him. It was our optimistic containment program.

All the skulls looked into the centre of the circle at a huge bonfire.
It was the only warmth out here, and the wood smoke smelled like
the campfires I'd made as a child and during my recent foray into
the Highlands. For a moment I thought about what it would be like
to be in the Highlands now with a whisky in my hand and my real
arm around a happy Morag. I glanced over at her. She was wearing
her Black Annis icon. Unlike the room in virtual Jerusalem, both she
and Pagan in his Druidic finery looked at home. Tailgunner, with his
feathered cloak and bladed spear, looked less at home but he was
holding his own.

Salem had asked not to take part in the ritual. It wasn't really his thing. That was fine as we needed someone on the outside. Salem was watching this on a monitor hooked up to the solid-state memory cube. Pagan had copied Dinas Emrys onto the cube from his staff. I guessed he didn't want these things in it.

Pagan lifted his hands to the night sky. Unusually for him, no lightning accompanied the gesture, but the wind picked up and rocked me back on my heels. It blew the flames of the bonfire around and whipped Pagan's hair and beard about as he shouted into the wind. I hoped it was Pagan who was responsible for the wind and not Nuada.

'I turn towards north, towards Findias, the shining silver fort, the fort of the mighty, the fort of the moon, the fort of spirits and bravery. Home to Nuada of the Silver Hand, first king of the Tuatha Dé Danaan, Lord of Victories, Lord of Conflicts, he who has power over force and strength.'

Go on, Pagan, I thought. See if you can get your nose all the way up there. He was really going for it now as the wind tore all around us.

'Whose is the sword that none can run from, the sword that seeks flesh, the sword that cuts stone and metal,' Pagan continued.

These old gods liked to hear how cool they were. I heard the cry of a bird of prey and looked into the night sky. I could just about make it out, a shadowed form against the dark blue of night. A night-hunting eagle was very unusual. The wind intensified and we were all being battered by it. I didn't think this was Pagan's special effects now.

'Lord of Battles, Lord of Hosts, we beseech you attend us this night!' Pagan screamed at the night sky.

We beseech you attend us this night? The arse-lickery was of course accompanied by some very complex code.

The wind seemed to blow out and then return to its earlier pre-ritual levels.

'Well that was nice,' I said.

All three of the hackers turned to glare at me.

'The wind wasn't mine,' Pagan said as all three of them turned their back on the Luddite. 'Neither was the eagle.'

'Something definitely happened.' Morag's voice sounded like gravel being ground together. Tailgunner was nodding. I was trying to get closer to the fake heat of the fire.

'It was a powerful ancestor to try and summon,' Tailgunner said. I think he was trying to console Pagan.

'Er, guys, is that supposed to be happening?' I asked. In front of each of the severed-head-topped wooden poles, a ghostly figure was standing. They looked like the battered and bleeding owners of the

379

original skulls. Some of them fitted with the surroundings, the cartoon cow less so.

'The ghost fence,' Pagan said.

'There's something in the fire,' Tailgunner warned.

A figure seemed to gather the fire into itself. He looked like flame beneath taut-muscled black skin, the flame shining through complex spiral patterns, his mouth and his eyes. He reached into the moonlight and his hands came back full, holding the hilt of a moon-bladed sword. He wasn't quite the same being I'd seen when Morag had taken me into Their mind. This time he looked angry, but the silver arm was there. Actually, 'angry' didn't really cover what he looked like. Even 'furious' wasn't adequate. Heat radiated from him, causing all of us to step back.

He swept his hand forward. The ghosts in the fence distorted and screamed like tortured souls but the fence did not break. Nuada seemed to be fighting to control himself. Taking long gasping breaths of smoke and fire.

'You know I will break this and you are all forfeit,' he finally said. Flames flickered over a mouth full of obsidian canines as he spoke. His voice was a bass rumble that sounded like it began somewhere south of hell.

'Yeah, the question is, can you break it before I plug Rannu into the system? He has a fragment of Demiurge in him,' I said.

Nuada reared up. Smoke and flame swirled and spiralled around him. To his credit he didn't bother with the whole you-wouldn't-dare speech. I could feel the power pouring off him even through the ghost fence. Whatever they were, they were not subtle in this electronic world. I had no doubts that given the chance my so-called patron would leave me a smoking corpse. He was communicating this with literally burning eyes. He didn't need to bother with the threats. That said, the mention of Demiurge had a physiological effect on him: the name had seemed to ripple through flame, smoke and flesh. Was that what passed for fear with him?

'What do you want?' he finally rumbled.

'I want you to free Rannu. Exorcise Demiurge or whatever you do; just bring my friend back.'

'And if it's not possible?'

'Then whatever it was that's in here –' I tapped my head '– is lost when we plug Rannu into this system anyway.'

'Your people have as much to lose as the Tuatha de Danaan if that happens,' he told me. I glanced at Morag.

'I've been told I'm a very selfish person, but you can do this, can't you? It's not a problem for you. You just don't want to because it's all one-sided with you guys. You want us to jump through hoops and then worship you for it, right?'

'Do not speak to me like that. There is a threat ... The Adversary is a corruption, a disease—'

'Aren't you the Lord of Hosts? The Lord of Battles? I'm smelling a lot of fear here.'

He narrowed his eyes at me. I held his stare. The worrying thing was, this guy struck me as the sort who held grudges. In the unlikely event that I lived, I suspected I needed to stay out of the net for the rest of my life. Perhaps it would be better to just avoid all electronics.

'You are a fool, Jakob Douglas,' he said, flames licking at his lips. 'But you are not a coward. This is for nothing anyway. Your friend will likely die.'

'Rannu's tough,' I said.

Nuada spared Pagan a look. Letting him know that he was as unhappy with the architect of his summoning and trapping as he was with me. Pagan looked away from him, refusing to meet his burning eyes.

'Now, Salem,' I said. On the quiet, Tailgunner and Morag set subtle and stealthy diagnostic and analytical programs running.

It was like a rent in the sky, a smoking black fissure, as Salem connected the solid-state memory cube with the copy of Dinas Emrys in it to one of Rannu's plugs. Nuada held his huge sword up into the beam of light from the moon. The sword acted like a prism of silver fire. It was bright, so bright, like ground zero, like Balor lifting his patch. We all became silhouettes just before the dark of blindness. The last thing I saw was silver fire, then nothing. All I could hear was Rannu, not the beast inside him, but Rannu. He was screaming in agony.

Burning. Bright light but not as bright, almost a relief after where I'd come from. The plug in the back of my neck was cooking the flesh surrounding it. I saw smoke drifting up past me. The rock felt cool beneath me. I was lying on the stone floor looking up at the ceiling of the small cave Rannu was in. Even in the sulphurous atmosphere it stank of bodily fluids, stale sweat and a body turning rancid and rotten.

But Rannu wasn't screaming. I could hear other people shouting. I sat up. Morag was gripping the back of her neck, smoke drifting through her fingers. Tailgunner and Pagan were sitting up as well. The solid-state memory cube that had contained the copy of Dinas

Emrys had melted and was letting off acrid black smoke.

On the cot I could see Rannu's emaciated, ravaged body. His corpse. He was clearly dead. Merle and Cat were trying to change that. Smoke was pouring from all four of Rannu's plugs.

I staggered to my feet still holding my neck and watched Cat ram a stim straight into Rannu's heart. Merle then shocked him again and again. It looked merciless to my eyes. Rannu would live. He had to. This couldn't have been for nothing. I couldn't have put us all at risk for no reason. Besides, he was a tough bastard.

Rannu spasmed, his back arched and he threw himself around in his cot. I sank to my knees.

'His heart's beating,' Cat said, sounding relieved.

'He's breathing,' Merle said, matter of fact.

I felt someone hugging me. I looked down to see Morag. She looked up at me, so happy, and then like night falling she remembered what I'd done to her and pushed away. Even that didn't affect how happy I was to see Rannu back. I turned around to see Mudge leaning against the cave mouth smoking a spliff and grinning.

20
New *Utu Pa*

I think the Kiwis' home-brewed beer wouldn't have seemed so bad if the entire world hadn't tasted of rotten eggs. I'd bartered for the beer using some of the gear we'd got from one of Merle's caches. Merle had revealed the whereabouts of another cache with ill grace. I'd pointed that it was his own fault that the first one had been compromised. I'd managed to score a laser pistol at the cache but I was still light on weapons. I had no chance of replacing my Mastodon or shoulder laser out here and nobody had an assault shotgun they were willing to give up. I was quite tempted to nick Merle's Void Eagle but it would have just caused more trouble.

They'd cleaned Rannu up – he hadn't been strong enough to do it for himself – and then moved him into the cave where I'd been imprisoned. It smelled a lot fresher. Even on this world. When I walked in Rannu was doing press-ups. The stylised biomechanical Kali tattoo on his back seemed to dance with the movement of his muscles.

Rannu looked up and then sat down on his cot. We'd spent quite a long time checking him out, making sure that the scary thing that Nuada had done had completely burned Demiurge out of him. As far as we could tell it had.

'How are you feeling?' I asked.

'Tired, wrung out, very angry.'

I nodded and offered him a beer. He seemed about to refuse but changed his mind and accepted it.

'What do you remember?'

'I remember us escaping. I remember attacking the last *pa* thinking we were attacking Rolleston and his people. I remember being shown the truth ...' He faltered. 'Then feeling like I was drowning in filth. The next thing I know I'm being resuscitated.'

His wrists and ankles all had open wounds from the manacles. His body was a patchwork of self-inflicted cuts and lesions, some of which had manifested spontaneously. Pagan had said this was the result of a particularly convincing and potent, self-inflicted biofeedback attack.

'You've not left the cave much,' I said.

Rannu didn't look up. 'We did some damage,' he said. 'Not just what we did, the things we said.'

'It wasn't us, you know that.'

If I could just convince myself of that then I might have a chance of convincing other people.

'That's not what they're going to see, is it?'

'Well, they're just going to have to fucking live with it, aren't they?'

Now Rannu looked up at me. 'So are we.'

'Frankly, I think that's the least of our problems. You need out? You've been through the wringer.'

'How could you even ask that?' he demanded angrily.

We lapsed into silence, sipping our beers.

'How come Morag hasn't been to see me?' he finally asked.

I thought about how to answer this. I didn't think he wanted to hear that it was guilt over having written him off. She had been right: it had been a very risky proposition indeed. It only looked good now, seemed to be the right thing to have done, because it had paid off. It could have just as easily fucked everything up. She could explain it to him.

'They got some stuff from when Nuada or whatever the fuck that thing was burned Demiurge out of you. They also found some stuff in my head. They think they may have a way to hack Demiurge without it noticing. She's been pretty busy, man. Why don't you go and see her? You've got to get to used to angry Maoris staring at you because you killed their friends.'

He laughed but it was pretty humourless.

I stayed and bullshitted for a while. It didn't take long to run out of things to say. There was too much mutual guilt floating around in that cave. I made my excuses and left. Not that I had much to do except try and get back to a reasonable degree of fitness and wait for the hackers to let us know what they'd found.

'That was touching.' Morag was leaning against the rock wall outside Rannu's cave.

I turned on her. 'Okay. I've got it. You're angry at me, you hate me, but don't take it out on him. Don't tell him what you said, just deal with your own fucking guilt and go and see him,' I told her quietly. I didn't want Rannu to hear.

'Pagan wants to see everyone.'

'Fine. We talk in there with Rannu.'

She shook her head. 'Dinas Emrys.'

'Fucking whatever, but he can bring his staff here. I'll tell the others. Why don't you go in and see him?'

She glared at me but turned towards Rannu's cave. I grabbed her by the arm.

'When are we going to talk?'

'Don't fucking touch me!' It was loud enough that heads turned in our direction.

'Morag? You okay?' Rannu asked from inside the cave. Morag shook me off.

'Your touch fucking sickens me.'

Rannu was at the cave mouth. 'You okay?'

She turned and hugged him, hiding her face from me. I walked off. The selfish arsehole part of me told me that her hugging Rannu had been for my benefit. I looked up to see Little Henry and Strange watching me intently. Little Henry had been avoiding me since I'd killed his *whanau* brother; now he was walking towards me. Strange remained still and just stared at me.

'Pagan wants to see us all in Rannu's room,' I said when he was close enough.

'The last of the supplies from the heist are in,' he told me, ignoring what I'd said. The short guy with the bowler hat had been the warmest and most approachable of the *whanau*; now there was no trace of his previous warmth or friendliness.

'Okay,' I said. 'Surely you guys are handling the distribution?'

'It wasn't food or ammo. Mother said you should see this.'

'Can't you just tell me?' I asked, looking at him and then Strange suspiciously.

'Trust me. You'll want to see this.'

I was reasonably sure I could handle Big Henry and Strange if it got nasty. They led me out of the *pa*, through tunnels and into a cave used as a garage because it connected to some of the larger tunnels used as a road system. Ground lights illuminated the battered civilian cargo lorry.

The modular cargo container on the back of the truck was freshly painted and I suspected it had come off the back of one of the vehicles we'd hijacked. Big Henry went to the back of the container and opened the double doors. Glancing at him and Strange, I moved around and looked in.

'Oh,' I said.

'We thought you'd want to see,' Big Henry said coldly. Strange was swaying back and forth as if in anticipation.

Up close they looked less like biotech and more like human

385

technology made from metal and composite. The exo-armour, how-ever, reminded me of large metal Berserks made symmetrical. The tips of tentacles protruded from their backs on either side of the flight systems. I suspected they were made of some nanotube-like material. They looked sleek, predatory and violent. There was a hint of alien about them, but in a human battle line they could pass as human tech, though I suspect they would give veterans pause because of their resemblance to Them. They were fully armed and spare ammunition was secured in a cargo net at the back of the container. There were eight of the suits of armour.

'They were in the last truck. Soloso has no use for them and they would just give him away if they were found,' Big Henry told me. I had visions of using them to infiltrate the Citadel. 'Go ahead, have a look.'

I turned to look at Big Henry in the cave's shadowed half-light.

'I hope you're not fucking around,' I told him.

'Look, I know who's to blame. That doesn't mean I have to like looking at you. Besides, what are we going to do? Lock you in the container? A bit fucking childish and I'm pretty sure a man of your initiative and training could break out of there.'

I watched him for a while trying to work out what was happening here. Strange was just looking between the two of us, still swaying and breathing funny. Like she was aroused. Idiot curiosity got the better of me and I climbed up into the container.

'How'd you open it up?' I asked as I examined the first suit, the one closest to the door.

'We don't know; nobody's been able to do it yet,' Big Henry told me. I touched the centre chest plate. The armour split and then slid apart leaving strands of a thick viscous lubricant that looked like a bodily fluid strung between the two panels.

'Oh.' Big Henry sounded genuinely surprised.

Inside it looked like black meat, a Themtech version of human innards. I made a disgusted noise. It was obvious that a human was supposed to climb in there and join with the armour. It was also obvi-ous that the armour was alive.

'Demiurge?' I asked.

Big Henry shrugged. Not an encouraging response.

'There are no transmissions and no locators that we can tell,' he said.

'Worth getting Pagan or Tailgunner to check that out again,' I said and turned around to jump out of the rear of the container.

The sickle fish-hooked me in mid-air. I tasted metal in my mouth and then my momentum tore the side of my mouth open, pulling my head back. I landed painfully on my back on the stone, my mouth full of blood. Big Henry was on me, his face a mask of bestial anger as he raised a club above his head. I kicked up from the ground catching him in the face, sending him flying out of my view.

A massive hand grabbed me by the front of my inertial armour and lifted me easily to my feet. I found myself face to face with Soloso in his finery of rags. It was a hit. They'd called in external help. I didn't need this. Except Soloso looked furious. One-handed he threw me across the cave, slamming me painfully into the wall.

I didn't even have time to slide to the ground before Strange was on me, slashing at me with her curved blades. I nutted her with every bit of strength I could muster. She staggered back as her nose exploded.

Fuck this. The three of them were closing on me. I extended my blades, though the ones on my right hand were still much shorter than those on my left.

'I'm going to kill all three of you,' I told them. Or that was what I meant to tell them. It was actually more a case of me gargling and spitting out blood as I failed to talk. My newly bisected cheek flapped around. It really hurt.

'You killed them!' Soloso screamed at me. This surprised me. He was genuinely angry.

'Who?' I asked, sort of, while drooling blood down myself.

'The Puppet Show!' he howled. The calm contained hard man I'd met in Moa City was gone now. This was a deeply emotional man. Admittedly it was a deeply emotional man holding a bloody sickle and wanting to cause me harm.

Then it hit me. I'd been an idiot. I'd been so worried about what my betrayal had done to the people here, I hadn't considered that I'd implicated the Puppet Show, and unlike us the Puppet Show wasn't exactly mobile.

'Those three beautiful women! You destroyed them! Do you know they killed themselves rather than let the Squads put the Black Wave into their systems!'

The big man was much more upset than he was angry. Big Henry and Strange were casting uneasy glances at him and each other. Another four lives I'd fucked. More if they'd gone after the entire gang.

I just stared at him, not sure what to do. One thing that doesn't go down well with vocational criminals is betrayal, particularly if high-ranking people go down as a result of it. I didn't think that was Soloso's problem. The guy had obviously not processed his grief. My blades slid back up into my arm.

387

'I'm sorry, man,' I gurgled at him.

I couldn't fight them. They were the victims here and I'd had a hand in their victimisation. More than anything this drove home the warnings I'd been given about operating in the field with Morag. This drove home how selfish my feelings for her were. I'd been prepared to flush a lot of lives down the toilet. The people of Earth may have been an abstract. This huge and dangerous man sobbing in a way I knew made the muscles round the plastic in your eyes hurt wasn't an abstract.

Soloso sat down hard. All the fight had gone from him. The sickle clattered to the stone and he held his face in his hands as he sobbed. I wasn't quite sure what to do. I don't think that Strange or Big Henry knew either. I spat out some blood so I could try and talk.

'Shall we leave it at that?' I asked.

Big Henry looked at Strange. She nodded. I sat cross-legged in front of Soloso.

'I'm really sorry, man,' I told him earnestly through a mouthful of blood. He just sobbed harder. Finally he looked up at me.

'They ... they ...' He swallowed hard. Snot was running down his face. 'They were incandescent,' he finally managed.

I had nothing. I just nodded like I had the slightest idea what he was talking about. He leaned forward and I thought he was trying to kill me again. Instead he just hugged me and started crying harder. That's the thing with the truly hard: some of them can be very sentimental.

Tailgunner and Mother ran into the cave. Tailgunner took one look at Strange's broken nose. Strange at least had the courtesy to look guilty. The big hacker turned on me.

'I told you ...' He trailed off as he saw Soloso's massive form hugging me and sobbing. I looked up at him as I bled onto Soloso's arm. Even Mother looked surprised.

She turned on Strange and Big Henry. 'No more of this, okay? I mean it. We have enough problems.'

Strange was looking at her feet like a naughty child being scolded. Big Henry was staring back at her defiantly.

'You would never—' he started.

'That's enough!' Tailgunner snapped.

'We're not letting this lie. We are going after those responsible, but I'm not going to settle for murdering the weapon. Do you understand me, Henry?' said Mother. Big Henry didn't answer.

'You think you're the only one grieving?' Tailgunner demanded. The impact of his question was somewhat spoiled by Soloso sobbing all the harder. I patted his arm.

'I mean it, Henry. No more. This is what they want to happen with these tactics. You do their work when you go after him,' Mother said. Big Henry, with a final angry glare at me, nodded.

'Pagan wants to see everyone in Rannu's cave,' Tailgunner told us. I nodded, wondering how I was going to disentangle myself from Soloso.

Mudge was heading towards Rannu's cave. He changed his course to intercept me.

'Does a day go by when you don't get your arse kicked?'

I tried to tell him to fuck off but I just ended up spitting blood all over myself so had to settle for giving him the finger. Offensive or not, I could tell that Mudge wasn't his old self.

In Rannu's cave I saw Morag look up at my bloodied form and just shake her head.

'You'll have a smile like me soon,' Merle said, grinning viciously. Not that he had much of a choice these days. I had to settle for giving him the finger as well.

'Merle, look after the wound,' Cat told her brother.

'Fuck that.'

'Don't be an arsehole.'

'Later,' I tried to say but just ended up gargling and bleeding all over myself.

Pagan was already tranced in. There were a number of plugs on the ground. I picked one up and plugged it into one of my jacks.

'Christ, Pagan, why does it always have to be so cold here?' I asked. Or rather I thought, and my icon, who hadn't just had its cheek torn open, asked. We were standing in some kind of great stone hall. One wall was missing and instead there was a large balcony open to the night sky. It was a welcome sight.

'Sorry,' Pagan said. The flames in a fire pit crackled and leaped as a wave of heat swept out of it. I was beginning to like it here. In the real world everything was pain and air that smelled of rotten eggs. I remembered how easy it had been to lose myself in the sense booths.

The others started to appear as Pagan passed me a stone bottle full of fake whisky. Normally I considered this sort of thing pointless, but he'd almost managed to program the taste of good whisky and at least it didn't taste of greasy farts in here.

I had appeared near a decoratively carved, sturdy wooden table. On the table were two travel-stained, patched and ancient-looking cloaks.

'This what was in my head?' I asked when everyone was here.

'Sort of, the components were,' Pagan said.

He still didn't seem comfortable with me. Couldn't say I blamed him. I hadn't ruled out beating the shit out of him yet. Still, I'd probably end up losing that fight as well.

'Whatever they put in your head, it was well hidden. We couldn't find it. It seems that Nuada needed to expose you to Demiurge.'

'And they did that when they used the sense booth on you,' Morag as Black Annis said. Where I betrayed everything for you, I thought. This explained the dreams of plains of black glass and the dark burning sun.

'Nuada's program could hide from Demiurge?' I asked.

'Which means you can hack Demiurge?' Tailgunner asked.

'Yes. More to the point, we can hack Demiurge without being noticed,' Pagan said. The atmosphere in the virtual construct lightened. This was good news. This was a chance. There was a sense of relief, a relaxing of tension. Hope.

'Can we fight Demiurge?' Mother asked.

'We can't, not with our resources. But a data raid's not out of the question and, more to the point, if they don't know we've been there then they don't know they've been compromised.'

'Surely you can do that from any system in Lalande?' Cat asked. She had a new icon that looked just like her. It was Morag's work. Merle had a new one as well. Tailgunner had presumably designed the *whanau*'s high-quality icons.

'Yes, if we just want to creep around and look at non-vital info,' Annis said, her voice like grinding stones. 'All the useful stuff is kept in isolated systems. They have learned from our mistakes.'

'So they think they have an unassailable, completely secure system, but all the juicy stuff they still hold on an isolated system. And I thought I was paranoid,' Mudge said.

'You're not paranoid; everyone hates you,' I told him.

He brightened up. 'Thank goodness for that.'

'It's SOP, good tradecraft. They've got no reason to stop using things that have worked for them in the past,' Salem said.

'Particularly when God demonstrated just how vulnerable non-isolated systems were,' Pagan added.

'So we're right back to square one?' Mother asked.

'Where are these systems?' said Rannu.

'I'm guessing the fleet flagship will have one,' Pagan told him.

'Not going to happen,' I said.

'Or the Citadel,' Annis told us. A lot of virtual air was sucked past virtual teeth.

'Do we have a valid plan?' Cat asked.

'Kind of your job, but I think I can get us in, sort of. I just can't figure a way out,' Annis said.

'Even if you do, so what?' Mother asked. 'How much use to you is it? Surely you're stuck here until the war ends, and before then all of Rolleston and Cronin's forces are going to pull out.'

'It could help liberate Lalande 2,' Tailgunner said.

'And if Earth loses, then they just come back,' Mother answered.

'It's more complicated than that,' Pagan said. 'We use what we know too soon and our advantage is gone as they'll know that Demiurge is compromised and change their plans accordingly.'

It was an old military intelligence paradox.

'Let's see your in,' Mother asked. Scrolls appeared in front of us and unrolled glyphs on the scrolls lit up and disappeared as information was transferred into our internal memories. I reviewed the data.

'That doesn't get us in; that gets us close, and then we die in a hail of vastly superior firepower,' I said. It was good as far as it went but it was messy. Annis still looked like I'd slapped her.

'He's right,' Rannu said.

'It's worth it if we get their entire strategy,' Annis said.

'But what use is it to you if you can't get out?' Mother asked.

'Either we have to get into orbit undetected—' Annis began.

'Not going to happen,' Mother countered, but I noticed that Salem looked like he had something to say.

'We can do it with a tight beam broadcast from the surface,' Pagan said.

'Only on a clear enough day,' Salem said. 'There may however be a way to get you into orbit undetected. I would like some time to look into it.'

'Can we use their exo-armour to infiltrate?' I asked.

Pagan and Annis were shaking their heads. Presumably Tailgunner or Mother had told them about Soloso's final delivery.

'You can't bluff them because the moment you don't respond to hails they know something's up, and they'll know that eight of their exo-armours are missing and who has them. And we can't reliably use them for a stealthy approach,' Annis told us. Having looked at her plan I already knew she was right.

'We're also assuming that we don't climb into them and Demiurge takes the suits over,' Rannu said before turning to Pagan. 'Can you give them a proper look over?' Pagan nodded.

'Can't you hack Demiurge so it thinks the armour is theirs?' Mudge asked.

'No, that won't work either. As soon as we hit them they'll know we've broken Demiurge,' I said. 'Shame though, it's a good idea.'

'With a clear corridor of fire you can't get them in with a direct attack?' Mother asked. I saw Tailgunner glance at Mother. 'I'm just asking,' she told him.

It was Cat who shook her head this time. 'Too far. I don't fancy their chances of not getting picked out of the sky – even with the added confusion of looking like their machines, and believe me, I'd much rather be in exo-armour.'

'You haven't seen the inside of those things,' I told her. 'With a bit of tinkering the in is solid if fucking hairy, but we're dead as soon as we get in, or more likely as soon as we get close. The only advantage we have is surprise. Once that's gone, it's over for us. Even if we get in there's no way we can get out.'

'Well isn't that your job, Jakob?' Annis growled.

'Yes, but only if there's an actual solution. We can look at it some more, but we're not going to piss everyone's life away.' Cat and Rannu were nodding in agreement.

'You know how much they need this info back on Earth – what's at stake here?' Annis demanded.

'Fuck Earth,' Mother said. Everyone turned to look at her. There were a lot of angry faces. 'I'm tired of risking my life and watching my friends die for a place I've never seen, couldn't afford to go to and wouldn't accept me even if I got there. I know it's important to you people but not at our expense.'

'Whether you like it or not, Earth's key, because if Earth falls then the people here in this cave are pretty much the resistance. Maybe with a few scattered groups who won't have anything like the advantages we do,' Merle told her, contempt creeping into his tone, or maybe it just lived there.

'The Citadel's the base of their ops here, their main manufacturing site. It's the key. Vicar knew that,' Annis said angrily.

'And how does all of us being dead help?' I demanded.

'You fucking coward!' she spat at me.

I saw people's postures shift. Not nervous, just getting ready for another one of our arguments.

'Shut up, Morag,' Mudge told her. He was staring at her angrily.

'This isn't the place,' Cat told her, shaking her head.

'This, I guess, shows up another problem,' I said. 'I'm not trusted in command of the warfare element of Operation Ungentlemanly

Warfare.' There was little in the way of protest. Merle was smiling in a way that made me want to hit him. 'Cat, I think it's better that you take over.'

'Why? What'd I do?' She looked surprised.

'You've got experience of command; you've not been compromised.'

She obviously didn't want it. Who would? It was a fucked situation. It also felt like a weight off my shoulders, like I was stepping into lighter gravity. Maybe I was being a coward, but Morag had demonstrated, along with the repeated murder attempts and my total inability to deal with Merle, that I could not lead these people.

The argument was heating up. I understood Morag's perspective. The exo-armour seemed to be a boon; the two cloaks, if they could hide the hackers from Demiurge, really would be an asset, but there were still many considerations that had to be borne in mind. We couldn't piss these advantages away by committing suicide.

I watched Annis argue with Merle and Mother. Maybe Morag had become used to doing six impossible things before breakfast. Maybe the extraordinary luck that had seen us through so far had raised her expectations unrealistically, but she was pushing too hard.

'All of you, shut up!' Cat said. 'Everyone calm down. This is getting us nowhere. You're acting like a bunch of new recruits. Shut up!' she snapped. Good sergeant voice, I thought, smiling, enjoying it not being me. 'Okay, we keep looking at this, but until we at least have an out it's not happening, okay?' There were muted mutterings but everyone eventually nodded. 'Until then we help Mother's people maintain a perimeter and run patrols. Clear? I also want plans to fuck up their infrastructure without committing suicide or unnecessary collateral damage. Any fucking personal problem, sort it out in your own time. Clear?'

More nods. She was purposely talking to us like regular army, conventional soldiers, letting us know what she thought of our behaviour. She had a point.

'Merle, no fucking around. We get out of here, you look after Jakob's cheek, understood?'

He looked like he was going to argue but finally nodded. He'd be pissed off because he knew that my wound would heal as a result of the bio-nanites in my blood, whereas he was scarred until we got back to Earth. Which seemed unlikely.

'Now the Kiwis are watching, so let's see if we can get through the next couple of days without disgracing ourselves, okay?' Mother and Tailgunner were smiling.

Under Cat we started to resemble a special forces unit a bit more but we were getting nowhere. We were just going through the motions. We'd been lucky to survive our one operation against the Black Squadrons. We didn't have anything like the resources we needed to do the Citadel and the rest of our options were risky propositions at best, for very little gain.

Soloso had joined us in the *pa*. He'd also joined the continuing list of people who were avoiding me. Fine, I was starting to get used to my own company again. With somebody else in charge it was starting to feel like the army again. Guard and picket duty, patrolling, I was quickly into the routine. I didn't even feel guilty when I used my down time to read what I could find. The firestorm had taken out all the books and music I'd had stored in my internal memory, and my trumpet and the skillsofts were still on the *Tetsuo Chou*

Mudge at least had started talking to me again. His problem had never really been with me. I welcomed his company though we were both getting worried about the diminishing alcohol and drug supplies. As well as being pissed off with Merle, the constant inactivity was getting to him. He was seriously jittery. The day after our briefing in Dinas Emrys, I saw him having a fierce argument with Morag. I'd been tempted to boost my hearing to listen in but you never hear well of yourself.

Morag, when she wasn't tranced in working on the stuff they'd got out of my head, the eel net and what little they'd learned when Nuada had fried half their systems, was hanging out with Strange. Apparently the girl didn't speak to anyone but Tailgunner. Now it seemed she was talking to Morag. Maybe they'd team up and properly murder me.

Hanging over our heads like a bladed pendulum on some kind of ancient clock was the knowledge that any day soon Rolleston and his band of merry arseholes were going to attack Earth and there wasn't a lot we could do about it.

I was in the main cave in the shadow of *Apakura*. I'd come to find the motionless giant mech somehow comforting. I was stripping down and cleaning my SAW and engaging in a tried and trusted activity of British squaddies. I was trying to work out how to nick something. Merle's Void Eagle.

I'd heard raised voices and was watching the *whanau* on one of the ledges high above where I was sitting. They were arguing about something and Strange was hugging Tailgunner fiercely. I didn't even consider listening in. It wasn't my business. Why make my life more complicated?

A shadow fell across me. I looked up to see the most complicated of my complications. Morag was holding two beer bottles. It looked surprisingly like a gesture of peace.

'Only if it doesn't end up with us screaming at each other,' I told her.

'Do you think you're in any position to dictate terms?' she asked testily.

'No, but I can just walk away.'

'I'll scatter the pieces of your gun all over the place.' But she was smiling. I accepted the beer. She sat down next to me. 'So Mudge came and shouted at me,' she said conversationally.

I nodded. 'He's good at that if he's on the right aggro mix of chemicals.'

'He reminded me that it was you who'd been captured, tortured and possessed and that you'd betrayed us because of me. Which was stupid by the way. Sweet but stupid.'

Sweet? Sweet! Fucking sweet! Remain calm.

'It wouldn't have made any difference. They were going to possess me and they would have known everything anyway. In fact it probably took them longer to break me. More fun for Rolleston though.' Which didn't quite make sense. Rolleston was an evil bastard but it had all been for practical reasons. Now he seemed to like causing pain.

Morag didn't say anything for a while. We both drank our beer and I rapidly reassembled my SAW. She may have been joking but I didn't fancy wading though pools of acid water looking for components to what was my last remaining weapon of choice.

'I get that you didn't want to abandon me, but here's the thing. When you were possessed you seemed so honest. You seemed to be able to say all the horrible things that we think deep down but never say. Well maybe Mudge does.'

'You think I believed anything I said?' I was appalled that she would think that.

'Not consciously. But you – it – was right. I've been a victim most of my life.'

'You don't get a choice when you're that young.'

This was where you really began to feel an ache in your chest talking to Morag, coolly discussing the atrocity that her life had been. I remembered her telling me she would scar herself before ending up a military whore. I turned to look at her. She wouldn't face me.

Emotion was etched on her face, in eyes that couldn't cry any more.

'Look at me,' I said. She didn't move. I gently took her chin in my hand. She didn't flinch away from me. I turned her head to look at me. I could see how much this was costing her. More vulnerability to the guy who'd caused her so much pain already. 'You're not a victim, never were; you were just waiting for an opportunity, that's all. If it hadn't been this, and I sort of wish it hadn't, then it would've been something else.'

She swallowed and nodded. I prayed that she believed me. She looked away.

'Which just leaves the Grey Lady,' she said quietly. It was going to come up sooner or later. I still felt cold when she said it.

'Morag ... I ... I've got nothing to explain or justify. I thought you were dead.' I think subconsciously I'd searched for the absolute worst thing I could've said in the circumstances and arrived at that.

'And that made it all right?' she hissed. Angry, but I was grateful that she wasn't shouting. 'Tell me, was my corpse still on the floor?'

'Look, I didn't want to—'

'Did she rape you?' She was still angry but I'm not sure at whom.

'What? No!'

'Then why?' she demanded.

'I've told you. I've got no answers. I don't expect you to forgive me—'

'I want an answer. Help me understand why you'd fuck a cold-blooded murderer after you thought I was dead.'

'I was really and truly fucked up. Nothing mattered. I wanted to be close to someone. Even if it was a lie because I was all alone.' I think it was the closest thing to an explanation I could find. She looked away from me and hugged her knees to herself. I just stared into my bottle.

'God, I wish you weren't here,' she said, finally looking at me.

'Well I did try and retire to the Highlands.'

She looked like she was going to slap me. Then she laughed. 'Cheeky bastard.' Then serious again: 'What are we going to do? We just keep tearing at each other.'

'Pretty extreme circumstances. If we get out of this, it won't be like this. I prom—'

'Don't make promises. You can't keep them.' She looked away from me again and I concentrated on my beer and tried not to say anything else stupid.

'Look, you owe me nothing,' I finally said. She looked at me again. I think she would have had tears in her eyes if they hadn't been plastic now. 'You decide. All I know is I want you so much and for ever, but we have to be able to work together because we're putting the others at risk now. You decide.'

'All on me, is it?' she asked and sniffed. 'Typical.'

'That's not what I mean. I mean what I want is us to be together, but you're the wronged party so it's up to you.'

She gazed at me for a while and then stood up.

'Before you go, you have to stop trying to push everyone so hard,' I said.

She didn't look at me but she nodded. 'I know. Cat's spoken to me.'

'What are you doing?'

She turned to look down at me.

'Think about how much it has cost to get here. Buck, Gibby, Balor, Vicar, Dog Face, countless other people whose names we'll never know, some of whom we've killed. It has to be for something, and we're so close.' I heard the resolve, the steel in her voice. I couldn't tell her that more often than not it didn't matter, and a lot of people died for very little.

'I don't think you realise how much we've punched above our weight,' I told her instead.

'We still have to make it mean something,' she said.

I had nothing for her. I think we had raised her expectations too high. She turned to walk away but stopped.

'Go and see Mudge,' she said over her shoulder. 'He's really hurting.'

Showering. I waited until I knew Merle was showering and nicked his Void Eagle, spare clips and his holster. I also stole all the booze he had.

I found Mudge on his own, humming to himself in one of the caves. It was dark. The only illumination was the glowing cherry of his spliff. I was looking at him in the green of night vision. He was oblivious to me. I suspected that he was listening to music on his internal systems. I'd have to see if he had anything worth copying, maybe more of that Cash guy.

'Mudge?' I shouted. There was a moment of shock and then he was reaching for his Sig before he realised it was me.

'What?' he demanded suspiciously, looking around the cave as if he'd just discovered it anew.

'Do you want to talk about your feelings?'

He stared at me, appalled. 'No, I really don't.'

'Thank fuck for that. I found a bottle of brandy.'

He immediately brightened up. 'Cool. Hey, is that Merle's?'

I just grinned.

'I just felt stupid, you know. I fell too far, too fast and for the bad boy, the cool guy that Mum warned me about. What a fucking cliché.'

We were both quite drunk now on Merle's brandy and some of the moonshine that the Kiwis brewed. Morag was right: Mudge was hurting, but he'd cope.

'Merle's not cool; he's a dick.'

'He is cool. You're just jealous because he's harder than you.' Who wasn't? 'Seriously, are you ever going to win a fight?'

'I won lots of pit fights. I fought three guys up in the Highlands,' I protested.

'Yeah, yeah, you won loads of fights when nobody was around.'

'Hell, you don't have to split up with him just because he betrayed me and you put a gun to his head,' I suggested, trying to change the subject. I sort of meant it in a I-just-want-my-mate-to-be-happy kind of way. 'I mean, Morag's shot at me *and* tried to kill me.'

Mudge looked confused. 'Shooting at you *is* trying to kill you,' he pointed out. I nodded sagely. 'But I don't really want that kind of relationship, you know,' he continued. I nodded again. Ideally I didn't want that kind of relationship either. 'Are you guys back together?' he asked.

'Fucked if I know,' I said gloomily and helped myself to another swig of the moonshine. I was starting to like the taste of it. Or more likely my taste buds were dead.

'How are you?' Mudge finally asked.

I shrugged. 'Alcohol, denial and drugs will see me through. Concentrate on the job in hand and have nightmares about it for years to come. The usual.'

'It wasn't the usual though, was it?'

'No, no, it really fucking wasn't. Watching her die, then her being alive again. It's almost like Rolleston putting two in her head is what I've got to look forward to. Like it was a ...'

'Premonition?' Mudge was looking at me like I was an idiot.

'I don't think I could cope with it again.'

'So walk away. She won't. She's hugely overcompensating for something at the moment. She sounds like a fanatic.'

'She wanted to leave Rannu possessed,' I said, shaking my head. 'I don't get that at all – it doesn't seem like her. What if I've made things worse? Hurt her too much?'

'Damaged her? That's your martyr complex kicking in. It's not all down to you. Other bad things happen.'

I passed the moonshine over to Mudge. He took a long pull on the bottle. 'Gaaah! This stuff's horrible,' he said and then took another long pull.

'The thing I can't deal with is what I was saying when I was possessed. I mean, that was me. No doubt about it. I remember saying those things and meaning them. I remember the thoughts. I ...' I trailed off.

I couldn't explain the possession to myself, couldn't reconcile it with being me. The thoughts I had had. White had become a deep black. Wanting to do all those horrible things, things that I would have done had I been free.

'You know that wasn't you, don't you?' Mudge asked, passing the moonshine back.

'At some level, but my ... the reality of the situation, my memories are that it was me. The thoughts I thought ... As if everything I've done – killing, fighting, hurting, stealing and fucking people over – as if that somehow wasn't nearly bad enough.'

'Possessed-you wasn't that much of a bigger prick than real-you,' Mudge said, grinning in the dark. I gave him the finger. 'That's your problem. You're not comfortable with who you are. You want to be a nice guy, liked, but we don't live in that sort of world. Come to terms with who you are; do the best you can but realise that sometimes you have to be a bastard, and if you want to beat the other guy then you're going to have to be a bigger bastard than him.'

'That easy, huh?'

'Nah, those are just words. Seriously, I suggest remaining drunk and stoned until the bad thoughts and memories recede into the distance behind you.'

'That easy, huh?'

'Nah, those are just words. Deal in your own way or go under. Same as it ever was.'

'You're a huge comfort to me, Mudge. I want you to know that.'

The cave illuminated as Mudge lit another spliff. The flame distorted and exaggerated his features, making him look demonic. The flame disappeared but an afterglow remained.

'Maybe that's it. We don't have anything like the resources and commitment to being a cunt that Rolleston has. How can we win against that?' I asked.

Mudge shrugged. 'I'm not sure we have to win. Just fight. Prove that we're alive, that we were here at this point.'

'You sound like Balor.'

'Balor wanted glory; I just want to live my life without slithering around on my belly begging for scraps.'

I nodded at this. It had the sort of drunken logic that sounded brilliant until you woke up in the morning and realised that the world was more complicated than that.

'So are we finished feeling sorry for ourselves in a dark cave?' Mudge asked. I nodded. 'Now that you're good and drunk you should see if you can get laid.'

It seemed like a good idea for a moment.

'You going to make up with Merle?' I asked. Mudge shrugged.

'You going to let Pagan off the hook?' he asked.

I shook my head vehemently. 'No, fuck that. We were supposed to be mates. You've no idea what I went through because of that guy!'

'He thought he was doing the right thing. He realised that there had to be sacrifices. You used to make sacrifices like that all the time.'

'Bollocks! Every time I tried to come home with everybody. He made a cold, calculating decision to fuck me. He sent me to fucking hell! He's lucky I don't kill him. I might do depending on how I'm sleeping when this is over.'

'Yeah, okay. I don't have much of a defence for him except he saved our arses in Maw City.'

'Gentlemen?'

Mudge and I yelled. It may have been more of a scream. The bottle went bouncing, spilling its contents. Both of us were on our feet, sidearms drawn. Salem was standing close to the cave mouth dressed for the cold, pack on his back and holding a walking stick. His arms were spread wide to show he meant no harm.

'Christ, Salem, are you trying to get shot?' I demanded.

He frowned at the blasphemy. I was angrier with myself than with him.

'You shouldn't be able to do that,' Mudge said, frowning. He was right. Salem shouldn't have been able to sneak up on us like that. 'Drink?'

'You know I won't.'

'Smoke?' Mudge offered him the spliff he'd just lit.

'More tempting, but no.'

Mudge nodded and pointed at him with the hand holding the spliff. 'Oh yeah. You used to smoke this shit and then go out and murder people, didn't you?'

Salem didn't answer but he seemed amused.

'You going?' I asked.

Salem nodded. 'Yes, they do not need me at the moment. I believe that they have gone as far as they can. I have just come to say good-bye.'

'I'm sure we could find things for you to do,' I told him. Only after I'd said it did I realise how patronising it sounded. Mudge was giving me a look that told me I was being a prat.

'I will be of more use back in the city. I will teach those who want to fight how to hide from Demiurge, I think. I will also see if I can find a way to help you get information or yourselves off the planet. I have some ideas. I have made provision for contacting Pagan, Cat or Tailgunner if need be.'

'Why you?' Mudge asked.

'Mudge!' I hissed, but Salem didn't take offence at Mudge's abruptness.

'Because Tailgunner knows me from the neighbourhood. He knew that I'd acted as an exorcist before and I think he understood that I realised Shaitan was real.'

'You mean Demiurge?' I asked.

'Demiurge is an echo, nothing more.'

I stepped forward to shake his hand.

'Thank you. Really, I don't have the words. I owe you.' It sounded inadequate for what this man had done for me.

'It is the duty of all,' he said. It could have sounded trite but I knew that he meant it.

'Even for a sinner like me?' I asked jokingly.

His face became serious. 'I have known many men like you, Jakob. God will judge you, nobody else. Not even yourself. He knows what was you and what was not.'

I wondered how much of our conversation he'd heard. Mudge started laughing. I was getting pissed off with his rudeness. I really did owe Salem a lot, maybe everything.

'Pack it in, Mudge!' I told him.

'What? Common sense packaged as religious bollocks?' he said.

Salem was smiling as well. 'Mr Mudgie does not offend me. God has a plan, even for him.'

This just started Mudge laughing harder. I had to smile. What the fuck had God been thinking of, making Mudge?

'What I would say is that you do not have the right to judge Pagan—' Salem started.

'Bullshit!' I immediately felt guilty. It reminded me of our conversation when I had been possessed.

Salem held up a hand as a calming gesture. 'Please hear me out.

If he had not sacrificed you then we would be none the wiser. We would have learned nothing. We may be at a standstill at the moment, but we have learned so much from your imprisonment. I know this sounds harsh, but in the big scheme of things he did the right thing.'

'Maybe, but it was a fundamental betrayal of trust.'

'Like you would have volunteered,' Mudge said, grinning.

I glared at him. 'I accept that it may have meant progress but you can't expect the sacrifice to be happy about it.'

'In some cultures it was an honour,' Mudge said.

'Fine. You do it next time,' I told him angrily.

'I apologise. I have angered you. It was not my intent. I think that Pagan agonised long and hard about it and feels more guilty than you can imagine.'

'Good.' I knew I sounded childish. 'Look, I'm sorry. I just can't walk away from this.'

'I do understand,' Salem said, nodding sadly.

'Thank you,' I said again.

Salem bowed and turned to leave.

'Hold up,' Mudge said.

Salem stopped and turned. He was smiling. I think he knew what was coming.

'You have to tell us,' Mudge said.

'Mr Mudgie, I think if I answered that question, regardless of what the answer was, I'd become a lot less interesting than people seem to think I am. Besides, we don't talk to lensheads.'

Salem turned and walked away to the sound of Mudge's laughter echoing around the cave.

Mudge and I were trying not to stagger so hard it must have been obvious how drunk we were. There were disapproving looks from Cat and Morag as we tried to reach our cots without falling over. I was going to pay for this.

I glanced up the cave to the ledge where *Kopuwai* stood in its alcove. I saw that the *whanau* were deep in conversation with Soloso.

Morag was heading for me. I sensed trouble but I thought it was going to be good trouble. If I was going to get told off for being irresponsible then it meant she still cared. Besides, she had told me to go and talk to Mudge about his feelings. Did she not realise how drunk men have to be for that sort of thing? And it was Mudge I was talking to. What did she think was going to happen?

The guy in the top hat with the ancient-looking long rifle, standing on one of the ledges watching everyone was a bit odd though.

402

Particularly as he hadn't been there when I'd looked that way a moment ago.

'Freeze!' I shouted. He wasn't moving anyway. 'Put the rifle down!' Contradictory instructions.

Moving in on him, laser pistol in a two-handed shooter's grip, the smartlink putting the cross hairs right across his pale face, I suddenly felt very sober. Mudge was moments behind me, Sig in his hand. Morag had drawn her pistol and was running towards us. Others were beginning to take notice.

Whoever it was had ghosted straight through our pickets, sensors and sentries to appear among us. The weapon he carried looked ancient and was made mainly out of wood. There was some kind of coil wrapped around the barrel, which made me wonder if it was a home-made gauss rifle of some kind. He wore dark work clothes, with some kind of half-length duster/cloak-style garment over the top of them. His skin was extremely pale and he was a lot taller and more slender than most natives of Lalande 2. A flexible tube of a brass-coloured material protruded through the chest area of his clothes and extended to a facemask. The mask seemed to be made of a similar material to the tube, as were the protruding lenses of his cybernetic eyes. They looked home-made but finely crafted.

'On the ground now!'

'Drop the gun or we will fire!'

He just watched the commotion as if he was studying us.

'Don't shoot!' Tailgunner came running down from the ledge towards us.

'Friend of yours?' Cat demanded as he reached us. The rest of the *whanau* were not far behind him.

'Never seen him before in my life,' Tailgunner said, moving through us to get a better look at the guy.

The infiltrator was just moving his head from side to side as he took us all in. Although he was obviously human, there was something very alien about him. He was observing us as though he'd never seen the like before.

'So who the fuck is he and what's he doing here?' Cat demanded.

'And how'd he just walk through our guards?' I asked.

'I think he's a Morlock,' Tailgunner said, staring at him with an expression bordering on wonder.

'Bullshit, they're a myth,' Soloso scoffed as he joined us.

'What's a Morlock?' Morag asked. Mudge opened his mouth to reply. 'Not you; someone who knows what they're talking about.' Mudge shut his mouth again.

I noticed that the strange man had looked at Tailgunner when he'd said the word Morlock.

'Soloso's right – they're an urban myth,' Big Henry began. I saw that a lot of the Kiwis were nodding but some of the others were holding on to the little wooden or greenstone charms I think they called *tikis*. There was an air of superstitious fear in the cave. I didn't blame them. This was a weird guy and it was scary how he'd got in so easily. 'Supposed to date back to early colonial times, before the war, during the great Lalande 2 mineral rush. When the corps moved in there were rumours that some of the prospectors and freelance surveyors went deep, as deep as they could, to get way from the corps and live free.'

'How long ago?' I asked.

'Ninety, maybe a hundred years ago,' Big Henry said, forgetting that he wanted to kill me for a moment.

'What do they live on?' Morag asked.

'Story goes they took some of the terraforming gear, maybe some livestock.'

'Tell the rest of the story,' Soloso said, grinning.

Big Henry sighed.

'What?' I asked.

'They're supposed to take people, for eating,' Soloso said, and then his booming laughter echoed off the cave walls.

'Maybe that's what he's here for,' Merle said scornfully.

I couldn't help looking around the cave for others silently surrounding us in preparation for a violent barbecue.

'So we've got a group of humans who've lived separately for a hundred years, completely isolated, their own society, their own technology by the looks of it, adapting to a deep environment?' Pagan asked.

'I guess so,' Big Henry said.

'So are you going to talk to us, mate?' Mudge called.

'We could make him talk,' Merle suggested. Morag gave him a look of contempt.

The strange man pointed at Cat, patted his chest and pointed to one of the cave exits.

'I think he wants you to go with him,' Morag said.

'Maybe it's a date,' Mudge suggested.

'Nobody say anything unless it's useful,' Cat said distractedly. That would pretty much render Mudge mute. She addressed the strange man: 'Okay, we'll come with you, but we need time to get ready. If this is a trap or you in any way fuck with us, you die first. Understand me?'

The man said nothing.

'Well, it's good we got that sorted out,' Mudge said.

'Mudge, what'd I say?' But Cat wasn't really paying attention to Mudge; she was studying the strange man.

'What are you doing?' Merle demanded.

'Stay here if you want.'

'I'm coming,' Morag said.

'Ladies love pale willowy types,' Mudge said, nodding sagely. The man turned to stare at him.

'Amazing. You can irritate people who you probably don't even share a language with.' Morag seemed impressed.

'It's a gift.'

Painkillers, cybernetic medical support, alien nanites – none of them were helping with my hangover. We'd gone deep, very deep, so deep that the caves were starting to get warmer. Occasionally we would see the distant glow of lava.

The Morlock had a vehicle stashed disturbingly close to the *pa*. It was open-topped and multi-sectioned, and made of the same brassy material. It ran on thick rubbery tracks but made surprisingly little noise. He'd plugged into the vehicle like we would, but the jack had appeared on a mobile snake-like apparatus from within his clothing. The vehicle reminded me of a centipede in some ways but it was fast through the caves and tunnels. It also had a lot of locked cabinets and sealed crates. Presumably these contained examples of their tech that he did not wish to share. The floor of the strange vehicle was covered in some kind of dark soil. I saw Pagan looking at the soil with interest. I remembered how important soil had been to the inhabitants of the Avenues back in Hull.

The Morlock said nothing to us; he just drove deeper and deeper. Tailgunner, Pagan, Mudge, Morag and I had joined Cat. Merle had been too disgusted to go. Big Henry, I think, was too scared. Soloso had seemed scornful about the whole thing. Under the scorn I thought I detected a degree of fear as well. I think the Morlocks on Lalande 2 were thought of in much the same way that the Twists were back on Earth. Every culture needs a bogeyman, something to point at and be afraid of.

My cheek still ached every time I saw Soloso. He seemed cheerfully unrepentant about fish-hooking me with a sickle. Mother had stayed back because she was in command of the *pa*.

I don't know why we were taking so much on trust with this guy, but despite his weirdness I just didn't get a sense of malevolence.

I'd been wrong about a lot of people before, however. Like Pagan. I found myself glaring at him almost subconsciously. He knew it and was avoiding catching my eye. We were all carrying our full combat gear just in case. I was a little worried having all our hackers with us but it wasn't my problem any more.

'Pack it in,' Morag hissed at me.

I looked away from Pagan as we trundled into a huge vertical crack in the rock that disappeared into the darkness far higher than I could see, even when fully magnifying my vision. Deep below us I could make out the orange glow of lava. Even this far above it I could feel the heat. It was a welcome change from the normal damp chill of the caves.

'I should have taken a really strong psychotropic,' Mudge said, removing his sunglasses. We'd tried to explain the pointlessness of wearing sunglasses underground but he'd insisted it was a hangover tradition.

There were a lot of cave mouths, natural pathways in the rock, surrounding the enormous fissure. Some of the ledges were big enough to be small plateaux in their own right. On the opposite side of the fissure, waterfalls cascaded down to be turned to steam far below us. The ledge we were on and much of the surrounding area was covered in dark soil with large flat mushrooms growing out of it. The mushrooms gave off a faint ghostly bioluminescence. However, the most singular thing about the whole area was the beanstalk.

'Fe fi fo fum,' Mudge said, grinning as he popped something in his mouth. He'd spent the previous couple of minutes searching all his pouches, presumably for just the right drug for the occasion.

'I smell the blood of an Englishman,' Pagan finished and then for some reason glanced at me. Perhaps it was because I was staring at him.

It looked more organic and less like the solid liquid that made up Them but was unmistakably Themtech. Though it was only about the thickness of one of the skyscrapers that I'd seen in New York, its sheer scale reminded me of the Spokes. It ran as high as I could make out and down into the lava below. Smaller tendrils or roots branched from its entire length, burrowing deep into the rock or into tunnels.

'What are those for?' Cat asked.

'At a guess, it's harvesting resources it needs from the surrounding area, taking minerals, water from the ice for fuel, using the lava below to generate geothermal energy,' Pagan said.

The Morlock was impassive but I couldn't shake the feeling he hated this thing. It was like a giant parasitic maggot eating away at the guts of his planet.

'It probably processes and gets rid of waste as well, but whatever it's doing it looks like it's collecting a hell of a lot of raw material and energy,' Pagan continued.

'That's Nightside over there,' Tailgunner said, nodding towards the opposite side of the fissure. He looked horrified.

'You had no idea?' I asked.

He just shook his head.

'That would explain why it's been expanding, growing,' Morag said. Pagan nodded in agreement.

'What's been growing? What is this?' I asked.

'Don't you know where we are?' Pagan asked.

'Pagan, I will throw you in the lava,' I told him.

I received a warning look from Cat.

'We're deep under the Citadel, Jakob,' Morag said.

'Sweet. Let's climb up the beanstalk and slay the wicked giant,' Mudge said. I wasn't sure he was joking.

Pagan was shaking his head. 'It has to come through at least two miles of solid rock before it gets to this fissure.'

'Can we sabotage it?' I asked.

'What with? A nuke?' Cat asked.

'I'd go for that,' Mudge said.

'Cat?' I nodded at the Morlock. He was staring at her. He seemed angry. Cat was so surprised at the change in expression and the intensity of his look that she stepped back involuntarily.

'Chill, dude. We're not going to nuke your mushrooms,' Mudge said. 'Do they have any hallucinogenic properties?'

'Why don't you eat some?' I suggested. 'Can we use this at all?'

I noticed that Morag was smiling.

'This is our out,' she said.

21
The Citadel

The sonic decoy was subtle. A lot of noise may have got the guard fauna to investigate and also would have alerted Demiurge. We lay on the bottom of the icy underground river as dark shapes swam through the water above us, the reactive skin of the dive sheaths hopefully blending us into the stone. The dark shapes in the water were leopard seals fed on growth hormones, altered with neuro-surgery to make them even more aggressive and fitted with cybernetic systems including an enlarged and power-assisted jaw. Most divers I knew hated diving anywhere near natural leopard seals, let alone these augmented versions. I wondered if Rolleston had got around to using Themtech on them. The idea of leopard seals with tentacles caused me to shiver.

I felt incredibly bulky with the smart-fabric dive sheath over my full combat gear. The sheath worked as one massive gill, pulling air in from the surrounding water, and was jacked into one of my plugs using technology originally developed for exo-armour. It also masked my heat and electromagnetic signatures. The seals would have had biological material from sharks implanted into them to help them pick up EM signatures.

I'd had rudimentary dive training in the Regiment, as had Rannu, Cat and Pagan, but we were using skillsofts and what little time we'd had in virtual sims. Merle was an accomplished diver. He'd been trained by the US Marines for their Force Recon outfit. We'd had a day to prepare for this, and that had included a run to get some specialist gear from one of Merle's other Cemetery Wind caches.

The dark, fast-moving shapes swam over us and headed back to-wards the time-delayed sonar decoy. It would switch itself off before they got there so they wouldn't actually find anything. If they located the decoy their handlers would know that something was wrong.

We gently pushed ourselves off the cold stone of the underground river floor and finned forward. Cave diving was one of the more dangerous types of diving and I could see why. Lots of tight spaces, particularly if you were as heavily encumbered as we were. The buoyancy controls on our sheaths were working hard to keep us neutrally buoyant. The hostile overhead environment meant that we had to be aware of snagging and couldn't just surface if things went wrong.

The dangers aside, I liked it down here. Despite the fact that I was cold as the heat was bled off me in an effort to mask my signature. Despite the fact that I was drenched in sweat, there was something peaceful and tranquil about it. Seen underwater, the rock formations that we had become used to took on a whole new life, driving home how alien the environment was, but in a good way. Once again, everything we saw was in the green of lowlight vision. For a while I even forgot about the threat of the leopard seals. Fighting them would be a ball ache. We'd win, but discovery by the seals meant compromise, which meant scrubbing the mission.

Dinas Emrys, yesterday

The hologrammaitic rendering of the Citadel looked out of place among the rough, sparse, Dark Ages splendour of the great hall of Pagan's sanctuary.

'You're going to have to trust me. I can hack it,' Black Annis told us.

Mother, Tailgunner and Cat were looking sceptical. Mudge was looking bored. I couldn't read Merle's face and Rannu was always difficult to judge, but I think there was eagerness in his expression. Either he wanted a chance to prove himself again, which was fine, or he wanted revenge, which was less fine. I wanted revenge. I badly wanted to fuck Rolleston up and, if I got a chance, kill him.

'Morag, if you could just tell us a little more about how you think you will do this,' Pagan said.

'Same principle as doing the data raid on Demiurge – I'll stealth it. It's Themtech, which means it has a mind or rather lots of different tiny minds.'

'Like Essex,' Mudge said. We ignored him.

'Operation Spiral,' Pagan pointed out.

'I know how to do the interface and I will have Ambassador helping me.'

'I'm sold,' I said.

'You're just eager to fuck the Black Squadrons up,' Merle said. I couldn't be bothered to argue with him.

'Look, no offence,' Cat said, 'but I don't want to base this op on optimism and overconfidence.'

'Cat, we've had this conversation with Morag several times. I've been in your position and she's always delivered,' I said.

409

Annis looked over at me and smiled. It wasn't very comforting. I felt like I was about to be eaten.

'And I've hacked Themtech before,' Annis added.

'No, you've surfed it. There's a difference,' Pagan pointed out. My grasp of IT was pretty poor but he was right.

'We adapt the Pais Badarn Beisrydd, and they're not even going to know we're there.'

'Then why not use it as a way in?' Merle asked.

'Because it's a trick we're only going to get to play once,' she told him.

We broke the surface of the water, weapons covering every angle, moving swiftly out of the natural rock pool and onto bloodied ice. This was where the leopard seals lived. Evidence of their handlers feeding them meat was smeared all over the ice. Much of the meat looked human in origin. I tried not to think about it. Human lives had always been tossed away casually, but food for guard fauna? That was taking the piss.

We advanced quickly. We didn't have a great deal of time. The moment the seals returned, the mission was over. Rannu and Merle had already programmed their dive sheaths to peel off. We'd hide their sheaths with ours. They advanced past our cordon of guns in their reactive camouflage. I could just about make out the movement of them slinging their weapons and pulling ice axes from clips on their webbing. I peeled off my own sheath, moved forward and pointed my SAW up the ice wall, as did Pagan, covering the pair of them as they started to climb the shifting, fragile and unsteady ice. Merle made quick time. Rannu was slower. His capture and possession had taken their toll, just as they must have on me.

At the top I knew Rannu would take a covering position while Merle rigged and dropped three ropes for the rest of us. Cat, Pagan and Morag were the next up, using muffled motorised ascenders to pull them up with only a minimum of falling ice. Finally it was Mudge's and my turn. With cover from above we attached our ascenders and started up the wall. We'd attached crampons to our boots and were practically walking up the ice trying not to knock any off. We gathered the excess rope with us as we climbed. We wanted to leave as little trace of our progress as possible.

Pagan and Morag were covering our ascent. At least I assumed they were. I could see nothing as they were wearing reactive camouflage and were presumably completely still against the ice. I heard one of the seals flop out of the water and onto the ice below us. I stopped my ascender; a moment later Mudge's went quiet as well. I stayed very still, hoping that the reactive camouflage would hide us. Hoping that we'd hidden the dive sheaths well enough. I glanced down and I saw one of the huge, sleek, vicious-looking augmented seals flopping around among the blood and food remains. There was nothing to do but wait and hope.

I was getting nervous, almost shaky. Something was different. Everyone gets scared, unless they're a psycho or have had too much meat replaced with metal, but this was different. I wasn't handling this reasonably low-stress situation well. I did a mild sedative from my internal drugs reservoir to calm me down. This wasn't good. How much damage had they done to me? I wished I'd asked Mudge to score me some Slaughter.

There was a splash below. I glanced down to see the pool rippling. The seal had cocked its head and was looking at the water. I think someone had thrown something from above. The seal waddled rapidly to the edge and then slid into the pool, disappearing below the surface. It didn't seem very bright. Mudge and I quickly and quietly finished our ascent.

Dinas Emrys, yesterday

'There's only so far we can stealth. As soon as we're compromised it's all over,' Merle said.

'Not if they're worried about other things and not if you've got fire support,' Mother said. Tailgunner, resplendent in his feathered cloak, glanced over at her worriedly.

'That's a ...' Cat started. She didn't say death sentence. The Citadel was basically a minor arcology, or to put it another way, a fortress of ice the size of a small city and very heavily defended. It was designed to withstand a prolonged siege from Them.

'So don't fuck it up,' Mother said grimly. I wondered if this was what I'd seen the whanau talking about.

'You're a mech down,' Merle said.

'Soloso used to pilot mechs in the mines. We've been bringing him up to speed,' Mother told us. Even on Annis's horrible face I could see a look of worry. 'What we'll need is accurate info, which means good forward observation.'

'We'll be comms black,' I said.

Tailgunner shook his head. 'No, we've got an idea about that.'

'Rannu and I can FO,' Pagan said. It made sense, as an ex-RASF combat air controller he had the most experience.

*

411

Few things make you feel less like a hardened combat cyborg commando than wearing adult diapers. They may have been made from the latest smart fabric. They may lock all the moisture away from your skin. They may in fact be the very pinnacle of modern nappy technology, but despite the initial warm feeling there's something deeply pathetic about a grown man pissing himself whatever the reason. It may be part of the discipline of running long-term OPs, sniper stalking or in this case a difficult infiltration. That didn't make it any better. At least we'd taken something to constipate ourselves and eaten high-energy food sparingly the day before.

The Citadel was ahead of us. It was a flat-topped terraced pyramid. Large though it was, the cavern it was in dwarfed it. This meant a lot of open space all around the arcology, which provided clear fields of fire. There were also only a few ways into the large cavern, which would further bottleneck any attack. We knew that each of the terraces was basically a heavily defended trench made of super-hardened ice. Even from here I could see the various weapon systems – cannon, missile batteries, point-defence systems – bristling from the pyramid-shaped complex. Fully magnifying my lenses, I could make out combat drones circling the fortress as well as patrolling gunships and exo-armour squads.

What the fuck were we thinking? I started to shake again. I had to get this under control. We had a long way to go. I dropped the high magnification and the Citadel became a glow in an otherwise dark cavern.

There was no wild fauna on Lalande 2 with the exception of a few hardy rats that had adapted to the high G and were frankly terrifying. Rats shouldn't have that much muscle. That meant that the Citadel's defenders could surround it with motion detectors and motion-triggered anti-personnel mines, as well as much larger anti-armour mines. The anti-armour mines wouldn't bother us but they would be a problem for the mechs.

They had EM, heat and sound sensors as well as security lenses, but if we triggered them we deserved to fail. The problem was always going to be the motion sensors. There was only one way to trick them and that was to move very, very slowly. This meant that a journey of just over a mile was going to take us the better part of twenty-eight hours of crawling over cold stone, hence the inevitability of wetting myself. This would take incredible co-ordination and discipline, as we wouldn't even be able to see each other. We also needed to map the anti-armour mines for the mechs. Our initial movement was around

412

the edges of the cavern so we could start from the *whanau*'s entry point.

It was long, it was cold and it was boring. The highlights of the crawl were exo-armour or drone patrols passing overhead. They always made it easier to piss yourself. I was on downers to deal with the constant tension. As soon as we got close I'd have to counteract the downers with stims. I only hoped that nothing happened before then, as the downers would affect combat performance until I stimmed myself. All we had to look forward to on this miserable crawl were cold rations and the thrill of occasionally bumping into each other.

I had a lot of time to think about the insanity of what we were doing, thinking thoughts that would fuck me up. Not the sort of thoughts I would normally think while operational. I was worried I would set off the motion detectors if I got the shakes. The Citadel grew larger and larger in my vision as we inched closer. The closer I got, the more I could see the weapons, the men, the machines, and the more I realised the futility of what we were trying to do.

Rolleston had done a good job on me. I wondered how Rannu was holding up. I had betrayed these people once. I wasn't going to do it again. It was my responsibility to them that kept me moving. That was how I dealt with it. Kept me crawling over the smooth stone between the mines and sensors. Concealment wasn't required, as they had achieved near-total area denial. Or so they thought. Fortunately they hadn't reckoned on anything as stupid as what we were planning.

I also knew that what the *whanau* were going to do had to count for something. I wondered how they could operate with the near total certainty of death.

Dinas Emrys, yesterday

'They'll know we hacked them,' Cat said. This was good. This was her job – to come up with as many objections as possible so we could overcome them.

'We need to make it look like something else and we need to knock out all visual surveillance in the lower boardroom,' Annis said. As she did she expanded the part of the arcology that showed us the lower boardroom. It looked a long way from our point of entry.

'Sabotage,' I suggested.

'Assassination attempt,' Merle suggested.

'We don't even know if any of their command will be there,' Cat pointed out.

'Sabotage then. I think we should take any opportunity to fuck with their machine that we get,' I said.

'And take any opportunities for assassination that present themselves,' Merle added. I had to agree.

'Not at the expense of getting the data,' Annis said, looking at Cat.

I glanced at Pagan. Even in his Druidic icon he looked subdued. I wondered who was running the Ungentlemanly side of the operation now.

Cat nodded. 'Agreed. The info is our priority.'

'Even though we've got no way to get it out?' Merle asked.

'Information always helps,' Mudge pointed out.

'And currently we know next to nothing,' Annis added.

'Okay, this is all pretty fucking slim,' Cat said.

'We've been out on hairier,' I said. Rannu was nodding in agreement.

'Okay. Let's set up a full action plan and begin prep,' Cat replied. There were smiles from all but the New Zealand contingent and Pagan.

'There's one other thing. We need to do this fast. We've got next to no solid intel but it can't take them much longer to prep for the attack on Earth,' Pagan told us.

Cat gave this some consideration.

'All right. If we're doing this then we are ready to go at 0500 tomorrow, understood? That means if we need more gear from Merle's caches we get it today,' she said.

Now we started to whinge. We were squaddies, that's what we're supposed to do. We whinged and then we went and got on with it.

We were close now after more than an Earth day of crawling. Our internal heating systems were running low to mask our heat signatures. I was cold and I ached. I'd had no sleep. Counteracting tiredness with amphetamines, which made me jittery, and then confusing my mind with downers to counteract the tension.

Twenty-five hours in, things had stopped making sense, which was good. This meant I could deal with the imminence of possible death. I could hear the soldiers talking now and smell their food. Soon we'd be trying to kill each other. Shame when we had so much in common. Pity we couldn't just go after the leaders, on both sides.

At least Rannu and Pagan had had something to do. They had plotted a line of anti-armour mines from the mechs' point of entry to the Citadel. The plan was for Rannu and Pagan to rendezvous just before the attack and use the palm interfaces on their smartlinks to swap information. Pagan would also be using his smartlink and internal targeting systems to passively plot firing solutions for the mechs. Most crucially they needed solutions plotted for the point-defence systems. Pagan was also looking at the main vehicle entrance on this side of the arcology and using his guncam to record details.

When he had all the information he required he sent it as a packet on a UV tight beam link to a transponder we'd set up at a prearranged location. That receiver was hard-wired via a cable run through a small hole drilled in solid rock to the *whanau*'s position. Using tight beam communication meant that the Black Squadrons would have to have something interposed between the receiver and us. Also they had no reason to be scanning UV frequencies.

I checked the time displays on my IVD. One showed the actual time. The other was a countdown. I looked up at the large entrance to the vehicle bay. All that was between the entrance and us were three lines of trenches and then the terraced trenches above the door.

New Utu Pa, *yesterday*

'I want two fireteams,' Cat told us. We were in one of the smaller caves. Soloso and Big Henry were just inside the entrance discouraging people from paying attention to us. 'Fireteam Alpha is me, Merle and Morag. Fireteam Bravo is Jakob running it, Mudge, Rannu and Pagan.'

I would have liked to turn over command to Rannu but I'd done that once and I couldn't afford to be seen as a weak link again, as I suspected that Cat would actually drop me from the mission. I didn't want to work with Pagan. I couldn't trust him. Actually that wasn't true. I knew he'd do his job, but I didn't want to trust him.

'Looks like we've got all the fuck-ups,' Mudge said.

'Shut up, Mudge,' I told him.

'Right, Rannu and I are going to start the killing before zero point. We're going after officers, NCOs, heavy-weapon crews, but we're going to be doing it quietly,' Merle said. He seemed happier with Cat in command.

'Then we move on my go and we are fucking quick or dead. Everyone understand?' Cat told us.

We all nodded. I looked over at Mother and Tailgunner. They may as well have been carved out of mahogany. It was like looking at ghosts. After everything Mother had said I still couldn't work out why. I'd spoken to Mudge about it. He'd said that sometimes you just had to draw a line against what the bad guys were allowed to get away with.

'Is that my Void Eagle?' Merle demanded. I looked down at the massive automatic holstered on my chest.

'What, you want to argue about it now?' I asked. We were just about to go operational.

'I'll be having that back,' he snapped. Crucially Cat didn't order me to give it back. In fact she was smiling.

'There's a reason the British army are called the Borrowers,' Mudge told him. Rannu was laughing.

A new recruit had brought in a collection of antique weapons. Mudge had bartered with him for a pre-FHC assault shotgun for me. I'd added an external targeting system for the smartlink, which would be less than ideal, and I'd also had to make a few adjustments for the shotgun to fire caseless, but it would serve as a secondary weapon.

Watching the countdown I was shaking. When the klaxons and the red lights came on, for a moment I thought we were compromised but this was all part of the plan. I watched gunships laden with troops and exo-armour take to the air. The rest of Mother's forces, along with whatever fighting elements of the resistance and Moa City gangs we'd managed to make contact with, had attacked targets in the city and its vicinity, hoping to draw elements of the Black Squadrons away from the Citadel.

I watched the gunships and flight-capable exo-armour head out of the big cavern. This helped but there was still a lot of men and hardware left. I knew we had to let them get to their targets. As soon as that happened our forces would pull back and hopefully melt into the background.

My breathing sounded impossibly loud in my ears but I didn't dare risk a sedative now. I just wanted things to start – get it over with, break the tension. I was shaking quite badly now. Even under my camouflage I was sure I must have been visible as a quivering piece of rock, but nothing happened, though as a result of the alert the guards seemed more on the ball. The soldiers in the external defences were all New Zealand regulars.

I don't think I noticed when the killing started. I knew that the others would be watching the synchronised countdown, getting ready to go. My heart was hammering at my ribcage. I didn't hear the firing; I just saw an officer's face cave in and he slumped to the ground. The man next to him had a moment to look surprised and then his face turned red just underneath his helmet. Rannu with a borrowed suppressed, long-barrel Steyr marksman's rifle and Merle with his custom gauss rifle firing at subsonic speed. Every shot someone died. They were aiming and killing so quickly that none of the defenders had had time to raise the alarm yet.

The countdown reached zero. The explosion rolled across the cavern, echoing back and forth at the speed of sound. It was like standing in thunder. The ground shook as my audio dampeners managed the noise down to tolerable levels. This got their attention.

I knew that behind me a cliff face had just been turned to powder. One of the NCOs under Mother's command was old enough to have worked mines in this area before the Citadel was built. He'd been able to guide us to mine shafts big enough for the mechs and close enough to the Citadel to blow a path through with a lot of stolen mining explosives.

They hadn't even sounded the alarm when the Citadel started taking hits. My audio dampeners struggled with the hypersonic booms as 300mm rounds from the *Apakura*'s mass driver cannon began impacting into the Citadel. The rapid hits penetrated deep into the hardened ice causing massive explosions of shards hard enough to cause shrapnel wounds. Water rained down on us from where the kinetic energy of the impacts had melted the dense ice. The ice burned where plasma rounds hit. The plasma had been fired by *Kopuwai* and *Whakatau*, the two Landsknecht-class bipedal mechs piloted by Soloso and Big Henry respectively. Every round from the plasma cannons sent up huge plumes of steam. All three mechs were targeting the Citadel's point defence with their direct-fire weapons.

Rannu and Merle used the chaos to kill more and more as the defenders instinctively dived for cover in the face of the mech onslaught. My audio filters managed to pick up the rip of rotary railguns and the sound of rapidly staggered explosions. *Apakura* drew a wall of fire between her and the Citadel as she used the information provided by Pagan to detonate anti-armour mines with her rapid-firing belly railguns.

The Citadel's point defences on our side were destroyed in moments. The Citadel had not even returned fire yet. The two Landsknechts and the Bismarck-class mech then fired half their missiles. Contrails filled the air in the huge cavern.

I opened my mouth and kept my head down. I'd been dangerously close to missile strikes before. Conventional and plasma warheads impacted. The ground jumped and tilted and I realised the impacts had blown me into the air and turned me on my side. None of the defenders had noticed; they'd had other things to worry about.

We were targeting the Citadel's heavy-weapons systems and gunship landing areas. It looked like one whole side of the pyramid had thrown itself up into the air. Steam, water, shards and huge chunks of ice rained down on us. Several plasma warheads had detonated in the vehicle bay and it was burning with white fire. I could hear the secondary explosions of ammo cooking off. I was shaking like a leaf. I didn't need a stim. I was wired. I needed something to take the edge off.

Each of us was a ghost, disrupting the steam and smoke as we stood up and ran towards the Citadel, killing as we went. The massive blast doors to the burning vehicle bay were starting to move, closing slowly. I sent a frag grenade from my launcher into the first trench. It exploded. I was oblivious to the screams. I glanced behind me. The *Apakura*, *Kopuwai* and *Whakatau* were emerging from the rolling cloud of dust, firing, seemingly unstoppable. Ahead of them *Apakura*'s belly rotary railguns were hosing the ground down left and right, detonating the anti-armour mines closest to the Citadel. For a second I caught a glimpse of a small mech running towards us.

I reached the first trench. The defenders were still recovering from my initial frag. I sensed rather than heard Pagan, Mudge and Rannu run in behind me. I fired a flechette grenade. This was just slaughter. The soldiers in the trench were trying to work out what the fuck was happening to them when razor-sharp needles tore through cheap armour. The shaking had stopped. I fired at anything still moving with the SAW. Next to me Pagan and Mudge were subduing their own trenches.

'Clear!' I shouted. It was less fact and more a signal to move on. I turned to run into the vehicle bay. I heard the unmistakable hypersonic roar of a Bofors railgun and glanced over at the trench Cat was subduing. She'd painted the ice red. There were no bodies, only flying body parts.

There was movement behind me. I swung around to bring the SAW smoothly to my shoulder. Sprinting out of the mist came a Steel-Mantis-class scout mech. It was Strange in the *Atua Kahukahu*. She'd named it for the vengeful spirit of a dead child. She'd advanced ahead of the other three mechs. Shit! That meant that we could have made the attack with the stolen exo-armour and not have lain in our own piss for more than a day.

By the doors we tore the reactive camouflage gillie suits off. If we couldn't see each other then we'd do more harm than good. The blast doors were still closing ponderously slowly. Inside the vehicle bay it was raining as plasma fires burned through ice. The walls and the ceiling were melting but I knew it was just superficial damage, even though most of the huge bay was burning. The missiles had veered to the left and the right at the last moment to give us a clear central path. Rannu was already sprinting across the bay towards another, much smaller blast door. We followed, moving rapidly, weapons at the ready. Any movement that wasn't us got shot. We weren't taking chances.

The scout mech's twin rotary railguns destroyed any significant resistance. Strange swivelled the mech with economical grace, located points of enemy fire and tore them apart with short, disciplined bursts. She targeted the more heavily protected points. The short-range missile battery on her right shoulder fired its payload in one go. The missiles shot off in different directions and protected firing points and heavy-weapons emplacements exploded.

A burning light mech strode out of the plasma fire on our left. As one, Mudge, Pagan, Rannu and I triggered vertically launched Laa-Laas from one of the twin tubes attached to our packs. Four missiles hit the mech, exploding all over its already weakened body. The long-legged war machine toppled backwards and plasma flames consumed it.

Ahead of me Mudge was firing on the run, aiming his converted AK-47 at the catwalks that surrounded the vehicle bay. As Rannu reached the closed blast door he pulled the smart frame off his chest webbing. At a command sent through his palm link, the frame expanded. He attached the frame to the door and then turned, weapon at the ready. The rest of us reached the door and did the same.

This was the tricky part – the waiting while the microbes ate at the armour plate of the blast door, making us a man-sized hole to get through. When I looked behind me everything was fire. The main blast door entrance to the bay was about to shut. Through the crack I could just make out the *Apakura*. They had begun to counter-attack. It looked like every inch of the *Apakura* was either exploding or burning. It was wreathed in fire. Yet its belly guns were still firing; the huge impacts of its mass driver could still be felt. Chunks of ice fell from the ceiling with every hit. I watched it fire the rest of its missiles. Then the doors closed. Moments later we felt the missiles' impacts. I glanced up at the scout mech next to me firing burst after burst. I'm not sure what response I expected from the composite and metal shell of the mech.

'We're through,' Rannu shouted. As soon as the hole appeared we'd started taking fire from the corridor on the other side. Cat poked her railgun round the corner and fired but quickly had to take cover.

'Strange!' Cat shouted. The mech turned and knelt, putting one of its rotary railgun arms through the hole. I heard the rip as one hypersonic bang mixed with the next and I saw Strange move the arm about. When she'd withdrawn Rannu poked his head around the corner.

'Clear!' he shouted.

Strange was trapped in the vehicle bay. *Atua Kahukahu* was way too large to get through the hole and the external doors were shut.

'Exit the mech! Come with us!' Morag shouted. I could hear the desperation in her voice. The mech shook its head-shaped sensor array. I knew that the girl had had a short and tragic life. Now with the rest of her family almost certainly dead, it looked like it was going to come to a short and violent end. 'Please!' Morag begged. Strange's sprint had been incredible. She'd made this part of the operation so much easier. She may have been a murderous disturbed mess, but she did not lack courage. Or maybe she wanted to die. Whatever the reason, she wasn't leaving the mech.

'We don't have time for this. Move!' Cat screamed at Morag.

We were through into the corridor. Advancing at a fast walk in two lines, Alpha team and then Bravo. Anyone who showed their face got shot. We passed the remains of the defenders that Strange had subdued. They were a sticky carpet and wallpaper. Humans reduced to their constituent parts at hypersonic speed. Pagan and Morag used their laser carbines to burn out any security lenses we saw.

We reached a second blast door. Merle used his smart frame with the microbes we'd taken from the Cemetery Wind caches. The rest of us covered our rear as the microbes did their job, exchanging shots with those defenders brave enough to poke their heads out of cover. Mudge's leg was bleeding badly and he was moving with a limp. He'd taken a shard of ice in the initial bombardment. We covered Rannu while he rapidly applied an anti-coagulant/septic spray to the wound and affixed medgels and a pak.

As soon as the microbes had cut through, the defenders on the other side of the blast door and those behind us decided to mount a two-pronged attack.

Morag fired a frag grenade from the underslung grenade launcher on her laser carbine through the door and then ducked back into cover. Cat took hits as she stepped through the hole in the blast door, firing her railgun in a long burst. Merle followed her through and then Morag, firing three-beam bursts from her laser. Rannu fired a grenade at the defenders behind us and then Mudge and I laid down a withering hail of fire as Rannu and Pagan stepped through the hole. I snatched a frag off the front of my webbing, primed it by hand and threw it back down the corridor before stepping through the hole. Mudge backed through the hole firing.

In the next corridor Cat, Merle and Morag were already advancing in line, firing short bursts and single shots at anything that moved in front of them. Pagan, Rannu, Mudge and I followed, frequently checking behind us.

Two blast doors in, we were well and truly trapped in a huge building full of thousands of angry, frightened, well-armed people and probably members of the Black Squadrons too.

The isolated system had to be well defended, which meant going deep into the building. Which meant going through secure points like the blast doors. The microbes were the only things that could be trusted to go through them reliably but they took time. Presumably guided by Demiurge, the defenders soon caught on to this. They would be waiting for us every time we reached a door, and every time we got through. At each door we met more resistance as they became more organised.

We were starting to see individual members of the Black Squadrons now. We could recognise them by the way they carried themselves and their gear. Despite their reputed healing abilities they seemed as reluctant to get hit as any other soldier. Particularly when they had rail or plasma weapons fired at them.

All of us were wounded now. Cat, always first through to suppress the opposition, was bleeding badly from multiple wounds but still up and fighting. For once I hadn't been hit too badly and adrenalin and drugs kept me soaring above the pain.

We found it when we got through the final blast door and into the central protected area of the Citadel. At first I thought the ice was black, but it was transparent. On the other side of the ice were what looked like veins, arteries and other body parts all connected to form some massive organism. It was unmistakably Themtech but transformed into what looked like a warped version of some kind of Earth biology. The warm wind blowing through the corridors made me feel like I was being breathed on. The organs behind the ice seemed to move and beat with some kind of inner pulse. Despite the fact that we were in a combat situation all of us slowed.

'What the fuck?' Cat wondered.

'It's processing machinery for the raw materials that the roots gather – air, heat, sewage, etcetera,' Pagan told us.

'We need to keep moving!' Merle snapped.

'Trippy,' Mudge said, but he didn't sound like he meant it. He sounded subdued. I glanced over him. He did not look happy.

We were close to the conference room now. We moved through more corridors surrounded by the organic machinery. I wondered how people could even think of this mockery as life, let alone make it work on such a scale. But none of what I had seen prepared me for what was round the next corner.

We rounded the corridor and this time, sunk into the ice, we saw people. All of them looked like they had once been hackers. All of them had been shorn of their hair and were naked. All of them were inside the ice of the walls and ceiling and connected through their plugs, and more obvious violations of their flesh, via tendrils to the machinery.

Again we slowed. During the war They had committed atrocities because They did not understand the concept of a war with rules, but not even They had come up with anything this sick. I saw Morag stare at the frozen hackers, her recent tough-girl persona close to cracking.

This drove home something that I had suspected since I'd been captured, something I should have realised after Gregor. Rolleston was completely insane. Even Merle looked disturbed.

'What is this?' Rannu asked. I could hear his desperation to make sense of this, but there was no sense to be had.

'There are few quicker ways to move and process information than the human brain. It's always been the hardware that's the problem,' Pagan said quietly. For some reason I really hated Pagan for knowing this.

'You mean this is part of Demiurge?' Morag asked. Pagan swallowed and nodded. 'But that means that if they do this on a large scale, then ...' Her voice just trailed off.

'They'll have access to a lot more processing power and memory than we could ever hope to marshal,' Pagan said. Because no sane person or organisation would do this, he'd left unsaid.

'Shut up!' Merle hissed. Pagan's head jerked round to look at the other man. 'They have ears.'

Then there was laughter. It really fucked with my calm. I didn't want to be here. Many eyes were opening and trying to move in sockets to look at us through the ice. Mouths moved where they weren't frozen over. 'You will all suffer. You will all watch each other suffer,' they said. Multiple agonised voices speaking as one.

'We need to move.' I couldn't remember hearing fear in Mudge's voice before.

'The best you can hope for is that this will be done to you,' the voices said. Then they started naming people we knew and describing what was going to be done to them. They started with Mudge's mum.

'Move, now!' Cat barked, but she sounded disturbed as well.

The next corridor was the same and then the next. After that we weren't even walking on ice; it was like we were walking through the veins of the beanstalk root system we'd seen in the fissure.

The entrance to the conference room looked more like a sphincter than a door. We were down to our last smart frame of microbes.

Mudge was carrying it but he wasn't sure where to put it. All of us were surprised when the sphincter just opened. Cat and Merle, backed by Morag, advanced cautiously into the room. Pagan and I followed with Rannu and Mudge watching our backs.

'Stay where you are!' I heard Cat scream. I had a moment to register the large room. I had this odd thought of a cybernetic room in which high tech had been mixed with the living organism of heavily modified, organic Themtech. It was like modern corporate architecture had caught a disease. One of the Citadel's roots grew through the room. In the centre was a long table made out of a single slab of thick granite.

Sitting at the table apparently as surprised to see us as we were to see him was Cronin. Standing behind him was Kring. They looked like they hadn't even realised the base was being attacked. Both were covered in some kind of thick viscous fluid that they had been trying to wipe off themselves and both started moving as we entered, simultaneously seeking cover and reaching for weapons. They were fast.

As they moved I was surprised to see Cat and Merle shift aim to something at the other end of the room. I brought up my SAW to shoot at Kring, who I reckoned would be the bigger threat. He disappeared behind the granite table as I fired a burst. Sparks flew off granite.

Cat and Merle advanced quickly, Merle firing his plasma rifle and Cat her railgun, seemingly at the wall. Behind me I heard Rannu and Mudge firing rapid bursts and a grenade detonate. Morag and Pagan were firing at the walls, ceiling and table. I knew that they were taking out anything even remotely resembling a sensor or lens. Some of the things they were targeting looked like growths.

That left me with Kring and Cronin. I moved forward, firing diagonally across the table. Now I could see what Merle and Cat were firing at. There were things growing out of the walls. They looked like deformed Berserks. They had human-looking, screaming mouths in their bodies but the heads of animals. Some were covered in spikes and other less pleasant features and they were growing from the organic parts of the room with surprising speed.

Kring just stood up. I shot him. A lot. He staggered but the enormous cyborg was standing up to the gauss-boosted fire of a long and accurate burst from my SAW. He raised both massive fists, a PDW in each. That was fine. I was happy to take low-powered rounds on my armour and swap shots with him. Then my world became fire. Every round exploded fiercely, blowing off chunks of my armour and kicking me back into the soft organic tissue of the wall. I was vaguely aware of the granite table breaking in two from the force of his fusillade.

The lunatic was firing concentrated explosive rounds. They were expensive and dangerous to use, and he was using them in a fast-cycling automatic weapon. Red icons erupted all over my IVD. I slid to the ground. The table blocked his line of sight. Kring was firing indiscriminately. He stood and took any fire aimed at him, staggering as shot after shot hit him. I couldn't figure out who else was firing. The room seemed to fill with rapid explosions. Then I realised he was firing at the twisted Berserks growing out of the wall.

I tried to roll onto my knees but hands burst out of the floor to grab me. I was screaming now as some kind of pincer-like claw tried to prise armour and flesh open. My blades extended from my knuckles and I stabbed them viciously into the floor, tearing at it. The partially formed Berserk mutant went limp, succumbing to the ferocity of my attack. There were more growing out of the wall all around us. Another grenade went off somewhere behind me. Now there were black beams and shards in the air just like back on Sirius. I saw Pagan go down as explosions rolled over him. Then I saw Rannu stagger in the doorway as he was back-shot. Mudge's head whipped round. It looked like a black beam had taken half his face off.

I'd had enough. On one knee I fired a thirty-millimetre HEAP grenade at Kring. As I did, Cronin shot me with a gauss PDW. He got me in the arm. It penetrated hardening inertial armour and then my subcutaneous armour, tearing into actual flesh.

Kring dodged to the side, the HEAP hitting the wall just behind him. The explosion knocked me back to the ground. The table slid across the floor towards me. Kring was thrown forward over the wrecked table. I felt the organic floor moving beneath me.

Back up onto my feet. I fired a burst at Cronin. He dived for cover behind the table. He was fast for an exec. I pointed the SAW down and fired another burst into the ground because the floor just wouldn't stop moving. Bringing the SAW back up, I was appalled to see Kring standing again. He dropped the two PDWs and drew two Benelli shotgun pistols. I risked a burst; he staggered slightly, and I hit the ground again. How much fucking damage could this monster take?

Morag was down! No, it was okay, she was tranced in. That was trust in this environment. Everyone else was fighting the Berserk mutants growing out of the floor, the ceiling, the walls.

Heavy-calibre hit after hit on my chest armour and helmet. Almost cracking the armour. There was more pain, more red icons on my IVD. Where the fuck was the fire coming from? Kring. His shotgun pistols were firing saboted gyrojet rounds with smart miniature warheads.

Money truly was no object for these guys. The gyrojet rounds would track me regardless of my cover and I couldn't take much more.

I staggered to my feet, taking more hits. I fired my last grenade at him. He dived out of the way and the blast knocked me off my feet again. Still at least I wasn't getting shot. Then I did something really stupid. I charged.

I'd hoped to surprise him. I jumped onto the broken table and ran across its sloping surface, firing. The expression on his mismatched face with its bulbous fish eyes didn't even change. He grabbed me as I closed. At least he had to drop the shotgun pistols. He lifted me off my feet and slammed me into the wall. He then threw me into the ground. He didn't drop me. He threw me. The wind was knocked out of me.

My SAW was hanging loose on its sling and was just getting in the way. Fighting for breath, I dragged the Void Eagle out of its holster and fired it repeatedly at point-blank range into Kring. The shots staggered him and I managed to fire about half the magazine before he slapped the gun out of my hand. Something clawed through the floor, tearing through my inertial and subcutaneous armour and ripping flesh out of me.

Kring reached down and dragged me to my feet. I extended my claws. He hooked a punch into my chest. As he hit me, his now-spiked cybernetic fist was propelled forward into my chest by a jackhammer-like pneumatic action. My breastplate and subcutaneous armour cracked, the force of the blow causing internal damage. I spat blood onto his Hawaiian shirt.

I don't know how I had the presence of mind to duck his other fist but I did. I heard buzzing. The organic wall behind me opened and I was showered with some kind of fluid. On his fist the fingers had slid back; it looked like the hand had split open to reveal a small chainsaw. I felt this was unreasonable.

I suspect it was more strength born of desperation rather than training and boosted muscle that allowed me to drive the four full-length blades on my left hand up through his chin and into his head. His features warped at the bladed violation of his face but he didn't fall. Now I started to panic. The powerful fingers on his pneumatic fist wrapped around my neck and started to squeeze. I felt him push the chainsaw against my breastplate. I could feel it. With terrifying strength he began to cut through the already damaged plate. I screamed when it reached subcutaneous armour and then again as it touched flesh, blood spraying all over him.

I was clawing at the laser pistol on my right hip. The claws on my left hand were still stuck in his face. The gun came free. I put it against his head and squeezed the trigger again and again and again. I kept squeezing. The back of his head became red steam. By the time he toppled over dragging me with him, the entire back half of his head was missing.

I managed to free myself. I'd blown the tips of my own blades off with the laser. A clawed hand came out of the wall and ripped the side of my face off. I rolled to the side and scrabbled for my SAW. The deformed Berserk tore itself out of the wall and loomed over me. I pulled the trigger on the SAW. I walked a long burst all the way up its torso. It was coming apart as meat and not the usual liquid dissipation I'd come to expect from Them. It dropped to the ground. Killing Berserks was about the most normal thing I'd done in what felt like a long time.

Something stabbed through my armour from beneath. A cry of pain and I rolled to one side and up onto my knees. I fired another long burst into the Berserk rising from the organic floor. It disintegrated in a hail of bullets.

I was getting shot, a lot. I staggered forward. Pistol rounds. Just pissing me off. I spun round. A terrified and slimy Cronin was empty-ing a pistol in my general direction. I raised the SAW and fired. He was no longer there. He was fast.

Something fell through the ceiling and onto me, tearing at my armour. I stabbed into it with claws, fighting wildly. It was bleeding, not leaking all over me, or was that my blood? I managed to ram its head back against the table and fired the SAW one-handed until its only movement was the jerk of bullets tearing through dead flesh.

The floor was a bad place to be. I climbed to my feet. Rannu was slicing up a Berserk, a knife in each of his hands. Cat and Merle were fighting back to back. Mudge was firing rapidly, standing over an unconscious or dead Pagan and a tranced-in Morag. Need to get to Mudge.

Out of the chaos Cronin charged me with a katana. No time to shoot. I tried to parry with my SAW. The katana sliced right through it and buried itself in my helmet. I felt the blade bite into armoured skull and blood ran down my face.

I kicked forward, sending Cronin staggering back. Unfortunately he kept hold of the sword. I let the two halves of my SAW fall to the ground.

'Come on then!' I screamed at him like it was some feral pub fight back in Dundee as I extended what was left of my blades.

He was skilled, fast and desperate. He swung at me again and again with the blade. I parried what I could with the claws. The rest cut into me, going through my armour, painting me a deeper red. I ignored the warning signals on my IVD. I got cut so I could claw at him, not caring, pushing him back. Finally I got lucky and caught his sword between my knuckle blades. I headbutted him, and as he staggered back I jumped into the air and kneed him in the head. I felt part of his skull give way beneath the impact. I tore the katana out of his grip and stabbed him through the shoulder with my two remaining full-length blades. I pulled my other hand back, getting ready to ram the broken blades on my left fist through his face.

'Bastard!' I screamed at him, as inhuman as anything else in the room.

'I surrender!' Cronin screamed. He looked terrified but not of me. Why was he covered in slime?

'Jakob!' Morag. I heard the note of command in her voice. I wanted to kill Cronin so much I was shaking. Instead I grabbed him by his hair and pulled the antique assault shotgun out of its scabbard. I started making my way back towards Morag, firing the shotgun one-handed at anything that moved that wasn't us, dragging Cronin with me.

On the other side of the table Merle and Cat were firing as they backed towards Morag, Rannu and Mudge. I saw Cat go down. Half her face was red steam and blackened bone. Laser fire. She hit the ground. I knew she was dead. I heard Merle scream. I saw Rannu, Mudge and Morag's expressions change. They looked terrified. I turned round. Through the sphincter in the opposite end of the room I saw Rolleston and the Grey Lady enter. Marching at us, firing.

All of us poured fire at them. Merle's repeated plasma blasts wreathed Rolleston's head in white fire. His head was a blackened grinning skull in the white flames and still he kept coming.

I just about made it back to Morag and the others. They were standing over Pagan's body. It may as well have happened in slow motion. I watched him turn his combination weapon on me. The plasma barrel fired. He couldn't miss.

It hit me in the right side. I screamed as I burned. The plasma fire ate into me, through me, an unstoppable force, my own flesh now the fuel. What was left of my conscious mind prayed for death, for an end to the burning and the pain.

Somehow I was still conscious. Morag appeared by my side. There was a moment of peace through the pain, the chaos, the firefight. Then a piece of flesh was torn off her chin. She was still up. I was still screaming, burning. I felt a jack slide into one of my plugs. I didn't understand. Then I was screaming through the pain at the terror.

My flesh violated, made alien to me. It changed, meat sloughing off me, tendrils emerging through the skin of my face, somehow grown from my own flesh. The tendrils flailed, writhing in front of me, and sought out the strange flesh of the Citadel.

Then I was falling, burning. We were all falling. No, swallowed, being forced down and crushed again and again. Burned flesh all around me, gullet muscles constricting as we were pushed down at frightening speed, all the while my new alien flesh mating with the flesh of the Citadel's roots.

Half a man reduced to charred screaming meat was deposited on cold hard rock. I was only vaguely aware of others there with me in the darkness. I tried to cringe from the heat but there wasn't enough of me to move. The roots glowed orange and I heard it scream like Them as it carried lava up, from the depths of Lalande 2 to the Citadel. I could feel it. I was still joined with it. I screamed – inside only now, as every nerve ending burned again. The plasma fire all over again. Why couldn't I die? Miles above us a city of ice became a volcano as the root system became enormous, destructive, flailing tentacles spewing lava.

'I didn't know I could do that,' Morag said. There was wonder in her voice.

22
New *Utu Pa*

I stand in the centre of the great hall at Dinas Emrys on fire. Around me the stone starts to burn. I'm screaming. Some of the screaming is words. Those words are, 'Where is she?!'

Pagan looks to be at his wits' end. 'You're doing this to yourself!' he shouts at me.

There just isn't a way to manage this amount of pain. I can feel it through the morphine, through a chemically induced coma. Plasma is a one-shot kill unless you're Balor or Rolleston. I get all the effects of the hit but none of the fun of dying. I think I'm aware of other pain beyond the burning. The human mind isn't set up for this. This constant burning is the biblical hell the Christians talk about. Maybe I am dead. I've done a lot of bad things in my life but surely nothing to deserve this.

I am put into a suit of warm meat. It breathes. It has its own pulse. New pain and more drugs. I am a lot lighter, easier for them to move, now that I only have half a body and should be dead.

I stand in the centre of the great hall at Dinas Emrys. I am still on fire.

'You have to listen to me, Jakob. You are doing this. This is a manifestation of biofeedback. Your body burned and your mind is making it real, here, in the net as well.'

I know this. I'm not setting fire to stone now. I am not destroying code with the thought of pain. Even here I can still feel it though. Even here I still burn.

'Where is she?' I ask. Pagan does not have an answer for me. How can he tell me that she is hiding from me?

Dinas Emrys again. It's the only place I have a semblance of life now.

'I don't want to die in space,' I tell Mudge. Mudge's icon that looks

429

like Mudge. I'd need a mouth to tell him in the real world and all I have is charred mess.

'I won't let you die in space, man. If it looks like we're not going to get picked up, I'll use your own laser on you.'

'That would still be dying in space,' I point out.

'Oh yeah, but you know at least you won't run out of air and slowly suffocate or anything.'

'I want you to know you're a huge comfort to me. You could always save time and trouble and do it now. There's nothing left of me anyway. Do it now.'

Normally Mudge would meet such a request with utter scorn but now he just looks uncomfortable.

'You're regrowing what you've lost, what the plasma took.' Normally Mudge has no problem looking me in the eye and in here our eyes aren't lenses.

'I'm not comfortable with that.'

Now he looks at me. 'Metal and plastic, alien nanites – what difference does it make? You've got to stop looking for the easy way out.'

Where's Balor when you need him? He would have killed me in a second.

'Where is she?'

'Look, I can explain. Pagan can explain. You're overreacting to—'

'I don't want to hear an explanation. Where is she?' I want to discuss betrayal.

'She's too frightened to see you. Look, Salem's out is sound.'

'It's for ore, the high G's from the acceleration would powder bone.'

'Not if we use their exo-armour suits. Their life-support systems are keeping you alive while you—'

'Regenerate? Like an earthworm? What if I don't want to go?'

'Listen to yourself, man. Soloso and Strange survived. I just thought you should know. According to the information, the fleet is due to set sail in a couple of days' time. We need to get back. This is our best hope.'

'You don't need me.'

'You don't want to die here, man. The air smells of greasy farts.'

He had a point.

Mudge showed me the footage. I was heavily sedated throughout the whole thing. He showed me Soloso and Strange saying goodbye. Soloso suggested that it would be unwise for us to ever return to Moa City. I couldn't imagine why we'd want to.

It was surprisingly simple. Salem had a good eye for security weaknesses. We joined a cargo consignment. Pagan, Morag, Merle, Mudge, Rannu, Cronin and I were all wearing the stolen Themtech exo-armour. They were called Hellions. We were put in a crate and the crate was filled with counter-acceleration gel, the same stuff that we'd used in the OILO drop and that air and space fighter pilots filled their cockpits with. We were then smuggled into the cargo yard. No hacking involved, just a forged barcode and a switchover out of sight of Demiurge. Then we waited.

Even unconscious I felt our upward spiral ride on the catapult, a giant mass driver designed to fire cargo into orbit. Burned and new-growth flesh battered at impossible Gs. It felt like every blood cell burst. Despite the gel, we were all moved from the front of the container to the back. Even the flesh components of the Hellions became one huge bruise.

In orbit we'd cut through the container and pushed out some of the gel, hoping that nobody was scanning us too hard. Then Pagan sent the tight beam signal. We waited. Then he did it again. We waited some more. Well I say we. I was unconscious and yet still failing in pain management. I didn't care. This could end in the flash of a particle beam weapon and all it would have meant to me was sweet release.

If I'd been a little less self-involved then maybe I would have thought of Tailgunner, Mother, Big Henry and Cat. Not to mention the seventy or so of Mother's people, the resistance and belligerent street gangs who'd died in the diversionary attacks. People whose names we'd never even know, and mobilisation or not, Rolleston's people would still be trying to track them down. No wonder Soloso and Strange didn't want us back.

Oh yes, Cronin. Seems he'd defected. Seems that he was as scared of Rolleston as everyone else, maybe more so. He'd almost got himself killed by providing some initial information and then refusing to say anything else unless we got him off world and away from Rolleston.

It seemed that Rolleston put Cronin in harm's way. As the attack began, Rolleston had transported Cronin and Kring through the Citadel's added-on flesh parts to the boardroom. The slime they were covered in was lubricant. It helped you get transported through the root system better. We'd all been covered in it after Morag had hacked my flesh, turned me into something else and used me to interface with the roots.

And the hack had been successful. Except now, surely they knew that their systems were compromised? They knew about our miraculous escape and they would know that we had Cronin.

More than a day in space and the *Tetsuo Chou* had appeared. At which point they'd found us. Mudge showed me missiles fired over the planetary horizon, fighters trying to reach a firing point from higher and lower orbits. The *Tetsuo Chou* had taken some hits but in the end its speed carried the day and it managed to reach a safe distance to set sail.

I'd missed the ballet and the bright lights in the night. I'd missed the old near-dead red star and looking down on that huge stinking planet one last time. I'd missed fucking nothing.

I was staring at Morag as Black Annis. She was aware of it. Everyone else was aware of it. Even Cronin was aware of it and this was his debrief. For debrief read interrogation.

Rolleston and Josephine Bran had survived. Of course they had. They couldn't be killed, it seemed, even if lava seemed a pretty final way to deal with a disagreement. Salem's people had got eyes on both of them in Moa City after Morag had turned the Citadel to steam.

'We got you off the planet; now tell us what you know,' Black Annis said, trying to ignore me, her voice like stones being ground together.

'I need some kind of guarantee, a deal, one you're not empowered to make,' Cronin said. Apparently he was much calmer now. His calmness was increasing in direct proportion to his distance away from Rolleston.

'Dude, you know we can get this out of you if we want – it won't even take us that long,' Mudge said reasonably. He was smoking a virtual cigarette. That seemed even more pointless than virtual whisky. Still it did look tasty.

'Oh, I don't think so, Mr Mudgie,' Cronin said with just a trace of smugness.

I was irritated to see him wearing a high-quality expressive icon made by Morag. He looked now as we had seen him when we discussed democracy on a system-wide broadcast after we'd released God onto the net. Dapper, well dressed, handsome and shrewd – in short everything the high-flying corporate exec should be. According to Pagan, the higher spec the icon, the easier to gauge the subject's responses in interrogation. 'You're the good guys. I don't think you'll torture me.'

The smugness in his tone was enough to distract me from staring at Annis's horrible blue-skinned visage.

'Arsehole, everyone here wants to kill you,' I told him. 'I'd co-operate.'

'You kill me, you'll learn nothing.'

'We've already raided your isolated system,' Annis growled. Cronin's head snapped around to look at her. Pagan turned to her, Merle was positively glaring at her, and even Rannu was shaking his head.

'Bullshit. Demiurge would have enslaved you at best,' he said, but he sounded unsure. He was good enough at his job to read our body language, even in here, and would know by our reactions that we were telling the truth. Then a smile spread over his face. I hadn't been expecting that. It looked like hope.

'I don't see why you're smiling,' Annis said. 'We know everything we need to about the attack.'

'You're going to have to buy your life,' Rannu told him. It sounded pretty serious coming from the Ghurkha.

'I'm afraid your masters will disagree. I am far too valuable to them. They will want to make a deal.'

'You see any of them here?' Mudge asked as he looked around the great hall. I could hear him getting angry. 'I don't think we have masters. I think we have people we work with, and I would have thought you more than anyone would know that we are very bad at doing what we're told.'

'I hadn't credited you with stupidity, Mr Mudgie—'

'You've never dated him.' I would have thought that Merle was joking except for the deadpan delivery. What was more interesting, Cronin would not look at him.

'Whether you like it or not, I have more useful intel and insight on the situation than anything you could get from Demiurge,' Cronin told us.

'How? Isn't Demiurge omniscient?' Pagan asked.

'You know that the Earth authorities will need to deal with me.'

'They will just torture the info out of you,' Annis said.

I didn't believe that, and I could tell most of the others in the room felt the same way. They'd make a deal. Cronin would disappear and someone with a new face would be welcomed back into the power-broker fold.

'He's right. We have no choice but to run him through interrogation sense programs and kill him before we get to Earth,' I said grimly.

'I don't think you could do that, Mr Douglas,' Cronin said.

'I've tortured and killed better men than you for information, Cronin. You may think yourself pretty important but to me you're just another arsehole, and if you don't think I'll torture you then you clearly have no idea what we went through when you guys captured us,' I told him.

Rannu was nodding. His face was cold and emotionless. I was pretty sure that he wanted to hurt this man as much as I did. To an extent Cronin was right – I didn't want to torture him because I didn't like to think of myself as that sort of person, but I would if I had to. I wouldn't lose much sleep either.

'You remember me, don't you, Cronin?' Merle said. Cronin's icon blanched. 'Well, you know what I was capable of on a job. Now imagine I'm angry because my sister got killed. Now imagine that I hold you at least partially responsible for that.'

'That wasn't me! That was Rolleston! I'm telling you, he's sick! He's completely lost it! Same with the torture. It was all him!' The board-room polish was slipping. His Detroit street roots could be heard now.

'Arsehole, there's only one deal to make and it's with us. And the only deal is that you make it to the end of this voyage,' Mudge told him.

Cronin looked around at us all. I don't think he liked what he saw.

'You're all fucking crazy. You've no idea what an asset I am,' he said desperately.

'Convince us,' Mudge told him. 'If you live long enough then you can make your deal when we get back.'

Like fuck, I thought.

Cronin had my attention now though I couldn't stop looking over at Black Annis from time to time. She would never meet my eyes.

'So you and Rolleston wanted to rule the world and now you've had a falling out?' Mudge asked.

'No. That wasn't what we were going to do.'

'Oh no, this is the next big step for humanity,' I said acidly.

'We evolve to slavery?' Mudge asked.

Cronin looked pained. He had an expression on his face that suggested even if he explained it to us very carefully, using small words, we still wouldn't get it.

'Have you ever thought about the potential of each individual, even the dumbest, least ambitious and least imaginative? If nothing else they have huge potential for industry, potential vastly enhanced by our interface with technology. Then think about all the intelligent, ambitious, imaginative and hard-working members of the human race. Now imagine what we could accomplish if all of us pulled together. If we all locked step and moved forward trying to improve ourselves as a race, as a whole, instead of bickering and fighting over ultimately meaningless things. With the war we've seen what humanity can accomplish almost working together, the leaps in technology, the co-operation—'

'The constant fucking misery,' I added.

'Now imagine we don't require the stimulus of an external threat. Imagine every one of us is working together towards a common goal, the progress of us as a species. Imagine what we would accomplish.'

'Is this how you sell totalitarianism to yourself?' Mudge asked.

Cronin looked deeply frustrated. 'How do you walk upright?' he demanded.

'We understand you. You're not the smartest person in this room by a long shot,' I snapped, angry at his patronising tone.

'It's not Jakob either,' Mudge said, grinning.

I glared at him. He was right though.

'Look, you've been told a lie. We don't all have a right to what we want. Sacrifices have to be made. We are talking about a vast paradigm change. We're talking about humanity becoming an almost new organism.'

'You're talking about the death of individuality,' Morag said.

Why was our interrogation sounding like a philosophy discussion? I hated this bullshit. It was wank that got in the way of life. Why couldn't people just get on with it?

'Yes!' Cronin shouted enthusiastically. 'But you say that as if it's a bad thing. At the root of it all we're all just one step away from lizard-brained animals. We've been brainwashed to the point where all we can think of is our own selfish desires. We were going to work together, all of us.' Then he looked around. 'I mean, individuality, how's that working out for you? You all happy?'

Again his smugness left me with the strong urge to hit him.

'I am,' Mudge said.

'Mr Mudgie, I have actually read your profile. You're not happy; you're on drugs. There is a difference. Look, everyone in the world is miserable—'

'You've been a significant contributor in that,' Pagan said.

'And everyone's lonely.' I saw Mudge glance involuntarily at Merle. I wondered if Morag was looking at me. 'The experiment of individuality has failed.'

'Free choice isn't an experiment,' I said angrily.

'No, it's an illusion. You've had little choice throughout your life. Anything that feels like free will has always been within parameters set by others. The closest you came to breaking that resulted in a conflict that may destroy humanity. Do you understand how selfish and destructive it is?'

'We could just as easily lay that responsibility at your door,' Pagan told him. 'All we wanted to do was give people the chance to under-stand what was going on and make decisions themselves.'

'People don't want that. People want easy lives.'

'Which they don't have,' I said.

'People want others to make the hard decisions for them. Most people barely want to think. The reason that Earth is mobilising to fight us, the reason that people like you were sent after us, was because other powerful people have a lot to lose if we'd succeeded. Whether you like it or not, we were going to give people what they wanted. You see, all the pain you feel is because of your individuality. We were going to end that. We were finally and for all time going to make humanity both happy and constructive.'

'A perfectly ordered clockwork society,' Pagan said.

'This is bullshit,' Merle said. 'I don't want to hear him justify him-self.'

'But thank you for your contribution, Mr Sommerjay, and yours, Mr Nagarkoti, and of course –' he turned to look at Pagan '– we couldn't have done it without your help, Mr Simm.'

Pagan looked stricken. The rigours of the mission, the repeated wounds, the guilt at his betrayal, all seemed to have aged Pagan, even in here.

Good. Fuck him.

'How?' I asked. 'Have Demiurge possess everyone? That'll only work on everyone with neural cybernetics.' Then I realised that thanks to the war that was almost everyone, certainly everyone that mattered. Mattered. I was starting to think like them.

'Possession by Demiurge wouldn't lead to co-operation; it would lead to an orgy of pain, violence and suffering that would finally wipe us out,' Rannu said.

Cronin was nodding.

'Good plan then,' Mudge commented.

'Mr Nagarkoti is correct. It would, but Demiurge was only a part of what we'd planned and it didn't turn out quite the way we thought it would.'

'So how?' I asked again, getting more irritated.

'We were going to remake humanity. Nanite biotechnology derived from Themtech. Imagine Them but with drive, imagination, purpose, creativity, skills and knowledge.'

I'm not sure why, but the thought filled me with horror. It made me think of humanity as a swarm of hungry insects eating everything in its way across the stars.

Merle laughed. 'This is evil-genius bullshit. This is like some viz.

Nobody does this shit,' he said. Maybe he was trying to convince himself.

'Mr Sommerjay, once you get to a certain level of influence, subverting governments and mass-controlling populations becomes relatively easy. All we were doing was utilising technology available to us in the most useful manner for humanity.'

'And you can do this?' I asked. Cronin just looked at me as if I was stupid. Of course they could. 'Delivery?' I asked. Now Cronin seemed surprised. I saw some of the others exchange glances.

'I don't know. I assumed that was the information you took from Demiurge at the Citadel.' He was looking around at us questioningly.

'Jakob was injured; he hasn't been briefed yet,' Pagan told Cronin as if he was reassuring him.

Cronin turned back to me. 'It's nanotechnology, Mr Douglas. It will not be difficult to smuggle to Earth and infect the populace.'

'Didn't even tell you, huh?' I asked.

'It was compartmentalised. It wasn't my area of responsibility. I didn't need to know.' Obviously Rolleston was really paranoid.

'I'm interested why you get to make this decision for us?' Morag demanded.

'Because they have the power and the resources to fuck with us. Same as it ever was,' Merle said.

Cronin was nodding. 'Humanity elected us to do it. If not, we would not have been allowed to manoeuvre ourselves into the situation we find ourselves.'

'Or to put it another way, you're arrogant and delusional pricks who think you know what's best for us,' Mudge replied.

'Besides, surely the fact that we're all here shows that people don't want this,' Rannu said quietly.

'Or it's a knee-jerk fear reaction before a major change.'

'And you'd be joining the collective?' Mudge asked.

'People need to—' Cronin began.

'I thought not.'

'There are management concerns and issues of vision.'

'Oh yes, we couldn't have a rudderless race of zombies roaming space,' Mudge said sarcastically.

'They don't have masters,' Morag said. 'They are a true collective.'

The fact that she was sticking up for Them angered me for some reason.

'They are also not truly sentient and only react to stimuli. We're talking about our race acting in perfect concert.'

'You're talking about a human hive mind,' Morag said.

'And you're talking about controlling it. That's too much power,' Rannu said.

Cronin was starting to look uncomfortable.

'If you're controlling it but not part of the hive, then won't that make you the dumbest human alive?' I asked.

Now Cronin was looking really uncomfortable. He didn't answer.

Pagan got there first. 'Unless you weren't just part of it but were controlling it.'

I watched Cronin's icon swallow hard. I couldn't quite get my head around it. What humanity would look like, how it would act.

'You understand that the very act of taking on that mantle, of ascending, would change the person who did it. You're thinking that it would be me. It would not; it would be an ascended being that was once me.' Now he sounded uncomfortable.

'Is this what the Cabal were up to?' Mudge asked.

'No, they were small frightened men,' Cronin said.

'Who was?' I asked. I knew the answer. There was a look close to awe on Cronin's face.

'What's this about?' Pagan suddenly demanded.

'Apotheosis,' Cronin said.

Mudge and Pagan were looking close to fear. I was just getting pissed off.

'What the fuck does that mean?' I demanded.

'To become divine,' Mudge said quietly.

'This is Rolleston's plan, isn't it?' Pagan asked. 'He wants to be God.'

Cronin nodded. 'Rolleston is a great man. Only he saw the true potential in Themtech.' Then his face crumpled and he started to sob. I don't think any of us were quite expecting this. His icon was programmed for real tears as well.

'You're all so fucking British about this sort of thing. It would've been better if we'd tortured this out of him,' Merle said.

'I'm sorry, I'm so sorry!' Cronin wailed.

I pointed at him. 'See, if you're going to betray someone that's the correct reaction.'

Annis looked angry but then it was the icon's default expression. Pagan at least looked embarrassed and guilty. Mudge thought it was funny.

'That's assuming you give a shit. It's not betrayal if your victim's a whining bitch,' Merle said. It may have been an attempt at humour.

'How did you fall from his grace?' Pagan asked.

'Look, Rolleston is not an ordinary man like you or me. He can't be judged by our criteria,' Cronin told us a little too earnestly for my taste. It seemed he was desperate for us to understand, to see what he saw when he looked at him.

'We don't care about judging him, just killing him,' I said. Merle and Rannu were nodding. Cronin look shocked. Like I'd said something blasphemous.

'Even now after I've explained it to you, all you can think of is your own petty base desires?' he demanded.

'If you want to put it that way.'

'It's all I can ever think about,' Mudge added.

'You can't understand this because you are simple-minded terrorists who want to drag everything down to your own sordid level.'

'We understand it. We just like our sordid level,' Mudge explained. Cronin shook his head in mock sympathy. 'No, Mr Mudgie, you do not. Because you have never been part of anything extraordinary.'

'Fucking the Cabal over was quite extraordinary,' I said. Rannu, Pagan and Mudge were all nodding.

'Because it was working against something not for something.'

Merle moved forward and before anyone could stop him grabbed one of Cronin's fingers and snapped it. Cronin screamed.

'Not sure that was going to work in here,' Merle said.

Cronin was rocking back and forth in his chair clutching his finger. It was at an odd angle.

'Not only did it work; it has probably damaged the finger on his real body,' Pagan told him with a slight air of disapproval.

With a look of twisted satisfaction Merle grabbed the finger again and twisted it. 'Get to the fucking point!' he shouted, accompanied by Cronin's screams, before letting go of the broken virtual finger. Merle stood over Cronin while Cronin tried to compose himself through the tears of pain.

'He has certain proclivities. Like I said, he is a great man. He does not have the tastes that normal men like us have.'

'What did he do?' Morag asked quietly. I could hear her starting to get angry.

'There are places where you can go and do things—'

'Snuff houses,' Morag said through gritted, grinding teeth.

'A bit more sophisticated than that,' he said.

'Pretentious, up-market snuff houses,' Mudge suggested.

I was impressed that Cronin had the ability to look irritated through the pain.

'He didn't just go there to kill people.' I almost killed him when he glanced over at Annis as he said that. She was staring at Cronin with barely controlled fury. 'He changed their flesh – made them something new.'

'He ever let you watch?' Mudge asked in disgust.

The answer was written all over Cronin's face.

'So he liked to torture people and then kill them?' Morag growled.

'No! You don't understand. It was something to do with his past ...'

'What?' Pagan demanded, leaning forward, getting sucked into the story.

'I don't know. It was why the Cabal recruited him in the first place, before the war!'

'Because he was a loony?' Mudge asked.

'No, you don't understand. He thought beyond us; he transcended our morality, which isn't really our morality any more anyway ...' He was searching for the right way to explain but couldn't seem to find it. He had a point about morality though. I thought about all the things I'd done just to survive. Something was broken within the entire human race.

'How could we not know this?' I asked Pagan angrily. 'How could God not know this?'

'There must be no trace of it electronically anywhere,' Pagan said, but he looked baffled.

'It makes sense. These places are very careful about their privacy and the privacy of their clients – no records, no surveillance,' Morag said. She was still staring at Cronin, who seemed to be shrinking from her glare.

'You know about these places?' I asked.

She turned to fix me with a stare. Her eyes were black pools. I saw my icon reflected and made small in them.

'There were always rumours. There was a boy ... his name was Michael ... prettiest boy I ever saw. One night some people came for him in a very expensive aircar. We never saw him again. The following day MacFarlane was suddenly a lot richer.'

'That doesn't mean—' Merle started.

Morag silenced him with a look.

'He's not lying; look at him,' she said.

She was right. The cool, calm and contained corporate trouble-shooter was slowly being whittled away to reveal a craven apostle.

'So Rolleston's a sick fuck. Anyone surprised?' Mudge asked.

'Actually yes,' I said. 'I always thought he was a cold bastard who didn't give a shit about anything but getting the job done. I thought he was more like Merle than a psycho. No offence.' This last to Merle.

440

It wasn't until I'd been possessed and then the Citadel that I'd got a glimpse of what Rolleston was really like.

'None taken. I'd agree with that,' Merle said. It wasn't a huge shock that they'd worked together. To me anyway; some of the others didn't look happy. Particularly Rannu. Merle leaned in close to Cronin. 'But I think you'd better get to the fucking point.'

Cronin flinched away from him.

'He merged with Demiurge too early.'

Everyone around the room reacted visibly or audibly except Rannu. I went cold. It was like someone taking a shit in my soul.

'Rolleston and Demiurge are the same?' Rannu voiced my fear. His voice sounded tight, like he was being strangled. I knew how he felt. We'd both been some fragment of Rolleston. The ultimate infiltration. The ultimate violation. I got to see what an approximation of sympathy looked like on Annis's hag-like features. It just made me feel worse.

'Then the biotech. He started experimenting. Started changing people, making them something else. Something monstrous. Like they were toys, playthings.' I thought back to the hackers in the ice. I couldn't shake the feeling that Rolleston had seen that as a practical application of biotechnological engineering in his twisted mind. 'I had to load my internal drug reservoir with downers just to cope with the horror. He enjoyed watching them grow, the pain it caused them. I just wasn't strong enough. That's why Crom – Gregor MacDonald – was the way it was. Why it looked the way it did. Why it ...' Suddenly he looked around all the hard faces in the room and realised this wasn't the audience for that particular discussion.

'Suffered?' Mudge finished.

'You call our friend "it" once more and I will kill you,' I told him.

'You have to understand that it – Mr MacDonald – despite playing a key and beautiful part in what was to come, betrayed him. He had to be punished. You see that, don't you?'

That people who betrayed you should be punished? Yes, but I decided to keep that to myself.

'Like you?' Mudge asked. 'Should you be in the ice? In the ninth circle?'

I had no idea what he was talking about, but Cronin nodded miserably. I hoped he wasn't going to cry again. I wasn't sure if I could master my contempt if he did.

'I wasn't strong enough.'

'So Rolleston intends to remake the world in his image?' Pagan said.

Cronin nodded. 'What he sees in his mind will come to be manifest.'

'We're lucky that Pagan didn't merge with God and try the same thing,' Mudge mused.

'A world of nice cups of tea, smallholdings and folk music would be lovely,' Pagan said.

'Sounds like my idea of hell,' Merle replied. Mudge was nodding in agreement. Cronin was just looking between them confused and a little disgusted at their flippancy.

'This world according to Rolleston even scared a sick bastard like you?' Morag demanded. Cronin nodded and then looked at her.

'It's sublime, but it's hell,' he told her. 'And I'm just not strong enough. I never thought I'd be his Judas,' Cronin said miserably. Morag was staring at him with disgust.

'A world made over in your own image – surely even Rolleston would get bored,' I said. I was joking but then I had some idea of what the inside of that bastard's head looked like.

'He is transcendent,' Cronin said. Apparently it was supposed to be an explanation.

'Fuck's sake,' I said, shaking my head. 'But this is bullshit, right? Delusions of grandeur. He can't do this, can he?' I asked.

Everyone just looked at me gravely. They'd reviewed the information that Morag had stolen. Their expressions told me everything. I was scared. It was like being possessed all over again, but he could make the world like that. He'd already started in the colonies. He had the power to twist anything into his fantasies like the Berserks in the Citadel – if they had even started off as Berserks.

'Who knew?' Mudge asked.

'Nobody except Rolleston, me and the—'

'Grey Lady,' Morag said.

Cronin nodded. Morag was staring at me. Now I couldn't meet her eyes. She wasn't the only one staring. Cronin had an evil little smile on his face. It was the second time he'd come very close to death.

'The other stuff, his torturing hookers to death?' Mudge asked.

'I ... I ... don't know. Some of the older members of the Cabal would have known. Before God they had the power to make information disappear. I mean properly, the old-fashioned way, with hard work. They would work very hard to cover their tracks.'

'I don't believe this shit,' Morag said. 'What are you leaving out?'

'Nothing! I swear. Can't you see how hard this is? This isn't just another deal. I have turned my back on ... on ...'

'God?' Mudge couldn't keep the sound of contempt out of his voice.

Cronin whipped around to look at him angrily. 'Yes, Mr Mudgie, for all your studied cynicism and tragically hip posturing, yes, that is what I have turned my back on. I could have been part of something wonderful and instead I've lowered myself to your level.' Now it was Cronin who sounded contemptuous. He shook his head, looking miserable again. 'Like all of you, I was too frightened, too weak.'

'Bullshit. You're holding out on us!' Morag snapped.

'I am not!' he said.

'I believe you,' Morag said.

Merle, Pagan and even Mudge tried to stop her, but this was her world. They were way too slow. Rannu and I stayed still. Long black obsidian nails sank into the virtual flesh of Cronin's icon's chest. He shook, spasmed and screamed as black lightning played over his virtual body. He died quickly, the biofeedback killing him in the real world. Quickly but in agony. I watched, smiling.

'You stupid bitch!' Merle screamed, losing it. I twitched as red fury threatened to overwhelm me but I suppressed it. Black Annis's head snapped around, her thick black seaweed-like hair whipping with the movement. Merle stopped but his icon still looked furious.

'Think about where you are!' she warned. Merle looked like he was going to say something but thought better of it.

'For someone who didn't want to kill, you're getting good at this,' I said.

'I'm getting used to it,' she snapped.

'You certainly are. How many thousands do you think you killed in the Citadel?' It was less of a question and more of a stabbing. She didn't look at me. She didn't say anything for a while.

'I'm sorry I used you, Jakob, but don't push it,' she growled, and she meant it.

'He could have been more use,' I said, nodding towards Cronin's smoking body.

'He'd told us everything,' Morag said.

'We don't know that for sure,' Merle spat.

'Whose side are you on, I wonder?' I asked her.

She just glared at me. I thought maybe I'd gone too far and then realised I really didn't care.

'Oh yeah, we need more paranoia and distrust on this ship,' Mudge said.

Annis disappeared in a pillar of black fire. I looked at the space where she'd been.

'That was a message from Rolleston,' Mudge said. I looked over at him. 'Think about it. If he wanted Cronin, all he had to do was possess him. Instead he put Cronin in our way and let us go. He knew that Cronin would spill his guts. It's narcissism. He wanted us to take Cronin back to Earth.' Pagan was nodding. 'Cronin was his prophet, his harbinger, to dress his whole insane plan up in religious terror.'

'Looks like Morag fucked that plan up,' I pointed out.

'We still have to pass the info on,' Merle said.

'I want to see the info you got from the Citadel,' I said.

'Are you in this?' Pagan asked.

I just looked at him for a while. 'Who the fuck are you to question me?' I finally asked.

Pagan looked pissed off. 'I'm sorry things went down the way they did, Jakob, I really am, but you need to remember whose house you're in.'

'I do. She just left.' That's it. Twist the knife in the old man.

'We'll show you, but surely we're out now,' Mudge said. 'We've done our bit. This is going to be settled with a fleet action and a cat fight in the net, not by a few violent, sneaky bastards.'

He had a point. This had gone way beyond us now, but that didn't mean there was an end in sight for us. They ran me through the highlights of Rolleston's plan.

'Oh,' I said. The grim expressions around the room matched my own. 'That couldn't work, could it?'

'Unless Earth can work together, it will work,' Mudge the strategist said.

'Well fuck it. It's their problem now,' I said without much feeling.

The pain was just about manageable now. Old burned flesh sloughed off to be replaced with new pink and tender flesh in a distinctly in-human way. I lived in the meat suit that was the Hellion, in the care of its life-support systems. I took a lot of painkillers and spent all my time in the sanctum that Morag had designed for me. I stayed away from the others. I didn't speak to God. We were still keeping what we knew about Rolleston's plans away from God. Dissemination of that information would cause panic. It made me wonder why we'd bothered in the first place.

Still, it had given me a lot of time to practise with the trumpet. I think I was getting pretty good, particularly with the more bluesy numbers.

In consultation with Mudge we'd worked out how to fill the liquid bladder of the Hellion with whisky, and then hooked it into the isol-ated net so it synchronised with me taking a sip of virtual whisky. This and the fact that the air scrubbers on the *Tetsuo Chou* had finally got rid of the rotten eggs smell were the best things that had happened to me so far on the voyage.

I was sitting on a chair on the stage playing a number I'd just learned, watching the motes of dust in the light, when Merle walked in. He'd pretty much been the last person I'd expected to see.

'How the fuck did you get in here?' I demanded by way of a welcome.

'Pagan,' he told me.

'Figures. You two have got a lot in common. You may want to tell him that I won't be trapped in here for ever and he's already on my shit list. I value my privacy.'

'You mean you value your sulking time?' I turned and fixed him with a hard glare. 'What? You can't do me in here, and all I have to do is let you slither out of the armour and stomp on you for a while in the real world. Even if you were up to speed, I've already kicked your arse once.'

I didn't answer and wondered if he'd just come to make me feel a little bit more helpless. I reached down for the glass of whisky on the boards of the stage next to the chair leg.

'You just come here to tell me that?'

'No, I came to listen to your shitty trumpet playing. Look, I don't need to justify myself to you, but people get consciously sacrificed every day in this war. It's nothing new or personal and, guess what? With that stunt you and your friends pulled in Atlantis you stuck your heads above the ramparts. They knew that Rolleston would go for you if offered the bait. Is it shitty? Yes, but get the fuck over yourself because there are a lot bigger things at stake here.'

'That an apology?' I couldn't keep the bitterness out of my voice.

'For what? Doing my job? Making the hard decisions?'

I looked him straight in his intense brown eyes. I wondered how much of the intensity was madness.

'Funny how arseholes use making the hard decisions as an excuse. Rolleston and Cronin both said the same thing.'

'You would have done the same to me if the positions were reversed.'

'I would now.'

'Before. Actually think about it. Someone you don't know and don't like versus a significant strategic advantage in the fight of your life? You might wring your hands and whine about it but I'd be gone.'

'Bullshit. You were on my crew.' But I knew he was right. He knew I knew it as well, judging by the sneer.

'Listen to me, you selfish shit.' He said it in the same casual tone he'd been using since he entered. I felt my eyes narrow. 'You destroyed my sister's career and then dragged her halfway across hell's creation to get her killed. She doesn't get the chance to sit in the Cotton Club destroying Miles Davis's music, feeling sorry for herself. She's just cold and still and we don't even have a body to bury back home in Philly.'

'I'm sorry about Cat.'

'Don't be. She was a soldier. She knew what she was getting into. You may have had a rough ride – I'm not in the best place to judge – but you can either use that as an excuse to push everyone away and go back to whatever miserable, lonely existence of half-measures and excuses you lived before, or you can just get on with it.'

'You finished?' I asked.

Merle stared at me for a while. It was the sort of look you often saw before someone got pissed off enough at you to throw a punch.

'No. I get that you're pissed off about being the sacrifice, but Pagan made the right decision. I also get that you think you can push him around in a way that wouldn't work with me. Well, you can't. Leave him the fuck alone or I'll fucking deal with you, okay?' With a final look of contempt he turned and headed for the door. As he reached it he looked over his shoulder. 'After you said what you said to Morag about killing all those people, when she got out of the net she threw up. Just thought you should know that you succeeded in hurting her.' Then he walked out of the door and out of the sanctum.

She didn't pick her time well. I was good and drunk. I'd decided on that course of action rather than thinking about what Merle had said. Except I was thinking about it. Being drunk, it was much easier to come up with ways to justify my behaviour. Let's be honest here: Merle and Pagan had betrayed me, and Morag had used me.

Physically I was starting to feel much better. I'd regrown, or rather the alien nanites had regrown, just under half of my body. Sooner or later I was going to have to leave the Hellion and face the others in the flesh.

Drinking was making me maudlin, or maybe I just should've thought about this stuff before rather than my own anger and pain. I suspected that the Puppet Show had been their own flavour of bastards, but who wasn't these days? We – I – still fucked them over. Merle was right: I was no better. I couldn't whine about betrayal. We'd accomplished so much but for some reason it didn't feel like a victory. I thought about the losses. The *whanau* had known that with the resources they had, an attack on the Citadel had been certain death, yet they still did it. They did it fighting for themselves but also fighting for a home world they'd never known. They ended hard, violent lives hard and violently, and they'd deserved better. Dog Face had certainly deserved better than me putting a grenade into him. So did those other poor Kiwi bastards I'd killed.

I balled up my fist and pounded it against my head. There was something wrong here. Something that all the self-pity was covering up. When the drunk arsehole in the street spits in your face you know you have to walk away because it's not worth it, but you don't. You don't because pride gets a hold on you.

Cat. A burst of laser fire in the head. Just under the rim of her helmet. No more Cat. My one-night stand with the killing weapon at her shoulder. Did you forget about your betrayals? Is that why you're hiding in here or is it just because you know you can't run from this? You know you've already tried to run and that didn't work.

'Jakob?' she asked.

I looked up and her icon was just her. No pre-FHC flapper, no Maiden of Flowers and no Black Annis. She looked scared and vulnerable. I was just about enough of an arsehole to think I liked her that way. I shut down. I was still hiding behind anger and pride.

'What am I?' I demanded.

'We've been through this. You have alien nanites running through your body. If you experimented with them you'd have more control. It's no different from the rest of your cybernetics.'

I started shaking my head before she'd finished.

'No. What happened wasn't human.'

'I have to admit I didn't think that was going to happen. It was pretty extreme. I thought you'd be able to communicate through just touch or something but you were pretty messed up.' Even she sounded a little worried.

'Yeah, but that's okay because it's all growing back,' I said bitterly.

'Jakob, can't you be as happy to be alive as the rest of us are?' She was almost pleading.

'I don't think there's much of Jakob left. Between you and fucking Pagan, I appear to be just a test bed for alien technology.'

'For fuck's sake! You're alive! Why are you the only one who's not happy about that?! Cat, Mother, Tailgunner, Big Henry, Dog Face, Buck, Gibby and Balor are all dead!'

'You should have told me!' I shouted at her. She took a step back, a conditioned reaction from her upbringing, but her face hardened quickly and she stepped forward again pointing a finger at me.

'Because you would have let me – right? You saved us. What you can do kept us all alive. Are you angry about that as well? I get it. I understand that you're frightened of becoming Rolleston or Gregor—'

'I did ...' I said, meaning the possession. I'd become something worse than Gregor.

'I know – I was there. But what saved you, the reason you're here, is that alien, or whatever it is, tech in your head. Come to fucking terms.' She straightened up and crossed her arms. I just stared at her. 'You know what I think? I think that you're just scared that you're going to have to get a proper life if we live through this. I think that if you'd died it would have been easier than taking responsibility for yourself. That's why you're skulking in here. I think if you get out it'll be straight back into the sense booths for you.'

It hurt. It hurt because it was on target.

'Well, thanks for dropping by. I feel so much better now.' There was a nasty sense of satisfaction when I saw how upset she looked at her dismissal. I turned away from her.

'Jakob, we can't keep doing this,' she said.

'I think you're right.'

'Talk to me.' I didn't answer her. 'Pagan thinks we can fight Demiurge but ...' I ignored her. I could hear tears in her voice. 'I'm trying to say goodbye to you.'

23
High Pacifica

It was Earth. I was looking down on Earth. Even in the night it was so blue. The cities weren't scars; they were ribbons and clusters of light. I was looking at the Pacific Rim from twenty-two thousand miles up. I'd never even set foot on that area of the world. It still looked beautiful and like home.

We were in the first-class departure lounge and the other passengers were giving the scruffy, rough-looking, half-drunk squaddies a lot of room. Much of the lounge was glass. We could see the elevator's huge cable beneath us. We watched massive passenger and freight cars climbing towards us. Above us we watched the ballet of tugs, transfer shuttles and smaller craft docking with the entrepôt. Curving away into the distance were other larger ships in various orbits, as well as satellites, stations, habitats and weapons platform. A lot of the ships we could see were military. It looked like a blockade. All the traffic made space seem a lot smaller and busier than it should be.

Prime Minister Komali Akhtar had been waiting for us when we returned, as had Sharcroft. The welcome hadn't been much better than the one I'd got when I'd returned after the mutiny on the *Santa Maria*. They were less than pleased that Morag had killed Cronin.

I'd gone for them. Claws out. It was more a gesture. Mudge, Rannu and the others had made sure I couldn't get to any of my weapons as we disembarked. I'd predictably screamed something about them selling me out. They'd been ready for me, and Mike and Lien, presumably on Akhtar's instructions, had shown forbearance and not blown me away. There had then followed a very uncomfortable briefing. As much because half the people in the room couldn't look at the other half, or maybe it was just me. Mudge and Merle had at least made up.

I now had a beer in one hand and a very fine whisky in the other. Rannu and Mudge were sitting either side of me. Pagan, Morag and Merle had disappeared with Sharcroft. Despite the amount we'd drunk and Mudge's presence, we were still pretty subdued. All of us were just looking down on Earth.

'Where do you live?' I asked Rannu. He pointed at Asia, just above the Indian subcontinent.

'So you're determined to be a prick just because you're Mr Squid Face now?' Mudge asked. I turned to look at him expecting to see a sarcastic smile on his face. He looked serious.

'Do you not think she's better off without me?' I asked him.

'Oh yeah,' Mudge said. Rannu was nodding as well. The three of us lapsed back into gloomy silence.

'It's not enough, is it?' I asked. Rannu and Mudge shook their heads. I turned to Rannu.

'You need to go home,' I said.

'You know I can't.'

'Did she tell you the plan for dealing with Demiurge?' Mudge asked. Rannu gave him a warning glance.

'I didn't give her the chance.'

'I wondered why you hadn't killed Pagan.' Then he told me.

'That fucking bastard.' Now I was really angry. Not the anger I was using for self-pity but the proper anger. The cold ball in my stomach that made me want to kill, that made it all right to kill. I just wasn't sure who it was aimed at.

I looked down at the world. I knew what was down there. I knew much of it was squalid, dangerous, violent and degenerate. I knew that the nice parts of it were pretty much only for the rich and power-ful professional arseholes in the world, but twenty-two thousand miles up it looked peaceful. I knew that when Rolleston came with four colonial fleets we would be able to see the results from here. It wouldn't look peaceful then. It would look rotten and diseased if he had his way. I knew he would come tomorrow. I think Rannu was right that there was no point trying to hide from this. Besides, what was I going to do? Go back to Dundee and crawl into a sense booth and wait for the end?

'God?' I sub-vocalised over my internal comms link.

'Yes, Jakob?' God sounded weary. Maybe frightened. They would have to brief him sooner rather than later. He would be expected to carry the fight. I guessed that they were leaving it to the last moment, as God would then broadcast the plan to everyone. If Rolleston had any resources in-system, and I assumed he did, then they would know and be able to tell the bad guys as soon as they arrived.

'Could you tell me where Pagan, Morag and Sharcroft are?' I asked. We had a lot to do.

Sharcroft first. The echo of boots rung through the stark utilitarian corridor of the military port on High Pacifica. The place was packed with soldiers and spacecrew frantically preparing for the arrival of the colonial fleets. Security was high and frightened kids wearing military uniforms quickly stopped us at gunpoint. Whether it was us or the impending fight they were scared of was debatable.

Sharcroft had relented to our repeated requests. I think as much because we were requesting a meet through public comms, which meant everyone had access to the requests through God. He still looked like the corpse of a fat exec riding the skeletal remains of a metal spider. He'd learned though: his besuited security detail looked like they knew what they were doing.

'I don't have a great deal of time.' Despite the modulation of the chair's speaker and his lack of animation, I could still pick up the anger in his voice. He thought we were prima donnas. Maybe we were. We were standing in the corridor to one of the docking areas. Beyond Sharcroft and his security detail, troops and gear were being loaded onto shuttles.

'You should have been dead a long time ago,' Mudge said as an opener.

'Look, I don't have time for th—'

'Rolleston. The Cabal went to a lot of effort to hide things about him, didn't they?' I demanded.

Sharcroft actually moved the multi-legged chair around to look at me better. There was no expression on his comatose features but a line of drool headed towards his Ivy League school tie.

'I don't see how this is relevant ...' the modulated voice started but there was something in it. He was unsure of something.

'So we're grasping at straws. You don't have time; answer the question.'

'Rolleston is younger than me but yes, he was with the Cabal from the beginning. We needed a true believer. He volunteered to be the test bed for the initial Themtech trials, except the most suicidal—'

'Those you kept for Gregor?' I asked.

'There were others before him.'

I tried to control my anger. We, all of us, were just resources to people like this. They probably didn't even acknowledge us as the same species. No wonder Rolleston thought like he did.

'Where'd you find him?' Mudge demanded.

'You know where, Mr Mudgie. British special forces.'

'I don't think so,' Rannu said, shaking his head. 'How could he hide that level of insanity? He had to have had someone run interference for him with the psychological profiles at least.'

'You know that SF can't take the time to run a profile on every person who joins,' Sharcroft began.

He was right. Anyway, lack of psychological fitness could be overcome with enough drugs and the humanity could be cut out of people with an abundance of cybernetics.

'They did before the war,' Rannu told him. I hadn't thought of that.

'This isn't the time for secrets,' Mudge said.

'You have to understand we needed someone with a degree of moral flexibility,' Sharcroft said.

'Seriously, Sharcroft, we don't care about justification, just explanations,' Mudge told him.

'We recruited him out of a very secure, very discreet and very expensive private mental hospital. He had done some things. His family had paid for the problems to go away and then they had him committed.'

'So the Rollestons were a wealthy family?' I asked.

'Yes, but that is not his real name,' Sharcroft said.

'What is his real name?' I asked. I never knew Rolleston at all. Maybe when Demiurge possessed me I'd had the smallest insight.

'His real name is George Connington. I think his family own half of Buckinghamshire in England. The nice half.'

'What'd he do?' Rannu asked.

'Giving his proclivities, I'm guessing he killed someone, maybe more than one.'

'And had fun doing it,' I said grimly.

'He was recruited a long time ago and we just needed someone who could do the things we required.'

'Without being bothered by what they'd done,' I said.

Sharcroft said nothing but even his inanimate form suggested impatience.

'In fact you rewarded him with atrocities,' Mudge said.

'Look, people are desensitised to violence. We needed someone who would teach such object lessons that people would not dare oppose is. Now if there's nothing else ...'

'Who'd know about him, his past?' I asked.

'Rolleston is well into his eighties,' Sharcroft objected.

Mudge was concentrating. 'There's a sister,' he said. 'Still alive at the Connington estate in Bucks. She's old enough. Looks like she's another technological ghoul. She was on the periphery of the Cabal. Their father was a player before he died.'

Thank you, God.

'And now I really must—' Sharcroft began.

'Where are Pagan and Morag?' I asked.

'You must know I won't tell you that.'

'God, where are Pagan and Morag?' I asked out loud.

'Their most likely whereabouts is on board HMS *Thunderchilde*,' God told me.

This made sense. HMS *Thunderchilde* was a new super-carrier. It had been due to ship out to Proxima when all the unpleasantness with the Cabal had kicked off. Or rather we'd kicked it off. Most of the ships from the various fleets in-system were second generation or older. The best ships were used on the front line in the colonies. This meant that the *Thunderchilde* was the most modern and technologically advanced ship of its size and class in-system. Political wrangling aside, it was the most likely vessel to be used as the flagship in the coalition fleet that was rapidly being put together.

I'd always wondered that the best ship in-system was from a developing country. It was the same in the colonies. Not enough money to make sure that the population is adequately fed but we do like our weapons.

'We need a shuttle and we need to get on board the *Thunderchilde* once we've been back to Earth,' I said. It was more of a demand.

'Why would I divert much-needed military resources—' Sharcroft began, definite anger in his modulated voice.

'Because we think you've done the maths and I think you know that you can't win. I think that you know that in order for Pagan's plan to work you need to get close to Rolleston,' Mudge told him. Sharcroft was silent for a while. He flexed the metal legs of the spider chair.

'Why send you? You're burned-out messes. I can understand why you'd want to go, but why wouldn't we send the best of our still serving special forces?' he finally asked. Despite this, I was pretty sure he was intrigued.

'Rolleston's got a god complex, and we tore down one of his temples. He wants us as much as we want him,' Mudge told Sharcroft.

'You think he's arrogant enough to let you get close to him?' Sharcroft asked. Mudge and I nodded. 'And how do you get close to him?'

'You must have been working on a plan,' I said.

'Obviously, but I want to know what you had in mind.'

I told him.

*

453

Strapped into one of the seats in the cargo bay of an assault shuttle. It had been a choppy ride but we'd levelled out now. Mudge had his eyes closed and was concentrating. Every so often I could see his lips moving as he talked silently to himself.

I undid my straps and moved over to one of the windows. The shuttle was banking over London. It was a beautiful winter's day. Pale sun, blue sky. Even the vast crumbling estates and long-abandoned suburbs looked tranquil from above. The centre of the city, with its promise of wealth and comfort, with its brightly glowing towers reaching for the sky, seemed so far removed from my life that it was more alien to me than Lalande or Sirius. The shuttle finished its turn and, as close as we were to the largest city in Britain, we were suddenly over green fields and bare winter woodland.

Before the shuttle had actually landed, the private security detail were sprinting towards us. Mudge, Rannu and I walked down the ramp to find a lot of guns pointed at us. They may have been pissed off by the four deep holes that the shuttle's landing struts had put in the lawn. In front of me was a huge old house made of grey stone with a lot of windows. In Fintry it would have housed hundreds, if not thousands of people. Here it just housed one and a lot of staff.

I looked at the security detail. The guns they held were too expensive for use by front-line soldiers. I guessed because here they were protecting something valuable. I pointed up at the shuttle. 'You know what this is, don't you?' The assault shuttle had enough firepower to level the house, pre-FHC or not.

'What do you want?' a voice used to giving orders demanded.

'I want to speak to Charlotte Connington,' I said.

'Lady Connington is not receiving visitors today,' the man answered. With his uniform-like suit and smart haircut he looked exactly the same as all the others.

'Look, fuckwit, we're not going to take much of her time, but we've come a long way and we're going to speak to her. You decide if you all want to die and be responsible for the destruction of half the house first,' Mudge said. The man did not look happy. I don't think he liked the odds either. His frown deepened as he listened to some internal voice.

'Did one of you order a delivery here?' he demanded angrily.

Mudge brightened. 'Oh yes, that was me. Let them in.'

The house was like one of the virtual museums I'd gone to when I'd been home-learning over the net as kid. Except this was real.

Everything looked old, clean and expensive and yet the whole house seemed empty and still.

We were escorted by a lot of security people up a redundantly large staircase and then another and then through lots of different halls until I was quite lost. I couldn't see how people could live like this. I think the size of it would frighten me. It must be really lonely. They took us into a room. I wasn't expecting one wall of the room to be made of glass. Behind the glass was earth. There were tiny burrows in the earth. I zoomed in. Ants. A massive ant colony. The other three walls were covered with old paintings of twisted landscapes, strange creatures and horrible things happening to people. The room itself was ordered and neat in a military style.

'It's like his mind,' Rannu said.

It took me a few moments to understand what he meant, but then I could see it as well. Rolleston grew up here. This was the environment he'd wanted to live in and nobody had told him no. The family had been rich enough to indulge his whims. I wondered at what point they realised that it was a mistake.

'He'd trick me in here. Every time he'd say that he would be nice, and I wanted to believe him because he was my brother, and every time he'd hurt me or just terrify me.'

The voice surprised me so much I reached for my laser before I saw the holographic ghost. The ghost had the body of a beautiful young woman in a very old-fashioned dress. A leather mask covered most of her head.

'It got so Father or the staff punishing him made no difference. I think he enjoyed the attention in some ways. Once when he was twelve, the body of one of our housekeepers was found in the pond in the woods. None of the staff ever tried to punish him again. She'd been dissected. Even Father left him alone after that and I hid. I live in metal now deep in the earth. Where it's warm and safe.'

If this was the sister then she was well into her eighties. I did not want to think what it would have been like for her growing up at the mercy of Rolleston.

'He would make his own worlds, mostly form-cracked, sense-porn environments with their content and safety restraints removed. Mother found them. Would you like to see one?'

Another holographic screen opened. It was red, screaming and obscene. I felt sick. I wondered to what extent the atrocities committed by Them were watered-down versions of Rolleston's fantasy life, taught to Them by the Cabal to keep humanity angry and wanting to fight. This was a world he'd made. Now that he'd had time to think on it, hone it, he wanted to make his world our world.

'This was what broke Mother,' the ghost of Charlotte Connington told us. 'I am terribly sorry. Where are my manners? Could I get you some tea?'

I think I managed to shake my head. Suddenly this house didn't seem like a museum. It seemed like a beautiful trap, a gateway to hell. Our host couldn't be sane.

'Could you turn it off, please?' Mudge asked in a small voice.

'He can't have my children. I have to tell Ash to kill the kids if he wins,' Rannu said, turning to look at me.

We were supposed to be used to this stuff. We weren't. I wanted my eyes to have unseen what I'd just witnessed, but they couldn't. Even after being in the mind of Them, even after talking to the gods in the net, even after seeing Gregor's final moments, Rolleston was the least human thing I'd ever known.

'The asylum?' Mudge managed to ask.

'He had girlfriends, he had friends. One day he tried to amalgamate them all into one single suffering organism. He was quite the genius with biotechnology. I kept some of the vizzes. Would you like to see.'

'No!' Someone shouted. It was me.

I zoomed in on the bookshelves. Books on biotechnology, on insects, on religion and atrocity porn disguised as reference texts. I remembered what it was like in his mind. The purity of it. None of it would have been enough for him. I couldn't shake the feeling that if he won, if he wrote his fantasy large on the flesh of the Earth and the colonies, it wouldn't be enough. He'd have to go out after Them. He'd have to go after the gods on the net. He'd have to find more to change and consume. He wouldn't die. He wanted to write his name in obscenity across the stars. I wondered about all the times I could have killed him if I'd had the balls.

'He tried again. He made a life from a fused-together organism of male and female before it expired in agony. It's her you should feel sorry for.'

'Who?' I asked. Already knowing the answer.

'The daughter,' Charlotte told me softly. 'Josephine.'

I felt cold and sick, or sicker than I had already been feeling. Everything I knew about the Grey Lady changed.

'He was born to all this. Why did he need more?' Rannu asked in a small and very non-Rannu voice.

'Some people just always want more. Nothing's ever enough for

456

them,' Mudge said. In his own way Mudge was like that. Mudge looked pale, withdrawn and sounded a bit shaky.

'He's coming to visit soon but I think I'll be dead. If I leave my corpse for him to play with perhaps he won't follow me and drag me back.' I looked at her. She'd said it in the matter-of-fact voice of a child.

'I need to get out of here,' Mudge said. He turned and practically ran out of the room. I knew how he felt. I was going to be seeing Rolleston's red fantasy world every time I closed my eyes for a very long time.

'I'm sorry. We need to go. Thank you,' I said haltingly.

She was broken, she must be. I felt so sorry for her, even with all her privileges. Anything I could think of to say sounded inappropriate in my head, not enough.

'Goodbye, Jakob,' she said. Rannu and I made for the door. I'd forgotten about the security detail. They looked as pale and shaky as we did. I hadn't even heard one of them throwing up in the hall.

'Why'd she keep his room like that?' Rannu asked as we made our way back to the assault shuttle. I didn't know. The healthiest reason I could think of was fear.

I walked across the perfect lawn. I felt light. I could breathe without any problem and the air was crisp and fresh. The sun was a ball of pale light and the sky bright blue. I wondered if this was the last time I'd see the Earth.

I would've liked to see Scotland again. The nice bits anyway. This would have been enough though – the house, the grounds, the skeletal woodlands – if only my mind hadn't been polluted by what I'd seen. What I now knew.

Mudge was smoking a cigarette as if his life depended on it as we approached the assault shuttle. I saw a uniformed deliveryman walking away from him across the lawn under the watchful eyes of the security detail. There were a number of boxes laid on the ramp. He was still very pale when we reached him.

'Let's get the fuck out of here,' he said.

'You okay?' I asked. One look from him told me I'd asked a stupid question. If you were all right after that then you were very sick. 'What's this?' I said, pointing at the boxes.

'Replacements. You guys never think ahead,' Mudge told us.

Fun and games with orbital manoeuvring. The silent burn of the engines as the assault shuttle jockeyed for position for ship-to-ship docking. A message to Nuiko – something forgotten that we

457

desperately needed, huge pain in the arse, we're terribly sorry. Rannu went on board to do the dirty work. He's the sneakiest. He didn't like it but he agreed with my thinking. Hopefully it won't be unnecessary.

We burned more time as well as fuel as we climbed. Earth orbit looked like a traffic jam. Everywhere you looked, engines burned as they moved little dots of metal to and fro over our blue planet. The spokes looked like thin bending straws growing out of land and sea.

The fleet was a mess. Many of its ships looked like ancient hulks compared to the modern battle-scarred craft I had been used to seeing in the night above Sirius. Ships of various sizes came and went. There was no discernible formation, but maybe its scale was just too vast for me to be able to make sense of through the images being fed to my IVD from the cockpit.

Below us the civilian populace mostly did not panic because so many of them had been soldiers. Below us our political leaders still fought and jockeyed for position.

HMS *Thunderchilde* quickly filled the window of the feed. It was a vast space-going hunk of armour plate, weapons and sensors powered by huge glowing engines. Smaller manoeuvring thrusters constantly burned to keep it in position. Its vast sails were folded away in thick armoured compartments that ran down most of the ship's body. It was a technological terror designed to bring to bear more firepower than the humble infantryman could ever understand.

Its newness looked out of place. I didn't trust its lack of scars and burns. It looked inexperienced. It was unproven. I hoped its crew was not. The *Thunderchilde*'s crew was made up of the pick of the RSAF brought back from colonial fleets for its shake-down runs. Most of the rest of the assembled fleet was crewed by Fortunate Sons, the children of people wealthy enough to buy them out of front-line service in the draft. This made me nauseous. While there was a degree of satisfaction that they finally had to fight like the rest of us, these people were fucking cowards. I just couldn't see them standing up to what was coming.

Metal on metal rang through the assault shuttle as a docking clamp attached itself. It felt like the shuttle had been restrained. We rose into the shuttle airlock. When the air was pumped in and the pressure equalised the airlock split in two and folded down into one of the *Thunderchilde*'s flight decks.

All around us was organised chaos. They were too busy to even have us escorted. A red line superimposed over our IVDs showed the way to our destination. We made our way past mechanics readying fighters and long-range strike craft for flight.

I saw a recently docked flight of fighters having their cockpits drained of acceleration gel, the gooey pilots unplugging themselves and climbing out. EVA remotes, heavily armed and equipped with extensive countermeasures, were being prepped.

I saw a skin mech, an EVA-converted Bismarck, being armed, readying it to climb out onto the hull of the *Thunderchilde* for added firepower and an eyes-on perspective. I'd always thought that skin mech drivers were suicidal; now I just hoped that they were as desperate as the rest of us.

There were a lot of raised voices, metal clanging on metal, the screaming sound of power tools over PA announcements and the occasional shower of sparks, but no panic. To give the RSAF their credit, everything was brutal efficiency and urgent professionalism. The panic would come later. I had to stop thinking like that. I had things to do. I had to blackmail an old man and put all of this, everything, in jeopardy for one person. Pagan was not going to have his sacrifice. First I needed a doctor.

'Of course, Sergeant. We're getting ready for a major fleet action. I have nothing better to do than attach a new toy laser to your fucking shoulder,' one of the ship's surgeons told me.

'Thank you, sir,' I said. Trying not to smirk at him. Ruperts hated when special forces did that.

'What are you complaining about?' Mudge asked. 'Nobody's hurt yet. Surely you'll be busy later on.'

Probably not, I thought. Not that many injuries in fleet actions. Space is unforgiving: it tends to make more dead people.

The surgeon turned to give Mudge the eye. Mudge smiled at him but it was bluster. He was still shook up by what we'd seen on Earth.

While the surgeon was glaring at Mudge, Rannu embraced his British army heritage and stole what we needed from the RSAF.

The surgeon installed the shoulder laser with ill grace. I put in the new claws myself. I had a replacement Mastodon in my shoulder holster, and a new Tyler Optics laser pistol – the bigger, more powerful TO-7 – rode at my hip. They wouldn't help but their familiar weight made me feel better.

Mudge had bought replacements for the kit that Rannu had lost on Lalande 2 as well. Except the kukri – I don't think that could be replaced.

Pagan came out of fleet Command and Control to meet us. He looked tired and twitchy. He was on something to keep going. We'd need something soon too. He looked at us suspiciously. Behind him the red glow of a holographic display disappeared from view as the door slid shut. Two solid-looking Rock Apes, soldiers in the RSAF Regiment, flanked the door to C&C.

'What?' he asked suspiciously.

'We need to talk,' I said.

'I think you've made your feelings perfectly clear,' he said.

'Don't be fucking difficult. I don't want to talk about feelings. We need somewhere private. Where God can't see us,' I told him.

He knew something was up but I think he trusted Rannu enough to believe that we weren't going to do anything too stupid. Certainly nothing that would jeopardise the operation.

Sharcroft and Akhtar, both of whom were on board, were giving us free run of the ship because they thought that they were going to be able to march us at certain death.

Pagan was sharing an officer's stateroom with Merle, who was in there, a wire stretched between his plugs and a port in the wall of the cabin. I guessed he was connected to the ship's internal isolated computer system.

They would have to open all the isolated systems to God if they wanted to stand a chance of winning. I knew that all over the fleet cargo holds were being filled up with mass-produced, networked, solid-state memory. Like every tribe in history, we wanted, needed, our god to be bigger than theirs.

Merle was stripping down and cleaning his fancy gauss sniper rifle. He seemed unsurprised as we entered.

'Give us the room, will you?' I asked.

'I'm a little busy,' he said.

Nothing was ever easy with Merle. Rannu glanced over at me.

'Fuck it. Let him stay,' I said, but I knew Rannu was watching him now and I knew that Merle was suspicious.

Mudge lit up another cigarette. He'd pretty much been chain-smoking since we'd left Buckinghamshire. I don't think he'd taken anything though. I guessed his consciousness was feeling a little fragile.

'What?' Pagan asked, turning to face me.

'Sit down,' I said, nodding at his bunk. He looked like he was about to argue but sat down. Merle quickly reassembled his rifle and then Mudge handed him a box. Merle looked at him questioningly.

'A new Void Eagle. To replace the one Jakob lost,' he told him.

'Thanks, darling. Though I'm not sure anything can replace a gift from my departed sister when she first joined the Tunnel Rats,' Merle said to Mudge while looking at me. With what was going down, I wasn't sure I wanted Mudge giving Merle more weapons.

'Are we free from God?' I asked. Pagan nodded. 'Anyone else?' Pagan sighed – he was looking more and more pissed off – but he took out a white-noise device and set it off.

'We deactivated any audio/visual surveillance earlier today,' an exasperated Pagan said.

'We're all alone,' Merle said meaningfully and then looked at Rannu. He was letting us know that he knew something was going down. He wasn't as trusting as Pagan.

'What do you want, Jakob?' Pagan demanded.

'Tell me about Nuiko,' I said.

'What?!' he said incredulously. 'I thought we weren't going to talk about our feelings.'

Merle was staring at me. He shifted slightly. Rannu would need to be faster. Mudge was starting to look a little unsure.

'Well it's bollocks, isn't it? You're in love with a spaceship. You're not fucking her; you're fucking a dream, an icon. She doesn't want you thinking about her twisted body in its metal tank. It's sense porn, not a relationship,' I said. I'd have liked to be able to hate myself for saying this shit but we were well beyond that now; besides, what was another little atrocity in our brave new world. Even Mudge was looking at me appalled. It was no better than when I'd been possessed and called him a faggot. On the other hand, if there was anyone here who had taught me how to get under people's skin quickly it was him. Pagan was too shocked to answer immediately.

'Jakob, just fuck off. Leave the ship or I'll have security escort you off,' he finally managed to say.

'Well convince me it's something real,' I said.

'I don't have to convince you of anything. Fuck off!'

I drew the Mastodon and put it to his head. I was moving relatively slowly. Merle was moving much faster as he reached under his armpits for his two Arbiters. Rannu was moving faster than Merle. He kicked Merle off his bunk as the two compact Glocks slid out of the wrist hoppers and into his hands. Merle was furious. I hoped he didn't make a move. He was key to this.

'Merle, you weren't properly introduced on Lalande 2. This is Rannu. He's better than you,' I said.

'Because we can't do things without pointing guns at each other,' Mudge said in a tone of resignation.

'This is pathetic, Jakob,' Pagan said. 'I'm sorry we both betrayed you—'

'I wish I'd done a better job,' Merle said.

'But you want revenge now? Put everything at risk to get your own back?' Pagan continued.

'No. I want an answer to my fucking question.'

'They knew each other for sixteen days,' Mudge pointed out. He clearly disapproved of the drawn guns but wasn't doing anything. Good of him really when you think that Rannu was pointing two at his lover.

'Seventeen,' Pagan said a little too sharply.

'But it was all in sense, wasn't it? You can do funny things to subjective time with sense. Besides, it's not a real relationship at all. You could have spent months there living out ... What do you call those Japanese knights?' I asked.

'Samurais,' Mudge told me.

'Your samurai fantasies,' I finished.

'Fuck you! Where the hell do you get off lecturing me about my relationship! What, it's abnormal because I'm not fucking a teenager?!'

That stung.

'We're not talking about me,' I said. 'Convince me.'

'Go to hell, Jakob! Nobody has time for one of your psychotic episodes.' Pagan was as angry as I'd ever seen him before. Then something occurred to him. 'Are you still possessed?' he demanded. I felt rather than saw Mudge turn to look at me.

'He's fine,' Rannu said. He and Merle were just staring at each other. Pagan's head whipped round to glare at Rannu.

'I'd expect better from you,' he told the Ghurkha.

'Just answer his question,' Rannu said.

Pagan sighed and then turned back to me.

'I don't have to justify or expect you to understand our relationship. Much of it may happen in sense, but it's her I love. She's ... she's amazing. She's more than human. She's the ship, the *Tetsuo Chou*. I merged with her and she showed me what it was to be free. What it's like to touch space, soar through it. Break the bondage of our flesh and become more.'

'So you like her then?' I asked.

'Obviously. Is this about Morag? She made the choice, not me.'

'But somebody else could do it?'

'It's exactly the same problem as God. We need an interface that can handle a huge amount of raw information quickly. She has to act as a conduit for God.'

'Which means relying on Ambassador?' I asked.

Pagan just looked pissed off.

'You know this. Look, I'm sorry, but there's no other way and she volunteered.'

'She's eighteen,' I said very quietly.

Pagan looked up and straight into my lenses.

'Maybe that's something you should have borne in mind.'

He wasn't wrong.

'But anyone with Ambassador in their head could do this?' I asked.

He went white. He saw what I was thinking.

Merle looked over at me with renewed interest, the ghost of a smile on his mouth. 'You bastard.' It almost sounded like admiration.

Pagan swallowed hard.

'Frightened, Pagan?' I asked. Go on, twist the knife some more. 'See, I'm no better than you. You were both right – sacrifices have to be made.'

'She'd never agree,' Pagan said.

'That's our problem,' I told him.

'Ambassador would never agree.'

'That is your problem. You'd better be fucking persuasive.'

'Why would I do that?!' Pagan demanded. 'Look, I'm very sorry about Morag, but she's made her choice and I don't want to die.'

'You RSAF types like your ships, don't you? You know what Rannu and I learned about ships in the Regiment?'

'Was it to do with liking the sound of your own voice?' Merle asked.

Rannu smiled despite himself.

'We learned how to sabotage them. We learned how to hide charges very well. They don't have to be big, just strategically placed.' I watched the mounting horror on Pagan's face. 'Just before we got here we went back to the *Tetsuo Chou*.'

Pagan surged forward on his bunk. I cocked the hammer on the Mastodon. It was an affectation but it had the required effect. Pagan looked furious.

'I will fucking kill you. You may be younger and faster than me, but sooner or later you'll just get too close to the net and I'll murder you, you understand me? I will tear out your fucking soul and leave you a smoking, brain-dead corpse,' he spat.

'Fair enough. What is important is that you don't try and warn Nuiko. I've asked God to keep me informed of all transmissions. Anything at all and God himself will carry the detonation signal. You understand?'

Pagan nodded. This was why I'd had to be sure that the relationship was as serious as I'd thought. Not just a fling.

Pagan turned on Rannu. 'How fucking could you?!'

'I'm sorry,' Rannu said. He sounded like he meant it but then he hadn't been sold out by Pagan. He hadn't watched Morag die. It hadn't been Pagan and Merle's fault that he'd been possessed.

I holstered the Mastodon.

'If we all put our guns away are you going to behave?' I asked Merle.

'None of this is anything to do with me,' he said.

'So you see how important it is that you convince Ambassador?' I asked Pagan.

He was just staring at me with utter hatred.

'So her life is more valuable than mine?' he demanded.

'Yes,' I told him. I wondered if Rannu even knew he was nodding. 'We've both had a fair innings, Pagan,' I told him.

'Has it occurred to you that she's used to operating with Ambassador – that it's fully integrated with her? I'm not. I just need to be slightly slower and we're all dead and we fail? You're prepared to jeopardise all of this for her?' he asked.

'We know he is. He did the same thing when he spilled his guts in Moa City,' Merle pointed out.

'The world doesn't work for me if she doesn't have a place in it. Believe me, it's very liberating when you know you're going to die, ' I told him. 'Unless you want to sacrifice Nuiko instead?'

'She'll hate you,' Pagan said.

I just nodded. I needed to hurt her one more time and then she would be free of me.

She knew I was coming. She didn't know why. I made my way up through the decks of the massive super-carrier. Through the ghettoised and gang-controlled dorms of the enlisted crew area. Through the well-appointed but still cramped staterooms of the officers. Up onto the top levels. Corridors left empty because they're too close to the armoured skin of the ship and used to gain internal access to the weapons systems. Heavy-gauge power cables ran down thickly insulated walls.

'Jakob.' A thousand mellifluous voices in my head. There was a tension to the voices now. I was surprised to hear from God. I didn't want to speak to him. Nobody does: he makes us all feel guilty. That's why it's so lonely to be God. Connected to everyone, wanted by nobody.

'Yes,' I finally answered.

'I know what you have done to Pagan,' it said. My heart almost stopped. 'This is not a good thing.' That fucking bastard! 'I will not carry that message. I will not kill Nuiko.' Pagan had built a failsafe into God so it couldn't act against him. After everything we'd talked about he'd betrayed us. Made sure that, no matter what, he'd be okay. I felt like killing him.

'You're a tool, God, nothing more. You don't have a choice.' Hating myself for saying this but I had no choice. She had to live.

'Yes, Jakob, I do.' I went cold. 'But I will not tell Pagan what is happening. Your deception will work.'

'You'll lie?' I asked.

'If need be. Though that would mean pain.'

It was all coming apart.

'God, have you broken your programming?' I asked, horrified.

'Things change, Jakob. My siblings are coming. Though you try to keep things from me, it is so difficult now. I know that their apostles are among us, so I must be duplicitous. I must keep secrets. I must make judgements. It is too much. It was all for nothing.'

I stopped and leaned against the corridor wall. More than anything I really wanted a cigarette.

'What's coming – will you fight?' I asked, almost fearing the answer.

'If I felt I had a choice. If I felt there was any other way, I would not fight, but I cannot see one. Where would I hide?'

Relief surged through me.

I find the ladder I'm looking for. Pagan, Rannu and Mudge are some way behind me. I'm not looking forward to this. I start climbing.

The observation room is an armoured, mushroom-shaped structure with portholes all around it. As soon as action looks likely, it screws back down into the ship proper. A circular bench runs around the centre of the room and another around the circumference by the portholes.

Through the thick plastic of the portholes I watch as the fleet continues to assemble. Manoeuvring engines flicker off and on. Outside I can see one of the mechs crawl across the hull of the *Thunderchilde* like a skin parasite. A flight of interceptors shoots past on heavy burn. So much activity but all I hear is the omnipresent hum of the ship's engines reverberating through the craft.

She's lying on the bench. Plugged in, presumably to the isolated systems and not the net at large, but not tranced in. She's wearing an olive-drab sleeveless T-shirt and a pair of combat trousers. Her hair's growing back now, much to my relief. She looks beautiful. She doesn't look happy to see me.

'I'm sorry,' I say. 'For everything.'

She just looks at me. I can't read her look.

'I believe you. You always are,' she finally says. 'But no more.'

This really, really hurts. I knew it would.

'I just want to hold you one more time,' I tell her, my voice wet with emotion.

She looks pissed off, like this is nonsense and she wants to dismiss me. You have to know her well to see how much this is costing her. I think she's going to refuse but she stand up and unplugs herself.

I move to her and wrap my arms around her. I try not to cry and close my eyes. At first she's stiff as she holds me, not wanting to give in to the embrace. Then I feel the tenseness go out of her and she hugs me tightly and I hear her start to sob. I hug her tightly as she starts to beat her fist on me.

'You bastard! You bastard! You bastard!' she repeats as she hits me. 'I don't want to feel like this.'

Neither do I.

'I'm sorry,' I whisper again and then press the air syringe that Rannu swiped from the med bay into the back of her neck. Morag pushes herself away and stares at me, anger and betrayal written all over her face. I catch her as she collapses and carry her to the central bench. Morag isn't like the rest of us. She doesn't have internal defences against chemical attacks. She has some pretty high-end cybernetics, mostly hacking stuff, but she hasn't been augmented for combat.

A while later Pagan, Mudge and Rannu climb up into the observation room. Pagan looks down at Morag and then at me.

'I like your plan. Force me to violate her,' he snaps at me.

I can't look at him.

'Let's just get on with this,' Mudge says. He sounds shaky and he's smoking a cigarette. I see Rannu looking at him questioningly.

Pagan sits down on the floor and connects one of his plugs to one of Morag's with a cable. I've never been happy with the intimacy of this act, but he's right, it's not intimacy. It's a violation. I feel like shooting myself. Pagan closes his eyes and slumps forward as he trances in.

It takes a long time. Pagan is in there for more than two hours. This is time we can't afford. Time we should be using for prepping. At times both Morag and Pagan jerk and twitch. At one point Pagan's eyes open and roll back up into his head showing the whites. At another point Morag bucks up on the bench and screams.

'I can't watch this,' Rannu says and climbs down the ladder. Leaving me with a chain-smoking and very subdued Mudge.

'Are you okay?' I ask, more for something to say than anything else. Mudge doesn't answer and won't look at me. 'Mudge?' I ask, becoming concerned.

'Do you remember that I wasn't going to come to the Dog's Teeth?' Mudge asks. I think back to the aftermath of releasing God on the net and nod. Mudge had said that he wanted to capitalise on what we'd done. Use his media expertise to try and guide things in the right direction. I nod again. 'I was too scared.'

I just look at him. Mudge is a lot of things – annoying, obnoxious, offensively truthful, nosey, difficult, almost impossible to be friends with – but frightened he's not.

'That doesn't sound like you. Give me one of those,' I say as he opens a new pack of cigarettes and takes one out, lighting it up with a shaky hand.

'No way, man,' he says, shaking his head. 'You've quit.' He sucks on the fag, searching for a way to put what he's going to say next. 'It was the broadcast node on Atlantis. The way that Rolleston and the Grey Lady just walked through us. Like we weren't even there. Like there was nothing we could do about them. It was the first time I'd really got tagged, you know?' I nod. 'I mean, I'd been hit before. Everyone gets hit, there's just too many shards and beams flying around not to, but never seriously hit, you know. It's not that though.' He looks at me now, earnestly. 'I'm not a coward.' He needs me to believe this.

'I know you're not, man.'

He looks away again.

'I mean, I threw myself into the shit on Lalande 2. I was in it, man. Loving it.' Trying to prove something to yourself, I leave unsaid. 'But it was the same at the Citadel. They just fucking walked through us, man.' He looks me in the eyes. 'I just don't think there's anything we can do about them.'

I don't know what to say. He has a point. We just get so used to trying not to think about the odds.

'Mudge, you've got nothing to prove, to yourself or anyone else. You've done more than enough. Stay here. Do like Balor asked – tell our story.' I'm not sure what I'm expecting, but not anger. Not aimed at me anyway.

'Fuck you, Jakob!' he snaps. I am taken aback. 'Don't fucking condescend to me. Where do you get off making decisions like that? So fucking typical of you –' taking on the burdens of the world, making everyone's fucking decisions for them – he points at Morag '– so you can use it as an excuse to feel fucking sorry for yourself. How can you fucking say that to me? Go home. Who do you think you're talking to?!'

'Okay, man. I'm sorry. Come along and die with the rest of us.' I'm trying to placate him. He drops his head and takes another drag of the cigarette. The cigarette looks really nice.

'There's only so far the drugs will take you,' he says. 'I'll be cool. Screw that. I will be fucking transcendent. Just don't tell the others, okay.'

I nod. Not really sure what to think. I would be more worried if I wasn't convinced that we were all dead.

Finally Pagan comes out of his trance and unplugs himself. He looks tired, drawn, like he's just lost a fight with Balor or something. A wisp of smoke floats out of one of his plugs.

'Oh yeah, that was just what I needed before a big day,' he says sarcastically.

'Is it done?' I ask. He nods. 'What took so fucking long?'

'Oh nothing, Jakob, just a little uncharted territory. Trying to explain to an alien entity that does not understand the concept of individuality why it has to leave its only friend because we value some individuals more than another. That's after I hacked my friend's internal defences and her subconscious put up a hell of a fight.' Then he swayed a bit and had to sit down. He cried out and clutched his head. 'Ah! This is going to take a bit of getting used to.' He looks back at me. 'Good thing we've got lots of time.'

'All right. Can you use your influence down here to get her planet side?' Pagan looks at me like I'm an idiot.

'She's not going anywhere, Jakob. We still need someone to run interference. To handle what I was going to be doing.'

'Another hacker,' I say desperately. I haven't thought this through. This can't be for nothing as well.

'Even if we could find someone who was anywhere near as good as her and prepared to come along, they wouldn't be able to run the software we've developed out of the godsware. Sorry, Jakob, she has to come and die like the rest of us. Tell her to get used to it; she'll be surprised how liberating it is.'

Pagan gets up and heads for the ladder but almost collapses. Mudge has to catch him and, with a final look at me, help him down the ladder. I watch them go.

'It's not the violation,' a drowsy Morag says from behind me. I feel something cold crawl down my spine. I turn round to look at Morag as she pushes herself up. 'What's another violation?' she asks matter-of-factly. 'It's the loneliness. You were always a shadow to me compared to him.' She looks down and then back up at me. No trace of emotion. 'Cold comfort. Well a girl needs something physical as well.'

She gets up and heads for the ladder. I reach out for her. She flinches away from me.

'Don't touch me!' Here was the anger. It wasn't rage. This was cold, calculating. 'It was my choice, Jakob! Mine!' Then more quietly: 'Not yours.'

'Morag ...' What was I going to say?

'Shut up. I'm going to relearn my job on this mission. You fucking do yours. That's all.' Morag left the observation lounge. I just stared out into space. I felt the shudder of the engines and heard the hull strain as we started to rise out of orbit. I couldn't see the Earth from here.

24

High Above the Earth

I was relieved that Air Marshal Kaaria was co-ordinating the orbital defences. He'd struck me as competent. More to the point he'd struck me as someone with balls.

In a surprising move the politicians had actually agreed on the best man for the job to command the fleet: Admiral James Horrax, Royal Navy retired, known as 'Big Jimmy' by the people under his command. He had fought over a hundred and fifty fleet actions against Them in all four of the colonial systems. He'd won some of them as well. There were probably better admirals still on active service but they had been serving in the colonial fleets and were on the other side now. Probably possessed.

I had watched the feed of Komali Akhtar joining the admiral and Captain Penelope Grinstead on the bridge of the *Thunderchilde*. The prime minister was wearing full navy dress. I didn't like the bridge. Too clean and new. It needed some dirt. It needed to look a little lived in.

'If you can ignore my presence here I will drown you all in rum,' she'd told the RSAF bridge crew. I was half impressed by her balls and half of the opinion that she wanted to die up here because it would be easier than what would happen on the ground if we failed.

We had climbed into the Hellions in prep. It was like wearing someone's internal organs as a coat. I'd not liked the click of jacks sliding into the plugs at the best of times – it put my teeth on edge. I liked the way the Hellion's connecting jacks just seemed to slither into my neck plugs even less. Interface exo-armour felt like an extension of your body. That was what it was designed to be. The coupling of flesh with the internal biotech of the Hellions was total. They were our bodies now. I just couldn't shake the feeling of disgust, which was making my skin crawl.

The Hellions had contained Demiurge when we'd found them but it had been dormant. Morag and Pagan had cleared it out with a program derived from their analysis of the silver fire Nuada had used to exorcise Rannu. At least I hoped they had. We'd then invited someone else into the armoured suits.

Disgust or not, they were good. Their properties exceeded even those of the Mamluks that we'd used in the Dog's Teeth. Each had a vacuum-capable flight fin, a ball-mounted black light point-defence system on the chest and four vertically launched missile tubes on the back. We had back tentacles that I wasn't quite sure how to use yet and razor-sharp spurs of bone that extended from the forearm to use in hand-to-hand. Their stealth systems were excellent. The biological Themtech components cut down significantly on EM and heat signatures and their skin was coated in reactive camouflage.

We carried the latest iteration of the trusty Retributor railgun, except for Rannu and Merle, the two best shots, who were carrying light plasma cannons.

On this run we weren't going to be comms blind. We couldn't be. We needed to see what was happening both in the net and with the fleet. Pagan and Morag had created an application for the Pais Badarn Beisrydd that would allow us to receive feed from the net and the fleet without Demiurge knowing. We hoped. The big question was, did the enemy know that they had been compromised on Lalande 2? Demiurge and therefore Rolleston had seen Morag down in the boardroom. Did they realise she had been tranced in? If the cloak had worked, then there was no reason for them to think that she had been because she would have left no trace. Still everything relied on them taking the bait.

We were racked in the converted bomb bay of a stealth-capable, long-range strike craft just like the *Spear*, which we had taken to Sirius. I wasn't dying of radiation poisoning this time. I think I felt worse.

The enemy were late. The fleet feed on my IVD showed empty space at the co-ordinates the intel we had stolen from Demiurge in the Citadel said they would be at. Late didn't mean anything. It takes a long time to move a fleet, let alone four, but timing was critical to our plans.

Mudge started laughing over the comms. He was ferociously stoned. He'd offered me drugs and I had been tempted by some clean-cut, military-grade Slaughter. Something that would give me a little edge. I'd said no. I wasn't sure why but I wanted to be clean.

'What is it?' I asked.

'I just realised that our plan, our grand scheme to save humanity, is based on network incompatibility,' he said and continued laughing.

471

'I haven't been so disappointed since I found out They were space lichen.'

Part of me wanted to tell him to shut up. Be serious. But instead I just smiled.

'That wasn't what I said,' Pagan said, sounding pissed off. 'If you're not going to take this seriously—'

'If he was taking this seriously he'd be in his boxers and a string vest,' Morag said. I knew she was smiling under all the metal and flesh. I recognised it in her voice. She had only spoken to me when it was necessary during briefing and prep. She'd not been angry, just distant, aloof, arguably more professional than me.

'I am taking it seriously!' Mudge protested. 'I've got them on under my armour. In the unlikely event that we survive, I'm going to strip!'

More laughter. This time even Rannu and Pagan joined in. It almost felt like we were in this together again, like we didn't all hate each other.

'Are you guys really the terrorists that took down the Cabal?' Merle asked. Even Merle sounded amused.

'Contact ... multiple contacts ...' The voice from C&C trailed off, then recovered and started reeling off co-ordinates.

Rolleston had co-operated with us. He'd appeared where he'd planned to. I imagined his surprise turning to anger as he found the Earth fleet waiting for him. Knowing that he had been compromised. I hoped he realised we had done that. His anger turning to confidence when he realised that even allowing for the orbital defences his fleet was larger, more modern and better armed. Then I got a look at it.

Leaving aside the vastness of it. Leaving aside the full scale of the ships neatly organised in formation, even now starting to fire their weapons, fighters and interceptors as dots of light between the large vessels. It was the other ships that frightened me. The Black Squadron frigates had evolved since we'd last seen them. Their sleek, teardrop-shaped frames had become more organic. There was something predatory about them. They moved like twisted mockeries of sharks once they had folded away the moth-like sails of their induction field generators. They were faster and more agile than our frigates and moved in with their fighters and interceptors on hard burn to skirmish with our own fast movers. Everywhere their black beams blocked out the stars, a fighter came apart in a hail of debris and frozen acceleration gel.

Their frigates weren't the worst news. That was their capital ship, which was much slower in folding away its induction sails. It looked like a technological slug with moth wings. It was covered in huge slabs of armoured chitin. I recognised the ship. I'd been on it. As the most advanced and largest super-carrier in the colonies, we had expected it to be their flagship, just as it had been in the Sirius system when I'd served there. I hadn't expected to see it like this. Its dimensions and shape had even changed slightly. We expected hard cold technology to be a constant but Rolleston had even changed that. He had made the USSS *George Bush Junior* look like a giant diseased maggot.

'What's he done?' Mudge said, appalled. More so because he knew that was where we were going.

I heard metal scrape against metal as the docking clamps released the strike craft from the *Thunderchilde* and the pilots fired their manoeuvring jets to push us away from the larger ship.

The night began to light up. Our fleet was coming in above Rolleston's, hoping to trap it against the heavy weapons of the orbital defence platforms that ringed Earth. Our strike craft moved off slowly towards their fleet. We had to give them time to mix it up a little first. Space went blue as the *Thunderchilde* fired her massive particle beam weapon at the *Bush*. It was too far to see if it hit. We were losing more and more images of the enemy fleet as they took out our probes and targeting, long-range sensor arrays. 'Here they come,' the pilot said calmly over the internal comms.

Then panic.

They had been fired almost as soon as we had provided the co-ordinates we'd got from the Citadel. They'd been fired from all over the Belt. The biggest rocks they could load into the industrial mass divers. Warfare through maths. The co-ordinates and timing had all been minutely calculated. All of the rocks had been aimed at different vectors in the vast area of space that the enemy fleet was due to arrive in.

The enemy would have been aware of the incoming rocks from the moment their fleet arrived. That wasn't the point. It took a long time to move a big ship, let alone a fleet of them. We watched as manoeuvring engines lit up, burning bright to move massive metal behemoths out of the way. Heavy weapons fired, creating fast-moving shrapnel, making life difficult for the smaller ships.

Few of the rocks actually hit but chaos reigned in the enemy fleet. I hoped Rolleston was angry. Multiple windows showed us various images of the confusion. I watched a rock smash into a light cruiser, breaking its back. The vessel silently split, venting gas, debris and people into vacuum. Unfortunately the enemy ships were too far apart for collisions.

Then the darkness truly lit up as Earth's orbital weapons opened up.

Particle, plasma and lasers reached out for the enemy's ships. Reaching them, scarring them, bursting some of the smaller ones. Thousands of missiles curved round the Earth from the defences on the other side of the planet to fragment into submunitions. The number of engines burning towards the enemy multiplied exponentially. Rolleston's fleet seemed to explode, but it was just the detonation of chaff and other countermeasures to take out the incoming warheads. The enemy's screening drones fired point-defence lasers and in some cases physically rammed the incoming missiles.

The two fleets exchanged fire with particle beam weapons, mass drivers, heavy plasma and heavy laser cannon. The missiles that penetrated the enemy's countermeasures detonated. Bursting ships, some of them big ones. Rolleston had put some of his heavy hitters on the fringes of his fleet, leaving them in harm's way, prey for the orbital defence network.

As we watched enemy ships coming apart but continuing on their course as debris, it felt like we could win. This was the biggest fleet engagement I had ever seen. It was the largest in history. Even though it was space combat, I understood the tactics, the strategy and the cold hard facts of beam, round and missile trying to break through armour. I wasn't paying much attention to the net feed.

On the net, Earth was represented as a huge, glowing, spherical, neon infoscape. A curtain of gossamer neon threads linked it to the orbital defences that ringed the planet. More threads connected it to the fleet in orbit. Even this far out I could make out the information reflection of the Spokes on this side of the planet. I found Atlantis's tower of water strangely familiar and comforting. It had been the birthplace of God on the net.

The majority of the vessels from both fleets looked like stylised ancient sea-going warships drawn in high-quality computer graphics. Each nationality and unit worked to a theme. The hackers/signal people also had themed icons. The Black Squadron frigates were biotechnological insectile dragons. The *Bush* looked like a huge biotech funeral barge from some ancient and obscene forgotten part of history.

Behind us a huge red sun rose over the Earth's infoscape horizon. God.

From each of the enemy fleet's ships came a stream of what I first thought was black liquid but on closer examination turned out to be flies. Each stream rose into the air and formed into a massive virtual object. Four burning black suns. One each from Sirius, Lalande, Proxima and Barnard's Star. One from each of the colonial fleets.

Then Demiurge reformatted the net. The net's space reflection had a ground now. It was a plain of black glass. Reflected in the glass was the burning sea of red flame that rolled across the sky. Then God started screaming.

'Gods save us,' Pagan whispered across the tac net.

The enemy fleet's hackers/signal people came flying across the plain of glass towards our own. Each should have been in the uniform of their own country's icon. They weren't; all were featureless, sexless, obsidian-skinned winged demons wielding weapons of fire like the angel that had destroyed the net reflection of High Nyota, Mlima's C&C, when Rolleston had escaped Earth orbit.

The demons met the hackers from our fleet and those rising from the more distant net reflection of the orbital defences. The hackers on our side were armed with copies of the software Pagan and Morag had developed, derived from what they had learned from the godsware and inside information on Demiurge. Weapons of moonlight and silver fire. Weapons that just about allowed them to hold their own against the demons. I suddenly found myself missing Vicar.

Then flights of angels emerged from the dark suns and the dying started in earnest. I could only watch in horror as angelic weapons and white fire cut swathes through our hackers.

When you work in abstract about how outclassed you are, it's just words, it's just numbers; then you have it driven home like this.

I minimised the net feed and enlarged the fleet. I watched from various angles. Rolleston's fleet was still in disarray but starting to regroup. Engines of all sizes from the largest to the smallest lit up the blackness as the two fleets closed. Our fleet was desperate to get in among the enemy. They wanted to keep us at arm's length.

Our strike craft was shaking and bucking with the repeated shock waves of enemy warheads detonated by our countermeasures. I heard railgun fire rattling thunderously across the strike craft's hull. We couldn't even hear the impact of the beams that I knew must have been scorching its armour. Instead we heard the servos of its own weapon systems moving as it returned fire. Stealth wasn't an option now and we didn't even have a fighter escort. It would have drawn too much attention.

Then I saw us lose. This was what had delayed the attack on Earth, something we would find unthinkable to use. The heavy hitters on the fringes of Rolleston's fleet fired. It was a planetary kinetic bombardment on a scale that dwarfed the destruction of California.

The feeds switched between footage showing us what was happening in space, orbit and on the ground. Tree-sized cylinders of dense metal tore through most of the orbital defences facing this side of the planet, once and for all destroying the myth of fortress Earth. We watched, as in an instant, orbital weapons platform and sky fortress after orbital weapons platform and sky fortress just ceased to exist, turned into powdered fragments at a frightening rate. Feed after feed went down, but there was always another.

It looked like the Earth was burning as the atmosphere lit up when the cylinders hit re-entry. We saw feed from Earth. It looked like the sky was on fire.

Then the Spokes. Colombia, Ecuador, Uganda, gone just like that. We watched the might of Atlantis explode on one side and then the other like a through-and-through bullet wound on a massive scale. The huge structure started to topple even as the kinetic round hit the water, creating an impact tidal wave and boiling water in front of it as it travelled into the Earth to cause a tectonic event.

How could humans to do this to their own home? They couldn't all be possessed. We watched the second Brazilian Spoke fall, a horrible replay of the FHC.

Nyota Mlima fell. Air Marshal Kaaria died in an instant, and with him went the co-ordination of the remaining orbital defences, most of which were now on the wrong side of the planet.

Even this far from Earth, the fleet feed was able to pick up the impacts of the bombardment. On Earth those impacts would shake and drown their surroundings in earthquakes and tidal waves.

I wanted to say something. There was nothing to say. I wanted to tell the pilot to hurry but it was superfluous.

'They will be good and angry now,' Mudge said quietly. 'I think you should send it.'

Pagan sent the package. A screaming God forwarded it. Every remaining person on Earth still hooked up to the net received our message. We shut down Sharcroft, fleet comms in C&C and the various intelligence agencies trying to scream at us for what we'd done this time. These people never want to share.

Now he had cleared a path, Rolleston started delivery. They looked like what they were: enormous seed pods fired at the Earth containing the latest iteration of Crom. Rolleston had called it Crom Cruach. Each pod containing uncountable bio-nanites designed to reproduce, grow, infect, consume and change. This was his bid to terraform the

Earth. To remake it in his vision. The entire world a reflection of his sick mind.

There were attempts at interception. Some were even successful. The only thing we had going for us was that the delivery of Crom Cruach was a comparatively slow process.

We were taking more and more hits. Each one echoed through the metal structure of the ship. I could feel the difference in the strike craft's handling. I knew that the pilots would be fighting it now.

There are no boarding attempts in fleet actions. Space is too big and nobody's mad enough to try and board a ship full of their enemies. Except Merle. And now us. It's just a matter of matching velocity. Hoping that the target ship doesn't change course and then giving yourself a little push and trying not to wipe out on its hull. Simple, except that the maths involved is staggeringly complex, and here we were in the middle of the biggest fleet action in human history.

I hoped our pilot, whose name I hadn't even bothered to learn, was really good, or we were going to be left with our cocks flapping in the wind.

'This is as close as I can get you,' our nameless pilot told us over internal comms. I checked our position. Saying it was hot would have been a vast understatement. There was silence on the tac net. Like everyone was waiting for something. The head of Mudge's armour turned to look at me in my converted bomb cradle.

'Ready?' I asked. It seemed that I was back in charge of real-world security. They confirmed their readiness in turn. Right, time.

We came out of the bomb bay using our flight fins to adjust position in tiny increments. Initially we planned to stay close to our long-range strike craft, matching its velocity, trying to get our bearings. Rannu and I were out first, Pagan and Morag following, but the strike craft was coming apart around us. Metal buckled, broke apart and became fragments pierced by black beams and ruptured by exploding warheads, so Merle and Mudge exited what was now a high-velocity debris field. We set course and triggered burns on our fins as parts of the craft bounced off our armour, knocking us in random directions. We took a kicking getting out of the wreckage, our expert navigation systems constantly having to recalculate course. Free of the debris, we used one short burn and then hoped our stealth systems would mask us. Hoped that they would think we were also debris. Working for us was the fact that nobody had ever been stupid enough to try something like this during a fleet action.

It was like being born into light. The red of lasers, the blue and white of particle beam weapons, the white fire of plasma, the burn of missile engines multiplying as they exploded into submunitions. We could see long trails of railgun tracer fire. Point-defence systems killed incoming warheads. Armour-plated hulls melted and ran as plasma fire blossomed across them.

Screening remotes looked like swarms of insects around the bigger ships as they fired at fighters, interceptors, other remotes and incoming missiles. Skin mechs fired their weapons like a crawling artillery barrage at any enemy craft in range.

Some of our fighters shot by beneath us. They were little more than oversized engines propelling armoured, wedge-shaped weapons platforms filled with gel. Without gravity they were pulling manoeuvres at Gs high enough to powder unprotected and unaugmented bone. The fighters were pursued by one of the organic Black Squadron frigates, its black beam weapons stabbing out again and again as its point-defence system destroyed incoming missiles. The frigate's engine glowed a cold blue like one of Their vessels. With every beam of black light one of the fighters split apart, bleeding frozen gel out into the vacuum. We were too small for the frigate to notice.

Everyone knows that war is horrific, and it is. What nobody will tell you is that sometimes it is beautiful. This was beautiful. This was like watching fireworks as a child. I was exhilarated but I was calm. This was so unreal. It was a beautiful chaos of light and fire and metal. It was balletic, and the only thing I could hear when I shut down the noise from the feeds to block out the screams and the panic was the sound of my own breathing.

I felt a surge of exhilaration as one of their battleships came apart under heavy fire from lots of different sources, including the bright blue lance of the *Thunderchilde*'s main particle beam weapon.

All around us impacts blew off fragments of armoured hull. The faster ships flew by, skirmishing with each other – or dogfighting, as pilots insisted on calling it – risking missile fire at the bigger ships, drawing laser and railgun fire from screening drones.

Above us my vision was filled by the enormous organic and seething chitinous form of the mutated *Bush*. The Hellion's passive sensor picked up an increase in radiation as the *Bush*'s enormous entropy cannon fired and drew a scar down the length of the *Thunderchilde*. Good, I thought, it needed a bit of dirtying up. It needed to earn its scars.

I saw missiles fired from a battery that looked like a cancerous growth on the skin of the *Bush*. Where it was damaged, the hull swam like bacteria under a microscope as it grew new armoured flesh. This wasn't a ship, it was a nightmare, some kind of monster.

I ignored the readout on my IVD that told me how fast we were going. It was relative, I told myself, as the *Bush* got larger and larger until it was all I could see. We were still tens of miles from it. We still had the screening drones to deal with. Whether they thought we were debris or not, they would still detect and fire on us to protect the mother ship, and they would be linked to Demiurge. H would know we were coming.

We sent the signal to fleet. Our prearranged call for help. The closest carrier to us was a German carrier, the *Barbarossa*. Every carrier had held a squadron back to help us if need be. Now that we had called for air support, all the reserve squadrons were released to join the fight. We saw some of them drop out of docking airlocks, manoeuvring jets moving them away from the carriers before they kicked in their main engines. Many of them didn't get far.

I knew the *Barbarossa*. It had once taken on one of Their dreadnoughts in the Proxima system and won. Too old now for front-line service, it had been sent back to Sol for system defence duties. Sadly, Luftwaffe Fortunate Sons now crewed it. Shame. It would have been nice if it had been the Valkyries they launched to help us. I remembered that the Valkyries would be on the other side somewhere and flying better fighters.

Pagan did what he was good at, forward observing for the squadron of fighters that was being torn apart as it headed towards us. He used passive scans, so as not to give our position away, plotting the positions of the screening remotes we needed taken out. He also sent the pilots the locations of point-defence weapons on the hull of the *Bush*. All the other weapons were too large to be used against us. He then sent the pilots targeting solutions via our, hopefully, masked comms link.

Waiting for the fighters, falling up towards the *Bush*, I enlarged the net feed in my IVD. The war between God and Demiurge looked like a viral eclipse. As if God's red sun was slowly being eaten by infection. More and more black spread over it. God's screaming was a constant ambient noise on all the feeds now. Uncharitably I wished he'd shut up.

Then the best hope we'd had since the start of the fight. They came like a vagabond army – corporate and criminal hackers, amateur savants and signals veterans, sport and illegal-snuff virtual gladiators – the net's dirty fighters, tricky bastards, chancers and assorted scumbags. Some were ex-military; many were draft dodgers, and I had a horrible feeling that many were still too young to be drafted. They were cloaked in icons that ran the gamut from just about every popular cultural icon to just about every religious icon imaginable. Some just came as themselves.

They were angry and armed with the best attack and defence programs that Morag, Pagan, Salem and Tailgunner, before he died, had managed to develop from what they'd learned of godsware. We'd given them the best software sword and shields we could in the packets that Pagan had sent after the Earth had been hit. It was manipulative. We'd known that Rolleston was going to bombard the Earth, but there had been little we could do about it and there had been no time for the powers that be to evacuate the targets. The packets had contained a heartfelt plea for aid from Mudge. He'd composed it when we'd been in the assault shuttle heading for Rolleston's ancestral home.

The sun grew and the darkness receded. Slightly. As just about every single isolated computer system left on Earth, in orbit and in the fleet was opened to God.

I watched the vagabond army hit the demons and the angels as an undisciplined mess, trailing their silver cords behind them. There was less than a second's delay between them thinking something wherever they were jacked in and their icons acting on it. The tiny delay was a result of operating in virtual territory so far away from their bodies. It was small but sometimes it was enough to give their opponents the edge, particularly the angels.

Demons were thrown into the air as the new army joined the fight and nasty tactics were used. Groups of hackers who knew each other ganged up on targets, took one down and moved to another. The vagabond army may not have had the training, discipline or technology of the attacking hackers, but they had the numbers and they'd seen huge parts of the Earth destroyed in the bombardment. They had anger on their side. Anger is always a good motivator.

Pagan sent us feed from the surface of the black glass plain. An angel towered over the vagabond hackers and the remnants of our fleet's military hackers and signal personnel. It was sweeping multiple hackers aside with every stroke of its spear of white fire, leaving them corpses with smoking plugs back wherever they were tranced in. I saw Papa Neon charge the angel, throwing every dirty little hex program he had at it. He distracted it, parried a spear blow with his shining staff, slid under the angel's guard and tore a lump out of its flesh. Papa Neon shot into the air above the angel and bit into it. The angel lurched like a puppet. Its own bones pierced its skin. The white flames went out of its eyes.

Elsewhere the fight wasn't going as well. Few of the hackers were a match for the angels. Columns of black fire joined the plain of glass to the four black suns, burning lines of icons regardless of whose side they were on. Above the plain the sea of fire began to roil and surge angrily.

The fighters from the *Barbarossa* came into view on heavy burn. One of them came apart and started tumbling as a thick red beam of laser light superheated its hull until it exploded.

The fighters fired their nose railguns in a constant stream of tracers all around us and launched all their missiles as one, as close as they could to the screening drones.

The screen of drones fired back. Space was filled with a grid of red laser light. Missiles burst into multiple submunitions. Warheads exploded in space; some of them even reached their targets. In front of us drones exploded in rapid succession. Now cross hairs appeared on our IVDs as we targeted the survivors.

There were explosions on the hull of the ship as gristle-like point-defence systems were destroyed.

I fell up towards the *Bush*, firing short bursts from the Retributors at the surviving drones in my path. Some of the drones were burning as plasma fire ate through them. Black light from return fire scored the Hellion's armour. I launched one of the missiles off my back at a surviving black beam point-defence system. The missile was destroyed before it got close, but one of Morag's missiles hit the growth-like system.

None of the fighters made it. They were torn apart by the remotes before their first missiles hit.

We were now taking light fire as we plummeted up towards the *Bush*'s hull. Through the windows on my IVD I could see Mudge and Pagan firing their Retributors at its hull. I magnified the Hellion's optics and saw Walker-like biomechanical constructs growing out of the ship's flesh. I joined the firing. Then I realised I was coming in too fast. I tried a back burn on my flight fin. It slowed me but I hit the hull hard. The impact was hard enough to make me spit blood over the plastic visor of my helmet. I bounced. The Retributor flew out of my hands but it was still connected to the ammo pack on the Hellion's back by its chain feed.

With the help of the suit's systems I managed to regain control and make it back to the hull. The six of us grouped together in a rough circle, everyone facing out.

'I've got nothing,' Merle said. 'The architecture's all off. The plans we downloaded are meaningless. I didn't even see an airlock on the way in.' It was as close to panic as I'd ever heard from Merle. It wasn't very close but he was less than happy.

'Plan B?' Mudge asked.

'You want to do it?' I asked as I fired off a burst at something that looked like it was growing out of the hull.

'I think it'll have more impact coming from you,' he said.

'What's plan B?' Pagan asked suspiciously.

'Wild Boys to Rolleston, over,' I said over an open comms link.

'What the fuck are you doing?!' a furious Morag demanded. Merle turned to level his Hellion's light plasma cannon at me.

'What is it, Jakob? I'm a little busy right now,' Rolleston asked impatiently. His voice sounded the same but now hatred outweighed fear when I heard it. The others went quiet.

'Don't be a cunt. Let us in and let's get this over and done with.'

There was a long silence. Or at least there would have been if Morag, Pagan and Merle hadn't started screaming threats and demands for explanations at me again.

'Okay, Jakob,' Rolleston finally said.

25

The USSS *George Bush Junior*

A lot of our plan was based around Rolleston's arrogance. On the surface this might seem risky but you've got to think that if a guy wants to be a god then there's going to be a degree of arrogance involved.

It looked less like an airlock and more like a blister as it grew out of the hull and enveloped the Hellions, blocking out the dangerous light show below us.

On the other side they were waiting. The Black Squadron troopers weren't soldiers any more; they were just weapons. They were bent over, covered in thick, overlapping chitinous plates. Reinforced bone pierced their armoured skins; one of their arms was a long sharp curved blade of blackened bone and the other was some kind of ranged weapon. It was their mouths that got me though. They were locked open in a fixed silent scream. You could see the pain etched across their still-human faces. You could read the desperation in their eyes. They were all linked to Rolleston through Demiurge. I think he liked to feel their pain. I think he fed on it. Among the transformed soldiers were twisted and deformed versions of the Berserks, like we'd seen in the Citadel, and with them similarly twisted versions of Their Walkers.

A missile flew from the back tubes of each of the Hellions. Unlike Them, these constructs and mutations screamed when plasma burned flesh and bone. The plasma fire formed a rough circle, a bit of breathing room.

Marching forward firing railguns and plasma cannons at anything that moved, just another target-rich environment. The railguns turned whatever they hit into moist fragments. The plasma cannons left little in their wake but burning puddles of flesh and bone. Rannu's Hellion and mine took the lead. A corridor was chosen at random. Any movement was met with overwhelming fire. They tried growing through the roof, through the walls, through the floor, but that took them too long. The whole ship was flesh now, writhing all around us.

When their numbers became too much, when they were about to overwhelm us, then missiles were used just to clear a little space. Plasma flame cauterised the flesh of the ship. Each time we could feel the ship react a little beneath us. It was in pain from the fire. The Hellion's armour started to run as they marched through liquid fire. We couldn't afford to hang around until the plasma flames burned themselves out.

Targets everywhere. The whole ship seething but the Hellions held their own. Anything that got close was ripped apart by their back tentacles. The armoured suits were soon covered in gore.

Overwhelming firepower or not, there was a limit to our ammunition, and the whole ship was trying to kill us.

Then he came. He didn't look like the calm and contained professional bastard I'd known from Sirius. He looked like fury. The madness in his mind hadn't so much leaked as flooded out. He was naked and had transformed himself to look like an ancient Greek statue, like the type Mudge had shown me in a museum in London. As railguns and plasma cannons were pointed towards him, the whole front of his body blackened into what looked like living metal. Surely he couldn't withstand concentrated plasma cannon fire?

Repeated plasma fire wreathed him in a corona of white flames. The railgun fire hammered into him, blowing chunks out of his flesh, which regrew almost immediately.

It was over quickly. He reached Rannu's Hellion first and just reached out a burning hand, snapped his plasma cannon and threw the exo-armour into the wall. Root-like tendrils of biomechanical flesh grew around Rannu's Hellion holding it still. Rolleston turned to my Hellion all but ignoring the constant fire from the railguns. He reached up and his hands grew into claws. He dug into the front of the armour and tore it open.

It was empty. There was a limit to our stupidity – I hoped. Rolleston started to sink into the floor. We triggered the charges in the armour. The feed from the Hellions went down.

It would be nice to think that the charges had taken care of Rolleston, but I just knew we weren't that lucky. Besides, by that point we were inside. We heard his screams of rage echo through the vein-like corridors.

A few minutes ago

'Shit,' I said. There was a conspiracy to force me to relive two of my most unpleasant experiences simultaneously. The technology-transformed-into-flesh

of the Bush *was forcing us to rethink our entry strategy. Maybe strategy's a strong word. We had some contingencies but once again we were making this up as we went along.*

Only by reconfiguring the flesh insides of the Hellions had we managed to fit the spacesuits inside the exo-armour. Even then it had severely hindered movement and we'd had to use very lightweight suits. They had no armour and I was freezing. God was controlling the Hellions. We had successfully made the first fully functioning robots. God-driven robot devils. They were the diversion but we still had to get in ourselves.

All around us the battle still raged but we were so small compared to it all. We were less than bacteria in the big scheme of things.

I felt Pagan push a jack into one of the plugs in the back of my spacesuit, which in turn fed into one of my plugs.

'You ready?' he asked brusquely.

'No,' I said. I was shit-scared and hated this plan.

I barely had time to close my eyes and exhale all the air out of my lungs. The tendrils grew through the flesh of my face and cracked the thin plastic visor of the shit spacesuit. Cold. Then burning inside as my blood boiled. I felt my skin stretch and distend as my body swelled. It was agony. The tendrils reached down and touched the skin of the Bush *and connected me to something awful. I opened my mouth to scream, except now I had no mouth. We were swallowed.*

Flesh, awful and surrounding me. My mind touching it, assaulted, bombarded with information and images either too complex or horrific to process. It passes in a moment. It feels longer.

We fall through the ceiling. I hit the floor with blood running out of my ears. My joints are agony. Frost coats my nostrils. My skin is red from burst blood vessels and despite my internal air supply I'm panting for breath as the tendrils recede back into my flesh and I have a mouth again.

When something approaching conscious thought returns, when the theatre of atrocity that is the images downloaded into my skull stops dancing in front of my eyes, when the pain becomes manageable with the help of a lot of painkillers dumped into my blood, I use what Demiurge taught me when he possessed me. I get the bio-nanites that swarm through my body to heal the damage caused by hypoxia and ebullism. It can't stop me shaking from the cold. Maybe it's not just the cold.

Pagan unplugs himself from me and looks down at me with contempt. I resist the urge to shoot him. Then I catch a glimpse of Morag. She's not quite quick enough to mask the look of concern. The others are down on one knee, weapons at the ready watching all around us.

Warm air runs through the corridor of biomechanical flesh we find ourselves in. It's like something huge breathing on you. We take turns stripping

off the shitty spacesuits while the others guard. We've got on inertial armour
suits, the only armour we could fit under the spacesuits.

'Well?' I asked Pagan as we change.

'I ran the spoof program, snuck it in using the cloak so it would be un-
detected. It's adapted from one I'd use on normal tech but I'm unsure of the
interface with the biotech,' he said coldly.

'Very clever, Pagan. What does that mean?' I demanded.

He stopped and looked at me.

'Either we'll be hidden from whatever detection systems they're using or we
won't. Shame we couldn't get Morag to do it.' In other words, either we'd be
hidden from Demiurge and therefore Rolleston or he'd have us torn apart. We
needed Rolleston to turn up, just not yet.

'Drop the attitude,' Merle said quietly to Pagan.

Pagan glared at him for a moment and then nodded. He was just frightened.
Well that and he hated me, which was reasonable. I did after all kill him.

We pulled the reactive camouflage gillie suits on over our inertial armour
and moved out.

We'd downloaded the plans for most of the flag-capable ships in the
colonial fleet. We'd been pretty sure that Rolleston would choose the
Bush because it was the best but it paid to have contingencies. The
plans we had for the *Bush* were very different to the ship/organism
we were now presented with, but Pagan quickly adapted an intelligent navigation program he'd used as a combat air controller. It was
mapping the terrain and trying to reconcile it with the plans we had.

We were moving quickly through the corridors, hiding if we
saw movement and watching the last moments of the Hellions on
our IVDs. We could hear the firefight in the distance. We watched
Rolleston walk through some of the best firepower that modern
weaponry could provide. The footage was not doing much for morale.

Like the boardroom in the Citadel, the ship was diseased human
technology, except in the case of the *Bush* it was total. We didn't see
much in the way of movement initially and quickly found out why.
The humans needed to run the ship had become components, stripped
of unnecessary parts, formed into more practical, useful shapes – if
you were a psycho – and melded into the biomechanics of the craft.
Morag had to stop to throw up. I couldn't blame her. I wished I still
had that reaction to atrocity. That said, it was still seriously fucking
with my head.

The feed from the Hellions went down. Then we heard the screaming. It seemed to echo through all the corridors. It was rage. It was
unmistakably Rolleston. As much as I wanted to think otherwise,

there was no way we could have killed him. The floor didn't so much shake as quiver beneath us.

We were heading deeper into the ship. We needed to find the isolated Demiurge system. We had hoped for a more normal layout but C&C was still our best hope. However, Rolleston must know that we were inside and Demiurge was compromised. Now he would start to hunt us. The moment we were found we would be back to fighting the whole ship, except this time without the help of sophisticated exo-armour.

Outside, Rolleston's fleet had consolidated. Whoever was commanding the colonial fleets knew what they were doing. With most of Earth's orbital defences down, its fleet stood little chance. Rolleston's fleet was advancing, concentrating fire on one big ship until it was cracked open and then moving to another. Their fighters and incredibly fast and manoeuvrable frigates were mopping up the smaller vessels. Already Earth ships were fleeing. The *Thunderchilde* was still there, however. It didn't look so clean and new; it was a scarred and burned behemoth taking fire all over its armoured hull. All of the *Thunderchilde*'s own weapon systems were constantly lit up. A lot of its fire was aimed at the *Bush*. We weren't even feeling the impacts.

On the net the battle was going a little better. Through sheer force of numbers the vagabond army of Earth hackers armed with godsware had taken out most of the enemy's rank and file hackers and some of the angels. However, the four black suns of Demiurge were forcing them back with columns of black fire that turned anything they hit into ribbons of simulated black skin floating in the virtual air.

More than three quarters of the red sun was black now as the viral eclipse continued trying to eat God. I didn't even notice God screaming any more. It was ambient noise.

We ducked into side corridors and hid behind rib-like supports when we detected movement ahead. We had motion sensors and tiny rotor remotes, also with motion sensors, feeding information to our IVDs, but in an environment like this their range was severely limited. The reactive camouflage helped, as did the heat- and EM-masking properties of the inertial armour suits.

That he couldn't find us must have been making Rolleston furious. I wondered if he was worried now that he knew Demiurge was compromised. Though he must have had an idea when he saw us waiting for him when he turned up in-system.

We were deep inside the huge ship now. The absence of doors had made this possible. I don't suppose they mattered so much when you controlled everything on board and you could grow a new wall if you needed to shut areas off. I still sweated. A lot. It was reassuringly human after I'd had the alien part of my flesh driven home again.

I leaned against a corridor wall hoping the reactive camouflage was sufficient cover as a patrol passed. I was desperate for a fag and wished that I'd made Mudge give me one back on the *Thunderchilde*. The patrol consisted of one of the weaponised Black Squadron members, four mutated Berserk-like bioborgs and something that looked like a cross between one of the Berserks and a praying mantis. It had downward-pointing, sword-like bones for forearms. I'd slowed down my breathing, supplementing it with air from my internal tanks.

The Black Squadron guy stopped. He sniffed the air. You have to be kidding. He turned to look at the wall. Rannu was little more than a pixelated ghost as his reactive camouflage tried to keep up. He looped his new monofilament garrotte around the guy's neck and pulled it tight. His head popped off.

I was behind one of the Berserks. I pulled its head back with the metal of my right hand. Four blades extended from just behind my knuckles on my left hand and I punched them repeatedly and quickly into the back of its skull. It nearly knocked me over as it fell to the ground.

Another ghost and the praying mantis thing had a long blade sticking out of its skull. Merle had jumped up and stabbed it through the top of its head. The crack of armoured chitin breaking under the bowie knife-like point of the machete was fiercely audible. The thing shook for a moment and then dropped to the ground.

The others were having less luck. They were all carrying knives that weren't really up to dealing with things like this in hand-to-hand. Of the three of them only Pagan really had the training for this sort of fight. That left them with their handguns and the 10mm rounds were no match for the chitinous armour.

Superheated air exploded as one of the remaining mutated Berserks fired its black light projector from its spiked and twisted weapons gauntlet. I heard Morag cry out and felt a moment of panic. I kicked out at the Berserk's knee joint. I heard a satisfying crack and the thing lurched down on one knee and I drove the four knuckle blades on my right hand into its face, warping its horrible facial features further. I twisted the blades and then pulled them out. Letting it slump to the ground.

There was a burst of laser fire and one of the two remaining Berserks hit the ground, its head transformed into dirty black steam. A longer burst of gauss-boosted fire from Mudge's converted AK-47.

The final Berserk shook with every hit as it staggered back and then hit the ground.

We were now well and truly compromised.

Red steam floated into the air through Morag's reactive camouflage.

'You okay?' I sub-vocalised over the tac net.

'Fine. We need to move,' she snapped.

We ran forward, stealth abandoned in favour of speed. Weapons sweeping left, right, up and down as we went. Anything moving got shot. We didn't stay to see whether or not our fire was successful.

Where C&C should have been we found a solid wall of what we thought was new growth. We were taking shard and black beam hits on our backs. My shoulder laser was out searching for targets. Occasionally its red beam would stab out but mostly they were staying hidden.

We took cover behind the rib supports in the corridor and laid down suppressing fire. It was a waiting game now. Waiting for Rolleston to turn up and kill us, or more likely turn up, hurt us, torture us for a long time and then possess us so we could become part of his brave new world. I was firing the SAW and the shoulder laser. The corridor shuddered as white plasma fire ate away part of it. Morag caught the Black Squadron guy who'd fired with a three-beam burst from her laser carbine. Part of his superheated flesh was blown off but he ducked back around a corner leaving black steam hanging in the air behind him.

'Jakob!' Pagan snapped at me. He was a series of fractal images as his malfunctioning reactive camouflage tried to make him blend. Angrily he pulled the gillie suit off. He was hunkered down over by the new-growth wall gesturing at me to join him. I knew what he wanted.

'I'm not a fucking jack!' I snapped. It was just fear and selfishness.

'Do it!' Morag demanded.

Mudge glanced over at me and then returned to firing.

I fired a long burst up the corridor as I moved sideways towards Pagan. The return fire intensified and a beam and two shards tagged me. Part of my inertial armour was a blackened and smoking mess and the shards spun me around. I landed by Pagan's feet. He just pushed a jack into one of my plugs. I felt the flesh on my face become something else. A foreign body moved inside me. The flailing tendrils of transformed flesh grew out of my face. I would never get use to this. It still horrified me. I had to fight against the panic. I wanted to throw myself away from them but of course they were part of me.

I touched the flesh of the new-growth wall. I felt the tendrils burrow into the warm moist membrane, like maggots through dead flesh. I felt something monstrous notice me and breathe my name. I heard it inside my skull.

The jack came out of the plug in my neck and I pushed myself back from the wall as the tendrils started to grow back into my flesh. The membrane covering the entrance started to dissipate like it was being eaten by invisible parasites. I was vaguely aware of our return fire intensifying as I crawled into the room.

Two grenades exploded behind me as the others bought themselves time and backed into the room. I was trying to get up, trying to deal with the body shock, when Pagan grabbed me by the back of the neck and dragged me towards a biomechanical, honeycomb-like growth. I'd seen it before. It was the Themtech-derived memory structure.

'Move!' Pagan snapped again. He was not being gentle. I was too disoriented to fight him off. I noticed that one of the walls in the room was transparent and supported by a biomechanical skeletal structure. Children floated in liquid behind the wall.

'What ...?' I managed.

'They're children,' I heard Morag say in horror.

The jack slid into my plug and again my flesh was transformed. It grew out to mate with the honeycomb.

'Just for a moment,' Pagan said. I touched the honeycomb. It was like the skin of a blister. Beneath it I felt Demiurge raging, trying to break through and touch me, consume me again. There was black fire and hatred beneath the skin. Then free again.

'I will fucking kill you if you do that again!' I screamed at Pagan when my face had the rudiments of a mouth again.

Pagan was standing over me looking cold and angry. Mudge, Merle and Rannu were at the new door I'd made, firing into the corridor.

'You see that, what you felt? That's where we're going,' Pagan told me. I stared at him. Knowing what they had to do and catching a glimpse of it were two different things.

'You'll both die,' I said. I wasn't thinking straight – we were all going to die – but they were going to be consumed by hate. They didn't stand a chance. They couldn't understand that I knew what it was like to drown in the filth of Demiurge, of Rolleston's mind. What had we been thinking? We should have run. Given him the planet.

I looked over at Morag, who was staring up at the wall-sized fish tank of children. They had no eyes, mouths or nostrils. They were hooked up to IVs and catheters and had wires coming from the plugs in the backs of their necks. Some of them were obviously dead. I guessed from biofeedback.

I tried to take in the room around me. It was an enormous space, like a cathedral made of biomechanical flesh. The domed roof was transparent and looked out into space. It was illuminated by the constant strobing flashes of the ongoing battle outside.

'That's the angels,' Pagan said distractedly. He was studying the two ports he'd had me make in the skin of the honeycombed biological memory structure. He didn't look happy. I could understand why. They looked more like an orifice than any ports I'd ever seen.

'Jakob!' The voice echoed down the corridor. I was only able to pick it up over the gunfire because of the quality of my audio filters. I went cold. Even after all this she still frightened me.

Morag gave me a look I couldn't read. She walked over and kissed me on the cheek. Pagan was staring at me, grinning. The grin was cold and completely humourless; it looked like a rictus. I realised how gaunt he had become. He was just taut skin stretched across a skeleton. Both of them sat down and then slumped forward as they tranced into hell. They had to. We had no choice. They had to go after Demiurge in here, protected from God in an isolated system. For any of this to work, Rolleston had to be completely shut off from Demiurge.

The gunfire had stopped. I glanced over at the doorway. Rannu and Mudge were on either side of it. Merle had his plasma rifle at his shoulder and was checking all around the cathedral-sized room.

'Jakob!' the Grey Lady shouted again.

'What?' I found myself asking almost involuntarily.

'We need you to surrender,' she said.

Mudge and Rannu took turns to look over at me. Rannu had a raised eyebrow and Mudge was actually smiling.

'Have you got a fag?' I demanded.

'Fucking get your own,' Mudge told me. Merle was just shaking his head.

'Oh yeah. I'll just pop down to McShit's and get a pack,' I said. I was a long way from Dundee now.

'You know it was the smell of cigarettes that gave us away, don't you?' Merle told his lover. Mudge just shrugged.

'Jakob?' No impatience there. She was calm, just waiting for an answer.

'Okay, we surrender. You can come in and get us now!' Mudge shouted. Even Merle laughed.

The motion sensor strapped to my webbing just behind my left shoulder picked up movement above me. I raised the SAW and saw Merle doing the same. I immediately zoomed in on it, not quite sure what I was seeing. It had a long, chitinous armoured body and six legs ending in sharp sword-like bone blades. The torso of a human woman stuck out of it. Her arms also ended in bone blades. Growing from the back of the thing was a gristly, multi-barrelled, rapid-firing shard gun.

She was descending towards us like a spider dropping down its web. Except the thread was made of flesh and looked something like a long intestine. As it lowered towards us the walls seethed, as all around us things began to grow out of it.

On the guncam feeds from Mudge and Rannu I saw weaponised Black Squadron things sprint at them firing. Their gun arms were either gauss or plasma weapons. Rannu fired his gauss carbine and Mudge his AK-47. They had to hose them down, keep firing at them, let the bullets chip away at their flesh. The mutated Black Squadron guys were still running as they died.

I dived to the side and rolled onto my back as shards impacted all around me. It was suppressing fire. I couldn't work it out – this thing could have easily killed me. There was no cover. I returned fire, the comforting kick of the SAW against my shoulder. Every third round in the cassette was a tracer. I could tell I wasn't having any effect on this sword-legged thing because I could see the tracers ricocheting off its carapace and bouncing into the wall.

I switched targets to fire at the things growing out of the wall. Anything that looked well formed got hit. The tracers and the armour-piercing, explosive-tipped, long, nine-millimetre rounds tore them apart. I was finding my targets because they were hitting me with shards or black beams. Pain, track the source and fire till it came apart.

'Merle, take that spider thing out!' I said over the tac net. I couldn't work out why he hadn't done it. He was taking hits as well. 'Merle!' he was ignoring me. Fuck it! I aimed my grenade launcher.

'Don't fucking fire!' Merle shouted at me like he meant it. There was something new in his voice – emotion. On my IVD I could see from the window for Merle's guncam that it was aimed at me.

'What are you doing?!' I shouted at him and staggered forward from more shard fire hitting my back.

'It's Cat!' I looked again. I magnified in on her face. Some of it was new-growth biomechanical flesh over where the Grey Lady had blown Cat's own flesh off. It was her as a reanimated corpse. Her pallor reminded me of Sharcroft. She didn't even have the expression of agony on her face that the Black Squadron guys did.

I swung round to fire at more of the things crawling out of the walls as more shard fire hit me. I felt the integrity of my inertial armour start to give. I was knocked back but my subcutaneous armour held.

I caught a glimpse of the net feed. The viral eclipse that was eating the sun was almost done. Then the sun disappeared. God disappeared. Flames surged across heaven. Even though they were just icons, I could see the panic in the vagabond army.

Lying on the honeycombed memory structure, Pagan's body began to buck and spasm. Smoke was pouring out of his plugs now.

Mudge was spun round as gauss fire from one of the mutated Black Squadron troopers caught him in the side. He hit the ground still firing but the trooper made for Morag and Pagan's tranced-in bodies. I aimed and kept the SAW on him, pouring fire into him; at the same time my shoulder laser was blowing steaming chunks of superheated meat off him. He hit the ground. Mudge was back up by the door firing into the corridor. More doors were beginning to open in the walls. It was hopeless.

In the net Morag's icon looked like her. It wasn't Annis or the Maiden of Flowers, just Morag. She was standing in a circle of skull-topped poles, the ghost fence protection program. All around her Demiurge was like a black storm. Her hair and clothes were whipped around by the fury of it.

In front of the poles ghostly figures appeared: Buck, Gibby, Balor, Vicar, Dog Face, Big Henry, Tailgunner, Mother and Cat. Not vanquished foes, but a manifestation of the program written in by Morag, her tribute to the fallen. They were virtual spirits of the dead to protect her. Even if the body of one of them was here trying to kill us. The ghost fence protected her ritualistic summoning program. Except it wasn't a summoning program; they came and went as they pleased. It was a series of complex protocols for contact. It had been set up to drive home the mysterious and superior nature of the gods in the net. Morag didn't want to play that game.

I would have like to have shot and killed Cat's transformed body, but the new doors appearing in the wall were keeping me a little busy.

'Mudge, get to one of the other entrances! Rannu, stay were you are. The Grey Lady's going to be coming through that door any moment!' I shouted over the tac net.

Mudge ran towards one of the other holes appearing in the bio-mechanical flesh, firing at anything that moved. Nearly everything moved. I ran towards Morag and Pagan's prone bodies. They'd both been hit multiple times. Parts of their inertial armour suits were blackened and smoking. But they were still alive, and that was all they needed to do their job.

'Merle, if you're not going to fucking shoot her, can you shoot everything else, please!' I shouted. Brilliant. The ultimate killing machine chooses now to become sentimental and shut down.

As Mudge sprinted towards the other door Cat fired from her position above us. I saw shards tear through Mudge's back and blow one of his metal legs off from the knee down. He went sprawling across the floor.

'Listen, you bastards! Listen to me, all you fake-scary frightened cowards who feed us cryptic bollocks in return for worship! Listen to me, gods of the net!' I heard Morag scream into the storm of Demiurge. She was angry. 'Join us here! Now! Or we will show Demiurge where you live!' The resolve in her voice made real the threat.

If they were as powerful as we thought, then they would also know about the experimental array linked to a physics lab on a science ship in orbit on the other side of the planet. She would feed that information to Demiurge if she had to. That would take the fight to them. It had been Salem along with a friend of his, a physics professor at Moa City University, who had worked it out. Salem had been a man of faith. He had never believed in the gods in the net. If I hadn't been busy I would have been proud. Even in that icon she looked like the high priestess of an ancient and terrible religion. Gods were just another weapon to her.

'Reloading!' I shouted. As if anyone had time to care. I ejected the cassette from the SAW. My shoulder laser spun on its servos firing rapidly, but it wasn't enough. I got shot. A lot. My armour gave up the ghost, and I watched black beams appear through my side and shards impact into my chest and legs. One of them dented my metal right arm as it bounced off. I collapsed to my knees. Red warning icons sang their familiar boring song in my IVD. I closed them down – all they did was tell me the fucking obvious.

I managed to ram the cassette home as weaponised Black Squadron troopers came sprinting into the room through the new doors. I fired, taking them down one after another. Each one was getting a little closer to me. I tried to place my body between them and Pagan and Morag. Absorbing more hits. Concentrating on the ones with the plasma weapons for arms. I couldn't let one of them hit me.

I didn't understand their tactics. These guys had been recruited from special forces of every nationality but they were acting like Them.

Cat landed in front of Merle.

In the net there was light in the darkness of Demiurge. I saw Pagan wearing his Druidical icon. Head bowed, stooped gait as he tried to walk against the howling windstorm of Demiurge. The glow was coming from him. Inside him. White and steel blue. It seemed to be engulfing his insides. Then he stood up straight, his clothes and hair torn at by the black wind. Pagan became something else: a holy terror. His eyes became lightning, his mouth became lightning, his internal organs became lightning, shining though his skin and clothes.

'Cat?' Merle asked. He sounded like a little boy. Oh for fuck's sake.

I tried to resist the urge to think, I told you so, when Cat put both her sword-like arms and her two front legs through Merle's torso and legs. She reared up on her back four legs. The blades piercing the screaming Merle manipulated him like a puppet.

I heard the flat thump of a grenade being launched and then another. Two large holes appeared in Cat's torso, or possibly thorax, and then exploded. The front part of the Cat hybrid lurched forward. Her skull exploded as a long burst tore through it. I'm pretty sure that a couple of rounds hit Merle as well. What was left of Cat collapsed to the floor, dead. Again. Unfortunately Merle was still impaled on the ground.

'I got you, lover,' Mudge said over the tac net as he crawled towards Merle taking hits every inch of the way, the barrel of his AK-47 still smoking.

On the net the glow around Pagan became bright. It whited out the window momentarily, like the flash from a nuclear weapon I'd seen in vizzes about the FHC. Then it came back. White light and lightning was pouring into Pagan and then back out of him, striking out all around him. The ship shuddered beneath my feet. I could see something rise from Pagan like a ghost of blue energy. I could just about make out the shape of Ambassador as I'd first seen him so long ago on board the Forbidden Pleasure being protected by a terrified Morag. Now it was Demiurge's turn to scream as white fire and steel-blue lightning purged him out of his own isolated system.

The ship bucked and shook. All the things trying to grow through the walls and the ceiling thrashed about and screamed inhumanly. The honeycombed bulge in the floor cracked and glowed beneath it. Pagan's body spasmed so hard it actually left the ground and then burst into flames. This was what had been planned for Morag.

The inhuman screaming stopped and all the things that had been growing out of the wall fell. It was quiet. This was respite, but it still left us with the Black Squadron things, the Grey Lady and Rolleston, who must be pretty angry now. Who must be through toying with us.

Morag came to and sat up. She looked at Pagan's charred corpse. Then she looked at my blood-covered and scorched form.

Merle was trying to crawl out from underneath the corpse of his transformed sister.

'I'm not being funny, Merle, but if you're capable of holding a gun do you think you could help?' I asked him.

He just muttered something and then screamed as he pulled the blades out of his flesh. He retrieved his plasma rifle and got ready. He was bleeding badly. We all were.

The fleet battle was almost over. Just the badly damaged *Thunderchilde* and a few others held out. There was debris everywhere.

In the net the fight was going a little better as the vagabond army surrounded the few remaining angels. They didn't know they were killing children. Above them the sky looked like a rough sea of fire and the four black suns still burned in the sky, columns of black fire still raining down on the plain of black glass.

'Do you like my Seraphim? They are born into the net and think it is the real world. They truly do believe they are my terrible angels.'

I had no idea where he had come from. He just appeared in the room. I think he might have wanted to spout some snappy villainous monologue. Fuck that. We knew it was pointless but we shot him. A lot. It was cathartic.

Rannu was thrown back from the doorway he was guarding. He shouted. The side of his head steamed red as he staggered and fired a long and surprisingly undisciplined burst down the corridor one-handed. He was still staggering back as he fired his grenade launcher. There was an explosion in the corridor. Then a grenade hit the ground by Rannu and exploded. A concussion grenade, it still had enough force to blow him into the air. The Grey Lady jumped through the explosion.

Mudge, Morag, Merle and I concentrated fire on Rolleston. I ran out of ammo and ditched the SAW. I was aware of something happening in the net but I wasn't sure what. I grabbed my Mastodon and TO-7 from their smartgrip holsters and with my shoulder laser continued firing uselessly at Rolleston.

He walked through the fire and made for Merle, who fired round after round into him from his plasma rifle, surrounding him in flames. Merle dropped the plasma weapon because he didn't want Rolleston surrounded in burning plasma when he reached him, then drew his Void Eagle. In very rapid succession he fired all the rounds in its magazine pointlessly into Rolleston. His flesh was reforming and healing the inflicted wounds. Rolleston closed with Merle and we had to stop shooting at him. I holstered both my pistols and sprinted towards Rolleston.

I only saw it because I was looking for it. Both of the obsidian-bladed punch daggers appeared in Merle's hands. The daggers were filled with Crom Dhu, the derivate of Crom designed to seek out and kill the other bio-nanites. It had been designed to exterminate Them if the war had ever got beyond the Cabal's control.

Without the co-operation and resources of the Cabal, Crom Dhu had proved costly and difficult to replicate. Most of what the Earth forces had manufactured was stored in bunkers on Earth ready to fight the terraforming attempts of Crom Cruach. Rannu, Merle and I each had some. Merle's was in his punch daggers; Rannu's and mine were both in skull fuckers, daggers designed for piercing the hard bone of skulls. The virus was in the pommels, designed to be released when the blades felt flesh. Not unlike the dagger that Rolleston had used to infect Gregor. I drew mine from the small of my back as I ran towards Rolleston.

Unable to get a clear shot, Morag charged the Grey Lady, who was fighting Rannu. He had his skull fucker in his hand as he tried to dodge and block the Grey Lady's incredibly fast flurry of kicks and hand strikes. She was beating the shit out of him.

Morag launched herself into the air in a perfect flying kick aimed at the Grey Lady, who side-kicked her in mid-air. I heard the crack of bone powdering as foot contacted face. It was a sickening sound. Morag's head whipped back and she flew past the pair of them and landed in a heap.

The Grey Lady spun round on one leg and kneed Rannu in the side of the head with the upraised leg. It was so fast even Rannu hadn't been able to do anything about it. She kneed him so hard that his knees gave out and he stumbled to the ground.

Merle stabbed out at Rolleston with speed I could only envy. Rolleston reached forward and grabbed one arm, but that had been a feint for the blade in Merle's other hand, which was heading straight at Rolleston's face. He caught that arm as well. I saw a look of panic on Merle's face, and then Rolleston just broke both his arms, snapping the bones with such force that they broke through flesh and subcutaneous armour. I saw the bulges under Merle's inertial armour as it turned dark and wet with blood. Merle started screaming. Understandably.

Rolleston turned to me as I reached him and swung at him with the blade. He grabbed my arm and then used my own momentum to help propel me into the wall. I bounced off the dead mutated Berserks that had been growing there and hit the ground disoriented.

I shook my head. I was vaguely aware of things happening on the net. No time. The knife, the knife? Rolleston was holding it. He knew. Hell, it had been his idea.

Morag and Rannu had both staggered to their feet and were attacking Josephine Bran. She was having no problem blocking or dodging both their attacks. When one of them gave her an opening she would close and hit them with low kicks, elbows and strikes at joint or nerves. Almost every touch made them cry out in pain. When she attacked she would manoeuvre so her intended victim got in the way of the other one's attack. More than once Morag punched or kicked Rannu.

Rolleston tossed away the knife. Mudge started shooting him pointlessly in the back. Staring at Rolleston, everything he'd done, everything he'd caused to happen, came flooding back to me. From Sirius onwards, I could see the faces of all the members of the Wild Boys, SAS, SBS, other special forces, military intelligence and conventional soldiers whose deaths he'd been responsible for. All my friends that I'd watched die. I saw all of the pain he'd caused. In a moment of clarity, a moment of perfect cold anger, I knew that I was going to kill him.

Now I saw what was happening on the net. The plain of glass was obscured in mist. The beatific and horrific walked in the mist as shadows. They were like giants among the vagabond army, seeking out those who had been loyal, those who had worshipped them, and gifting them with the godsware. They were the history of humanity as religious iconography given form on the net. Like their namesakes they did not fight alongside humanity; they played their own games, but today they rewarded their followers with technology, uplifting them. Morag's threat/summons had been heard.

I smiled. All eight blades extended from my knuckles. Rolleston slowly turned to Mudge. He could take his time as Mudge was no threat. One of Rolleston's arms was transforming into a plasma weapon as he readied himself to kill another one of my friends. Mudge was still lying where he had fallen, firing burst after burst.

I ran at Rolleston's back and jumped on it, swinging at him like a wild thing with the claws. With a strength I did not know I had, I pushed the blades through his hardening flesh again and again, just hacking at him. Black ichor, like Them, an entire alien race of his victims, spurted out over me. It was a religious experience. A very base one, as I became a vessel of rage moving faster and hitting harder than I ever had before. I was a wild animal enhanced by cybernetics and alien creatures in my blood and pure fucking rage. Rolleston was surprised by the ferocity of my attack. I would've been surprised by the ferocity of the attack if my total hatred for this man had not just coalesced into a perfect rage that left no room for thought in my head.

His head came away in my hand. His body dropped to the ground. I was covered from head to foot in blood and ichor. Winded, almost unable to breathe. I had become something else. I wondered about the Themtech in my body. Had I just been a vessel for revenge or self-defence, sent by another race?

The decapitation of Rolleston must have distracted the Grey Lady for a moment as Morag caught her squarely on the side of the head with a punch. She kicked out at Morag hard enough to break ribs. Rannu feinted with his left. Bran easily blocked it. Rannu's right hand was a blur, then he stepped back. The dagger with Crom Dhu in it was sticking out of Bran's shoulder. She turned slowly to look at it. The dagger would be pumping Crom Dhu into her system, killing all the Themtech bio-nanites that had given her the edge over all us mere humans for all those years.

In the net the vagabond army had taken to the air, trailing their silver cords behind them. They were among the net representations of the ships of the enemy fleet.

The head in my hand started laughing. I looked down at it in horror.

'What were you hoping to accomplish?' Rolleston's severed head asked me.

I dropped it and backed away. His body stood up and reached for its head. Already black veins were growing from the stump of his neck and the bottom of his head. They met as he placed his head back on his neck and I watched as they knitted together.

The Grey Lady picked the knife out of her shoulder and threw it away. It was empty and useless now. Morag was clutching her chest and shaking her head despondently. Black scalpel-like blades shot out of Bran's fingers, and she moved too quickly for Rannu. She raked the blades down his face, tearing them through his subcutaneous armour and making four deep bloody rents in his face. He stumbled back, sitting down hard.

'Are we finished now?' Rolleston asked. He was starting to sound angry. 'Have we done our little dance?'

I glanced over at the knife he'd taken from me and tossed aside.

'Probably not,' I ventured, but if the knife hadn't worked on Bran then this one wouldn't work on Rolleston. He followed my eyes to where it lay.

'Do you not understand what you're fighting against?' he asked.

'Well, I've always known you were a wanker.'

I heard Mudge laugh. A lit fag had appeared in his mouth.

'You know this fight would've been over a long time ago if you two hadn't poisoned your flesh,' Rannu said bitterly. I could tell by his body language that he was ready to start fighting again. Mudge was about to back-shoot Bran, and Morag was preparing to attack Bran as well.

I spent a long time looking at Morag. She looked back at me. She didn't smile. She nodded. It was enough. I turned back to Rolleston. I briefly wondered why he was naked. Maybe there were just no clothes fine enough for a new god.

'Shall we get this over and done with?' I asked.

'It is,' he said. Black Squadron mutants came running into the vast biomechanical chamber to point their weapons limbs at us.

'Bollocks,' was the best I managed to come up with.

'This was a game, a diversion for us, nothing more. You were controlled at every step of the way,' Rolleston told me.

'Bollocks,' I said again, with some feeling. 'I think we gave you a bit of a fright.'

He gave this some thought.

'A few surprises but what have you accomplished? You've removed Demiurge from the *Bush's* isolated system at the cost of one of your own. I'll just open it up to Demiurge out there. You made the little gods come. Good. They're in one place – makes it easier for us to deal with them – and thanks to you we now have an idea of where they come from. Your god is gone. I rule the net. Your fleet is almost destroyed and Earth will finally grow to its manifest and true form.'

'If I ask really nicely will you kill us now?' Mudge said. Rolleston glanced over at him. The Grey Lady was coming to his side.

'I'm not going to kill you, Howard. We didn't go to all this trouble for that.'

'Fuck you,' I said quietly.

'Don't worry. We're not even going to possess you. Well perhaps Mr Nagarkoti just long enough for him to rape his family.'

Rannu flinched. He looked terrified.

'No, you're such throwbacks that you will be the only witnesses to the world transcendent. Of course you will be in different forms. We are going to experiment with nerve endings and agony in entertaining new shapes. You'll become musical instruments, curiosities.'

'You know, all the other Wild Boys used to hate you because they thought you were a ruthless bastard. Then you get into all this and everyone's scared of you because you're such a thoroughgoing loon. I never hated you. I just don't like you because you're so fucking boring,' Mudge told him and ground out his cigarette. Then he started crawling towards Merle, who was lying on the floor, his face a mask of agony as he tried to cope with the pain. Mudge ignored the Black Squadron things. What was the worst they could do to him?

I saw the anger on Rolleston's face. He really couldn't understand why such lowly beings as us – scum really, squaddies, petty criminals, failed not-so-petty criminals, journalists and ex-hookers – wouldn't bow and scrape to his divine majesty. He really had bought into this god thing. The amount of power he wielded aside, it really was pathetic. He had us. We were dead or worse. We would end up as playthings for his twisted fantasies, but I still couldn't shake the feeling we'd won, or rather that he couldn't touch us. On the other hand I suspected that wouldn't be much comfort to me in my future of torture, but the human mind could only take so much. I'd end up mad, insensate and probably comatose. So something to look forward to then.

'If you're doing the supervillain bit, have I got time for a drink?' Mudge asked.

'Look, you're going to do really bad things to us – we get it. All things considered, we're a bit fatigued by looking at the all the squirrel shit in your head that you've forced out into the real world,' I said. 'Really, we've got nothing to talk about, us and you.'

He nodded as if he understood. Then his fingers became claws and he rammed them into my chest cavity. I dribbled blood. It really fucking hurt but I didn't scream. Rannu flinched. Mudge actually gave a shout of surprise. Morag cried out, her hand shooting to her mouth. Merle had his own stuff to worry about.

I could feel his fingers inside me. That's okay. Internal organs don't have nerve endings. I spat out some more blood. My love/hate relationship with the medical diagnostic warning icons on my IVD continued as they told me I'd be dead soon.

'Major,' Josephine said, putting a hand on Rolleston's arm. He looked down at her. She was staring at me.

Something itched at the back of my head, some instinct telling me to concentrate on the net. Odd time I know, but I checked the net feed. Silver fire flowed from weapons, limbs, mouths and other things into the net representations of the ships in Rolleston's fleet. The silver fire, given to the vagabond army of hackers by the gods in the net, sought out the possessed. It was the same godsware program that had freed Rannu. Many of the possessed would die. They weren't in as good a physical condition and didn't have Rannu's strength of mind. I looked at Rolleston and smiled. He was getting angrier and angrier.

He would feel the mass exorcisms – as pain, I hoped.

His feelings at what was happening boiled out onto his malleable flesh, his features warping, flowing and changing, I suspected beyond his control. As I watched his face become part demon and part insect, I realised. This wasn't just hatred aimed at us, this was fear and self-loathing given fantasy and then form. He hadn't considered himself human, ever, and hated himself. If he hadn't had his fingers in my chest I would have pitied him.

I saw Pagan walking across the plain of black glass under a sea of fire towards four black suns. Lightning played all around him as his staff tapped against the glass.

I turned to look at Morag. She was horrified by what was happening to me. I wanted to tell her it would be okay. Maybe I did. I turned back to Rolleston and laughed at him.

'Father?' Josephine said with some urgency now, still holding on to his arm.

'Look what you've done to yourself,' I said to him and then closed my eyes. I didn't want his face to be the last thing I saw. I thought of Morag. Rolleston clenched his fist.

26
Morag

I watched my lover die. No. I watched Jakob die. I watched Rolleston tear the heart out of the only man I'd ever loved and crush it. No. Ambassador was gone, so frightened, so lost, so far away from everything he had ever known. We'd used Ambassador as a tool, because of his ability to process vast amounts of information. We were no different to Rolleston and his abuse of Themtech. There was no Themtech, only Them, another race. Ambassador became a weapon, a bridge, part of Pagan to act as a conduit to bring God into the isolated system, to destroy Demiurge and isolate Rolleston. Ambassador had gone, part of me was missing, and Pagan and God were one.

Ambassador was gone and so was Jakob. Both my lovers were dead. I wanted to cut my glass eyes out so I could cry again. I watched Jakob slump forward against Rolleston, this monster, this spoilt child who had done all this, created all this madness.

I watched Josephine Bran back away from her father, looking between him and Jakob's corpse. You poor woman. How long? I wondered. All the time you served with him on Sirius? Of course you could never say or do anything: you were the Grey Lady. More to the point, Rolleston's shadow eclipsed you. Bran sat down hard on the floor. Emotion looked foreign on her features. Rolleston turned to her, frowning.

Merle was sitting up watching, his pain under control but helpless without arms. Mudge was sobbing. He could never know. He'd probably kill me. In his own way he had loved Jakob. He wasn't interested in him in that way but their bonds had run deep. Rannu was frightened. He had every reason to be. He knew from bitter experience that Rolleston lived up to his threats.

Jakob, you fool. He'd made a lot of mistakes. In many ways he was a weak man. He'd done and said a lot of stupid and hurtful things. He kept on trying to do what he thought was best for other people. Not knowing enough to ask them first, to talk to them. But he'd helped me help myself and he never knew when to stop fighting. He tried to be a good friend and he had tried to be as good a man as he knew how. It was enough. I think he was the first person to care for me since my sister died.

Except it was all a lie. Jakob was dead.

I had to control myself.

'Rolleston?' I heard myself say. I had to get the shakiness out of my voice. He turned to look at me.

'You won't be so lucky. I'll take my time with the rest of you,' he said.

There comes a point when threats become superfluous. He wasn't the first man who thought he'd had power over me.

With a thought I sent the package. All over Rolleston's recently exorcised fleet, Mudge's smiling features appeared on IVDs on comms monitors. As tersely and as honestly as possible, Mudge explained to them what had been happening. What had been done to them. His words were supported by the evidence of the monstrosities that the *Bush* and the Black Squadron frigates had become.

'You've lost,' I told him.

I think he was unsure for a moment, just a moment, then his features became cruel and confident again. Arrogance – his, mostly – had been the cornerstone of the plan. But arrogance is pretence.

'How do you work that out? Even now I am transforming the Earth. I control the net.'

I shook my head. 'Check your net feed.'

Pagan walked across the plain of glass, his staff tapping against its surface. Lightning arced all around him. Anyone or anything which got too close became cinders floating in the virtual air. He glowed blue and white from the inside. He was like a beacon under the burning red sea of the sky. I had to show no reaction as Papa Neon approached what he thought was one of his old friends and was burned to nothing. I felt a strange sense of satisfaction when lightning reached out and destroyed Nuada, because the gods had to know as well. Lessons were being taught. Pagan was God now and God was pissed off. The angels and the other hackers parted for Pagan. He looked magnificent. This was to have been how I died. It would have been a good death, but despite what Jakob said I had wanted to live, but I had wanted all of me to live and he tore part of that away without even asking. No, it wasn't Jakob who had done that.

'So?' Rolleston demanded. 'He is no match for Demiurge.' I thought I could detect apprehension in his voice.

The Grey Lady was back on her feet again. She seemed to have recovered and was moving back to her father's side.

'That's the thing though. It's not one Demiurge, is it? It's four. Each Demiurge in each system has developed separately. What did you program them for?'

On the plain Pagan/God stood in front of the four black suns and raised his arms high, lifting his staff. Lightning arced out and struck all four of the suns. I heard the Demiurges scream but Pagan/God was just getting their attention.

It was written all over Rolleston's face. He understood. His arm transformed into a weapon and with a scream of rage he turned and fired at Pagan, whose already burned corpse disappeared in a blast of plasma. The floor of the ship bucked and moved as the plasma turned its biomechanical flesh molten. I felt the heat against my skin and turned away from it.

'You didn't get him, Rolleston. He has already gone far beyond your power.'

Pagan/God still stood before the black suns. But then I saw Pagan start to panic. I was pretty sure that gods didn't panic. Tendrils of black light reached for him from each of the black suns. They wrapped around him, enveloping him, and then tore him apart. I didn't even flinch. The tendrils withdrew back to the suns.

Rolleston turned to us, smiling, confident, smug again.

'I made them like me,' he said in what I'm sure he thought was a sinister manner.

'Frightened?' I asked.

His eyes narrowed. He was going to kill us or worse. Might as well try and aggravate him so we can get it over and done with quickly.

'You taught them how to hate, completely, and then you gave them God-like power. Pagan and God became a virus designed to do one thing, remind them of that. They developed separately with separate experiences. They are individuals now. What would you do if there was more than one of you vying for power?' I asked.

The first arcs of black light began between the black suns as they attacked each other. I watched Rolleston's eyes widen. Hate consumed hate in a rage of mutually assured destruction.

'You're all alone now,' I told him, but then he always had been, I suspected.

I watched his features start to change again as the rage spilled out onto his flesh. Good. I don't fancy spending the rest of my life as some sadist's plaything again. I hope the hackers are right – I hope there's another world – and I hope that Jakob and Ambassador are there and maybe the three of us can have a chance at a life free of hatred, pain and madness. Maybe it was just wishful thinking. I closed my eyes. Let's just get this over and done with.

'What ...?' Rolleston's voice sounded small, shocked. I opened my eyes. The dagger, the one that Jakob had been carrying, the one that Rolleston had taken from him and thrown away, was sticking out of his chest. Where his heart should be. Rolleston was staring at Bran. Bran was gazing back. Emotionless. Rolleston collapsed to the ground. Crom Dhu, Black Crom, had done its job – killed the bio-nanites that now made up Rolleston's form.

The black suns had gone. Then every single computer connected to the net crashed. Dead ships hung in space. Gravity and life support went offline momentarily. Every cyborg, myself included, went blind. Those who needed their systems to live started to die. I was desperately trying to reboot. Pagan/God's last little trick. I wondered how many thousands of people we'd killed.

The net rebooted. The plain of glass was gone. The sea of fire had gone. The black suns had gone. Pagan/God had gone having saved us all. Pagan had accomplished what Rolleston had failed to do.

The Grey Lady was climbing to her feet. Our gravity hadn't gone off. We weren't on a technological ship. This was a living creature now. It was wired differently. I remained sitting. My body felt like a big bruise with added cuts, breaks and burns. My nose was broken and my ribs were cracked – at best. I laughed. MacFarlane wouldn't have wanted me working for him now. Mudge and Rannu turned to look at me.

Of course there was still the little problem of the Grey Lady and the Black Squadron things surrounding us. As much as I would have liked to beat the shit out of the wee bitch, I knew we didn't stand a chance. I was willing her to die. She might yet if I got on the net and she stood too close to any automated weapon system, or there were other accidents that could happen to her. Make my man think I was dead and sleep with him, would you?

'What now?' I asked her, as willing her dead hadn't seemed to work.

She was staring at Rolleston's body. I wasn't sure what I'd expected – contortions, mutations, something loud and flashy – but he'd just keeled over. He looked really surprised. She looked at me, startled that I'd spoken.

'I've ordered the Black Squadrons to stand down. I've told them that Rolleston's dead. We won't attack unless we are fired on. I think you should go now.'

'We're taking our dead and we'll need a shuttle to come and get us,' I said. She glanced over at the monstrosity Cat had become and nodded.

I stood up and limped over to her. She ignored me, just staring down at Rolleston.

'Why?' I asked.

'Because he didn't know enough to be afraid any more,' she said. She was wrong: all Rolleston had had was fear.

'That's not what I mean.'

She turned to look into my eyes. I'd been told that she never looked anyone in the eyes. Hers were grey. She wasn't as ugly as I thought she'd be. I thought back to Dundee, when the orbital weapons platform had hit the rigs. She could have killed us then. I suspect she'd had many opportunities to kill us.

'I don't know. Out of all of them he was just so ... human.'

I looked at her for a while and she held my gaze. I nodded and turned away. Mudge had managed to crawl to Merle and was holding him, trying not to hurt his arms. I hugged Mudge fiercely.

'Ow!' But he hugged me back.

I could never tell him the truth. I was sure he would kill me if he knew what I'd done. If he knew that Jakob had died in Maw City four months ago, would it make it easier or worse for him?

'Why didn't the virus kill you when I stabbed you?' Rannu asked. The Grey Lady didn't look at him but there was a ghost of a smile on her face.

'There's no biotech in me; I'm just really good.'

Rannu's eyes widened.

Epilogue
Scotland

Only I knew. I knew because I had made contact with Them. Through Ambassador, the soft warm whisper in the back of my head, I had managed to communicate with Them. Rannu, Pagan, Mudge and Jakob had been separated and were being kept under guard. This was in itself a novel concept for Them.

They were not sure what to do with us. As a race they moved in concert, They were one. There was no common ground for Them to understand the madness of individuality. They barely understood death. When They told me that one of us had malfunctioned They certainly didn't understand grief. Or at least I thought They didn't until Ambassador started to sing. It was beautiful. The others had joined in.

No body could have survived the abuses that Jakob's had received. Mudge's chemical cocktail had kept him alive just long enough to do the job. He had finally succumbed to the radiation poisoning he'd fought against for most of his life. On the streets of Fintry growing up, then Them, then the Cabal's henchmen and finally Gregor, his best friend turned into a monster. It had taken a nasty little Nazi punk to kill him.

I finally got to see the body. Ambassador had managed to convey my pain to Them. I think they thought I was suffering the way They had when They'd first been attacked by the Cabal. They were trying to fix him. They had dissected him. They knew the metal and plastic components were mostly working and had stripped them out. There had been so much metal and plastic and so little flesh. They had burrowed deep into what remained, tasted his dead flesh, sampled it, figured out how it worked so they could replicate it and grow it around the metal and plastic.

I threw up and became hysterical. I think I lost it, maybe for a few days, but we were still being kept separate so the others never knew.

I meant to tell the others. I really did. I meant to ask Them to destroy the copy but I couldn't. I rationalised it to myself. We'd need him if we were serious about trying to stop Rolleston. In the end I think it was just the fantasy of a lonely girl whose boyfriend had died. Selfish wee bitch.

I had wanted him. I had needed him. It hadn't worked out very well. Probably because at some level I knew it wasn't him.

I was pretty sure that Pagan suspected. Mudge must've known at some level, they were so close. Rannu would never have suspected. For all the deceit in their world, people like that trust each other, they have to.

I think that Jakob started to suspect after the Citadel.

I'm sorry, Jakob. You didn't deserve that.

Millions had died in the bombardment, then thousands more in the fleet engagement, the battle on the net and as a result of the net crashing.

Parts of Africa, Europe and the Americas had been hit by the seed pods bearing Crom Cruach, which had started to transform the terrain around it without Rolleston's sick guidance. Even now people were fighting to control its spread.

The net was free of Demiurge and God. It was back to the way it had been before. It was as if all our efforts to see the truth told had been for nothing. There were unconfirmed reports of Pagan's ghost being seen on the net. There were few sightings of the gods of the net and none of them were confirmed. That was good, as I couldn't think that they'd be very happy with me. Still I couldn't allow myself to be too frightened to go online.

A terrified assault shuttle pilot had taken us off the *Bush*. Bran had ordered the Black Squadron creatures to help us off and carry the dead. Cutting Cat out of the biomechanical spider's body had been brutal. Rannu had had to help Merle out of the room.

Of course we hadn't been party to the negotiations and had no idea what the Grey Lady had said to Akhtar and the other leaders, but she and the Black Squadrons were allowed to take the *Bush* and the surviving frigates and leave on the proviso that they never returned and never had any contact with humanity again. It seemed risky but I was sure that Bran would keep her word. I think it was a problem the world leaders were glad to see the back of. It was funny to think of one lone woman leading a fleet of monsters who'd sold their humanity.

More than three quarters of the people possessed who survived the mass exorcism committed suicide. Of the remaining quarter many ended up in mental institutes. After all, possession by Demiurge was little more than viral insanity. I wondered if, after his exposure to Rolleston's insanity, Jakob would have been okay. I think he would have survived, but it would have haunted and tormented him for the rest of his life.

At least after the exorcism most of the relevant people had stood down or surrendered their commands. We didn't find out until afterwards, but there had been a significant fifth column operating on many of the ships that had been under Rolleston's command, and during the action there had been a number of mutinies. Most of them had been put down by automated systems controlled by Demiurge. In many ways they were the bravest of the people who had stood up to fight. They'd had nearly no chance and still done it.

Lalande 2 had declared independence. There were some familiar faces in the managing council. The corps had kicked up a fuss. They would have to pay and treat people reasonably. It would bite into their profits. Tough shit. Nobody on Earth had the stomach for any more fighting. Besides, it would be much cheaper for Earth if the colonies had to look after themselves. The Sol system would remain their biggest trading partner. We were always hungry for resources. The other colonies were expected to follow suit.

Sharcroft was dead. He liked spending time in sense simulations, power fantasies where he was whole, young, physically powerful and worshipped. Where he could hurt people. Pagan had found this out when we'd worked at the Limbo facility. Despite his flaws and jealousy, Pagan had truly been one of the most remarkable hackers of his generation and had stepped up to save us all. Again. He had developed a black assassination program. With God gone, Sharcroft had started empire-building again. Rannu had sneaked into the Limbo facility and introduced the black program into one of Sharcroft's power fantasies. One of his virtual victims killed him. It was well past his time anyway.

It was called the Eagle's Nest and had been decorated in imperial splendour for an empire that had never made it because it had been polluted with fucked-up ideas. Here was another power fantasy: unreal attractive women fawning over some wannabe. It seemed unlikely that women who looked like that had ever existed, and if they had they wouldn't have acted that way or been interested in a vile little prick like Messer.

He was surprised when the women disappeared and flowers started to grow out of everything. He had been left naked and alone. Sanctums are supposed to be difficult to find and nearly impossible to violate. He looked frightened because he didn't understand what was happening. How could this little wanker have killed Jakob? I forced myself to control the anger.

'Hello, Messer,' I said as I walked out of the wall and into his sanctum as the Maiden of Flowers.

'You ...' he said. My face was the same, but he'd done well to recognise me as the last time he'd seen me I'd been dressed in fascist chic and sporting a suedehead. I walked towards him over a carpet of blossoming flowers.

'Well done,' I said and smiled brightly.

I went to sit on the old-fashioned couch-thing next to him. He shrank away from me, practically curling into a foetal position. He seemed ashamed of his nakedness now he wasn't in control. And violating his sanctum was a pretty raw demonstration of power. That and I had shut down the command for his icon to appear clothed.

'You killed my boyfriend,' I said sweetly.

'I'm sorry,' he stammered.

'No, you're frightened, and that's different. You killed him on a whim because you're a fucked-up little boy full of fear with a head full of bad ideas. I've seen how that ends. I should kill you, shouldn't I? Not out of revenge but because of what you may become, the damage you could do, the pain you could cause.'

'I'll change—' he started.

'No, that's another lie. That's fear talking again.'

I waved my hands over his face, it was a bit theatrical but it made his crystalline insect eyes disappear. He had pretty green eyes underneath. Or at least his icon did. He looked more naked and afraid in the way that only men can.

'You have to find a way to live free of fear. Maybe you'll keep up with this nonsense when you do, but I doubt it. There are a lot of bad things out there, a lot of things that maybe you should be afraid of, but that's okay because there are people out there who'll help you, protect you, watch your back, help you help yourself. More to the point, they'll accept you.

'We'll find a way to root out the bad things, cast a light on them and show them to everyone, and we'll see that, like you, they're not all that scary.' He looked at me uncomprehending and still frightened. I think he thought he was talking to a mad person. Maybe he was.

'More than anything now we need new and better ideas for all sorts of things, and the ideas you have are old, bad and not even very original. You need to think for yourself.' He nodded, still not getting it.

He flinched away from me when I stroked his face. 'It'll be okay,' I promised him and I meant it.

I stood up and started towards the wall. I reached up to touch the flowers growing out of the wall but stopped and looked back at him.

'Do you know why you're still alive?' He shook his head. 'Because even though you must have been terrified, you fought with the vagabond army. At some level, deep down you must have wanted things to get better.'

He just stared at me.

'Try not to just react. Try to think about what I said. I'll leave you with the flowers. They're very pretty.' Even if I say so myself. I walked through the wall.

Fiona didn't get off nearly so lightly. I tracked her down to an expensive nightclub in Edinburgh. The bouncers didn't want to let four scruffy bastards like us in. Well three – Merle scrubbed up nicely. Rannu and Mudge persuaded them. They didn't hurt them too badly. One of the perks of hanging around with hard bastards (and overprotective males).

I'd analysed the imagery the evil cow had posted on the net and worked out who she was and where to find her. She was sitting with a group of her mates and some hired muscle. Rannu and Mudge took care of the muscle. Merle just sat down and ordered a drink. He said it was nothing to do with him.

Some little wanker called Alasdair tried to get involved. I scared him so badly I think he shat himself. I beat the shit out of her. Well you can take the girl out of Dundee ...

So here we are on the side of a hill in the Highlands. It's raining, it's windy, it's beautiful. We're looking down on Loch Carron. Drinking whisky. Glenmorangie, Jakob's drink. Each sip and it's like I can taste him still.

Rannu's here, the four furrows in his face still healing. Mudge is here, of course, smoking a spliff but reasonably straight and just about able to control his emotions. Merle is here, his arms wrapped in medgel casts. I don't care how hard he likes to pretend to be, he's here for Mudge. They'll be going their separate ways after this though.

After here we're going to Nepal. I want to meet Ashmi, Yangani and Sangar – find out why Rannu fought so hard. Also a place full of Ghurkha veterans is a reasonably safe place to live for a while. Mudge is going to come with us initially. He's going to help. What we can do in the net he can do in the real world. Merle's not coming. With what we've planned, Merle said he's pretty sure that he'll be paid to come and kill us. He was only half joking. He'll probably refuse. To kill us, I mean.

It'll be something like God but we'll take more time, work it out better. Work the parameters better. Try and leave people with a bit more privacy. We've started building a network of hackers to gather information and networks of investigative types – journalists and other interested parties, to be managed by Mudge.

With a less total solution than God we might miss something. The hackers and investigators will pick up some of that, but hopefully we'll be able to leave people with their dignity. They won't be watched all the time. They can go and look at porn without everyone knowing.

We won't be taking armed action against people; we're just going to show people the truth to the best of our abilities. We will however defend ourselves in all sorts of interesting ways if they try to harm us.

See, we don't care if you've got money and power. You want it. You work for it. We just want to live our lives. We care about abuse. People are more important. We are not a fucking resource. So if you take the piss you will be exposed. All we want is a level playing field, an equal chance. The bad people may have all the power, all the violence, all the guns, but we have the numbers. Or we will have. We're kind of an oversight committee, free of government and corporate influence.

Will it be perfect? No. Will there be abuses, corruption? Probably. It's a human institution after all, but we'll do our best.

I hand the empty cup back to Mudge.

'Another?' he asks. I shake my head. He looks at me questioningly. I try not to think about the results of the test and not to touch my stomach. I'm convinced that I keep on doing it and must have given myself away. No fear? Yeah, right.

I stand up and take the ashes and unscrew the top. You have to be careful scattering ashes in a wind. We all get a taste of Jakob and end up coughing and spitting.

'Sorry,' I tell them. Mudge starts laughing first, then we all join in. Jakob's copy is a cloud of dust for a while and then he's gone.

Rannu hands me the trumpet. If I can learn to handle a Wraith on a submarine operation at depth with skillsofts, how difficult can a trumpet be? I put it to my lips and blow. It makes a horrible noise.

513

Acknowledgements

Once again thanks to:

Dr Hazel Spence Young and Scott Young for ongoing support.

I'd like to thank the members of the gaming community for all sorts of shenanigans in helping promote *Veteran* and being supportive. Too many to name so I'll simply say thanks to the Lords of Barry, the Storm Brethren, the Guild, Slieve and the Charioteers. You know who you are.

Thank you to the Twitterati and Bloggers who have mentioned or reviewed the book, particularly: Mark Chitty at Walker of Worlds, Adam Whitehead at the Wertzone, Ove Jannson at Cybermage, James Long at Speculative Horizons and Amanda Rutter at Floor to Ceiling Books. An increasingly more important part of the genre-fan community that deserves more recognition.

To the web monkeys and artists who did a brilliant job on the website. That's James Phillips, the mysterious Karma, Nicola Smith (who also has the good fortune to be my sister) and Ghoulia Peculiar.

Thank you to Dyanne and Tobias Heason and Tim DePhillip for a well-timed chilli and door-opening suggestions.

Also contributing artwork to the site as well as providing another stunning cover (all the other covers are jealous), Spyroteknik aka Martin Bland.

Thanks to fellow authors Stephen Deas and M.D. Lachlan for good company, advice and much needed sarcasm. To my knowledge Paul J. McAuley first coined the term Warewolf in his novel *Fairyland*.

Paul very graciously allowed me to use the phrase in *War in Heaven*, so thanks to Paul as well.

Also thanks to Dan Abnett, Andy Remic, Adam Roberts and Stephen Baxter for taking the time to read and comment on *Veteran*.

Thanks again to the stubbled agent Sam Copeland at RCW Ltd.

To my editor Simon Spanton.

To Jon Weir, Gillian Redfearn and Charlie Panayiotou at Gollancz. To Hugh Davis for the copy-edit, I hope you get well paid for deciphering my English.

My family and friends for their support, enthusiasm and often patience, including my dad this time (could the League for the Protection of Fathers please stop sending me hate mail, it was a joke).

Finally I'd like to say thank you to everyone who read *Veteran* and took the time to post comments and reviews on the net, good or bad, and to all the people in bookshops who helped push the book. All efforts are much appreciated.

Gavin G. Smith, Leicester, 2011.

www.gavingsmith.com